CENTAURUS

TOR BOOKS BY DAVID G. HARTWELL

NONFICTION
Age of Wonders

AS EDITOR
The Ascent of Wonder (with Kathryn Cramer)
Centaurus
Christmas Forever
Christmas Stars
The Dark Descent
Foundation of Fears
Northern Stars (with Glenn Grant)
Northern Suns (with Glenn Grant)
The Science Fiction Century
Visions of Wonder (with Milton E. Wolf)

CENTAURUS

THE BEST OF

AUSTRALIAN SCIENCE FICTION

edited by

David G. Hartwell
Damien Broderick

TOR

A TOM DOHERTY ASSOCIATES BOOK
NEW YORK

For the whole crew who did the *Australian SF Review*, one of the magazines that inspired *The New York Review of Science Fiction*.

—DAVID G. HARTWELL

For Jonathan Strahan and Jeremy G. Byrne, and the rest of the wonderful Perth SF Renaissance.

—DAMIEN BRODERICK

CENTAURUS: THE BEST OF AUSTRALIAN SCIENCE FICTION

Copyright © 1999 by David G. Hartwell and Damien Broderick

This book is printed on acid-free paper.

A Tor Book
Published by Tom Doherty Associates, LLC
175 Fifth Avenue
New York, NY 10010

www.tor.com

Designed by Lisa Pifher

Tor® is a registered trademark of Tom Doherty Associates, LLC

Library of Congress Cataloging-in-Publication Data

Centaurus : the best of Australian science fiction / edited by David G. Hartwell
    and Damien Broderick.—1st ed.
              p.   cm.
    "A Tom Doherty Associates book."
    ISBN 0-312-86556-2 (acid-free paper)
        1. Science fiction, Australian.   I. Hartwell, David G.
II. Broderick, Damien.
PR9617.35.S33C46   1999
823'.0876208994—dc21   99-21936
                                                                   CIP

First Edition: July 1999

Printed in the United States of America

0   9   8   7   6   5   4   3   2   1

CONTENTS

INTRODUCTION

Damien Broderick

Australia is ... *different*. Even the stars dusted on the Aussie sky are different, as you gaze up into the great southern darkness.

These are not the constellations known by most humans throughout history, the hundred millennia of prehistory. High in the southern sky, invisible from London or Saint Petersburg or Chicago, two bright stars point to the five comprising a slightly dented Southern Cross. Australia's flag shows that cross, and one of the pointers—the less interesting one, oddly enough. The brighter of the Pointers, farther from the cross, is actually not one star but three, locked in mutual orbit: Sunlike Alpha Centauri A and B, and dim, red Proxima, closest to our world of all suns except the Sun.

To grow up under the light of the nearest stars, under Centaurus, is ... *magical*. Better yet—it's *science fictional!*

Alpha Centauri, that bright composite light, has another name: Rigil Kent. Few know that, though once the secret knowledge of stars was hugged to the breast of all who stood watch on cold nights. Aborigines, with their hundreds of separate tongues, use many names for the nearest star. For the Boorung people (from the southeastern part of the nation, the rich farmland that white people choose to call Victoria), Cross and Pointers are *Tchingal* and *Bunya,* an emu and possum from the spirit Dreaming. If science fiction mythmakers tell different tales, perhaps those are potentially no less resonant for the new composite culture of 20 million people that has taken command of the continent and is in the process of being reshaped by its immense, austere power.

It's been called the last continent—or the second-last, if we count Antarctica under all that ice and snow. But Australia was by no means the most recent great expanse of sovereign land found and inhabited by humans walking out of Africa. They did so fifty thousand years ago at least, perhaps more, tens of millennia before humans trudged into the Americas. By that calendar, European settlement—some call it invasion, and certainly the native peoples were trampled and murdered in dreadful numbers—was the merest blip in the past. Whites have remade the rediscovered continent in little more than two centuries—but it has remade them in turn. Australians are *different*. Ask any of us.

It is notorious that the first European painters who tried to render the intractable Australian landscape uttered curious chimeras: soft, deciduous dales and soft, woolly skies, complete with half-remembered Grecian ruins. Nothing could be further from the experience of the outback, the numinous hard, blue heavens, the hot sun, the lashing downpours, animals that hop and bear their young in pouches, snakes and insects that sicken or kill with venom so poisonous it seems like a biblical retribution. The same kinds of perceptual blunders happened for a long time in writing produced by English-speaking Australians. Writers and readers in the "last continent" are denizens of two worlds, and only slowly is Australia's fiction bringing the two into meaningful conjunction. For a long time it has seemed that Jewish intellectual New York, say, or white-bread roller blading Los Angeles, are more vividly recognizable and germane than Sydney or the bush.

Unlike the ancient teachings and songs of the first peoples, SF (science fiction, speculative fiction, even sci-fi if you absolutely must) is not much more than a century old. H. G. Wells called his pioneering efforts "scientific romances," still a good name, and his wonderfully fecund *The Time Machine* and *War of the Worlds* were published as late as 1895 and 1898. So Australia as a Europeanized nation—it became a federation, a unified nation, as recently as 1901—is even younger than this Space Age genre. Still, if you push SF's birth back to Mary Shelley's *Frankenstein* in 1818, it coincides with white settlement. Time enough, you'd think, to grow plenty of Aussie SF.

In fact, though, it has seemed rather thin on the ground. In 1982, Dr. Van Ikin gathered a swag of futuristic, Lemurian, satirical, and utopian tales from 1845 to 1947 and placed them (in his landmark anthology *Australian Science Fiction*) side by side with a selection of recent generic SF and fringe surreal fiction. Ikin argued at length for this inclusive eclecticism, but perhaps not persuasively. Science fiction is hardly achieved by the simple act of supposing that the world differs slightly from the consensus version. Many of the early tries were crudely wrought and depressingly racist, with titles like *The Yellow Wave* (1895) and *The Colored Conquest* (1904). Erle Cox's *Out of the Silence* (serialized in a newspaper in 1919) *is* authentic SF and troublingly nasty: a farmer finds a beautiful white superwoman from an earlier civilization preserved underground in suspended animation as lower races wrought ruin upon her ancient world. On the other hand, feminist utopias suggested new paths: Mary Ann Moore-Bentley, in 1901, adventured with *A Woman of Mars, or Australia's Enfranchised Women*. Despite some controversial highlights and flurries—notably, *Tomorrow and Tomorrow* (1947) by M. Barnard Eldershaw (solo, Marjorie Barnard sans Flora Eldershaw), politically censored for subversive views—most of the century saw little SF from Australians and most of that derivative and third-rate. The population was very small, and access to publication extremely limited.

In the last decade, happily, we have seen a burst of talented activity in both SF proper and commercial fantasy (usually fat novels or trilogies set in a variant of Middle Earth, with dashing derring-do among semidivine characters enacting mythic themes). Still, you could easily get the impression than Australians don't care to dream about the stars and the strange inhabitants of alien worlds—unless those aliens speak in American accents, in which case Aussies eagerly gulp down *X-Files*, *Star Wars*, *Star Trek*, a hundred gaudy movies, a thousand imported paperbacks.

It comes as some surprise, therefore, that Australians are at least notable SF *critics*—not just carping complainers, either, but astute anatomists and cataloguers of these strange new literary fruit. The first major encyclopedia of SF, in three parts (1974, 1978, 1983), was written by a Tasmanian amateur scholar. Indeed, Don Tuck gained the 1984 Hugo, SF's premier award, chosen by its fans assembled in their thousands at the World Science Fiction Convention—held, of course, as usual, in one of the large cities of the United States.

The field's most important critical volume ever, *The Encyclopedia of Science Fiction*, was also the brainchild of an Australian, Peter Nicholls, who got a Hugo in 1980 and then again, for its even larger revision, shared one with John Clute in 1995. (But Australia being a provincial little universe, Nicholls failed to be nominated for the equivalent local award for SF criticism—an award named, in an inevitable irony, for the nom de plume of pioneering American SF critic James Blish, who wielded his sharp scalpel as William Atheling Jr.).

"We are the Smart Alecks," Nicholls had stated more than two decades ago, in a feisty lecture at London's Institute of Contemporary Arts. "We take our metaphors from all over, from geology, dress design, traditional literature, or relativity physics. We feel free to mix our fundamentally academic observations with an ironic raciness of manner."

To the haughty academic world of criticism and theory, SF smacked of acne cures and lonely Saturday nights. That estimate was not altogether wrong then, and has become more apt since the triumph of *Star Wars*, *The Terminator*, and groaning bookshelves of lucrative consumer fantasy fodder. "Academic readers dislike us for our vulgarity"—Nicholls, the wry scholar, observed, drawing deeply on an experience of exclusion known keenly by SF fans everywhere, but most sharply, perhaps, in Australia—"while ordinary readers dislike us for our constant display of our own cleverness."

Wishing to advance the prospects of his chosen genre, Nicholls sought ways to cut through prejudice and self-erected hazard alike. Everyone would benefit, he decided, if he and his smart-aleck mates made their judgments "in a level, friendly tone, veering neither toward condescension on the one hand nor obscurantism on the other." He had in mind especially his terrifyingly dithyrambic Anglo-Canadian colleague Clute, who had written previously, with resigned contempt, of genre SF's "mild ignorant readership." Wearying of spilling their esoteric seed on barren ground, Nicholls and Clute joined forces at the end of the 1970s (together with thirty-one others of like mind, age, and gender, plus one woman) to produce the first edition of their encyclopedia.

Yet the genre itself remains a problem for many sophisticated adult readers. SF—not the vile "sci-fi," which is more aptly applied to media fodder—continues to be ignored or disliked by readers trained to enjoy literary or "canonical" texts while detesting anything else. I'm inclined to view this disdain as a kind of learned incompetence, a bigotry that wounds its practitioners as much as its victims. More than one literary Australian journalist has asked me, in genuine puzzlement, "Why do you like science fiction when everyone else hates it?" This strange claim flies in the face of solid sales of SF and fantasy in a time when literary fiction struggles to survive. Worse, it ignores the striking realities of popular culture. Of the top-earning movies of all time, the majority are science fiction or fantasy. True, this is largely "product" tailored for unreflecting and sentimental teen consumers. But it can hardly be said that everyone hates SF when there's scarcely anything that viewers love more.

SF's delight in sheer imagination blends magical escapism with an all-too-realistic awareness of the impact on our world of incessant technological upheaval. Mass-media versions of SF inevitably debase any subtle play with either component, so it is not surprising that huge success at the box office fails to translate into fame, fortune, or even critical esteem for SF's best artists. After all, periods when the whole family routinely settled down to watch the latest Western did not produce a surge of nuanced novels about existential cowboys. With SF, it is more complicated. Despite spectacular epiphanies of shaped light, no Spielberg movie of UFOs or dinosaurs can approach the cognitive delights of print SF, from A. E. van Vogt's baffling superintelligent protagonists to William Gibson's cyberspace.

That is no less true of Australia's science fiction, which at its best (which, admittedly, is seldom) is among the finest ever written in any country. This should not be surprising. Australians no longer live under what historian Geoffrey Blainey memorably dubbed the "tyranny of distance." It costs a little more to freight books and magazines across the vast oceans, to airmail stories out to the metropolitan centers of the world, but it can be done with only an extra week's lag. Today, of course, even that rupture is healing, as instantaneous everywhere-at-once is made real by the Internet and E-mail. A vivid, local SF magazine like *Eidolon,* where some of Greg Egan's first stories were published by editors Jonathan Strahan and Jeremy Byrne, can be sampled on the World Wide Web, and subscriptions are no harder to arrange than those for *Asimov's* and *F&SF* in the U.S.A. or *Interzone* in Britain. Australians travel prodigiously and are as likely to meet by accident in a small town outside Boston or in a pub in London as in their home suburb. (Australia, remember, is *big,* and the locals find it almost as easy and cheap to fly to Portugal or Madras as to cross their own red-desert nation's heartland from one green coastal patch to another thousands of kilometers distant. The late, very funny fan Roger Weddall had no difficulty convincing those he met overseas that it is a legal requirement, like military conscription, for all young Australians to leave the country for two years.)

Strikingly, a university press has published an entire *Encyclopaedia of Australian Science Fiction & Fantasy* (1998), edited by Paul Collins, Steven Paulsen, and Sean McMullen, yet the names of the writers of Australia's science fiction are perhaps still not known well to most of the greater world's SF enthusiasts. Egan, of course, is a wonderful exception, the *wunderkind* who startled U.S. and UK audiences so acutely that for a time *Year's Best* anthologies were incomplete without *two* stories apiece by him; I consider him currently the most important SF writer in the world. At a quite different angle, Peter Carey is another exception, much admired by literary readers, from his earlier fabulations that borrowed SF tropes to his parabolic invented history, *The Unusual History of Tristan Smith.* Other authors have made a mark, more often among SF's specialist critics than with mass readerships. George Turner came to SF late, at sixty-two after middling success as a mainstream novelist of manners (he shared the 1963 Miles Franklin Award, a distinguished mainstream prize). *Beloved Son* made a powerful impression, and 1987's *The Sea and Summer* won the Arthur C. Clarke Award and was in the running for the Commonwealth Prize. Before his death in 1997, he produced a body of mature work that is still finding a worldwide audience comparable with, say, Stanislaw Lem's.

Frank Bryning, attracted to SF around the time of World War One, had published a notable series of tales about a Commonwealth space station, and SF that introduced Aboriginal characters. Lee Harding, John

Baxter, and David Rome (David Boutland) virtually colonized John Carnell's English magazines *New Worlds* and *Science Fantasy,* and his original
anthology series, *New Writings in SF,* in the early-to-mid 1960s, but have
since moved to other genres or fallen silent. Jack Wodhams's dementedly
inventive and popular japes appeared regularly while he had the tutelage
of John Campbell at *Analog,* but with the great editor's death his work
sprawled into indiscipline and near-illiteracy. Wynne Whiteford sold his
first SF stories in the U.S.A. to *Amazing* and *Fantastic Universe* in the early
1950s, and in the 1980s returned to form with a number of routine adventure novels.

And, of course, the most well-known Aussie SF writer of all was merchant navy captain A. Bertram Chandler, known confusingly as "Jack" to
his wife and friends and "Bert" to the SF fans. Guest of honor at the
Chicago World Science Fiction Convention, and several times at Japanese
conventions, he was the only Australian member of that Golden Age generation who got their start in John W. Campbell's famous *Astounding Science Fiction.* Or is that a misleading claim? After all, Chandler was
forty-four years old when he emigrated from Britain in 1956, and his most
famous stories (such as the much anthologized "Giant Killer," from 1945)
were sold *before* he moved to Australia. By comparison, Arthur C. Clarke
became a resident of Colombo in the same year Chandler settled in Australia; one might doubt that Clarke is known as the finest Sri Lankan SF
writer.

By the same token, should we regard Neville Shute, author of the most
famous after-the-bomb novel (surely a SF theme, even though *On the Beach*
is hardly SF), as an Aussie writer? He arrived in 1950 and left a decade
later. John Brosnan, born in Australia, has been expatriate (like Baxter)
for nearly thirty years. Cherry Wilder, a fine writer represented in many
Aussie anthologies, is actually a New Zealander who lived in Australia for
twenty-two years of her young adulthood before moving with her husband,
Horst Grimm, to Germany, going home recently to her birthplace. Call
her an honorary Aussie. Jack Dann, Aussie SF's most illustrious adopted
son, arrived as recently as 1993, aged forty-eight, married an Australian,
awaits dual citizenship, and is as purely an upstate New York writer as the
world will ever see.

David Lake, however, clearly *is* best seen as an Australian SF writer.
An academic raised in India, he settled in 1967 at the age of thirty-eight,
becoming an Australian citizen. Victor Kelleher lived for the early years of
his maturity in Africa, settling in Australia at thirty-seven, in 1976; like
Lake, his work was written in his adoptive homeland. At the furthest extreme, consider the odd case of Dr. Paul Myron Anthony Linebarger, god-

son of Sun Yat-sen, psychological warrior, and author under the name Cordwainer Smith of the most memorable science fiction short story sequence ever conceived. Smith lived in Canberra, the Australian capital, for extended periods during several stints at the Australian National University, and his Instrumentality tales, with their refrains from the planet Old North Australia, stand near the heart of world science fiction mythology. It would not be realistic, alas, to conscript Smith to the roster of local talent.

Terry Dowling is among the best-loved local writers and most-awarded in and out of Australia, a writer who stubbornly hews his own path (one mapped ahead, it's true, by Cordwainer Smith, J. G. Ballard, and Jack Vance), no doubt to the detriment of his appeal to the larger commercial audience. My own novels and stories have sold modestly and gained awards in Australia and the U.S.A. (My 1980 *The Dreaming Dragons* was selected by British scholar David Pringle as one of the best one hundred SF novels in English since Orwell's *1984*.)

In the late 1990s, newer writers are exploding into existence. Some of them, finally, are women, although successful Australian women fantasists, including Sara Douglass, Rosaleen Love, Isobelle Carmody, Lucy Sussex, Jane Routley, Kim Wilkins, Beverley Macdonald, and Shannah Jay (Sherry-Ann Jacobs) have tended to prefer varieties of heroic or gothicized fantasy (also favored by Keith Taylor, Garth Nix, Dirk Strasser, and several other male writers), ghost stories, or the uncanny. Other women of considerable gifts have written little, regrettably: these include the superb Philippa Maddern, Yvonne Rousseau, and Petrina Smith. Among the best of the newcomers, some prolific, are Sean McMullen, Stephen Dedman, Sean Williams, Paul Voermans, Tess Williams, Simon Brown, Richard Harland, Andrew Whitmore, and Russell Blackford. Children's and Young Adult SF or fantasy—long ago colonized by veterans Mary Pratchett, Patricia Wrightston, and Ivan Southall—is booming again and attracting awards from such authors as John Marsden, Paul Jennings, Gillian Rubinstein, Victor Kelleher, Catherine Jinks, Gary Crews, Sophie Masson, Brian Caswell, Caroline Macdonald, Rory Barnes, and Sue Isle. Some of those names are just now starting to become familiar to readers in the U.S.A., the UK, and Europe; but most are still performing their impressive pyrotechnics in an off-off-off Broadway dive south of the equator, where the seasons are reversed and the local heroes are heralded more for their sporting prowess, their golden swimsuited bodies, and their awesome capacity for beer than for their brilliant imagination.

There are varieties of dispossession. I'd like to show you some snapshots of this metaphoric subcontinent of the main, where the great world is the Future itself, as seen by those who have seized it: *America,* as H. Bruce Franklin termed it in the telling subtitle to his fine study of the SF of Robert A. Heinlein, *as science fiction.*

In 1985, in an anthology dedicated to Ursula Le Guin and Gene Wolfe—two wonderful writers and American (of course) guests of honor at AussieCon II, the second World Science Fiction Convention held in Australia—I tried to position that moment against local generic history:

Here is an odd fact. I encourage you to marvel at it: Not until twenty years ago was the first mass-market SF collection by an Australian published in Australia.

Why is this surprising? Well, after all, science fiction was hardly brand new in the world at large twenty years ago. H. G. Wells, its major innovator, had been dead since 1946. Hiroshima and Nagasaki, by 1965, were already ash two decades past. So was the fabled American Golden Age of SF.

Indeed, at that very moment the New Wave of rebellion against Golden Age science fiction was beginning to roll in Britain. Brian Aldiss and Cordwainer Smith and Samuel R. Delany and Tom Disch were recasting the nature of the genre. And we in Australia were . . . what? Sending out our first collection to sniff the air. (As it chanced, this novelty was a small pulpy gathering of my own small, inept stories.)

Thirty years ago, a biological generation or more, three years after that embarrassing collection had appeared, Australian SF writer and editor John Baxter compiled *The Pacific Book of Australian Science Fiction,* also the first of its kind. He was coolly ironic, as is his way (as is the Australian way, indeed):

Nobody has ever been able adequately to define the dimension and effect of the sense of wonder; like a trace element, it is only noticeable when it is not there. One could be sure, however, that Australia did not have it. The science fiction produced here was weak stuff, feeble, derivative, lacking the spark of imagination, of wonder, which enlivened that written in Britain and the United States. Worse, there was no strong national character in what was produced. It might as well have been written by people *from* another planet as *about* them.

That was a candid admission for the second paragraph of such a volume. Luckily, Baxter found matters had improved since the late fifties:

> . . . Australian artistic life has renewed itself in a wave of innovation and experiment. Patrick White, Sidney Nolan, Richard Meale, and Judith Wright have provided us for the first time with a legitimate national voice. . . . The stimulus of their work has penetrated into many areas, one of the most unexpected of them being science fiction.

Even so,

> There is a colony of new and imaginative writers, a mild climate of acceptance, and a measure of support here and abroad, but that is all.

A colony within a colony, of course. Nearly a decade later, in 1977, I introduced a comparable anthology thus:

> Science fiction in Australian?
> Why, yes. It burgeons and thrives . . . in 1975—*annus mirabilis!*—the prestigious World Science Fiction Convention itself, snatched like the America's Cup from its traditional trustees, enlivened the Southern Cross Hotel. . . .
> Yes indeed. Warm-blooded, clawed and billed, it hatches and suckles its young, glides daringly from tall eucalyptus trees. . . . Alas, it carries a Qantas ticket in its pouch.

That was true then, piercingly so, as a generation and more of cultural expatriates testify. To remain in this wide, brown land was to be subject to that tyranny of distance I cited earlier, to suffer exclusion (it was an agony) from the company of true adults, artists, wheelers and dealers. It seems hard to imagine, a mere two decades on. But that was an epoch before wide-bodied jets carried off annually a tenth of the population of the land (or whatever the staggering figure is), before the same jets, and a score or two of wretched, sinking fishing boats, fetched to Australia in their hundreds of thousands the multicoloured, many-voiced people of all the suffering on ambitious earth. People coming of their own free choice! Amazing! And with their arrival they made up for the departed, who themselves, of course, returned for Christmas and arts festivals to be lionized, bearing Magi word from the centers of metropolitan culture. In 1977, then, matters hung at this crux (or so it seemed to me, who'd never left Australia's shores even on a pilgrimage, except endlessly in mediated imagination):

> Australians subsist, as everyone agrees, in a hand-me-down culture. It is of the essence of culture, admittedly, as much to be transmitted as to be renewed, but ours is curiously threadbare and ill-fitting. If a son asks for bread, the odds are high indeed that his father will give him a stone (or a lamington). It's an inevitable irony, then—and so, perhaps, no irony at all—that the world's finest science fiction to date was forged to a significant degree in the Australian experience. . . .

Of an American writer, Cordwainer Smith.

I had gone in search of Cordwainer Smith in 1965, when his second collection of SF stories, *Space Lords*, revealed that he was living at the time in Canberra. It named his stockbroker. A penniless student, I flew at once to find him out and found only that I had missed him.

His last book was *Nostrilia*, about the boy Roderick Frederick Ronald Arnold William MacArthur McBann from the immensely rich world Old North Australia. Here is how he described that planet:

> Somebody once singsonged it up, like this:
> "Gray lay the land, oh. Gray grass from sky to sky. Not near the weir, dear. Not a mountain, low or high—only hills and gray gray. Watch the dappled dimpled twinkles blooming on the star bar.
> "That is Nostrilia . . .
> "Beige-brown sheep lie on blue-gray grass while the clouds rush past, low overhead, like iron pipes ceilinging the world . . ."

"It is incantatory stuff," I commented, "taking us away from ourselves (if we allow it to) to bring us back. No Australian employing the multiple tongues of science fiction has written so well out of his native experience as Linebarger did from several visits. Nor is it sufficient to retort that the genre is, after all, an instrument for amplifying American accents. It *is* that, but more deeply it's a transducer of the technological experience: the myth of the man/transistor interface. Our aspirations are linked ineluctably with the machine, with what the machine has done to and for us, and our world. We all press our mouths to the grease-nipple; for us, pity and terror are newly shaped, and can benefit from new means of expression."

The colonial experience roars like a flame in my two-decades'-old words. Not the colonialism that whites (my immigrant forebears) imposed upon those native to the gray gray land (as they saw it, blinded by the antipodean light and memories of impossible wet green), but what we already knew poignantly as the same Coca-Cola–nization that was winning the East as it had won the West. My myth, as you'll have noticed, was not yet the *human/chip* interface, but its parochial and unthinkingly sexist grammatical predecessor. For all that, my lament was not I think, just a whine of exclusion. There were indeed attempts at an Aussie SF, I noted:

> They spring sometimes direct from the American vocabulary and syntax; sometimes from the electrical/chemical revival of *fin-de-siècle* voyage into sensory derangement; sometimes from the still-fruitful exercise of surrealist confrontation with irrational realities our bureaucratic enterprise would prefer to obliterate. Our second-hand culture may be dull and anxious to remain dull, but the implosions and exhalations of radical change are seldom contained for long by the strictures of rule-book efficiency experts.

In such a climate (the leftish arts–encouraging Whitlam government of 1972–75 had been voted out resoundingly after what amounted to a constitutional coup, perhaps connived at by covert U.S. interests), could SF be, in any sense, authentically, peculiarly Australian? I thought it might and said so with all the dubious hauteur of a colonial factor for finer values from elsewhere:

> We are, on the whole, raw, vulgar; our communal tastes lack any hint of genuine cultivation. We excuse this coarseness by appeal to "bush mateship," a pragmatics of social accord rendered in a crucible of harsh geography, scant resources, the root-severing distance from Europe.
>
> All this special pleading is, of course, mendacious. Last time I looked at the figures, we were the most urbanized culture on earth: 86 percent of the population in cities, suburbs, largish towns. Electronic communication grids us so uncompromisingly into the globe that in one recent notorious epiphany the Australian public was told of important U.S. military plans before the President managed to inform his American constituency. We are, if anything, the victims of technological triumph. If the bush once spoke to our shearers and poets, its voice is now hardly audible

over the crash and screech of process-line, office equipment, television commercials, overpowered motor cars, and jet-lagged impresarios.

Five years later, in his *Australian Science Fiction,* Van Ikin found a tradition steeped in anxieties of race, of loneliness, of utopian romance, and of political hope. Turning his pages, it is easy to agree with the concluding words of his historical introduction:

> Never afraid to tackle the topical and controversial (although sometimes unable to deal with such material effectively), Australian SF has mirrored the nation's apprehensive fascination with its own unexplored emptiness, and its fear of forfeiting its never-too-clear racial identity. If the nation's early SF reveals Australians to have been racist, sexist, and materialistic, it also reveals their more altruistic utopian aspirations, and the more recent offerings of Australian SF show that ignoble attitudes are receding.

That was 1982. It is notable that as Australians approach the second century of federation in 2001, there's been a resurgence of bigotry and sometimes violent hatred for non-British and more broadly non-European new arrivals. A melting pot like the U.S.A, but in thrall to any number of overseas owners, investors, gamblers, and ideologues, Australia is the very model of a postmodern landscape. One might argue, of course, that ructions over small, venomous pockets of racist ardor prove the wholesome generosity, or at least live-and-let-live, fair-go ethos, of a genuine emerging multicultural, stranded community. One might hope so, at least. Certainly that is the future that recent significant science fiction has emphasised.

Yet Australian SF writers and editors cannot avoid a nagging sense of insignificance, worsened by a perennial background drone, the mocking suggestion (as Ikin and Dowling note in their 1993 anthology *Mortal Fire*) that "It's kids' stuff really, isn't it; I mean you don't see adults reading it, do you?" Even granting that SF is not always kids' stuff, Ikin and Dowling find recurrent misunderstandings even among enthusiasts for the genre: "Why do we need Australian SF when Australia is such a small-time player in technology and has no real part in the space-race?"

Dowling makes the obvious rejoinder: "The central issue here is really the assumption that science fiction must always be about space or technology. That's wrong . . ."

Ikin adds,

> It's also wrong to assume that science fiction is written by and for
> the big players. When science fiction deals with technology, it
> looks at its impact upon people and society, and that involves
> looking at the impact of small-time player-nations like Australia.
> Contemporary SF in particular will frequently align itself with the
> underdogs, looking at whiz-bang new development from the per-
> spective of those on the receiving end . . .

Big time, small time, those who deal from power, those at the receiving
end "down under" (destable phrase): all the vivid bruises, the flinching and
defiant postures, of living and writing at the edge of the world, it is inescapable, even in attempted epiphany. I will close with one final characteristic snapshot from my 1988 anthology *Matilda at the Speed of Light:*

> It is 200 years since whites brought the seeds of an English-
> speaking culture to Australia; it is a suitable time for us to burst
> free, at last, from the twin tyrannies of distance and difference. If
> the past is another country, where they do things differently, so is
> the future—and we shall *all* be living there. It is suitable, as we
> hump our blueys to the strains of "Waltzing Matilda," that the
> songs we sing by the hot blue light of the late twentieth-century
> furnace should be songs in that boundary-less tongue, that voice
> of fecund fiction, which is framed by science.

Matilda, as I said then, is waltzing no longer. Matilda is rushing into
tomorrow, beneath the blazing sign of Rigil Kent, the Centaurus stars invisible from those shores that gave science fiction birth, and we are rushing
into tomorrow with her, at the speed of light.

THE OTHER EDITOR'S INTRODUCTION

David G. Hartwell

This anthology is a showcase of the best Australian science fiction, and that requires immediate qualification and explanation. First and foremost, this volume is devoted to science fiction, not to other genres such as fantasy or horror, and to writers who live and write in Australia. The timing of the book is the occasion of the third World Science Fiction Convention ever to be held in Australia, the 1999 convention in Melbourne.

Some other exclusions: these writers herein are in our opinion the best of the lot; there aren't many others in Australia who have written any SF works that measure up to these writers, and best doesn't mean much if good works and good writers are not excluded in favor of better. And while we did figure in slippery factors such as importance and influence and popularity, we went with our taste, argued and discussed the writers and the stories for a couple of years, and came up with, in our opinion, a very strong book. We intend it to be read by SF readers all over the world who want the pleasure of absolutely first-rate stories (no matter who wrote them or where) and who might want in addition a clear view of the real achievements of Australian SF. We are well aware of Paul Collins's *Metaworlds*, Terry Dowling and Vera Ilkin's *Mortal Fire*, and Peter McNamara & Margaret Winch's *Alien Shores*, three good anthologies that have a claim to representing Australia's best in SF, but we believe our book is better.

And we are not afraid to get shot at for our taste; we have included both famous and influential writers, and one first story by a relative unknown from a packaged series, another story from manuscript (sold but not yet published by a magazine at the time of consideration), and at least one story that may be challenged as not science fiction, in spite of its selection years ago for Terry Carr's *Year's Best SF* volume when it first appeared.

And yet, and yet . . . another book this size could be done, just as good, with only a few names overlapping. This is not all the best, but all the best that fit. At the moment this is the better "best of," but in the coming years, who knows?

Australian SF did not spring up recently, but for complex reasons it did not really begin as a separate segment of the growing world of SF literature in the twentieth century until the late 1960s. Some kind of threshold was crossed in 1966 when John Bangsund, with John Foyster and Lee Harding, began to publish the critical fanzine *Australian Science Fiction Review*, aimed at literate readers of science fiction everywhere in the world. In 1969, Bruce Gillespie founded *SF Commentary* to continue the flow of critical writing from Australia into the world community after the demise of *ASFR*, and in that year the Ditmar Awards were founded, given annually to the best SF in the world and in Australia. Shortly after, the William Atheling, Jr. Award for Criticism (in honor of James Blish, who had borrowed for his magazine criticism that pseudonym from Ezra Pound) was associated with the Ditmars (in 1976), still the only popular award for SF criticism in the world. So by the early 1970s there was an established punishment and reward system in place for SF writing in Australia, a world-famous community of cutting-edge SF reviewers and critics. But not many writers.

Unfortunately, there was not yet a professional market on the Australian continent to support writers of fiction. But there were some fans, and some writers, and in part because of the famous critical fanzines, the first Australian World Science Fiction Convention was held in 1975 in Melbourne, and that event generated a spectrum of related activities—the first major SF writing workshop held by Guest of Honor Ursula K. Le Guin; the founding of a number of small presses, the first real local markets for writers who were (with the exception of A. Bertram Chandler and Jack Wodhams) sometimes published but virtually unnoticed in the rest of the world. They were certainly not particularly noticed as Australian writers. Cordwainer Smith was the only SF writer of the first rank identified with Australia before the mid 1970s, and he wasn't Australian.

There was no need felt to institute a Ditmar Award for Australian short fiction until 1978 (stories by John Foyster, Cherry Wilder [twice], Philippa Maddern, and Kevin McKay had in earlier years occasionally been nominated in competition with novels, but never won), and the category was skipped in 1979, '80, and '83. All the stories nominated in 1984 were from one original anthology *(Dreamworks)*, and five of the six nominated in 1986 were from two different original anthologies *(Strange Attractors* and *Urban Fantasies)*. You might say with some justice, though, that by the mid-1980s Australian science fiction writing was alive and well. And it should be no surprise that many of the writers were also nominees for the William Atheling, Jr. Award. It is interesting to note that writer/critic or writer/editor/critic was the identifier for perhaps a majority of

Australian SF writers until the 1990s—James Blish was certainly an influential model—and certainly most of the major ones.

It appears that the history of contemporary Australian SF is the history of the original anthologies that, more than magazines, are and have been its lifeblood. With few exceptions, the SF writers of Australia have published in small press books and magazines, and occasionally in the British and American magazines. There are some outstanding novels, and fewer single-author collections, of distinction. But there are a lot of anthologies ranging from the good to the excellent, and even the worst are still better than the average anthology today in the U.S.

Back in the 1960s, before John Baxter's *The Pacific Book of Science Fiction* (1968), the first of contemporary times, Australian writers were appearing regularly in E. J. Carnell's anthology series, *New Writings in SF* (which produced one or two hardcover volumes a year in the sixties and early seventies filled with original SF stories). The first professional SF magazine in Australia was not published until 1981–87 (*Omega Science Digest*) and the second two, still publishing, commenced in 1990 (*Aurealis: The Australian Magazine of Fantasy & Science Fiction*, and *Eidolon, The Journal of Australian Science Fiction & Fantasy*). It is worth noting that these two current magazines publish a mix of fantasy, horror, and science fiction, and provide in the 1990s a stable market for Australian writers for the first time. A third, *Altair*, was launched in 1998.

But having spent more than a year, with the assistance of my co-editor, surveying the last three decades of Australian SF, it is clear that the magazines do not approach the anthologies in importance during the last twenty years. The list of anthologies from 1976 onward yields at least one a year: Lee Harding's *Beyond Tomorrow* (1976), *The Altered Eye* (1976), and *Rooms of Paradise* (1978); George Turner's *The View from the Edge* (1977); *Transmutations*, edited by Rob Gerrand (1979); Damien Broderick's *The Zeitgeist Machine* (1977), *Strange Attractors* (1985), and *Matilda at the Speed of Light*(1988); Paul Collins's *Worlds* books (*Envisaged Worlds* [1978], *Other Worlds* [1978], *Alien Worlds* (1979), *Distant Worlds* [1981], *Frontier Worlds* [1983], and others, perhaps culminating in *Metaworlds* [1994]); David King's *Dreamworks* (1983), and King and Russell Blackford's *Urban Fantasies* (1985); *Glass Reptile Breakout*, edited by Van Ikin (1990), and Ikin and Terry Dowling's *Mortal Fire* (1993); Leigh Blackmore's *Terror Australis:Best of Australian Horror* (1993); Peter McNamara & Margaret Winch's showcase *Alien Shores* (1994); Judith Raphael Buckrich and Lucy Sussex's impressive feminist fantasy anthology, *She's Fantastical* (1995); and, finally, a new *Year's Best Australian Science Fiction and Fantasy* edited by Jonathan Strahan and Jeremy G. Byrne in 1997 and 1998. The magisterial *Dreaming Down Under* (1998), edited by Jack Dann and Janeen Webb, is the biggest and most impressive collection of fantasy, SF, and horror yet done in Australia.

And that leads me to the observation that genre mixing among fantasy, SF and horror is operating in Australia as it does in, say, *Interzone* in the UK or *On Spec* in Canada (and for perhaps the same reasons—there is not a large enough pool of writers and stories of high quality to fill markets and keep genres separated). Any book or magazine published as SF may also contain pure fantasy and/or horror. If it is labeled fantasy, you'll get fantasy; horror, horror; but if it is SF, you may get something of all three, and perhaps some fabulation or speculative fiction or non-genre literary experimentation. Certainly many of the anthologies mentioned above contain all three genres (one of the criteria for inclusion in Collins's *Metaworlds: Best Australian Science Fiction* is that one story received an Honorable Mention in Datlow & Windling's *Year's Best Fantasy & Horror*).

As an outside observer, does there seem to me to be anything essentially Australian about Australian science fiction, any special aesthetic that separates it from literary production in other geographic locations? Basically, no, and I did not anticipate finding one. Is there, then, any reason for focusing attention on it the way we do in this book? Yes, because the best Australian SF writers play the international game of SF writing in the English language as well as any writers anywhere in the world, and better than many. That critic's training and attitudes mentioned above help the writers to aspire to a high standard of excellence. And this is special, and worthy of praise and attention, in a time when many writers aspire only to the standard of publishable prose. As if it didn't matter to readers.

But the aspiration to excellence that is a necessary (though not sufficient) condition for achieving excellence does matter to readers, and we offer in this anthology writers who have aspired and stories that in our opinion do achieve a share of science fictional truth and literary beauty, conceived under different constellations, under Centaurus.

David G. Hartwell
Pleasantville, NY

GEORGE TURNER

The review of George Turner's novel *Brainchild* in 1991 in the *New York Times* states: ". . . The Australian George Turner joins a hand-ful of writers—names like Stanislaw Lem and J. G. Ballard come to mind—whose works transcend national and genre boundaries and who deserve to be known by readers who would not ordinarily pick up a book labeled science fiction." Turner, who had won the Arthur C. Clarke Award for best novel for *The Sea and Summer* (aka *Drowning Towers*) in 1988, was an established novelist in Australia before turning to science fiction writing in the 1970s. He was also, from the late 1960s onward, one of the strongest and most opinionated of lit-erary critics in the SF field, to which he had a life-long attachment. And he was particularly supportive of younger writers in SF, such as Lucy Sussex and Leanne Frahm. At the time of his death in 1997, he was certainly the best known living SF writer in Australia, a ma-jor figure in the SF world. He was working on a new novel, despite stating that *Down There in Darkness* (Tor 1999), which he had writ-ten during 1995 and 1996, would be his last.

In the "Envoi" of *A Pursuit of Miracles*, his only short story col-lection, he repeated the call he had made to science fiction writers in his autobiographical book on SF, *In the Heart or in the Head*, for a "literature of considered ideas." The ideas that most engaged Turner concerned overpopulation, the widening gap between rich and poor, and the ambiguity of the state that controls most people's lives—and the possibility of a catastrophic human dieback caused by pollution, war, and/or disease. His short fiction was often the ker-nel of one of his novels.

FLOWERING MANDRAKE

Go, and catch a falling star,
Get with child a mandrake root . . .
—From the poem "Go and Catch a Falling Star," by John Donne

FOUR STARS MAKE CAPELLA: two g-type suns sharing between them five times the mass of Terra's Sol and two lesser lights seen only with difficulty from a system so far away.

Two of the fifteen orbiting worlds produced thinking life under fairly similar conditions, but the dominant forms that evolved on each bore little resemblance to each other save in the possession of upright carriage, a head, and limbs for ambulation and grasping.

When, in time, they discovered each other's existence, they fought with that ferocity of civilized hatred that no feral species can or needs to match.

The Red-Bloods fought at first because they were attacked, then because they perceived that the Green Folk were bent not on conquest but on destruction. The Green Folk fought because the discovery of Red-Blood dominance over a planet uncovered traits deep in their genetic structure. Evolution had been for them a million-year struggle against domination by emerging red-blooded forms, and their eventual supremacy had been achieved only by ruthless self-preservation—the destruction of all competition. They kept small animals for various domestic and manufacturing purposes, even ate them at times for gourmet pleasure rather than need, and feared them not at all; but the ancient enmity and dread persisted in racial defensiveness like a memory in the blood.

The discovery of a planet of Red-Bloods with a capacity for cultural competition wreaked psychological havoc. Almost without thought the Green Folk attacked.

Ships exploded, ancient cities drowned in fresh-sprung lava pits, atmospheres were polluted with death.

Beyond the Capellan system no sentient being knew of species in conflict. Galactic darkness swallowed the bright, tiny carnage.

Capella lay some forty-seven light-years from the nearest habitable planet, which its people called, by various forms of the name, Terra.

Only one member of the crew, a young officer of the Fifth Brachiate, new to his insignia and with little seniority, but infinitely privileged over the Root-kin of his gunnery unit, escaped the destruction of *Deadly Thorn*. His name (if it matters, because it was never heard anywhere again) was Fernix, which meant in the Old Tongue, "journeying forest father."

When the Triple Alert flashed he was in the Leisure Mess, sucking at a tubule of the stem, taking in the new, mildly stimulating liquor fermented from the red fluid of animals. It was a popular drink, not too dangerously potent, taken with a flick of excitement for the rumor that it was salted with the life-blood of enemy captives. This was surely untrue but made a good morale-boosting story.

Triple Alerts came a dozen a day and these bored old hands of the war no longer leapt to battle stations like sprouts-in-training. Some hostile craft a satellite's orbit distant had detected *Deadly Thorn* and launched a missile; deflector arrays would catch and return it with augmented velocity and the flurry would be over before they reached the doorway.

There was, of course, always the unlucky chance. Deflector arrays had their failings and enemy launchers their moments of cunning.

Fernix was still clearing his mouth when an instant of brilliant explosion filled space around *Deadly Thorn* and her nose section and Command Room blew out into the long night.

He was running, an automation trained to emergency, when the sirens screamed, and through the remaining two-thirds of the ship the ironwood bulkheads thudded closed. He was running for his Brachiate Enclave, where his Root-kin waited for orders, when the second missile struck somewhere forward of him and on the belly plates five decks below.

A brutal rending and splintering rose under him, and at his running feet the immensely strong deck timbers tore apart in a gaping mouth that he attempted uselessly to cross in a clumsy, shaken leap. Off balance and unprepared, he felt himself falling into Cargo Three, the Maintenance Stores hold.

At the same moment ship's gravity vanished and the lighting system failed. *Deadly Thorn* was Dead Thorn. Fernix tumbled at a blind angle into darkness, arms across his head against crashing into a pillar or bulkhead at speed. In fact, his foot caught in a length of rope, dragging him to a jarring halt.

Spread arms told him he had been fortunate to land on a stack of tarpaulins when it might as easily have been the sharp edges of toolboxes. Knowledge of the Issue Layout told him precisely where he was in the huge hold. There was a nub of escape pods in the wall not far to his left. He moved cautiously sideways, not daring to lose contact in null-gravity darkness but slithering as fast as he safely might.

Bulkheads had warped in the broken and twisted hull; both temperature and air pressure were dropping perceptibly.

He found the wall of the hold at the outer skin and moved slowly toward the vanished fore section until he felt the swelling of the nub of pods and, at last, the mechanism of an entry lock. Needing a little light to align the incised lines that would spring the mechanism, he pumped sap until the luminescent buds of his right arm shed a mild greenish radiance on the ironwood.

He thought momentarily, regretfully, of his Root-kin crew able to move only a creeper-length from their assigned beds, awaiting death without him. In this extremity he owed them no loyalty and they would expect none, but they would, he hoped, think well of him. They were neuters, expendable and aware of it, whereas he, Officer Class, free-moving breeder, carried in him the gift of new life. There could be no question of dying with them though sentimental ballads wept such ideas; they, hard-headed pragmatists, would think it the act of an idiot. And they would be right.

He matched the lock lines and stepped quickly in as the fissure opened. As he closed the inner port, the automatic launch set the pod drifting gently into space.

He activated fresh luminescence to find the control panels and light switch. A low-powered light—perhaps forty watts—shone in the small space. To his eyes it was brilliant and a little dangerous; to a culture that made little use of metals, the power-carrying copper wires were a constant threat to wood, however tempered and insulated.

To discover where he was with respect to *Deadly Thorn,* he activated an enzyme flow through the ironwood hull at a point he judged would offer the best vision. As the area cleared he was able to see the lightless hulk-occulting stars. The entire forward section was gone, perhaps blown to dust, and a ragged hole gaped amidships under the belly holds. If other pods floated nearby, he could not see them.

Poised weightless over the controls, he checked the direction of the three-dimensional compass point in its bowl and saw that the homing beam shone steadily with no flicker from intervening wreckage. His way was clear and his duty certain, to return to the Home World carrying his spores of life.

A final, useless missile must have struck *Deadly Thorn* as he stretched for the controls and never reached them. A silent explosion dazzled his eyes, then assaulted his hearing as the shock wave struck the pod. A huge plate of *Deadly Thorn*'s armor loomed in the faint glow of his light, spinning lazily to strike the pod a glancing blow that set it tumbling end over end.

He had a split second for cursing carelessness because he had not strapped down at once. Then his curled-up, frightened body bounced back and forth from the spinning walls until his head struck solidly and unconsciousness took him.

He came to in midair with legs bunched into his stomach and arms clasped round his skull. There was no gravity; he was falling free. But where?

Slow, swimming motions brought him to a handhold, but he became aware of a brutal stiffness in his right side. He pumped sap to make fingerlight, bent his head to the ribplates, and saw with revulsion that he was deformed; the plates had been broken and had healed while he floated, but had healed unevenly in a body curled up instead of stretched. Surgery would rectify that—but first he must find a surgeon.

He was struck unpleasantly by the fact that even this botched joining would have occupied several months of the somatic shutdown that had maintained him in coma while the central system concentrated on healing. (He recalled sourly that the Red-Bloods healed quickly, almost on the run.)

Deity only knew where in space he might be by now.

But what had broken his body?

There were no sharp edges in the pod. Something broken, protruding spikes?

Shockingly, yes. The compass needle had been wrenched loose and the transparent, glassy tegument, black with his sap, lay shattered around it.

He thought, *I am lost,* but not yet with despair; there were actions to be taken before despair need be faced. He fed the hull, creating windows. Spaces cleared, opening on darkness and the diamond points of far stars. He found no sign of *Deadly Thorn*; he might have drifted a long way from her after the blast. He looked for the HomeWorld, palely green, but could not find it; nor could he see the bluer, duller sister-world of the red-sapped, animal enemy.

Patiently he scanned the sky until a terrifying sight of the double star told him his search was done. It was visible still as a pair but as the twin radiances of a distant star. Of the lesser companions he could see nothing; their dimness was lost in the deep sky.

He had drifted unbelievably far. He could not estimate the distance; he remembered only from some long-ago lecture that the double star might appear like this from a point beyond the orbit of the outermost planet, the dark fifteenth world.

The sight spoke not of months of healing but of years.

Only a brain injury . . .

Every officer carried a small grooming mirror in his tunic; with it Fernix examined the front and sides of his skull as well as he was able. Tiny swellings of healed fractures were visible, telling him that the braincase had crushed cruelly in on his frontal lobes and temples. Regrowth of brain tissue had forced them out again but the marks were unmistakable. In the collision with the wreckage of *Deadly Thorn* he had crashed disastrously into . . . what?

The whole drive panel was buckled and cracked, its levers broken off or jammed down hard in their guides. They were what had assaulted him. Acceleration at top level had held him unconscious until the last drops in the tank were consumed, releasing him then to float and commence healing.

Fearfully he examined the fuel gauges. The Forward Flight gauge was empty, its black needle flush with the bottom.

The Retro fuel gauge still showed full, indicating precisely enough to balance the Forward gauge supply and bring the pod to a halt—enough, he realized drearily, to leave him twice as far from home as he now was, because the buckled panel had locked the steering jet controls with the rest. He could not take the pod into the necessary end-for-end roll. Only the useless deceleration lever still seemed free in its guides. The linkages behind the panel might still be operable, but he had no means of reaching them and no engineering skill to achieve much if he did.

He was more than lost; he was coffined alive.

Something like despair, something like fear shook his mind as he eased himself into the pilot's seat, bruises complaining, but his species was not given to the disintegrative emotions. He sat quietly until the spasm subsided.

His actions now were culturally governed; there could be no question of what he would do. He was an officer, a carrier of breeding, and the next generation must be given every chance, however small, to be born. *Very small*, he thought. His pod could drift for a million years without being found and without falling into the gravity field of a world, let alone a livable world, but the Compulsion could not be denied. The Compulsion had never been stated in words; it was in the genes, irrevocable.

Calmly now, he withdrew the hull enzymes and blacked out the universe. He started the air pump and the quiet hiss of intake assured him that it was operative still. As the pressure tank filled with the withdrawn atmosphere, he made the mental adjustment for Transformation. As with the Compulsion, there were no words for what took place. Psychologists theorized and priests pontificated but when the time and the circumstance came together, the thing happened. The process was as intangible as thought, about whose nature there was also no agreement. The thought and the need and the will formed the cultural imperative, and the thing happened.

Before consciousness left him, perhaps for ever, Fernix doused the internal heating, which was not run from the ruined drive panel.

Resuscitation he did not think about. That would take place automatically if the pod ever drifted close enough to a sun for its hull to warm appreciably, but that would not, could not happen. Deity did not play at Chance-in-a-Million with His creation.

Consciousness faded out. The last wisps of air withdrew. The temperature fell slowly; it would require several days to match the cold of space.

The Transformation crept over him as a hardening of his outer skin, slowly, slowly, until his form was sheathed in seamless bark. Enzymes clustered at the underside of his skin, fostering a hardening above and below until tegument and muscle took on the impermeability of ironwood. Officer of the Fifth Brachiate Fernix had become a huge, complex spore drifting in galactic emptiness.

He was, in fact, drifting at a surprising speed. A full tank expended at full acceleration had cut out with the pod moving at something close to six thousandths of the speed of light.

The pod's automatic distress signal shut down. It had never been heard amid the radio noise of battle fleets. The interior temperature dropped toward zero and the vegetal computers faded out as ion exchange ceased. The pod slept.

Nearly eight thousand Terrestrial years passed before the old saying was disproved: Deity did indeed play at Chance-in-a-Million with His creation.

Vegetal computers were more efficient than a metal-working culture would readily believe, though they could not compete in any way with the multiplex machines of the animal foe—in any, that is, except one.

The pod's computers were living things in the sense that any plant is a living thing. They were as much grown as fashioned, as much trained as programmed, and their essential mechanisms shared one faculty with the entity in Transformation who slept in his armor: They could adopt the spore mode and recover from it in the presence of warmth.

They had no way of detecting the passage of millennia as they slept, but their links to the skin of the pod could and did react to the heat of a g-type sun rushing nearer by the moment.

As the outer temperature rose, at first by microscopic increments, then faster and faster, the computer frame sucked warmth from the hull and, still at cryogenic levels, returned to minimal function.

At the end of half a day the chemical warming plant came silently into operation and the internal temperature climbed toward normal. Automatically the Life Maintenance computer opened the air tank to loose a jet of snow that evanesced at once into invisible gases.

The miracle of awakening came to Fernix. His outer tegument metamorphosed, cell by cell, into vegetal flesh as his body heat responded; first pores, then more generalized organs sucked carbon dioxide from the air and return from Transformation began.

Emergence into full consciousness was slow, first as an emptiness in which flashes of dreams, inchoate and meaningless, darted and vanished; then as a closer, more personal space occupied by true dreams becoming ever more lucid as metabolism completed its regeneration; finally as an awareness of self, of small pressures from the restricted pilot's seat, of sap swelling in capillaries and veins, of warmth and the sharp scent of too-pure air. His first coherent thought was that a good life caterer would have included some forest fragrance, mulch or nitrate, in the atmosphere tank.

From that point he was awake, in full muscular and mental control, more swiftly than a Red-Blood could have managed. (But the Red-Bloods had no Transformation refuge that the scientists could discover; in deep cold or without air they died and quickly rotted. They were disgusting.)

He knew that only rising warmth could have recalled him.

A sun?

The Great Twin itself?

That was not possible.

Thanking Deity that the computers were not operated from the drive panel, he directed them to provide enzyme vision and in a moment gazed straight ahead at a smallish yellow sun near the center of the forward field.

So Deity did . . . He wasted no time on that beyond a transient thought that every chance must come to coincidence at some time in the life of the universe—and that he might as well be winner as any other.

He asked the navigating computer for details: distance, size, luminescence. Slowly, because vegetal processes cannot be hurried, the thing made its observations and calculations and offered them. Obediently it unrolled the stellar chart and almanac—and Fernix knew where he was.

And, he thought, *little good* that *brings me.*

This was a star not easily naked-eye visible from the Home World, but the astronomers had long ago pinpointed it and its unseen planets. He was forty-seven light-years from home (his mind accepted without understanding the abyss of time passed) on a course plunging him into the gravity well of an all-too-welcoming star at some thirty-two miles per second. The computer assured him that on his present course this yellow sun, though a child by comparison with the Great Twin, was powerful enough to grasp him and draw him into its atmosphere of flame.

But he had not come so far across time and space to die sitting still, eaten alive by a pigmy star.

He needed to buy time for thought. Deceleration alone was not enough for useful flight.

There was a blue-green planet, the almanac told him, which might possibly offer livable conditions. The hope was small in a universe where minute changes of temperature, orbit, or atmosphere composition could put a world forever beyond life; but the Deity that had guided him so finely and so far could surely crown His miracle with a greater one.

If he could achieve steering . . .

He was tempted to jemmy the cover off the Drive Panel and expose the linkages, but common sense suggested that he would merely cause greater damage. He was coldly aware of ignorance and lack of mechanical talent; the maze of linkages would be to him just that—a maze, impenetrable.

Because he was untrained he failed for several hours to hit on the possibility that the computer, once programmed to act rather than simply inform the pilot, might operate directly on the machine structures, bypassing linkages and levers. The entertainment media had imprinted him and all but those who actually operated spacecraft with a mental picture of pilots working by manual control, whereas it might be necessary only to tell the computer what he wanted.

That turned out to be anything but simple. As a gunnery officer he considered himself computer competent, but he slept several times before he penetrated the symbols, information needs, and connections of the highly specialized machine. Like most junior officers he had been rushed through an inadequate basic training and sent into space innocent of the peacetime auxiliary courses, with no expertise in other than visual navigation.

But, finally, the steering jets turned the pod end for end, the main jet roared triumphantly, and the little craft slowed at the limit of deceleration his consciousness could bear. Held firmly in his straps with an arm weighing like stonewood, he questioned the computer about trajectories and escape velocities and how it might take him to the third planet of the yellow star.

It balanced distance against fuel and calculated a slingshot rounding of the central sun, which would bring him economically to his goal, his destiny. There would be, Fernix knew, only a single chance and choice.

A Miner's Mate is, more correctly, an Asteroid Mining Navigational and Mass Detection Buoy. One of them sat sedately above a group of fairly large iridium-bearing "rocks" in the Belt, providing guidance for the occasional incoming or outgoing scow and warning against rogue intruders—meteorites or small asteroids in eccentric orbits. It carried a considerable armament, including two fusion bombs capable of shattering a ten-million-ton mass, but large wanderers were rare and collision orbits rarer still. Its warnings commonly did little more than send miners scurrying to the sheltered side of their rock until the danger passed.

Since space debris travels at speeds of miles per second, the sensitivity radius of the Mate's radar and vision systems was necessarily large. It registered the incoming pod at a million kilometers. Being fully automatic, it had no intelligence to find anything peculiar in the fact that it saw the thing before the mass detectors noted its presence. It simply radioed a routine alert to the mines and thereafter conscientiously observed.

The Shift Safety Monitor at the communication shack saw the tiny, brilliant point of light on his screen and wondered briefly what sort of craft was blasting inward from the outer orbits. Scientific and exploratory probes were continuously listed, and there were none due in this area of the System. Somebody racing home in emergency? Automatically he looked for the mass reading and there was none. What could the bloody Mate be doing? The mass of metal that put out such a blast must be easily measurable.

The Monitor's name was John Takamatta; he was a Murri from Western Queensland. This particular group of mines was a Murri venture and he was a trained miner and emergency pilot, now taking his turn on the dreary safety shift. Like most of his people he rarely acted without careful observation first; he waited for the Mate to declare or solve its problem.

The Mate's problem was that it could not recognize timber or any substance that let most of its beam through and diffused it thoroughly in passage. There was metal present but not enough to contain the tubes for such a drive blast and there was ceramic, probably enough for linings, but the amorphous mass surrounding these was matter for conjecture and conjecture was outside its capacity.

However, it tried, feeding back to the Mines computer a flicker of figures that mimicked a state of desperate uncertainty and gave the impression of a large, fuzzy thing of indefinite outline secreting within it some small metal components and ceramic duct lining.

Takamatta tried to enlarge the screen image but the size of the light did not change. It was either very small or far away or both.

The Mate's hesitant figures hovered around something under a ton, but no mass so slight could contain such brilliance. Yet it could only be a ship and there were no ships of that nursery size. He rang the dormitory for the off-duty, sleeping Computer Technician. Albert Tjilkamati would curse him for it, but they were related, men of the same Dreaming, and the curse would be routinely friendly.

Albert came, cursed, watched, sent a few test orders to the Mate, and decided that it was not malfunctioning, yet the oscillating, tentative figures suggested a human operator floundering with an observation beyond his competence. Once the analogy had occurred to him, he saw the force of it.

"Something it can't recognize, John. Its beam is being diffused and spread from inner surfaces—like light shining into a box of fog. The receptors don't understand. John, man, it's picked up something new in space! We'll be in the newscasts!"

He called Search-and-Rescue's advance base in the Belt.

The Search-and-Rescue Watch Officer knew Albert Tjilkamati; if he said "strange" and "unusual," then strange and unusual the thing was.

"OK, Albert, I'll send a probe. Get back to you later."

He eased a torpedo probe out of its hangar, instructed its computers, and sent it to intercept the flight path of the stranger. The probe was mainly a block of observational and analytical equipment in a narrow, twelve-meter tube, most of which was fuel tank; it leapt across the sky at an acceleration that would have broken every bone in a human body.

Starting from a point-five-million kilometers retrograde from the orbit of the Murri Mines, it used the Miner's Mate broadcast to form a base for triangulation and discovered at once that the incoming craft was decelerating at a g number so high that the probe would have to recalculate its navigating instructions in order to draw alongside. It would, in fact, have to slow down and let the thing catch up with it.

The Watch Officer asked his prime computer for enhancement of the fuzzy mass/size estimates of the Mate, but the machine could not decide what the craft was made of or precisely where its edges were.

At this point, as if aware of observation, the craft's blast vanished from the screen.

The Watch Officer was intrigued but not much concerned; his probe had it on firm trace and would not let go. He notified HQ Mars, which was providentially the nearest HQ to him, of an incoming "artificial object of unknown origin," accompanied by a full transcript of the Mate's data, stated, "Intelligence probe dispatched," and sat back to contemplate the probable uproar at HQ Mars. The lunatic fringe would be in full babble.

The computer, not Fernix, had cut the pod's blast because its velocity had dropped to the effective rate for rounding the system's sun. There would be corrections later as approach allowed more accurate data on the star's mass and gravity, but for two million kilometers the pod would coast.

Fernix drifted into sleep. Transformation sleep conferred no healing, being essentially a reduction of metabolism to preservative zero; nothing was lost or gained during the hiatus. So he had awakened still in reaction to the stress of escape from *Deadly Thorn* and now needed sleep.

He woke again to the stridency of an alarm. The computer flashed characters in urgent orange, proclaiming the presence of a mass in steady attendance above and to the right of the pod and no more than twice its length distant.

He realized sluggishly that the mass must be a ship; only a ship equipped with damping screens could have approached so closely without detection.

The thought brought him fully alert. He opened a narrow vision slit and at first saw nothing; then he observed the slender occulting of stars. The thing was in darkness and probably painted black, else the central sun should have glinted on its nose.

If this was an artifact of the local life, he needed to find out what he could about it, even at the risk of exposing himself—if that was indeed a risk. The crew might well be friendly. He primed a camera for minimum exposure and, to aid it, turned the pod's lighting up full and opened the vision slit to his head's width for a tenth of a second.

It was enough for the camera to take its picture. It was enough, also, for the other to shoot through the gap a beam of intense light to take its own picture and blind Fernix's weak eyes. He flung his arms across his face and grunted with pain until his sight cleared. He stayed in darkness with the slit closed. He reasoned that he had been photographed by a race whose vision stretched farther into the shortwave light spectrum than his and not so far into the gentler infrared.

When the ache in his eyes subsided, he examined his own infrared picture. It showed a slender needle of nondescript color, dull and nonreflective, without visible ports. The small diameter of the craft inclined him to think it was an unmanned reconnaissance probe. His evolutionary teaching dictated that an intelligent life-form must perforce have its brain case and sensory organs raised well above ground level, and no such entity could have stood upright or even sat comfortably in that projectile.

He considered what action he might take.

He had been outplayed at the observation game and could do nothing about that. His weaponless pod was not equipped to fight, which was perhaps as well; nothing would be gained by antagonizing these unknown people. Evasive action was out of the question. His fuel supply was low and his computer's decisions had been made on limits too tight for any but last-ditch interference from himself; there was none for ad hoc maneuver.

He could take no action. The next move must come from outside.

Conclusion reached, he slept. The Search-and-Rescue call sign squealed in the shack, the screen cleared, and Takamarra looked up from his novel as the Watch Officer hailed him. "John, oh, John, have we got something here! This one will puncture holes in your Dreaming!"

John said coldly, "Indeed." He was no traditionalist but did not appreciate light handling of his cultural mores by a white man.

Some fifteen seconds would pass before his reply reached SAR and fifteen more for the Watch Officer's response. In that time he digested the message and concluded that the unlikely was true, that the intruding craft was extrasystemic. Alien. And that the existence of life among the stars *could* have some effect on the credibility of Murri Dreaming.

Then he decided that it would not. Incursion of the white man and knowledge of a huge world beyond the oceans had altered most things in his people's lives but not that one thing, the Dreamings around which the Murri cultures were built. Science and civilization might rock on their foundations as the word went out, *We are not alone*, but the ancient beliefs would not shift by the quiver of a thought.

Willy Grant's voice said, "Get this carefully, John. Make notes. We need the biggest scow you've got because yours is the nearest mining group. We want to pick this little ship out of the sky, but we can't get a magnetic grapple on it because what little metal there is appears to be shielded. The best bet is to clamp it in the loading jaws of your Number Three scow if it's available. The thing is only ten meters long and three wide, so it will fit in easily. The scow can dawdle sunward and let the outsider catch up with it until they are matched for speed. Forty-eight hours at one-point-five g should do it. This is an Emergency Order, John, so time and fuel compensation will be paid. Relay that to your Manager, but pronto. The scow's computer can talk to mine about course and speed, and we'll have your Manager's balls in a double reef knot if he raises objections. Got it?"

"Got it, Willy." He repeated the message for check. "Hang on while I pass it." Minus the threat; the Elder might not appreciate blunt humor.

The Murri Duty Manager preserved the Old Man routine of unimpressed self-possession, which fooled nobody. He turned his eyes from his screen, contemplated infinity in his fingernails for a respectable sixty seconds, raised his white-bearded head with an air of responsible decision making, and said, "Number Three scow is empty and available. It shall be floated off. The SAR computer can then take over." He would not have had the nerve to say otherwise; nobody in space flouted SAR.

Grant, on the other screen, heard the message and beat down the temptation to wink at John; the tribal old dear would be outraged and so would his miners. The Murri were good blokes but in some areas you had to tread carefully. When the Manager had cut out, he said, "Now, John, this'll rock you from here to Uluru. Look!"

He displayed a picture of the intruder illuminated by the probe's beam. It was shaped roughly like an apple seed, symmetrical and smooth, its line broken only by what must be a surprisingly narrow jet throat. Its color seemed to be a deep brown, almost ebony.

"Now, get this!" He homed the viewpoint to a distance of a few inches from the hull. "What do you make of it?"

What John saw surprised him very much. The hull surface was grained like wood; there was even a spot where some missile (sand-grain meteoroid?) had gouged it to expose a slightly lighter color and what was surely a broken splinter end.

Willy carried on talking. You do not wait for an answer across a thirty-second delay. "Looks like wood, doesn't it? Well, see this!" The view roved back and forth from nose to tail, and the wave pattern of the grain flowed evenly along the whole length. "You'd think they grew the thing and lathed it out of a single block. And why not? A ship doesn't have to be built of steel, does it? I know timber couldn't stand the takeoff and landing strains, but how about if they are ferried up in bulk in a metal mother ship or built on asteroids and launched at low speed? Or there could be means of hardening and strengthening timber; we don't know because we've never needed to do it. But a race on a metal-poor world would develop alternative technologies. I'd stake a month's pay the thing's made of wood, John."

In John's opinion he would have won the bet.

Willy did not display the other picture, the shocker taken when the alien tried to photograph the probe. Under instruction he had given Takamatta enough to satisfy immediate curiosity without providing food for the idiot fantasy that flourishes when laymen are presented with too much mystery and too few answers.

Alone he studied the startling hologram, at lifesize, which his computer had built for him.

It seemed that the alien had also taken a shot of the probe just as the automatic camera took advantage of the widening slit in the intruder's hull. The thing's face—"face" for want of a word—stared at him over what was surely a camera lens.

The alien—being, entity, what you would—seemed generally patterned on an anthropoid model with a skin dappled in gray and green. The head and neck protruded above shoulders from which sprang arms or extensions of some kind—probably arms, Willy thought, because on the thing's camera rested what should be fingers, though they looked more like a bunch of aerial roots dropped by some variety of creeper but thicker and, judging by their outlandish grasping, more flexible than fingers.

In the narrow head he could discern no obvious bone structure under thick—flesh? The face was repulsive in the vague fashion of nightmare when the horror is incompletely seen. There was a mouth, or something in the place of a mouth—an orifice, small and round with slightly raised edges where lips should have been. He thought of a tube that would shoot forward to fix and suck. Nose there was none. The eyes—they had to be eyes—were circular black discs with little holes at their centers.

He guessed hazily that black eyes, totally receptive of all wavelengths of light, could be very powerful organs of vision, given the outlandish nervous system necessary to operate them. Or, perhaps, the central holes were the receptors, like pinhole cameras.

Ears? Well . . . there were flaps on the sides of the head, probably capable of manipulation since the hologram showed one raised and one nearly flush with the gray-and-green flesh. A third flap, partly open, in what must be called the forehead and revealing under it an intricately shaped opening reminiscent of the outer ear, suggested all-around hearing with a capacity for blocking out sound and/or direction finding. A useful variation.

Hair there seemed to be none, but on the crown of the bud-shaped skull sat a plain, yellowish lump like a skittish party hat, a fez six inches or so high and four wide. Yet it seemed to be part of the head, not a decoration. He could make nothing of it.

There remained the faintly purplish cape around the thing's shoulders. Or was it a cape? It hung loosely over both shoulders and its lower edges fell below the rim of the vision slit, but it was parted at the throat and he had an impression that what he saw at the parting was dappled flesh rather than a garment. On closer examination he thought that the "cape" was actually a huge flap of skin, perhaps growing from the back of the neck. He thought of an elephant's ears, which serve as cooling surfaces.

An idea that had been knocking for expression came suddenly into the light and he said aloud, "The thing's a plant!"

At once he was, however unwarrantably, certain that he looked on the portrait of a plant shaped in the caricature of a man. The "cape" was a huge leaf, not for cooling but for transpiration. The seemingly boneless skull and tentacular hands made vegetable sense; the thing would be infinitely flexible in body, acquiring rigidity as and where needed by hydrostatic pressure. He pondered root systems and acquired mobility as an evolutionary problem without a glimmer of an answer, but his impression would not be shifted.

The thing from out there was a motile vegetable.

The setting up of ore refineries on asteroids that were usually worked out in a few years would have been prohibitively expensive, so the main refinery had been located on Phobos, and there the output of all Belt companies was handled without need for the scows to make planetfall. The saving in expensive fuel was most of what made the ventures profitable. Nor was there any waste of manpower on those lonely voyages; the scows were computer-directed from float-off to docking.

An empty scow, not slowed by several hundred tons mass of ore, could accelerate at a very respectable g-rate. Number Three scow from the Murri outfit caught its prey dead on time, forty-eight hours after float-off. Forty-eight hours of silent flight, accompanied by a probe that made no move, took toll of nerves. Fernix slept and wondered and theorized from too little knowledge and slept again. At the second waking he fed, sparsely, not knowing how long his supplies must stretch; he injected a bare minimum of trace elements into the mulch tray with just enough water to guarantee ingestion, and rested his feet in it. The splayed pads protruded their tubules like tiny rootlets as his system drew up the moisture. He preferred mouth feeding but in the pod he had no choice.

The brief euphoria of ingestion passed and his mood flickered between fear and hope. Did the probe accompany him for a purpose unknown or did its controllers watch and wait to see what he would do?

He would do nothing. The vacillations of mood rendered him unfit to decide with proper reason. He writhed internally but sat still, did nothing.

His people, slow-thinking and phlegmatic, did not slip easily into neurosis but he was muttering and twitching when new outside action came. He switched into calm observation and appraisal.

The alarm indicated a new presence in space, ahead of him but drawing close. He chanced a pinhole observation in the direction of the new mass but could see nothing. Whatever the thing was, either he was closing on it or it waited for him. His computer reported that the mass was losing some speed, and he decided that it intended to match his course.

His instruments described it as long in body and large in diameter but not of a mass consistent with such size. An empty shell? Such as a cargo vessel with cleared holds?

Shortly he found that the probe had vanished and a quite monstrous ship was slipping back past him; the light of the system's sun shone on its pitted, blue-painted nose. It was old in space and about the size of a raiding destroyer but showed no sign of armament.

It slipped behind him and took up a steady position uncomfortably close to him. He was tempted to discover what it would do if he accelerated or changed course, then thought of his thin-edge supply of fuel. Do nothing, nothing; pray for friendly beings.

He saw with a frisson of tension that it was moving swiftly up to him.

Looming close to collision point, it opened its forward hull in a vast black mouth and gullet, like the sea monsters of his baby tales.

Its forward surge engulfed his pod, swallowed it whole, and closed about it as something (grasping bands?) thudded on the pod's shell and held captor and prey to matched speeds. He was imprisoned in a vast, empty space, in darkness.

After a while he cleared the pod's entire shell, turning it into a transparent seed hanging in a white space illuminated by his interior lights. White, he thought, for optimum lighting when they work in here.

The space was utterly vacant. At the far end, roughly amidships he calculated, vertical oblong outlines were visible against her white paint— entry hatches. So the entities stood upright; he had expected no less. Evolutionary observation and theory (formulated so long ago, so far away) suggested that an intelligent, land-based being must stand erect, that it should carry brain and major sensory organs at its greatest height, that it should possess strong limbs for locomotion and grasping in limited number according to the law of minimum replication, that it—

—a dozen other things whose correctness he should soon discover in fact.

He saw that his pod was clamped above and below in a vise powerful enough to hold it steady in a turbulent maneuvre. It was, his instruments told him, basically iron, as was the hull of the ship.

He was not sure whether or not he should envy a race that could be so prodigal of metal. Their technologies would be very different from those of the Home World.

He waited for them but they did not come.

Could their ship be unmanned, totally remote-controlled? His people had a few such—had had a few such—but their radio-control techniques had been primitive and doubtful. Given unlimited iron and copper for experiment . . .

He waited.

Suddenly the pod was jerked backward as the captor vessel decelerated at a comfortable rate; he could have withstood twice as much.

Homing on a world nearby? He could not tell; his instruments could not penetrate the metal hull.

He thought, *I am learning the discipline of patience.*

The crew of a ship approaching Phobos would have seen few surface installations though the moonlet housed the HQ Outer Planets Search and Rescue, an Advanced College of Null-Gravity Science, the Belt Mining Cooperative Ore Refineries, a dozen privately owned and very secretive research organizations, and, most extensive of all, the Martian Terraforming Project Laboratories and Administrative Offices.

All of these were located inside the tunneled and hollowed rock that was Phobos.

It had been known for a century or more that the moonlet was slowly spiraling inward for a long fall to Mars, and Martian Terraforming did not want some six thousand cubic kilometers of solid matter crashing on the planet either before or after its hundred-year work was completed. So the interior had been excavated to the extent of nearly twenty percent of the total mass (the engineers had vetoed more lest stress changes break the rock apart) and the detritus used as a reaction mass, fired by a barrage of electromagnetic catapults into space in trajectories exquisitely designed to miss the Martian horizon. The slow change in delta-v had corrected the inward drift, but more subtle measures would eventually have to be taken, and one College research unit was permanently engaged in deciding what such measures might be (subtle measures is easily said) and how they might be applied (less easily said).

Phobos, swinging six thousand kilometers above the Martian surface, was a busy hive where even gossip rarely rose above the intellectual feuds and excitements of dogged dedication—

—until a junior ass in SAR cried breathlessly, careless of eager ears, "Bloody thing looks like a lily pad with head and chest. A plant, bejesus!"

After that, SAR had trouble preventing the information being broadcast throughout the System, but prevent it they did. The last thing a troubled Earth needed as it emerged from the Greenhouse Years and the Population Wars was the political, religious, and lunatic fringe upheaval expectable on the cry of *We are not alone*.

Possum Takamatta, John's younger brother, a Communications Operative with SAR, pondered the hologram transmitted from the Belt and asked, "Just what sense do they think an ecologist might make of that?"

"God knows," said ecologist Anne Spriggs of Waterloo, Iowa, and Martian Terraforming, who was as pink-and-white as Possum was deep brown-black, "but I know some botany, which is more than anyone else around here does, so I just might make a useful contribution, read guess."

"With no tame expert at hand, they're desperate?"

"Possum, wouldn't you be desperate?"

"Why? I'm just interested. My people knew that 'more things in heaven and earth' line twenty thousand years before Shakespeare. You got any ideas?"

"No, only questions."

"Like?"

"Is it necessarily a plant because it reminds us of a plant? If it is, how does a rooted vegetable evolve into a motile form?"

"Who says it's motile? We've only got this still picture."

"It has to be to go into space. It couldn't take a garden plot with it."

"Why not? A small one, packed with concentrates, eh? And why should it have to become motile? Might have descended from floating algae washed up in swamplands with plenty of mud. Developed feet instead of roots, eh?"

Anne said with frustration, "So much for the ecologist! The local screeneye has more ideas than I do."

He tried soothing because he liked Anne. "You're hampered by knowledge, while I can give free rein to ignorance."

She was not mollified. "Anyway, is it plant or animal? Why not something new? Who knows what conditions formed it or where it's from?"

"From at least Alpha Centauri; that's the nearest. It came in at thirty k per second, and decelerating; if that was anything like its constant speed it's been on its way for centuries. That's a long time for one little lone entity."

"Why not FTL propulsion?"

"Come off it, girl! Do you credit that shit?"

"Not really."

"Nor does anyone else. If it came from anywhere out there, then it's an ancient monument in its own lifetime."

"In the face of that," she said, "I feel monumentally useless. What in hell am I good for?"

"Marry me and find out."

"In a humpy outside Alice Springs?"

"I've a bloody expensive home in Brisbane."

"And I've a fiancé in Waterloo, Iowa."

"The hell you say!"

"So watch it, Buster!" She planted a kiss on the tip of his ear. "That's it. Everything else is off limits."

"In Australia we say out of bounds."

"In Australia you also say 'sheila' when you mean 'pushover.' "

Not quite right but near enough and she certainly made better viewing than the mess on the screen.

In another part of the cavern system the Base Commander SAR held a meeting in an office not designed to hold thirteen people at once—himself and the twelve managers of the moonlet's private research companies. Commander Ali Musad's mother was Italian, his father Iraqi, and himself a citizen of Switzerland; SAR took pride in being the least racially oriented of all the service arms.

He had set the office internal g at one-fifth, enough to keep them all on the floor, however crowded; it is difficult to dominate a meeting whose units sit on walls and ceiling and float away at a careless gesture.

He said, "I have a problem and I need your help. As Station senior executive I can give orders to service groups and enforce them; of you ladies and gentlemen representing civilian projects, I can only ask."

They resented his overall authority. They remained silent, letting him wriggle on his own hook, whatever it was. Then they might help, cautiously, if advantage offered.

"Some of you will have heard of a . . . presence . . . in space. A foolish boy talked too loudly in a mess room and no doubt the whisper of what he said has gone the rounds."

That should have produced a murmur but did not. Only Harrison of Ultra-Micro asked, "Something about a green man in a sort of lifeboat?"

"Something like that."

"I didn't pay attention. Another comedian at work or has someone picked up a phantom image from a dramacast?"

"Neither. He's real."

Someone jeered softly, someone laughed, most preferred a sceptical lift of eyebrows. Chan of Null-g Germinants suggested that managers had low priority on the rumor chain. "Ask the maintenance staff; they're the slush bearers."

Musad told them, "It isn't silly season slush; it's real; I've seen it. Talk has to be stopped."

Still they did not take him too seriously. "Can't stop gossip, Commander."

"I mean stop it getting off Phobos."

"Too late, Commander. If it's a little green men story, it's gone out on a dozen private coms by now."

He said stiffly, "It hasn't. I've activated the censor network." The shocked silence was everything he could have desired. "Every com going out is being scanned for keywords; anything containing them is being held for my decision."

He waited while anger ran its course of outrage and vituperation. They didn't give a damn about little green men but censorship was an arbitrary interference guaranteed to rouse fury anywhere across the System. The noise simmered down in predictable protests: ". . . abuse of power . . . justifiable only in war emergency . . . legally doubtful on international Phobos . . ."

Melanie Duchamp, the Beautiful Battleaxe of Fillette-Bonded Aromatics, produced the growling English that browbeat boardrooms: "You will need a vairy good reason for this."

No honorific, he noted; Melanie was psyching herself for battle. "It was a necessary move. Now I am asking you to ratify it among your company personnel."

"Fat chance," said one, and another, "We'd have mutiny on our hands."

He had expected as much. "In that case I shall order it as a service necessity and take whatever blame comes." And leave them to accept blame if events proved his action the right one. "I can promise worse than mutiny if the news is not controlled."

At that at least they listened. He told them what he knew of the intruding ship, its contents, and the speculation about its origin, and then, "Let this news loose on Earth and Luna and we'll have every whining, power-grabbing, politicking ratbag in the System here within days. I don't mean just the service arms and intelligence wood beetles and scientists and power brokers; I mean the churches and cults and fringe pseudosciences and rich brats and with nothing better to do. I also mean your own company executives and research specialists and the same from your merchant rivals—to say nothing of the print and electronic media nosing at your secrets. How do you feel about it?"

It was Melanie who surrendered savagely. "I will support you—under protest."

"You don't have to cover your arse, Melanie. I'll take the flack."

"So? There will be lawsuits, class actions that will cost the companies millions."

"No! I will declare a Defence Emergency."

"Then God or Allah help you, Commander."

Harrison said, "You can't do it. You say the thing seems to be unarmed; how can you invoke defence?"

"Possible espionage by an alien intruder. If that won't do, the Legal Section will think up something else."

In the end they agreed if only because he left them no choice. Satisfied that they would keep the lid on civilian protest, he threw them a bone: He would call on them to supply experts in various fields not immediately available among the service personnel on Phobos, because he intended to bring the thing inside and mount as complete an examination as possible before allowing a squeak out of Phobos Communications.

They brightened behind impassive agreement. With their own men at the center of action, they would be first with the news as history was made in their particular corners . . . with profit perhaps . . . and wily Musad was welcome to the lawsuits.

When they had gone he summoned his secretary. "All on record?"

"Yes, sir."

"Am I covered?"

"I think so. They will cooperate in case you retaliate by leaving them out of the selection of expert assistance. Which means that you must take at least one from each firm, however useless."

"Yes. Many messages intercepted?"

"Seven for your attention. Three to media outlets. It seems we have some unofficial stringers aboard."

"The buggers are everywhere. I don't want media complaints when they find out that their lines were stopped. They stir up too much shit." He recalled too late that Miss Merritt was a Clean Thinker. "Sorry."

She was unforgiving. "Nevertheless there will be complaints." Her tone added, And serve you right. Clean Thinkers held that censorship was unnecessary in a right-minded community—and so was crude language.

"I think the courts will uphold me."

"No doubt, sir. Will that be all?"

"Yes, Miss Merritt." And to hell with you, Miss Merritt, but you are too efficient to be returned to the pool.

The Number Three scow drifted down through darkness to hover over the moonlet's docking intake, a square hole like a mineshaft that came suddenly alive with light.

The docking computer took control, edged the huge scow, precisely centered, through the intake, and closed the entry behind it.

A backup computer waited, ready to take over in the event of malfunction, and a human operator waited with finger on override, prepared to assume manual control at an unpredictable, unprogrammable happening. This was a first in the history of the human race and almost anything, including the inconceivable, might occur.

Nothing did.

The computer took the scow evenly through the second lock, closed it, moved the vessel sideways through the Repair and Maintenance Cavern to the largest dock, and set it smoothly bellydown on the floor. Then, because nobody had thought to tell it otherwise, it followed normal procedure and switched on one-eighth g in the floor area covered by the vessel, sufficient to ensure cargo stability.

Watching in his office screen, Musad cursed somebody's thoughtlessness—his own, where the buck stopped—and opened his mouth for a countermanding order. Then he thought that any damage was already done. Anyway, why should there be damage? No world with an eighth g would have produced a life-form requiring an atmosphere, and the probe had certainly reported an atmosphere of sorts. Whatever lived inside the . . . lifeboat? . . . should be comfortable enough.

He shut his mouth and called Analysis. "Full scan, inside and out. There is a living being inside; take care."

Analysis knew more than he about taking care and had prepared accordingly. The first necessity was to establish the precise position of the thing inside—being, entity, et, what you would—and ascertain that it was or was not alone. So, a very delicate selection of penetrating radiation in irreducibly small doses, just enough to get a readable shadow and keep it in view.

Analysis had far better instrumentation than the comparatively crude probe and established at once that the thing was alive and moving its . . . limbs? . . . while remaining in seated position facing the nose of the vessel. Able now to work safely around the thing, visitor, whatever, Analysis unleashed its full battery of probe, camera, resolution, and dissection.

The results were interesting, exciting, even breathtaking, but no scrap of evidence suggested where the little ship might have come from.

Musad was an administrator, not a scientist; Analysis gave him a very condensed version of its immensely detailed preliminary report—blocked out, scripted, eviscerated, rendered down, and printed for him in under three hours—highlighting the facts he had called for most urgently:

The living entity in the captive vessel would be, when it stood, approximately one and a half meters tall. It showed the basic pentagonal structure—head and four limbs—which might well represent an evolutionary optimum design for surface dwellers in a low-g Terrene range. There was a rudimentary skeletal structure, more in the nature of supportive surface plates than armatures of bone, and the limbs appeared tentacular rather than jointed. This raised problems of push-pull capability with no answers immediately available.

Spectroscopic reading was complicated by the chemical structure of the vessel's hull, but chlorophyll was definitely present in the entity as well as in the hull, and the bulky "cape" on its shoulders showed the visual characteristics of a huge leaf. It was certainly a carbon-based form and seemed to be about ninety percent water; there was no sign of hemoglobin or any related molecule.

The atmosphere was some forty percent denser than Terrene air at sea level, a little light in oxygen but heavy with water vapor and carbon dioxide.

Tentative description: Highly intelligent, highly evolved, motile plant species.

We always wondered about aliens and now we've got one. What does he eat? Fertilizer? Or does that snout work like a Venus's-flytrap?

The small amounts of iron in the vessel—tank linings and a few hand tools—argued a metal-poor environment, ruling out any Sol-system planet as a world of origin.

As if they needed ruling out!

The ceramic lining of the jet would require longer evaluation but appeared to be of an unfamiliar crystalline macrostructure. All the other parts of the vessel, including the hull, were timber. There was nothing unusual about the composition of the various woods but a great deal unusual about the treatments they had undergone, presumably for hardening and strengthening; no description of these could be hazarded without closer examination. (There followed a dissertation on the possible technology of a timber-based culture. Musad skipped over it.)

Dating procedures were at best tentative on materials whose isotopic balance might not match Terrene counterparts, but guesstimates gave a pro tem figure of between seven and ten thousand Terrene years. The signatories declined to draw any conclusions as to the age of the vegetal pilot or where he might have originated.

And all it does is sit there, sit there, sit there, occasionally moving a tentacle in some unguessable activity. So, what next?

He was taken by an idea so absurd that it would not go away, an idea that might, just might stir the creature into some action. It was a sort of "welcome home" idea—rather, an introduction . . .

He called the Projection Library.

Fernix slept and woke while the deceleration held him comfortably in his seat. He slept again and woke, nerves alert, when deceleration ceased.

He opened a tiny vision hole but saw only his prison still closed around him.

Shortly there was a perceptible forward motion and the slightest of centrifugal effects as the direction changed several times. Then his captor ship settled, gently for so large a transport. His pod shook momentarily and was still.

Suddenly there was gravity, not much of it but enough to aid balance and movement.

Not that he had any intention of moving; he could not afford movement. He needed energy. Food alone was not enough; his thousands of chloroplasts needed sunlight for the miracle of conversion to maintain body temperature, muscle tone, even the capacity to think effectively. There was a spectrum lamp aboard but its batteries would operate for only a limited time; a pod was not intended for pan-galactic voyaging.

Yet full alertness could be demanded of him at any moment; he must pump his body resources to a reasonable ability for sustained effort. He used a third of the lamp's reserve, switched it off, and continued at rest in the pilot seat.

There was little assessment he could make of his position. His captors had demonstrated no technological expertise (beyond a squandering of metal) that could not have been duplicated on the Home World, nor had they attempted to harm him. So they were civilized beings, reasonably of a cultural status with which he could relate.

On the panel, radiation detectors flickered at low power. He was, he guessed, being investigated. So, this race was able to operate its instruments *through* the metal hull outside. That proved little; a race evolving on a metal-rich world would naturally develop along different lines of scientific interest from one grown from the forests of Home. Different need not mean better.

It was an exciting thought, that on another world a people had emerged from the nurturing trees to conquer the void of space.

The thought was followed by another, more like a dream, in which his people had traversed the unimaginable distance between stars to colonize this faraway system, facing and overcoming the challenges of worlds utterly variant from their own, inventing whole new sciences to maintain their foothold on the universe.

The open-minded intelligence can contemplate the unfamiliar, the never-conceived, and adapt it to new modes of survival.

He had arrived by freakish accident; could not his people have made the crossing during the eons while he crept through space in free fall? The idea of using Transformation for survival while a ship traversed the years and miles had been mooted often.

His reverie was broken by a squealing hiss from outside the pod.

Outside. They were supplying his prison with an atmosphere.

Chemist Megan Ryan was the first to curse Musad for mishandling the approach to the alien ship. Suited up and ready to examine the hull, she heard someone at the closed-circuit screen ask, "What the hell's going on? They've let air into the scow."

She clawed the man out of the way and punched Musad's number to scream at him, "What do you think you're bloody well doing?"

"And who do you think you're talking to, Captain-Specialist?"

She took a deep, furious breath. "To you . . . sir. Who ordered air into the scow?"

"I did." His tone said that if she objected, her reason had better be foolproof.

"But why, why, why?" She was close to stuttering with rage.

His administrative mind groped uneasily at the likelihood of an error of unscientific judgment and decided that this was not a moment for discipline. "To provide air and temperature for the investigating teams to work in. What else?"

She swallowed, conscious of a red face and tears of frustration. "Sir, that ship has been in space for God only knows how long, in the interstellar deep. Its timber hull will have collected impact evidence of space-borne elements and zero-temperature molecules. That evidence will by now have been negated by temperature change and highly reactive gases. Knowledge has been destroyed."

She was right and he would hear about it later from higher echelons; he simply had not thought from a laboratory standpoint. "I'm sorry, Meg, but my first priority for investigation is the traveler rather than the ship. He represents more urgent science than a little basic chemistry."

The wriggling was shameful and he knew it; he had forgotten everything outside the focus of his own excitement, the alien.

She was glaring still as he cut her off. He spoke to the Library: "Have you got much?"

"A good representative selection, sir. Vegetable environments from different climates. As you requested, no human beings."

"Good. I don't want humans presented to him in stances and occupations he—it—won't understand. Get a computer mockup ready—a naked man, good physique, in a spacesuit. Set it up so that the suit can be dissolved from around him. I want a laboratory effect, emotionally distancing, to reduce any "monster" reaction."

"Yes, sir," the screen murmured.

"He's put out a probe of some sort," said another screen. "Sampling the air maybe."

Musad turned to screen 3 and the alien ship. The temperature in the hold had risen to minus thirty Celsius and vapor was clearing rapidly from the warming air. Visibility was already good. When the air reached normal temperature and pressure for their planet, Fernix reasoned, they would come for him.

They did not come, though temperature and pressure leveled off. He was disappointed but accepted that there would be circumstances that he could not at present comprehend.

He extended a hull probe for atmosphere analysis, to find the outside pressure very low while the water vapor content hovered at the "dry" end of the scale and the carbon dioxide reading was disturbingly light. He could exist in such an atmosphere only with difficulty and constant reenergizing. Acclimatization would take time.

Through the generations, he reasoned, his people would have made adaptation, for the vegetal germ was capable of swift genetic change. There would be visible differences by now—of skin, of stature, of breathing areas—but essentially they would be his people still . . .

He saw a flash of colored movement outside his spyhole and leaned forward to observe.

In the prison space, a bare arm's length from the pod's nose, a silver-green tree flickered into existence, took color and solidity to become a dark, slender trunk rising high before spreading into radiating fronds. His narrow field of vision took in others like it on both sides and beyond, ranged at roughly equal distances. Beyond them again, a broad river. The palmate forms were familiar (mutations, perhaps, of ancestral seeds carried across the void?) as was the formal arrangement on a riverbank, the traditional files of the rituals of Deity.

As he watched, the scene changed to a vista of rolling highlands thickly covered with conical trees of the deep green of polar growths, and in the foreground a meadow brilliant with some manner of green cover where four-legged, white beasts grazed. Their shape was unfamiliar, but his people had used grazing beasts throughout historical time; children loved them and petted them and wept when they were slaughtered. Only the anthropoid monsters from the sister world could terrify the young and rouse the adults to protective furry.

As the picture faded he wondered had the man-beasts been utterly destroyed. Some would have been preserved for study . . . mated in zoos . . . exhibited . . .

A new view faded in and the hologram placed him at the edge of a great pond on whose surface floated green pads three or four strides across their diameter. He recognized water-dwelling tubers though the evolved details were strange, as were the flitting things that darted on and above them. Forms analogous to insects, he guessed, thinking that some such line was an almost inevitable product of similar environment.

Cautiously he opened the vision slit wider and saw that the huge picture extended away and above as though no walls set limits to it. He looked upward to an outrageously blue, cloudless sky that hurt his eyes. This world, without cloud cover, would be different indeed.

He realized with a burst of emotion, of enormous pride and fulfillment, that he was being shown the local planet of his people, accentuating the similarities that he would recognize, welcoming him Home as best they could.

The picture changed again and this time he wept.

His pod lay now in the heart of a jungle clearing, brilliant-hued with flowers and fungi that stirred memory though none were truly familiar. Tall, damp trunks lifted to the light, up to the tight leaf cover where the branching giants competed for the light filtered down through cloud cover. For there was cloud cover here, familiarly gray, pressing down and loosing its continuous drizzle to collect on the leaves and slide groundward in silver-liquid tendrils. Bright insect-things darted, and larger things that flapped extensions like flattened arms to stay aloft in surprisingly effective fashion. These were strange indeed as were the four-legged, furry things that leapt and scurried on the ground, chewing leaves and grubbing for roots.

The whole area could have been a corner of his ancestral estate, transformed yet strangely and truly belonging. He had been welcomed to a various but beautiful world.

With the drunken recklessness of love and recognition, he activated the enzyme control and cleared the entire hull of the pod for vision. It was as though he stood in the heart of a Home playground, amid surroundings he already loved.

Soon, soon his people of these new, triumphant years must show themselves . . .

. . . and as though the desire had triggered the revelation, the jungle faded away and a single figure formed beyond the nose of the pod, floating in darkness as only a hologram could, hugely bulky in its pressure suit, face hidden behind the filtering helmet plate but wholly human in its outward structure of head and arms and motor limbs.

He left the seat to lean, yearning, against his transparent hull, face pressed to the invisible surface, arms spread in unrestrained blessing.

The figure spread its arms in a similar gesture, the ancient gesture of welcome and peace, unchanged across the void and down the centuries.

The outlines of the pressure suit commenced to blur, to fade, revealing the creature within.

The naked body was white, stiff-limbed, fang-mouthed, bright-eyed with recognition of its helpless, immemorial foe.

It floated, arms outstretched, in mockery of the ritual of peace.

The Red-Blood.

The enemy.

When the first hologram appeared—the Nile-bank scene of the planting program for binding the loosening soil—Musad watched for reaction from the ship but there was none.

The Swedish panorama, its forest of firs contrasted with the feeding sheep, pleased him better. On any habitable world there must be some environment roughly correlating with this, some scene of bucolic peace.

Then came the Victoria lilies and their pond life—A screen voice said, "It's opened the vision slit a little bit. It's interested."

It? Too clinical. Musad would settle for he. Could be she, of course, or some exotic gender yet unclassified.

The fourth scene, the jungle display, brought a dramatic result. The entire hull of the ship became cloudy, then translucent and—vanished. The interior was revealed from nose to jet.

Musad did not bother scanning the internal fittings; a dozen cameras would be doing that from every angle. He concentrated on the alien.

It—*he* rose swiftly out of his chair, head thrust forward in the fashion of a pointing hound, and stepped close to the invisible inner hull. He was not very tall, Musad thought, nor heavily muscled but very limber, as though jointless. (But how could a jointless being stand erect or exert pressure? His basically engineering mind thought vaguely of a compartmentalized hydrostatic system, nerve-operated. Practical but slow in reaction time.) He lifted his tentacular arms, spreading the great "cape" like a leaf to sunlight, and raised them over his head in a movement redolent of ecstasy.

Could jungle, or something like it, be the preferred habitat? *He* was plainly enthralled.

The jungle scene faded and the hold was in darkness save for the low-level radiance of the little ship's interior lighting.

The computer's creation, man-in-space-suit, appeared forward of the ship, floating a meter above the floor. *He* leaned, in unmistakable fascination, close against the inner hull. *He* pressed his face against the invisible timber like a child at a sweetshop window and slowly spread his arms. His "hands" were bunches of gray-green hoses until the fingers separated and stiffened. Musad could see that the tubular members straightened and swelled slightly; he could detect no muscle but they had plainly hardened as they pressed against the wood. It seemed to Musad that he stood in a posture of unrestrained, longing welcome.

The Library operator must have caught the same impression and in a moment of inspiration had the space-suited figure duplicate the outspread stance of friendship. Then he began to fade the armor, baring the symbolic man within.

He remained perfectly still.

Musad advanced his viewpoint until the alien's face dominated his screen. The face changed slowly. Thin folds of skin advanced across the huge black eyes, closing until only small circles remained. The mouth tube retracted and simultaneously opened wide in another circle, a great "Oh!" of wonder and surprise. The face resembled nothing more than a child's drawing of a happy clown.

Musad pulled back the view and saw that the "cape" was now fully raised behind the head, like some vast Elizabethan jeweled collar, save that the leaf veins shone bright yellow.

"He's happy," Musad said to anyone who might hear him. "He's happy!"

He stepped slowly back from the hull, lowered an arm to one of the panels—and the dark hull was there again, lightless, impenetrable.

Musad could not, never did know that what he had seen was a rictus mask more deeply murderous than simple hatred could rouse and mold.

For Fernix, recognition of the Red-Blood was more than a cataclysm; it was a trigger.

On the Home World, when the end came it was recognized.

An end was an end. Intellect lost overriding control and biological forces took over. Genetically dictated reactions awoke and the process of Final Change began.

Pollination, initiated in the peak years of adolescence and suspended until the Time of Flowering, was completed in a burst of inner activity. At the same time stimulant molecules invaded his cerebrum, clarifying and calming thought for the Last Actions. In the domed crown of his skull, the bud stirred; the first lines of cleavage appeared faintly on the surface as the pressure of opening mounted. His people flowered once only in life—when, at the moment of leaving it, the pollen was gathered by exultant young partners while the dying one's children were born.

There would be none to gather pollen from Fernix, but his salute should be as royal as his lineage.

The initial burst of killing rage against the Red-Blood ebbed slowly. Had the projection been indeed a physical Red-Blood he would have been unable to master the urge to murder, he would have been out of the pod and in attack without conscious thought, obeying an impulse prehistorically ancient. The fading of the thing helped return him to reason.

It had shown him in the opening of its mouth, in what the things called a "smile," that he was the helpless captive of enemy cruelty. The display of fangs had been the promise of the last insult to honorable extinction, the eating of his body before Final Change could translate him to Deity.

It did not seem to him irrational that he had so simply projected as fact his people's conquest of space and the new worlds; his psychology carried no understanding other than that the vegetal races were naturally dominant in the intellectual universe. The Home World scientists found it difficult to account for the evolution of thinking Red-Bloods on the neighbor planet; such things, they reasoned, could only be sports, the occasional creations of a blind chance, having no destiny.

Fernix, orthodox because he had no training beyond orthodoxy, could only grasp that his people must have been totally destroyed in that long-ago war, overwhelmed by unimaginable disaster. Not they had conquered interstellar space but the Red-Bloods. He, Fernix, was alone in a universe empty of his kind.

He knew, as he regained mental balance, that Final Change had begun. There was no fear of death in his people's psychology, only an ineradicable instinct to perpetuate the species; Fernix felt already the changes in his lower limbs heralding the swift growth of embryonic offspring, motile units in one limb, rooted slave-kin in the other.

That they would be born only to die almost at once did not trouble him; he could not abort births governed by autonomic forces and he was not capable of useless railing against the inevitable. He had seen the terror of Red-Bloods as death came to them and been unable to comprehend the working of brains that in extremity rendered their possessors useless and demented. How could such creatures have mastered the great void?

He settled again into the pilot's seat and with quick actions emptied the whole store of trace elements into the feeding bed and thrust his feet deep into the mulch.

With triumphant pleasure he opened the emergency carbon dioxide cock and drained the tank into the pod's atmosphere. His death would be such a flowering of insult as few had ever offered the Red-Bloods. The burst of mocking blossom, in the color of their own life fluid, would take his people out of history in a blaze of derisive laughter at their barbarian destroyers.

That was not all. One other gesture was possible—the winning of a last battle although the war was long over.

The alien had shut himself in. The shortwave team reported that he had resumed the pilot seat and as far as they could determine had moved little in several hours.

Anne Ryan blamed Musad and was careless who heard her. "It's a vegetable form and he lulls it into euphoria with holograms of arboreal paradise, then confronts it with a bone-and-meat structure as far outside its experience as it is outside ours! It's probably half-paralysed with shock. It needs time to assimilate the unthinkable. We need a brain here, not a bloody bureaucrat."

Melanie's contribution seemed more vicious for being delivered in a strong Breton accent. "The thing showed its teeth! The plant was terrified. It has no teeth, only a sucking tube! So you bare teeth at it and it runs to hide! Who would not?"

Musad thought the women had a point and that he had acted with more authority than prudence. But, what should be done on first contact with the unknowable? The only certainty had been that he must take some action; if he had ordered the scientists to leave the thing alone, he would have had rebellion on his hands and eventually questions asked in political arenas; if he had given them their heads, they would have mauled each other in battles for priority and he would have ended up cashiered for inefficient management of an undisciplined rabble.

Now, when he had no idea what to do, help came from his own SAR, from the shortwave investigation team. "Something's going on inside, sir, but we don't know what it means. In the first minutes after it closed off the vision we could see it—the shadow of it, that is—gesturing like an angry man. Then it went back to the seat and made motions like pressing little buttons or flicking small levers—maybe. We can't be sure because with so much wood it's hard to get even a shadow picture. At any rate it made some adjustments because the carbon dioxide component in its air went up eight per cent. The water vapor content seems to have increased, too, and the temperature has risen from thirty-five degrees to forty-six."

"Hothouse conditions!"

"Superhothouse, sir."

"What's he up to? Forcing his growth?"

"We think more likely some other growth it carries in there. Maybe it has seeds in that thing like a tub at its feet. That's if the things make seeds."

Seeds or sprouts or tubers or buds . . . What do you do when you don't know what you're dealing with? How do you even think?

The different, careful tones of the radiographer said, "Sir, it doesn't want any part of us."

"Seems so."

"If it won't come to us, sir, shouldn't we go to it?"

Musad had no false pride. "You have a suggestion, Sergeant?"

"We could put a duroplastic tent around its ship, sir, big enough to allow a bunch of scientists to work in space suits, and fill it with an atmosphere matching the alien's."

"Then?"

"Cut a hole in the hull, sir, and get it out. Cut the ship in half if necessary."

That should at least keep everybody quiet until the next decision—except, perhaps, the alien—and anything he did would be marginably preferable to stalemate. And—oh, God!—he would have to decide who to allow into the tent and who must wait his or her turn.

He noted the Sergeant's name; one man at least was thinking while the rest boiled and complained. Yet he hesitated to give a command that in itself would be controversial.

He was still hesitating when the Analysis team gave an update: "It hasn't moved from the chair in two hours. Now chest movement has ceased; it is no longer breathing. It is probably dead."

That settled it. He ordered positioning of the tent and matching of atmospheres. That done, they must recover the body before serious deterioration set in.

Fernix was not dead. Not quite. The complex overlapping of birth and death made the passing of his kind a drawn-out experience.

Fully aerated, he had ceased to breathe. The new ones in his lower limbs drew their nourishment from the mulch and no longer needed him, were in the process of detaching themselves. When they dropped free, his life's duty, life's story, life's meaning would be complete . . .

. . . save for the one thing more, planned and prepared.

Now he could only wait with tentacle/finger curled for tightening, remaining perfectly still, having no reason to move, conserving strength for the final action.

His quietly sinking senses told him dully of sounds outside the pod and a fading curiosity wondered what they did out there. He thought of activating hull vision but the thought slipped away.

A sword of white fire cut a section from the hull alongside the control panels a long arm's length from him and he was aware, without reacting as alertness ebbed (only the last command holding strength for its moment), of a suited figure entering the pod, followed by another. And another.

Red-Bloods. He no longer hated or cared. They would be dealt with.

One knelt by his lower limbs and unintelligible sounds dribbled from the grille in its helmet. He could not tell what it did.

Came the Last Pain, the splitting of cleavage lines in his bud sheath as the death flower swelled and bloomed from his ruined head.

At the moment of brain death his body obeyed the command stored in its nervous system for this moment. The curled tentacle/finger retracted, giving the computer its last command.

Under the tent the science teams went at it with a will. A small piece to of timber was carved, with unexpected difficulty, from the alien craft's hull and rushed to a laboratory. The preliminary report came very quickly: ". . . a technique of molecular fusion—everything packed tight in cross-bonded grids. Not brittle but elastic beyond anything you'd believe. Take a real explosive wallop to do more than make it quiver and settle back."

The ceramic jet lining seemed impervious to common cutting methods, and nobody wanted to use force at this stage. Soft radiation told little and they agreed that hard radiation should not be risked until they had found a means of excising small samples.

Chemanalysis had managed to create a computer mock-up of the contents of the fuel tank, derived from hazy shortwave and sonar pictures, and was excited by a vision of complex molecular structures that promised incredible power output but must remain illogical until their catalysts were derived.

Carbon Dating, on safer ground with a piece of timber more or less analysed, certified the ship as eight thousand years old, give or take a hundred, which made no sense at all of the presence of a living thing within.

Well, it had been living, in some fashion, perhaps still was—in some fashion. But, centuries?

Then the section of hull was cut out and the first group went in. There was surprisingly little to see. The cabin was small because most of the vessel's volume was fuel storage and the living space was parsimoniously uncluttered. There was a timber panel with wooden keys midmounted like tiny seesaws, which might be on-off controls, another console-type installation that could reasonably be a keyboard, and clusters of incomprehensible recording instruments—some circular, some square, and some like bent thermometers. There was also a sort of dashboard set with small levers, badly smashed.

Ecologist Anne Spriggs of Waterloo, Iowa, surveyed the alien with the despair of a preserver arrived too late. The creature was an unpleasant sight, its gray-and-green skin muted in death to patched and streaky brown, its slender body collapsed upon itself until it resembled nothing so much as a stick-figure doll. It had died with a tentacle resting loosely—round one of the on-off seesaw controls.

A tiny movement, low down, brought her kneeling cumbersomely to scrutinize the container of mulch on the floor beneath the creature's lower limbs. The limbs hung oddly above it, their exposed, footless termini lighter colored than the body, as if only recently exposed. Broken off? Cut off? How and why?

Several brown sticks lay on the surface of the mulch. One of them wriggled. Despite an instant revulsion she reached a gloved hand to pick it up. It was a tuber of some kind, like a brown artichoke formed fortuitously with nubs for vestigial arms and legs and head, and spots for eyes.

Musad spoke in her helmet. "What have you there, Anne?"

"I think it's an embryo alien. It's like—" she shrugged and held it up.

He suggested, "A mandrake."

That was a somehow nasty idea, smelling of small evil.

A rending crack from the dead creature itself startled the suited figures crowding into the hull and those who watched through screens.

They were offered a miracle. The excrescence on the thing's skull opened flaps like huge sepals and a blood-red crimson bolt shot a meter's length of unfolding bloom free of the body. It unfurled not a single flower but a clustered dozen packed in and on each other, each opening the flared trumpet of a monstrous lily.

The flowers expanded in a drunken ecstasy of growth, bending down and over the dead thing that fed them until it was wrapped in a shroud of blood. From the hearts of the trumpets rose green stamens like spears, each crowned with a golden magnet of pollen.

And not another, Anne thought, for such a flourish of procreation to attract and join.

In the surprised stillness someone, somewhere, whistled softly and another hissed an indrawn breath of wonder. Melanie's voice spoke from her office deep in the moonlet, Breton roughness smoothed in awe, "I have never seen so lovely a thing."

An unidentified voice said, "Like a salute from somewhere out there."

And that, Musad thought, would be the line the media would fall on with crocodile tears: A Dying Salute from Infinity. . . .

Then Anne Spriggs said with a touch of panic, "It moved!"

"What moved?"

"The body. It moved its hand. On the lever."

"A natural contraction," Musad said. "The whole external form appears to have shrunk."

Fernix had placed a slight delay on the ignition. He wanted the Red-Bloods to see his derisive flowering, but he also wanted to be decently dead before the fury struck.

When the fuel spark finally leapt the ignition gap, his life was over; he had timed his going with dignity. Home World would have honored him.

The jet roared, filling the scow's hold with a sea of fire before the craft skidded across the floor to crash through the soft steel of the imprisoning hull.

Those outside the scow had a microsecond's view of death in a blinding, incandescent torpedo that struck the rock wall of the Maintenance Cavern and disintegrated. The cloudburst of fuel from the shattered tank burgeoned in a twenty-thousand-degree ball of fire, engulfing and destroying the watchers in a hell-breath and licking its tongues of bellowing flame into the adjoining corridors and tunnels, a monstrous blast of heat driving death before it.

Thirty-seven scientists died and more than three hundred general personnel. Nearly a thousand others suffered serious burns.

The material damage ran to the total of a dozen national debts, and the lawsuits of the private companies on Phobos made the fortunes of the lawyers on both sides.

Heads fell on the political chopping block, Musad's first among the offerings to the smug virtue of scapegoating.

First contact between intelligent cultures had been made.

A. BERTRAM CHANDLER

A. Bertram Chandler, writer and sea captain, was already established as a science fiction writer in John W. Campbell's *Astounding* and the other genre magazines in England and America by the time he moved from England to Australia in 1956. (Well-known stories from 1945–1955 include "Giant Killer," "Boomerang," and "Jetsam.") But his major reputation followed the publication of his novels, beginning in the early 1960s, and for at least the next two decades, from the early '60s to the early '80s, he was the most famous Australian SF writer. His "Rim of Space" series, featuring the heroic Commodore John Grimes, the suave, wry, competent space officer, was his most popular work. He was certainly the most prolific Australian SF writer, the author of forty-four novels and over two hundred short stories, published worldwide in genre magazines. And he was the only Australian SF writer ever to be guest of honor at a World Science Fiction Convention outside of Australia (Chicago, 1982). This story was first published in *Galaxy* in 1971, and later collected in *The Hard Way Up* (1972).

THE MOUNTAIN MOVERS

OLGANA—EARTH-TYPE, REVOLVING around a Sol-type primary— is a backwater planet. It is well off the main Galactic trade routes, although it gets by quite comfortably by exporting meat, butter, wool, and the like to the neighboring, highly industrialized Mekanika System. Olgana was a Lost Colony, one of those worlds stumbled upon quite by chance during the First Expansion, settled in a spirit of great thankfulness by the personnel of a hopelessly off course, completely lost emigrant lodejammer. It was rediscovered—this time with no element of chance involved—by the Survey Service's *Trail Blazer*, before the colonists had drifted too far from the mainstream of human culture. Shortly thereafter there were legal proceedings against these same colonists, occupying a few argumentative weeks at the Federation's Court of Galactic Justice in Geneva, on Earth; had these been successful they would have been followed by an Eviction Order. Even in those days it was illegal for humans to establish themselves on any planet already supporting an intelligent life-form. *But*—and the colonists' Learned Counsel made the most of it—that law had not been in existence when *Lode Jumbuk* lifted off from Port Woomera on what turned out to be her last voyage. It was only a legal quibble, but the aborigines had no representation at Court—and, furthermore, Counsel for the Defense had hinted, in the right quarters, that if he lost his case he would bring suit on behalf of his clients against the Interstellar Transport Commission, holding that body fully responsible for the plight of *Lode Jumbuk*'s castaways and their descendants. ITC, fearing that a dangerous and expensive precedent might be established, brought behind-the-scenes pressure to bear and the case was dropped. Nobody asked the aborigines what they thought about it all.

There was no denying that the Olganan natives—if they were na-tives—were a backward race. They were humanoid—to outward appear-ances human. They did not, however, quite fit into the general biological pattern of their world, the fauna of which mainly comprised very primitive egg-laying mammals. The aborigines were mammals as highly developed as Man himself, although along slightly different lines. There had been sur-prisingly little research into Olganan biology, however; the Colony's highly competent biologists seemed to be entirely lacking in the spirit of scientific curiosity. They were biological engineers rather than scientists, their main concern being to improve the strains of their meat-producing and wool-bearing animals, descended in the main from the spermatozoa and ova that *Lode Jumbuk*—as did all colonization vessels of her period—had carried under refrigeration.

To Olgana came the Survey Service's Serpent Class Courier *Adder,* Lieutenant John Grimes commanding. She carried not-very-important dis-patches for Commander Lewin, Officer-in-Charge of the small Federation Survey Service Base maintained on the planet. The dispatches were deliv-ered and then, after the almost mandatory small talk, Grimes asked, "And would there be any Orders for me, Commander?"

Lewin—a small, dark, usually intense man—grinned. "Of a sort, Lieu-tenant. Of a sort. You must be in Commodore Damien's good books. When *I* was skipper of a Courier it was always a case of getting from Point A to Point B as soon as possible, if not before, with stopovers cut down to the irreducible minimum. . . . Well, since you ask, I received a Carlottigram from Officer Commanding Couriers just before you blew in. I am to inform you that there will be no employment for your vessel for a period of at least six weeks local. You and your officers are to put yourselves at my disposal. . . ." The Commander grinned again. "I find it hard enough to find jobs enough to keep my own personnel as much as half busy. So . . . enjoy yourselves. Go your merry ways rejoicing, as long as you carry your personal transceivers at all times. See the sights, such as they are. Wallow in the fleshpots—such as *they* are." He paused. "I only wish that the Com-modore had loved me as much as he seems to love you."

"Mphm," grunted Grimes, his prominent ears reddening. "I don't think that it's quite that way, sir." He was remembering his last interview with Damien. *Get out of my sight!* the Commodore had snarled. *Get out of my sight, and don't come back until I'm in a better temper if ever. . . .*

"Indeed?" with a sardonic lift of the eyebrows.

"It's this way, Commander. I don't think that I'm overly popular around Lindisfarn Base at the moment. . . ."

Lewin laughed outright. "I'd guessed as much. Your fame, Lieutenant, has spread even to Olgana. Frankly, I don't want you in my hair, around my Base, humble though it be. The administration of this planet is none of my concern, luckily, so you and your officers can carouse to your hearts' content as long as it's not in my bailiwick."

"Have you any suggestions, sir?" asked Grimes stiffly.

"Why, yes. There's the so-called Gold Coast. It got started after the Trans-Galactic Clippers started calling here on their cruises."

"Inflated prices," grumbled Grimes. "A tourist trap. . . ."

"How right you are. But not every TG cruise passenger is a millionaire. I could recommend, perhaps, the coach tour of Nevernever. You probably saw it from Space on your way in—that whacking great island continent in the Southern Hemisphere."

"How did it get its name?"

"The natives call it that—or something that sounds almost like that. It's the only continent upon which the aborigines live, by the way. When *Lode Jumbuk* made her landing there was no intelligent life at all in the Northern Hemisphere."

"What's so attractive about this tour?"

"Nevernever is the only unspoiled hunk of real estate on the planet. It has been settled along the coastal fringe by humans, but the outback— which means the Inland and most of the country north of Capricorn—is practically still the way it was when Men first came here. Oh, there're sheep and cattle stations, and a bit of mining, but there won't be any real development, with irrigation and all the rest, until population pressure forces it. And the aborigines—well, most of them—still live in the semidesert the way they did before *Lode Jumbuk* came." Lewin was warming up. "Think of it, Lieutenant, an opportunity to explore a primitive world while enjoying all mod. cons.! You might never get such a chance again."

"I'll think about it," Grimes told him.

He thought about it. He discussed it with his officers. Mr. Beadle, the First Lieutenant, was not enthusiastic. In spite of his habitual lugubrious mien he had a passion for the bright lights and made it quite clear that he had enjoyed of late so few opportunities to spend his pay that he could well afford a Gold Coast holiday. Von Tannenbaum, Navigator; Slovotny, Electronic Communications; and Vitelli, Engineer, sided with Beadle. Grimes did not try to persuade them—after all, he was getting no commission from the Olganan Tourist Bureau. Spooky Deane, the Psionic Communications Officer, asked rather shyly if he could come along with the Captain. He was not the companion that Grimes would have chosen—but he was a telepath, and it was just possible that his gift would be useful.

Deane and Grimes took the rocket mail from Newer York to New Melbourne, and during the trip Grimes indulged in one of his favorite whinges, about the inability of the average colonist to come up with really original names for his cities. At New Melbourne—a drab, oversized village on the southern coast of Nevernever—they stayed at a hotel that, although recommended by Trans-Galactic Clippers, failed dismally to come up to Galactic standards, making no attempt whatsoever to cater for guests born and brought up on worlds with widely differing atmospheres, gravitational fields, and dietary customs. Then there was a day's shopping, during which the two spacemen purchased such items of personal equipment as they had been told would be necessary by the office of Nevernever Tours. The following morning, early, they took a cab from their hotel to the Nevernever Coach Terminus. It was still dark, and it was cold, and it was raining.

They sat with the other passengers, all of whom were, like themselves, roughly dressed, in the chilly waiting room, waiting for something to happen. To pass the time Grimes sized up the others. Some were obviously outworlders—there was a TG Clipper in at the spaceport. Some—their accent made it obvious—were Olganans, taking the opportunity of seeing something of their own planet. None of them, on this dismal morning, looked very attractive. Grimes admitted that the same could be said about Deane and himself; the telepath conveyed the impression of a blob of ectoplasm roughly wrapped in a too gaudy poncho.

A heavy engine growled outside, and bright lights stabbed through the big windows. Deane got unsteadily to his feet. "Look at that, Captain!" he exclaimed. "Wheels, yet? I expected an inertial drive vehicle, or at least a hoverbus!"

"You should have read the brochure, Spooky. The idea of this tour is to see the country the same way as the first explorers did, to get the *feel* of it . . ."

"I can get the feel of it as well from an aircraft as from this archaic contraption!"

"We aren't all telepaths. . . ."

Two porters had come in and were picking up suitcases, carrying them outside. The tourists, holding their overnight grips, followed, watched their baggage being stowed in a locker at the rear of the coach. From the PA system a voice was ordering, "All passengers will now embus! All passengers will now embus!"

The passengers embussed, and Grimes and Deane found themselves seated behind a young couple of obviously Terran origin, while across the aisle from them was a pair of youngish ladies who could be nothing other than schoolteachers. A fat, middle-aged man, dressed in a not very neat uniform of gray coveralls, eased himself into the driver's seat. "All aboard?" he asked. "Anybody who's not, sing out!" The coach lurched from the terminus on to the rain-wet street, was soon bowling north through the dreary suburbs of New Melbourne.

Northeast they ran at first, and then almost due north, following the coast. Here the land was rich, green, well-wooded, with apple orchards, vineyards, orange groves. Then there was sheep country, rolling downland speckled with the white shapes of the grazing animals. "It's wrong," Deane whispered to Grimes. "It's all wrong. . . ."

"What's wrong, Spooky?"

"I can feel it—even if you can't. The . . . the resentment. . . ."

"The aborigines, you mean?"

"Yes. But even stronger, the native animals, driven from their own pastures, hunted and destroyed to make room for the outsiders from beyond the stars. And the plants—what's left of the native flora in these parts. Weeds to be rooted out and burned, so that the grapes and grain and the oranges may flourish. . . ."

"You must have felt the same on other colonized worlds, Spooky."

"Not as strongly as here. I can almost put it into words. . . . *The First Ones* let us alone."

"Mphm," grunted Grimes. "Makes sense, I suppose. The original colonists, with only the resources of *Lode Jumbuk* to draw upon, couldn't have made much of an impression. But when they had all the resources of the Federation to draw upon . . ."

"I don't think it's quite that way . . . ," murmured Deane doubtfully.

"Then what *do* you think?"

"I . . . I don't know, Captain. . . ."

But they had little further opportunity for private talk. Slowly at first, and then more rapidly, the coachload of assorted passengers was thawing out. The driver initiated this process—he was, Grimes realized, almost like the captain of a ship, responsible for the well-being, psychological as well as physical, of his personnel. Using a fixed microphone by his seat he delivered commentaries on the places of interest that they passed, and, when he judged that the time was ripe, had another microphone on a wandering lead passed among the passengers, the drill being that each would introduce himself by name, profession, and place of residence.

Yes, they were a mixed bag these tourists. About half of them were from Earth—they must be, thought Grimes, from the TG Clipper *Cutty Sark* presently berthed at the spaceport. Public Servants, lawyers, the inevitable Instructors from universities, both major and minor, improving their knowledge of the worlds of the Federation in a relatively inexpensive way. The Olganans were similarly diversified.

When it came to Grimes's turn he said, "John Grimes, spaceman. Last place of permanent residence St. Helier, Channel Islands, Earth."

Tanya Lancaster, the younger and prettier of the two teachers across the aisle, turned to him. "I thought you were a Terry, John. You don't mind my using your given name, do you? It's supposed to be on the rules on this tour. . . ."

"I like it, Tanya."

"That's good. But you can't be from the *Cutty Sark*. I should know all the officers, at least by sight by this time."

"And if I were one of *Cutty Sark*'s officers," said Grimes gallantly (after all, this Tanya wench was not at all bad looking, with her chestnut hair, green eyes, and thin, intelligent face), "I should have known you by this time."

"Oh," she said, "you must be from the Base."

"Almost right."

"You are making things awkward. Ah, I have it. You're from that funny little destroyer or whatever it is that's berthed at the Survey Service's end of the spaceport."

"She's not a funny little destroyer," Grimes told her stiffly. "She's a Serpent Class Courier."

The girl laughed. "And she's *yours*. Yes, I overheard your friend calling you 'Captain' . . ."

"Yes. She's mine. . . ."

"And now, folks," boomed the driver's amplified voice, "how about a little singsong to liven things up? Any volunteers?"

The microphone was passed along to a group of young Olganan students. After a brief consultation they burst into song.

" 'When the jolly *Jumbuk* lifted from Port Woomera
Out and away for Altair Three
Glad were we all to kiss the tired old Earth good-bye—
Who'll come a-sailing in *Jumbuk* with me?

" 'Sailing in *Jumbuk*, sailing in *Jumbuk*,
Who'll come a-sailing in *Jumbuk* with me?
Glad were we all to kiss the tired old Earth good-bye—
You'll come a-sailing in *Jumbuk* with me!

" 'Then there was Storm, the Pile, and all the engines dead—
Blown out to Hell and gone were we!
Lost in the Galaxy, falling free in sweet damn all—
Who'll come a-sailing in *Jumbuk* with me?

" 'Sailing in *Jumbuk*, sailing in *Jumbuk*,
Who'll come a-sailing in *Jumbuk* with me?
Lost in the Galaxy, falling free in sweet damn all—
You'll come a sailing in *Jumbuk* with me!

" 'Up jumped the Captain, shouted for his Engineer,
Start me the diesels, one, two, three!
Give me the power to feed into the Ehrenhafts—
You'll come a-sailing in *Jumbuk* with me!' "

"But that's *ours!*" declared Tanya indignantly, her Australian accent suddenly very obvious. "It's our 'Waltzing Matilda!' "

" 'Waltzing Matilda' never was yours," Grimes told her. "The words—yes, but the tune, no. Like many another song it's always having new verses tacked on to it."

"I suppose you're right. But these comic lyrics of theirs—what are they all about?"

"You've heard of the Ehrenhaft Drive, haven't you?"

"The first FTL Drive, wasn't it?"

"I suppose you could call it that. The Ehrenhaft generators converted the ship, the lodejammer, into what was, in effect, a huge magnetic particle. As long as she was on the right tramlines, the right line of magnetic force, she got to where she was supposed to get to in a relatively short time. But a magnetic storm, tangling the lines of force like a bowl of spaghetti, would throw her anywhere—or nowhere. And these storms also drained the micropile of all energy. In such circumstances all that could be done was to start up the emergency diesel generators, to supply electric power to the Ehrenhaft generators. After this the ship would stooge along hopefully, trying to find a habitable planet before the fuel ran out. . . ."

"H'm." She grinned suddenly. "I suppose it's more worthy of being immortalized in song than our sheep-stealing Jolly Swagman. But I still prefer the original." And then, aided by her friend, Moira Stevens—a fat and cheerful young woman—she sang what she still claimed was the original version. Grimes allowed himself to wonder what the ghost of the Jolly Swagman—still, presumably, haunting that faraway billabong—would have made of it all. . . .

That night they reached the first of their camping sites, a clearing in the bush, on the banks of a river that was little more than a trickle, but with quite adequate toilet facilities in plastic huts. The coach crew—there was a cook as well as the driver—laid out the pneumatic pup tents in three neat rows, swiftly inflating them with a hose from the coach's air compressor. Wood was collected for a fire, and folding grills laid across it. "The inevitable steak and billy tea," muttered somebody who had been on the tour before. "It's *always* steak and billy tea . . ."

But the food, although plain, was good, and the yarning around the fire was enjoyable, and finally, Grimes found that the air mattress in his tent was at least as comfortable as his bunk aboard *Adder*. He slept well, and awoke refreshed to the sound of the taped Reveille. He was among the first in line for the toilet facilities and, dressed and ready for what the day might bring, lined up for his eggs and bacon and mug of tea with a good appetite. Then there was the washing up, the deflation of mattresses and tents, the stowing away of these and the baggage—and, very shortly after the bright sun had appeared over the low hills to the eastward, the tour was on its way again.

On they drove, and on, through drought-stricken land that showed few signs of human occupancy, that was old, old long before the coming of Man. Through sun-parched plains they drove, where scrawny cattle foraged listlessly for scraps of sun-dried grass, where tumbleweed scurried across the roadway, where dust devils raised their whirling columns of sand and light debris. But there was life, apart from the thirsty cattle, apart from the gray scrub that, with the first rains of the wet season, would put forth its brief, vivid greenery, its short-lived, gaudy flowers. Once the coach stopped to let a herd if sausagekine across the track—low-slung, furry quadrupeds, wriggling like huge lizards on their almost rudimentary legs. There was a great clicking of cameras. "We're lucky, folks," said the driver.

"These beasts are almost extinct. They were classed as pests until only a couple of years ago—how they've been reclassed as protected fauna. . . ." They rolled past an aboriginal encampment where giant gaunt, black figures, looking arachnoid rather than humanoid, stood immobile about their cooking fires. "Bad bastards those," announced the driver. "Most of the others will put on shows for us, will sell us curios—but not that tribe. . . ."

Now and again there were other vehicles—diesel-engined tourist coaches like their own, large and small hovercraft, and, in the cloudless sky, the occasional high-flying inertial-drive aircraft. But, in the main, the land was empty, the long, straight road seeming to stretch to infinity ahead of them and behind them. The little settlements—pub, general store, and a huddle of other buildings—were welcome every time that one was reached. There was a great consumption of cold beer at each stop, conversations with the locals, who gathered as though by magic at each halt. There were the coach parks—concentration camps in the desert rather than oases, but with much appreciated hot showers and facilities for washing clothing.

On they drove, and on, and Grimes and Deane teamed up with Tanya and Moira. But there was no sharing of tents. The rather disgruntled Grimes gained the impression that the girl's mother had told her, at an early age, to beware of spacemen. Come to that, after the first two nights there were no tents. Now that they were in regions where it was certain that no rain would fall, all hands slept in their sleeping bags only under the stars.

And then they came to the Cragge Rock reserve. "Cragge Rock," said the driver into his microphone, "is named after Captain Cragge, Master of the *Lode Jumbuk*, just as the planet itself is named after his wife, Olga." He paused. "Perhaps somewhere in the Galaxy there's a mountain that will be called Grimes's Rock—but with all due respect to the distinguished spaceman in our midst he'll have to try hard to find the equal to Cragge Rock! The Rock folks, is the largest monolith in the known Universe— just a solid hunk of granite. Five miles long, a mile across, half a mile high." He turned his attention to Tanya and Moira. "Bigger than *your* Ayers Rock, ladies!" He paused again for the slight outburst of chuckles. "And to the north, sixty miles distant, there's Mount Conway, a typical mesa. Twenty miles to the south there's Mount Sarah, named after Chief Officer Conway's wife. It's usually called 'the Sallies,' as it consists of five separate domes of red conglomerate. So you see that geologically Cragge Rock doesn't fit in. There're quite a few theories, folks. One is that there was a submarine volcanic eruption when this was all part of the ocean bed. The Rock was an extrusion of molten matter from the core of the planet. It has been further shaped by millions of years of erosion since the sea floor was lifted to become this island continent."

As he spoke, the Rock was lifting over the otherwise featureless horizon. It squatted there on the skyline, glowering red in the almost level rays of the westering sun, an enormous crimson slug. It possessed beauty of a sort—but the overall impression was one of strength.

"We spend five full days here, folks," went on the driver. "There's a hotel, and there's an abo settlement, and most of the boos speak English. They'll be happy to tell you *their* legends about the Rock—Wuluru they call it. It's one of their sacred places, but they don't mind us coming here as long as we pay for the privilege. That, of course, is all taken care of by the Tourist Bureau; but if you want any curios, you'll have to fork out for them. . . . See the way that the Rock's changing color as the sun gets lower? And once the sun's down it'll slowly fade like a dying ember. . . ."

The Rock was close now, towering above them, a red wall against the darkening blue of the cloudless sky. Then they were in its shadow, and the sheer granite wall was purple, shading to cold blue. . . . Sunlight again, like a sudden blow, and a last circuit of the time-pocked monolith, and a final stop on the eastern side of the stone mountain.

They got out of the coach, stood there, shivering a little in the still, chilly air. "It has something . . ." whispered Tanya Lancaster. "It has something . . ." agreed Moira Stevens.

"Ancestral memory?" asked Deane, with unusual sharpness.

"You're prying!" snapped the fat girl.

"I'm not, Moira. But I couldn't help picking up the strong emanation from your minds."

Tanya laughed. "Like most modern Australians we're a mixed lot— and, in our fully integrated society, most of us have some aboriginal blood. But . . . Why should Moira and I feel so at home here, both at home and hopelessly lost?"

"If you let me probe . . ." suggested Deane gently.

"No," flared the girl. "No!"

Grimes sympathized with her. He knew, all too well, what it is like to have a trained telepath, no matter how high his ethical standards, around. But he said. "Spooky's to be trusted. I know."

"You might trust him, John. I don't know him well enough."

"He knows *us* too bloody well!" growled Moira.

"I smell steak," said Grimes, changing the subject.

The four of them walked to the open fire, where the evening meal was already cooking.

Dawn on the Rock was worth waking up early for. Grimes stood with the others, blanket-wrapped against the cold, and watched the great hulk flush gradually from blue to purple, from purple to pink. Over it and beyond it the sky was black, the stars very bright, almost as bright as in airless Space. Then the sun was up, and the Rock stood there, a red island in the sea of tawny sand, a surf of green brush breaking about its base. The show was over. The party went to the showers and toilets and then, dressed, assembled for breakfast.

After the meal they walked from the encampment to the Rock. Tanya and Moira stayed in the company of Grimes and Deane, but their manner toward the two spacemen was distinctly chilly; they were more interested in their guidebooks than in conversation. On their way they passed the aboriginal village. A huddle of crude shelters it was, constructed of natural materials and battered sheets of plastic. Fires were burning, and gobbets of unidentifiable meat were cooking over them. Women—naked, with straggling hair and pendulous breasts, yet human enough—looked up and around at the well-clothed, well-fed tourists with an odd, sly mixture of timidity and boldness. One of them pointed to a leveled camera and screamed, "First gibbit half dollar!"

"You'd better," advised the driver. "Very commercial-minded, these people. . . ."

Men were emerging from the primitive huts. One of them approached Grimes and his companions, his teeth startlingly white in his coal black face. He was holding what looked like a crucifix. "Very good," he said, waving it in front of him. "Two dollar."

"I'm not religious . . ." Grimes began, to be cut short by Tanya's laugh. "Don't be a fool, John," she told him. "It's a throwing weapon."

"A throwing weapon?"

"Yes. Like our boomerangs. Let me show you." She turned to the native, held out her hand. "Here. Please."

"You throw, missie?"

"Yes. I throw."

Watched by the tourists and the natives, she held the thing by the end of its long arm, turned until she was facing about forty-five degrees away from the light, morning breeze, the flat surfaces of the cross at right angles to the wind. She raised her arm, then threw, with a peculiar flick of her wrist. The weapon left her hand, spinning, turned so that it was flying horizontally, like a miniature helicopter. It traveled about forty yards, came around in a lazy arc, faltered, then fell in a flurry of fine sand.

"Not very good," complained the girl. "You got better? You got proper one?"

The savage grinned. "You know?"

"Yes. I know."

The man went back into his hut, returned with another weapon. This one was old, beautifully made, and lacking the crude designs that had been burned into the other with red-hot wire. He handed it to Tanya, who hefted it approvingly. She threw it as she had thrown the first one—and the difference was immediately obvious. There was no clumsiness in its flight, no hesitation. Spinning, it flew, more like a living thing than a machine. Its arms turned more and more lazily as it came back—and Tanya, with a clapping motion, deftly caught it between her two hands. She stood admiring it—the smooth finish imparted by the most primitive of tools, the polish of age and of long use.

"How much?" she asked.

"No sale, missie." Again the very white grin. "But I give."

"But you can't. You mustn't."

"You take."

"I shouldn't, but . . ."

"Take it, lady," said the driver. "This man is Najatira, the Chief of these people. Refusing his gift would offend him." Then, businesslike, "You guide, Najatira?"

"Yes. I guide." He barked a few words in his own language to his women, one of whom scuttled over the sand to retrieve the first, fallen throwing weapon. Then, walking fast on his big, splayed feet, he strode toward the rock. Somehow the two girls had ranged themselves on either side of him. Grimes looked on disapprovingly. Who was it who had said that these natives were humanoid only? This naked savage, to judge by his external equipment, was all too human. Exchanging disapproving glances, the two spacemen took their places in the little procession.

"Cave," said Najatira, pointing. The orifice, curiously regular, was exactly at the tail of the slug-shaped monolith. "Called, by my people, the Hole of Winds. Story say, in Dream Time, wind come from there, wind move world. . . . Before, world no move. No daytime; no nighttime. . . ."

"Looks almost like a venturi, Captain," Deane remarked to Grimes.

"Mphm. Certainly looks almost too regular to be natural. But erosion does odd things. Or it could have been made by a blast of gases from the thing's inside . . ."

"Precisely," said Deane.

"But you don't think . . . ? No. It would be impossible."

"I don't know what to think," admitted Deane.

Their native guide was leading them around the base of the Rock. "This Cave of Birth. Tonight ceremony. We show you. . . . And there— look up. What we call the fishing net. In Dream Time caught big fish. . . ."

"A circuit . . ." muttered Grimes. "Exposed by millennia of weather- ing . . ." He laughed. "I'm getting as bad as you, Spooky. Nature comes up with the most remarkable imitations of Man-made things . . ."

So it went on, the trudge around the base of the monolith, under the hot sun, while their tireless guide pointed out this and that feature. As soon as the older members of the party began to show signs of distress, the driver spoke into his wrist transceiver and within a few minutes the coach came rumbling over the rough track and then, with its partial load, kept pace with those who were still walking. Grimes and Deane were among these hardy ones, but only because Tanya and Moira showed no signs of flagging, and because Grimes felt responsible for the women. After all, the Survey Service had been referred to as the Policemen of the Galaxy. It was unthinkable that two civilized human females should fall for this unwashed savage—but already he knew that civilized human females are apt to do the weirdest things.

At last the tour came to an end. Najatira, after bowing with surprising courtesy, strode off toward his own camp. The tourists clustered hungrily around the folding tables that had been set up, wolfed the thick sandwiches, and gulped great drafts of hot, sweet tea.

During the afternoon there were flights over the Rock and the countryside for those who wished them, a large blimp having come in from the nearest airport for that purpose. This archaic transport was the occasion for surprise and incredulity, but it was explained that such aircraft were used by *Lode Jumbuk*'s people for their initial explorations.

"The bloody thing's not safe," complained Deane as soon as they were airborne.

Grimes ignored him. He was looking out and down through the big cabin windows. Yes, the Rock did look odd, out of place. It was part of the landscape—but it did not belong. It had been there for millions of years—but still it did not belong. Mount Conway and Mount Sarah were natural enough geological formations—*but*, be thought, *Cragge Rock is just as natural.* He tried to envision what it must have looked like when that upwelling of molten rock thrust through the ocean bed.

"It wasn't like that, Captain," said Deane quietly.

"Damn you, Spooky! Get out of my mind."

"I'm sorry," the telepath told him, although he didn't sound it. "It's just that this locality is like a jigsaw puzzle. I'm trying to find the pieces and to make them fit." He looked around to make sure that none of the others in the swaying, creaking cabin was listening. "Tanya and Moira . . . The kinship they feel with Najatira . . ."

"Why don't you ask them about it?" Grimes suggested, jerking his head toward the forward end of the car, where the two girls were sitting. "Is it kinship, or is it just the attraction that a woman on holiday feels for an exotic male?"

"It's more than that."

"So you're prying."

"I'm trying not to." He looked down without interest at Mount Conway, over which the airship was slowly flying. "But it's hard to."

"You could get into trouble, Spooky. And you could get the ship into trouble. . . ."

"And you, Captain."

"Yes. And me." Then Grimes allowed a slight smile to flicker over his face. "But I know you. You're on to something. And as we're on holiday from the ship, I don't suppose that I can give you any direct orders . . ."

"I'm not a space-lawyer, so I'll take your word for that."

"Just be careful. And keep me informed."

While they talked the pilot of the blimp, his voice amplified, had been giving out statistics. The conversation had been private enough.

That night there was the dance.

Flaring fires had been built on the sand, in a semicircle, the inner arc of which faced the mouth of the Cave of Birth. The tourists sat there, some on the ground and some on folding stools, the fires at their backs, waiting. Overhead the sky was black and clear, the stars bitterly bright.

From inside the cave there was music—of a sort. There was a rhythmic wheezing of primitive trumpets, the staccato rapping of knocking sticks. There was a yelping male voice—Najatira's—that seemed to be giving orders rather than singing.

Grimes turned to say something to Tanya, but she was no longer in her place. Neither was Moira. The two girls must have gone together to the toilet block; they would be back shortly. He returned his attention to the black entrance to the Cave.

The first figure emerged from it, crouching, a stick held in his hands. Then the second, then the third . . . There was something oddly familiar about it, something that didn't make sense, or that made the wrong kind of sense. Grimes tried to remember what it was. Dimly he realized that Deane was helping him, that the telepath was trying to bring his memories to the conscious level.

Yes, that was it. That was the way the Marines disembarked on the surface of an unexplored, possibly hostile planet, automatic weapons at the ready . . .

Twelve men were outside the Cave now, advancing in a dancelike step. The crude, tree-stem trumpets were still sounding, like the plaint of tired machinery, and the noise of the knocking sticks was that of cooling metal. The leader paused, stood upright. With his fingers in his mouth he gave a piercing whistle.

The women emerged, carrying bundles, hesitantly, two steps forward, one step back. Grimes gasped his disbelief. Surely that was Tanya, as naked as the others—and there was no mistaking Moira. He jumped to his feet, ignoring the protests of those behind him, trying to shake off Deane's restraining hand.

"Let go!" he snarled.

"Don't interfere, Captain!" The telepath's voice was urgent. "Don't you see? They've gone native—no, that's not right. But they've reverted. And there's no law against it."

"I can still drag them out of this. They'll thank me after." He turned around and shouted, "Come on, all of you! We must put a stop to this vile performance!"

"Captain Grimes!" This was the coach driver, his voice angry. "Sit down, sir! This sort of thing has happened before, and it's nothing to worry about. The young ladies are in no danger!"

"It's happened before," agreed Deane, unexpectedly, "with neurotic exhibitionists, wanting to have their photographs taken among the savages. But not *this* way!"

Then, even more unexpectedly, it was Deane who was running out across the sand, and it was Najatira who advanced to meet him, not in hostility but in welcome. It was Grimes who, unheeded, yelled, "Come back, Spooky! Come back here!"

He didn't know what was happening, but he didn't like it. First of all those two silly bitches, and now one of his own officers. What the hell was getting into everybody? Followed by a half-dozen of the other men, he ran toward the cave mouth. Their way was barred by a line of the tribesmen, holding their sticks now like spears (which they were)—not like make-believe guns. Najatira stood proudly behind the armed men, and on either side of him stood the two girls, a strange, arrogant pride in every line of their naked bodies. And there was Deane, a strange smile on his face. His face, too, was strange, seemed suddenly to have acquired lines of authority.

"Go back, John," he ordered. "There is nothing that you can do." He added softly, "But there is much that I can do."

"What the hell are you talking about, Spooky?"

"I'm an Australian, like Moira and Tanya here. Like them, I have the Old Blood in my veins. Unlike them, I'm a spaceman. Do you think that after all these years in the Service I, with my talent, haven't learned how to handle and navigate a ship, any ship? I shall take my people back to where they belong."

And then Grimes *knew*. The knowledge came flooding into his mind, from the mind of Deane, from the minds of the others, whose ancestral memories had been awakened by the telepath. But he was still responsible. He must still try to stop this craziness.

"Mr. Deane!" he snapped as he strode forward firmly. He brushed aside the point of the spear that was aimed at his chest. He saw Tanya throw something and sneered as it missed his head by inches. He did not see the cruciform boomerang returning, was aware of it only as a crashing blow from behind, as a flash of crimson light, then darkness.

He recovered slowly. He was stretched out on the sand beside the coach. Two of the nurses among the passengers were with him.

He asked, as he tried to sit up, "What happened?"

"They all went back into the cave," the girl said. "The rock . . . The rock closed behind them. And there were lights. And a voice, it was Mr. Deane's voice, but loud, loud, saying, 'Clear the field? Clear the field! Get back, everybody. Get well back. Get well away!' So we got well back."

"And what's happening now?" asked Grimes. The nurses helped him as he got groggily to his feet. He stared toward the distant Rock. He could hear the beat of mighty engines and the ground was trembling under his feet. Lights flashed here and there on the surface of the monolith. Even with the knowledge that Deane had fed into his mind he could not believe what he was seeing.

The Rock was lifting, its highest part suddenly eclipsing a bright constellation. It was lifting, and the skin of the planet protested as the vast ship, that for so long had been embedded in it, tore itself free. Tremors knocked the tourists from their feet, but somehow Grimes remained standing, oblivious to the shouts and screams. He heard the crash behind him as the coach was overturned, but did not look. At this moment it was only a minor distraction.

The Rock was lifting, had lifted. It was a deeper blackness against the blackness of the sky, a scattering of strange, impossible stars against the distant stars, a bright cluster (at first) that dimmed and diminished, that dwindled, faster and faster, and then was gone, leaving in its wake utter darkness and silence.

The silence was broken by the coach driver. He said slowly, "I've had to cope with vandalism in my time, but nothing like this. What the Board will say when they hear that their biggest tourist attraction has gone I hate to think about . . ." He seemed to cheer up slightly. "But it was one of *your* officers, Captain Grimes, from *your* ship, that did it. I hope you enjoy explaining it!"

Grimes explained, as well as he was able, to Commander Lewin. He said, "As we all know, sir, there are these odd races, human rather than humanoid, all through the Galaxy. It all ties in with the Common Origin of Mankind theories. I never used to have much time for them myself, but now . . ."

"Never mind that, Grimes. Get on with the washing."

"Well, Deane was decent enough to let loose a flood of knowledge into my mind just before that blasted Tanya clonked me with her boomerang. It seems that millions of years ago these stone spaceships, these hollowed-out asteroids, were sent to explore this Galaxy. I got only a hazy idea of their propulsive machinery, but it was something on the lines of our Inertial Drive, and something on the lines of our Mannschenn Drive, with auxiliary rockets for maneuvering in orbit and so forth. They were never meant to land, but they could, if they had to. Their power? Derived from the conversion of matter, any matter, with the generators or converters ready to start up when the right button was pushed—but the button had to be pushed psionically. Get me?"

"Not very well. But go on."

"Something happened to this ship, to the crew and passengers of this ship. A disease, I think it was, wiping out almost all the adults, leaving only children and a handful of not very experienced ratings. Somebody— it must have been one of the officers just before he died—got the ship down somehow. He set things so that it could not be reentered until somebody with the right qualifications came along."

"The right qualifications?"

"Yes. Psionic talents, more than a smattering of astronautics, and descended from the Old People . . ."

"Like your Mr. Deane. But what about the two girls?"

"They had the Old Blood. And they were highly educated. And they could have been latent telepaths . . ."

"Could be." Levin smiled without much mirth. "Meanwhile, Lieutenant, I have to try to explain to the Olganan Government, with copies to Trans-Galactic Clippers *and* to our own masters, including *your* Commodore Damien. All in all, Grimes, it was a fine night's work. Apart from the Rock, there were two TG passengers *and* a Survey Service officer . . ."

"*And* the tribe . . ."

"The least of the Olganan Government's worries, and nothing at all to do with TG or ourselves. Even so . . ." This time his smile was tinged with genuine, but sardonic, humor.

"Even so?" echoed Grimes.

"What if those tribesmen and women decided to liberate—I suppose that's the right word—those other tribespeople, the full-blooded ones who're still living in the vicinity of the other stone spaceship? What if the Australians realize, one sunny morning, that their precious Ayers Rock has up and left them?"

"I know who'll be blamed," said Grimes glumly.

"How right you are," concurred Lewin.

PHILIPPA C. MADDERN

Philippa Maddern attended the famous and influential SF writing workshop, led by Ursula K. Le Guin in Australia in 1975, that resulted in the anthology *The Altered I*. This marked a significant moment in Australian SF, the first of the two workshops that produced an aggregation of new writers, some of whom are still coming into international prominence in the 1990s (even as another group of newcomers such as Sean McMullen, Sean Williams, Greg Egan, and Stephen Dedman emerge to give them competition). Maddern made an immediate impression with her short fiction, commencing with three stories selected by Le Guin in *The Altered I*: "The Ins and Outs of the Hadya City State," "Broken Pit," and an untitled story. A fourth story, "Wherever You Are," appeared in *The View from the Edge*, another significant anthology, and others followed in anthologies and magazines. The best known may be "Inhabiting the Interspaces," which appeared in the anthology *Transmutations* (1981). She also lived in England for a while and was talked about as a bright new writer. She seemed on the brink of international success. But Maddern went into college teaching and published only two stories after "Inhabiting the Interspaces" in the 1980s: "Confusion Day," in King and Blackford's *Urban Fantasies* (1985), and "Things Fall Apart," in Broderick's *Matilda at the Speed of Light* (1988). And in the 1990s she has published one story in *Eidolon*, "The Subconscious Computer" (1990), and another, "Not With Love," in the Sussex and Buckrich anthology *She's Fantastical* (1995). She is therefore still relatively unknown outside the Australian community, where she had such a profound initial impact.

THINGS FALL APART

Wardour came to Leong's private viewing clad in strict black and silver, his thick silver-rope necklace encircling the black collar of his shirt and his face gray with illness. As he walked through the door there was not so much a silence as a momentary hush preceding an outbreak of louder and more extravagant conversation, the corner of every eye upon him, in hope of either amusement or approval. He saw with foreboding that young Danny Considine, having snatched an untasted glass of champagne from his companion's hand, was rushing to offer it with much-practiced artlessness.

"My dear, you look *marvelous*. Quite *en grande tenue*," said Danny, as soon as he was within earshot.

Wardour looked at him as if assessing his authenticity, waved aside the wine, took up the nearest glass of chilled herb tea, and replied, "Surely the current phrase is 'tarted up like the president's robot.'" Danny produced a creditable laugh. Wardour turned away to the exhibition. He never, in public, accorded patrons precedence over art, saying that he earned his fee with books, programs, and advice on art purchases, and anything more was subject to further negotiation. Lazarini, the principal patron present, thought it dignified and cultured to submit to this treatment, and went on talking kindly to the artist. Two of Wardour's old friends greeted him quietly as he passed, but only Danny, chattering desperately, accompanied him. Wardour kindly refrained from dispensing with him.

A predictable show, he thought. Here were the two mandatory social-realism set pieces, displaying hunched and smelly citizens, government-clothed, against a background of government housing, munching govern-

ment handouts, and staring blankly across what Leong evidently imagined
to be a government parkland. There were several bad slick portraits of
patrons and their patronal enterprises, and a selection of excellent imaginative works presumably done in Leong's spare time. As Wardour halted,
peering shortsightedly at each of these, he heard the talk at his back not
precisely directed toward him, but swiveling, like a loudspeaker, to follow
his progress.

"Five million if you count the government holding."

"Won't they abstain?" "They'll be bleeding-well squeezed out of CoBia
if they do." "Good. Good."

". . . knew he'd been ill, but I just assumed it was AIDS." "No, definitely leukemia, his patron's doctor says so." "But surely—you know—gene
washing?" "At his age? They wouldn't do it."

"And he said . . ." "Yes, I was there. . . ." *(Ha ha ha.)* "Who?" (Deep
voice, imitating someone else.) "I'll have the whisky" *(Ha ha ha ha)* "And
afterward at the house . . ." *(Ha ha ha.)* "Yes, I know—" *(Ha ha ha ha ha.)*

Wardour dodged back and forth in front of a holo of two entwined
athletes. There was something odd on the left face. Then looking more
closely, he saw that Leong had suspended a series of magnifiers to enlarge
one segment of one flawless profile of one beautiful boy. As he came closer
he could see, as through an undiminishing tunnel, first the exquisite golden
surface of his skin, then its individual pores and flakes, then each of its
cells, then the nuclei, and hints of molecules and proteins. He watched
the cells swim and shiver under the magnifier. A crowd of vague, black,
fuzzy things was infiltrating cells in the upper-right quadrant of the circle.
He could see the cells begin to split and collapse, consumed by disease. His
body shook with sympathy, as if each drop of his blood jumped in terror
at the sight of its own death. He clutched his shuddering glass more firmly
and swung round so abruptly that his sleeve whisked a plate clear out of
the hand of the man standing next to him.

Wardour opened his mouth to apologize and left it open in astonishment; for the young man, quick as thought, dropped to one knee, caught
the tumbling plate elegantly on the tips of his fingers, and, tilting back his
head, grinned in shy triumph at him. Then he climbed back to his feet
and resumed the appearance of a nondescript onlooker in overalls holding
his crumb-covered plate.

Enchanted by such insouciant skill, Wardour exclaimed, "You're a juggler! A performing artist! Just what Lazarini needs. Shall I introduce you?"

The young man retreated even farther, if that were possible, into his
protective imitation of the ordinary. "Actually, I'm a scientist," he said;
and then, as if making a gallant attempt to help out the conversation, "a

biochemist." Wardour waited. The young man turned around to Danny. "Well aren't you going to introduce us?"

This surprised Wardour greatly; usually Danny's companions were even worse than himself. Yet here was Danny, with relentless charm, explaining that Patrick was a *brilliant* scientist and an old school friend of his, and *what* good fortune that he and Wardour should have met. Patrick was apparently struck dumb by this, though the mention of Wardour's name raised no trace of comprehension in him. Wardour, really curious to hear the opinion of so surprising a person, said to him. "What do you think of this then?"

"The exhibition?"

Wardour nodded. Patrick looked perplexed. He ran his hand over his furry, cropped hair, carefully, as if stroking a nervous cat, and said at last, "It's a wank, I reckon. Well, most of it. This one here's okay, with the viruses. They do that sort of thing, you know." (He sounded reproachful of the moral state of viruses.) "And a couple of others. But all those por-traits—I don't know. If they were experiments, I wouldn't do them."

"Quite right," said Wardour, immensely cheered; but Patrick just said, "I think your patron's trying to get hold of you."

Sure enough, Lazarini was approaching with Leong in tow, evidently bent on introducing the new artist to the established critic. Wardour col-lected his concentration onto Leong and began in his best public style. There was no point in attempting private conversation; inevitably it would become a lecture delivered to Leong by Wardour in a glare of attention from the rest of the party. Already heads were turning, and conversations stopping short in anticipation of the performance.

By the time Wardour had dissected her showing into its three parts, almost nobody except the patrons were talking. After a brisk passage of arms against social realism ("If you must attempt to portray people who are, effectually, as unknown to you as chimpanzees, surely you should do so either as comic genre, abstraction, or allegory"), he proceeded to what he called "the only serious part of the exhibit. You agree with me?" Before his fascinated audience, he laid out his array of comments like sharp and shining crystals. "In holo four, you take the easy way. Why? Where you opt for the complex, as in holo seven, you reward your viewers if they pay attention. Thus you integrate them into your work. They add meaning to it by their perception, and it contributes to their perception. This is why we come back to it again and again (look at the floor in front, that tells its own tale)." Obediently, that part of the crowd nearest to it leaned over to inspect the scuffed floor at the feet of the gilded, decaying youth in holo seven and nodded wisely. So quiet was the hall that one could hear Danny's voice from the back, vibrant with champagne and venom.

"Of course it's all right if you've *got* a patron; you can say what you like *then*, about *anyone*, Peter included. Not that I dislike him at all, I'm very fond of Peter, but you *must* admit that in *this* instance he's behaved like the most *arrogant, windy, pissy, self-satisfied* little *bastard* who ever . . ."

"And I mustn't forget the portraits," said Wardour plaintively. "Why are they so bad?" He paused, but Leong would not venture on an answer. "It's not good enough, after all, to say that we don't like the patrons; Goya's portrait of the family of Charles V is not a product of liking, but it is a masterpiece. Nor is it useful to say that an artist must be free from all external constraint to do good work. The Van Eycks, Rembrandt, Michelangelo produced some of their best art on commission. I see no reason why we shouldn't regain the knack. After all, it is no credit to oneself or one's patrons . . ." (for the first time his eye sought Lazarini in the crowd) "in fact, it is shameful and disgusting—to flatter them with words and dishonor them with bad painting."

Lazarini politely interrupted a *sotto voce* conversation on currency regulations to nod back. Wardour said to Leong, "Thank you. A good exhibition. I enjoyed it," and turned away. Patrick was nowhere to be seen. Behind him, a steady shuffle had started toward holo seven. Resisting the temptation to scan the room, he made his way to the door. The voices pursued him out as the door slid shut.

". . . if the government fell?" "No chance." "Yes, *wonderful*, social realists, patrons, and artists all in one hit." "No, Helen says definitely leukemia." "But surely—gene washing?"

He felt appallingly tired and very angry. Surely they knew, these people? How could they ignore, how could they be so blind or careless as not to see the bills for their own children's gene reconstruction? How did they think that those huge sums of money could be met by most of the population? He knew, he, crafty Wardour, who had seen his name six thousandth on a line at the government hospital, who had seen what was coming, and sweated out the accounting part of a Fine Arts and Economics degree, who had bluffed and weaseled and dazzled his way into the pay of the first patrons. He knew. What excuse was there for the others to be blind? It would have been better if he had had AIDS. Some workers still got it; some of the companies put money into improving the treatment for it. Nobody bothered to market cures for leukemia for those who couldn't pay for them. A blood transfusion tomorrow. Virotherapy the week after. Death coming soon, as sure as water runs downhill.

There was a bus phone at the end of the foyer, he knew. Better than begging a lift in one of his patron's cars. At the thought of the bus, the malignant hallway extended itself a farther twenty meters again in front of him. Was it really possible to stagger so far? Or would he end up crawling over that shiny gray marble desert? But, no. Here he was, walking upright, chatting urbanely to Matthew, who had come out after him—once (long ago) a lover, now an old if not a close friend—and the expanse of floor was diminishing steadily in front of them.

"Not an uncommonly bad exhibition, but the standard of public criticism continues to appall me," he told Matthew. And then prompted to a confidence he hardly understood himself, said, "I heard only one decent comment, and that was from a young man who is apparently a scientist. Patrick, or some such name. I don't know where he came from."

"Patrick Teague," said Matthew unerringly. As one of Lazarini's businessmen, his acquaintance was wide. He glanced curiously at Wardour, who, to his own annoyance, found himself saying, "He came with young Considine, I see. Rather a curious partnership, surely."

"No, it's the other way round," said Matthew. "He and Teague were at school together. Teague does some work for the gallery, I believe—scaffolding, hanging, something like that. They all get complimentary tickets, and, of course, Considine edged his way in on it. That boy's nothing but a leech."

"So unlike the rest of us," murmured Wardour dryly, as a burst of pain grabbed his spine.

Matthew hitched his eyebrows in a resigned way and said, "How's work? Do you get any time off?"

"I find work very soothing," said Wardour, and normally it would have been true; not only did the subject matter delight him, but there was the added joy of secrecy. No one knew, not Matthew, not even Lazarini, the treasure he was unearthing from the dingy bundles of Lazarini's last manuscript purchases. Yet tonight his own critical ear detected the echo of a lie in his voice. For a moment he thought with longing, not of parchment and gold leaf and lapis lazuli, but of Patrick's close, dark hair and quiet, well-trained body. He thought of waking in the night, in the dream-ridden darkness, of turning over and finding the smooth warmth of someone else there, and of going to sleep again, comforted. But, but, the boy hardly knew him, probably would hate condescension from an elderly notable, but there was no time, no time to do even a tenth of the things he had planned. Not a twentieth. "Very soothing," he repeated firmly as the bus arrived to take him home.

Home. Two rooms in a tied block of flats. No room even for Patrick, even if . . . And yet there was an obscure comfort still in his desk, his well-designed study chair, his terminal, his books and fiches, and the vellum pages that were arguably—no, certainly—the last unfinished work of Renee of Anjou, King of Sicily and Jerusalem. His patron had bought them by money without knowing of their existence. He, Wardour, alone understood what they were. Truly, they were his own privacy; to turn to the smooth, white vellum sheets, to spread out his colored fiches of comparative illuminations was as good as a journey back home to childhood. Even the colors had a long familiarity to him—the women's robes as blue as the sky above the curve of a water tank, the reds as deep as old tin roofs, the wheatfield golds. Only one page had its full two columns of text, but it was enough. He knew the pictures had been meant to illustrate the tale of the journey of the esquire Ame, the esquire Soul, from birth to salvation. He could show which was the first scene, the birth of Soul, with Reason and Knowledge as midwives. He had the last of the series, unfinished but unmistakably the picture of the justified Soul standing at the entrance to the glorious blaze of the Heavenly City. He had only to identify and order the inner pages; only a few months' work. Surely death could be staved off so long? The page of text must be early in the story. It told of the battle between Soul and the dragon Anger. Anger was a young man's sin in Renee of Anjou's time. What about the rest? Was there a picture for every cardinal sin, or did the fight against the others appear in the wounded figures in the background of the dragon picture? (There was a fat, beheaded figure that might be Avarice, the greed of the soul or simply the more commonplace Gluttony.) In another picture, Soul stood in the center of a forest, reading from a book; but the pages of the book were blank. What was it? What was the meaning of the illustration with Soul sitting his horse and looking at a lion curled in a hollow in the ground? Was the dark castle to which Soul came, armed and visored, on another page, the Keep of Despair? The artist had painted rooms seen through the windows of the castle. In one was a hanged man—Judas? A woman sat, savage and brooding, in the gateway of the castle. Could she be linked typologically to Dürer's *Melancholia?*

The hours passed; Wardour had forgotten even to be tired and had only once remembered Patrick.

Because she was so nearly not employed at all, Sanova worked in an office opening onto the foyer of the building. It was a poor area. Very little light came in, and that cold and dusty. For some reason, it seemed to Sanova like looking out of a beleaguered castle. Today, the feeling was especially strong. She leaned her elbows on her knees, and pondered how on earth she could present her research as in any way essential to the work of Consolidated Biochemicals.

If Bob would only agree to call it Defence Systems Efficiency . . . but he wouldn't, too many people clamoring to squeeze under that umbrella already. Then what was a study of replicability relevant to? The answer, unfortunately, was either nothing, or almost everything. Even if she could prove that certain scientific experiments were not replicable—not just hard to test, like evolution, but not replicable, so that one could repeat the experiment exactly, and still not have the same result—would the company care? Or would they simply pay to shut her up?

At this point Patrick walked past and, in his polite way, stopped to say hello and could he do anything for her?

"Nothing at all. Why?" said Sanova, surprised. For Patrick, though phenomenally even tempered, was rarely forthcoming. Their conversations were usually confined to exchanges of information about their work. Patrick studied viruses, and had what were held to be brilliant but eccentric beliefs about the self-determination of virus behavior. Since this led him into extrascientific models of explanation, he and Sanova had a good deal in common. But Patrick was, in an unconcerned way, successful. His disease-control plans seemed to work, and there was a general feeling in CoBia that a lot of money could be made out of and by him. Sanova, clinging to the very edge of lukewarm managerial favor, would have hated him had he not been so patently unimpressed with his prospects. He continued to take on odd jobs in the city, in the underground, in art galleries, as the moods took him; and to stroll around other people's offices to see what was going on, stopping now and then to chat with someone and juggle deftly with their pens and paper clips, as he was doing now with three dead batteries from Sanova's desk top.

Now he said simply, "You look like despair. What's wrong?"

"Oh, it's only budgets coming up again. I suppose it'll be okay." Sanova was unable to prevent herself sounding both dreary and pathetic.

"Why? They won't dump you."

"They certainly might."

"Not a chance. They need their bright young scholars."

"I'm neither very bright nor very young."

Patrick rubbed his hair up backward and frowned. He said at last, "You make too little of yourself. You could ask for more than you get, and they'd probably give it to you. They don't respect people who don't ask. That's why I ask for the world all the time, and look what happens. I can't get them off my back, offering to get things for me."

Sanova, controlling her irritation with difficulty, said, "Well what would you do then? Who would you ask?"

"Anyone. Marketing Research. They do contingency maths; they'd be falling over backward to get you. Or go out and get a patron; there're lots of them out there. I tell you, I went to a private viewing on the weekend, and there were three patrons I could have had for the picking up. Anyone could, I mean. Well, there were two, anyway. I think the other one was a critic or something, but he was a good bloke; he'd help you all right. And you don't have to stick to science, come to that. You could do other things."

"Like juggling, I suppose."

"Yeah, it's a good living, juggling," said Patrick, impervious to disbelief. "I made a lot of money over the weekend, juggling down in the Dorms."

Sanova, horrified, said, "You don't juggle for money down there? They haven't got enough to live on anyway."

"Why not? They don't have to pay me if they don't want to."

"But you don't need it."

Patrick looked mildly irritated. "Sure, but that's not the point. They wouldn't want to watch if they didn't pay. It's like your lectures. You lecture down there, don't you? And you get paid? So what's the difference?"

"But the lecture's really useful. It—it gives them something they wouldn't get otherwise. I . . ." She hesitated before Patrick's patent skepticism. He said, kindly changing the subject, "Want me to introduce you to a patron? Herds of them in the galleries. Just waiting to be picked up. Like a lot of little lap dogs. Woof woof." He held his hands up, paw fashion, under his chin, and let his tongue hang out winsomely. Unwillingly, Sanova smiled at him and said, "You really think market research might do something?"

"Sure. Try Alice. She's good. Do you know her?"

"Well . . . yes, sort of. I doubt if she'd remember me."

"You just try," said Patrick tolerantly, and walked off.

Ame sat his horse in the shadow of the forest. Ivy curled at its margins, entwined with solemn flowers; silent birds perched in its curly tendrils. Before him, the green hillside sloped away, drawing him toward, toward whatever it was, what place, what bright city whose white towers and wide, light-filled streets he had never seen, and yet longed for always. His horse, Cors, cropped at the grass. Cors could be a willing ally; together they had fought the dragon Ire. He could be willful; given a chance, he would take his master to the whorehouse or the tavern. Now he seemed undecided, and Ame himself was strangely unable to fathom the way. The city over the hilltop was his destination—but what of the forest? Its twisted paths might be as good a way to the city as any—better, indeed, than the straight, green way before him. The forest was more than a random collection of trees. The paths were more than random. Each track was there because someone had chosen to follow it. Each tree was as much the same as, and as much different from, its neighbor, as the words of an unknown language, arranged in curling sentences by the purposeful paths. It was a language he could learn; he was certain of it. In his mind he saw the wood as a book and himself the reader. He saw himself following its cryptic paragraphs, which might tell him—who knew?—the way to his perfect city. He was sure he should go through the forest.

And yet—the hillside. Looking more closely, he saw that it was not a simple sweep of turf. There was a spot of color in one of the shallow, grassy hollows to his right. It was a smooth, tawny gold, like ripe wheat. It filled the hollow with a solid mass of velvety fur. As he looked, a fierce, frowning yellow eye opened in it. It was a lion.

He might have been afraid of the lion; it was a huge, fearsome, dangerous beast. Yet he felt sure that it was not his enemy. It stared at him, unblinking and unafraid. "We two will fight together," it seemed to say, just as the dragon had spoken to him in his own voice, saying, "You will kill me or I will kill you." The lion stretched one huge golden paw toward him, claws extended, indolent and luxurious. Cors saw it and gazed intently, excitedly, at it; but did not plunge and snort as he had at the dragon, though the dragon had faced them with just such cruel, spiked claws. Cors too felt the lion was a friend. "Whom shall we fight?" asked Ame silently of the golden beast. But it shut its eye and never answered.

He sat at the edge of the forest, trapped. He thought he saw that the lion and the dragon belonged together, in one class of beings—the deadly, bestial fighter, who spoke to him from inside his own head. That being so, he should ride to meet the lion and take the adventure. But then how would he ever come to the forest and read his way through it? Or would the lion come with him through the wood? One glance at it was enough to tell him it would not. It was too bold, too bright, to track those labyrinthine paths. There might be beasts who would guide him there—peacocks to lecture from every tree, the wise white deer with the crucifix between its antlers to light the way—but the lion would not be there.

The wood and the lion were equal ways to reach the city. He did not know how to choose which one should come next. He could not go on. Before him in his mind, two roads opened out, as blank as two white pages.

On Tuesday evening, Sanova gave her lecture in the Ballan Dorm. She and her students met in a corner of the Barter Market. If she was lucky, and business was particularly slack, one of the stall holders would lend her a table. She could then set it on end, and draw calculations and diagrams on its peeling laminex surface. If not, she simply sat on the pavement and talked. Her students almost never had any money to spare, but they paid in kind as well as they could, and sometimes she managed to resell what they gave her for hard currency. Today, she was finishing a series of lectures on replication theory. The group in front of her, down to about seventy-five now that the less enthusiastic had dropped out, squatted dead still, following her every gesture with rigid attention. Some, she knew, would memorize the lecture entire, to take on to other markets. Others were intent from the sheer effort to comprehend; eight years in a government school was hardly adequate preparation for understanding an esoteric philosophy of science. As usual, on the completion of the lecture, she allowed the first comers, squashed together in the center of the front row, to make comments or raise questions. They spoke in the abbreviated jargon of street debate, knowing that the rest of the crowd, impatient to get their own say in, would allow no hesitation or oratory.

"Too much evidence against you," said the first. "For one hundred, two hundred years, scientists replicate experiments. How you account for it?"

"Contrary," said the huge, goitered woman on his left. "Replications can be faked, juggled. Who says experiments were done same all the time? Lack of rigorous checking could give two hundred years—quote scientific quote—success. Anyway, suppose two hundred years' replications. Sanova's case's still the exception. Explaining exceptions often leads new understanding, example, anomaly of speed-of-light observations to Newtonian physics leads to Einstein, right?"

"Support second commentator, both points. Besides, Sanova's theory worth testing. What if causation dependent on analogical, not logical sequences, as in medieval correspondence theory? Example, experiment done under astrological sign Taurus might not be replicable under Virgo, get me? Worth trying."

"Objection, third commentator—basically says only that up till now scientists concentrate some variables, ignore others, example astrological sign. Doesn't constitute different scientific method, only extension of method.

"Amendment fourth commentator's objection. Only goes to show that notions of cause determine sorts of variables tested. For sure Sanova suggests new variables to test; she's on about new notions of cause. Logical and it corresponds, right? So pro-Sanova."

"Okay, new objection for Sanova. Replication science predicts, example tachyons predicts before found in fact. Does nonreplication science predict? If not, what bloody good's it to us? You tell us when the lights'll be on next week, that'd be good science, eh?" The speaker cocked his bright-eyed, withered little face over his shoulder and grinned at the audience, who laughed at him. He was an old hand; anyone who ever went to street lectures knew him. Jocular and serious comments floated over the mass of heads toward him.

"Come on, Harry, you don't want to predict the lights; you want to predict the dogs." "So who wants to predict tachyons. That any more use to us?" "Dumb talk. If we were only interested our stomachs, wouldn't be here. Sanova wouldn't be here. Be licking a patron's bum instead."

Sanova grinned back at Harry and said loudly, "It's a good objection, in that maybe nonreplicatory science can't predict. But then it's becoming increasingly clear that replicating science predicts only in very narrow limits. Maybe prediction isn't a good way of understanding the world, get me?" Over the heads of the crowd, she saw a group of young people with gloves and padded jackets and sticks bearing down on them and added wryly, "But if it is, I predict the lights are going to be cut about one second from now."

Her students needed no time. They had already followed her gaze, and the Clubbers got a scatter of good-humored abuse as they came up. "Can't you do better than that?" yelled one backbencher. "Over in Melton they have lights seven nights a week."

"Not our fault," said one of the Clubbers. "We squared it with the Melton bastards. Power station shutdown at Portland. You'd better get moving."

Reluctantly, they got to their feet. Several came up to shake hands with Sanova and pay their dues of home-grown veggies, bottles of government orange juice, sheets of capsules. Some asked when and where she would be lecturing next. As she moved away to the pub to ring a bus, she found Harry walking beside her. His shoes were made from pieces of plastic carton, he walked with a chronic arthritic jerk, his thin, gray hair was tied back with an old piece of printer ribbon. But he grinned up at her cheerfully and shrewdly and said, "And what about it, eh? This company of yours employ you again next year? You think?"

"I don't know," said Sanova. "You're quite right; they want predictions. If they knew what I was doing, I wouldn't see the door they'd shove me out so fast. I asked the Market Research manager if she'll protect the project. She said she might."

"Pressure on her?"

"Yeah. Things are pretty tight." She hesitated a moment and said, "A guy upstairs suicided the other week, because he couldn't get his group any

more money to work on, and no one else would take them on. Alice—
she's the Market Research woman—told me to try for government grants
as well. So there you are; it might go either way."

Harry stretched his eyebrows comically up away from his eyes, as if
with incredulous innocence, then closed one eyelid with a parody of cunning. "Govament!" he said. "Govament! Nah. Govament won't have any
money soon. Bankrupting, they are. You listen to me. If they toss you out,
you come to us. We'll look after you. You'll see."

Sanova felt a burst of affection from him, for all her hungry, dilapi-
dated, keen-witted students. Of course they could not help. No amount of
improvisatory scrounging could provide the equipment to test the limits of
replicability in any fashion that would hold water. But they meant the offer
all the same. She smiled at Harry and patted his arm. She said, "Yes, I'll
remember."

Harry smiled back. They were standing at the door of the pub. "Got
some cash to buy me a drink?" he asked hopefully. Sanova gave him all
but her bus fare.

She went on down the street to ring for the bus. Already the lights
were cutting out in some of the side alleys. The phone booth, when she
reached it, was fortunately still functional, though the slime on its floor
and the smell of it showed clearly that its main use was as a public urinal.
Sanova balanced distastefully on the driest patch of the floor and waited
for the bus signal to come through. Another light went out. Soon it would
be dangerous to stay around alone, especially with a purse in hand. And
Alice, though she had been kind enough, had not rung back . . . all very
well for Patrick to be so unconcerned, he really did not care whether CoBia
employed him or not. *What shall I do?* she thought.

Because of the virotherapy, Wardour missed two of his patron's weekly
drinks parties, and he was too proud to ask whether anyone had seen Patrick or not. When he arrived at the third, he was given no chance to look
out for him. A furor of unexplained origin was taking place, and Danny
Considine again rushed to meet him. "Wardour, have you heard the news?
The government's fallen."

Wardour would have replied, "Again?" but had no time. Two of his
fellows came and swept him into the center of a serious discussion, presided
over by Lazarini. It appeared that the problem was not that the government
had fallen, but that no party or combination of parties could be persuaded
to take over the departed government's huge debts and increasing obligations. What would happen if this state of affairs were to continue was the

theme of the second patron's pontifications. What would happen to the Dorms, the Schools, the Hospitals? "I predict," said he, confidently ominous, "that there'll be anarchy, simple anarchy. Unless CoBia can put pressure on the New Liberals...."

"Anarchy?" said Wardour, as of a new and interesting word.

"In the Dorms, of course, in the Dorms. Among the unemployed," said the patron kindly.

"But my dear fellow (no, no sherry thanks; tea if there is some), my dear fellow, you speak as if people *like* anarchy, *want* anarchy, are only waiting for a chance to *exercise* it. Where did you pick up such a ridiculous idea? Now I know *nothing* about politics, nothing at all, but surely we can all see that some of the best brains of the last hundred years have *tried*, have attempted diligently to persuade people of the virtues of anarchy, and gotten absolutely nowhere. People will set up *any* sort of order rather than have none. It may not be the sort of order we like, but order of some sort in the Dorms there will be. Now tell me—do you seriously think the so-called government has in fact been running the Dorms for the last twenty years or so? Hm? Of course not. As I hear it, almost all institutions are now run of the Dorms by the Dorms for the Dorms—especially when it comes to law and order. So I really can't see that a lack of government will make so much difference."

There was a hush. The patron said, "Er, yes. Well," and appeared to lose all sense of direction. Matthew said, "You really are wonderful, Wardour. You make it sound so much less important than the authenticity of one of your medieval manuscripts."

"So it is," said Wardour happily, thinking of his unknown treasure. Lazarini laughed heartily and buffeted him painfully on the upper arm. The group split up, some attending the patron in another low-voiced doom discussion, others with Wardour, or chatting idly. Wardour prattled artlessly about sequence and symbolism in manuscripts, trying not to look across his listeners' shoulders as new arrivals came in the door. But Matthew had implied the boy was not a client of Lazarini, and he was undoubtedly right. ... "The dragon of Wrath, for instance, very interesting, is matched, I would hypothesize, by the Lion of Righteous Rage, neither precisely *heavenly*, if you see what I mean, but one considerably better than the other. Really, such a complicated view of the world. Everything with its counterparts in the various spheres." Someone quoted psychotherapy on rage and libido; someone else mentioned Dante. Wardour listened gracefully, but he felt immeasurably lonely. None of them, he thought confusedly, really knew what had happened. Governments, all governments, gone; a change that had never been seen, a world as it had not existed for what? ... ten thousand years? And all they could think of was their own safety. Perhaps they still thought they had safety to preserve. Surely Patrick would not say such stupid things, if one could ask him? And then suddenly he wondered if he were not so sad, so immensely miserable, because he, Wardour, would never see the new world, would die before he could observe it, he who had always loved new things, while the cowards, who were afraid of it, would live and never know what had been given them. Everything would go on, but he would not be there.

"Very plausible," he said. "Now Lawrence would say . . ."

He left the party early, as was increasingly his habit, and went downstairs intending to do no more than glance at the latest extension to Lazarini's gallery. Lazarini, for obscure reasons probably connected with the fall of the government, was anxious to have it opened to selected visitors as soon as possible. Lazarini's decorator, an unimaginative woman, immediately buttonholed him for detailed instructions on the lighting of various exhibits. Exasperated as he was by this triviality, Wardour was constrained to stand talking with her and marking-up the hanging diagram in detail. As he did so, someone walked by carrying a load of glass plates; and as if his nose or his ears telegraphed to his unconscious eyes, he looked up and saw Patrick. Patrick was wearing the same overalls as before, as if he had no other style of dress. He carried the heavy, brittle sheets unconcernedly, whistling softly the while, and set them down gently and precisely in their place. As he came back, he turned aside and stood patiently, evidently waiting for some further order or explanation from the decorator. She ignored him and Wardour, who had previously set her down as simply pompous, was now furious with her as a snob. Pointedly, he stopped talking and waited, hand on keyboard. She turned to Patrick with bad grace and asked him what he wanted.

"Nothing actually," said Patrick in his light, carefree voice. "It's the blokes downstairs. They've got another job to go to, and they say if they're not given parking room they'll take the whole load back to the warehouse. They're getting stroppy."

The director, with an air of self-righteous disgust and a hasty apology to Wardour, bustled off. Wardour and Patrick turned to watch her out of sight, shoulder to shoulder as if they were in collusion. Patrick said contentedly, "Thought that would get her off your back."

Wardour gaped at him. "My dear boy, how did you know? That I, er, that . . ." He had not been reduced to stammering since boyhood.

Patrick looked surprised. "Well, you did want her to stop going on about all that crap, didn't you?"

Dumbly, Wardour nodded. Patrick said cheerfully, "Well, I'd better get going. And I guess you want to get home." They turned together and ambled toward the door, Wardour, for the first time in his remembered life, with more will than power to speak. The doorway loomed ahead. He would have to turn one way, down the marble entrance corridor, and Patrick would go the other, to the loading bay, and there was nothing he could think of to say. At the last minute, desperately, he said, "This government bankruptcy—I trust it won't affect your prospects at all? I presume science is still safe in the hands of business?"

Patrick stopped, considering. "I think so," he said at last. "I expect there'll be lots of refugees crowding in, but I think CoBia'll keep me. They may want someone a bit keener, that's all. You know, run round after the project manager and look eager. I'm no good at that sort of thing. But I'll manage."

"If there's anything I can do—a recommendation . . . ?" said Wardour, and cursed himself for sounding so eager, like that classic figure of fun, the ancient lecher. But Patrick smiled at him and reached out to touch his arm. "That's good of you," he said. "That's nice. But I'll be okay, I don't care a lot what I do." He nodded good-bye and turned away.

Mercy, in her severe blue gown, was talking. "Forgiveness of all these you ask of me, and I will give you. Freely and unstintingly you are forgiven all your sins. For I, Mercy, have watched you in all your journey, have longed after you as a mother after her child. I watched you in your battle with Ire; I saw you lead Luxuria on a leash, as a tamed lion. You wandered in the thickets of worldly knowledge, and I saw you. You turned away from the poor man in his need, and I wept for you . . ."

Ame, his knees sore from the stony ground at Mercy's feet, felt a sudden alarm. What poor man? The other adventures he remembered, but what was this? Should he have seen something? Had he or Mercy got it wrong, and if so, how?

"Now at this time when you must be torn for a little while from the body that you have mastered, ask of me, and my sister Grace, and you shall have entrance to the holy city. . . ."

Ame looked round anxiously, but was relieved to see Cors stuffing himself with grass as usual. If a poor man was still to be found, he might need Cors. But how was he to explain this to Mercy, who apparently did not see the need at all? Could this indeed be Mercy, who stood before him as blind as Justice, never knowing that something was wrong, that he could not rise from his knees, that he was trapped again in a hiatus of indecision?

He closed his eyes against the aching of his legs and pressed his hands together to endure.

When Sanova got into work the next day, there was a notice on the terminal to contact the Marketing Manager. Sanova's stomach jumped. She had heard of the fall of the government on the bus news and expected no good things of it. It was possible that Alice had known it was impending when she suggested government grants, in which case it had been no suggestion but a clear warning. But if not? She picked up the phone and got the line message. After several agonizing minutes, Alice's voice said impatiently, "Yes, who's there?"

"Sanova. You asked me to call."

"Sanova, Sanova, oh yes, published a paper on reliability theory. Look, we can't get you in. This government crash will overload us ten applicants to each place."

Sanova said nothing. It was no worse than she had expected. Alice paused and went on, "I have got a suggestion. It's not much, but it's worth trying. You know Wardour?"

"Who?"

"Wardour. Art critic, journalist. Big name. Client of Lazarini's. He's dying, or so they say. AIDS probably. He's as gay as a gamer, but that's beside the point. There'll be a client vacancy. Lazarini's a generous patron. I can put a word in for you if you like."

"Please. Please do. Thank you," said Sanova. Alice had switched on to the next call before she finished. She put down the phone and was immediately stabbed through by a piercing blow of guilt. Be a client? Never go down to the street lectures? Leave brave Harry and fat Martha and all the rest just when the government money that gave them all their margin between desperation and livelihood was gone too? Never, and she had done it.

She went slowly back to her desk, and sat staring at the offprint on it. She had requested it some time ago. It was unpromisingly titled "Some notes Toward a Critique of the Theory of Experimental Practice." Unwillingly, she began to cry.

When Wardour came at last to the hospital, even Lazarini visited him. He had been given a single room. He had a console and desk beside his bed, but complained that the keys were too stiff to be used. It was a standard console. Only Matthew told him that there was nothing wrong with it.

In the intervals of typing, he arranged and rearranged his folder of illuminations. He was almost sure they were right, almost certain that the figure dividing his cloak with the beggar was, unlikely as it seemed, Ame rather than St. Martin. He was dressed in Ame's colors; and the beggar, oddly enough, had a twisted face a little like the juggler's in the feast scene. And all the while he pored over the paintings, he was nerving himself to ask a favor of Lazarini. He had never done it. Illogically it seemed to him worse than ordinary clientage, to take gifts and beg for more. But (he sometimes thought) there would be no shame to bother him after he was dead. And it was for Patrick. And he had, in his hand, a gift for Lazarini that would sell for millions.

When Lazarini arrived, Wardour was sitting propped up with the folder of illuminations in front of him. He said, without preamble, "These are yours. I had hoped to give them to you in a proper order, with a sufficient commentary. But I shan't have time. You'd better take them as they are." He held them out, open to the page of the feast of the humors and elements, white and green and gold and red and blue. Behind the high chair, where Ame sat, half-lord and half-subject of his strange guests, a jester with cropped hair and a twisted face juggled forever with five colored balls. Lazarini took it carefully, real delight on his face.

"What do you mean mine? I haven't seen this, have I?"

"Possibly not. It was in the Sikoyo collection you bought—in fragments, not as you see it here. I admit, I may have been wrong to keep my counsel all this while, but it was with the best intentions. It's certainly Renee of Anjou. A hitherto unknown work. It's worth millions to you, of course, even if you choose to sell it now."

Lazarini said nothing, turning the leaves carefully, by their edges, with his clean fingers. He noticed that Wardour's hands were covered with tiny blood blisters. There were slight smears of blood on the turned-back sheet, but none on the vellum pages. Wardour had used a cloth to handle the manuscript. There was a long silence. When he reached the end, Wardour said carelessly, "I hope you like it?"

"Like it! Well, yes, I—you old bastard," said Lazarini, and laughed. "You stupid, amazing old bastard; just shut up and let me look at this again."

Satisfied, Wardour watched him scrutinize the manuscript closely, giving little grunts of appreciation. *He pretends to know nothing but the value, but it's a pose,* thought Wardour, as if seeing the man for the first time. He waited, tensing himself for the right moment. Now, in a minute, in a minute more, he could get a job for Patrick—if he were careful. Lazarini looked up, and Wardour said, "So where will you sell it, do you think?"

But Lazarini for once did not answer. He smiled at Wardour, looking almost shy. He said at last, "I won't sell this. I can't do that. It's your life's work. What do you want done with it?" And then, the old habit of command reasserting itself, "No, don't tell me—I know. I'll set up an institute—with a gallery and school—I've been meaning to do something like that. I'll call it after you. We'll have every good young artist in the country trained there, and we'll have this manuscript there on display all the time. How about it?" He reached out and took Wardour's hand.

There was silence. Wardour was too moved and grief-stricken to speak. He saw Lazarini's face lightened and eager with rare affection and generosity and knew that he had lost, that he could never now throw back that offer and ask another favor. His throat swelled; he supposed it was a fair appearance of incredulous gratitude. He managed to shake Lazarini's hand and croak, "And scientists. We'll get a few good scientists as well." But that was all he could do.

In the morning, Sanova, bleary with crying, read on the message screen, "Contacted Lazarini. Reckon you're in. Alice." Wardour closed his folder and died, hemorrhaging. Harry took an overdose, reckoning correctly that his family could no longer afford to feed him. Ame stood on the threshold of a new city, white and gold under a new heaven, and heard the eternal music call him in.

C H R I S   L A W S O N

Chris Lawson is a relatively new writer who has published several times in *Eidolon,* now the leading Australian magazine in the genre, and in the ambitious original anthology *Dreaming Down Under* (1998). Now a medical doctor in Melbourne, he grew up in New Guinea on a crocodile farm. He says, "The writers who have most influenced me are the ideas men in SF: Bester, Asimov, Clarke, and Benford. It was George Turner, though, who showed me that it was possible to conjoin ideas and traditional narrative values, and I wish I'd had an opportunity to thank him properly." This story appeared in 1999 in *Asimov's.* "Occasionally," says Lawson, "in moments of extreme self-confidence, I even hope to change the way people think about the world."

CTA TAA CAG TGT AGC GAC GAA TGT CTA
CAG AAA CAA GAA TGT CAT GAG TGT CTA
GAT CAT AAC CGA TGT AGC GAC GAA TGT
CTA CAA GAA AGG AAT TAA GAG GGA TAC
CGA TGT AGC GAC GAA TGT CTA AAT CAT
CAA CAC AAA AGT AGT TAA CAT CAG AAA
AGC GAA TGC TTC TTT

In the Name of God, the Merciful, the Compassionate

THESE WORDS OPEN THE Qur'an. They were written in my father's blood.

After Mother died, and Da recovered from his chemotherapy, we went on a pilgrimage together. In my usual eleven-year-old curious way, I asked him why we had to go to the Other End of the World to pray when we could do it just fine at home.

"Zada," he said, "there are only five pillars of faith. It is easier than any of the other pillars because you only need to do it once in a lifetime. Remember this during Ramadan, when you are hungry and you know you will be hungry again the next day, but your *hajj* will be over."

Da would brook no further discussion, so we set off for the Holy

Lands. At eleven, I was less than impressed. I expected to find Paradise filled with thousands of fountains and birds and orchards and blooms. Instead, we huddled in cloth tents with hundreds of thousands of sweaty pilgrims, most of whom spoke other languages. As we tramped across a cramped and dirty wasteland, I wondered why Allah had made his Holy Lands so dry and dusty, but I had the sense even then not to ask Da about it.

Near Damascus, we heard about the bloodwriting. The pilgrims were all speaking about it. Half thought it blasphemous; the other half thought it a path to Heaven. Since Da was a biologist, the pilgrims in our troop asked him what he thought. He said he would have to go to the bloodwriters directly and find out.

On a dusty Monday, after morning prayer, my father and I visited the bloodwriter's stall. The canvas was a beautiful white, and the man at the stall smiled as Da approached. He spoke some Arabic, which I could not understand.

"I speak English," said my father.

The stall attendant switched to English with the ease of a juggler changing hands. "Wonderful, sir! Many of our customers prefer English."

"I also speak biology. My pilgrim companions have asked me to review your product."

I thought it very forward of my father, but the stall attendant seemed unfazed. He exuded confidence about his product.

"An expert!" he exclaimed. "Even better. Many pilgrims are distrustful of Western science. I do what I can to reassure them, but they see me as a salesman and not to be trusted. I welcome your endorsement."

"Then earn it."

The stall attendant wiped his moustache and began his spiel.

"Since the Dawn of Time, the Word of Allah has been read by mullahs. . . ."

"Stop!" said Da. "The Qur'an was revealed to Muhammad fifteen centuries ago; the Dawn of Time predates it by several billion years. I want answers, not portentous falsehoods."

Now the man was nervous. "Perhaps you should see my uncle. He invented the bloodwriting. I will fetch him."

Soon he returned with an older, infinitely more respectable man, with gray whiskers in his mustache and hair.

"Please forgive my nephew," said the old man. "He has watched too much American television and thinks the best way to impress is to use dramatic words, wild gestures, and, where possible, a toll-free number."

The nephew bowed his head and slunk to the back of the stall, chastened.

"May I answer your questions?" the old man asked.

"If you would be so kind," said Da, gesturing for the man to continue.

" 'Bloodwriting' is a good word, and I owe my nephew a debt of gratitude for that. But the actual process is something altogether more mundane. I offer a virus, nothing more. I have taken a hypoimmunogenic strain of adeno-associated virus and added a special code to its DNA."

Da said, "The other pilgrims tell me that you can write the Qur'an into their blood."

"That I can, sir," said the old man. "Long ago I learned a trick that would get the adeno-associated virus to write its code into bone marrow stem cells. It made me a rich man. Now I use my gift for Allah's work. I consider it part of my *zakât.*"

Da suppressed a wry smile. *Zakât*, charitable donation, was one of the five pillars. This old man was so blinded by avarice that he believed selling his invention for small profit was enough to fulfill his obligation to God.

The old man smiled and raised a small ampoule of red liquid. He continued, "This, my friend, is the virus. I have stripped its core and put the entire text of the Qur'an into its DNA. If you inject it, the virus will write the Qur'an into your myeloid precursor cells, and then your white blood cells will carry the Word of Àllah inside them."

I put my hand up to catch his attention. "Why not red blood cells?" I asked. "They carry all the oxygen."

The old man looked at me as if he noticed me for the first time. "Hello, little one. You are very smart. Red blood cells carry oxygen, but they have no DNA. They cannot carry the Word."

It all seemed too complicated to an eleven-year-old girl.

My father was curious. "DNA codes for amino acid sequences. How can you write the Qur'an in DNA?"

"DNA is just another alphabet," said the old man. He handed my father a card. "Here is the crib sheet."

My father studied the card for several minutes, and I saw his face change from skeptical to awed. He passed the card to me. It was filled with Arabic squiggles, which I could not understand. The only thing I knew about Arabic was that it was written right-to-left, the reverse of English.

"I can't read it," I said to the man. He made a little spinning gesture with his finger, indicating that I should flip the card over. I flipped the card and saw the same crib sheet, only with Anglicized terms for each Arabic letter. Then he handed me another crib sheet, and said, "This is the sheet for English text.

AAA a	AG	q	ATA	[–] dash	ACA
AAG b	AG	r	AT	[/] slash	ACG
AAT c	AG	s	ATT	{stop}	ACT
AAC d	AG	t	ATC	{stop}	ACC
GAA e	GG	u	GT	['] apostrophe	GCA {stop}
GAG f	GG	v	GT	["] quotation	GCG
GAT g	GG	w	GT	[(] open	GCT 0
GAC h	GG	x	GT	[)] close	GCC 1
TAA i	TG	y	TTA	[?] question	TCA 2
TAG j	TG	z	TT	[!]	TCG 3
TAT k	TG	[ ] space	TTT	[•] end verse	TCT 4
TAC l	TG	[.] full	TCC	[¶] paragraph	TCC 5
CAA m	CG	[,] comma	CTA	{cap} capital	CCA 6
CAG n	CG	[:] colon	CT		CCG 7
CAT o	CG	[;] semi-	CTT		CCT 8
CAC p	CG	[-] hyphen	CTC		CCC 9

"The Arabic alphabet has twenty-eight letters. Each letter changes form, depending on its position in the word. But the rules are rigid, so there is no need to put each variation in the crib sheet. It is enough to know that the letter is *aliph* or *bi,* and whether it is at the start, at the end, or in the middle of the word.

"The [stop] commands are also left in their usual places. These are the body's natural commands and they tell ribosomes when to stop making a protein. It only cost three spots and there were plenty to spare, so they stayed in."

My father asked, "Do you have an English translation?"

"Your daughter is looking at the crib sheet for the English language," the old man explained, "and there are other texts one can write, but not the Qur'an."

Thinking rapidly, Da said, "But you could write the Qur'an in English?"

"If I wanted to pursue secular causes, I could do that," the old man said. "But I have all the secular things I need. I have copyrighted crib sheets for all the common alphabets, and I make a profit on them. For the Qur'an, however, translations are not acceptable. Only the original words of Muhammad can be trusted. It is one thing for *dhimmis* to translate it for their own curiosity, but if you are a true believer you must read the Word of God in its unsullied form."

Da stared at the man. The old man had just claimed that millions of Muslims were false believers because they could not read the original Qur'an. Da shook his head and let the matter go. There were plenty of imams who would agree with the old man.

"What is the success rate of the inoculation?"

"Ninety-five percent of my trial subjects had identifiable Qur'an text in their blood after two weeks, although I cannot guarantee that the entire text survived the insertion in all of those subjects. No peer-reviewed journal would accept the paper." He handed my father a copy of an article from *Modern Gene Techniques*. "Not because the science is poor, as you will see for yourself, but because Islam scares them."

Da looked serious. "How much are you charging for this?"

"Aha! The essential question. I would dearly love to give it away, but even a king would grow poor if he gave a grain of rice to every hungry man. I ask enough to cover my costs, and no haggling. It is a hundred U.S. dollars or equivalent."

Da looked into the dusty sky, thinking. "I am puzzled," he said at last. "The Qur'an has one hundred and fourteen suras, which comes to tens of thousands of words. Yet the adeno-associated virus is quite small. Surely it can't all fit inside the viral coat?"

At this the old man nodded. "I see you are truly a man of wisdom. It is a patented secret, but I suppose that someday a greedy industrialist will lay hands on my virus and sequence the genome. So, I will tell you on the condition that it goes no further than this stall."

Da gave his word.

"The code is compressed. The original text has enormous redundancy, and with advanced compression, I can reduce the amount of DNA by over 80 percent. It is still a lot of code."

I remember Da's jaw dropping. "That must mean the viral code is self-extracting. How on earth do you commandeer the ribosomes?"

"I think I have given away enough secrets for today," said the old man.

"Please forgive me," said Da. "It was curiosity, not greed, that drove me to ask." Da changed his mind about the bloodwriter. This truly was fair *zakât*. Such a wealth of invention for only a hundred U.S. dollars.

"And the safety?" asked my father.

The old man handed him a number of papers, which my father read carefully, nodding his head periodically, and humming each time he was impressed by the data.

"I'll have a dose," said Da, "then no one can accuse me of being a slipshod reviewer."

"Sir, I would be honored to give a complimentary bloodwriting to you and your daughter."

"Thank you. I am delighted to accept your gift, but only for me. Not for my daughter. Not until she is of age and can make her own decision."

Da took a red ampoule in his hands and held it up to the light, as if he was looking through an envelope for the letters of the Qur'an. He shook his head at the marvel and handed it back to the old man, who drew it up in a syringe.

That night, our fellow pilgrims made a fire and gathered around to hear my father talk. As he spoke, four translators whispered their own tongues to the crowd. The scene was like a great theater from the *Arabian Nights*. Scores of people wrapped in white robes leaned into my father's words, drinking up his excitement. It could have been a meeting of princes.

Whenever Da said something that amazed the gathered masses, you could hear the inbreath of the crowd, first from the English speakers and then, in patches, as the words came out in the other languages. He told them about DNA, and how it told our bodies how to live. He told them about introns, the long stretches of human DNA that are useless to our bodies, but which we carry still from viruses that invaded our distant progenitors, like ancestral scars. He told them about the DNA code, with its triplets of adenine, guanine, cytosine, and thymine, and he passed around copies of the bloodwriter's crib sheet. He told them about blood and the white cells that fought infection. He talked about the adeno-associated virus and how it injected its DNA into humans. He talked about the bloodwriter's injection and the mild fever it had given him. He told them of the price. And he answered questions for an hour.

The next day, as soon as the morning prayers were over, the bloodwriting stall was swamped with customers. The old man ran out of ampoules by midmorning and only avoided a riot by promising to bring more the following day.

I had made friends with another girl. She was two years younger than I was, and we did not share a language, but we still found ways to play together to relieve the boredom.

One day I saw her giggling and whispering to her mother, who looked furtively at me and at Da. The mother waved over her companions and spoke to them in solemn tones. Soon a very angry-looking phalanx of women descended on my unsuspecting father. They stood before him, hands on hips, and the one who spoke English pointed a finger at me.

"Where is her mother?" asked the woman. She was taller than the others, a weather-beaten woman who looked like she was sixty but must have been younger because she had a child only two years old. "This is no place for a young girl to be escorted by a man."

"Zada's mother died in a car accident back home. I am her father, and I can escort her without help, thank you."

"I think not," said the woman.

"What right have you to say such a thing?" asked Da. "I am her father."

The woman pointed again. "Ala says she saw your daughter bathing, and she has not had the *khitan*. Is this true?"

"It is none of your business," said Da.

The woman screamed at him. "I will not allow my daughter to play with harlots. Is it true?"

"It is none of your business."

The woman lurched forward and pulled me by my arm. I squealed and twisted out of her grasp and ran behind my father for protection. I wrapped my arms around his waist and held on tightly.

"Show us," demanded the woman. "Prove she is clean enough to travel with this camp."

Da refused, which made the woman lose her temper. She slapped him so hard she split his lip. He tasted the blood, but stood resolute. She reached around and tried to unlock my arms from Da's waist. He pushed her away.

"She is not fit to share our camp. She should be cut, or else she will be shamed in the sight of Allah!" the woman screamed. The other women were shouting and shaking their fists, but few of them knew English, so it was as much in confusion as anger.

My father fixed the woman with a vicious glare. "You call my daughter shameful in the sight of Allah? I am a servant of Allah. Prove to me that Allah is shamed and I will do what I can to remove the shame. Fetch a mullah."

The woman scowled. "I will fetch a mullah, although I doubt your promise is worth as much as words in the sand."

"Make sure the mullah speaks English," my father demanded as she slipped away. He turned to me and wiped away my tears. "Don't worry, Zada. No harm will come to you."

"Will I be allowed to play with Ala?"

"No. Not with these old vultures hanging around."

By the evening, the women had found a mullah gullible enough to mediate the dispute. They tugged his sleeves as he walked toward our camp, hurrying him up. It was obvious that his distaste had grown with every minute in the company of the women, and now he was genuinely reluctant to speak on the matter.

The weathered woman pointed us out to the mullah and spat some words at him that we did not understand.

"Sir, I hear that your daughter is uncircumcised. Is this true?"

"It is none of your business," said Da.

The mullah's face dropped. You could almost see his heart sinking. "Did you not promise . . ."

"I promised to discuss theology with you and that crone. My daughter's anatomy is not your affair."

"Please, sir . . ."

Da cut him off abruptly. "Mullah, in your considered opinion, is it necessary for a Muslim girl to be circumcised?"

"It is the accepted practice," said the mullah.

"I do not care about the accepted practice. I ask what Muhammad says."

"Well, I'm sure that Muhammad says something on the matter," said the mullah.

"Show me where."

The mullah coughed, thinking of the fastest way to extract himself. "I did not bring my books with me," he said.

Da laughed, not believing that a mullah would travel so far to mediate a theological dispute without a book. "Here, have mine," Da said, as he passed the Qur'an to the mullah. "Show me where Muhammad says such a thing."

The mullah's shoulders slumped. "You know I cannot. It is not in the Qur'an. But it is sunnah."

"Sunnah," said Da, "is very clear on the matter. Circumcision is *makrumah* for women, it is honorable but not compulsory. There is no requirement for women to be circumcised."

"Sir, you are very learned. But there is more to Islam than a strict reading of the Qur'an and sunnah. There have even been occasions when the Word of Muhammad has been overturned by later imams. Muhammad himself knew that he was not an expert on all things, and he said that it was the responsibility of future generations to rise above his imperfect knowledge."

"So, you are saying that even if it was recorded in the Qur'an, that would not make it compulsory." Da gave a smile—the little quirk of his lips that he gave every time he had laid a logical trap for someone.

The mullah looked grim. The trap had snapped shut on his leg, and he was not looking forward to extricating himself.

"Tell these women so we can go back to our tents and sleep," said Da.

The mullah turned to the women and spoke to them. The weathered woman became agitated and started waving her hands wildly. Her voice was an overwrought screech. The mullah turned back to us.

"She refuses to share camp with you and insists you leave."

Da fixed the mullah with his iron gaze. "Mullah, you are a learned man in a difficult situation, but surely you can see the woman is half-mad. She complains that my daughter has not been mutilated and would not taint herself with my daughter's presence. Yet she is tainted herself. Did she tell you that she tried to assault my daughter and strip her naked in public view? Did she tell you that she inflicted this wound on me when I stood between her and my daughter? Did she tell you that I have taken the bloodwriting, so she spilled the Word of God when she drew blood?"

The mullah looked appalled. He went back to the woman, who started screeching all over again. He cut her off and began berating her. She stopped talking, stunned that the mullah had turned on her. He kept berating her until she showed a sign of humility. When she bowed her head, the mullah stopped his tirade; but as soon as the words stopped she sent a dagger glance our way.

That night, three families pulled out of our camp. Many of the others in camp were pleased to see them go. I heard one of the grandmothers mutter, *"Taliban,"* under her breath, making a curse of the words.

The mood in camp lifted, except for mine. "It's my fault Ala left," I said.

"No, it is not your fault," said Da. "It was her family's fault. They want the whole world to think and to do what they do. This is against the teaching of the Qur'an, which says that there shall be no coercion in the matter of faith. I can find the sura if you like."

"Am I unclean?"

"No," said Da, "you are the most beautiful girl in the world."

By morning, the camp had been filled by other families. The faces were more friendly, but Ala was gone. It was my first lesson in intolerance, and it came from my own faith.

———————————

In Sydney, we sat for hours, waiting to be processed. By the third hour, Da finally lost patience and approached the customs officer.

"We are Australian citizens, you know?" Da said.

"Please be seated. We are still waiting for cross-checks."

"I was born in Brisbane, for crying out loud! Zada was born in Melbourne. My family is Australian four generations back."

His protests made no difference. Ever since the Saladin outbreak, customs checked all Muslims thoroughly. Fifty residents of Darwin had died from an outbreak of a biological weapon that the Saladins had released. Only a handful of Saladins had survived, and they were all in prison. It had been years ago, but Australia still treated its Muslims as if every single one of us was a terrorist waiting for the opportunity to go berserk.

We were insulted, shouted at, and spat on by men and women who then stepped into their exclusive clubs and talked about how uncivilized we were. Once it had been the Aborigines, then it had been the Italian and Greek immigrants; a generation later it was the Asians; now it was our turn. Da had thought that we could leave for a while, go on our pilgrimage, and return to a more settled nation; but our treatment by the customs officers indicated that little had changed in the year we were away.

They forced Da to strip for a search and nearly did the same for me until Da threatened them with child molestation charges. They took blood samples from both of us. They went through our luggage ruthlessly. They X-rayed our suitcases from so many angles that Da joked they would glow in the dark.

Then they made us wait, which was the worst punishment of all.

Da leaned over to me and whispered, "They are worried about my blood. They think that maybe I am carrying a deadly virus like a Saladin. And who knows? Maybe the Qur'an *is* a deadly virus." He chuckled.

"Can they read your blood?" I asked.

"Yes, but they can't make sense of it without the code sheet."

"If they knew it was just the Qur'an texts, would they let us go?"

"Probably," said Da.

"Why don't you give it to them then?"

He sighed. "Zada, it is hard to understand, but many people hate us for no reason other than our faith. I have never killed or hurt or stolen from anyone in my life, and yet people hate me because I pray in a church with a crescent instead of a cross."

"But I want to get out of here," I pleaded.

"Listen to me, daughter. I could show them the crib sheet and explain it to them, but then they would know the code, and that is a terrifying possibility. There are people who have tried to design illnesses that attack only Jews or only blacks, but so far they have failed. The reason why they have failed is that there is no serological marker for Jewish or Negro blood. Now we stupid Muslims, and I count myself among the fools, have identified ourselves. In my blood is a code that says that I am a Muslim, not just by birth, but by active faith. I have marked myself. I might as well walk into a neo-Nazi rally wearing a Star of David.

"Maybe I am just a pessimist," he continued. "Maybe no one will ever design an anti-Muslim virus, but it is now technically possible. The longer it takes the *dhimmis* to find out how, the better."

I looked up at my father. He had called himself a fool. "Da, I thought you were smart!"

"Most of the time, darling. But sometimes faith means you have to do the dumb thing."

"I don't want to be dumb," I said.

Da laughed. "You know you can choose whatever you want to be. But there is a small hope I have for you. To do it you would need to be very, *very* smart."

"What?" I asked.

"I want you to grow up to be smart enough to figure out how to stop the illnesses I'm talking about. Mark my words, racial plagues will come one day unless someone can stop them."

"Do you think I could?"

Da looked at me with utter conviction. "I have never doubted it."

Da's leukemia recurred a few years later. The chemotherapy had failed to cure him after all, although it had given him seven good years, just long enough to see me to adulthood and enrolled in genetics.

I tried to figure out a way to cure Da, but I was only a fresher. I understood less than half the words in my textbooks. The best I could do was hold his hand as he slowly died.

It was then that I finally understood what he meant when he said that sometimes it was important not to be smart. At the climax of our hajj we had gone around the Kaaba seven times, moving in a human whirlpool. It made no sense at all intellectually. Going around and around a white temple in a throng of strangers was about as pointless a thing as you could possibly do, and yet I still remember the event as one of the most moving in my life. For a brief moment I felt a part of a greater community, not just of Muslims, but of the universe. With that last ritual, Da and I became hajj and hajji and it felt wonderful.

But I could not put aside my thoughts the way Da could. I had to be smart. Da had asked me to be smart. And when he died after four months and two failed chemo cycles, I no longer believed in Allah. I wanted to maintain my faith, as much for my father as for me, but my heart was empty.

The event that finally tipped me, although I did not even realize it until much later, was seeing his blood in a sample tube. The oncology nurse had drawn 8 mls from his central line then rolled the sample tube end over end to mix the blood with the anticoagulant. I saw the blood darken in the tubes as it deoxygenated, and I thought about the blood cells in there. The white cells contained the suras of the Qur'an, but they also carried the broken code that turned them into cancer cells.

Da had once overcome leukemia years before. The doctors told me it was very rare to have a relapse after seven years. And this relapse seemed to be more aggressive than the first one. The tests, they told me, indicated this was a new mutation.

Mutation: a change in genetic code. Mutagen: an agent that promotes mutation.

Bloodwriting, by definition, was mutagenic. Da had injected 114 suras into his own DNA. The designer had been very careful to make sure that the bloodwriting virus inserted itself somewhere safe so it would not disrupt a tumor-suppressor gene or switch on an oncogene—but that was for normal people. Da's DNA was already damaged by leukemia and chemotherapy. The virus had written a new code over the top, and I believe the new code switched his leukemia back on.

The Qur'an had spoken to his blood, and said:

He it is Who created you from dust, then from a small lifegerm, then from a clot, then He brings you forth as a child, then that you may attain your maturity, then that you may be old—and of you there are some who are caused to die before—and that you may reach an appointed term, and that you may understand. He it is who gives life and brings death, so when He decrees an affair, He only says to it: Be, and it is.

I never forgave Allah for saying, "Be!" to my father's leukemia.

An educated, intelligent biologist, Da must have suspected that the Qur'an had killed him. Still, he never missed a prayer until the day he died. My own faith was not so strong. It shattered like fine china on concrete.

Disbelief is the only possible revenge for omnipotence.

An infidel I was by then, but I had made a promise to my father, and for my postdoc I solved the bloodwriting problem. He would have been proud.

I abandoned the crib sheet. In my scheme the codons were assigned randomly to letters. Rather than preordaining *TAT* to mean *zen* in Arabic or "k" in English, I designed a process that shuffled the letters into a new configuration every time. Because there are sixty-four codons with three {stop} marks and eight blanks, that comes to about 5×10^{83} or 500, 000,000, 000,000,000,000,000,000,000,000,000,000,000,000,000,000,000,000,000,000, 000,000,000,000,000,000,000,000 combinations. No one could design a virus specific to the Qur'an suras anymore. The *dhimmi* bastards would need to design a different virus for every Muslim on the face of the earth.

The faith of my father was safe to bloodwrite.

In my own blood I have written the things important to me. There is a picture of my family, a picture of my wedding, and a picture of my parents from when they were both alive. Pictures can be encoded just as easily as text.

There is some text: Crick and Watson's original paper describing the double-helix of DNA, and Martin Luther King's "I Have a Dream" speech. I also transcribed Cassius's words from *Julius Caesar:*

> The fault, dear Brutus, is not in our stars,
> But in ourselves, that we are underlings.

For the memory of my father, I included a Muslim parable, a *sunnah* story about Muhammad: One day, a group of farmers asked Muhammad for evidence on improving their crop. Muhammad told the farmers not to pollinate their date trees. The farmers recognized Muhammad as a wise man and did as he said. That year, however, none of the trees bore any dates. The farmers were angry, and they returned to Muhammad, demanding an explanation. Muhammad heard their complaints, then pointed out that he was a religious man, not a farmer, and his wisdom could not be expected to encompass the sum of human learning. He said, "You know your worldly business better."

It is my favorite parable from Islam and is as important in its way as Jesus's Sermon on the Mount.

At the end of my insert, I included a quote from the *dhimmi* Albert Einstein recorded the year after the atomic bombing of Japan.

He said, "The release of atom power has changed everything but our way of thinking," then added, "The solution of this problem lies in the heart of humankind."

I have paraphrased that last sentence into the essence of my new faith. No god was ever so succinct.

My artificial intron reads:

```
CTA  AGC  GAC  GAA  TGT  AGT  CAT  TAC  GGA
AGC  TAA  CAT  CAG  TGT  TAC  TAA  GAA  AGT
TGT  TAA  CAG  TGT  AGC  GAC  GAA  TGT  GAC
GAA  AAA  AGG  AGC  TGT  CAT  GAG  TGT  GAC
GGA  CAA  AAA  CAG  TAT  TAA  CAG  AAC  TGC
```

Eight words, 45 codons, 135 base pairs that say:

The solution lies in the heart of humankind.

I whisper it to my children every night.

KEVIN McKAY

James Kevin McKay was born in a small town in the state of Victoria, where his father owned the local newspaper and printing shop. He passed a Commonwealth Public Service entrance examination and became a telegraph boy (telgraph services were part of the federal postal system), and this set him on his career course: "Over the years I was a mailman, sorter, postal clerk, telegraphist (both Morse and teleprinter), and later, in administrative jobs . . . finally I found my true postal *métier*, the Stamps and Philatelic Section." He retired from this creative job after more than fifteen years involved in designing stamps, aerograms, special postmarks, etc., in 1976, due to heart problems. And in that year he wrote his first SF and fantasy stories. He'd liked SF from childhood. He lived in a remote country town until the age of twenty, where very few books or magazines were available, but nevertheless he has been an SF reader since the 1930s—Wells, Verne, the usual suspects. And when he moved to a larger country town, Mildura, he found some secondhand U.S. magazines—*Amazing, Astounding*. His writing somewhat overlapped his BA studies, starting in 1976 when he retired from work, and ceased about a decade later.

"Pie Row Joe" was politely bounced by the editor of *Fantasy & Science Fiction* before McKay entered it in a short story contest at Unicon IV, the Australian National Convention in 1978, where the guests of honor were Brian Aldiss and Roger Zelazny; he won first prize (George Turner was a judge), and was approached by Lee Harding, who took the piece for *Rooms of Para-*

dise. Then it was reprinted in Terry Carr's influential *Best SF of the Year,* and was nominated for a Ditmar Award in competition with four novels. Later, he was asked for stories by the other editors he sold to, but he published only four SF stories. He never attended another convention. He knows they exist but has never been part of fandom. He has read very little Aussie SF, or any other kind in recent years, although he still subscribes to *F&SF*—he misses clever tales with a twist in the tale, or sociological commentary. "Style is everything."

I DON'T WANTA FINISH up in the cold, mate, so 'scuse me if I don't get up to shake 'ands.

I know what's wrong with you; I seen 'em bring you in with a busted leg, 'n' I 'eard the doc and the nurses talkin' about you fallin' orf a tractor. I'm dyin' for a smoke—spose ya wouldn't 'ave one on ya? No—the big dame woulda taken 'em offa ya.

This ain't a bad 'ospital for a little country joint like this, 'cept for them two: the whoppin' big sheila like a white-painted paddle steamer, and the skinny dried-up little dame like a nole thistle ready to blow away, or burn up. Starch 'n' Husk, I call 'em. Got them names from the TV down the pub.

Bloody freezin' in 'ere. Ya'd think they'd 'ave a bit o' fire. You like fires? I do. Always 'ave done, ever since I can remember, even before I went to school. We 'ad wood fires in them days. My ole man usta cut 'is own firewood; usta put on big logs and stumps. I usta sit, watchin' 'em burn. They all made diffrunt pikshers like.

Big long logs, they go in gray color, with long wavy cracks right down 'em. 'N' at first, ya think they never gonna burn, cos the pale yella flame is breathin' over 'em, 'n' nothin' 'appens. 'N' then, gray smoke starts comin' out the cracks, 'n' they start, real slow, sorta goin' black. 'N' then little red glowworms starts creepin' over the surface, just like when a dry leaf starts to catch.

Y'ever start a campfire out in the bush? with a handful uv dry leaves fer kindlin'? Ya start 'er up, 'n' ya think she's not gonna go, but then them little red worms starts crawlin', and the wind huffs on 'er 'n' she flares and crackles, 'n' ya say, "She's right now," and ya put on some bigger stuff.

Look—pay a-bloody-tention when a man's talkin' to ya. Stick ya bloody book away, 'n' ya might learn somethin'. Wish I 'ad a smoke. Any-'ow, I know where I can get one.

Them big logs, once they was really goin', they'd give orf gray smoke and then clear bright yella flames. 'N' then—pfft—a little pocket of gas or sumpin 'ud burst out and send out a clear jet of flame, clean as anything ya ever see. But she wouldn't last; she'd die out, like the arse end o' one o' them moon rockets I seen on telly; then she'd fizzle. Like everything a man ever tries to do.

I done lotsa things in me time; I've worked up 'n' down this river all me life. I've picked t'bacca up Myrtleford 'n' t' matters at Shepparton; I've snatched grapes every summer year after year, on me knees in red dirt, with burnin' sun on me bare back and cuts all over me bloody 'ands. I've shore sheep up the Darling, till I never want to smell that stink o' sheep shit and wet wool again. They can shove their wool. . . .

Y'ever see wool burnin'? It don't burn proper, like wood. Kind of comes up in black bubbles, and stinks, and crawls over itself like.

Got a cig? No, I ast ya that. 'N' I told ya, taint polite to read when a man's talkin' to ya. What was I sayin'? Yeah, about fires.

Funny 'ow a log goes into the fireplace all of one piece like, but after she's burnt a bit she starts to cut up into little squares, like snake skin. Ya can watch them little bits, and they go gray outside, but in the cracks in between it's red as guts, like when ya butcher a bunny.

'N' finally, she gets a crawly kinda gray ash all over, and ya start askin' yaself, will she fall this second? the next? the one after that? But she always beats ya; just when ya thinks she's never gonna fall, away she goes.

Up go the sparks, like the souls of all the inseks what ever lived in the wood when she was alive—termites, ants, grubs. Where do they go? Up the chimney, sure, but after that?

Bugger it, listen, willya? I'm tryin' to tell ya how to start a fire. You're like the young bucks up the pub, know every bloody thing. I gave up tryin' to watch TV after they put in the pool table. Man couldn't hear 'imself think for smart alecks yellin' and shoutin' out what shots they gonna play next—and then missin' 'em.

I seen Walter Lindrum play up the Cliffs once. You wouldn't even know who 'e was, mate. Only the best player 'Stralia ever 'ad, that's who—'e could play all these young sods on a break with both 'ands tied be'ind 'im.

Talkin' about 'ands, I can still shut me eyes and see Gerald's 'and the day that schoolteacher bastard 'it 'im. It was in the wintertime, cos I remember we 'ad a fire in the classroom, and I was watchin' it, in between doin' me school work, 'cos I like fires. When I was real young, before I went to school, I usta go out in the bush and start me own fires.

When me old man went farmin', only land 'e could afford was way out in the never-nevers, where a bloody lizard couldn't live unless 'e 'ad 'is own lunch 'n' water bag. The ole man 'ad to clear the bush with two 'orses. 'Nuther thing you wouldn't know nothin' about, 'cept 'ow it runs at Flemington. We 'ad two great big Clydesdales, Punch and Judy. 'Itch a chain to 'em, and the other end round a tree stump. Never 'ad to use the whip, just yell out to 'em, and they'd belly down and 'eave, 'n' out she'd come clean as a whistle. We'd burn orf the small branches 'n' keep the logs and big stumps fer firewood fer the winter. She could get real cold out there in that Mallee country.

You still listenin', mate? I'll go and get us both a smoke when I finish what I wanta tell ya. Any'ow . . .

When I was three or four, the ole man was still clearin' the land. Much good it did 'im. Bloody sand country it was; only thing 'eld it together was the scrub what 'e was doin' 'is best to get rid of. When 'e took it all orf, and got the paddicks plowed, the first good breeze sent the topsoil airmail to Noo Zealand.

That Husk, the nurse, she's like a bloody dried-up thistle, all gray and skinny and prickly. I seen thistles like that out in the Mallee. In the middle of a paddick, one lousy little thistle, maybe only a foot 'igh, what stopped the grains o' sand when the wind blew, and built up a sand 'll three foot 'igh and six foot long downwind of itself.

I seen fences, mate, built on top o' one another. The first'd stop the sand, and evenchally get buried; then the poor bastard farmer'd afta build another, nailin' the new droppers to wotever was left stickin' up. 'N' they reckoned it was wheat land!

Ever seen a fire in a paddick uv ripe wheat? She really goes; not much smoke then, mate, only whirls of orange-red fire, goin' maybe forty miles a nour if there's a good wind be'ind 'er.

Any'ow, I was tellin' ya, I like fire. Before I went to school, and me dad and mum was busy on the farm, I usta go walkabout in the scrub. 'N' I usta siddown and look at a patch of dry grass, and think 'ow nice it'd be if I 'ad a little fire, like. I didn't want it for warmth, y'understand, just wanted to look at 'er, 'n' maybe play with 'er a bit.

'N' a coupla times, or maybe more—I dunno, I'm talkin' about fifty year ago—I started some fires that burnt through into where the ole man was workin', or maybe toward the hut, cos I can remember 'im sayin' to me mum: "Girl, I dunno where 'e gets them matches, but for Gawd's sake keep the things away from 'im, cos 'e is a pie row maniac." 'N' me mum said, "I swear I have every match in this house in my apron pocket."

Any'ow, I was tellin' ya about me friend Gerald. 'E was me best school-mate, although I got along with the other kids alright, 'speshly when I usta start a bit uv a campfire for 'em after school. We 'ad a real nice lady, Miss Sims, for a teacher. It was only a bit of a country school like, with little and big kids all mixed up together, but it was all OK till I was in sixth grade, when they sent Miss Sims orf to another school, and we copped this bastard Searce.

'E was a washed-out gingernut, hair like a dead fox, eyes like a dead codfish, eyelashes like dead fishes' bones.

"DISSIPLINE!" he says. "That is what is needed here. When I come into the room, you all sit at attention," 'e says. "Ow can ya *sit* at attention, mate? But 'e knew. When 'e come in, we was all sposed to sit upright, feet together, backs straight, eyes front, 'ands joined be'ind backs. 'N' ya dare not look sideways, cos 'e 'ad this great big strap.

It was made, I reck'n, from draft 'orse 'arness—double-sided leather, with a packing piece in between, stitched all round, and weighin' about a pound and a 'alf. 'E always carried it, and 'e could be quicker on the draw than Tom Mix.

Me and me mate, Gerry, sat in the desk right next to the door. Like I told ya, I was writin' a bit, and lookin' at the fire, and thinkin' to meself, "I'll make that log bust in half NOW," when I look from the fire to dead in front of me, and there 'e is. Searce, the sod. Rubber soles, 'e wore, 'n' sneaked around like a black fella creepin' on plovers. Outa the corner of me eye I see all the other kids sit at attention, and so do I.

Poor ole Gerald, 'e was a good kid, 'e's still workin', con-she-enshus like. Got 'is left 'and 'oldin' down the left page of 'is ecker book, 'n the pen in 'is right 'and, and so wrapped up in what 'e's doin' that 'e wouldn't wake up if a dunny fell on 'im.

I dare not look up in case I meet them fish eyes. I stare straight in front at the leather buttons on the sports coat and the end o' the strap stickin' outa the pocket. I think as hard as I can to Gerald: "Wake up, mate, wake up!" but I never was any good at thinkin' at people. I'm fright-ened to give 'im a poke with me knee, cos Fisheyes can see me legs. So I sit like a statchoo, tryin' to think at Gerald. No good. That's one of the few things in me life, mate, that I'm sorry for.

Fisheyes stan's there for what seems like 'alf a nour. Then 'e slowly pulls out the strap, slowly, as if 'e's lickin' 'is chops. And BANG! 'e gets Gerald right acrost the back of the left hand.

Poor Gerry nilly shit 'imself. Up 'e jumps, and mita gorn through the ceilin' 'cept that 'is knees comes ker-runch up against the bottom of the desk. Back of 'is 'and goes white, and then red, and starts palpitatin'. "That's for not sitting to attention when I come in."

Searce goes over to warm 'is arse at the fire. I knew 'e smoked, 'n kept a tin o' wax matches in 'is 'ip pocket, cos I'd seen 'em. 'N I thought, "Wouldn't it be beaut if 'is matches caught fire?"

All uv a sudden 'e screamed, 'n' jumped 'igher than Gerry, 'n' grabbed at 'is pocket. I 'ope those bloody matches burned a foot into 'im. 'Is pants caught fire, and 'e whacked at 'em like a wheat lumper with a mouse up 'is leg.

Talkin' about legs, yours is bust in two places, I 'eard Starchy say. So I'll be outa 'ere afore you, mate. I'm only burnt a bit, that's all; be right as rain soon. I'll tell ya 'ow I come to be in 'ere if you'll put that book away. It's all bullshit any'ow.

Any'ow, as I was sayin', I'm burnt a bit. It was me own fault, so I gotta take me medicine.

I didn't leave meself a way out, see? That was me trouble. But 'e never shoulda sooled them dorgs onto me; that's when 'e really arst for it. 'E was worse than Starchy, 'n' she's bad enough. What's more, even ya bed ain't ya own in this bloody 'orspital. I got outa mine awhile ago and, bugger me, when I tries to get back in, there's some other joker in it!

I felt like goin' to 'ave a pee, see, 'n' when I turn around and look back, 'eres this other bastard in me bed. Real crook 'e 'is—looks like a roast duck. 'Is skin's nicely browned all over, 'e's got choobs stuck up 'is snout and other places, 'n' Starchy 'n' Husk is messin' around 'im like crows around a dead lamb.

"Strike me 'andsome," I says to meself, "a man better go back or 'e'll finish up out in the cold" so I moved in again, and some'ow they got this other joker out.

Any'ow, what was I sayin'? Aw yeah, out.

That's 'ow I moved out uv school. Searce's pants were on fire, see, and 'e's jumpin' up and down like a frill-neck lizard. I 'adn't learnt then to keep me face closed, and I dunno 'ow 'e guessed, but 'e looked straight at me and picked me for settin' fire to the wax matches. 'E just went plain berserk, comin' at me with the strap up.

I raced fer the door 'n' out I went, straight for 'ome. When I get there I kep' goin' into the scrub, but I 'ung around the edges of the bush to see what'd 'appen. Presently, up 'e comes in 'is 1928 Ford, 'n' I could see 'im layin' down the law to me ole man.

'N I got to thinkin', "What if 'is petrol tank 'sploded?"

BLOOOOM! Fisheyes and the ole man are runnin' for their lives.

Fisheyes walked orf, offa our property; me ole man come lookin' for me. 'Venchally, of course, 'e caught me.

"But 'e hit Gerry, Dad," I said. "Fer nothin'. Nothin' a tall!"

"I believe you, son," me dad said. "But you know I'm gonna hafta hit you for somethin'. You got this pie row mania, and I gotta try to cure it." So 'e cut a four-foot len'th of whipstick Mallee, and 'e let me have it. That night I left, in the dark.

Soon as it gets a bit darker in 'ere, I'm gonna go 'n' get a smoke, and I ain't forgot ya. Getcha one too. Smoke's a funny thing. Ever noticed 'ow, no matter what side of a campfire ya sits on, the smoke always seems to come your way? One of the laws o' Nachur, I reckon. Wind's from the south, so ya sits on the south, and still ya cop it, because she goes and switches.

That's what buggered me. She switched from the north to the south, and I didn't leave meself no way out.

I did leave me mum a note. I said I loved 'er and Dad, and I'd come back when the schoolteacher bizness died down. Well, ya know what they say 'bout good intentions. I never did get back there before me mum and dad died. I've seen the old 'omestead, but it's like what I told ya, mate, just all sand blowin'.

Any'ow, I was tellin' ya, campfires. I've sat round thousands of 'em, Myrtleford to Renmark, Mildura to Bourke. I never carried matches; wasn't no need to. I c'd always rake up a few dry leaves 'n' sticks, and think 'ow nice it'd be if I 'ad a little fire. 'N' next thing ya know, there she was, cracklin' away like a beauty. Sometimes, even, if I was real tired, I wouldn't even bother to carry the bigger bits of wood; I'd just think 'em over to the fire, like.

'N' sometimes, if I'd been on the booze and I was showin' orf, I'd do me little tricks for me mates, wantin' to show 'em how to start a campfire, 'n' bring some wood, without matches or sweat. But they was mostly dopey; they could never catch on to the way of it. Some of 'em knew the same words as me old man, and that's why they call me "Pie Row Joe."

Good mates, they was. I never 'urt nobody after that schoolteacher bastard, till just afore I got shoved in 'ere.

That Starchy can shove—she could push Jack Dempsey around. "Turn Mister Burns over," she says. "Mister Burns"—strike me lucky, that's me! I never been called that afore in me life. The doc is talkin' some garbage about critical loss of fluids. 'E could lose some 'imself, 'e's still wet be'ind the ear'oles.

I'm still cold. It was bloody hot that day. I was humpin' me swag, comin' down through Karamull. On the hoof, 'opin to 'itch 'ike a bit, when

I sees a shortcut acrost the paddicks. I been there before, so I knows the owner is a bastard, and a lucky one at that. In the drought, when 'is neighbours was flat out like a lizard drinkin', every bloody thunderstorm, the only rain in it would fall on *his* paddicks, but 'e wouldn't help nobody.

But I didn't want nothin' from 'im. I was just takin' a shortcut. 'Is wheat was four foot tall, and ripe, 'n' Blind Freddy could see 'e was gonna get twenty bags to th' acre while the other poor sods wasn't even gonna get their seed back.

The road went a mile that way, and then a mile back, 'n' all the time I could see the pub only two 'undred yards away acrost the crop. It was buh-luddy 'ot. 'Undred and twenty in the shade, 'cept there wasn't none, and a 'owlin' north wind right in me face. I was chewin' sand between me teeth, it was in me eyes, I was 'angin' onto me 'at, 'n' them dry roley-poleys, big as sheep, was bowlin' along and stingin' me in the face like flyin' barbwire. I kep' thinkin' of a big cold beer, so I decides to risk it through the fence.

Well, 'e'd ploughed a firebreak right along the wire, so I does the right thing; I sticks to the break 'stead o' trampin' down the ripe crop. Next thing I knows, 'e's yellin', "Get to buggery outa there," and soolin' his bloody dorgs on to me. Bastards, they was, like 'im. Yellow, like dingoes, like Fisheyes's hair. So I runs, and scrambles through the other fence, and rips me last decent pair of strides.

The pub was just up the road, so I got a beer, and then some more. One led to another, like. Was just the day fer it—'undred and twenty, and red 'ot wind like a furnace blast, and dust and dirt, and the sky fulla curlicue clouds.

Any'ow, where was I? Yeah, 'ow I got into 'orspital.

So, the sun went down, like a ball o' fire, 'n' I got to thinkin', oo's that bastard to sool the dorgs on to me? Never done 'im no 'arm. Be nice if 'is wheat caught fire.

So I started back up the track in the dark. Dark in 'ere; soon be safe to go and pinch some smokes, even if we can't find no booze.

Boy, was I boozed that night. I c'n just remember wheat paddicks each side of the gravel road, 'n' scrub and dry grass between the wire fences right up to the edge of the gravel.

I leaned on the top wire of 'is north fence 'n' thought about a little fire. Only a little 'un. Lovely little yellow flames, lickin' round the bottoms of the wheat stalks. Next thing I knows, it's roarin' through the crop, yellow and red and orange and twistin' in the dark, with wriggly burnin' stalks flyin' up in the air and droppin' back ahead of the main fire to start new 'uns. 'N' the north wind, still blowin' a red 'ot gale, right be'ind the lot.

Beautiful, she was. Beautiful, mate. You never seen nothin' so lovely.

'N' the farmer's out there, like a madman, with a little squirt 'stinguisher on 'is back; 'n' when that's done, with green boughs ripped offa the scrub trees beside the road.

'N' I'm laughin'. Laughin' fit to kill.

Kill? I never meant to kill the sod. Jus' made a bit o' a mistake, that's all. 'N' I know where I made it.

All uv a sudden I felt that the hot northerly had dropped. Died stone dead it 'ad, and there was a smell like wet dirt, like maybe a few spots o' rain in the air. Just all kinda quiet for a minute, with this earthy smell, 'stead o' the stink o' burnin' grass. I knew what I'd forgot.

But I shoulda known it. The signs 'ad been there all day—the northerly, the curling-up long white clouds. There was gonna be a cool change, with a roarin' southerly buster. 'N' there I was, with dry grass, dry scrub 'n' dry wheat all around me, and the fire on me wrong side. I starts to run for me life.

I knew e-zackly where I was goin'. Back two 'undred yards along the road was a storm-water drain, a three-foot concrete pipe under the gravel. It 'ad white posts, so people wouldn't drive cars into it, and there was some kind o' notice board. If I was lucky, I might get to it. 'F I was real lucky, might even be water in it.

The wind shifted, bang! from north to south. The flames came back on theirselves; the wheat crackled and twisted in corkscrews of fire. The Mallee scrub along the sides of the road was lit up for two 'undred yards, redlike, and balls uv burnin' wheat and roley-poleys like Catherine wheels was jumpin' the road, and startin' up flames on the other side. The tops of the trees was burnin', too.

A rabbit ran acrost the road. 'S fur was smokin'. 'S eyes was lit up, orange. They reckon rabbits can see backward as well as forward. What was you lookin' at then, little fella? Your past life? I never meant to get ya, pal.

I c'd see the signpost at the drain. 'Twas one of them stupid things the fire brigades puts up ter try to stop people from startin' bushfires. It was white paint, shinin' orange; it said, "FIRE IS A GOOD SERVANT BUT A BAD MASTER."

I was lookin' at it in a funny way, like, from face down in the gravel. The white paint was all bubblin' and blisterin', and so were me 'ands 'n' arms.

So that's 'ow I come 'ere, and that's all I can remember, mate, till I woke up in this 'orspital. But I'll soon be out, be out afore you, pal. Getcha that smoke now. The doc keeps 'is in 'is desk. I don't like 'is brand—

they're them brown things, like little cigars, like rolled-up used crap paper. But I'll getcha one.

I gets outa me bed. Bit wobbly on the old pins, like. I floats down the corridor, and I grabs one of the quack's smokes. I goes back to the ward, and bugger me! Starchy has done it again. The ole roast duck is back in me bloody bed.

"Bugger you, mate," I says. "Move over."

'E don't move, 'e's still got all this junk shoved up 'is snout, and what's more, 'e looks bloody near dead.

"OK," I says, "I'm comin' back in," 'n' so I do.

I think how it'd be (cos I got no matches, ya know) if this stinkin' little cigar had a red end on it, glowing, like. 'N' I take a draw.

Next thing I knows, the young joker with the busted leg is yellin', "Nurse, Nurse," 'n' Starchy steams in with Husk in tow. "His bedclothes are on fire!" the young fella yells. Sure enough, the ole roast duck has set me bed on fire, and Starchy makes a great thing of chuckin' water around. The silly old sod; some people just can't manage fire at all. Starchy pulls the choobs outa me nose, and draws the curtins round me bed.

I mean, the old roast duck's bed. So, whatta I care, any'ow? This joint is only for sick people. Sooner I'm outa 'ere, the better.

So I wander back down the corridor, out the front door. Over the other side of the road, there's some kind of barbecue or picnic, with camp-fires 's far 's I can see. Lovely fires. They're chuckin' on big logs, 'n' the coals are shinin' red and orange, 'n' the flames are leapin' up toward 'eaven. There's lots of me old mates there.

"Come on, Joe," they're shoutin'. "Over 'ere, mate!"

So I starts to go acrost the road.

Then. Then. I sees two bastards I never wanted to lay eyes on again. Fisheyes the schoolteacher, and the Karamull farmer. Last time I seen 'im, 'e was rollin' in the dirt, tryin' to put out 'is burnin' clothes. But they was wool, and kept bubblin' and crawlin' like big black caterpillars.

Fisheyes 'n' the farmer are wavin' their arms, too, for me to come over their way.

Be damned to 'em.

I'll see them in Hell first.

SEAN WILLIAMS

Sean Williams has published over fifty short stories since "Light Bodies Falling" (*Aurealis*, 1991). This productive writer of SF and horror is one of the dominant Australian writers in the field in this decade, with story collections—*Doorway to Eternity* (1994), *A View Before Dying* (1998), *New Adventures in Sci-Fi* (1999)—and three novels, *The Unknown Soldier* (with Shane Dix, 1993), *Metal Fatigue* (1996), and *The Resurrected Man* (1998), the latter two long SF mysteries; all have been published in Australia. The first of the novels is now forthcoming from a U.S. publisher as the first of a projected trilogy, and Williams is another writer who seems poised to escalate into the larger SF world of international publishing. Thus far his fiction is more notable for its engaging imagery than its coherent plotting, but his imagery is truly wonderful and his storytelling compelling. "The Map of the Mines of Barnath" is perhaps typical, and is arguably his best story to date.

A MAP OF THE MINES OF BARNATH

THE MANAGER OF THE mines was a small, gray man named Carnarvon, wiry with muscle and as tough as old boots. A slight accent betrayed his off-world origins; one of the older colonies, I thought, or perhaps even Earth. He was sympathetic in a matter-of-fact way, as though my position was far from unique.

"What was your brother's name?" he asked.

"Martin Cavell. Do you remember him?"

Carnarvon shook his head, tapping into a terminal. "No, but his records should . . . yes. This'll tell us something."

I tried to wait while he read the file, but impatience soon got the better of me. "What happened?"

"It seems he took a three-day pass to the upper levels, then chose to continue deeper when the pass expired." Carnarvon skimmed through the file to the end. "Your brother died on the fifth level."

"How?"

"The exact details are unknown. There was no body, no witnesses, and no inquiry. Assumption of death is automatic under these circumstances."

"A pretty large assumption, I would've thought."

"Nevertheless."

He seemed quite content to leave it there, but ten thousand kilometers of travel prompted me to dig deeper.

"Would it be possible to see the place where he died?"

"Possible, yes, but . . ." He looked at me oddly. "You don't know the mines, do you?"

"No. This is my first time here."

"Nobody's said anything?"

"I only flew in this afternoon." It was my turn to look puzzled. "Is there something I should know?"

Carnarvon shook his head slowly. "You wouldn't believe me if I told you."

"So show me. Or have me shown. You don't have to take me personally—"

"No, I'll take you. It's been awhile since I went all the way." He looked around the office, eyes itemizing the contents one by one until they finally came back to me. "If you want a Grand Tour, I'll give you a Grand Tour."

"Thank you." His capitulation was both unexpected and total; he made me feel slightly guilty for inconveniencing him. "As soon as I find out what happened to Martin, I'll be out of your hair, I promise."

"That could take longer than you think."

"I'm in no hurry."

He sighed and called his deputy into the office. "I'm going Down, Carmen," he told the woman. "You're in charge until I get back."

They shook hands gravely and I thought for an instant that she was about to say something. But she didn't. She just watched as we left the office, her eyes filled with something oddly like grief.

Carnarvon led me to an elevator shaft, handed me a hard hat and a dirty blue overcoat. He looked around the surface level—at the swarming clerks and technicians, at the administration buildings and bulk-transport containers—and shook his head a third time.

"Let's go," he said wearily, and hit DOWN. The cage door closed and the floor fell away.

The mines of Barnath are the biggest in known space and rumored to be inexhaustible. Discovered a century ago, they have turned our previously struggling, pastoral world into a major mineral exporter. The five thousand people—according to the unofficial tourist brochure—who work its seven levels are capable of extracting over a million tons of any given ore per month, plus the same again in refined materials, most of which is exported off-world.

Yet, strangely, the mines are completely independent of the rest of the planet, like a distant country or a very large corporation. Visitors are rare, especially to the deeper levels, and the flow of information to the world outside is often restricted, as it was regarding my brother's fate. But the official policy on the surface is to let the status quo remain. The fate of the planet depends on a constant if not large supply of Barnath metal—

so, while ore comes out of the upper shaft, any situation, no matter how unusual, can be tolerated.

Carnarvon, if he was aware of his awesome responsibility, didn't let it show. "We don't get many people here," he said, pausing to light a cigarette. "Usually from off-planet—those who have heard rumors and want to check for themselves. Most are satisfied with a few pamphlets and a quick tour of the upper levels."

"What about Martin?"

"He was an exception, like you."

I nodded, allowing him the point. "What about the other miners, then?"

"A handful—the ones called 'skimmers'—live nearby, drifters and no-hopers, usually. They only go as far as the third level, where we do the refining. More permanent miners work the deeper levels. The deepest ones never come Up at all."

"So some actually *live* down there?"

"Of course. They're the ones who work best."

My surprise was mild but genuine. This was a rumor I had heard and dismissed as unlikely. I had never been in a mine before, but the thought of crawling for any length of time along what I imagined to be cramped, poorly lit tunnels made me feel claustrophobic.

"Why?" I asked.

Carnarvon looked me in the eye, studying my reaction with interest. "Surface people from 'round here, apart from the skimmers, don't work below ground because they're afraid of the mines. They're scared that if they go inside, they'll get caught."

"Gold fever?" I joked.

"No,"—there was little humor in Carnarvon's eyes—"*caught.*"

I waited, but he did not explain further. If he was trying to scare me off, or warn me, it didn't work. I had come too far to be deterred by vague superstitions.

The cage rattled to a halt. The doors swung open and Carnarvon waved me ahead. "After you."

I nodded and entered the mines.

One & Two

The sparsely populated first and second levels are almost identical and usually regarded as a single unit. These were what greeted the first settlers when they discovered the mines and sent the first of many expeditions into the depths of the planet. Carved from the bedrock, at 575 meters, respectively, the two upper levels were found to be empty of ore and life, little more than half-submerged tunnels littered with rubble and dirt. That they had been fashioned by ROTH—Races Other Than Human—was obvious, however. Mankind had not been on Barnath long enough to begin such an ambitious project, let alone subsequently abandon it. Another species had therefore established the mines, emptied them of all valuable minerals, and left. Or so it appeared at first.

When I arrived, new tunnels were being carved by skimmers in a half-hearted attempt to reopen the upper levels. The air was full of dust and the screaming of pneumatic and sonic drills. The weight of the rock above and around me was almost palpable—a feeling compounded by the stifling half-light. Flickering electric arcs swung from carelessly looped cables draped along the tunnels. It was unexpectedly hot and uncomfortably damp. In some tunnels it almost seemed to be raining.

Jean Tarquitz, the supervisor of the upper levels, greeted us as Carnarvon showed me around. She was an attractive woman, although filthy, grimed with moisture-streaked dust. When Carnarvon explained that we were heading on a Grand Tour, she looked surprised.

"Why?" she asked, as I had earlier, staring at us both with naked curiosity.

"I've been topside long enough," Carnarvon explained, "waiting for an excuse to come back Down." Even I, who had known him little more than an hour, could tell that his casual words hid a more complex reason. "I thought it was about time."

"And you?"

"Looking for my brother."

There was both amusement and pity in her pale orange eyes as she snorted disdainfully and waved us on.

My tour of the first level passed quickly. Tarquitz accompanied us to the second, which had little new to offer and bade us farewell as we reentered the shaft to the third. A load of processed ore climbed past us, deafening all those nearby with the sound of laboring machinery.

"The Director has been active in the lower levels," she said. "I've heard rumors—"

"I know," said Carnarvon wearily. "We'll be careful."

"If it comes for you," she asserted, "it comes regardless of care."

"I haven't forgotten."

"Who's the Director?" I asked, but Carnarvon shook his head and motioned me into the cage.

"Take your time," said Tarquitz.

"I will," Carnarvon replied, and the doors closed.

The lift fell, swaying gently from side to side, and although the first two drops had lasted little more than sixty seconds each, this descent took us at least ten minutes.

Three

The third level held the first of many surprises to greet the settlers. Its heart is an enormous chamber as large as five Old Earth cathedrals stacked one on top of the other, crisscrossed by ladders and pipes and startlingly well-lit—a brilliant contrast to the upper levels. Its walls are orange and thickly veined. The air is full of the rumbling of machinery and echoing explosions. Huge ROTH artefacts, inactive for the most part, cling to the walls and ceiling; some are mounted like stalagmites on the "floor," around which cluster the refineries brought Down a piece at a time by human settlers. Green-clad miners swarm like ants along the walls and walkways, issuing from the myriad tunnels that lead deeper into the earth.

"How many people work here?" I asked, left almost breathless by the sheer scale of the chamber. Too large to be fully comprehended in even a series of glances, it provoked a feeling of vertigo so powerful as to dull the mind.

"On this level, something like six thousand; most of them in side cuts rather than the actual core. Your brother was one of them, for a while."

I shook my head. The figure didn't make sense. It was larger than the one I'd been given earlier for the population of the entire mine, and there were still four more levels to go. But I chose not to pursue the matter then and there; I supposed that I'd misheard him through the constant noise echoing in the chamber.

I tried to imagine Martin working here, and failed. We had spoken briefly before his departure for the mines, but he had said nothing about intending to seek employment. Just a holiday, he had said, to satisfy his curiosity. I wondered what had happened to change his mind.

The lift ended halfway down the chamber.

We stopped there to procure water bottles, to exchange a handful of words with a taciturn attendant, and to admire the view. Huge ore-lifters floated past us—up, full; down, empty. Carnarvon informed me that protocol forbade us taking such a direct route to the base of the third level. Between the midway point of the third level and its rock floor were only ladders.

"Nothing else can truly do this place justice," he said, and I believed him.

By then I had an inkling that the Grand Tour was far more than a quick circuit of faces and off-cuts—hence Carnarvon's initial reluctance to take me. I was glad that I had no one waiting for me aboveground.

It took us three hours to reach the base of the chamber and the first of many way stations. We rested there for an hour or so, meeting a few of the deeper miners—called "moles"—who were heading Upward for a stint in the refineries and, ultimately, the surface. They were uniformly dirty, but only two-thirds were pale skinned. The rest were deeply tanned, which I found strange. All shared a peculiar dullness of stare, a strain of world weariness, which I later learned was called "miner's eyes." As though nothing more could surprise them, they regarded the world with patient, cynical skepticism.

I asked them about my brother but received only quizzical stares in reply.

"Tourist," explained Carnarvon patiently. Some laughed openly; others touched my shoulder in sadness and went to sit elsewhere.

"Why is everyone so . . . ?" I struggled for the word, but couldn't find it.

"Unconcerned?" suggested Carnarvon, a wry smile twisting his rubbery features. "If they are, it's because they know something you don't."

"Which is?"

"Don't ask now. You'll—"

"I know, I know. I'll find out later."

His smile broadened. "Exactly."

When we had rested, Carnarvon showed me some of the machinery that fills the third level. The purpose of the ancient ROTH mechanisms eluded me then, just as it has eluded human researchers for one full century.

Then it was time to enter the Shaft, the central column that plummets downward through the four remaining levels. The cage was three times as large as the lift by which we had previously descended. Low benches lined two of the walls.

A crowd of miners spilled from the cage, dressed in unfamiliar white uniforms. They stared at us, but said nothing. When they had gone, Carnarvon turned to face me. "The journey really begins here," he said, on the threshold of the cage. "If you want to turn back, it's not too late."

I shook my head. "I need to know what happened to Martin."

"Why?" He seemed genuinely unable to understand.

"Because he was important to me," I said. "Am I in danger?"

"Yes." His honesty was both dismaying and thrilling. "Everyone who enters the mines is at risk—and the deeper, the more so."

It was my turn to ask, "Why?"

But Carnarvon, waving me inside, refused to answer.

He stood silently by my side as the cage fell, not meeting my stare. Five minutes passed without a word spoken by either of us. If Carnarvon didn't want to talk, I wasn't going to make him.

Then, after fifteen minutes, the floor lurched, and I felt momentarily light-headed. Only then did Carnarvon speak, as though we had passed some unannounced barrier. "The last time I passed this way was twelve years ago—heading Up from the fifth level, swearing that I would never come back." He took off his hard hat and slicked back his wiry gray hair. "But part of me always knew I would, one day. And the same part knows that there's no going back this time. You only get out once. If you return, the mines have you forever."

I studied him closely. If this was a confession, then I failed to comprehend it. " 'Caught' ?" I asked, using his own word.

He laughed softly. "Well and truly. I hate this place, but I love it, too. And the people who work here, mad bastards that we are."

His attention wandered back to his own thoughts. Reluctant to let the silence claim us again, I asked him a question that had been troubling me for some time. "Why are we the only ones going Down?"

Carnarvon laughed again. "You noticed? Good. If you can answer that question, my friend, you'll be one step closer to grasping the truth about the mines."

And he would speak no more until the cage bumped to a halt and we stumbled from it.

Four

Imagine a grey plain at midnight, rippled in a series of low, undulating hills and valleys. The plain is in complete darkness, except for an area as large as a small town illuminated by powerful, white spotlights. In this lighted area sits an open-face mine, hacked into a hillside like a weeping sore. It is so dark in this place that nothing else can be seen: no stars, no horizon, just one patch of brilliant light and a slender line rising upward into blackness. Now imagine the plain buried four thousand meters underground in a chamber so large that the walls and ceiling are invisible. This is the fourth level.

A faceless technician handed me a pressure suit. A clumsy outfit of rubber and carbon fibres, it stank of sweat and grease, as though worn by thousands of people in its lifetime. Puzzled, I followed Carnarvon's lead and shrugged into it, leaving my outer garments in a locker. I felt oddly light, and wondered if the air had a higher oxygen content than I was accustomed to. Carnarvon led me to an air lock and cycled the pair of us through.

"Poisonous atmosphere," he said via the suit radio, explaining the suits if not the sight that lay before me. I watched as cranes swung and powerful vehicles unloaded their burdens beneath the spotlights. The miners swarming across the face looked like dark animals in their gray suits—hence, I supposed, the nickname "moles."

"What are they mining for?" I asked.

"Here, iron ore," replied Carnarvon. "There are other faces nearby cut for strontium and uranium."

I hunted for a reference point, some means of guessing the size of the space around me, but failed. "How big is this level?" I asked, admitting defeat.

"Bigger than you think, I promise you."

We headed through the gloom toward a row of huts, where Carnarvon introduced himself to the level supervisor, a portly man called Stolle whose suit resembled a blowfish with stumpy arms and legs. Still dazzled by the strangeness of the fourth level, I was content to let them do the talking.

"I remember you," said Stolle to Carnarvon, squinting through his plastic visor. His voice was liquid with static. "Two years ago—three, maybe?—you worked here for a while."

"Twelve," corrected Carnarvon.

"Christ." Stolle winked at me dryly, as though sharing a joke I failed to understand. "Time flies down here."

"Any news of the Director?" asked Carnarvon.

"It's out there," said the supervisor, shrugging. "Definitely out there. We've lost a few on this level, but not many. Usual story. That, and the rumors of an eighth level, are about the only things we can depend on down here."

He invited us to join him for a drink, but Carnarvon explained that we were tired. This wasn't a lie, as far as I was concerned; my watch told me that eight hours had passed since my arrival at the mines, and my eyes were thick with fatigue. So Carnarvon made excuses, and we bunked down in a crowded dormitory wing with a dozen off-duty moles, clipped by air hoses to a communal tank, our radios silenced.

Thus I spent my first night in the mines of Barnath: in a rubber suit, breathing air that stank of *human,* wondering what the hell I was doing. And when I dreamed, it was of Martin walking ahead of me along a dark, stone tunnel, forever out of reach.

A dull explosion woke me an unknown time later. When we stumbled out of the wing, a new hole had been added to the scarred hillside. The ever-present glare of the spotlights seemed brighter and the ceaseless activity of the open-face mine more feverish than before.

We dined on preprocessed slop in one of the few pressurized compart-ments of that level. The moles around us eyed us curiously, and a moment or two passed before I realized what it was that distinguished us from them. It was, quite simply, that we were talking. On the fourth level, where communication is only practical via intersuit radio, casual conversation is discouraged. Even in the mess-hall.

"How much farther?" I asked Carnarvon, regardless. The night's sleep had left me irritable, rather than refreshed. I was impatient to make some progress on my quest to find Martin.

"Forever and a day, as they say." He glanced at me in amusement. "You still think you'll be leaving here in a hurry?"

"Why shouldn't I be?"

"Because these are the mines of Barnath, my friend. They're not like anywhere else. Where you come from, everything's the same—it never changes; it'll be there tomorrow, forever. But here . . . if the Director doesn't get you, then you're caught anyway."

I put down my spoon, appetite forgotten. There was a new strength in Carnarvon's eyes that bothered me, left me feeling like an intruder, un-wanted. His stare was almost a challenge, defying me to unravel the riddle of the mines on my own.

"Who is the Director?" I asked, pacing my words deliberately.

Perhaps he saw the growing frustration in my eyes and the anger that lurked behind it. Or he, too, was tired of his own guessing game. Either way, he also put down his spoon and finally began to explain, after a fashion.

"The Director lives in the mines," he said. "Or else it's an integral part of them. Either. We don't know much about it, except that it can go anywhere anytime it wants to. We don't even know where it goes between

+appearances—I've never heard of it being seen topside—but we always know when it's been."

"It?" I asked. "I thought you were talking about someone in particular. Your superior, perhaps."

"No. One of the early explorers coined the name, for whatever reason, and it's as good as any other."

He paused, watching me closely, waiting for a response.

"So what is it? A machine?"

"That's certainly possible. The mines aren't human-built. The ROTH made them; the ROTH left them here for us to plunder. Maybe they switched on some sort of security system before they left, and the Director is its enforcer." He shrugged. "But few people really believe it's an alien artifact."

"Then *someone* must know about it, surely?"

"Just think for a second before you jump to conclusions. It should be obvious. What if the ROTH *didn't* leave? What if they're still in here somewhere?"

I stared at him. "Are you suggesting that the Director is an alien?"

"That's the most popular explanation. More than one ROTH, perhaps. No one's seen it and lived. All we know is that it takes people working in the mines—usually the best, most talented. Those it comes for and doesn't take, it kills."

"You're kidding?"

Carnarvon shook his head gravely. "It's no joke down here. Deeper still, it's positively morbid. Live in the mines for a while and the fact starts to get to you. You never know if it'll come for you, or if you'll be taken when it does."

"I never heard any of this before."

"Of course not. Word doesn't get out because hardly anyone who comes this deep leaves again. Those few who do leave hang around the surface for a while and then go back Down. The Director is all part of the lure and the trap of Barnath, you see. No one knows *where* it takes the ones it doesn't kill." He picked up his spoon and attacked his breakfast viciously. "That's why I'm here. The mystery has me hooked."

"And me? Why am I here?"

"To find your brother, of course."

"Did the Director take *him?*"

Carnarvon paused between mouthfuls. "If you meet it, you can ask it yourself."

I pushed my bowl aside and sealed my suit.

"Going somewhere?" asked Carnarvon, amused.

"Outside," I said. "I need to think."

I shouldered my way through a crowd of miners and headed out into the darkness. The face of the cut was hidden behind a low hill; the only light came from reflected haze and a crooked line of beacons strung across the gray-green dust that served for a floor on the fourth level.

I squatted on my haunches and regarded the empty view for a long while. It was like sitting on the face of a starless moon. I didn't hear Carnarvon approach.

"Time to go," he said, putting his hand on my shoulder. "Coming?"

I raised my head wearily. "You say Martin disappeared from the next level?"

"Yes, the fifth. That's what the records said, anyway."

"Then I'm coming. At least that far."

Even through the visor I could see his skeptical smile, curled like a question mark as though he doubted my motives.

"He's alive," I insisted. "I can feel him."

"If you say so."

"All I want to do is find him and take him home. Is that so difficult?"

Carnarvon helped me to my feet, and we trudged back to the Shaft building. I expected to don our old clothes, but we didn't.

"Pressure suits from here on," he explained, as we waited for the cage to reach our level. "Just in case."

The cage rattled to a halt and the doors opened. I regarded the interior with foreboding. Carnarvon didn't hesitate, however, so I followed reluctantly.

The cage dropped downward. Again I felt that strange sensation of giddiness halfway, but this time my companion chose to remain silent for the rest of the journey, lost in thought.

Five

I was definitely lighter when I stepped from the cage. The disembarkation bay was an enormous room, sterile white and brilliantly lit. Behind me, six identical air locks opened into the wall; we had entered the chamber via the second from the right. A large section of the floor was transparent, and Carnarvon gestured that I should look down through it.

It took me a minute or so to find a sense of perspective. The view was surreal. Great blue sheets of energy slashed and hacked at something I couldn't quite identify. A hill, I thought at first, then a mountain. It wasn't until I realized that the dots drifting over the surface of the object were ore-lifters—themselves so huge they made men look like specks—that I guessed the incredible truth.

Trapped within the mines, orbiting slowly beneath my feet, was an entire planet.

"That's impossible," I breathed, as bolts of stupendous energy sheared free continent-sized chunks of rock. My vantage point was high—at least thirty thousand meters—and the view spectacular.

"I know," said Carnarvon. "But we're mining it anyway. And it's not that large, really—barely the size of Mars. Completely dead, of course, and metal-rich. It'll keep the mines active for a century or two at least."

My gaze wandered from the planet across the roof of the incomprehensible chamber. Giant habitats clung to the naked rock of the "roof" like shellfish, upside down. Huge docking grapnels awaited ore-lifters ferrying material from the scarred surface below. Everywhere I looked were men and women in white pressure suits, crawling like flies over an unimaginable carcass.

"How many?" I asked, almost afraid of the answer.

"Two and a half million," replied Carnarvon, and I swallowed. I had in mind the unofficial government estimate of five thousand, which now seemed ludicrous in the face of what I was seeing.

"Surely someone must have noticed?"

"To date, no one has." Carnarvon unsealed his suit, crooking the helmet over his forearm like an old-timer. "As I said, people this deep rarely leave."

"But still, they had to come from *somewhere*—"

"Exactly. A few, like your brother, come from the surface, drifting down through the levels over the years, but that still leaves us quite a large number short of the real population of the mine."

"Where, then?" I had a vision of the miners raising families, which I immediately discredited. Only an idiot would have children in a place like this.

"We may never know the full answer to that question," Carnarvon said. "Some miners come Up from the deeper levels without ever having gone Down in the first place."

I studied him suspiciously, wondering if he was playing me for a fool. He wasn't. He was deadly serious.

But he had to be lying.

I, too, shucked my helmet and breathed the air of the fifth level. It tasted faintly electric and of the population that had breathed it before me. I could still feel the weight of rock around me, defying the view through the window at my feet. A planet *within* a planet . . . ?

I turned away from the sight. It was too much.

"Come on," said Carnarvon. "We have to log ourselves in." He took my arm and led me along the bay, toward a corridor. The narrow passageway ended in a desk.

A clerk behind a computer terminal greeted us patiently. "Names?" he asked.

Carnarvon gave him mine and added, "Skimmer," when asked for my profession. The ease with which my identity had been redefined did not escape me: from quester to tourist to skimmer in less than two days. Had something similar happened to Martin? The clerk handed me a white, plastic ID card, which I absently tucked into a ziplock pouch.

Then it was Carnarvon's turn. The clerk accepted the title, "Manager," with little sign of being impressed.

"When?" he asked, tapping at the keyboard.

"Forty-five to Fifty-five."

"We had your predecessor through here last year," said the clerk. "He lasted a month."

"Taken?"

"Killed." The clerk handed him a red card, which Carnarvon stuck to the front of his suit. "You have a fortnight's grace, you and your friend, after which you'll have to find work."

"Of course," said Carnarvon, not at all fazed by the apparent insubordination. "Thank you."

He commandeered an electric cart and drove me deeper into the habitat. Occasionally we passed a circular window in the floor, reminding me that beneath my feet lay not the solid rock my apparent weight suggested, but empty space and then something far more remarkable.

"You'll probably be asking yourself the same questions I asked when I came here." Carnarvon smiled at me sympathetically as he drove. "I was a fusion technician from Earth, so the first thing I said when I looked out that window was, 'How do you pay your fuel bill?'" He chuckled self-deprecatingly. "It wasn't until two years later that I learned where the energy actually comes from."

"And where does it?" I croaked.

"Deeper still," he said. "The next level powers the entire mine. The ROTH were far more advanced than we are. All the equipment in this chamber and the sixth were just lying around, waiting to be used. So we used it. We didn't have to understand how it worked."

Memory prompted me to ask, "I thought there were seven levels?"

"There are," he said, but I could draw him no further on the issue of the last. Instead, he described life in the fifth: the way most of the mining on the planet is teleoperated; how the miners spend nearly all of their time in the ceiling habitats, only venturing to the surface to deal with circumstances that cannot be handled by automatics or remotes. The energy-lances are directed from a cluster of habitats in a segment of the level that has been designated North, coinciding with the magnetic field of the planet.

It was there, I learned, Martin had worked. When I asked to be taken there first, Carnarvon smiled grimly.

"You haven't grasped the scale yet, have you? It'll take at least three days to get there by cart; one if we can requisition a shuttle."

The corridor widened, became a busy thoroughfare. Miners in clean uniforms walked or drove by on unknown errands, and I watched them in silence, trying to remember what the surface—"home," I reminded myself—looked like. But I couldn't. It was too far away.

Carnarvon pulled us to a halt outside a small door.

"Clothes, food, and rest," he said. "And then we keep going."

I nodded numbly, and let myself be led inside.

Standard uniform on the fifth level is a white, cotton one-piece, fitted with numerous pockets and pouches. The outfits are comfortably simple—almost spartan. The food, however, is an order of magnitude better than that of the previous level, being the product of hydroponic gardens scattered across the "roof."

"The ROTH left them, too," said Carnarvon, as we ate our way through real vegetables and soy-base steak.

"And the habitats?"

"Yes." Carnarvon smiled wryly. "They were more like us than we give them credit for, most of the time."

"What do you mean?"

"Well, everyone down here regards the Director as almost godlike," he said, "when it's probably just a ROTH that eats the same food as us and stands only a little taller."

I finished my meal in silence, bothered by that thought. I put myself in the shoes of those first colonists, stumbling upon this tremendous cavern and its contents. What had they imagined they had found? And why hadn't research teams descended upon the mines from all corners of the inhabited galaxy?

I knew better than to ask for answers to these questions. All I could do was wait until the truth became clear on its own, however long that took.

When we had finished our meal, Carnarvon drove us to a transport dock, where we caught a shuttle halfway to the northern quadrant. The stubby craft swooped low over the planet below, granting me an unequaled view of the mining operations taking place. From this angle, the sprawl of habitats above resembled a colony of small, white mushrooms suspended from a distant ceiling—or a world of sealed cities, turned inside-out.

As we left the shuttle, a party of miners came toward us through the air lock umbilical. One of them called for my attention as he approached.

"Cavell, you old bastard, where've you been? It's been ages, and you still owe me for Carole."

"I'm sorry," I said, staring at him. He was short, grizzled, and completely unfamiliar. "You must be thinking of my brother. We look the same."

"No," he said. "I remember you. We worked—"

One of his companions nudged him in the ribs.

"Oh, right," he said. "You're on your way Down." He reached out for my hand and shook it. "The name's Donahue, anyway. I guess I'll meet you later."

He entered the shuttle with his workmates. The doors closed on his smiling face, shutting out my confusion.

"What the hell?"

"It happens," said Carnarvon. "You'll get used to this sort of thing."

"I don't *want* to get used to it." Mental exhaustion—too many riddles in too short a time—was taking its toll. "I just want to find out what happened to Martin and get out of here."

"A little more patience." Carnarvon smiled, a mixture of amusement and sympathy. "Not far now."

We took another cart the rest of the way, through a network of evacuated tunnels that crisscrosses the roof of the fifth chamber. Like insects, we crawled for seven hours along this hollow web, inch by strange inch, while the world-within-a-world turned implacably below us.

Above the planet's north pole, vast forces crackle through the dust-filled vacuum. Enormous bolts of static electricity split the nether sky. The habitats echo with the thunder of mighty energies. Martin's old home, amidst all of this, trembles on the edge between stone and fire—just as many homes did, and still do, on this level.

A security officer showed us Martin's file. It stated that he had worked in the habitat for no less than two years.

"There must be some mistake," I said. "He's only been missing for six weeks."

She handed me a photo. "Is that him?"

I looked carefully. The man in the hologram was older than I remembered, but definitely Martin.

"Yes, it is," I admitted, grudgingly. "But how do you explain—?"

"We don't," she said. "We just accept."

Carnarvon took the file from her, winking. "Come on," he said to me. "Let's go see where he was taken."

I followed him out of the administration building, hating the curl of amusement I saw in his profile. With the end of my quest in sight, the last thing I wanted to hear was more nonsense.

"This is crazy," I stated.

"Sure," he agreed pleasantly. "But blame the ROTH if you have to blame someone." We headed to a nearby building, where the files told us Martin had lived.

"He left his room at midnight," read Carnarvon. "Going to meet a lover, apparently."

We followed a series of corridors, all equally unremarkable, until Carnarvon brought me to a sudden halt.

"The cameras tracked him as far as here, then lost him."

I looked around. The corridor was empty and featureless. There was no sign that anybody had passed this way at all, let alone died here.

"What else does the file say?" I asked, staring at the blank, polished floor.

"Not much. Martin turned a corner, walked four steps, and vanished. The general consensus is that the Director took him."

"Where?"

"No one knows." Carnarvon put a hand on my shoulder. "I'm sorry."

I shrugged his hand away. "I don't believe you're telling me everything."

"Of course not. But I don't know everything, do I?"

"Bullshit." His flippancy annoyed me, fueled my growing frustration. "This has been one long smoke screen right from the beginning. You told me I'd understand when I saw the fifth level. Well, I'm here and I've seen it, but I still don't understand. Why can't you just tell me?"

"I—"

"My brother's disappeared, for God's sake!"

"Look around you. Can *you* understand what's going on here? No one can. Your brother was taken in full view of a security camera, and it saw nothing. Four steps—zap—gone. Where? If I knew, I'd tell you, I swear. We lose something like three hundred people a year under similar circumstances, and nearly triple that many are killed—"

"So why doesn't somebody do something?"

"Such as? What do you suggest? This has been happening for one hundred years; if something could have been done, we would have done it already."

"So close the mines."

"We can't. They're too productive. And the odds of the Director striking are statistically insignificant anyway. You've more chance of dying on the surface."

I felt caged in and wanted to strike something. "You're lying."

"Not at all—"

"You think you can palm me off with false records and insanities—"

"If you'll just calm down—"

"No! I refuse to believe that Martin is dead. He's down here somewhere, and I'm going to find him."

I turned on my heel and angrily walked away.

"How?" Carnarvon called after me. "You're not the first to have tried, you know!"

I ignored him. Grief, anger, and a sense of betrayal fought for control of my mind, clouding my thoughts and judgment. I knew that Martin was alive somewhere; I could feel it in my bones. I wasn't going to let the matter go so easily. Martin would have done the same for me, I was sure, had our roles been reversed.

I wandered the corridors, losing myself in the maze of the habitat, not caring if Carnarvon followed. Ten minutes passed before I regained my senses and realized that I was alone. When I did, I set out to begin my own investigation.

I was allocated a room near Martin and started asking questions.

No one could give me hard facts about my brother. Few people remembered him, as though years had passed since his disappearance. One even went so far as to suggest that it *had* been years, but I dismissed her as a liar, part of the conspiracy keeping me from the truth, even though she insisted that she had been his lover.

My two weeks of grace passed quickly and fruitlessly, spent for the most part in mess halls and recreation facilities, always asking questions. The citizens of the fifth level, although sympathetic, were victims of the same passivity to fate espoused by the security officer who had shown me

Martin's file. I despaired of ever learning the truth, but for the wrong reasons: I wondered what Martin had done to warrant such a thorough whitewash of his sudden departure.

And always, everywhere I looked, was the strangeness of the mines, the sheer improbability of it all, from the planet below to the habitats above. I felt overwhelmed by odd details gleaned from the people I interviewed: the way power was beamed by maser from the south "pole" rather than sent along cables; the slag pit, an apparently bottomless hole in the "ceiling" that was used to dispose of waste materials; the odd discrepancy between the mass of minerals extracted from the planet and that which arrived on the surface of Barnath, the latter being roughly one-sixth of the former; and the cluster of ROTH artifacts on the planet itself, which, although active, seemed to serve no other function than to send bright sparks of ball lightning hurtling around the sundered crust. But I refused to submit to the disorientation; I vowed that I would remain undistracted until I knew the truth. My life on the surface was waiting. I had to find Martin and bring him back, no matter how long it took.

So great was my blindness that I disregarded what was staring me in the face: that, in order to comprehend what had happened to Martin, I would first have to comprehend the mines themselves, a task for which I was both physically and mentally unprepared.

It wasn't until I met a man called Azimuth, a well-tanned mole from the sixth level, that I learned what fate was really awaiting me.

I happened across him him in a bar on the northeast quadrant of the fifth level—a dirty man, dressed in his stained undersuit from farther Up. He recognized my face and came to join me at my table.

"I remember you," he said. "You came here looking for your brother, right?"

"That's right. Do you know anything about—?"

He laughed, anticipating my question. "No, no. I never met him. But I heard about you on the news circuits topside before I came here."

I frowned. "When was that?"

"Well, let me see now. I came here five years ago, and I'd heard the story six months before that. Five and a half years then. Sure, that'd be about right."

I must have gaped at his words, for he laughed again at my confusion.

"You haven't noticed yet?" he asked. "Time is all fucked up down here. You arrived, what . . . ?"

"Fourteen days ago," I forced out.

"And I'm in my sixth year, with the Director's grace. Topside, it could've been centuries. You never know how long until you look."

Azimuth didn't stop there, but I hardly heard what he said. According to Martin's records, he had worked in the mines for two years—a fact I had initially dismissed as ridiculous. If time really was askew deep in the mines—a possibility I could not discredit, given the other wonders I had already witnessed—then the obstacles facing me were greater than I had imagined. But there was still hope.

I forced myself out of my daze. "The newscast," I said. "What did it say?"

Azimuth hesitated. "You sure you want to know?"

I gripped him firmly on the arm. "Tell me."

"All I remember is the headline: 'Brothers separated, then reunited by death.' Very tragic. I don't know whether that helps you, or makes things worse, but there you go. You wanted to hear it."

I gaped incredulously. "Reunited," I echoed to myself, "by *death?*"

He obviously interpreted my stunned silence as a sign of comprehension and barreled upward from his seat, chuckling deep in his belly. "Be seein' you, maybe."

When he had gone, I regarded my drink with despair, thinking dull, slow thoughts. The truth was like a heavy weight—the weight of miles of solid earth—settling upon my shoulders.

When my glass was empty, I wandered "home," alone.

That evening, I tracked down Carnarvon. He was still in the northern habitat, easily reached by internal vidcom.

"I've been waiting for you to call," he said. "I knew you would."

I hesitated for a moment, balanced on the edge of total acceptance. When the words eventually came, it didn't sound like me speaking. "Who did *you* lose?"

"My wife." His voice was even; his eyes reflected the sympathy I offered, unwanted. "It took me a month to realize, I'd never find her by looking. When I tried to escape back to Earth, I ended up on Barnath, where I decided to stay. For all the years I've been manager, I've been waiting for someone like you to bring me back."

"And here we are."

"Yes. Here we are. Looking without finding again."

The silence claimed us again. I had only one question left.

"Do you want to come with me?"

"Sure." He smiled. "The Grand Tour isn't over yet."

We met the next day and logged out of the fifth level. The Shaft accepted our pressure-suited bodies indifferently, and we dropped like stones into the depths of an impossible earth.

Six

The sixth level opens onto the fiery face of a sun.

Our period of grace had expired. I found work as an energy-scoop operator and met the man called Donahue who had greeted me in the embarkation bay of the fifth level. He didn't remember me, of course, but we quickly became friends. He helped me adjust to the artificial gravity of B Station and taught me everything I needed to learn about my new job. He also introduced me to his sister, Carole. It wasn't long before my tan was as deep as theirs and my acceptance of the impossible almost as automatic.

The sixth level does that to you. It overwhelms, it terrifies, it can even drive a person mad. But those who make it this far and stay for any length of time tend to have been a little crazy in the first place.

Carnarvon's time as surface manager served him in good stead, even though the post was irrelevant to the deeper levels. He worked in administration, somewhere in the heart of the central gravity-platform. We met once a week to discuss our progress.

Progress where? It didn't matter. We were both marking time before the inevitable.

Then, six months after Carnarvon and I had entered the mines, he didn't show for our weekly meeting. I dug around for information and eventually learned that the Director had come for him during the week. His body was never found.

I waited a month before moving on. My link with the surface had been severed; there was no point staying any longer than I had to. As though I had oscillated until then from a stretched rubber band, I suddenly found myself cut free. I started to fall.

The level supervisor was sympathetic.

There was only one way left to go at the very end.

Seven

The cage opens and I float into a transparent sphere nearly one hundred meters across, fixed to the base of the Shaft like a bubble on a straw.

There is no one present to watch or to censure me as I drift through the zero gravity, press my face against the surface of the bubble, and stare outward.

My eyes adjust eventually. Instead of darkness outside the bubble, I see stars.

Stars . . .

The Shaft ends here. There is no Downward path anymore—only Up, and Up, and Up. Forever.

There appears to be no way to leave the bubble, but part of me wonders what would happen if I could. Could I travel through space and reenter the mines from above, thus completing a strange loop of navigation?

Even here, it seems, there are no answers. There are only questions—and me, staring apelike at the stars. What could be stranger than this? Like the first colonists, I have stepped into the alien mines of Barnath and found everything I didn't expect: space beyond comprehension, time in disarray, resources without end, and . . .

I suddenly realize what *else* the first colonists found, what prevented word from spreading across the galaxy, and what halted the scientific jihad aimed like an arrow at the heart of the mines. Only one discovery could have been sufficient.

People. People have always been here, wandering twisted loops through time, crossing and recrossing, occasionally colliding. They greeted the first explorers of the deeper levels and integrated them seamlessly into a pre-existing society. Later arrivals were likewise assimilated, lured by mysteries and wonders in abundance, by a curiosity so great that not even the threat of death deterred them.

Whether the mines themselves are from the future or from the distant past or whether they exist entirely beyond time doesn't matter. Nothing here is certain, except that humanity has moved in and has therefore been here forever, entangled in some unknowable cosmic scheme.

Maybe the ROTH never existed at all. Even the Director might be human, with a purpose of his own.

My skin crawls, as though across an incomprehensible distance I am being watched.

On the heels of that thought comes an impatience, a need to move—in any direction. Time is passing around me like the heavy surges of a deep sea. A minute here might be a million hours on the surface, for all I know, or a heartbeat a whole lifetime. I want to travel, to be taken farther. *Now.*

But the Director will come, I remind myself, only when it comes. Not before. Of that I am reasonably certain, if nothing else.

My ghostly reflection stares back at me with Martin's face—the face of my other half, my twin.

A not-so-distant light in the alien starscape moves like a tear down the face of my reflection, and I sense that he is waiting for me, wherever he is.

LUCY SUSSEX

Lucy Sussex emerged from the 1979 writers workshop led by George Turner and Terry Carr. Notwithstanding the respect in which Leanne Frahm is held and the two novels published by Paul Voermans in the early 1990s, Sussex is now the most successful writer from the 1970s workshops. Relatively little of her work is SF, as opposed to fantasy or horror, but she has been an important presence in the Australian SF community, undoubtedly one of the most important female writers of SF in Australia, and, is beginning to be recognized worldwide. Her first story, "The Parish and Mrs Brown," was in *Dreamworks* (1983), followed by stories in King and Blackford's *Urban Fantasies* (1985) and in Broderick's *Strange Attractors* (1985). She was a co-editor of *Australian Science Fiction Review* (Second Series)—arguably the most ambitious critical SF magazine of the 1980s—for its first two years (1986–87). Then, in 1988, she published two more stories, including the title story of her 1990 collection, *My Lady Tongue and Other Stories*, the book upon which her reputation rests. She has edited three anthologies, including the notable *She's Fantastical* (1995, with Judith Raphael Buckrich, another attendee at the 1979 workshop), the first anthology of SF and fantasy by Australian women and two others for young adults. Sussex has published three fantasy novels in the 1990s: *Deersnake*, for young adults; *The Scarlet Rider* (1996), a ghost story for adults; and *Black Ice* (1997), another juvenile. She has continued to write short fiction, most often fantasy or horror; of her SF stories, "My Lady Tongue" is still her high watermark.

HONEYCOMB, MY HONEY, SWEET Honey Coombe. I love her so much I daubed her name on the biggest white wall in the ghetto and round it a six-foot heart. The paint was shocking pink, and it dribbled, when I so wanted my ideogram to be perfect! She passed by that wall every day, but unfortunately so did others, and that was how the trouble started.

"Vandalism!" That was the Neighborhood Watch, our ghetto guards. I was minding my own business, thinking of Honey, but cat curious I followed the groups of womyn drifting toward the clamor. It was only when I was in the main square that I realized the offence was mine. Ah well, I'd brazen it out—I'm nothing if not brazen.

There was a crowd in the square, which included the off-duty Watch and most of the powers-that-be in Womyn Only. One of the most dignified of these Elders was actually atop a stepladder inspecting my splash.

"Honeycomb," she announced to the groundlings as if every womyn Jill of them couldn't already read. "Possibly male reference to our genitals?"

"Ishtar!" cried the Watch Chief. "They got in this far?" There was a horrified mumble from the masses.

"Tsk tsk. Sleeping on the job," I said, just loudly enough for the Watch to hear and not pinpoint me. Zoska, who'd reared me, came forward, trailing her youngest.

"Not quite down to their usual standard, is it?" she said.

"Bar the color."

It was strident, but that's my style.

"They go in for dribbling cocks usually, not dribbling hearts."

Some of the hearers drew in their breaths hard, and she snapped:
"Don't be silly, this isn't the Hive."

"You think it's a Sister?" asked the Watch Chief, catching on at last.

Zoska nodded her coif of plaits and I cursed silently; if she got much
warmer things would be not for me.

"Our vandal," said Zoska, "loves Honeycomb."

"There aren't any Sisters of that name," said the ladder climber. "Unless you mean Marthe's daughter Honey . . ."

Their heads followed one direction and I thought I saw my sweeting,
so I waved my floppy hat at her. But it was only her grim mamma and I
knew I was for it.

"I own up! I did it, I did it!" I shouted, jumping up and down.

"Thought so," said Zoska.

Marthe was looking black and I was beginning to realize why.

"Sister Raffy," said the Chief, "Womyn Only supports artistic expression, but isn't this over the top?"

"Shucks, Officer, I'm in love."

"Honeycomb," said Marthe, as though that sweet name was wormwood
in her mouth, "is that your name for her?"

I nodded, thinking uh-oh! My darling's name was Honey Marthe, the
mother's name affixed to the daughter's, as is ghetto custom. Me, I'm Raphael Grania, but I only answer to Raffy. Coombe had been Honey's father,
a sperm donor anonymous except in the genetic profile of his daughter.
Hard-core dykes like Marthe (who never ventured from the ghetto nor
indeed much from the Hive, our inner sanctum) detested the profiles—but
kept them in case of genetic disorders. Honey had found the document
and discovered her humorless mother had made an accidental pun. I had
laughed at that, at Marthe, but now I had made a laughing stock of her,
and worse. It was bad taste to remind Womyn Only that its girl children
were not spontaneously generated.

Me and my big paintbrush. There was a long, really nasty silence,
during which I mentally gave myself a hundred lashes, and crossed miles
of paving on my knee bones.

"You'll never call her that again," said Marthe, and strode off followed
by a curious knot of Elders. The crowd was staring and Zoska had piggy-
backed her child and was pushing toward me. I didn't need comfort now,
just action! So I pretended not to see her and nipped around the corner
and over a couple of back gardens, shortcutting to Honey's home. It was
empty, and I stood outside and thought of the hydroponic flowers I had
thrown through her window. Then I embarked on a long and increasingly

desperate tour of our trysting places. I found nobody waiting, alas! and at
the last the Watch Chief found me. She was embarrassed but stern.

"Marthe and Honey are in the Hive, from which the Elders have
banned you until further notice."

I lay down by *our* fountain and imitated it for a while. Then I recovered
and went to see Zoska.

"Ninny," she said.

We sat in the sunny, brick courtyard behind her little house, she at
her embroidery frame and Basienka, who had accompanied her to the meeting, wandering around the confined space in her enigmatic two-year-old's
way.

"Oh, I agree absolutely. Now what do I do?"

"Go to Bozena at Haven, until the fuss dies down."

Haven was the refuge we dykes were building in the country. I had
scouted the site and normally would go there gladly.

"Can't leave Honey." Puck puck puck went the needle into the stiff
linen cloth. "I get soppy just thinking about her."

"Creamy, you mean," said Zoska. "I know you."

"No, this is the real thing. I'm so sentimental I could die."

Zoska sighed.

"You're old enough to be her mother."

"Not quite. Honey may be sixteen, but I—as you ought to remember—
had a late menarche."

She did the sums with her lips.

"So you did. I was confusing you with Boz."

"Quite a party we had for it," I said, hopping over a wall in my mind
into memory lane.

"Was it ever! You tore up the poem Grania had written for the occasion, and when she created lit out with Boz. The pair of you didn't come
back until six the next morning, when you burst into my bedroom shouting
you were in love with each other. I haven't had intoxicants at a menarche
party since. Won't have it at hers either."

She grinned at Basienka.

"Look at her. Aren't I clever? Forty-eight years and three months I
was when I bore her. Broke the ghetto record."

I recollected that Zoska had begun the career of mothering with Bozena and had had thirty-two years at it since. Some daughters were hers;
others came from Sisters who, like Grania, preferred not to have the rearing
of their young.

She looked at me, reading my face.

"You and Boz may have had your adventures with Haven, but I've reared seven fine womyn. Mind you, it's early days with Basienka and with Urszula I'm not sure."

I stirred, perceiving how my least favorite sister might help my purpose.

"You could use Urszula as an example to Marthe. She's not much older than Honey; she's taken up with Bea, who's my age . . ."

"I've got enough chickens to take chances with them. Marthe's only got one."

"Let me finish. And Urszula's leaving the ghetto!"

"Oh, Ishtar, don't even think of saying that to Marthe!"

"Why not? Honey wants to."

"After she's been reared hard core? To go among *men*? Raffy, she really must love you."

"I want to swear committal."

She reached into the basket between us for a new skein of wool, the colors jewel bright against her fingers.

"Wow, Raffy settling down at last. Okay, I'll talk to Marthe." She snipped off a length of wool viciously.

"It won't be easy."

Her gaze was like a mirror, in which my scarecrow image—in old camouflage duds from Haven (worn to annoy the hard cores, who never went Outside), lurid pink shirt, embroidered scarf, and old hat—was reflected with censure.

"Raffy, you're disreputable. You'll have to smarten up if I'm to get anywhere with Marthe, and while I'm at it also stop teasing the Elders and getting into fights with the Watch. You're the last match Marthe wants for Honey."

"I'm the daughter of a famous poet."

"Yes, and Grania denounces you in verse for being undutiful."

"We never ever got on."

"So I got the rearing of you, half my luck. Raffy, I can't win Marthe without Grania's help. You'll have to make up with her."

" 'I'll put a girdle round about the earth in forty minutes!' "

"What's that? What do you mean?"

"It's poetry. Shakespeare, a man. I mean, I'll do it."

She was looking puzzled and I got up to stretch my skinny legs in the courtyard, puzzled myself. I keep my Shakespeare well hid in Womyn Only, because of what it means to me: lost time with Benedict, a man. Swashbuckling Raffy might have had a child, a son even, and not by donor but by the old way, which Shakespeare writes about a lot.

There was no telling what a hard-core dyke would do if she knew her daughter was marrying tainted flesh. But Marthe would never hear of it, would she?

In my perambulations I nearly tripped over Basienka, who looked up from trying to unpick a wool flower on the skirt of the little peasant dress all Zoska's daughters, even tatty Raffy, wore. On her face was the same knowing smile as the Cumaean Sibyl, whose painting adorns a wall in the Hive, and I was suddenly afraid. Marthe could discover Raffy's little secret from Grania, who might tell her if we two were unreconciled.

I looked away from Basienka to Zoska.

"Can you talk to Marthe? I'll do Grania."

She nodded her silver-brown head, and I took leave of her. Grania lived outside Womyn Only, in a small brick house with a studied bohemian air. There was a hammock on the front verandah with a huge hole in it; the garden was a careful mixture of weeds and color-clashing flowers; the brass nameplate said "Poet's Corner." Before I could knock, the door was opened by Bea, lover of my foster-sister Urszula. She carried a carton of books for her shop, my mother's literary children, new branded with her squiggly signature.

"Hi, Raffy, surprise to see you . . ."

"Here?" I asked dangerously.

She looked embarrassed.

"I'll get out of your way. Raffy . . . do you really want Marthe for a mum-in-law?"

"Anything for Honey."

She walked down the pathway with my brothers and sisters. I waved, then went noisily inside. Grania was in her visitor's chair, a monster of carved mahogany chosen to diminish the bulk of the womyn within it. From my mother I had my height, but I blessed her donor for a lithe figure, for his genes dominated over those that would have made me resemble a hippo. She batted not an eyelid as I sauntered in.

"Come to your mummikins, lambie-pie," she said icily. It was the standard greeting and as usual I kept my distance, leaning against a wall of this book-lined grotto, with its troll-queen enthroned.

"What, no fond greeting?"

Go cautiously, I thought.

"Did you ask Bea about me?"

"Of course. She said you were in trouble, big trouble if you come and visit me. There was mention of a sweet young thing locked away from your wickedness. Then she spied your approach and bolted, leaving me in a state of gossipus interruptus."

"I shall bring you to climax."

"This sounds like the tale of your lost month. The one time you confided in me."

I stared at her.

"Mother, we are of one mind. I want you to recall the incident."

She grinned evilly.

"How could I forget Raphael's *True Confessions?*"

My lost time had been thirteen years back, before Haven even, but it was vivid to me. When I dipped into the past with Zoska, I had half-seen the brickwork and moss beneath my feet strewn with colored streamers and crushed paper cups. Now, instead of books, I could see pollution-bleached grass, weird trees, and eroded hills with knob rocks sticking out. She's very visual, Honey's Raffy.

I had been Outside both ghetto and City, sussing out a site for Haven in the countryside. When I remember, the mind's eye comes through first, then later the body with what my past self was feeling. I had been happy, despite the desolation, which was coldly beautiful, and the dangers. The country had unmarked pollution dumps, which had already claimed one scout, wild dogs, and, of course, the bogey of man.

Ah, who cared! I was wearing camouflage clothes that were weather-proof; I had survival rations, weapons, minicommunicator, compass, heat detector, Auntie Cobley, and all. The paraphernalia fitted neatly into a five-kilo pack on my shoulders that left me unencumbered, feeling free. There was a wild wind blowing, early spring sunlight, and Raffy, who had lived behind walls, was madly in love with wide open spaces.

This was my first solo voyage. Previously I had gone with senior members of the Watch, who were supposed to restrain young hotheads like Boz and me, and then with Boz. That trip had been a mistake, for in the excitement we had revived our first love, only to quarrel so bitterly we resolved: never again. We were too alike, and I crave opposites, Honey.

I was walking through a narrow valley peaceful even though bisected by a service road, when I heard a droning roar, steadily increasing in volume. Diving into the nearest cover, a ditch curtained with green weed, I checked the heat sensor, which registered zero. My fears of a behemoth mutant vanished and I peered through the green to see a robotruck on the road, making its slow thunder from a macrofarm somewhere. False alarm; but nonetheless I left the road and went cross-country, moving swiftly until I came to a patch of burnt-out ground.

I started to weep then, and my future self, standing in Grania's study, sought for a reason. There was a memory within the memory and it was red, the color of the fire that had engulfed a house on the edge of the ghetto. Five womyn had been inside and there were more dead, Watch members who had surprised the arsonists. "Men did it," Zoska had explained to little Urszula, who had only stared at her uncomprehendingly.

After the fire had been doused there had been more red, with a torchlit meeting in the main square I was later to defile with my "Honeycomb." The Elders had argued and argued what to do and slowly a consensus was reached. We were easily attacked within our enclosure; we needed to go beyond the city, found a city of our own. And so the Haven movement began and changed the lives of Boz and me. We had been feckless ghetto girls, too wild for the Watch and too hard core to find work in the straight world. Now we had a goal in life.

Standing among charcoal and singed trees, I wept for the dead, until it occurred to me that were it not for them I would still be cooped up in Zoska's living room. There was a site for me to look at; I went on.

Our Haven was defined by a list of desiderata, a majority of which had to be ticked before the Elders would approve the site. My destination had already accrued some ticks, if we were to believe the intermediary feminists who had investigated the site in the guise of a macrofarm consortium. They had liked it. Yet the site needed to be seen with a dyke's eyes and secretly. The memory of the incinerated house still burned.

I spent a day at the prospective site, being thorough. Womyn Only looked at many locations, finding some too marshy, too polluted, too grim, et cetera. I was writing the report in my head as I trudged: "Eminently suitable for our queendom, our newfoundland"—words Grania had used when she heard of my vocation, laughing all the while—"except . . ." It was insufficiently secluded, being too close to the farm I had seen the truck trundling toward earlier. And this farm, as the intermediaries had discovered, was not staffed entirely by robots.

I inked in the last mental full stop of my report and turned to go, when the late afternoon light caught a spot of color on a distant hillside. When I pulled out my viewfinder I saw a scrawny blossom tree in its spring best. The flowers were chalky pink, beautiful.

I glanced at the sun and again at the tree, estimating it was a kilometer away. Why not? I could take a pressed flower home for Zoska to copy and maybe another for a young lady of the Watch I had my eye on. What I had not expected, though, was the macrofarm's fence between me and tree, impenetrable even for a Scout equipped to the eyeballs. I followed it hopefully and came at last to a spot where an animal had burrowed beneath it. There was just room for Raffy, but not if she were humpbacked: I had to discard the pack in order to squeeze through.

The detour had eaten at the daylight, and the hill was dusked over by the time I arrived at the tree. Feeling uneasy, I decided not to stay long and reached for a blossom. There was a growl and automatically I jumped into the branches as a low shaggy shape came up the slope toward me. It was a feral dog, and it was followed by its brethren.

They clustered snarling around the base of the tree and I climbed higher. Hormones from the macrofarm had affected this tree's growth: it was some seven meters high, with sturdy branches. I sat in the highest of these, watching the dogs leap upward, snapping teeth on air and scrabbling their paws on the bark before falling to earth again. I was well out of reach, but I cursed, the dogs replying in their language. Any idiot would have checked the heat sensor for these pests or considered that they might have dug under the fence. Any idiot, but not Raffy.

Packless I was not quite defenseless, wearing under my camo shirt a weapon as unphallic as a dyke could make it. I took out the gun and shot experimentally at the dog chieftain, remembering my target practice with the Scouts. It was close: there was a smell of singed hair and the pack ran off a little, yelping. I gloated until I registered another smell, that of singed tree. The shot had nicked a lower bough, had almost cut it through.

Rather than whittle my sanctuary away I stopped, and the dogs settled under the tree for a long wait. I considered my options: the gun had a limited number of charges and the waning light would not improve my aim. Better to wait until the morning. I ate a couple of blossoms and found them tasteless, then had the joy of a half-eaten lolly Urszula had dropped in my pocket during the farewell. Lest I fall in sleep, I buckled my belt around flesh and tree trunk. The sun set and like the dogs I waited.

In the darkness maybe I slept, for when I awoke suddenly it was moon-rise and all the landscape silvery. There was a pawing and moaning at the foot of the tree, as the dogs milled around something strange—a metal canister. As I watched it emitted white mist; the dogs sniffed at it and whined. I could smell chemicals now, stupefying, and below the dogs were staggering like drunks. I pulled my scarf over my face for a filter, feeling weak and glad of the belt that bound me.

Walking among the fallen, twitching forms was a figure oddly distorted around the face. It stopped and stared upward at my form outlined against branches and sky.

"Here, catch!" and it threw a package to me expertly. The gift was a mask like the mask, I saw now, of the giver. I pulled it over my head and breathed freely again.

"You can come down now."

For the first time I noticed the lower timbre: a man's voice. Was I going from frying pan to firing squad? I began to pick at my self-made bonds watching *him* all the while. The canister had disgorged its drug and he was walking from dog to dog, pressing a rod against each head. There was a faint click, then death.

A deep-voiced thank you, I decided, then scram! I rebuckled my belt and clambered down, too fast, for in the haste I put foot to the half-severed branch. It cracked beneath me and I fell in a shower of pink flowers made silver. With a splintering crash, bough, Raffy, and all hit earth, just missing the hillock of a dead dog.

"Are you all right?"

He was bending over me now, and I heard him draw his breath in deep. I looked and noticed my leg caught between wood and ground. Funny, it never used to bend that way.

"If you don't mind me saying so, that's a godawful break. I'll have to take you back to the farm."

He was fumbling in a pocket of his coat.

"Can't have you screaming blue murder all the way there . . . sorry about this, mate."

His hand emerged from the pocket with another canister, and simultaneously he reached forward and snapped my mask off.

"Sorry," he repeated and cracked the canister under my nose.

Much later I awoke in yellow artificial light and found myself lying on a table, head propped up on foam. There was a machine covering one leg.

"Robo doctor," he said, from where he sat watching. "They gave me one 'cos I'm all alone here."

I stared at him; a smallish man with a lined, weary face, not young, not particularly muscled, and not threatening at the moment, although you never could trust them.

"Well, say something! Think you'll give yourself away? I can tell you're a woman."

"Womyn."

"And that you're one of those."

"I'm Raphael."

"That's a man's name, an archangel's."

"My mother says angels don't have gender, so there."

"Your mum knows her theology, Raphael. I'm Benedict. That means blessings, and I don't mean you harm. I even left your toy with you."

Sure enough, my right hand had been folded around the gun. I lifted both cautiously.

"Don't burn me," he said, and I lowered my hand.

"We aren't all beasts," he said seriously, and at that moment the machine on my leg thrummed. He got up to inspect it and, satisfied, lifted it off. Revealed were my camo pants cut off at midthigh and the rest encased in pale, stiff plastic.

"Like I said, bad break, and you'll find bruises and cuts, too. To get you down to my transport I had to hook your belt onto the branch and drag it behind me like a peacock's tail."

Our gaze met.

"You're bigger than me, in case you hadn't noticed."

Perhaps he expected me to smirk. I merely changed the subject. "Can I have some water? That mist dehydrates."

"I'll make some coffee; grow it myself. Ambrosia!"

I looked puzzled, and he added, "Food of the gods."

"Goddesses."

He disappeared from my view, and I got up on one elbow to see where I was. From the curving plastic walls I guessed I was inside a housing module, but the high-tech was offset by an incredible mess. There was furniture, mainly in disrepair, plants in pots, odd bits of machinery, some half-dismantled, tools, rusty wire, music tapes, collections of colored stones—clutter everywhere. Vaguely I wondered how Benedict had managed to bring me in here, then realized, with a grimace, that he must have carried me.

When he returned from the small cook-unit set against one wall he handed me a cup, taking care our flesh never touched in the transaction.

"How did you find me?"

"I'm the caretaker. I know what goes on down the farm. The dogs showed up on the heat sensor when they broke in and so did you. When all the blips were grouped round the old cherry, I could kill two jobs at once: get the pack and see who you were. From the wavelength I knew it was a human."

"*Homo sapiens.*"

He put his cup down on the table hard. "Raphael, I've been talking to you fifteen minutes and this is the third time you've corrected me!"

"It offends my sensibilities."

"And being corrected offends mine!"

We glared at each other and he sighed. "Sorry, I'm not used to *people* much. Maybe I'll leave you and your leg alone for now."

He went over to a packing case and dragged out a blanket, which he draped carefully on the table beside me.

"I sleep in the next module. If you want something, scream."

He shuffled away, following some invisible path that led him to the door without falling over anything. Pausing at the threshold, he put his hand to a knob in the plastic and the yellow glare dimmed down to night-light.

"Thanks for the rescue," I said, and threw the blanket over my head before he could respond.

Daylight shining through the translucent plastic woke me, that and a pain in my groin.

"Benedict!"

He appeared in the doorway, in a change of clothes, but unshaven.

"I wanna piss!"

"Oh, gawd," he said, looking from door to table and at the mess in between. I flung off the blanket and slid to a one-legged stop on the floor, forcing the issue.

He bent down and rose with a large broom, which he used to clear a haphazard path from me to the exit. Experimentally I hopped, and nearly went face first into a robot of some kind, its sharp guts exposed for maintenance. As I wobbled, he restored my balance with a hand to my sleeve.

"Can you lean on me, perhaps?"

Once Boz and I had gone out of the ghetto to visit Bea, now Urszula's Bea, and a man had grabbed at me. After we had rubbed his face in a mud puddle, it had vaguely registered that his flesh felt no different from a womyn's. Then, as now.

Benedict lived in three small modules, living, sleeping, and bathroom, all detached from each other and set in a circle. Although the day was overcast and chill it felt good to be outside, so afterward I let go of him and sat on the little grass courtyard between the ovals of plastic. He brought coffee and insta-bread from the module and we breakfasted.

"Raphael . . ."

Only Grania called me that, and now Benedict. After his outburst I did not want to correct him again, to say, *Just Raffy*.

"What's to be done with you?"

"I'll contact the Sisters. There's a communicator in my pack."

"Pack, where?" and I said, "By the hole under the fence."

He groaned.

"Knew I'd have to fix it sometime. Okay, I'll kill two jobs again: get your handbag and seal the fence."

It was starting to drizzle, so he helped me inside again, then left. I very soon got bored silly in the crowded room and gazing around spotted a fat old book. After one glance I dropped it—full of strange words. Then I thought to clean my gun and found that Benedict had removed the charges when I was unconscious.

When he came back I threw it at him, shouting, "Pig!"

The impact left a white mark on his face, but he stood still as the gun clattered to the floor.

"How was I to know you wouldn't fry me for laying hands on you?"

"I don't care! Pig!"

His gaze flitted about the room.

"You've been at my Shakespeare."

I recalled the name on the old book.

"I'd have ripped it to shreds if I'd known you valued it."

He lunged forward and grabbed the volume. "For that I'd have killed you."

I had never cared for poetry, thanks to Grania, and so was struck mum by his feeling.

"You've never heard of Bill," he said sadly and opened the book. Seeing him distracted, I snatched at the pack, but he deftly kicked my good leg from under me. I fell heavily, breath and pride knocked out of me. While I lay, he began quietly to read:

" 'O, she doth teach the torches to burn bright!
It seems she hangs upon the cheek of night
Like a rich jewel in an Ethiop's ear—
Beauty too rich for use, for earth too dear!
So shows a snowy dove trooping with crows,
As yonder lady o'er her fellows shows.
The measure done, I'll watch her place of stand,
And, touching hers, make blessèd my rude hand.
Did my heart love till now? forswear it, sight!
For I ne'er saw true beauty till this night.' "

I was a captive audience, but it was words rather than a shackle of plastic that held me. Words that summoned memories: in front of me was the beautiful face of a dark girl who had come just once into the ghetto. I had made enquiries about her and found her irrevocably straight, so I kicked a wall and went on living.

(Never would a face have the same effect on me until, years later, I came back from Haven to find little Honey had grown up. But by then I knew Romeo's speech by rote.)

Benedict stopped, and spoke his own words:

"See, it's not all rapes."

I was sitting up by then; he dropped the pack into my lap and went out. I opened it, found the communicator and began to cry.

"What is it?" he asked from the doorway.

"I—can't. I've blown it; I'm better off dead."

He sat down on the arm of a laden armchair.

"Have you noticed, Raphael, that I've never asked you what you're doing out here? You lot haven't been careful enough. For months now there have been rumors on the computer of walkers in the waste, consortiums nobody's heard of waving big money, a girl dressed like you found dead in a dioxin dump . . ."

I scowled, remembering how the Scouts had ascribed the death to inexperience, "Poor thing, let her go alone too soon." Now they would say the same about Raffy.

"Stop crying. I don't care what you're up to so long as I'm left alone. And I never dob in anyone. Call the ladies!"

Maybe I trusted him, but the Sisters never would. Besides . . .

"I'd be a laughing stock, skiving off after flowers and having to be rescued—by an andro! They'd never let me scout again."

"So," he said, "I'm not going to tell my bosses, and you're not going to tell your bossesses. What then?"

"How long before I walk?"

"Coupla months. The robo gave you a calcium accelerator, but you can't hurry *Mother* Nature."

He was looking glum and the emotion was infectious; the consequences of our silence were an unwanted guest for him and dependence on a man for me.

"I can modify a robo into transport for you," he said. "But it'll take time."

"Gimme materials and I'll make crutches."

He fished in the litter behind the chair, emerging with an all-purpose kit, its plastic grimy and dented.

"You can make one crutch from the broom—never use it anyway. I'll see what's handy for the other."

He was half out the door when I yelled at him, "Benedict! I want something else."

He turned and I tapped the gun meaningfully.

"Promise you won't burn me?"

"I promise only if you promise not to . . ."

I stopped, for an extraordinary expression of grief had taken hold of his face. "Lord, what we've done to deserve this, and rightly too!"

He took the charges from his coat pocket and rolled them across the floor to me, where they were stopped by my leg in its plastic chitin. I picked them up, counted them, slotted them into their pods—and looked up to see that Benedict had gone.

Good, because I needed to consider the strange situation we had fallen into. An analogy came to mind: Edge City, when two wildly differing ghetto factions united against the middle ground. Just because their interests coincided did not mean opportunities were lost for mischief to each other; I should remember that. He had several Edges on me: mobility and his computer, wherever it was, with which he could summon his bosses if the guest proved irksome. On the other hand I had the Edges of a gun and my communicator, for a last-resort SOS.

Thinking of a Mayday caused me to remember that I had not given my daily position report to the ghetto. I glanced at my watch, noting I was several hours late. If I didn't send the Scouts off on a wild-gorse chase, they would go straight to my last location, just south of the site, and from there track me to the macrofarm. Loss of face for me, but of life for Benedict, who, despite his hospitality, would be killed out of hand.

I unfolded my map, looking for a labyrinth or tanglewood and found a marsh, probably once a sewage farm. It was off-course; perfect. I fed its coordinates into the flute, a coding device that unraveled information into its component yarns and sent it across space, to be knit up only at the other end. "Chased by wild dogs," I added for explanation, and flicked the communicator to receiving mode.

A jumble of symbols appeared on the little screen, resolving first into letters, then words. "OK. Come on home." Whoever was on the other end was in a laconic mood. I had a moment of conscience, as I remembered Zoska, Boz, and my other foster sisters, even despised Grania—then I turned the communicator off.

" 'The rest is silence,' " I said, as I returned the communicator to my pack.

Benedict spoke from the doorway, and I jumped:

"Do you know where that comes from?"

"How long have you been there?"

"Only long enough to hear you quote Bill."

He came in lugging a collection of staves.

"Any of these do?"

"Yeah, the longest," and we set to woodwork. Our hands dipped in and out of the kitbox, never coinciding.

After a while he returned to the quotation.

"Where'd you hear that?"

"Probably my mother."

"The authority on angels?"

"Yeah, I've got two mothers." He blinked. "One gave birth to me; the other reared me."

"So which knows Bill?"

"My blood mother, Grania Erato."

"Poetry woman, eh?"

Now I blinked; then I remembered that he read.

"You know her?"

He shook his head.

"I only read one book. See, Raphael, I decided long ago that a man, begging your pardon, didn't have time to read everything. There're too many people writing and nearly all of them are mediocre. There ought to be a pogrom—they hide the really good writers with their verbiage. So I just stuck with the very best."

He gestured at the book.

"Before you flare up at me again, I'm not saying your mum's no good. I never read her . . . I'm restricted in my reading."

"But how do you know she writes verse?"

"Erato's the muse of love poetry."

"How pretentious," I said without thinking, and bit my lip, too late.

He looked at me, reading more than I wished him to, so I bent over the crutch and worked like a machine. After a pause, he followed suit. Even when we broke briefly for more bread and coffee, we did not speak—until the crutches were finished.

"Yeay!"

I pulled myself up to standing and fitted the pads under my arms. Suddenly Raffy metamorphosed from crawling caterpillar to a mummy-long-legs, with limbs of wood, plastic and flesh. It was fleet, in a lurching fashion, for with three long steps I was down Benedict's pathway and outside, being buffeted by the late afternoon wind.

"Whee!"

He had followed me outside protectively.

"Don't overdo it. Years ago I was on those things and took days getting used to them. Don't think because you're muscled like a racehorse that you won't be sore."

Just for that, I left the courtyard, hopping through the gaps between the modules to the farm proper. It consisted of more modules, but giant, in row after row with tidy concrete paths in between. I lolloped to the nearest and stared through the plastic opaqued by my breath, like a child at a shop window. There were many green plants, and the glint of steel as a robot gardener rolled up and down.

I glanced behind me and saw Benedict watching like a guardian angel. Irritated by his solicitude I swung away from the wall and went for a long walk along concrete, walled in always by plastic. He did not follow, perhaps expecting a clout over the head with a crutch.

When I returned, doused in sweat and radiating heat like a boiler, I found the courtyard littered with Benedict's junk. Dust blew like a mist from the door of the living module.

I sat down with a thump on the packing case and at the noise he came out, wearing a faded red scarf over his grizzled hair.

"You want your broom back for the spring cleaning?"

He scowled. "I'm making space. If you're living here you'll need territory of your own. For *my* sanity I'm making a moiety of the living room."

"Need help?"

He stared at me. "Move furniture when you've buggered yourself with the most strenuous walk you could manage? Braggadacian!"

He disappeared inside again and I, feeling parched, went to the bathroom to get a drink without disturbing him. There was a mirror there, overlooked previously, and it reflected the new face like a stranger. I saw a girl, weary and strained, with twigs in her brown hair and smears from bark on her face. The man's glass told me what I had not noticed in his gaze: this girl was attractive.

The water splashed into my hands and I longed for a bath, but only cleaned my face. To strip, and to have him sneak up behind me . . .

When I went out it was sunset, and I shivered at the memory of dogs and flowers. I sat on the crate again and watched lights come on inside the living module. It resembled a giant phosphorescent slug.

"You can come in now, Raphael."

Within, a low wall had been built of odds and ends; on one side was Benedict's clutter, on the other was an area cleared of all save a mattress with my pack and blanket set neatly upon it.

"I'll make the wall higher, give you privacy, promise. I'm just out of energy now."

"It's not urgent," I lied politely.

He grunted and dodged effortlessly to the cook-unit, where a saucepan bubbled. I looked for the table and found it pushed against the wall, at the end of the path. There were two chairs by it; I sat down and noticed the Shakespeare on the table, like a second guest for dinner.

Benedict brought stewpot, cutlery, and crockery to the table.

" 'Let good digestion wait on appetite!' "

"I suppose that's in your book too," I said.

"Bill says something about everything."

Chitchat was forgotten then, as we ate like a pair of wild beasts. When the meal was over, I reached for the book.

"What are you doing?" he asked suspiciously.

"Seeing what he says about the likes of me . . . them, as you put it. What's this, The Taming of the . . ."

"I doubt you'll find it there," he said and pulled the book from me. "How 'bout this: 'Would it not grieve a woman to be overmastered with a piece of valiant dust? to make account of her life to a clod of wayward marl?' That's feminist at least."

"Nice. Who is she?"

"Lass called Beatrice. A bit like you: fierce."

I twitched the book into my grasp again, accidentally losing the place. In front of me was a list of names followed by their speeches and I looked for Beatrice.

"Phooey. Here she's saying: 'I love you with so much of my heart that none is left to protest' to a clod named . . ."

"Benedick," he finished. Picking up the book, he walked to the door.

"Good night," he said, without turning.

"Good night."

I fidgeted for a while then shoved the robot against the door and went to sleep. In the morning I was awakened by the sound of an electric motor. Moving, I found my muscles sore (prophetic Benedict!), but pushed the robot aside and swung out. The courtyard was empty, but through the gap I could see Benedict atop a squat vehicle with fat rubber wheels. He zoomed it down a pathway and out of sight.

Tied to the largest bit of the courtyard junk was a note: "Off to check fences. Back late today. Place yours."

I stood there like a tripod, listening to the motor fade out of earshot. How lovely to be alone again! Then my solitude was interrupted by the tock of rain—within moments my hair was soaked and drops trickled down my neck. I laughed, throwing my head back to drink rain, and went to the bathroom module to finish what the cloudburst had begun. Only the mirror marred my mood; its big round eye seemed prurient so I made it stare at the wall.

Showered, I went searching for Benedict's computer and found the console behind a filing cabinet that looked as if the robot had kicked it in a pet. Raffy was never a hacker, except for a romantic summer with the ghetto's computer whiz, yet the sight revived memories. Benedict was no hacker either, for log-on instructions were taped to the keyboard. There was no password, but I guessed "Shakespeare" and guessed right.

The screen lit up with a list of options and I choose "Security" and after that "Heat Sensor." An infrared picture of the farm covered the screen, with the small blips of wildlife and one big blip moving slowly around the perimeter. It would appear Benedict was truthful. I returned to the original list and took the option "Maintenance." This killed the curious kitten for diagram after confusing diagram of the giant modules appeared. The care involved indicated that the green crop I had glimpsed so briefly was highly lucrative. What was it? Best not ask. The seclusion of the farm and the fact that the intermediaries had not been able to discover the names of its owners argued a need for secrecy.

Benedict returned after dark, to the lukewarm half of a meal I had concocted from various odd edibles found around the cook-unit. He devoured it, then looked closely at me.

"Good, you had a bath. Thought if I went away you would—you were starting to pong."

I was silent, and he gazed around the module. After my hacking, I had got sick of having to weave through his mess like a drunkard, so had added the more maneuverable furniture to the wall.

"And you made space! I can work in here."

"What on?"

"Robo-digger. To modify for *your* transport."

"I've got the wood legs."

He shook his head.

"Very soon you'll find them restricting."

He spread a plastic groundsheet on the floor and wheeled in the digger, which—shovel apart—was the baby of his transport. I opened my mouth and he said, raising his voice an octave, "Need help?" Then, in his normal pitch, "No thanks, Raphael, unless you're an expert on robotics."

I shook my head, reluctantly. He grinned, then saw my expression and pulled the corners of his mouth down.

"Why don't you talk to me while I work?"

"About what?"

"The ghetto. See, I'm curious—it's natural with something that excludes you. Years ago, before your wall went up, I walked through the ghetto fringes. Dirty looks galore, but nobody beat me up. I suppose being a little tich saved me."

I agreed silently.

"What did you see, Benedict?"

"Nothing much, just no men."

I snorted and he blushed rosy pink.

"I was only there five minutes, girl."

I gazed at him, gauging what information to give and what to withhold. At Bea's house I had met straight women who would politely, deviously, direct the conversation to my lifestyle. All I needed do was think of the most unsound of them, add a dash of caution, and I would have a recipe for Benedict.

"Why are you staring at me?" he asked.

Just for a moment, the image of a woman had flickered on his face.

"It's just a place where womyn live. We have the wall, and beyond that are 'suburbs,' where feminists and dykes who don't mind mixing"—like Bea and Grania—"live. The Watch, that's our police, call them the first line of defence. Soft cores live just inside the wall, hard cores farther in."

"What's them?"

"Degrees of ideological rigidity."

"And what are you?"

"Guess," I said coldly.

"In between, I'd say."

Correct, but he needn't know that. He waited, then ventured: "What about the money, economy, sort of thing, eh?"

"The suburbans pay tithes from their work in the andro's world." Grania had been bankrolling the ghetto for decades, to name one prominent instance. "There're also workshops, factories, where goods are made to sell Outside."

"Like what?"

"I'm not going to tell you."

"Knitting," he fished, half-seriously. I smiled at his little joke and also at the thought of the systems that my old hacker love marketed to a lot of blissful ignoramuses.

"The ideal is self-sufficiency," I said, imagining the walled Haven in the country, our City of Womyn.

"In more ways than one," he muttered. "I've heard talk of a Hive."

Loose lips! I thought, but continued, trying not to let the exchange become an Edge Game.

"It's the center for us. To stay there long is to forget that your kind exist. Call it an editing device."

Any mention of andros was forbidden in our temple to the Gyn principle, which caused some bizarre conversations. Once Urszula, being a brat, had asked Zoska in front of hardcores where babies came from. ("Yes, Mama, but what makes the baby grow in your belly? Why aren't I growing one now?") She had got a flustered answer about cabbages and my accompanying raucous laughter got me thrown out of the Hive for the very first time. It had been "unseemly," in this quiet place decorated with murals of

Ishtar, Athena, and Joan of Arc sans Ur-Nammu, Zeus, and the English clerics. I could feel uplifted, even refreshed in the Hive, but ultimately it was claustrophobic. All restrictions annoy Raffy.

Benedict should not hear criticisms, but neither could I voice vague platitudes. I clammed up. The cessation obviously irritated him, for he began to quote his Bill, half to himself, a quarter to the digger, and a quarter to me. I listened until we parted for the night.

In the morning it rained again, and Benedict's robotics were interrupted by the visit of a truck. He dealt with it, returned and worked with a mixture of care and haste. By a happy coincidence the sun poked out moments after the contraption was finished. He pushed it out into the courtyard and through a gap to the start of a sloping path.

"Hop on."

He took the crutches, slotting them into a niche at the back of the transport.

"Oh, so that's what it's for."

"That, by your hand, is direction and this is speed. This starts the motor."

I forestalled him and switched it on myself. As the machine purred he grinned at his handiwork. Seeing him off guard I put my hand hard on the speed button.

"Hey, wait! Whoa!"

"Wowee!"

The machine shot down the path straight for one of the giant modules, and I grabbed the steering just in time to execute a two-wheeled turn. To show Benedict I had mistressed the vehicle, I did a circuit of the module and risked glancing behind for his reaction. He was open-mouthed like a yokel, so with a wave I disappeared around the module again.

When I had explored on crutches I had found the farm monotonous; riding, it was the same, although I passed a processing plant and the road for the trucks, which relieved the uniformity. There was more fun in being Raffy the speed maniac, careering around like a pinball. Pride cometh before a crash, of course, and I was sobered by a near collision with a robot gardener.

"Road hog!" I shouted at its featureless metal carapace, largely to cover the pain from my leg, which had been jarred. Then I continued down the path and found I was free of modules, in open, tussocked country. Still adventurous, I rode to the fence and back, but at an invalid's pace.

It was late when I puttered nervously up to Benedict's home, and to my relief he was not waiting outside. I parked the transport and became a stick insect again.

He was sitting at the console.

"Have a nice time?"

"Yes, thank you."

"I watched your blip until it slowed down. Then I did some hacking."

I poled to where I could see the screen, which resembled the old samplers displayed in the Hive: across the screen was verse, Grania's verse:

> Battersea blues couldn't keep me apart
> I got to play songs in a grimy gutter
> With you along—your clutter.
>
> There're leaves in your hair, have you
> been dancing with your old man again?
> Walk on the wind of September evening
> Don't come down until I've finished playing.
>
> Lend me a mood, oh no
> I'm not wistful, not jealous.
> I have the music and you have the heart
> Battersea blues couldn't keep me apart."

"She was very young when she wrote that," I said. "She still had her father's name."

"So I saw."

"You didn't get far with her verse."

"On the contrary. I accessed the biography first, which was mainly a list of prizes, then the contents page of the *Collected Works*. There were lots of poems about R. and Raphael, but I thought you'd thump me if I read them. So I accessed the cheapest poem about anything else."

"Thanks."

"Amazing! She's said thank you to me twice in one conversation."

There was a round scrap of plastic temptingly near; I leaned on one crutch and savagely batted it across the module with the other. It hit the wall with a satisfying clunk.

"I live in glass. Anything she hears about me goes into her verse! Vampire!"

"The parent feeds the child and then feeds off him . . . her."

I stared at him.

"You're not unique," he said. "With me it was my father."

"My father was 10-cc of sticky fluid," I said viciously. He ignored the goad.

"Lucky you."

He switched off the console.

"Dad was a drunk. Only good thing he did was desert the family. Trouble was he kept coming back."

I, too, had been incompletely deserted.

"Mum was all right," he said. "Earth Mother type."

"Like my foster mother."

"That's right," he recalled. "You said you had two."

"She says the world's oldest profession isn't whoring, it's motherhood. That's what she does."

"She good at it?"

I laughed. "You think so, on the evidence of me?"

"I meant, is she respected for it?"

"It's high status in the ghetto."

Zoska had been nominated as an Elder, but had dodged the election by beginning Basienka.

"That's how it should be," he said.

Both of us had become embarrassed by the confessions, and so gravitated to the table, where there was a bowl of fresh greens.

"Grow it myself," he said proudly. "One of the perks of the job."

"That and being alone," I said, and he nodded, a little too emphatically. We sat and ate, crushing crisp leaves between our teeth. The crunching made me aggressive, revived my daredevil high with the transport. Foolhardy as ever, I decided on an Edge Game. If Benedict was in a confessing mood, he might give information valuable to the ghetto and my curiosity.

I waved a strip of bok choy: "You grow other greens in the modules."

"You noticed?"

This was not a good sign, but I persisted, "I don't know botany, but they're like no plants I've seen."

"They're intoxicants. The only other perk of the job."

I had not expected him to fold so easily. Careful, a biochemical sensor warned.

"They come from what used to be the Amazon rain forest. Got saved from extinction when a scientist ate one and had a nice time. They're still only quasilegal, like the other substances that relax society's rules a little. That's why this farm is far from awkward questions."

He paused. "Except when asked by Raphaels. You want to try some?"

We were both on the razor's edge now. His suggestion had caught me off guard, but to signal that might be dangerous. I had to answer quickly.

"Sure."

He went out and I grinned like a wedge of cheese. Free intoxicant!

Benedict was gone a long time and returned, not with the expected green sheaf, but carrying a small box.

"Could have got raw stuff, just pull if off the vine, but it's rough. This is processed, ready for the truck."

He opened the box, to reveal gray crystals, more intoxicant than I had ever seen before. I nodded warily, thinking about dosages—in the ghetto only Boz had had a stronger head than Raffy for the drug. He set the box on the table and to my surprise ignited the crystals. A soft gray smoke, reminiscent of Zoska's old homespun shawl, drifted upward.

"This is freebasing. Extravagant, but the best."

I attempted the worldly wise expression of a drug savant, and obviously failed, for he continued: "This extract's euphoric. Other types make people concentrate, make 'em sexy, send 'em to sleep . . . the many words that describe emotions, they're all covered by the drug. It's a universal, like Bill."

The smoke swirled round me, like the three witches on a panel in the Hive.

"Weird sisters," he said, and I goggled: did the drug cause telepathy?

"From the book," he explained. "Want to hear it?"

"Yes."

He read from his memory, speech after fantastical speech, and I savored them. All, except for the initial extract from *Macbeth*, were descants on the theme of heterosexual love, which might have been oppressive had not the language transcended gender. I heard the love-talk of men and women and interpreted it as that of womyn.

He stopped, dried out, and an eerie silence descended. The room was a ball of smoke and we were silhouettes to each other. Feeling nervous, I moved closer to him, and he turned his head.

"Did that upset you?"

"No."

"Very sexist. I'm sorry. I forgot with you it was girl and girl."

"It's much like the other," I said, recalling the language.

"Really? You've tried?"

I was feeling pleasantly confused.

"No, although Grania said I'd try anything except incest and folk dancing."

He had never seemed threatening; that was his advantage, or Edge. Perhaps to convince myself he was still there, in this witches' brew, or perhaps for Raffy's damned curiosity, I reached out and touched him. His chest was as hard as that of a prepubescent girl.

"Is this an advance?" he said, cautiously flattered.

It was now. Raffy is also tactile.

He put his hand reverently over mine—they were almost the same size.

"Who'd have thought it? An old man like me."

Actually he was younger than Grania. Our other hands were grappled now.

"I'm out of practice," he said, and glanced around. The smoke had cleared a little.

"Not on that hard little mattress," I said.

We stood up, and I teetered as I tried to fit the crutches.

"Are we ever stoned!" he said. "You'll never make it out the door."

He tried to life me but got hopelessly tangled with a crutch, and nearly fell over himself.

"Any suggestions?"

"Pig-back," I said muzzily.

He laughed: "Yeah, appropriate for a pig."

He knelt in front of me and I stood on my good leg, tucking the crutches under one arm.

"Hupsy-daisy," he said, and I rode him out the door to the sleeping module.

I awoke, again to daylight diffused through module plastic, and looked into the face of Benedict. Asleep, he looked like something the cat had dragged in: a little beat-up mouse.

As if on cue he opened his eyes.

"Raphael, that was sweet."

I rolled over on my back, to get the weight off my cast and also to escape his sooky expression. There, above me, was flesh, holos of naked women, all breasts, buttocks, thighs, taped to the module ceiling. They had a look of vacuous unreality suggesting the counterfeit; if not, they were like no womyn I had ever seen.

It had been dark in here last night. Intentionally? He saw my expression and groaned like a creaky door. I shot up and began to extract my clothes from the mess around his bed, swearing under my breath. Pulling on a garment I overbalanced and fell on top of him; he lay still beneath me. I scrambled up again and finished dressing. Then I found my crutches at the foot of the bed and poled furiously for the living module. There was a box of gray ash on the table and I knocked it to the floor, before grabbing my pack and heading for my transport.

He was standing in the courtyard, wrapped in a blanket.

"Raphael!" he shouted. "I'm only human and I mean a man!"

"That's no excuse!"

I started the motor and sped away, making a grand exit. Moments later I remembered my gun: should I return and use it? No. I never wanted to see him again.

My intent had been to follow the roboroad to the gate, the weak spot in most defences. However in my haste I had made a wrong turning and was as lost among identical paths and modules as an ant on a checkerboard. The sun was out; I estimated east and headed that way. The maze of modules ended and I continued toward the fence, thinking to circumnavigate to the farm entrance. Idly I noticed the tracks of a larger transport on the grass before me. Then there was a cherry bough, its flowers withered and dry, and beyond it, up a steep slope, the rock-a-bye-Raffy tree.

I pulled out the communicator and held it in my hand like a shell. It was no use, for the same restrictions still applied. If I returned to the ghetto on a stolen transport, questions would still be asked about my leg. For expediency's sake I would have to return and make peace with Benedict.

I drove along the fence to the gate, as planned, and found it open. Was this an invitation to leave? If so, I refused it and took the road back to Benedict.

He was waiting outside this time, looking worried.

"Why didn't you go?"

Dismounting, I tapped the cast with a crutch in answer: it made a dull sound, like a prison door slamming.

"Yes, but after what we did? I did?"

His tone was guilty and something occurred to me: he had mentioned that the drug could make people "sexy."

"Benedict, was there aphrodisiac in that blend?"

"A little," he said sheepishly, a repentant ram. "Didn't think it'd work."

I struck him with a crutch, not hard, but sufficient to send him reeling back against the nearest piece of junk. He hit it at an angle, gashing his scalp. Blood dribbled down like water into his eyes.

"I can't see! Raphael, help!"

He was crouched on the ground, both hands over the wound. There was no way I could lift him.

"Stand up!" I said like the Watch Chief and he obeyed.

"Easy. I'm here."

He reached one blood-sticky hand out to the voice. I anchored the crutches and took hold of it.

"Inside," he said. "Doctor!"

Now I had the problem of getting him to the living module, for while he clasped me as though drowning I could not use the crutches. They required both hands. A sudden gust of wind flapped my scarf, left untied in the hasty dressing, and I had an idea.

"Benedict, let go!"

Very slowly, he complied.

"Now take this," I said, and brushed one fringed end of the scarf against his fingers. He took it, and I wrapped the other end around one crutch handgrip. Carefully I swung into the module, leading him by an embroidered tether.

"The lame leading the blind," he said.

Inside I sat him down at the table and found the doctor unit. When I activated it, the optical sensors swiveled and it made a clicking noise, tsk, tsk, tsk. Metal hands shot out of the body and began to minister. Within minutes the blood had been cleaned from him and the hair shaved from around the gash, which was staunched with a dab of sealant. The robot went into inert mode and I switched it off.

He opened his eyes and stared down at an anthill of split ash. Absently he smoothed it with the side of his hand.

"Raphael . . ."

"Yes?"

He doddled in the ash with a forefinger, then erased the design.

"Don't hit me again, but I'm not protected against fertility. Are you?"

I sat down too, feeling sick to my boots.

"Of course not. And I'm at full moon."

He sighed, and as if his head was suddenly too heavy, rested his cheek on the ashy hand. Realizing too late, he withdrew the hand and stared at it glumly.

"Next it'll be sackcloth."

I made no reply.

"Say something. Laugh at slapstick old me."

"The doctor," I said incoherently.

"They programmed it for a man on his own, no gynecology. I've heard that jumping with your legs in splints . . ."

"Very funny."

"Well, surely the ghetto has herbal remedies."

"No need."

"No, I suppose not."

"I'm *not* speaking to you," and with that I retired behind the wall of China, or rather of junk, and huddled under the blanket. After a pause he went out, and I heard the noise of his transport, moving away.

He did not come into the living module the rest of that day, nor did

I go out—thus we avoided each other. The following day the pattern was reversed: I took the little transport out around the farm while he was a stay-at-home. In this way we had the necessary illusion of being alone. If our paths crossed the junctions were marked by a chilling silence.

The routine was finally aborted one rainy morning, as we breakfasted— he on fresh-brewed coffee and I on food-concentrate from the pack. An electronic whine crossed the wall.

"The heat sensor!" he said, and dashed to the console. I followed in seven-league strides.

"What is it?"

He jabbed a stubby finger at the screen.

"Figures, just north. Your mates?"

I leaned closer to stare at the sexless blobs. The marsh had been north of the farm.

"Relax, this isn't the dyke cavalry. They're just being curious."

(Taking a look at the farm and also the site, but I couldn't say that.)

He frowned.

"Don't think much of their tracking. You and the tree were on the other side."

"I gave them a position reading for the marsh center."

"Gulper? They could have been killed looking for you there."

After all that had happened since I had crawled under the fence, I should have been immune to shock. Yet that jarred me. With my luck it would probably be Boz.

"Well, I didn't know it was dangerous. If I hadn't they'd have burst in here thinking I'd been kidnapped for a sex slave—which is partly true."

He winced.

"Take the cart and catch up with them."

They would come back and kill you, I thought, but only said, "I'd be pitied for the rest of my life."

"A fate worse than death," he said drily.

"And what if I were carrying?"

We had agonized silently about that question for three days now, but to voice it hurt not at all. He took the cue quickly.

"Any reason you might not?"

"I never tried. And you?"

"The ladies all took precautions. I never got close to one so she'd stop using them and have my baby . . . have a child with me."

I rocked on the crutches and considered.

"What are our options?"

"One—nothing's cooking. Two, there is, but you want to stop it."

That option was tricky: the knowledge lay outside the ghetto and I would have to consult with feminists, who might blab.

"Three, you don't."

"It might be a boy!" I cried. How unpleasant, to have the enemy growing inside me.

"Can't see him being reared by manhaters," he said.

"I suppose you'd want to keep him."

"I just remember," he said reasonably, "the one nice thing my dad did with me, which was fishing. Sitting by a stream, if I can find one unpolluted, teaching a small me . . ."

"Small you!"

He looked at me.

"He might take after his tearaway mum."

There was a pause while I tried to imagine a male Raffy.

"You'd not let me keep a girl?" he said.

I shrugged, recalling Grania's poems about father-daughter incest. On the other hand, the idea of returning to the ghetto with a female infant, claiming to have found her in bulrushes—the idea was preposterous.

"Look Benedict, aren't we counting chickens before they're hatched? There might be nothing in the eggshell."

"True," he said dubiously, and we left it at that. At least we were talking again, but the cautious camaraderie was gone. In the days that followed we ate together, did odd jobs around the farm together, but were emotionally apart. The book remained a common ground but we read it to ourselves separately.

Time passed in this waiting game. One day he put in hours at the terminal, while I hogged the book, enjoying the three witches and disagreeing with their images in the Hive (not evil enough). Sensing from his absorption that this was no farm matter, I sneaked up behind him, as quietly as a Woodeny could.

He was searching scientific literature, combining the terms "calcium accelerator" and "embryology."

"Raphael, quit reading over my shoulder," he said mildly.

"Tell me what you found first."

"See for yourself," and he dodged past me. I sat down at the terminal and saw that he had accessed several articles, full-text. One dealt with white mice, the other with monotremes.

"What about people?"

"I tried that," he said from the other side of the room. "No research reports."

The door of the module slammed and I began to read the articles. The monotreme one was inconclusive and the white mice had eaten their young—not an encouraging prognosis.

I glanced back and saw that Benedict had snaffled the Shakespeare. Ah, well, it was his turn for it. To complete the reversal I began hacking myself, first checking the account to which the searches were credited. It worried me that Benedict's bosses might smell a lady rat if their employee ticked up searches unconnected with their product. However, the account was private, its searches—until recently—solely of the database Shaklit.

I returned to the original enquiry and discarded "embryology" to concentrate on the drug that was healing my leg. After an hour I knew that in the young and healthy the period of accelerated cure could be as short as one month. I patted the cast thoughtfully; it would be rushing things, but if Option One occurred I could be away much sooner than Benedict expected. A quick getaway was desirable—he was starting to look sooky again.

He made one more attempt to discuss our possible parenthood:

"Have you decided yet?"

"On what?"

"Options Two or Three?"

"Oh, Ishtar, it might well be neither!"

I stormed off, more bluster, for I was late and I think he knew it. Of course, the upsets I had experienced this month would have disturbed the cycle of a she-elephant. . . .

One pale spring dawn I woke up very early and found it was Remembrance day, as in Grania's famous poem. Her words had never bobbed up in my mind much before, but now I was thinking in a mixture of Grania and Bill. I activated the Doctor and addressed it to my leg. It whirred, clicked again, shone lights, prodded me here and there—and then it extruded a nozzle that sprayed the cast with pink mist. The plastic melted away as I watched, leaving not even a discarded cocoon to mark my change. The leg underneath was scaly and looked strange; I cautiously tried exercises then shuffled up and down. It was whole.

Much of my silence had been put to the devising of contingency plans, and I knew what to do. I laid the crutches aside and *walked* to the console, where I instructed the gates to open. Then I shouldered my pack and left, pausing only to streak blood on the door of the sleeping module: my explanation.

He must have slept late that morning, for I had escaped the farm and was following the road through thickets of yellow gorse before he came after me. Hearing the motor, I moved to the roadside. Prickly leaves brushed my bare new leg—if I hid there I would be scratched raw. Instead I pulled out the gun, hating to use it.

Benedict was astride the little transport and for the first time I noticed, as he must have before, that riders of the converted digger looked absurd. He brought it to a stop on the other side of the road, several meters from me. Now I was in sight he seemed unable to speak.

"You got the message," I finally said.

He nodded. "Raphael! Not a word good-bye."

A buzzing insect shot past my head, going from gorse bush to gorse bush and incidentally from Raffy to Benedict. He continued:

"Oh I know that you couldn't predict what I'd do. Suspicious minds! I'm not here to compel you."

"What then?"

"I'm worried. What if you meet another pack of dogs? I know you accessed CA data, and that you think the leg's sound. But you could refracture if you run on it, and this time nobody might help you."

He was right: although I had paced myself carefully over the distance, I had developed a limp.

"Do you want to guard me back to the ghetto?"

"And ruin your reputation? No, girl, just take the transport."

I started to demur, but he kept speaking:

"You can ditch it near the city. There's a homing circuit and it'll make its way back down the road."

"I can't."

He looked astounded.

"How do I repay you? I've taken and given nothing in return."

"But you have."

He clambered off the transport.

"Raphael, you've not been easy to live with. I cannot endure my Lady Tongue, not lately. But I've fallen in love with her."

He stopped.

"My first love! A lesbian who won't be tamed, won't play Beatrice with Benedict."

Slowly he moved away from the vehicle.

"It's a gift to me if you take it, stops me imagining you et by dogs."

There was no real answer to this speech, not one that would satisfy him. I took one step, then two, toward the transport.

"Thank you," he said, when I got onto it.

"Thank you! Good-bye."

"Good-bye," he replied, his expression bleak. I started the motor and coasted away, glancing back now and then to see him standing there against the yellow like a spoon in mustard. A bend of the road hid him, and I never saw him again.

Now I knew how he had felt. Oh, Honey! The emotional ache had become physical—I stared at Grania and suffered.

"How could I forget?" she said. "You limped in here like a wounded belletrice, expecting me to shred the—quite good—elegy I'd written for you. When I didn't, you told me what you thought of me. It was a strange speech, first ghetto-gutter, then becoming arcane and archaic. 'Cacodemon' was one word used—I had not heard it outside *Richard III*. How strange to hear it from my Raphael's foul mouth. When you finished, your womynly chest panting up and down like a bellows, I remarked, quoting as is my way . . ."

" 'She was wont to speak plain and to the purpose . . . and now is she turned orthography, her words are a very fantastical banquet—just so many strange dishes.' "

"And you turned to the bookshelf, and following the alpha-beta around, you discovered Shakes-rags and opened it."

"I said, '*Much Ado About Nothing*, act 2, Scene 3, nyaagh!' "

"Whereupon I remarked that while missing, presumed dead, you had attended classes on Shakespeare."

"And I told you the whole story."

"Which made me wonder why you, so secretive—"

"Because you write about me!"

". . . should spiel the most profound experience of your life. Raphael, I know a dare when I see one. You were daring me to write that Raphael Grania had fornicated with an andro. Being contrary, a trait you have inherited, I didn't."

"Would you, now?"

"It's stale bread news. Haven's half-completed and I doubt anyone would murder that poor man for slipping you a mickey thirteen years ago. The hard cores wouldn't like it, but you dislike them."

"I intend to marry into them."

This time she did blink.

"Oh, the sweet young thing. What's her name?"

"Honey Marthe."

"Is she pretty?"

"Very. And with a mother like a meat-ax."

She put her pink hands to her mouth. "So that's why you want my silence!"

"I want a vow of it."

"On one condition."

"What?"

"Raphael, on that night you withheld information from your dear mamma. You never said what you thought of the heterosexual act."

I considered.

"Very well, but you must swear first."

"On something sacred. I know you."

Feeling foolish, as she no doubt intended, I knelt down by the chair and she put her heavy hand on my head. An opportunity for caress, I realized.

"I swear, on Raphael, not to tattle."

I stood up.

"That promise covers what I shall tell you."

She nodded.

"Spit it out, this byte, this titbit."

I was silent, thinking of words.

"Mumchance! I see I must interrogate you. Was it pleasurable?"

"Of course. But not the real thing. Hence Honey."

She stored the information away.

"Well, my heretic, we both lose by this transaction, you some privacy, I for not being able to put this grain through the art mill."

"Crushing me," I said, continuing the conceit.

"You exaggerate, nothing could do that. I know being muse-food, muesli, was irksome, but it cracked your indifference wonderfully. Naughty of me, but fun—you always bit."

"No more."

"No, if we are to be at peace. Allow me at least an epithalamium."

"You do that. Make it good."

Interview concluded, I strolled down the hall and out. The garden summoned memories of other flowers, but I brushed them away. Benedict, my apologies . . .

I returned to the ghetto, encountering the on-duty Watch at the gate. Considering my scuffles with that body, they were friendly, which made me suspect some support. This inkling and the news of Grania I wanted to share with Zoska, but when I returned to her little house, she was out. From Basienka's room came a voice singing lullabies, probably Urszula bullied into baby-sitting. Not wanting questions, I raided the larder, mouse-quiet, and went to bed. Sated physically but not emotionally, I slept.

In the morning Basienka awakened me by crawling into my bed with a huge rag doll.

"You want breakfast, kid?"

She considered it like a duchess.

"Yes."

"Well, we'll make some for everyone."

We brewed coffee, chopped fruit, and toasted bread rolls, then I carried the tray into the bedroom. Zoska was weeping.

"What is it? Row with your lover again?"

In answer she waved her hand at the little radio beside the bed, which received only the ghetto's weak FM signal. I listened, to an Elder talking excitedly about—

"Parthenogenesis! They've done it at last!"

Zoska blew her nose loudly.

"And it's too late for me. Curse the biological clock!"

With exquisite timing, Basienka plonked herself in her mother's lap. Zoska hugged her.

"Still, you two will benefit. No more seed and egg, just egg and egg."

"Omelette."

"Don't be facetious, you dreadful child. Other dreadful child, don't spill my coffee!"

Complete independence, I thought, as she fussed over Basienka. It had been the inevitable consequence of the Sisters' path, an ideal from the beginnings of the ghetto. Just because I had once been friendly with a man did not mean I regretted this innovation, that cast my kind adrift from his. Benedict, I was a Sister first, and there was no changing it.

"How did it go last night?" asked Zoska, munching fruit.

"All fixed."

"Good girl."

"How about you?"

"I talked my head off, first to Marthe, then I had tea with the Scouts and dropped in on the soft-core leaders. On the way home I was met by the faction of hard cores at odds with Marthe. We're getting an Edge City."

"There's still the Elders."

"A Scout talked on the flute with Boz, and she sent the Elders a rocket, saying Marthe was behaving like a heavy father. I thought that too, but it takes the Head of Haven to say it and remain unscathed."

She gestured at the radio.

"But this news has done it."

I finished my coffee and lounged back.

"Sure it's wonderful, but how does it affect Raffy 'n' Honey?"

"Well it's like I'm fighting with the baby and the sky rains honey apples. Instant end to hostilities as we gorge."

"Honey apple," said Basienka.

"Silly," I said. "Now you'll have to get her one."

"Honey apple."

"Later, sweet tooth," said Zoska. "Talking of H-O-N-E-Y, I saw her."

I sat up straight, rocking the bed.

"What she say, what she say?"

"She loves you."

I jumped off the bed and capered around it, followed by the imitative Basienka.

"She got Marthe out of the room to tell me that. Not as submissive as I thought."

"My bad influence."

"No doubt. But I still think you'll be doing the fighting when that girl leaves the ghetto."

"What if I take her to Haven?"

"A good compromise."

She paused.

"Is it as utopic as Boz claims?"

"We're working on it," I said.

"You do that. I'll stay at home, old imperfect ghetto, in case Haven goes . . ."

"Dystopian?"

"Dystopian. Forget I said that. I just realized I'm being thrown out with the bathwater. Still, it's the best way to get Marthe out of your hair, which now I think of it—"

She put her head on one side.

"—needs a cut."

She hopped out of bed.

"Let me bully you for the last time."

First she made me wash in the little bathroom cluttered with watertoys, then combed down my damp mop and trimmed it. With an air of relish, she next produced respectable clothes, bought in between the visits of the day before. There were gray pants, gray shirt, smart black boots, and a stiff, sobersides hat. As I admired my well-behaved self in the bedroom mirror, I noticed her sidling out the door with my old gaudy rags.

"What are you doing?"

"Throwing these out."

"Including the scarf, your handiwork?"

She pulled it out and inspected it.

"No! But it's filthy, I'll get you another."

She rummaged in her workbasket and withdrew a strip of linen em-broidered with pink cherry blossoms. I wondered vaguely if there was a cosmic conspiracy to remind me of Benedict—Zoska had never seen the flowers; the dogs had prevented me plucking one for her. Smiling wryly, I put the scarf on.

"You look very eligible," she said and kissed me.

"Honey apple," said the repeating machine.

"Come on," I said. "Let's buy one for her."

Outside the little street was bustling with womyn, some carrying flow-ers and all smiling.

"What's this?" I said to nobody in particular and a passing soft-core replied:

"Party in the main square. To celebrate!"

We strolled toward square and Hive, infected by the festive mood. A junior Scout dashed by, came to a dead stop, twirled round and gaped at me. Recovering, she ran off in the opposite direction and returned with two giggling girlfriends, and the Watch Chief.

"Lay off," I said, embarrassed.

"Well," said the Chief, "you are nicely turned out."

"For the books," I muttered.

"Doesn't she look fine?" said Zoska.

"My word yes. Almost unrecognizable."

I clenched my fists behind my back, momentarily regretting that all my rowdiness must be past. To my annoyance, the Watch Chief fell into step with us, chatting to Zoska about weddings:

"I cried and cried when my eldest . . ."

"Honey apple," said the tireless Basienka.

"Soon, when we reach the square," I said. The Watch Chief bent close to me:

"We whitewashed your graffiti."

"Censorship."

"It benefits you. Marthe was turning cartwheels every time she passed it."

"What a sight. Well, thank you."

But she was not finished yet. "One of my lasses let in Bea this morning with a message for Marthe. From Grania."

She eyed me, awaiting the reaction.

"How nice," I said blithely. Maybe it was the festival ambience, but I felt as if I was riding the crest of a wave, which would not suddenly dump me in a welter of foam and sand. We were nearly at the square now, its proximity marked by music, the whiff of intoxicant, and thankfully for the little girl clasping my hand, a sticky-sweet smell.

"There you are, persistent child," said Zoska. "Raffy, do you want one?"

"Not in these clothes."

The Watch Chief had already, incongruously, been tempted by the confection.

In a procession of four, and attracting more womyn in our wake, hard cores, soft cores, stray lovers, friends, and the curious, we crossed the square to the Hive, our sunken fortress. The girl on guard was unexpectedly confronted by her superior, sticky.

"Tell Marthe she has visitors," said the Chief.

We waited, the crowd jostling and muttering around us. After a suitable delay, the door at the foot of the ramp opened and Marthe, flanked by the two hard-core Elders, ascended.

"Greetings, Raphael Grania," she said formally.

"Greetings, Marthe Maria," I replied, tit for tat.

I saw her gaze roll down my attire, but being as good an actor as Grania, she made no verbal or physical comment.

"I have received a verse letter from Grania Erato. It commends our alliance."

Behind me, I heard Zoska intake breath in gleeful surprise and then let it out slowly, as if she would have liked to whoop. Several of the rowdier Scouts actually cheered, and this was picked up by the young, the noisy, and the disaffected. It was in the end an impressive sound, threatening even. Marthe suddenly looked, and I think felt, vulnerable.

"I am, of course, honored to communicate with the great poet."

And mediocre parent, I thought.

"Having long admired her verse, I am pleased—my words can't express how much—to be given a holograph sample of it."

And to be the subject of it, I thought. Vanity! I could tell her it was no pleasure.

"For some reason," she added, her tone changing, "it's called 'To a Fellow Widow Twankey.'"

She looked flustered; the crowd, equally puzzled, was silent.

"I never understand all her allusions," I said quickly, well-knowing Grania's dangerous humor. "Marthe Maria! Has my mother's intervention changed your mind?"

She regained a little of her dark composure.

"The Elders have informed me that in a day of such celebration, Hive cannot be off-limits. In view of that, the letter, and other factors . . ."

She looked pointedly at someone behind me, from the opposite faction of hard cores, I presumed.

"I have no choice but to withdraw the prohibition."

Zoska hugged me, releasing Basienka, who for some time had been tugging at her mother's hand. Seizing the opportunity, she ran down the ramp and through the slit of door held open by the Watchgirl. There were stairs behind that door—Zoska looked over my shoulder and screamed. The guard started and let the door clang shut.

There was a moment of agony and then the door opened slowly again. My Honey came out cradling my foster-sister.

Beautiful Honeycomb! I wanted to shout it, but that would have ruined everything. Instead I stood silent as a doll, watching Basienka offer Honey some of her apple. Honey, smiling, took a bite and the crowd went "Ooh!"

"Little scene-stealer," muttered Zoska. She walked halfway down the ramp and collected the baby. Marthe took *her* baby by the hand for a moment: good-bye. Then we faced each other, with no womyn between us.

"Get a move on," yelled somebody.

So, shyly, we met at the top of the ramp and kissed. The ghetto cheered and we parted, half-embarrassed by the noise. Her lips had tasted sweet from the candied fruit.

"Honeymouth," I said.

"Yes, that is her name," said her mother. "Honey Marthe."

And I laughed, and Honey laughed, and it was all right.

GREG EGAN

If George Turner was the most prominent SF writer from Australia on the world stage from the late 1970s to the mid-1990s, Greg Egan at this moment looks like the best bet to follow. Already internationally famous for his stories and novels, he seems to have hit his stride in the early 1990s and to have become one of the two most interesting new hard SF writers of the decade (the other is Stephen Baxter). His first novel was published in 1983, but his writing burst into prominence in 1990 with several fine stories that focused attention on his writing and launched his books. His SF novels to date are *Quarantine* (1992), *Permutation City* (1994), *Distress* (1995), *Diaspora* (1997), and *Teranesia* (1999); his short story collections are *Our Lady of Chernobyl* (1995), *Axiomatic* (1995), and *Luminous* (1999). Significant indicators of his attitudes toward writing are the fact that he remains socially isolated from the SF field—no one has met him in person—and he has written a strongly worded attack on national identities in SF. He does not identify himself as an Australian SF writer, but as a writer of SF in the English language who happens to live in Australia. "Wang's Carpets" first appeared in Greg Bear's flagship hard SF anthology, *New Legends* (1995), and is one of Egan's finest stories to date.

WANG'S CARPETS

Waiting to be cloned one thousand times and scattered across ten million cubic light-years, Paolo Venetti relaxed in his favorite ceremonial bathtub: a tiered hexagonal pool set in a courtyard of black marble flecked with gold. Paolo wore full traditional anatomy, uncomfortable garb at first, but the warm currents flowing across his back and shoulders slowly eased him into a pleasant torpor. He could have reached the same state in an instant, by decree—but the occasion seemed to demand the complete ritual of verisimilitude, the ornate curlicued longhand of imitation physical cause and effect.

As the moment of diaspora approached, a small gray lizard darted across the courtyard, claws scrabbling. It halted by the far edge of the pool, and Paolo marveled at the delicate pulse of its breathing, and watched the lizard watching him, until it moved again, disappearing into the surrounding vineyards. The environment was full of birds and insects, rodents and small reptiles—decorative in appearance, but also satisfying a more abstract aesthetic: softening the harsh radial symmetry of the lone observer; anchoring the simulation by perceiving it from a multitude of viewpoints. Ontological guy lines. No one had asked the lizards if they wanted to be cloned, though. They were coming along for the ride, like it or not.

The sky above the courtyard was warm and blue, cloudless and sunless, isotropic. Paolo waited calmly, prepared for every one of half a dozen possible fates.

An invisible bell chimed softly, three times. Paolo laughed, delighted.

One chime would have meant that he was still on Earth: an anticlimax, certainly—but there would have been advantages to compensate for that. Everyone who really mattered to him lived in the Carter-Zimmerman polis, but not all of them had chosen to take part in the diaspora to the same degree; his Earth-self would have lost no one. Helping to ensure that the thousand ships were safely dispatched would have been satisfying, too. And remaining a member of the wider Earth-based community, plugged into the entire global culture in real time, would have been an attraction in itself.

Two chimes would have meant that this clone of Carter-Zimmerman had reached a planetary system devoid of life. Paolo had run a sophisticated—but nonsapient—self-predictive model before deciding to wake under those conditions. Exploring a handful of alien worlds, however barren, had seemed likely to be an enriching experience for him—with the distinct advantage that the whole endeavor would be untrammeled by the kind of elaborate precautions necessary in the presence of alien life. C-Z's population would have fallen by more than half—and many of his closest friends would have been absent—but he would have forged new friendships, he was sure.

Four chimes would have signaled the discovery of intelligent aliens. Five, a technological civilization. Six, spacefarers.

Three chimes, though, meant that the scout probes had detected unambiguous signs of life—and that was reason enough for jubilation. Up until the moment of the prelaunch cloning—a subjective instant before the chimes had sounded—no reports of alien life had ever reached Earth. There'd been no guarantee that any part of the diaspora would find it.

Paolo willed the polis library to brief him; it promptly rewired the declarative memory of his simulated traditional brain with all the information he was likely to need to satisfy his immediate curiosity. This clone of C-Z had arrived at Vega, the second closest of the thousand target stars, twenty-seven light-years from Earth. Paolo closed his eyes and visualized a star map with a thousand lines radiating out from the sun, then zoomed in on the trajectory that described his own journey. It had taken three centuries to reach Vega—but the vast majority of the polis's twenty thousand inhabitants had programmed their exoselves to suspend them prior to the cloning and to wake them only if and when they arrived at a suitable destination. Ninety-two citizens had chosen the alternative: experiencing every voyage of the diaspora from start to finish, risking disappointment, and even death. Paolo now knew that the ship aimed at Fomalhaut, the target nearest Earth, had been struck by debris and annihilated *en route*. He mourned the ninety-two, briefly. He hadn't been close to any of them, prior to the cloning, and the particular versions who'd willfully perished two centuries ago in interstellar space seemed as remote as the victims of some ancient calamity from the era of flesh.

Paolo examined his new home star through the cameras of one of the scout probes—and the strange filters of the ancestral visual system. In traditional colors, Vega was a fierce blue-white disk, laced with prominences. Three times the mass of the sun, twice the size and twice as hot, sixty times as luminous. Burning hydrogen fast—and already halfway through its allotted five hundred million years on the main sequence.

Vega's sole planet, Orpheus, had been a featureless blip to the best lunar interferometers; now Paolo gazed down on its blue-green crescent, ten thousand kilometers below Carter-Zimmerman itself. Orpheus was terrestrial, a nickel-iron-silicate world; slightly larger than Earth, slightly warmer—a billion kilometers took the edge off Vega's heat—and almost drowning in liquid water. Impatient to see the whole surface firsthand, Paolo slowed his clock rate a thousandfold, allowing C-Z to circumnavigate the planet in twenty subjective seconds, daylight unshrouding a broad new swath with each pass. Two slender ocher-colored continents with mountainous spines bracketed hemispheric oceans, and dazzling expanses of pack ice covered both poles—far more so in the north, where jagged white peninsulas radiated out from the midwinter arctic darkness.

The Orphean atmosphere was mostly nitrogen—six times as much as on Earth; probably split by UV from primordial ammonia—with traces of water vapor and carbon dioxide, but not enough of either for a runaway greenhouse effect. The high atmospheric pressure meant reduced evaporation—Paolo saw not a wisp of cloud—and the large, warm oceans in turn helped feed carbon dioxide back into the crust, locking it up in limestone sediments destined for subduction.

The whole system was young, by Earth standards, but Vega's greater mass, and a denser protostellar cloud, would have meant swifter passage through most of the traumas of birth: nuclear ignition and early luminosity fluctuations; planetary coalescence and the age of bombardments. The library estimated that Orpheus had enjoyed a relatively stable climate, and freedom from major impacts, for at least the past hundred million years.

Long enough for primitive life to appear—

A hand seized Paolo firmly by the ankle and tugged him beneath the water. He offered no resistance, and let the vision of the planet slip away. Only two other people in C-Z had free access to this environment—and his father didn't play games with his now-twelve-hundred-year-old son.

Elena dragged him all the way to the bottom of the pool, before releasing his foot and hovering above him, a triumphant silhouette against the bright surface. She was ancestor-shaped, but obviously cheating; she spoke with perfect clarity; and no air bubbles at all.

"Late sleeper! I've been waiting seven weeks for this!"

Paolo feigned indifference, but he was fast running out of breath. He had his exoself convert him into an amphibious human variant—biologically and historically authentic, if no longer the definitive ancestral phenotype. Water flooded into his modified lungs, and his modified brain welcomed it.

He said, "Why would I want to waste consciousness, sitting around waiting for the scout probes to refine their observations? I woke as soon as the data was unambiguous."

She pummeled his chest; he reached up and pulled her down, instinctively reducing his buoyancy to compensate, and they rolled across the bottom of the pool, kissing.

Elena said, "You know we're the first C-Z to arrive, anywhere? The Fomalhaut ship was destroyed. So there's only one other pair of us. Back on Earth."

"So?" Then he remembered. Elena had chosen not to wake if any other version of her had already encountered life. Whatever fate befell each of the remaining ships, every other version of him would have to live without her.

He nodded soberly, and kissed her again. "What am I meant to say? You're a thousand times more precious to me, now?"

"Yes."

"Ah, but what about the you-and-I on Earth? Five hundred times would be closer to the truth."

"There's no poetry in five hundred."

"Don't be so defeatist. Rewire your language centers."

She ran her hands along the sides of his rib cage, down to his hips. They made love with their almost-traditional bodies—and brains; Paolo was amused to the point of distraction when his limbic system went into overdrive, but he remembered enough from the last occasion to bury his self-consciousness and surrender to the strange hijacker. It wasn't like making love in any civilized fashion—the rate of information exchange between them was minuscule, for a start—but it had the raw insistent quality of most ancestral pleasures.

Then they drifted up to the surface of the pool and lay beneath the radiant sunless sky.

Paolo thought, *I've crossed twenty-seven light-years in an instant. I'm orbiting the first planet ever found to hold alien life. And I've sacrificed nothing— left nothing I truly value behind. This is too good, too good.* He felt a pang of regret for his other selves—it was hard to imagine them faring as well, without Elena, without Orpheus—but there was nothing he could do about that now. Although there'd be time to confer with Earth before any more ships reached their destinations, he'd decided—prior to the cloning—not to allow the unfolding of his manifold future to be swayed by any change of heart. Whether or not his Earth-self agreed, the two of them were powerless to alter the criteria for waking. The self with the right to choose for the thousand had passed away.

No matter, Paolo decided. The others would find—or construct—their own reasons for happiness. And there was still the chance that one of them would wake to the sound of *four chimes*.

Elena said, "If you'd slept much longer, you would have missed the vote."

The vote? The scouts in low orbit had gathered what data they could about Orphean biology. To proceed any farther, it would be necessary to send microprobes into the ocean itself—an escalation of contact that required the approval of two-thirds of the polis. There was no compelling reason to believe that the presence of a few million tiny robots could do any harm; all they'd leave behind in the water was a few kilojoules of waste heat. Nevertheless, a faction had arisen that advocated caution. The citizens of Carter-Zimmerman, they argued, could continue to observe from a distance for another decade, or another millennium, refining their observations and hypotheses before intruding . . . and those who disagreed could always sleep away the time, or find other interests to pursue.

Paolo delved into his library-fresh knowledge of the "carpets"—the single Orphean life-form detected so far. They were free-floating creatures living in the equatorial ocean depths—apparently destroyed by UV if they drifted too close to the surface. They grew to a size of hundreds of meters, then fissioned into dozens of fragments, each of which continued to grow. It was tempting to assume that they were colonies of single-celled organisms, something like giant kelp—but there was no real evidence yet to back that up. It was difficult enough for the scout probes to discern the carpets' gross appearance and behavior through a kilometer of water, even with Vega's copious neutrinos lighting the way; remote observations on a microscopic scale, let alone biochemical analyses, were out of the question. Spectroscopy revealed that the surface water was full of intriguing molecular debris—but guessing the relationship of any of it to the living carpets was like trying to reconstruct human biochemistry by studying human ashes.

Paolo turned to Elena. "What do you think?"

She moaned theatrically; the topic must have been argued to death while he slept. "The microprobes are harmless. They could tell us exactly what the carpets are made of, without removing a single molecule. What's the risk? *Culture shock?*"

Paolo flicked water onto her face, affectionately; the impulse seemed to come with the amphibian body. "You can't be sure that they're not intelligent."

"Do you know what was living on Earth, two hundred million years after it was formed?"

"Maybe cyanobacteria. Maybe nothing. This isn't Earth, though."

"True. But even in the unlikely event that the carpets are intelligent, do you think they'd notice the presence of robots a millionth their size? If they're unified organisms, they don't appear to react to anything in their environment—they have no predators, they don't pursue food, they just drift with the currents—so there's no reason for them to possess elaborate sense organs at all, let alone anything working on a submillimeter scale. And if they're colonies of single-celled creatures, one of which happens to collide with a microprobe and register its presence with surface receptors . . . what conceivable harm could that do?"

"I have no idea. But my ignorance is no guarantee of safety."

Elena splashed him back. "The only way to deal with your *ignorance* is to vote to send down the microprobes. We have to be cautious, I agree— but there's no point *being here* if we don't find out what's happening in the oceans right now. I don't want to wait for this planet to evolve something smart enough to broadcast biochemistry lessons into space. If we're not willing to take a few infinitesimal risks, Vega will turn red giant before we learn anything."

It was a throwaway line—but Paolo tried to imagine witnessing the event. In a quarter of a billion years, would the citizens of Carter-Zimmerman be debating the ethics of intervening to rescue the Orpheans— or would they all have lost interest, and departed for other stars, or modified themselves into beings entirely devoid of nostalgic compassion for organic life?

Grandiose visions for a twelve-hundred-year-old. The Fomalhaut clone had been obliterated by one tiny piece of rock. There was far more junk in the Vegan system than in interstellar space; even ringed by defenses, its data backed up to all the far-flung scout probes, this C-Z was not invulnerable just because it had arrived intact. Elena was right; they had to seize the moment—or they might as well retreat into their own hermetic worlds and forget that they'd ever made the journey.

Paolo recalled the honest puzzlement of a friend from Ashton-Laval, *Why go looking for aliens? Our polis has a thousand ecologies, a trillion species of evolved life. What do you hope to find, out there, that you couldn't have grown at home.*

What had he hoped to find? Just the answers to a few simple questions. Did human consciousness bootstrap all of space-time into existence, in order to explain itself? Or had a neutral, preexisting universe given birth to a billion varieties of conscious life, all capable of harboring the same delusions of grandeur—until they collided with each other? Anthrocosmology was used to justify the inward-looking stance of most polises: if the physical universe was created by human thought, it had no special status that placed it above virtual reality. It might have come first—and every virtual reality might need to run on a physical computing device, subject to physical laws—but it occupied no privileged position in terms of "truth" versus "illusion." If the ACs were right, then it was no more *honest* to value the physical universe over more recent artificial realities than it was honest to remain flesh instead of software, or ape instead of human, or bacterium instead of ape.

Elena said, "We can't lie here forever; the gang's all waiting to see you."

"Where?" Paolo felt his first pang of homesickness; on Earth, his circle of friends had always met in a real-time image of the Mount Pinatubo crater, plucked straight from the observation satellites. A recording wouldn't be the same.

"I'll show you."

Paolo reached over and took her hand. The pool, the sky, the courtyard vanished—and he found himself gazing down on Orpheus again . . . nightside, but far from dark, with his full mental palette now encoding everything from the pale wash of ground-current long-wave radio, to the multicolored shimmer of isotopic gamma rays and back-scattered cosmic-ray *bremsstrahlung*. Half the abstract knowledge the library had fed him about the planet was obvious at a glance, now. The ocean's smoothly tapered thermal glow spelt *three hundred Kelvin* instantly—as well as backlighting the atmosphere's tell-tale infrared silhouette.

He was standing on a long, metallic-looking girder, one edge of a vast geodesic sphere, open to the blazing cathedral of space. He glanced up and saw the star-rich dust-clogged band of the Milky Way, encircling him from zenith to nadir, aware of the glow of every gas cloud, discerning each absorption and emission line, Paolo could almost feel the plane of the galactic disk transect him. Some constellations were distorted, but the view was more familiar than strange—and he recognized most of the old signposts by color. He had his bearings now. Twenty degrees away from Sirius—

south, by parochial Earth reckoning—faint but unmistakable: the sun.

Elena was beside him—superficially unchanged, although they'd both shrugged off the constraints of biology. The conventions of this environment mimicked the physics of real macroscopic objects in free fall and vacuum, but it wasn't set up to model any kind of chemistry, let alone that of flesh and blood. Their new bodies were human-shaped, but devoid of elaborate microstructure—and their minds weren't embedded in the physics at all, but were running directly on the processor web.

Paolo was relieved to be back to normal; ceremonial regression to the ancestral form was a venerable C-Z tradition—and being human was largely self-affirming, while it lasted—but every time he emerged from the experience, he felt as if he'd broken free of billion-year-old shackles. There were polises on Earth where the citizens would have found his present structure almost as archaic: a consciousness dominated by sensory perception, an illusion of possessing solid form, a single time coordinate. The last flesh human had died long before Paolo was constructed, and apart from the communities of Gleisner robots, Carter-Zimmerman was about as conservative as a transhuman society could be. The balance seemed right to Paolo, though—acknowledging the flexibility of software, without abandoning interest in the physical world—and although the stubbornly corporeal Gleisners had been first to the stars, the C-Z diaspora would soon overtake them.

Their friends gathered round, showing off their effortless free-fall acrobatics, greeting Paolo and chiding him for not arranging to wake sooner; he was the last of the gang to emerge from hibernation.

"Do you like our humble new meeting place?" Hermann floated by Paolo's shoulder, a chimeric cluster of limbs and sense organs, speaking through the vacuum in modulated infrared. "We call it Satellite Pinatubo. It's desolate up here, I know—but we were afraid it might violate the spirit of caution if we dared pretend to walk the Orphean surface."

Paolo glanced mentally at a scout probe's close-up of a typical stretch of dry land, and expanse of fissured red rock. "More desolate down there, I think." He was tempted to touch the ground—to let the private vision become tactile—but he resisted. Being elsewhere in the middle of a conversation was bad etiquette.

"Ignore Hermann," Liesl advised. "He wants to flood Orpheus with our alien machinery before we have any idea what the effects might be." Liesl was a green-and-turquoise butterfly, with a stylized human face stippled in gold on each wing.

Paolo was surprised; from the way Elena had spoken, he'd assumed that his friends must have come to a consensus in favor of the microprobes—and only a late sleeper, new to the issues, would bother to argue the point.

"What effects? The carpets—"

"Forget the carpets! Even if the carpets are as simple as they look, we don't know what else is down there." As Liesl's wings fluttered, her mirror-image faces seemed to glance at each other for support. "With neutrino imaging, we barely achieve spatial resolution in meters, time resolution in seconds. We don't know anything about smaller life-forms."

"And we never will, if you have your way." Karpal—an ex-Gleisner, human-shaped as ever—had been Liesl's lover last time Paolo was awake.

"We've only been here for a fraction of an Orphean year! There's still a wealth of data we could gather nonintrusively, with a little patience. There might be rare beachings of ocean life—"

Elena said dryly, "Rare indeed. Orpheus has negligible tides, shallow waves, very few storms. And anything beached would be fried by UV before we glimpsed anything more instructive than we're already seeing in the surface water."

"Not necessarily. The carpets seem to be vulnerable—but other species might be better protected, if they live nearer to the surface. And Orpheus is seismically active; we should at least wait for a tsunami to dump a few cubic kilometers of ocean onto a shoreline, and see what it reveals."

Paolo smiled; he hadn't thought of that. A tsunami might be worth waiting for.

Liesl continued, "What is there to lose by waiting a few hundred Orphean years? At the very least, we could gather baseline data on seasonal climate patterns—and we could watch for anomalies, storms and quakes, hoping for some revelatory glimpses."

A few hundred Orphean years? A *few terrestrial millennia?* Paolo's ambivalence waned. If he'd wanted to inhabit geological time, he would have migrated to the Lokhande polis, where the Order of Contemplative Observers watched Earth's mountains erode in subjective seconds. Orpheus hung in the sky beneath them, a beautiful puzzle waiting to be decoded, demanding to be understood.

He said, "But what if there *are* no 'revelatory glimpse'? How long do we wait? We don't know how rare life is—in time, or in space. If this planet is precious, *so is the epoch it's passing through.* We don't know how rapidly Orphean biology is evolving; species might appear and vanish while we agonize over the risks of gathering better data. The carpets—and whatever else—could die out before we'd learned the first thing about them. What a waste that would be!"

Liesl stood her ground.

"And if we damage the Orphean ecology—or culture—by rushing in? That wouldn't be a waste. It would be a tragedy."

Paolo assimilated all the stored transmissions from his Earth-self—almost three hundred years' worth—before composing a reply. The early communications included detailed mind grafts—and it was good to share the excitement of the diaspora's launch; to watch—very nearly firsthand—the thousand ships, nanomachine-carved from asteroids, depart in a blaze of fusion fire from beyond the orbit of Mars. Then things settled down to the usual prosaic matters: Elena, the gang, shameless gossip, Carter-Zimmerman's ongoing research projects, the buzz of interpolis cultural tensions, the not-quite-cyclic convulsions of the arts (the perceptual aesthetic overthrows the emotional, again . . . although Valladas in Konishi polis claims to have constructed a new synthesis of the two).

After the first fifty years, his Earth-self had begun to hold things back; by the time news reached Earth of the Fomalhaut clones' demise, the messages had become pure audiovisual linear monologues. Paolo understood. It was only right; they'd diverged, and you didn't send mind grafts to strangers.

Most of the transmissions had been broadcast to all of the ships, indiscriminately. Forty-three years ago, though, his Earth-self had sent a special message to the Vega-bound clone.

"The new lunar spectroscope we finished last year has just picked up clear signs of water on Orpheus. There should be large temperate oceans waiting for you, if the models are right. So . . . good luck." Vision showed the instrument's domes growing out of the rock of the lunar farside; plots of the Orphean spectral data; an ensemble of planetary models. "Maybe it seems strange to you—all the trouble we're taking to catch a glimpse of what you're going to see in close-up so soon. It's hard to explain: I don't think it's jealousy, or even impatience. Just a need for independence.

"There's been a revival of the old debate: should we consider redesigning our minds to encompass interstellar distances? One self spanning thousands of stars, not via cloning, but through acceptance of the natural time scale of the light-speed lag. Millennia passing between mental events. Local contingencies dealt with by nonconscious systems." Essays, pro and con, were appended; Paolo ingested summaries. "I don't think the idea will gain much support though—and the new astronomical projects are something of an antidote. We have to make peace with the fact that we've stayed behind . . . so we cling to the Earth—looking outward, but remaining firmly anchored.

"I keep asking myself, though: Where do we go from here? History can't guide us. Evolution can't guide us. The C-Z charter says *understand and respect the universe* . . . but in what form? On what scale? With what kind of senses, what kind of minds? We can become anything at all—and that space of possible futures dwarfs the galaxy. Can we explore it without losing our way? Flesh humans used to spin fantasies about aliens arriving to 'conquer' Earth, to steal their 'precious' physical resources, to wipe them out for fear of 'competition' . . . as if a species capable of making the journey wouldn't have had the power, or the wit, or the imagination, to rid itself of obsolete biological imperatives. *Conquering the galaxy* is what bacteria with spaceships would do—knowing no better, having no choice.

"Our condition is the opposite of that: we have no end of choices. That's why we need to find alien life—not just to break the spell of the anthrocosmologists. We need to find aliens who've faced the same decisions—and discovered how to live, what to become. We need to understand what it means to inhabit the universe."

Paolo watched the crude neutrino images of the carpets moving in staccato jerks around his dodecahedral room. Twenty-four ragged oblongs drifted above him, daughters of a larger ragged oblong that had just fissioned. Models suggested that shear forces from ocean currents could explain the whole process, triggered by nothing more than the parent reaching a critical size. The purely mechanical break-up of a colony—if that was what it was—might have little to do with the life cycle of the constituent organisms. It was frustrating. Paolo was accustomed to a torrent of data on anything that caught his interest; for the diaspora's great discovery to remain nothing more than a sequence of coarse monochrome snapshots was intolerable.

He glanced at a schematic of the scout probes' neutrino detectors, but there was no obvious scope for improvement. Nuclei in the detectors were excited into unstable high-energy states, then kept there by fine-tuned gamma-ray lasers picking off lower-energy eigenstates faster than they could creep into existence and attract a transition. Changes in neutrino flux of one part in ten-to-the-fifteenth could shift the energy levels far enough to disrupt the balancing act. The carpets cast a shadow so faint, though, that even this near-perfect vision could barely resolve it.

Orlando Venetti said, "You're awake."

Paolo turned. His father stood an arm's length away, presenting as an ornately clad human of indeterminate age. Definitely older than Paolo, though; Orlando never ceased to play up his seniority—even if the age difference was only twenty-five percent now, and falling.

Paolo banished the carpets from the room to the space behind one pentagonal window, and took his father's hand. The portions of Orlando's mind that meshed with his own expressed pleasure at Paolo's emergence from hibernation, fondly dwelt on past shared experiences, and entertained hopes of continued harmony between father and son. Paolo's greeting was similar, a carefully contrived "revelation" of his own emotional state. It was more of a ritual than an act of communication—but then, even with Elena, he set up barriers. No one was totally honest with another person— unless the two of them intended to permanently fuse.

Orlando nodded at the carpets. "I hope you appreciate how important they are."

"You know I do." He hadn't included that in his greeting, though. "First alien life." C-Z *humiliates the Gleisner robots, at last*—that was probably how his father saw it. The robots had been first to Alpha Centauri, and first to an extrasolar planet—but first life was Apollo to their Sputniks, for anyone who chose to think in those terms.

Orlando said, "This is the book we need, to catch the citizens of the marginal polises. The ones who haven't quite imploded into solipsism. This will shake them up—don't you think?"

Paolo shrugged. Earth's transhumans were free to implode into anything they liked; it didn't stop Carter-Zimmerman from exploring the physical universe. But thrashing the Gleisners wouldn't be enough for Orlando; he lived for the day when C-Z would become the cultural mainstream. Any polis could multiply its population a billionfold in a microsecond, if it wanted the vacuous honor of outnumbering the rest. Luring other citizens to migrate was harder—and persuading them to rewrite their own local charters was harder still. Orlando had a missionary streak: he wanted every other polis to see the error of its ways and follow C-Z to the stars.

Paolo said, "Ashton-Laval has intelligent aliens. I wouldn't be so sure that news of giant seaweed is going to take Earth by storm."

Orlando was venomous. "Ashton-Laval intervened in its so-called 'evolutionary' simulations so many times that they might as well have built the end products in an act of creation lasting six days. They wanted talking reptiles, and—*mirabile dictu!*—they got talking reptiles. There are self-modified transhumans in *this polis* more alien than the aliens in Ashton-Laval."

Paolo smiled. "All right. Forget Ashton-Laval. But forget the marginal polises, too. We choose to value the physical world. That's what defines us—but it's as arbitrary as any other choice of values. Why can't you accept that? It's not the One True Path that the infidels have to be bludgeoned into following." He knew he was arguing half for the sake of it—he desperately wanted to refute the anthrocosmologists himself—but Orlando always drove him into taking the opposite position. Out of fear of being nothing but his father's clone. Despite the total absence of inherited episodic memories the stochastic input into his ontogenesis, the chaotically divergent nature of the iterative mind-building algorithms.

Orlando made a beckoning gesture, dragging the image of the carpets halfway back into the room. "You'll vote for the microprobes?"

"Of course."

"Everything depends on that now. It's good to start with a tantalizing glimpse—but if we don't follow up with details soon, they'll lose interest back on Earth very rapidly."

"Lose interest? It'll be fifty-four years before we know if anyone paid the slightest attention in the first place."

Orlando eyed him with disappointment, and resignation. "If you don't care about the other polises, think about C-Z. This helps us; it strengthens us. We have to make the most of that."

Paolo was bemused. "The charter is the charter. What needs to be strengthened? You make it sound like there's something at risk."

"What do you think a thousand lifeless worlds would have done to us? Do you think the charter would have remained intact?"

Paolo had never considered the scenario. "Maybe not. But in every C-Z where the charter was rewritten, there would have been citizens who'd have gone off and founded new polises on the old lines. You and I, for a start. We could have called it Venetti-Venetti."

"While half your friends turned their backs on the physical world? While Carter-Zimmerman, after two thousand years, went solipsist? You'd be happy with that?"

Paolo laughed. "No—but it's not going to happen, is it? *We've found life.* All right, I agree with you: this strengthens C-Z. The diaspora might have 'failed' . . . but it didn't. We've been lucky. I'm glad, I'm grateful. Is that what you wanted to hear?"

Orlando said sourly, "You take too much for granted."

"And you care too much what I think! I'm not your . . . heir." Orlando was first-generation, scanned from flesh—and there were times when he seemed unable to accept that the whole concept of generation had lost its archaic significance. "You don't need me to safeguard the future of Carter-Zimmerman on your behalf. Or the future of transhumanity. You can do it in person."

Orlando looked wounded—a conscious choice, but it still encoded something. Paolo felt a pang of regret—but he'd said nothing he could honestly retract.

His father gathered up the sleeves of his gold and crimson robes—the only citizen of C-Z who could make Paolo uncomfortable to be naked—and repeated as he vanished from the room: "You take too much for granted."

The gang watched the launch of the microprobes together—even Liesl, though she came in mourning, as a giant dark bird. Karpai stroked her feathers nervously. Hermann appeared as a creature out of Escher, a segmented worm with six human-shaped feet—on legs with elbows—given to curling up into a disk and rolling along the girders of Satellite Pinatubo. Paolo and Elena kept saying the same thing simultaneously; they'd just made love.

Hermann had moved the satellite to a notional orbit just below one of the scout probes—and changed the environment's scale, so that the probe's lower surface, an intricate landscape of detector modules and attitude-control jets, blotted out half the sky. The atmospheric-entry capsules—ceramic teardrops three centimeters wide—burst from their launch tube and hurtled past like boulders, vanishing from sight before they'd fallen so much as ten meters closer to Orpheus. It was all scrupulously accurate, although it was part real-time imagery, part extrapolation, part *faux*. Paolo thought, *We might as well have run a pure simulation . . . and pretended to follow the capsules down.* Elena gave him a guilty/admonishing look. *Yeah—and then why bother actually launching them at all? Why not just simulate a plausible Orphean ocean full of plausible Orphean life-forms? Why not simulate the whole diaspora?* There was no crime of heresy in C-Z; no one had ever been exiled for breaking the charter. At times it still felt like a tightrope walk; though, trying to classify every act of simulation into those that contributed to an understanding of the physical universe (good), those that were merely convenient, recreational, aesthetic (acceptable) . . . and those that constituted a denial of the primacy of real phenomena (think to think about emigration).

The vote on the microprobes had been close: seventy-two percent in favor, just over the required two-thirds majority, with five percent abstaining. (Citizens created since the arrival at Vega were excluded . . . not that anyone in Carter-Zimmerman would have dreamt of stacking the ballot, perish the thought.) Paolo had been surprised at the narrow margin; he'd yet to hear a single plausible scenario for the microprobes doing harm. He wondered if there was another, unspoken reason that had nothing to do with fears for the Orphean ecology, or hypothetical culture. *A wish to prolong the pleasure of unraveling the planet's mysteries?* Paolo had some sympathy with that impulse—but the launch of the microprobes would do nothing to undermine the greater long-term pleasure of watching, and understanding, as Orphean life evolved.

Liesl said forlornly, "Coastline erosion models show that the northwestern shore of Lambda is inundated by tsunami every ninety Orphean years, on average." She offered the data to them; Paolo glanced at it, and it looked convincing—but the point was academic now. "We could have waited."

Hermann waved his eye-stalks at her. "Beaches covered in fossils, are they?"

"No, but the conditions hardly—"

"No excuses!" He wound his body around a girder, kicking his legs gleefully. Hermann was first-generation, even older than Orlando; he'd been scanned in the twenty-first century, before Carter-Zimmerman existed. Over the centuries, though, he'd wiped most of his episodic memories, and rewritten his personality a dozen times. He'd once told Paolo, "I think of myself as my own great-great-grandson. Death's not so bad, if you do it incrementally. Ditto for immortality."

Elena said, "I keep trying to imagine how it will feel if another C-Z clone stumbles on something infinitely better—like aliens with wormhole drives—while we're back here studying rafts of algae." The body she wore was more stylized than usual—still humanoid, but sexless, hairless, and smooth, the face inexpressive and androgynous.

"If they have wormhole drives, they might visit us. Or share the technology, so we can link up the whole diaspora."

"If they have wormhole drives, where have they been for the last two thousand years?"

Paolo laughed. "Exactly. But I know what you mean, *First alien life . . .* and it's likely to be about as sophisticated as seaweed. It breaks the jinx, though. Seaweed every twenty-seven light-years. Nervous systems every fifty? Intelligence every hundred?" He fell silent, abruptly realizing what she was feeling: electing not to wake again after first life was beginning to seem like the wrong choice, a waste of the opportunities the diaspora had created. Paolo offered her a mind graft expressing empathy and support, but she declined.

She said, "I want sharp borders, right now. I want to deal with this myself."

"I understand." He let the partial model of her that he'd acquired as they'd made love fade from his mind. It was nonsapient, and no longer linked to her—but to retain it any longer when she felt this way would have seemed like a transgression. Paolo took the responsibilities of intimacy seriously. His lover before Elena had asked him to erase all his knowledge of her, and he'd more or less complied—the only thing he still knew about her was the fact that she'd made the request.

Hermann announced, "Planetfall!" Paolo glanced at a replay of a scout probe view that showed the first few entry capsules breaking up above the ocean and releasing their microprobes. Nanomachines transformed the ceramic shields (and then themselves) into carbon dioxide and a few simple minerals—nothing the micrometeorites constantly raining down onto Orpheus didn't contain—before the fragments could strike the water. The microprobes would broadcast nothing; when they'd finished gathering data, they'd float to the surface and modulate their UV reflectivity. It would be up to the scout probes to locate these specks, and read their messages, before they self-destructed as thoroughly as the entry capsules.

Hermann said, "This calls for a celebration. I'm heading for the Heart. Who'll join me?"

Paolo glanced at Elena. She shook her head. "You go."

"Are you sure?"

"Yes! Go on." Her skin had taken on a mirrored sheen; her expressionless face reflected the planet below. "I'm all right. I just want some time to think things through, on my own."

Hermann coiled around the satellite's frame, stretching his pale body as he went, gaining segments, gaining legs. "Come on, come on! Karpal? Liesl? Come and celebrate!"

Elena was gone. Liesl made a derisive sound and flapped off into the distance, mocking the environment's airlessness. Paolo and Karpal watched as Hermann grew longer and faster—and then in a blur of speed and change stretched out to wrap the entire geodesic frame. Paolo demagnetized his feet and moved away, laughing; Karpal did the same.

Then Hermann constricted like a boa and snapped the whole satellite apart.

They floated for a while, two human-shaped machines and a giant worm in a cloud of spinning metal fragments, an absurd collection of imaginary debris, glinting by the light of the true stars.

The Heart was always crowded, but it was larger than Paolo had seen it—even though Hermann had shrunk back to his original size, so as not to make a scene. The huge, muscular chamber arched above them, pulsating wetly in time to the music, as they searched for the perfect location to soak up the atmosphere. Paolo had visited public environments in other polises, back on Earth; many were designed to be nothing more than a perceptual framework for group emotion-sharing. He'd never understood the attraction of becoming intimate with large numbers of strangers. Ancestral social hierarchies might have had their faults—and it was absurd to try to make a virtue of the limitations imposed by minds confined to wetware—but the whole idea of mass telepathy as an end in itself seemed bizarre to Paolo . . . and even old-fashioned, in a way. Humans, clearly, would have benefited from a good strong dose of each other's inner life to keep them from slaughtering each other—but any civilized transhuman could respect and value other citizens without the need to have *been them* firsthand.

They found a good spot and made some furniture, a table and two chairs—Hermann preferred to stand—and the floor expanded to make room. Paolo looked around, shouting greetings at the people he recognized by sight, but not bothering to check for identity broadcasts from the rest. Chances were he'd met everyone here, but he didn't want to spend the next hour exchanging pleasantries with casual acquaintances.

Hermann said, "I've been monitoring our modest stellar observatory's data stream—my antidote to Vegan parochialism. Odd things are going on around Sirius. We're seeing electron-positron annihilation gamma rays, gravity waves . . . and some unexplained hot spots on Sirius B." He turned to Karpal and asked innocently, "What do you think those robots are up to? There's a rumor that they're planning to drag the white dwarf out of orbit and use it as part of a giant spaceship."

"I never listen to rumors." Karpal always presented as a faithful reproduction of his old human-shaped Gleisner body—and his mind, Paolo gathered, always took the form of a physiological model, even though he was five generations removed from flesh. Leaving his people and coming into C-Z must have taken considerable courage; they'd never welcome him back.

Paolo said, "Does it matter what they do? Where they go, how they get there? There's more than enough room for both of us. Even if they shadowed the diaspora—even if they came to Vega—we could study the Orpheans together, couldn't we?"

Hermann's cartoon insect face showed mock alarm, eyes growing wider, and wider apart. "Not if they dragged along a white dwarf! Next thing they'd want to start building a Dyson sphere." He turned back to Karpal. "You don't still suffer the urge, do you, for . . . *astrophysical* engineering?"

"Nothing C-Z's exploitation of a few megatons of Vegan asteroid material hasn't satisfied."

Paolo tried to change the subject. "Has anyone heard from Earth, lately? I'm beginning to feel unplugged." His own most recent message was a decade older than the time lag.

Karpal said, "You're not missing much; all they're talking about is Orpheus . . . ever since the new lunar observations, the signs of water. They seem more excited by the mere possibility of life than we are by the certainty. And they have very high hopes."

Paolo laughed. "They do. My Earth-self seems to be counting on the diaspora to find an advanced civilization with the answers to all of transhumanity's existential problems. I don't think he'll get much cosmic guidance from kelp."

"You know there was a big rise in emigration from C-Z after the launch? Emigration, and suicides." Hermann had stopped wriggling and gyrating, becoming almost still, a sign of rare seriousness. "I suspect that's what triggered the astronomy program in the first place. And it seems to have stanched the flow, at least in the short term. Earth C-Z detected water before any clone in the diaspora—and when they hear that we've found life, they'll feel more like collaborators in the discovery because of it."

Paolo felt a stirring of unease. *Emigration and suicides? Was that why Orlando had been so gloomy?* After three hundred years of waiting, how high had expectations become?

A buzz of excitement crossed the floor, a sudden shift in the tone of the conversation. Hermann whispered reverently, "First microprobe has surfaced. And the data is coming in now."

The nonsapient Heart was intelligent enough to guess its patron's wishes. Although everyone could tap the library for results, privately, the music cut out and a giant public image of the summary data appeared, high in the chamber. Paolo had to crane his neck to view it, a novel experience.

The microprobe had mapped one of the carpets in high resolution. The image showed the expected rough oblong, some hundred meters wide—but the two- or-three-meter-thick slab of the neutrino tomographs was revealed now as a delicate, convoluted surface—fine as a single layer of skin, but folded into an elaborate space-filling curve. Paolo checked the full data: the topology was strictly planar despite the pathological appearance. No holes, no joins—just a surface that meandered wildly enough to look ten thousand times thicker from a distance than it really was.

An inset showed the microstructure, at a point that started at the rim of the carpet and then—slowly—moved toward the center. Paolo stared at the flowing molecular diagram for several seconds before he grasped what it meant.

The carpet was not a colony of single-celled creatures. Nor was it a multicellular organism. It was a *single molecule*, a two-dimensional polymer weighing twenty-five-million kilograms. A giant sheet of folded polysaccharide, a complex mesh of interlinked pentose and hexose sugars hung with alkyl and amide side chains. A bit like a plant cell wall—except that this polymer was far stronger than cellulose, and the surface area was twenty orders of magnitude greater.

Karpal said, "I hope those entry capsules were perfectly sterile. Earth bacteria would gorge themselves on this. One big floating carbohydrate dinner, with no defenses."

Hermann thought it over. "Maybe. If they had enzymes capable of breaking off a piece—which I doubt. No chance we'll find out, though: even if there'd been bacterial spores lingering in the asteroid belt from early human expeditions, every ship in the diaspora was double-checked for contamination *en route*. We haven't brought smallpox to the Americas."

Paolo was still dazed. "But how does it assemble? How does it . . . grow?" Hermann consulted the library and replied, before Paolo could do the same.

"The edge of the carpet catalyses its own growth. The polymer is irregular, aperiodic—there's no single component that simply repeats. But there seem to be about twenty thousand basic structural units—twenty thousand different polysaccharide building blocks." Paolo saw them: long bundles of cross-linked chains running the whole two-hundred-micron thickness of the carpet, each with a roughly square cross-section, bonded at several thousand points to the four neighboring units. "Even at this depth, the ocean's full of UV-generated radicals that filter down from the surface. Any structural unit exposed to the water converts those radicals into more polysaccharide—and builds another structural unit."

Paolo glanced at the library again, for a simulation of the process. Catalytic sites strewn along the sides of each unit trapped the radicals in place, long enough for new bonds to form between them. Some simple sugars were incorporated straight into the polymer as they were created; others were set free to drift in solution for a microsecond or two, until they were needed. At that level, there were only a few basic chemical tricks being used . . . but molecular evolution must have worked its way up from a few small autocatalytic fragments, first formed by chance, to this elaborate system of twenty thousand mutually self-replicating structures. If the "structural units" had floated free in the ocean as independent molecules, the "life-form" they comprised would have been virtually invisible. By bonding together, though, they became twenty thousand colors in a giant mosaic.

It was astonishing. Paolo hoped Elena was tapping the library, wherever she was. A colony of algae would have been more "advanced"—but this incredible primordial creature revealed infinitely more about the possibilities for the genesis of life. Carbohydrate, here, played every biochemical role: information carrier, enzyme, energy source, structural material. Nothing like it could have survived on Earth, once there were organisms capable of feeding on it—and if there were ever intelligent Orpheans, they'd be unlikely to find any trace of this bizarre ancestor.

Karpal wore a secretive smile.

Paolo said, "What?"

"Wang tiles. The carpets are made out of Wang tiles."

Hermann beat him to the library, again.

"*Wang* as in twentieth-century flesh mathematician, Hao Wang. *Tiles* as in any set of shapes that can cover the plane. Wang tiles are squares with various shaped edges, which have to fit complementary shapes on adjacent squares. You can cover the plane with a set of Wang tiles, as long as you choose the right one every step of the way. Or, in the case of the carpets, grow the right one."

Karpal said, "We should call them Wang's Carpets, in honor of Hao Wang. After twenty-three hundred years, his mathematics has come to life."

Paolo liked the idea, but he was doubtful. "We may have trouble getting a two-thirds majority on that. It's a bit obscure . . ."

Hermann laughed. "Who needs a two-thirds majority? If we want to call them Wang's Carpets, we can call them Wang's Carpets. There are ninety-seven languages in current use in C-Z—half of them invented since the polis was founded. I don't think we'll be exiled for coining one private name."

Paolo concurred, slightly embarrassed. The truth was, he'd completely forgotten that Hermann and Karpal weren't actually speaking Modern Roman.

The three of them instructed their exoselves to consider the name adopted: henceforth, they'd hear "carpet" as "Wang's Carpet"—but if they used the term with anyone else, the reverse translation would apply.

Paolo sat and drank in the image of the giant alien: the first life-form encountered by human or transhuman that was not a biological cousin. The death, at last, of the possibility that Earth might be unique.

They hadn't refuted the anthrocosmologists yet, though. Not quite. If, as the ACs claimed, human consciousness was the seed around which all of space-time had crystallized—if the universe was nothing but the simplest orderly explanation for human thought—then there was, strictly speaking, no need for a single alien to exist, anywhere. But the physics that justified human existence couldn't help generating a billion other worlds where life could arise. The ACs would be unmoved by Wang's Carpets; they'd insist that these creatures were physical, if not biological, cousins—merely an unavoidable by-product of anthropogenic, life-enabling physical laws.

The real test wouldn't come until the diaspora—or the Gleisner robots—finally encountered conscious aliens: minds entirely unrelated to humanity, observing and explaining the universe that human thought had supposedly built. Most ACs had come right out and declared such a find impossible; it was the sole falsifiable prediction of their hypothesis. Alien consciousness, as opposed to mere alien life, would always build itself a separate universe—because the chance of two unrelated forms of self-awareness concocting exactly the same physics and the same cosmology was infinitesimal—and any alien biosphere that seemed capable of evolving consciousness would simply never do so.

Paolo glanced at the map of the diaspora, and took heart. *Alien life already*—and the search had barely started; there were nine hundred and ninety-eight target systems yet to be explored. And even if every one of them proved no more conclusive than Orpheus . . . he was prepared to send clones out farther—and prepared to wait. Consciousness had taken far longer to appear on Earth than the quarter-of-a-billion years remaining before Vega left the main sequence—but the whole point of being here, after all, was that Orpheus wasn't Earth.

Orlando's celebration of the microprobe discoveries was a very first-generation affair. The environment was an endless sunlit garden strewn with tables covered in *food.* and the invitation had politely suggested attendance in fully human form. Paolo politely faked it—simulating most of the physiology, but running the body as a puppet, leaving his mind unshackled.

Orlando introduced his new lover, Catherine, who presented as a tall, dark-skinned woman. Paolo didn't recognize her on sight, but checked the identity code she broadcast. It was a small polis; he'd met her once before—as a man called Samuel, one of the physicists who'd worked on the main interstellar fusion drive employed by all the ships of the diaspora. Paolo was amused to think that many of the people here would be seeing his father as a woman. The majority of the citizens of C-Z still practiced the conventions of relative gender that had come into fashion in the twenty-third century—and Orlando had wired them into his own son too deeply for Paolo to wish to abandon them—but whenever the paradoxes were revealed so starkly, he wondered how much longer the conventions would endure. Paolo was same-sex to Orlando, and hence saw his father's lover as a woman, the two close relationships taking precedence over his casual knowledge of Catherine as Samuel. Orlando perceived himself as being male and heterosexual, as his flesh original had been . . . while Samuel saw himself the same way . . . and each perceived the other to be a heterosexual woman. If certain third parties ended up with mixed signals, so be it. It was a typical C-Z compromise: nobody could bear to overturn the old order and do away with gender entirely (as most other polises had done) . . . but nobody could resist the flexibility that being software, not flesh, provided.

Paolo drifted from table to table to table, sampling the food to keep up appearances, wishing Elena had come. There was little conversation about the biology of Wang's Carpets; most of the people here were simply celebrating their win against the opponents of the microprobes—and the humiliation that faction would suffer, now that it was clearer than ever that the "invasive" observations could have done no harm. Liesl's fears had proved unfounded; there was no other life in the ocean, just Wang's Carpets of various sizes. Paolo, feeling perversely even-handed after the fact, kept wanting to remind these smug movers and shakers, *There might have been anything down there. Strange creatures, delicate and vulnerable in ways we could never have anticipated. We were lucky, that's all.*

He ended up alone with Orlando almost by chance; they were both fleeing different groups of appalling guests when their paths crossed on the lawn.

Paolo asked, "How do you think they'll take this, back home?"

"It's first life, isn't it? Primitive or not. It should at least maintain interest in the diaspora, until the next alien biosphere is discovered." Orlando seemed subdued; perhaps he was finally coming to terms with the gulf between their modest discovery, and Earth's longing for world-shaking results. "And at least the chemistry is novel. If it had turned out to be based on DNA and protein, I think half of Earth C-Z would have died of boredom on the spot. Let's face it, the possibilities of DNA have been simulated to death."

Paolo smiled at the heresy. "You think if nature hadn't managed a little originality, it would have dented people's faith in the charter? If the solipsist polises had begun to look more inventive than the universe itself . . ."

"Exactly."

They walked on in silence, then Orlando halted and turned to face him.

He said, "There's something I've been wanting to tell you. My Earth-self is dead."

"*What?*"

"Please, don't make a fuss."

"But . . . why? Why would he—?" *Dead* meant suicide; there was no other cause—unless the sun had turned red giant and swallowed everything out to the orbit of Mars.

"I don't know why. Whether it was a vote of confidence in the diaspora"—Orlando had chosen to wake only in the presence of alien life— "or whether he despaired of us sending back good news, and couldn't face the waiting, and the risk of disappointment. He didn't give a reason. He just had his exoself send a message, stating what he'd done."

Paolo was shaken. If a clone of *Orlando* had succumbed to pessimism, he couldn't begin to imagine the state of mind of the rest of Earth C-Z.

"When did this happen?"

"About fifty years after the launch."

"My Earth-self said nothing."

"It was up to me to tell you, not him."

"I wouldn't have seen it that way."

"Apparently, you would have."

Paolo fell silent, confused. How was he supposed to mourn a distant version of Orlando, in the presence of the one he thought of as real? Death of one clone was a strange half-death, a hard thing to come to terms with. His Earth-self had lost a father; his father had lost an Earth-self. What exactly did that mean to *him*?

What Orlando cared most about was Earth C-Z. Paolo said carefully, "Hermann told me there'd been a rise in emigration and suicide—until the spectroscope picked up the Orphean water. Morale has improved a lot since then—and when they hear that it's more than just water . . ."

Orlando cut him off sharply. "You don't have to talk things up for me. I'm in no danger of repeating the act."

They stood on the lawn, facing each other. Paolo composed a dozen different combinations of mood to communicate, but none of them felt right. He could have granted his father perfect knowledge of everything he was feeling—but what exactly would that knowledge have conveyed? In the end, there was fusion, or separateness. There was nothing in between.

Orlando said, "Kill myself—and leave the fate of transhumanity in your hands? You must be out of your fucking mind."

They walked on together, laughing.

Karpal seemed barely able to gather his thoughts enough to speak. Paolo would have offered him a mind graft promoting tranquillity and concentration—distilled from his own most focused moments—but he was sure that Karpal would never have accepted it. He said, "Why don't you just start wherever you want to? I'll stop you if you're not making sense."

Karpal looked around the white dodecahedron with an expression of disbelief. "You live here?"

"Some of the time."

"But this is your base environment? No trees? No sky? No *furniture?*"

Paolo refrained from repeating any of Hermann's naive-robot jokes. "I add them when I want them. You know, like . . . music. Look, don't let my taste in decor distract you."

Karpal made a chair and sat down heavily.

He said, "Hao Wang proved a powerful theorem, twenty-three hundred years ago. Think of a row of Wang tiles as being like the data tape of a Turing machine." Paolo had the library grant him knowledge of the term; it was the original conceptual form of a generalized computing device, an imaginary machine that moved back and forth along a limitless one-dimensional data tape, reading and writing symbols according to a given set of rules.

"With the right set of tiles, to force the right pattern, the next row of the tiling will look like the data tape after the Turing machine has performed one step of its computation. And the row after that will be the data tape after two steps, and so on. For any given Turing machine, there's a set of Wang tiles that can imitate it."

Paolo nodded amiably. He hadn't heard of this particular quaint result, but it was hardly surprising. "The carpets must be carrying out billions of acts of computation every second . . . but then, so are the water molecules around them. There are no physical processes that don't perform arithmetic of some kind."

"True. But with the carpets, it's not quite the same as random molecular motion."

"Maybe not."

Karpal smiled, but said nothing.

"What? You've found a pattern? Don't tell me: our set of twenty thousand polysaccharide Wang tiles just happens to form the Turing machine for calculating pi."

"No. What they form is a universal Turing machine. They can calculate anything at all—depending on the data they start with. Every daughter fragment is like a program being fed to a chemical computer. Growth executes the program."

"Ah." Paolo's curiosity was roused—but he was having some trouble picturing where the hypothetical Turing machine put its read/write head. "Are you telling me only one tile changes between any two rows, where the 'machine' leaves its mark on the 'data tape' . . ." The mosaics he'd seen were a riot of complexity, with no two rows remotely the same.

Karpal said, "No, no. Wang's original example worked exactly like a standard Turing machine, to simplify the argument . . . but the carpets are more like an arbitrary number of different computers with overlapping data, all working in parallel. This is biology, not a designed machine—it's as messy and wild as, say . . . a mammalian genome. In fact, there are mathematical similarities with gene regulation: I've identified Kauffman networks at every level, from the tiling rules up; the whole system's poised on the hyperadaptive edge between frozen and chaotic behavior."

Paolo absorbed that, with the library's help. Like Earth life, the carpets seemed to have evolved a combination of robustness and flexibility that would have maximized their power to take advantage of natural selection. Thousands of different autocatalytic chemical networks must have arisen soon after the formation of Orpheus—but as the ocean chemistry and the climate changed in the Vegan system's early traumatic millennia, the ability to respond to selection pressure had itself been selected for, and the carpets were the result. Their complexity seemed redundant, now, after a hundred million years of relative stability—and no predators or competition in sight—but the legacy remained.

"So if the carpets have ended up as universal computers . . . with no real need anymore to respond to their surrounding . . . what are they *doing* with all that computing power?"

Karpal said solemnly, "I'll show you."

Paolo followed him into an environment where they drifted above a schematic of a carpet, an abstract landscape stretching far into the distance, elaborately wrinkled like the real thing, but otherwise heavily stylized, with each of the polysaccharide building blocks portrayed as a square tile with four different-colored edges. The adjoining edges of neighboring tiles bore complementary colors—to represent the complementary, interlocking shapes of the borders of the building blocks.

"One group of microprobes finally managed to sequence an entire daughter fragment," Karpal explained, "although the exact edges it started life with are largely guesswork, since the thing was growing while they were trying to map it." He gestured impatiently, and all the wrinkles and folds were smoothed away, an irrelevant distraction. They moved to one border of the ragged-edged carpet, and Karpal started the simulation running.

Paolo watched the mosaic extending itself, following the tiling rules perfectly—an orderly mathematical process here: no chance collisions of radicals with catalytic sites, no mismatched borders between two new-grown neighboring "tiles" triggering the disintegration of both. Just the distillation of the higher-level consequences of all that random motion.

Karpal led Paolo up to a height where he could see subtle patterns being woven, overlapping multiplexed periodicities drifting across the growing edge, meeting and sometimes interacting, sometimes passing right through each other. Mobile pseudoattractors, quasistable waveforms in a one-dimensional universe. The carpet's second dimension was more like time than space, a permanent record of the history of the edge.

Karpal seemed to read his mind. "One-dimensional. Worse than flatland. No connectivity, no complexity. What can possibly happen in a system like that? Nothing of interest, right?"

He clapped his hands and the environment exploded around Paolo. Trails of color streaked across his sensorium, entwining, then disintegrating into luminous smoke.

"Wrong. Everything goes on in a multidimensional frequency space. I've Fourier-transformed the edge into over a thousand components, and there's independent information in all of them. We're only in a narrow cross-section here, a sixteen-dimensional slice—but it's oriented to show the principal components, the maximum detail."

Paolo spun in a blur of meaningless color, utterly lost, his surroundings beyond comprehension. "You're a *Gleisner robot*, Karpal! *Only* sixteen dimensions! How can you have done this?"

Karpal sounded hurt, wherever he was. "Why do you think I came to C-Z? I thought you people were flexible!"

"What you're doing is . . ." *What?* Heresy? There was no such thing. Officially. "Have you shown this to anyone else?"

"Of course not. Who did you have in mind? Liesl? *Hermann?*"

"Good. I know how to keep my mouth shut." Paolo invoked his exoself and moved back into the dodecahedron. He addressed the empty room. "How can I put this? The physical universe has three spatial dimensions, plus time. Citizens of Carter-Zimmerman inhabit the physical universe. Higher dimensional mind games are for the solipsists." Even as he said it, he realized how pompous he sounded. It was an arbitrary doctrine, not some great moral principle.

But it was the doctrine he'd lived with for twelve hundred years.

Karpal replied, more bemused than offended, "It's the only way to see what's going on. The only sensible way to apprehend it. Don't you want to know what the carpets are *actually like?*"

Paolo felt himself being tempted. Inhabit a *sixteen-dimensional slice of a thousand-dimensional frequency space?* But it was in the service of understanding a real physical system—not a novel experience for its own sake.

And nobody had to find out.

He ran a quick—nonsapient—self-predictive model. There was a ninety-three-percent chance that he'd give in, after fifteen subjective minutes of agonizing over the decision. It hardly seemed fair to keep Karpal waiting that long.

He said, "You'll have to loan me your mind-shaping algorithm. My exoself wouldn't know where to begin."

When it was done, he steeled himself, and moved back into Karpal's environment. For a moment, there was nothing but the same meaningless blur as before.

Then everything suddenly crystallized.

Creatures swam around them, elaborately branched tubes like mobile coral, vividly colored in all the hues of Paolo's mental palette—Karpal's attempt to cram in some of the information that a mere sixteen dimensions couldn't show? Paolo glanced down at his own body—nothing was missing, but he could see *around* it in all the thirteen dimensions in which it was nothing but a pinprick; he quickly looked away. The "coral" seemed far more natural to his altered sensory map, occupying sixteen-space in all directions, and shaded with hints that it occupied much more. And Paolo had no doubt that it was "alive"—it looked more organic than the carpets themselves, by far.

Karpal said, "Every point in this space encodes some kind of quasi-periodic pattern in the tiles. Each dimension represents a different characteristic size—like a wavelength, although the analogy's not precise. The position in each dimension represents other attributes of the pattern, relating to the particular tiles it employs. So the localized systems you see around you are clusters of a few billion patterns, all with broadly similar attributes at similar wavelengths."

They moved away from the swimming coral, into a swarm of something like jellyfish: floppy hyperspheres waving wispy tendrils (each one of them more substantial than Paolo). Tiny jewel-like creatures darted among them. Paolo was just beginning to notice that nothing moved here like a solid object drifting through normal space; motion seemed to entail a shimmering deformation at the leading hypersurface, a visible process of disassembly and reconstruction.

Karpal led him on through the secret ocean. There were helical worms, coiled together in groups of indeterminate number—each single creature breaking up into a dozen or more wriggling slivers, and then recombining . . . although not always from the same parts. There were dazzling multi-colored stemless flowers, intricate hypercones of "gossamer-thin" fifteen-dimensional petals—each one a hypnotic fractal labyrinth of crevices and capillaries. There were clawed monstrosities, writhing knots of sharp insec-tile parts like an orgy of decapitated scorpions.

Paolo said, uncertainly, "You could give people a glimpse of this in just three-dimensions. Enough to make it clear that there's . . . *life* in here. This is going to shake them up badly, though." Life—embedded in the accidental computations of Wang's Carpets, with no possibility of ever relating to the world outside. This was an affront to Carter-Zimmerman's whole philosophy: if nature had evolved "organisms" as divorced from re-ality as the inhabitants of the most inward-looking polis, where was the privileged status of the physical universe, the clear distinction between truth and illusion?

And after three hundred years of waiting for good news from the di-sapora, how would they respond to this back on Earth?

Karpal said, "There's one more thing I have to show you."

He'd named the creatures squids, for obvious reasons. *Distant cousins of the jellyfish, perhaps?* They were prodding each other with their tentacles in a way that looked thoroughly carnal—but Karpal explained, "There's no analog of light here. We're viewing all this according to ad hoc rules that have nothing to do with the native physics. All the creatures here gather information about each other by contact alone—which is actually quite a rich means of exchanging data, with so many dimensions. What you're seeing is communication by touch."

"Communication about what?"

"Just gossip, I expect. Social relationships."

Paolo stared at the writhing mass of tentacles.

"You think they're *conscious?*"

Karpal, pointlike, grinned broadly. "They have a central control struc-ture with more connectivity than the human brain—and which correlates data gathered from the skin. I've mapped that organ, and I've started to analyze its function."

He led Paolo into another environment, a representation of the data structures in the "brain" of one of the squids. It was—mercifully—three-dimensional, and highly stylized, built of translucent colored blocks marked with icons, representing mental symbols, linked by broad lines indicating the major connections between them. Paolo had seen similar diagrams of transhuman minds; this was far less elaborate, but eerily familiar nonetheless.

Karpal said, "Here's the sensory map of its surroundings. Full of other squids' bodies, and vague data on the last known positions of a few smaller creatures. But you'll see that the symbols activated by the physical presence of the other squids are linked to these"—he traced the connections with one finger—"representations. Which are crude miniatures of *this whole structure* here."

"This whole structure" was an assembly labeled with icons for memory retrieval, simple tropisms, short-term goals. The general business of being and doing.

"The squid has maps, not just of other squids' bodies, but their minds as well. Right or wrong, it certainly tries to know what the others are thinking about. And"—he pointed out another set of links, leading to another, less crude, miniature squid mind—"it thinks about its own thoughts as well. I'd call that *consciousness,* wouldn't you?"

Paolo said weakly, "You've kept all this to yourself? You came this far, without saying a word—"

Karpal was chastened. "I know it was selfish—but once I'd decoded the interactions of the tile patterns, I couldn't tear myself away long enough to start explaining it to anyone else. And I came to you first because I wanted your advice on the best way to break the news."

Paolo laughed bitterly. "The best way to break the news that *first alien consciousness* is hidden deep inside a biological computer? That everything the diaspora was trying to prove has been turned on its head? The best way to explain to the citizens of Carter-Zimmerman that after a three-hundred-year journey, they might as well have stayed on Earth running simulations with as little resemblance to the physical universe as possible?"

Karpal took the outburst in good humor. "I was thinking more along the lines of the *best way to point out* that if we hadn't traveled to Orpheus and studied Wang's Carpets, we'd never have had the chance to tell the solipsists of Ashton-Laval that all their elaborate invented life-forms and exotic imaginary universes pale into insignificance compared to what's really out here—and which only the Carter-Zimmerman diaspora could have found."

Paolo and Elena stood together on the edge of Satellite Pinatubo, watching one of the scout probes aim its maser at a distant point in space. Paolo thought he saw a faint scatter of microwaves from the beam as it collided with iron-rich meteor dust. *Elena's mind being diffracted all over the cosmos?* Best not think about that.

He said, "When you meet the other versions of me who haven't experienced Orpheus, I hope you'll offer them mind grafts so they won't be jealous."

She frowned. "Ah. Will I or won't I? I can't be bothered modeling it. I expect I will. You should have asked me before I cloned myself. No need for jealousy, though. There'll be worlds far stranger than Orpheus."

"I doubt it. You really think so?"

"I wouldn't be doing this if I didn't believe that." Elena had no power to change the fate of the frozen clones of her previous self—but everyone had the right to emigrate.

Paolo took her hand. The beam had been aimed almost at Regulus, UV-hot and bright, but as he looked away, the cool yellow light of the sun caught his eye.

Vega C-Z was taking the news of the squids surprisingly well, so far. Karpal's way of putting it had cushioned the blow: it was only by traveling all this distance across the real, physical universe that they could have made such a discovery—and it was amazing how pragmatic even the most doctrinaire citizens had turned out to be. Before the launch, "alien solipsists" would have been the most unpalatable idea imaginable, the most abhorrent thing the diaspora could have stumbled upon—but now that they were here, and stuck with the fact of it, people were finding ways to view it in a better light. Orlando had even proclaimed, "*This* will be the perfect hook for the marginal polises. 'Travel through real space to witness a truly alien virtual reality.' We can sell it as a synthesis of the two world views."

Paolo still feared for Earth, though—where his Earth-self and others were waiting in hope of alien guidance. Would they take the message of Wang's Carpets to heart and retreat into their own hermetic worlds, oblivious to physical reality?

And he wondered if the anthrocosmologists had finally been refuted . . . or not. Karpal had discovered alien consciousness—but it was sealed inside a cosmos of its own, its perceptions of itself and its surroundings neither reinforcing nor conflicting with human and transhuman explanations of reality. It would be millennia before C-Z could untangle the ethical problems of daring to try to make contact . . . assuming that both Wang's Carpets, and the inherited data patterns of the squids, survived that long.

Paolo looked around at the wild splendor of the scar-choked galaxy, felt the disk reach in and cut right through him. *Could all this strange haphazard beauty be nothing but an excuse for those who beheld it to exist? Nothing but the sum of all the answers to all the questions humans and transhumans had ever asked the universe—answers created in the asking?*

He couldn't believe that—but the question remained unanswered. So far.

SEAN McMULLEN

Sean McMullen is one of the new breed of Australian hard SF
authors to emerge in the late 1980s. He comes from a family of
engineers and works as a computer professional in Melbourne. He
also studied English literature and history at university, and sang
for two years with the Victoria State Opera. He is in addition one
of the leading bibliographers of Australian SF, and has won the
William Atheling, Jr. Award three times in the 1990s. His bibli-
ographies are an essential underpinning of the *Melbourne University Press Encyclopaedia of Australian Science Fiction & Fantasy*
(1998). His first story was "The Pharaoh's Airship" (1986). Nine
early stories (including "The Dominant Style") are collected in
Call to the Edge (1992), and taken together they give evidence of
an impressive and wide-ranging SF storytelling talent. His first two
novels, *Voices in the Light* (1994) and *Mirrorsun Rising* (1995), were
part of the projected Greatwinter series. The third has not yet
appeared because the Australian publisher ceased publishing novels, but a novella, "The Miocene Arrow," which contains a kernel
of the third book, was published in 1994. McMullen's latest novel,
The Centurion's Empire (1998), was published by Tor in the U.S.
an ambitious novel that should establish McMullen as a major SF
writer on the world SF stage.

THE DOMINANT STYLE

A SERIES OF WILD skids and near misses nearly ended my mission at the very beginning. It taught me, though, that a real car handles very differently to the simulator that I had been trained on. Thus, even though Lindenville was not far from where I had bought the 1934 MG Magnette, I kept to the back roads for most of the morning. Slowly, slowly, I built up a semblance of the easy familiarity that the owner of such a car should have. Fourteen years is a long time to be away, and both the roads and cars had changed a lot. The big engine growled its breath of warm, sweet alcohol, and balmy air tumbled past me as I explored the forest-lined mountain roads.

I drove wearing goggles, shivering irrationally behind glass disks that seemed to grant some relief from the immense, blue, open dome of the sky. By late morning I could no longer blame my driving for postponing the inevitable meeting. I would have to choose a house at random, crash through into lives that would have nothing in common with mine, and so raise suspicion in a deadly guardian for which I would be bait.

A wing swooped through the sky ahead of me, circling one of the houses. A wing, nothing more. Pillar-box red with a rear propeller driving it through the air. A small sports plane: that meant an aircraft enthusiast, a welcome for my background.

I found the driveway, slowed and turned off the road. Gravel crunched under the narrow, cross-ply tires as I came up to a multilevel white house built into a hillside. The driveway skirted the base of the hill, around an area of lawn the size of a football field, then terminated where a small hangar and double garage sat together near stone steps that led to the house.

At the base of the steps stood a woman, watching the sky. She paid me little attention, other than to wave. As I switched the engine off, I heard the small aircraft approaching in the distance. The flying wing cruised into view, made a wide, leisurely circuit of the field, then landed and taxied to the hangar. A mental command to myself invoked my RAM-cache, which identified the design. The name would guarantee me a welcome.

Guarantee? Apprehension crawled over me as I got out of the car. How would these people react to me? What would I feel when I removed the goggles? Could I bear to? Suddenly annoyed with my fears, I swept the goggles from my head. The world rushed away into vast, limitless space, and I fought, hopelessly, with the notion that my head was exploding. Total exposure to blue, open sky, sweeping wooded hillsides, the piping of wild birds: all utterly foreign, yet home.

I took a firm hold of myself, climbed over the low stone wall that circled the lawn, then walked across to the aircraft.

"Works like a charm now, Lyndal," said the well-groomed yet weatherworn man who emerged from the cockpit. "The trouble was with the fuel mixture, just as I thought."

"Very good, Will," she said, with a toss of fluffy curls. "And just in time for our guest."

"I hope you don't mind me just driving in like this," I said, as I walked over to them, "but I had to have a closer look at your flying wing. It's modeled on Soldenhoff's A2 of 1929, isn't it?"

"Well, yes, but the wings are Professor Ackerman's 1936 design, and the engine is a Salmson 9: Swiss body, American wings, and French engine, and built by Chomleigh of Bristol."

His smile was broad. I had his full attention and he was anxious to be friendly—because I had driven up in the right sort of car and displayed a common bond of interest.

"Do you do any flying in your spare time?" he asked.

"Not in my spare time." I laughed, already relaxing. "I'm a flying boat captain with Pan American."

"Pan American? So you would fly those new Boeing Clippers, forty-two tons and six-dozen passengers?"

"That's right. I'm on the Los Angeles to Sydney route, and I mainly fly the leg from Fiji to Sydney. My name is Colin Strathlen, by the way."

I extended my right hand to him, my skin crawling with fear again. For me, first contact. Did I have the gesture right? Was there some subtle movement that I had missed—obvious to them yet lost to me? He reached out and shook my hand with no hesitation at all, almost before I knew he was doing it.

"Aitkins, Will Aitkins," he declared. "And this is my wife, Lyndal."

She smiled at me. Cumulus clouds of loose blonde curls framed green eyes that were very nearly blue. "So where do you live, Colin?" she asked.

"My house is in Los Angeles, but I spend most of my spare time in Fiji."

"Wonderful," she breathed—and there was no feigning the sincerity.

"Not so wonderful. Los Angeles is all rush, while Fiji is too slow and . . . well, paradise can be a boring place to live in. I was told that the country is good just west of Sydney, so here I am, checking the real estate."

"Well, why not check Lindenville from the air?" exclaimed Will, flattered that a professional pilot was admiring his hobby aircraft. For an excuse to put the goggles back on and escape the openness, I almost agreed. Lyndal intervened, taking me by the arm and talking Will into inviting me for lunch. We ascended the blue stone garden steps through meticulously sculpted terraces.

My uneasiness returned as we entered the house, which was a stack of offset concrete and glass disks. The whole design emphasised openness and light, the very things that I found most disturbing. The dining room looked out over the wooded hillside that was their garden. Tiled floor, a curving, marble-top bar, a matching dining table, with bentwood and red leather chairs: it was an art deco interior that might have been designed by Jacques Meistermann in the early thirties. I could see that even without consulting my RAMcache. I had once been an architect, after all.

"So you don't like Fiji?" asked William, as we took our coffee and macaroons out onto the patio.

"It's a place to visit, not to live." I sat with my back to the view, comforted by the solidity of the walls. The choice of an international pilot as a persona covered a multitude of sins. One could know a lot of places superficially, yet not have to know any one place really well. Small errors would be understandable, would be overlooked.

I washed my hands in cool, clean running water in a basin cut from green marble. The black tiles of the floor and walls reflected my image almost as well as the oval, chrome-edged mirror. Again the style was thirties art deco—after Robert Pommier perhaps. Everything had the look of being no more than two or three years old, pleasingly new, yet, comfortably worn in. Looking around as I fumbled with a towel to dry my hands, I shivered as I wondered who or what was in charge of maintenance. I was a feral intruder, and the two who had gone before me had been killed.

During lunch Will had talked about my MG Magnette with such sincere admiration that I had to insist on him taking it out for a drive. Lyndal and I watched from the patio as he roared off down the driveway amid showers of gravel. Within moments the gardeners were there, raking the surface back into order. Turning away, I now saw that a maid was removing the plates and cups. Her uniform blended with the wall behind; her face, her figure, her very being was . . . elusive. She existed to make food appear while calling no attention to herself. I realized that all the servants I had seen thus far had that faded, nondescript appearance and manner.

Lyndal taught French at a nearby boarding school, but only for two days in the week. She loved Hawaii; she loved anything to do with tropical islands.

"I've traveled by cruise ship," she told me. "The voyages are nothing to me though. It's *being* there. Swimming in warm lagoons, cold roast snapper, and salad in open restaurants, blazing red sunsets and palm trees . . . what are flying boats like compared to a ship?"

"I can't make a comparison; I know only flying boats."

"But are they stylish and comfortable, or like Will's red flying wing, all wind and noise?"

"Well, I fly Boeing 314 Clippers. They are noisier than a ship and a lot smaller; but they have Pullman interiors, a dozen crew, and even a chef. The trip from Melbourne to Hawaii is two days."

"Two days! That settles it then," she said, reaching out to squeeze my hand. "Next time I'll fly—and with you as captain."

There was little sense of schedule in this place, although they had a strongly developed sense of diurnal time. Will returned, and as he stood there running his hands along the Magnette's polished curves, we went down to join him. He offered to take me on a tour of the area in his own car, so we spent the afternoon driving through the forested hills along wide, black, curving roads. The houses of their neighbors hinted at their presence with flashes of white, red, and gold amid the green. Diligent but disturbingly neutral servants and tradesfolk from the Lindenville township manicured the lawns and tended the gardens, while the owners worked at being rich, leisured and, gracious.

Late in the afternoon we stopped at a restaurant with a view of the sprawling patchwork of parks, lakes, gardens, and occasional houses that was Sydney. As we dined, we watched the sparse lights of the city become alive in the distance. The interior was all thick black carpets, chrome railings, darkened glass vistas, and feature walls of carved greenstone. Beer and cocktails were brought by waiters whose existence seemed no more than a puff of smoke, as if they had been bred merely to make the right drinks appear in the right place without intrusion. After a tender fillet steak washed down with Hunter Valley claret, I was guided back to the car. I dozed with my head on Lyndal's shoulder as we sat three abreast in the front seat, and Will flung his Chevron tourer down the wide, twisting roads.

Before sleep finally claimed me for the night, I lay on the firm, wide bed in a guest room, uneasily luxuriating in cream-and-ginger-brushed flannel pajamas, and looking out over the dark forms of the hills. I shivered a little, with pleasure and fear. All these houses were organic wholes, all consistent works of art, masterpieces maintained to perfection . . . under whose direction?

The dim glow of the turquoise night lamp outlined the scars displayed by my open pajama. I had been torn to pieces; I had been tortured beyond imagining in many accidents, then stapled and force-grown back together again each time. My home for fourteen years had been a small, squalid room, paint peeling from the metal walls and the air as fetid as a cesspool. Soon I would have to return to it, yet for now I was living as humans ought to. I slid between the sheets with a shivery sigh of pleasure, then clicked off the nightlamp and reveled at being pulled down into the mattress by my own weight. Here was silence, darkness, clean air, and good food. Here was paradise.

Even after a week I had not outstayed the welcome of my hosts. Will spent a few days managing his fuel alcohol plant, and once he even made the trip in my Magnette. My *Magnette.* It was all that I had to make me real. Lyndal played bridge with me, and tried to teach me tennis, all the while talking about visits to the Mediterranean and the South Sea islands on luxurious cruise ships, and about what they had seen, who they had met. More than five years back, and there was no fine detail in her memories.

I watched, observed . . . particularly the dedicated, doggedly particular tradesfolk. They had no smalltalk; they had no interests outside their own specialties. Some were gardeners, others cooked and cleaned, and still others did repairs and kept the house frozen in stylistic perfection. They observed me, too, most likely in that same particular detail, and they seemed to find me wanting. Scowls flickered across the bland neutrality of their faces as I failed unknowable tests.

My hosts' only child was boarding at the school where Lyndal taught.

Out of their nine servants, two had children, both living in, and both apprenticed to their parents' trades. One afternoon as I sat watching the children play, I noticed how all their games related to work and trades, as if their apprenticeship was inbuilt . . . which it was!

Suddenly I saw it all clearly, an absurdly simple explanation. There was no overseer, the only regulator here was style—and style was inbuilt. I hurried inside to the guest room, took a small, black case from the dresser, and babbled my theory into it. It replied by requesting more data. Data on style, data on art, data on design, and sample genetic material.

Each day I examined a different part the house. Sometimes a particular room, sometimes the garden paths and outbuildings. I took samples: tiny slivers of wood, hair, and even blood, when a gardener cut his hand on a spade. I took the samples to the small, black case locked in my dresser; and there the secrets of the house reluctantly displayed themselves. I reserved time for work and worked in secret, but otherwise I played the part of an honored guest. Day after day I spoke with my black case, and my unease grew as the length of my stay approached fourteen days. Soon I would be either gone or dead.

On the evening of the eleventh day, Lyndal had gone to bed early with a pulp detective novel, leaving Will and me in his study. We were drinking port from fine crystal.

"I must leave tonight," I announced as he poked at the fire. "You can keep my MG."

He straightened, his eyebrows raised. "You . . . are welcome to stay as long as you like," he said hesitantly. "Is something the matter?"

"Look at me, Will. Thin, well-healed scars on my face and hands. What does all that suggest?"

"Ah, nothing." There was a pause while the polite stupidity of his own reply did its work. "Oh, a plane crash, I suppose."

"Not a soldier? Or a newly released criminal?"

The last two concepts ran against internal barriers that I now knew to exist within him. He did not, perhaps could not, reply.

"What year is it?" I asked. He brightened at once, released from my unthinkable questions.

"Dates, how I hate 'em. Oh, I'd say 1937 or 1938."

"Are you sure?"

"Of the year? Well, as sure as the next man would be."

"The next man would not be sure at all. Neither would the next woman. The year is of no consequence to you, yet it has been in the region of 1938 for over seven hundred centuries."

I allowed the shocked silence to age and mellow before I continued. I have always had a flair for the theatrical. He sat forward with his mouth open. The polished Domzeise mantle clock ticked sedately. Fifteen ticks. Suddenly he relaxed and laughed, but I was not joking. His smile faded.

"Aren't you going to ask?" I prompted quietly.

"Ask?"

"Who I am."

"Who are you?"

It was my turn to pause, stupidly lost for words after leading him to this point so dramatically. I took a deep breath.

"I am an architect . . ." That was an absurd way to begin. Try again. "Late in what you think is the next century, a very advanced spacecraft was built as part of a scheme to move industries off earth. Something went wrong on the test voyage, but now we are home again. Because of relativistic effects, only fourteen years have passed for us. I was recruited to help plan the new colony."

"Spacecraft?" stammered Will. "But even our best planes can't fly higher than eight miles. You're . . ."

"A fake? I could take off my shirt, show the scars where I was blown apart then stapled back together. I could take down my trousers, show you radiation scars not possible in 1938." I removed my shirt. He goggled, gripping the arms of his chair. My injuries would have meant certain death to someone depending on 1938 medical techniques.

"Modern technology did some terrible things to the Earth in the twelve decades that you think are still to come. The air was heating up, the sea level rose by two meters, croplands were becoming deserts, and toxins from industrial pollution were in everything. One group wanted to move all industry to other worlds, to let the earth recover. They must have been discredited when our ship vanished, and there was another faction promoting a more drastic solution. Genetic tailoring can alter the form and destiny of any species, Homo sapiens included. Its supporters seem to have won, from what I've found. Your whole society is based on genetic tailoring."

"Genetics? What do you mean? Our bodies are still the same."

Enthusiasm now outweighed my caution. I forgot who and what I was talking to. Mistake.

"The structures of beehives are encoded in the bees' genes, along with their daily and seasonal routines. Humans are more than bees, yet . . . the skills to build a certain type of house, to keep it in good repair, to want no more than that out of life: all that could be genetically encoded too— and has been. Throughout history people have lived out lives as happy, fulfilled servants and artisans, so why not take it a stage further and supply inbuilt skills? Will, the design of your houses and furniture, and the main-tenance of your life style, has been artificially encoded into human genes. The wherewithal to live graciously in a house like this is within your own particular genes. Tradesfolk, servants, they all have genetically inbuilt skills to preserve and maintain their own piece of your lifestyle. The European-American art deco style has come to dominate by now, although there may have been dozens of others to begin with."

The words took a moment to register with him, then, "Damn you. I'm not an insect!" he shouted, surging up out of his chair with his fists clenched.

"Please sit down."

"I have you here as my guest, I drive you around, I introduce you to my neighbors—and now you call me a parasite."

"Will, that's not what I said."

"A bee then—and not just a bee, a bloody drone!"

"The analogy was unfortunate—"

"Stand up! I'm going to run you out of here with my bare hands."

I stood up as he advanced on me. His hands came up, full of the confidence of a proficient boxer, yet with none of what had been built and trained into me. I held out an open hand and kept him from coming closer. He tried to push my arm away, tried very hard.

"I'm four times stronger than you, Will. About half of me was not there when I was born, and the replacement parts are much better."

He sat down. "You're real," he breathed in wonder.

I nodded. He shakily poured port into a wine glass, drained it. "So why are you here? To study us? To help us?"

"True, we are studying you. I have a small laboratory and radio in my luggage, and I have been in constant contact with the starship. My reports concur with those of two earlier observers: all humans alive on Earth today have been genetically tailored to maintain their civilization in balance with the environment. Women control their estrus, and they can ovulate at will until they have two children—three if a child dies. There were 15,000 million people when we left, but now the population is barely thirty mil-lion. Fuels are grown as crops, industry is based on maintenance and re-cycling. You live well, but without change."

"Isn't it the same everywhere?" he asked, pouring out a fourth glass of port. "Is the world just one huge hive?"

"Not a hive, but a species in harmony. Really, this world is just so beautiful now. When we first scanned it from space, we stared in wonder at the restored wilderness, the clean oceans, and at the wonderful archi-tecture in your towns. Your house is two thousand years old, and parts of the walls are ten times older. Your car has been rebuilt nineteen times in the six hundred years of its life so far; my instruments show it all. Maintenance is a genetic trait now, along with industry based on recyclable and renewable resources. No war, no crime; in fact, those very concepts have been blocked out of your mind genetically. The Earth has been healed from being the poisonous slag heap that I remember."

Try as I might, I could not make him share my enthusiasm for his own world.

"Harmony without humanity," Will muttered. "I'm a drone bee, with everything that I stand for coded into me and nothing open to my choice. *You* are really human; you are free in your starship. We're *Homo art deco!*" His words trampled thoughtlessly over exposed nerves and unspeakable memories. It was my turn to be annoyed.

"Human? When most of me is powered by a fusion resonance pack in my chest? When my muscles are collagen biosubstrate, and my spinal cord is a bundle of spun fluoride glass fibers? I'm *Homo cyborg*, not *sapiens*."

I stood with my back to the fireplace. Leaning against the mantelpiece and sipping my port, I looked across the room through the French windows to the moon rising behind the hills. Enchanting.

"We will soon take a vote," I announced. "I have recommended that we journey on."

"Who is 'we'?"

"The 105 men and 90 women of our vessel's crew. The Earth is a closed and stable ecology; we should not violate it. We remember what the Earth was like when people like us were dominant: exploitation, pollution, climatic change, catastrophic wars—we caused it all."

He poured out yet another port. The crystal decanter was emptying fast.

"But you had progress, too," he said, pleading but hopeless.

"Progress, but at a price—and there's another factor, a more important one. Strangers who do not fit the genetically determined styles of your art deco ecology are killed."

"Now that's crazy; I'd never—"

"Not you, but your servants and artisans. Their genes have been altered to maintain your society as well as your buildings. My two predecessors from the starship were killed after a fortnight of hospitality. The first seemed to die in an accident, but the second was beaten to death by the gardeners on an estate in Virginia. I was permitted to volunteer because I am expendable."

"Expendable? Why?"

"Don't ask, Will. My studies and observations have worked out why your tradesfolk kill true outsiders. A genetic sword of Damocles hangs above visitors to Earth, and unless they can fit within your style as well as someone born to it, the sword falls after about two weeks. My welcome has nearly run out, so I am leaving."

"No! Stay here, build a new city in the wilderness areas, where our servants could not see you. Help us to break our genetic chains."

"That would return nightmares to the Earth. We *could* establish a settlement in some remote area, but your maintenance people would attack us whenever contact was made. We have brought many of the old weapons back with us, and we would annihilate you, make no mistake. There is a faction on the starship that wants to do just that; and if you are really unlucky, they will win the vote. As I have said, my recommendation is that we move on, as much as I love it here. We know of another world: a cold, bleak place but still habitable. A shuttle craft will pick me up an hour before dawn; then we shall take our starship on its last journey."

He drained his glass again—he was drinking only in single gulps now. I sipped nervously at my own port, still on my first glass.

"You show us what we are, then leave! How do you think I feel after what you have told me? Why tell me in the first place? Is this part of your studies?"

"No, no." I sighed, unbearably tired now. "I . . . perhaps I wanted to . . . to share this with you, to speak to you as an equal. I'm very lonely, Will, and you have been a friend. I didn't mean to be cruel."

He buried his face in his hands and sat very still.

"But I have been cruel, unspeakably cruel. I'm sorry. You will forget, though. More than just mechanical skills and style have been built into you. You are also tailored to forget noncyclic events like this after a few years. Writing it down will not help. Your paper is always made to degrade in the same period."

Will was not used to heavy drinking. Without warning he lurched off to that exquisite bathroom, to be sick in the basin cut from green marble. He did not make it. I tried to clean him up, then called the footman. Hostility already burned bright in the normally dull eyes of the servant. I was a pathogen within the veins of their world, and the antibodies were massing to attack.

As Will was being cleaned up for bed, I slunk away to pack. After about half an hour there were raised voices from the direction of the master bedroom, punctuated by the tinkle of breaking glass. Another half hour passed in silence. I would be gone by the time the morning came with its recriminations, and it was barely 10:00 P.M. The bed was inviting, and gravity would not pull me down into the firm softness of a mattress for many years to come.

I lay naked with the window open, watching the night sky and listening to the sounds of an Earth forever barred to me. Agoraphobia was no longer a problem, not when the open spaces were so beautiful. I was not prepared for the click of the door opening and hurriedly pulled the sheet across myself.

"The man's a pig!" sobbed Lyndal, anger stiffening her gasped breaths. "I've always told him that if he wanted to drink, then I didn't want to know about it."

"I . . . may have upset him with some of my stories. My scars—"

"I don't care! He should have sent a note with the maid, then spent the night on the sofa. He reeked of vomit; and he, he . . . he finally fell asleep, snoring like the swine that he is."

More tears, more recriminations. She sat on the bed, I held her hand. We talked as moonlight streamed in through the open window, silver and seductive. Lyndal shifted, crouched lower when I pointed to the gleaming disk that was now above the lintel of the windows. Her head touched my shoulder. I hesitated, then slid my arm around her waist.

"I'm not very good at this," she confessed, pulling back the sheet, hesitating, then shedding frothy silk lace. "You don't have the wrong idea, do you? I mean, after years of behaving himself he suddenly . . . I . . . just don't want to feel trapped with him."

Being seduced for the sake of revenge may not be the most flattering of seductions, but it is better than not being seduced at all. Just after 3:00 A.M. she left, with an awkward yet affectionate kiss. I showered, savoring it as my last shower on Earth. Slow and cautious in the darkness, I made my way down the stone steps of the garden to the little airfield. A familiar warbling whine announced the approach of the starship's shuttle.

As I walked out onto the circular lawn, brilliant light splashed out behind me. I turned. The house was bathed in spotlights, gleaming white against the black sky. Will and Lyndal were standing on the patio, arms around each other! Waving. He—*they*—knew! The shuttle descended—a battered wedge on cushions of invisible force.

They must have discussed what I had told him, then staged the sound effects of an argument. Why? Perhaps she adjusted her estrus cycle to ovulate for a second time. There was I, with genes that could break the genetic mold that held them in serene stasis. His child can break the mold around our world, they must have decided. A brave, desperate, yet very human gesture. They would forget all this, but my genes would spread out and change their world, for better or worse.

I scratched at the radiation scars on my legs, reminded myself of my own hopelessly irradiated testicles as the shuttle nestled down into the grass with a crackle of electric buffer fields.

Will and Lyndal had tried to break their genetic shackles; but although they had failed, there was hope. Mutation and genetic drift were already eroding the foundations of *Homo art deco*, but even when change began again, it would be slow. The human race was resting, pausing for breath after the headlong dash from chipped flint to the threshold of space. I had paused to rest too, but I was barred from being anymore than a guest. If I were to pause for more than a fortnight in that world of exquisite guest rooms . . . an idea flashed in my mind, brighter than the gleaming white house at the center of the spotlights. I scooped my dark plastic commdee out of a pocket and called the shuttle on a local beam.

"Drop 3 to Jaybird, drop 3 to Jaybird!"

"Jaybird, Drop 3. You're cleared to board."

"Lift butt, Jaybird. I'm carrying a Trojan virus. Only just discovered it with the biopack. Influenza based; it'd go through our ship in hours. Biopack projection is fatal without genetic armor."

"Jaybird to Drop 3. Get into the airlock; I'll hold you there until we get back. I can't just leave you."

"Negative, Jaybird, I'm a dead man already. It's a biowar Trojan, probably left around to wipe *us* out if we ever came back."

"Jaybird to Drop 3—"

"Drop 3 to Jaybird. Tell them up there that this place may be pretty, but it's a killer. Good-bye and good luck."

I broke the link and ran. The shuttle stayed for another minute as the pilot tried to call me; and by the time he finally lifted, I had reached Will's garage and was starting my MG Magnette. The shuttle rose slowly, drawing every eye to the sky and drowning my car's engine as I drove down the driveway with my lights still off. Once on the road, the twin cones of my headlights lanced out through a thin mist, and I was just another traveler on the road.

The shuttle streaked through the sky ahead of me, and was gone.

LEANNE FRAHM

Leanne Frahm was, by the early 1980s, initially the most successful writer to come out of the two Australian writing workshops of the 1970s. Her second published story won a Ditmar Award in 1980 (and she won another in 1994 for "Catalyst"). U.S. editor and writer Terry Carr, who visited Australia to teach at the workshop she attended, was impressed enough by her talent to agent her work in the U.S.A. throughout the early 1980s. By 1985, she had published twelve stories, most of which first appeared in the United States. She was the first of the Australian writers of her generation to build an international career with her short fiction. But by that time she had ceased to write, following an operation for a brain tumor, and a crisis in her family's small business that required full-time work for a few years.

Her return to writing, around 1990, has resulted in a small stream of stories. A significant amount of her fiction is horror or speculative fiction. Her only book is a limited-edition collection, *Borderline* (1996), which includes the original title story reprinted in this book, an informative interview, and a bibliography. "Borderline" is set in her characteristic North Australian geography, but the intrusion of wonder is in the grand tradition of science fiction invasions from another dimension.

Dad!" KIM'S VOICE WAS bright and clear coming down the phone line. Jack smiled at the sound of it.

"G'day, Kimmie," he answered. "How are you, love?"

There was a moment's hesitation. Then, "I'm fine, Dad, fine. It's about this coming week, though . . ."

Jack pursed his lips. "Yes," he said guardedly.

"Look," Kim went on, "I know Chris and I were supposed to come up to the beach house with you, and Jack Jr's still coming, as far as I know, but . . ."

"What's up, Kim?" said Jack, sighing. He should have guessed. Kim was always going to visit from the city, but so often something happened to prevent it. Jack thought of his daughter, with immense affection and pride. She had the brains in the family, all right. Went through Uni, and had a flash job as a research chemist for a big drug company. Research chemist. Jack savored the words every time he said them, rolling the rich ringing sound of it around his tongue. Her mother would have been proud.

But the job meant he hardly ever saw her and her husband Chris. Sydney was a long way from a North Queensland beach. And now, when it looked like they'd finally managed to take some time off to visit, along with her brother Jack Jr. which would make it a real family reunion, here she was trying to cancel yet again . . . Jack felt a stab of irritation. "Well, go on," he said brusquely.

"Something's come up," said Kim. "I know that sounds vague, but it's important."

"You mean you're working," said Jack.

"No, not exactly."

"Then what's the problem?"

Jack could hear her searching for the right words. "I might be working," she said at last. "If there's anyway I can get involved with something really exciting and important, I want to be here."

"How likely is that?" said Jack.

"I . . ." she stumbled. Jack grinned to himself. Kim could never lie to him successfully.

"I just don't know," she said finally. "The government's involved, so we're only hearing rumors, but . . ."

"So you're not working, and not likely to be, but you'll miss our week because of a rumor," Jack said relentlessly. Kim's sigh was audible. "That's not fair, Dad," she said. "Putting it like that."

Jack made his voice sound guileless. "How should I put it, Kimmie?"

Kim laughed suddenly. "Oh, Dad," she said, "you're hopeless. All right, we'll be there. I suppose I'm grasping at straws, hoping I'll be called in, and not even sure what I'd be called in for. But I'll be bringing a mobile phone and fax, and if . . ."

"Okay, Kim," said Jack. "Mind you don't miss that plane now. And give my regards to Chris."

"Love you, Dad."

Jack shook the thick mangrove mud from his sandshoes as he climbed up the grassy bank from the creek. He put a certain amount of venom into each kick. The crab pot he'd left in the creek last night baited with a fine meaty bone was empty, but the bone was stripped right down to gleaming white. That meant that at least one big buck—maybe two—had feasted during the night. And now they were gone.

He wondered grimly if it had been that bloody Bill Haskins, who lived farther along the beach. Bill was a bit of a sneak, lied like a pig in mud about the fish he claimed he caught. And whinge! Always complaining up at the pub that he never got any decent muddies. But no, Bill was one of the old school, an old codger. *Like me*, thought Jack. He wouldn't stoop that low. Still, he'd keep it in mind . . .

Jack hefted the coil of rope attached to the wire crab pot around his shoulder and straightened up. He'd really wanted those mud crabs, wanted to surprise the kids with a real seafood dinner—fresh, like they never got down south, Kim and Chris in Sydney and Jack Jr. in Melbourne. He wanted the visit to be special, because they hardly ever got together now, and he was getting on, certainly getting on . . .

He was glad they were all settled, although he still had reservations about Kim's husband Chris. He was clever, no doubt about that, but Jack couldn't get used to the idea of a man staying home and writing things for a living. Writing for newspapers was all right, newspaper writers were pretty informed and brainy, but somehow writing articles for fancy magazines wasn't a real man's job, not the way Jack thought. Still, Kim seemed happy with him, and Jack had to admit that was all right by him. . . .

Jack Jr. now. Jack was more than a little in awe of his successful son. Jack Jr. was in business, although Jack could never quite work out exactly what he did. The few times Jack Jr. had tried to explain, it had all got so complicated that Jack had lost the thread. Kim once said Jack Jr.'s career was "opportunism," but Jack didn't think that was its real title, not the way Kim said it.

Jack spat, hefted the pot more comfortably on his back, and set off. His house faced the sea, protected from the sea wind by scraggly she-oaks. Between it and the mangrove-lined creek was a long meadow spotted with tussocks of salt grass. The sun was already biting hot, making him squint through the heat waves.

A couple of questing gulls circled over him, then flew off across the dunes with guttural cries.

Their calls faded with distance, and as they did, Jack became aware of another sound, a different sound, surfacing. It was a soft hissing, like dry sand blown against corrugated iron, nearby, just behind him. It ended with a sound like a sharp in-drawn breath that cut off abruptly as he swung round, the crab pot bumping painfully into his hip.

At first Jack was unable to register what he was seeing. He had no point of reference that would allow his mind to say, "Well, that's like a . . ." or "Oh yes, that's a bit similar to . . ."

It reminded him of the time a cyclone had passed over the coast and the tidal surges had dragged something from the absolute depths of the ocean and flung it onto the nearby beach. When the wind and rain had died down they'd all gone to look at it. It was the most silent Jack could remember a crowd being. Even Bill Haskins was mute. They stood in small tight groups, staring.

Jack heard later that the CSIRO bloke they sent out to check decided it was a giant deep-sea squid, but Jack and the others felt that was only as good a guess as any, considering the condition of the thing.

For the fury of the cyclone and the decrease in pressure as it was wrenched from its habitat so far below the surface had turned it inside out. At least that's what they'd assumed. Whether through its arse or its mouth, no one could say. Jack had been as totally perplexed as the others, and there was a camaraderie of bafflement in the situation . . .

That was lacking now. He was alone, staring at an object that had suddenly appeared behind him, an object that left him groping desperately for recognition. The crab pot fell to the ground and the rope snaked unheeded from his shoulders.

It was motionless. That was the only good thing about it. Jack's first coherent thought was that if it hadn't been, he didn't know whether he would have been able to summon the will to run. He felt his lungs start to work again, and was grateful, because he realized he'd stopped breathing when he first saw the thing, and if it had been up to him, and not purely an automatic process, he mightn't have thought to start again. He noticed these things with a deep and slow intensity, because it was easier to observe them than to contemplate the thing in front of him.

It was almost a cube, about five feet square on a side, but more of a squashed cube. Its sides bulged slightly. But cubes were generally, as far as Jack knew, artificial things, like children's alphabet blocks or concrete building blocks. This cube didn't look artificial, although its shiny surface could have been made of plastic. It looked like—meat, or something that should have been made of meat, something alive, but with a look of complete nonaliveness.

Jack's mind began to hurt, trying to make sense of his thoughts. He licked his lips, forcing himself to study it more intently.

The shininess seemed to be caused by a covering of tiny scales that glistened in the sun, with a look about them of oil streaks on water. But he thought he could see through them, into the matter of the thing, where it seemed to be slightly luminous, like storm clouds when lightning flashes beyond them and their walls and valleys and rifts are illuminated briefly against a black sky—it was like that, like looking into a thunderhead. But it was hard to tell in the brightness of the sun. . . .

And beyond that—Christ, looking into this thing was like looking into a picture puzzle—pale red streaks cleaved its heart . . . Jack blinked rapidly, as if he'd been staring into infinity and getting dizzy from it. Meat shouldn't look like that. He took a step back.

Jack rued that step the moment he took it. Because the thing moved too. It trembled slightly, slid a few inches, and was still. The movement startled Jack, just when he'd become more or less confident that the thing was permanently fixed to the ground. "Damn blast it!" he muttered, growing angry. It wasn't as if this was a croc or something that could bite and scratch, something dangerous, at least not in the sense that Jack understood danger—just a jellyish lump that sat there looking odd. And moving a bit.

He stroked his stubbled chin with callused fingers, thinking hard. Suddenly inspired, he took a few mincing steps toward the house and stopped. The thing moved again, in the same direction, and halted too. Jack felt a wave of jubilation coupled with a shiver of fear. All right. It only wanted to follow him. Why, Jack had no idea. It didn't seem to want to do anything with him, just to sit there and look like a faintly lit nightmare. But at least Jack was regaining control.

He bent down to grab the crab pot—not taking his eyes off the thing— and set off toward the house with strides as long as he could make them. Glancing back, he saw the thing following, gliding over the sand and stubbled patches of grass, silent as a lizard on glass.

He passed the few stunted bush-lemon trees and snake-limbed guavas that marked the boundary of his yard. A wide verandah encircled the house, which perched on low stumps. There were two sets of three-step stairs, front and back. Jack ran up the back steps, dumped the crabbing gear on the verandah and turned, panting. The thing had stopped at the bottom of the stairs.

Jack congratulated himself. The stairs were only three feet wide, and it couldn't squeeze through that, no normal thing that wide could fit. . . . But it was trying. Yes, it was definitely trying.

Jack was surprised at how calm he was, watching it, and thinking about the fat lady at the turnstiles in the flashy new supermarket he'd visited in the big town thirty miles down the road. He'd chuckled then (and he was damn near chuckling now, which was odd) watching the fat lady squeeze and squeeze, sucking her breath in so her enormous bosom rolled high onto her chest and her huge stomach compressed to make her half as wide by twice as broad and her immense bum had sort of pulled itself in and down and she'd turned sideways . . . Yes, he was chuckling now, his face all stiff and feeling paper-lined. No normal thing, but then this wasn't what he'd generally call normal, and he'd been so sure that once he reached the verandah it wouldn't be able to follow, that home was "bar" like in tag. . . .

His grin was so rigid it threatened to pull his throat muscles out of his neck and he backed into the doorway.

The thing stopped. Jack didn't know if it had a brain inside it somewhere to work it out, or eyes to measure the distance, but it stopped trying to come up the stairs. With a slight vibration, it settled near the bottom of the steps, silent under the bright sun. Far away, a gull cried.

Once inside the kitchen, Jack's legs almost crumpled with relief. "Jesus," he whispered, wiping at the sweat on his forehead he hadn't even known was there till now. Abruptly he saw himself very clearly—a gnarled, slightly stooped old man who was gasping and quivering with fear. It was a sorrowful sight, and he felt a surge of raw childish anger at the thing that had conjured it. It wasn't an emotion of much permanent use, but it stopped the trembling and allowed him to think.

The logical thing to do would be to phone the police—Stan Hollis at the small one-man Kuttabul station. He was closest. After all, reasoned Jack, if a wild animal escaped from the circus, that's what he'd do. Police handle that sort of thing. Stan would know what to do.

But a beer would be nice, while he was phoning Stan. The morning was warm, and he'd been out in the sun. A Stubby would be great.

The first draft was delicious. He hadn't realized how thirsty the morning's events had made him. He went to the back door to check on the thing, and it was still there. So it wasn't leaving (that was a pity, that was) or moving.

He finished the Stubby and opened a second on the way to the phone. He grinned as he picked up the receiver, picturing Stan's face when he told him that a . . . what? His grin dissolved. *Hey, Stan, there's a big square thing, maybe made of meat or jelly or plastic, with a light inside, that followed me home from the creek.* How much have you had this morning, Jack? Stan would say . . . No, maybe not Stan.

Who then? And it burst on him as blazingly as a 'roo-shooter's spotlights on a cornered wallaby. Not Stan. Not when he had Kim and Jack Jr. and Chris coming this afternoon.

Joy spilled over him as coolly and refreshingly as the beer. They'd know what to do. Kim was a *scientist,* by God. She'd know what it was. And how to get rid of it.

He opened his third beer and went out to the verandah, where he could keep an eye on the thing till they came. He sank back in the old wicker armchair and stretched his legs out, eyeing the faintly changing luminescence boldly.

"Just wait," he said out loud. "Just wait till they get here."

The sound of an engine revving over the sandy road at the front of the beach house roused Jack. "Fell asleep, by God," he muttered, levering himself stiffly out of the chair. "Must be the kids."

His foot knocked an empty beer bottle that bounced down the steps with a glassy pinging sound, onto the sand in the dazzling afternoon sunlight. Jack squinted after it, noting the slant of the sun's rays. He must have been asleep for a while . . .

Then he saw it again. The thing. It hadn't been a dream.

He swallowed a surge of beer-tasting bile, realizing he'd fallen asleep right in front of it . . . All at once the weight of his years and the knowledge of his vulnerability felt like a large stone crushing his chest.

"Dad!" he heard in Kim's clear voice. "Where are you, you old bugger?" That was Jack Jr.'s cheerful basso. The kids were here, and they'd help him. Tears of relief bleared his eyes.

Hurrying down the hallway to the front door, he saw a white car with a rental company's name on its side. Then their heads (Jack Jr.'s distinctive flaming red hair), then their bodies as they climbed the three steps (Kim in a pretty orange sun frock), and finally they were all crowding the front verandah, laughing and talking as he bowled out of the door at them.

"Dad," said Kim, dropping her bag and reaching for him. He hugged her fiercely. She laughed and put her hands on his shoulders and pushed him back a little—she was taller than him, but he'd never minded that, not a bit. Her mother's, Myra's, genes, Kim always said. Myra came from a tall family, and now tall Kim was looking down at him, surprise on her face.

"Dad, you've been drinking—it's a bit early, isn't it?" Then she looked more closely into his eyes, still rheumy with tears. He made an ineffectual movement to wipe them, but she was too near. So near he could see the small lines that were starting to show at the corners of her eyes and the merest sprinkling of gray in the hair above her ears.

Her voice softened. "What's the matter, Dad?"

I'm afraid, Jack thought with unusual clarity. More afraid than he'd admitted to himself. That's why he'd slept so long, so he wouldn't have to wake up and face . . . it.

Jack Jr. and Chris were standing behind Kim, both wearing expressions of concern and, perhaps, a touch of wariness. *They're seeing a drunken old codger,* thought Jack miserably. *That's all.* They looked so relaxed and casual, strong in colorful open-necked shirts and smart slacks, Chris's hair a bit more gray behind his glass's frames . . . "Look," was all he could manage, pulling away from Kim. "Come and look!" He caught their puzzled glances at each other, Jack Jr.'s shrug and "I don't know" expression at Kim.

"Just . . . Look!" he said more strongly.

They followed him along the hallway, the unpolished timber floorboards creaking. The afternoon sun slanted in through the back door, making a rectangle of brightness on the floor. For an awful instant Jack wondered if it would still be there. What if it had gotten bored and wandered off, or just disappeared as mysteriously as it arrived? They would never believe him; it would be a drunken hallucination. Jack's face flamed scarlet with anxiety as he went out the back door and halted on the verandah. He swung back to the others as they emerged.

"See?" he said triumphantly. "See?"

Kim brushed by him, shading her eyes against the sun, her mouth open just a fraction. Chris and Jack Jr. joined her at the railing.

"Holy shit!" exclaimed Jack Jr. "What the hell is that?"

Chris looked at Kim. "What on earth is it? Do you know? It looks almost alive . . ."

"Hell no," said Jack Jr. He gripped the verandah railing and leaned out, staring down on it. "It looks like some kind of polymer—look at the sheen on it." He laughed uneasily and turned to Jack. "Okay, Dad, we give in. The council's supplied you with state-of-the-art rubbish bins? It's a nuclear-powered incinerator? Come on, Dad."

They were all looking at Jack now, and he realized they all thought he knew. That it was some sort of outrageous gadget he'd found—Kim still frowned at him, though. Maybe they just wanted him to know, because then they wouldn't have to be afraid of it, like he was.

He looked at the thing in dismay. The sun angled across it, making it shinier than before, giving it a blue-green patina like an opal, and obscuring the faint lights inside unless you really looked for them . . .

"It's not any of those things," Jack managed at last. "It just turned up, down near the creek. It followed me home."

"Followed you?" said Chris, grinning disbelievingly.

"How can—?" Jack Jr. began, but Kim cut across him.

"Then it's organic?" she said.

Jack shook his head. He didn't understand the question.

"Is it alive?" she amended.

Jack shrugged irritably. They were asking him too many questions that he didn't have answers to. They were the smart ones, the ones with an education. *They* were supposed to know.

Kim saw his frustration. "Sit down, Dad," she said, leading him to the chair. She positioned herself where she could both see him and watch the thing. Jack saw she was trembling slightly. Chris and Jack Jr. remained at the railing, examining it with cautious fascination.

"Tell us about it," Kim coaxed.

So Jack told them. About the crabs that weren't there, and his disappointment. About the walk home, and the odd sounds. About standing frozen as an ice block, about it moving and following him home. He told them how he had nearly rung Stan. (Jack Jr. laughed at this point and said, "Jesus—a Queensland country cop!" in a sarcastic way and Kim told him to shut up.) He told them about falling asleep, but he left out the beer, and the stultifying fright. What they saw on his face they saw—he couldn't do much about that. But he didn't intend to magnify it by talking about it; a man had his pride.

When he finished there was silence for a few minutes. Then Kim spoke. "Well?" she said to Chris and Jack Jr. "Do either of you recognize this at all or know of anything like it?"

Chris shook his head emphatically. Jack Jr. murmured, "Well, there was this movie called *The Blob* . . ."

"Shut up, Jack!" Kim said again. Jack could feel the tension in the air increase like a pulley's rope tightened another notch.

Kim's voice was loud and brittle with excitement. "If I said I knew what it was, I'd be lying. But I think I know *of* it."

"Oh yeah," said Jack Jr. Chris looked at her inquiringly.

She nodded slowly, eyes still fixed on the thing. "Chris, you know I've mentioned the rumors I've been hearing—mysterious reports about large organisms being discovered at various locations during the last month." She glanced at Jack Jr. and bit her lip. "I don't know if I should be saying anything, the government's put a blanket on it."

"Go on, don't mind me," said Jack Jr. "After all, whatever this is, it happens to be on my father's property and I think I have a right to know about it."

Jack thought privately that he did too, being the father in question. They all stared at Kim.

"Well," she said, opening her palms, "I don't really know much. As I said, it's been very secretive, and the stories that are getting out are pretty bizarre. There's talk that some of us," (*she means us scientists*, thought Jack proudly), "are being commandeered for government research." She gestured to Jack. "That's what I meant when I rang and tried to . . ."

"Put off this holiday," said Jack dryly.

She had the grace to blush. "I was hoping . . . I know it's not likely, but my specialty is drug-related effects on genetic material, and the rumors are saying . . ." Her reddened face paled suddenly.

"What?" said Chris quickly.

She stared at the thing in silence so long Jack thought she'd fallen asleep with her eyes open.

"What?" Chris demanded again. Jack Jr. was frowning at her. "Yes, what?" he repeated.

She dropped her gaze. "Oh, all sorts of things. You know how gossipy science is."

"So this is probably just a rumored 'large organism,' " said Chris, "about which you know nothing. And where does this large organism come form?"

"I honestly don't know," said Kim.

Jack was nonplussed. While they seemed to have concurred on a name for the thing, "large organism" didn't seem to be much more descriptive than "thing." And naming it hadn't lessened the tension that hung around them like smoke from a bushfire, and naming it hadn't decreased the feeling that was growing in him that Kimmie was lying about something, or at least not being completely open.

"You say the government's in on this thing," he said to her.

She nodded. "Yes, Dad. If this is the same thing I've heard about."

"Then the government needs to know about it," he said, raising himself from the chair. "I'll ring Stan Hollis after all."

Kim grabbed his arm. "No, wait, Dad!" Chris and Jack Jr., who had been leaning on the railing, straightened.

Kim stood up as Jack sat back in his chair. "Look," she said, "this thing is pretty unusual and pretty exciting—we can all see that. I'd really like the chance to look at it by myself first, Dad. And it mightn't have anything to do with the reports I mentioned; it could be something quite different and new. 'Large organism' could cover anything, couldn't it?" She looked at the younger men for support.

Jack Jr. nodded vigorously. Chris was more hesitant. "I'm not sure," he said. "We don't know how dangerous this thing could be. It's a total unknown . . ." He trailed off, looking questioningly at Kim.

"It's been here, according to Dad, for a while," she said. "It's done nothing untoward so far."

"That we know of." Chris looked pointedly at Jack.

"I'm all right," flared Jack. He was mulling over the phrase "according to Dad," and he didn't like it very much. It seemed to be saying that they weren't convinced that what he had told them was true. And there was a gleam in Kim's eyes that was mirrored in Jack Jr.'s. It looked very much akin to greed.

Jack chewed his lip, thinking it over. Of course Kim would want this to herself. If this was something unknown, as Chris put it, and if she could convince herself that the government didn't know about it already, wouldn't she want the glory of discovering it? Of examining it and becoming famous? Of course she would.

And Jack Jr. was a businessman. You could make lots of money from scientific discoveries, it was in the papers all the time. And Jack supposed that this, this thing that had frightened him so much could, in its purest form, be termed a scientific discovery.

It niggled at him. He wasn't sure it was right, but he finally nodded.

"All right," he said. "You lot can have a look at it first." He had a feeling that they would have done just what they wanted anyway, his permission or no, but it was nice they at least acted as if they were deferring to his age and wisdom . . .

"Thanks, Dad," said Kim, jubilantly.

"Just a minute," said Chris, his voice anxious. "What are you planning to do? You've got no idea what this is, no equipment, no lab—how can you possibly investigate anything?"

Kim looked perplexed and irritated, both at once. "I'll just . . . I don't know. Make it up as I go along. But I'm not letting this chance go by."

"Right," nodded Jack Jr. "After all, if the government's interested, then we should be too."

Chris shook his head. "Well, be careful."

"Of what?" said Kim.

"Chris, I give up. Explosions? Laser rays? How would I know?"

"Exactly," said Kim. "We don't know. So we'll be careful. But look at it—it hasn't moved a centimeter since we've been here. You've been writing too many speculative articles."

There was a hard edge to Kim's voice that Jack had never heard before. This was what Kim-the-scientist was like, then. It scared him a little, for her sake. He sat forward on the edge of his chair, hands clasped and dangling between his legs, and watched as they made their way down the stairs toward it. They grouped in a cluster on one side of the thing, staring at it. He heard indrawn breaths, and knew they could now see into it, and were as astonished as he had been.

"*Is* it alive?" said Chris.

Kim shook her head wonderingly. "I don't know. It has absolutely no features, not on any side. That translucent outer coat looks hard, like Perspex." She put out her hand tentatively.

"Don't . . ." said Chris, ". . . touch it! Not yet."

Kim laughed, a trifle nervously, and pulled her hand away. "All right, all right. What do you think, Jack?"

"My money's on an organic supercomputer—you know, a combination of organic brain cells and electronics. See, those lights are the neural synapses firing . . ."

"Then where are the connections for a screen or printer? That's only theoretical, anyway."

"Theoretical here—on Earth," said Chris in sepulchral tones.

They all laughed, less nervously. *They were beginning to relax with it,* Jack thought incredulously. Christ, young people can get used to anything nowadays.

"Of course, if it is manufactured, then that means it belongs to some-one," Chris pointed out. They glanced around involuntarily—Chris looked up, Jack noted. But the road and foreshore and the bush behind them were deserted.

Jack Jr. shrugged. "It's on Dad's property, came willingly, apparently. Possession is et cetera, et cetera."

"Right," said Kim. "Let's check the mobility Dad said it showed." She turned to Jack. "Come on, Dad. It's seeming fairly harmless."

She has to reassure me, Jack thought sadly.

"Come and walk away . . ." She pointed along the track to the creek, ". . . a hundred meters or so."

There was no help for it. He had to join them in their silly games, or they would come to perceive the depths of his fear, and despise him.

"Why me?" he said testily, joining them, closer to it than he had been before.

"It might only respond to you, Dad," Jack Jr. said. "Maybe you're the only one who can lead it around."

Jack trudged off through the sand, refusing to look back, until he heard Kim call, "Okay, Dad. You might as well stop. It's not moving."

He turned to watch them. There was a brief discussion, then all three of them set off in his direction.

They had gone only a few steps when the thing moved. They stopped, surprised, and watched it stop too. Then they began walking toward Jack again, backward, so they could see it, halting as they came abreast of him.

"I just can't believe this," Kim said breathlessly as the thing came to rest near them. "It didn't turn, did it?" She looked questioningly at the others. They shook their heads. "Just moved straight in this direction. But why?" No one answered.

"Now," she went on, "let's everyone move back to the house, but one at a time. You first, Dad."

Jack obligingly moved off, thinking as he looked out to the line of breakers beyond the house how easily Kim had assumed command over her husband and brother. There was a queer kind of vindication in that. *Always knew she had the brains,* he mused.

He halted at the steps, and observed the others following him, one by one, as Kim had instructed. Kim came last, and of course the thing followed her, as Jack had known it would. It seemed a bit obvious, but then he guessed that scientists needed to spell it out plainly.

Kim was flushed as she joined them, with the thing trailing behind. It stopped near the steps again. Jack didn't think he'd ever seen Kim look so pretty and vivacious, not even at her wedding to Chris.

"Point number one," she said. "It targets human beings. Nonspecific. Chris, have you got your laptop with you?"

"It's in the car."

"Remind me to get it out for notes. Now, we've got to test it on animals, too. Other mammals and reptiles, whatever we can find here. So point number one is amended to: *at present* it targets human beings."

The men nodded and she went on. "Point number two. It moves, but with no observable means of locomotion. It just—wafts."

" 'Waft' is not a scientific term," said Chris.

"It might be after this," rejoined Kim.

"Perhaps we just can't see it," said Jack Jr. "Maybe there are little wheels or treads in the bottom. Maybe it's a costume and there's actually a little person in there who walks—"

"For Christ's sake, be serious," Kim snapped. "I checked for tracks while it was moving—didn't you?" She pointed to the sandy soil that clearly showed only the deep depressions of their footsteps.

"No, not really . . ." muttered Jack Jr. He had the grace to look shuffle-footed. Jack suppressed a cackle at Kim's cleverness.

"Actually," offered Chris, "none of the grass stalks it moved over are broken. It'd be interesting to see how much it weighs."

"Good point," said Kim briefly. "We'll check on that later. Now— point number three. The only obvious sign of any sort of metabolism is that faint glowing effect." She glanced at Jack and he knew she was keeping it simple for him. "No observable functions such as breathing, digestion, heartbeat or pulse, no sweating, nothing."

"What does that mean?" said Chris.

"It means we still don't know if it's organic or nonorganic."

"Or both," said Jack Jr. stubbornly.

"Or neither," Kim flashed. "And now for point number four." She turned to Jack. "Dad, have you got a really sharp, thin knife?"

"There's my filleting knife," Jack began, then realized what she meant to do with it. "You going to cut that thing?"

Kim's face set in hard lines at the accusatory tone in his voice. "I'm going to take a sample, yes."

"Jesus, Kimmie," said Jack Jr. "Do you think that's a good idea?"

"Don't be so bloody inane," Kim flared.

"But why?" said Chris, trying to be reasonable. "You can't do anything with it, no lab, no microscope . . ."

Kim's response was almost a shout. "I just want to see!"

"It could be dangerous," Chris faltered.

"What? Toxic fluids, rays from outer space?" Kim's eyes were narrowed and grim, reminding Jack of the half-closed eyes of a mean little shovel-nose shark that had caught itself up in his fishing net once. It wounded him to see the same expression on the face of his daughter.

"You could hurt the creature, girlie," he said gently. "It might bleed to death."

Kim's voice was tight. "There is no evidence of a circulatory system in that thing. Look. See how far you can see into it. No veins or arteries. No blood. And I'll bet there's no nervous system to make it hurt."

All three men were silent, staring at her. Jack had the sudden thought that she looked old, more like forty than . . . but when he added it up, she was thirty-nine. *Silly of me*, he thought. *Must be what'sisname's disease. But I never think of Kim as getting old, not old like me . . .*

"God damn it!" she exploded at their grave expressions. "Look at me! I'm nearly forty . . ." Jack started at the coincidence of their thoughts, ". . . and I've done nothing but pedestrian work all my life! This is a chance to get involved with something I'd never dare dream of. If this is what I've heard about, if any of the rumors are even remotely close to the truth, then I have to go as far as I can, so they can't ignore me, they'll have to let me in on the research."

She looked round them all, and there was a hint of pleading in her eyes so small and slight that anyone who didn't know her would have missed it. To Jack, it was as evident as a shag on a rock. He cleared his throat, and turned to hawk phlegm behind a grass tussock. "I'll fetch the filleting knife."

Relief sparkled in her eyes. "Thanks, Dad," she said.

Kim stood by the thing, the three men grouped behind her. The sun was westering now, imparting a rich misty glow to the air and striping the sand with deep blue-gray shadows. Jack thought longingly that this was the best time of the day to be fishing, and wished he could have been somewhere else, just him and a line and a hook . . .

Kim had changed from her bright dress into a shirt and jeans, in case there was a mess. She wore cheerful pink rubber gloves, new from a packet that Myra had never used. She held the filleting knife (which had been soaking in raw Dettol for a while) poised. The tableau they made with the thing looked to Jack like some weird ritual, as if Kim was about to make a sacrifice for one of those groups of crazies that you read about in the papers. A deeper part of his mind wondered if she was . . .

"There seems to be at least three layers," Kim said, jerking Jack back to reality. *Like one of those TV stories*, he thought. Giving a running commentary while the blood spurts and you can hardly eat your dinner with close-ups of all the mucky inside stuff."

"I don't know if I can separate them, so I'm aiming for a cone-biopsy— a big one." She smiled at her joke, which Jack didn't understand.

She pushed the knife gently into the outer layer. It disappeared to the hilt, and she drew it back a little, catching her breath.

"What's wrong?" said Chris sharply.

"Nothing. It's just that I wasn't expecting it. It's softer than butter." She pushed the knife in again. "Any reaction?"

Jack Jr. was standing back a little. "No, nothing on this side. Nothing we can see. Hang on!" He hurriedly circumnavigated the object. "Not a whisker's movement."

"No," she murmured. "No, vibration, nothing. I might as well be cutting into cheese."

Jack looked at Chris. His face was wet with sweat. "Heat getting to you?" he whispered, unable to stop that particular imp of malice. Chris frowned at him abstractedly and looked back to his wife.

"This is going to be so easy," said Kim. She worked the thin blade around till she had completed a circle.

"No fluids," said Chris.

She nodded. "I noticed."

She used the knife as a lever, and the conical section slipped out. Kim studied it as she withdrew it, cradling it in her free hand. "There's the outer layer. Like a rind, isn't it? And the secondary one."

They peered over her shoulder. "Rind" was a good word for it. And "cheese," like Kim said. It reminded Jack of a fancy cheese that was served at the end of a meal he and Myra had in a restaurant once—the one with the flaky white hard shell that you cut into, revealing a sloppy cream stuff . . . "Cheese?" he'd said in disgust. "That isn't cheese. Don't they have any decent cheddar?" Myra had shushed him, her embarrassment in what was only a tarted-up café almost comical . . .

Only this cheese had an opalescent shell, and the inside stuff—well, the closest thing to it that Jack had seen was a lump of raw fish flesh, and fish on the turn at that. It was whitish and slightly transparent, with no light in it at all, and despite the fact that he was more than familiar with raw fish flesh, the sight of that conical curd of repellent colorless matter made his gorge rise. He stepped back as Kim placed the sample on a scrubbed side table they'd brought down to use.

"There's another unusual aspect," she said.

"What's that?" said Chris, moistening his lips.

"It's mass. I might as well be handling air. There's no feeling of weight at all. It must be incredibly light, despite its bulk. We still haven't got to the third layer—at least it looks like a third layer. I'll have to enlarge this and cut some of that secondary integument away."

Jack flinched. "Kimmie," he said, "don't you think that's enough for the thing to take? You might be about killing it."

"Oh, Dad," she said impatiently. He waited for Jack Jr. to come to his defence, or even Chris, but although they seemed, by the looks on their faces, as repulsed as he, there was a curious avidity in their expressions that also said loud and clear, "Oh, Dad." His cheeks burned.

Kim was busy cutting into the cavity, enlarging it, standing back to allow scraps of stuff to fall to the ground and trampling on them as she moved forward again. Jack gritted his dentures, wishing for a moment he still had real teeth to grind, it was so much more satisfying. He hated seeing this, and yet it didn't seem to be hurting the thing. Maybe it wasn't alive, couldn't feel the slicing and scraping. Jack hoped so.

It took awhile. Kim was in up to her elbow when she suddenly slowed down, and began to maneuvre the knife more delicately. She eased a piece out as expertly as an oyster-catcher winking a snail from its shell and held it up. If anything, this part of the thing was more revolting than the rest of it.

Kim's eyes shone as she looked at the substance in her hands. There was no light in this, or even the hint of one. *If someone had a heavy head cold*, thought Jack, *and a really dirty nose, this would be what came out*. Thick gray sticky-looking strands of stuff gave the impression that Kim was playing cat's cradle with a skein of slimy wool.

"Jesus!" said Jack Jr., taking two steps back. "Put it down, Kim!"

But Kim stood with it, fascination glowing in her face.

Chris looked at her, frowning. "You know what this is, don't you?" he said.

Kim half-nodded, then shook her head. "Only what the rumors were saying . . ."

"What?" Chris and Jack Jr. spoke together.

"Well," she began, and hesitated, clearing her throat, and started again. "All I can do is quote. The outer layer is a lipid sheath—fats and carbohydrates. The second layer is composed of blocks of protein . . ."

"Protein?" interrupted Jack. "Knew it looked like fish!"

The others looked at him. "Well," he said defensively, "isn't that what protein is—meat and fish and chicken?"

Kim smiled at him. "Yes, Dad. Pretty well."

Chris still frowned. His eyes behind the lenses of his glasses seemed enlarged with impatience at the interjection.

"Go on," he urged. "The third layer . . ."

The words came out in a whisper. "Double-stranded RNA—ribonucleic acid."

"But that's . . ." The color drained from Chris's face.

Kim nodded. "Yes. I thought you'd recognize it. You did that article awhile ago."

"What!" shouted Jack Jr., angry at being left out of it, and showing it. He echoed Jack's opinion exactly.

"The stories I've heard indicate that this might be a virus," said Kim matter-of-factly. "More particularly, a viron, being an individual particle . . ."

"A virus?" Jack Jr.'s mouth gaped, and his angry expression melted like ice cream in the sun. Kim placed the sample on the table with the first one and stripped off the pink gloves.

"I'm only repeating what I've heard," she said. "I don't have an electron microscope to examine this—" she pointed to the pieces on the table—"so I can't confirm it, but the gross structural characteristics are similar. The lipid sheath is most commonly found in virii that infect animal cells, and you can have nucleic acid consisting of DNA, and the strandedness of the nucleic acid varies. But basically, that thing may be an enormously magnified virus."

Chris looked incredulous. "And you're saying there are more of these things; they've just started popping up around the place?"

Kim nodded. "Quite randomly, apparently. Not many. I didn't know what they looked like, only that there was this incredible speculation that giant virii had appeared and were being investigated."

"A virus!" said Jack Jr. "But Jesus, Kim, you touched it, you had it all over your hands! And we've all been near it, breathing around it." Jack watched the businessman disappear, leaving a frightened boy, like the skeleton of a leaf when the good greenness has withered.

Kim tried to put a hand on his shoulder, but he shied away.

"No, Jack," she said. "I don't believe it's harmful."

"Believe?" Jack Jr. exploded. "What *do* you believe, then?"

"Don't tell me the supercomputer salesman is having second thoughts," murmured Chris. Jack Jr. looked very much as if he would have liked to hit him, but was scared of catching something.

Kim came between them and said with all the firmness she could muster (which to Jack didn't seem like a hell of a lot, and that made him wonder how certain Kim herself was), "Jack, you haven't heard me. This is an individual particle, a discrete unit. A virus is harmful when it invades a cell—your cells." Jack Jr. winced. "This one can't invade anyone's cells—

it's too big. There are no cells in the world it can invade . . ." She shook her head. "This thing shouldn't exist. A virus is the smallest living organism, so stripped of functions that it's questionable whether it is alive. It's somewhere on the borderline between animate and inanimate. But a virus is measured in millionths of a millimeter, and this one is . . . 'huge' doesn't do it justice. Of course we're not even sure that it is a virus."

"But suppose it bursts, and explodes into millions of virus particles— Christ, you cut into it!" Jack Jr. was pale.

"No! This is one organism. One organism, possibly a virus, expanded to a colossal size. It can't subdivide."

Chris cut in. "Maybe that explains why it follows people, us, around, if it's programmed to invade a human cell. It knows we have them, but it can't proceed, so it just stays there waiting for conditions to become favorable."

"You might be right," said Kim. "It would indicate a human-invasive virus, not one that attacks plants or animals. But where does it come from?"

"It came for me," said Jack loudly.

Kim turned to him. "Why yes, it did. And—that's the one thing we've ignored all along." She looked thoughtful. "Dad, you're sure it wasn't around earlier? You couldn't have missed it?"

"No." Jack shook his head, certain of one fact in this rigmarole. "There was a sound like when you open a tin of baked beans, and I turned around, and there it was."

"So," said Chris, "It suddenly appeared, as if it was emerging . . ."

"From another dimension?" said Kim.

"Oh Christ, a giant virus from another dimension," groaned Jack Jr. "I can't believe this is happening."

"I think we've reached the nadir of speculation," Chris said abruptly. "It's late. You can't do much more now, Kim. Let's think about it tomorrow."

The others nodded, Jack Jr. unhappily, and they climbed the stairs to the verandah. Jack lingered behind them. The sun was setting and the daylight was dimming into dusk. He watched the glow in the virus thing brighten, marred only by a jet black patch where the hole was. The evening air was still warm and humid, but Jack shivered as he studied it. The children seemed to have forgotten one thing.

Myra had died of a virus.

They ate their evening meal on the verandah, with the thing brightly visible in the darkness, still motionless. Jack could offer only ham sand-

wiches—with all the drama of the afternoon he'd forgotten to defrost the
fish he'd meant to use in place of the crab.

There was some talk of keeping watches through the night, but everyone was tired, and the proposal lapsed through lack of volunteers. They
were subdued, whole minutes passing without a word.

In the silence, it occurred to Jack that he hadn't got around to making
up the spare beds for them, either. Myra always made up the spare beds; it
was a ritual if visitors were coming. Making them up with clean sheets,
and even if they were used for only one night, whipping off the sheets and
washing them again, ready for the next guest. Jack had always thought—
and said—it was a terrible waste of energy, but the habit had rubbed off,
and now he felt a vague guilt that the beds weren't made up with snowy
spotless bedclothes as Myra would have wanted . . .

Jack faltered from his half-drowse as Kim stood up. "I'm off to bed—
we could all do with a good night's sleep. In the morning we can decide
what to do." She smiled at him. "I'm sorry this has been such an upset for
you, Dad."

"Not to worry," said Jack. "Doesn't bother me at all." They murmured
good nights and went inside.

He looked out past the thing toward the blacker bulk of the mangroves,
whose canopies were visible above the grassy rise. He ought to be feeling
a measure of contentment by now. After all, he had wanted the kids to
come and solve the problem for him. But it seemed worse than ever. His
guts turned slowly inside him like an unsettled dog. "Blasted ham," he
muttered, and made his way to his bedroom.

The thing was still by the back steps as the next morning dawned bright
and still. Jack had hoped it might be gone. There was a touch of copper
in the sky that foretold heat, and gulls wheeled and squabbled over the
dunes. And the kids were just as bad, he thought acidly after breakfast.
He'd kept quiet, but the other three had argued for half an hour.

Jack Jr. wanted to ring the government straight away—for a while Jack
considered Kim might rip the telephone cord right out of the wall to stop
him. Kim, with a look of wide-eyed stubborn desperation, didn't want to
ring anyone—yet. Chris looked pompous and kept asking why not. They
had long involved conversations in which Jack understood maybe two
words in twenty.

He stood on the back verandah, frowning down at it, and listening to
the others who were still in the kitchen. He found its unchanging aspect
becoming more infuriating by the minute, sitting with a dull gray hole in

the middle of its nacreous lustre like some heathen idol whose diamond eye had been stolen.

"I'm going to do a bit of fishing," he announced as Jack Jr. began a lecture on the ethics of treason for the third time. He went to fetch his tackle, thinking with relish of the point at the mouth of the creek where the mangroves petered out, unable to establish a footing on the granite boulders that emerged from the sea, tossed and jumbled and slippery with the algae that attracted the fish . . .

"I'll come too," offered Jack Jr., coming to the door.

"No," said Jack, immediately changing his mind. "Going surf fishing. Only got one surf rod."

Jack Jr. shrugged and turned away, but not before Jack caught a smile directed at the others that looked distinctly patronizing to him. He pulled the lid of the freezer open, letting it thump against the wall, and rummaged through the frozen packets inside, clattering them and bringing the conversation to a stop.

He found the pack of bait and let the lid come crashing down as he stalked to the back verandah again. The silence behind him was immensely pleasing.

The surf rod, a twelve-foot length of finely finished bamboo, lay against the wall of the house at the back of the verandah. Jack scooped it up along with his tackle box and expertly maneuvered it around the railing as he went to the top of the stairs.

He heard Kim's voice as she walked out from the kitchen and turned to look back over his shoulder, holding the rod parallel to the ground.

"What is it?" he said.

"Dad, I'm terribly sorry things are turning out this way," she said. "But this thing is so important."

He was in no mood to be cajoled. He started down the steps, still looking back at her. "If you had any sense, girlie," he said, "you'd ring Stan Hollis and be done with the whole . . ."

Kim's cry was shrill. "Dad! Stop!"

He did. Immediately. And stood as frozen as if ice water had been dashed over him from an enormous bucket. The thing was behind him. Kim was staring past him at it. Her mouth was open. He could see the dim bobbing shapes of the men hurrying down the hallway in response to her call. Slowly he turned to face—what? Whatever it was, he'd rather know about it before it happened . . .

Jack was nonplussed. All that had happened was that because he hadn't been looking, he had speared the thing with the surf rod. Roughly five feet of it was still on his side, and what with the softness of the thing's shell he hadn't even noticed he'd done it. He looked back at Kim.

"What's the matter?" he said. "You put a bloody great hole in it. This shouldn't hurt it."

He started to back up the steps, to pull the rod out of it. "No, don't!" said Kim sharply. "How long is that rod?"

Jack placed the tackle box on the step beside him with an elaborate show of precision. Then he straightened and put his free hand on his hip. "I am on my way to go fishing. Why do you suddenly need to know how long my bloody rod is?"

"How long?" It was a breathy scream.

A chill came with it. Suddenly Jack was unsure, wavering beneath the intensity of her gaze. The hand holding the rod tingled, as if it expected the thing's insides, those nasty ropes of gray matter, to come creeping along the rod, engulfing his hand, then him . . .

"It's about . . . twelve feet or so," he said. He looked back at the creature, to assure himself that it and its insides were stationary.

Kim slipped lightly past him and ran round to the other side of it. "Then where's the rest of it?" she said.

The men reacted at once. Chris gave a long drawn-out "What?" and Jack Jr. said, "Hey?" and they both barged past Jack to join her.

Jack stood alone on the steps. Disbelief brought a deep flush to his face. "You mean," he said loudly, "You mean that bloody mongrel of a thing has et my rod?"

Kim waved at him distractedly. "Just a minute, Dad." She and Chris and Jack Jr. stared at their side of the thing, while Jack felt the uncertainty and fear of the previous day coalesce into a dull fury.

"Dad," called Kim, "Just back up slowly and pull the rod out as you go." Jack obliged, steeling himself for the sight of his prized, and now, in all likelihood, mangled rod. He backed up the stairs, across the verandah. The rod kept coming. He was just inside the hallway when its tip emerged, the rod whole and unscathed. Even the ferrules weren't bent, the line still threaded through them. He was relieved.

The other three watched silently. He waggled the tip of the rod at them triumphantly. "There," he said with satisfaction, "it wasn't et after all. Just as well. Good rods like this are scarce . . ."

Kim's voice sounded a little strangled as she broke in on him. "Could you bring the rod down here to us, Dad?"

Jack clutched it more tightly. "You're not going to do anything foolish with it, are you?"

"No, it'll be all right. Just bring it down here."

She wore that peculiar look of excitement again, as she had when she cut into the thing. Reluctantly Jack obeyed.

Chris took the rod as Jack came up to him, and Kim nodded. Without a word, Chris backed up and, placing the point of the rod in the center of the thing's side, walked slowly forward. It disappeared inexorably into it. Chris continued until the reel touched the surface.

He stood nose-to-nose with it, eighteen inches of handle in his hands, and looked questioningly at Kim and Jack Jr. They walked slowly around the thing while Jack watched, totally at a loss.

"Nothing," whispered Kim as they rejoined Chris. Jack Jr. nodded, bug-eyed.

"Where does it go?" said Kim, and there was such a wonderment in her eyes that Jack almost felt like weeping.

Kim and Chris and Jack Jr. sat in a tight circle in the sand near the thing, oblivious of the hot tropical sun arrowing its rays almost directly down on them. Jack had rescued his rod from Chris before they could think of any more experiments with it, put instead of going fishing, he had placed it back in its position on the verandah near the wall. He'd dumped his tackle box and, without a word to them, walked into the kitchen to replace the bait in the freezer, only more quietly than when he had got it out.

Now he sat on the top step of the back verandah smoking a cigarette, staring sometimes at the thing, which showed no sign of having had a bamboo rod thrust through its middle, and sometimes across to where the deep green mangrove leaves waved and an osprey glided regally along the creek, following its winding ways.

He was close enough to hear most of what his son and his daughter and her husband were saying, and somehow it was more frightening than the thing was, because there was even less in their talk that he could fathom, and it seemed to deal with things that were right outside the pale of nature as he understood it. This was a different fear, one that coiled coldly into a small bundle in the pit of his stomach, like a small fat death adder waiting to strike. It was like this with Myra . . .

"Granted it comes from somewhere," Kim was saying grimly. "If it comes from another dimension, then the rod must have gone into that dimension."

"*If*. Multiple dimensions are science fiction fodder," Chris objected. "Along with multiple realities and other escape clauses."

"So they are," said Kim. "So far. You can't test the reality of something until you have access to it. This thing is it. This is the entrance to the borderline between our universe, and someone else's."

"Look," said Chris, "there could be a hundred simple explanations—well, maybe not so simple, but convincing—explanations for what we saw. And that's all it was. Just us seeing something. No controlled laboratory conditions, no scientific measurements. We haven't even examined the rod to see if it's been altered internally, or on a molecular level."

(Jack hoped Chris didn't mean what it sounded like he meant.)

Kim raised her eyebrows. "All right," she said. "You're the writer. Give us an explanation."

Chris sat looking at his hands laced over his knees for a moment. "Well, maybe the interior of that thing reacts with the solidity of the rod . . . Maybe it makes it become soft and it curls round rather than goes through."

"It wasn't curly when we took it out," Jack Jr. pointed out.

"Maybe contact with the air makes it rigid again," said Chris, sweating. "Maybe lots of things." His voice rose. "So many things you just can't sit there and insist this thing leads to another dimension or reality or whatever."

Kim looked at him levelly. "It's the only thing that makes any sense."

Jack Jr. cleared his throat. Jack had been surprised by the change in Jack Jr. since this latest incident. He was less nervous, more interested. Even though he sat there in a T-shirt and shorts, Jack could see the businessman in him, calculating and speculating. He had found something here that he could connect with, something that might mean dollars, or whatever it was in business that Jack Jr. prized most highly. There was just a hint of that shark gleam in his eyes that Kim had worn earlier. It made Jack uncomfortable, and a bit sad.

"I think I'm on Kimmie's side," Jack Jr. said slowly. "If the rod didn't come out on the other side, then it went somewhere else." He held up his hand as Chris started to object. "No, I'm not saying it went into another dimension or shit like that. That's for you scientists and writers to theorize about. But there may be a coolie in China or a commuter in New York with a very sore arse because the rod went up it. That's what I'm interested in."

"Christ!" exclaimed Chris in disgust. "Now he wants to set up a fucking franchise in instantaneous teleportation!"

Jack, still on the steps and into his third cigarette, recoiled at the language. In front of Kim. *They should both be ashamed*, he thought. But it didn't seem to faze her, went right over her head . . . Jack sighed with regret for the loss of old-fashioned manners.

Chris tried once more. "Did your precious rumors say anything about other dimensions?" he challenged.

"No," said Kim. "Maybe I've gone further already than the researchers have."

"You!" Chris laughed bitterly. "Your father's found everything, and what he didn't find was accidental. You haven't had anything to do with it."

Kim went as white as a sheet with anger. Her voice was as tightly controlled as a bedspring as she turned her back on Chris and said loudly to the others, "What I want to do next is send something organic through it."

"Jesus no!" Chris was aghast. "You can't . . ."

Kim looked at him over her shoulder, and her face softened. "Not me—that's what you thought, didn't you?" she said. "You thought I wanted to go . . ."

A wave of sympathy rolled over Jack. He knew how Chris felt, because that's what he'd thought she meant, too.

"Silly," said Kim to Chris, although her eyes were on the thing, not on him. "I don't intend to do anything that crazy." *Not right now*, thought Jack, *but maybe later. . . .*

"Look, Kim," said Chris earnestly. "This independent stuff has gone on long enough. You've got something really weird here, and yes, maybe you've already found out some important stuff about it. So please—let's just report it and let someone else worry about it."

There was a regrouping in the circle, although no one moved. It looked to Jack now that Kim and Jack Jr. were on one side, Chris on the other. *I wonder if I should go down and even things up?* he mused. But a deep weariness in his heart told him that, in their eyes, he wouldn't count.

"Someone else worry about fame?" said Kim softly. She threw a fleeting sideways glance at Jack Jr. "And money?"

Oh, she knows the strings to pull, thought Jack dully. He got up, intending to check out the amount of beer left in the fridge, which seemed the only sensible thing to do at this stage.

Kim rose too, and ran up the steps to him. "Dad," she said, "I need an animal. Are there any cats, or maybe dogs around here?"

Jack stopped and stared at her, truly shocked. "You're not going to put a good animal into there!" he said.

Kim put an arm around him. "It's for science, Dad." Her voice was low and wheedling. "It's worth it."

Jack pulled away, disgusted that at the age of almost forty, she would act like a child to get her way with him. Disgusted with himself, because he knew it worked.

"Never mind cats and dogs," he said gruffly. "Would a toad do?"

"Yes, fine," she said, her eyes gleaming again.

He walked stiffly round to the shady side of the house where the rain-water tank sat on a wooden stand. The dripping from the tank kept the sand moist and clumps of grass grew more greenly here. He thrust his hand into the dimness and straightened. "Here," he said.

The toad blinked itself out of sleep, its golden eyelids half-closed. It squirmed in his grip, huge and fat as lard, the lumpy glands behind its head weeping a thick white poisonous syrup.

"The rod's too flexible," said Kim. "It won't take its weight. Do you have a longish piece of timber around, Dad?"

Jack sighed. If there was only something he couldn't supply them with, then maybe they'd quit this nonsense. But if he said no, they'd scout around and jury-rig something up.

"Under the house," he said. "There's a good long plank from when I painted the house last. Send Jack in for it. He might as well do some of the dirty work."

Jack Jr. found the sawhorses, too. Jack had known he would. They made it easier still. He sat on the top step again, this time cradling a Stubby, and watched.

Kim said they were testing whether going through to the "other side," as she called it, would harm a living creature. Jack hoped fervently that it would. That the toad would come back squashed, or maybe suffocated because the air was bad there, or just keeled over from shock. Anything that would discourage Kim . . .

The toad was in a cage of chicken wire nailed to the end of the plank by Jack Jr.—a sloppy job, but the toad was neither slim nor agile enough to slip out. Once settled in the hot sun, it dozed off again.

Jack watched as Chris—reluctantly—and Jack Jr.—more eagerly—slid the plank across the sawhorses. The toad disappeared into the virus-thing without opposition; its surface molded neatly around the plank without gaps. The men pushed until only a foot of the plank rested on the second sawhorse. It was a fourteen-foot piece of timber, and heavy. They had to push down to keep it from tipping up, now that there was—supposedly—no support at the other end. The muscles in their arms corded, and even Jack Jr. was sweating, though nothing like Chris.

"Give it ten seconds," said Kim, standing to one side like an army instructor.

It was a long ten seconds.

Then they pulled the timber back, and the wire and the toad emerged. They set the plank down and clustered silently with Kim at the cage. Jack could see nothing. *God damn*, he thought. *They could at least tell me . . .* Curiosity overcame his reluctance, and he went down to join them.

It was the worst possible result. The toad blinked as Kim shoved a twig through the wire and poked it. When she persisted, it opened and closed its mouth, made ineffectual hopping movements with its back legs, and its poison glands swelled.

Kim's expression was exultant, and Jack Jr. grinned broadly. "Son of a bitch!" he exclaimed. Chris darted quick glances at them, his face white, and Jack realized the man was terrified. Jack wondered if it was because he was a writer that he knew this was a bad thing. His respect for his son-in-law grew.

"Twenty seconds," commanded Kim. Jack looked at Chris, hoping he'd object, say a flat "No." But that wouldn't work; if Chris refused, Kim would take his place with her brother, hefting the plank into position . . . It wouldn't change a thing. Chris joined Jack Jr. at the end of the plank.

The same result. The toad returned unhurt and functioning. To Jack, its squat ugly face wore an expression of mystification and exasperation, that was all.

Kim took a deep breath. "Once more, a minute," she said.

This time, Chris did try to argue.

"Listen," he said rapidly. "You can't surmise anything from this. You know that; you're trained. Surface appearances mean nothing. Its insides might be ruined, its brains scrambled. It could be poisoned right this minute, dying. It could have picked up a bacterium that's killing it while we're watching. Damn it, you know that!"

There was the tiniest flicker of doubt in Kim's wide eyes. Then she shook herself. "One minute," she repeated.

Evening approached. They sat at the kitchen table drinking coffee. A cooling southerly breeze had sprung up; it came through the front door and brushed past them on the way to the back steps and the virus-thing.

They were still talking. It seemed to Jack he had never heard so much talk in one day, especially so much that went right over his head. But he thought he was getting the general drift.

"Well, suppose just for now that it is a virus," Chris was saying. "There are several different theories on the source of viruses. No one's satisfactorily explained their place in the scheme of things yet.

"There's one school that explains them as genetic material gone astray in early evolution, another that they drift down constantly from space. They're an enigma because they don't quite fit the labels 'living' and 'non-living' and are hard to classify. I don't know if anyone's seriously proposed that they come from another dimension, probably because there's never been any proof that alternate dimensions exist."

"Hang on," interjected Jack Jr. "Aren't you the one who was arguing against other dimensions before?"

Chris nodded, wiping his forehead with his handkerchief and meticulously refolding it. "That's right. And I'm still certainly not convinced they exist. I'm not convinced that thing is a gigantic virus, either. But we have a situation here with several inexplicables, and I'm trying to tie them together in a way that makes sense of them."

Jack thought that was clever. If Chris could explain things with words, maybe Kim would stop her investigations.

Chris continued, "This thing is an entrance to somewhere—on the borderline between us and somewhere else. Objects go through this . . . virus to a place we can't see—call it another dimension, another plane of reality, an alternate universe, whatever. That means that not only is it connected to this other dimension, but it's probably the thing's place of origin."

Kim said "I think we can discount Earth—anywhere on Earth—as its source. But why would a virus—if it is a virus—come from there, from this other dimension? And one like that, so large it's functionless?"

"I think it was a mistake," said Chris.

"Why would you call it that?" asked Kim, watching Chris with utter fascination.

"Well," he said with a shaky laugh, "now it's 'what-if' time. What if there are beings in this other place who are responsible for sending viruses into our world—hell, maybe the viruses are the beings. But if our viruses come from there, maybe they dispatch viruses to other worlds or realities or whatever. What if that virus was meant for somewhere else, where it would be the right size to infect a cell?"

Jack got up quietly and went to the fridge for a beer. There was only one left, and he opened it at the sink with a loud pop and a fizz that reminded him of the virus-thing coming up behind him. . . .

"Hush, Dad," said Kim absently.

"Or what if their machinery went haywire, and produced a virus that's no use to them at all?" Chris shook his head, his mouth stretched into a painful grin. Drops of sweat fell onto his shirt, dissolving into dark, spreading spots. "Viruses. We've been fighting back over the last hundred years. New drugs, vaccines, interferon. But as we overcome one, like smallpox with vaccine, new and more insidious ones appear. Suddenly. Look at the Kawasaki syndrome. And they mutate, as with AIDS. It isn't too hard to imagine viruses doing so well if there's intelligence behind their creation, is it?"

"Bullshit," said Jack Jr. belligerently. "You catch viruses from other people."

"Of course you do," Chris said impatiently. "That's part of their very efficient mechanism. Their only goal is to create more viruses to infect more people. But the original virus, the archetype . . . Like the ones that are turning up here now . . ."

"Still bullshit," said Jack Jr. But it looked to Jack that he believed it enough to be frightened.

Kim was gazing into the distance. "The virus is open-ended," she said slowly. "If we can send objects through it into that dimension . . . Oh, that reminds me, where is that toad?"

Jack took a long swig of beer. "I let it go," he said.

"Let it go? Oh, Dad!" Kim's shoulders slumped. "A million toads out there and he lets this one go . . ." She shook her head and resumed. "Maybe all viruses are open-ended—the ones that get into our cells and give us diseases. Maybe they transfer the energy of the dying cell to the other dimension. Maybe we're just an energy source, tapped by the beings in the other dimension . . ."

Jack put his empty Stubby on the table and stood up abruptly. The others glanced up. "Are you all right, Dad?" said Kim.

"Fine, fine," he muttered. There was no Fourex left in the fridge, he remembered. "I'm going into Kuttabul to the pub."

Kim looked apprehensive. "You won't say anything about this, will you?"

Jack snorted. Little green men—well, nobody had said exactly that, but that was what they meant—little green men sending viruses into the world . . . "No, Kimmie," he said at last. "It's not something I'd want to talk about."

He descended the front steps and went toward the shed where the ancient Ford ute was parked. Bullshit, all of it. Jack Jr. was right. He revved the old engine angrily, clashed it into gear and wavered down the road, past the beachfront where the outgoing tide had left the yellow sand damp and fresh and unmarked except for the tracks of a questing curlew.

Bullshit, but that didn't mean Kimmie didn't mean to try to go through the thing, the virus, like the rod and the toad had. She meant to go, he knew that, into a place where little green men made viruses to torment real people. And she was stubborn, he knew that, too.

Sand sprayed from the wheels as he jammed the accelerator to the floor.

Jack was on his fourth beer, comfortably propped at the bar. He took long, easy drafts and thought back to the hospital.

The doctor had said, and Jack remembered it very clearly, even if his memory wasn't so hot on other things nowadays, that if it had been a bacteriological infection, which Jack took to mean an ordinary germ, they could have fought it. But it was a virus. Viruses couldn't be fought.

Sure, transplant a liver, operate on a *heart*, that was okay, that was *easy*. Jack had said that to them, angry at them with a fury underpinned with grief. But fight a virus? No, too hard. He had hated that doctor.

And so Myra had died . . . of a virus.

He slammed the glass on the counter and called Ron, the publican, for another. Stan Hollis came through the door. Jack glanced at his watch and saw it was okay, afterhours for the policeman. Good old Stan, always honest. No drinking while on duty for him, not like that sod before him who just about lived at the pub—that's where you rang first if you wanted a policeman then . . .

Jack wondered idly if things would have turned out differently if he'd followed his instincts and rung Stan when the virus-thing first arrived. He picked up his beer and went over to the table where the policeman was sitting and settled himself into the opposite chair.

"Hi, Stan," he said.

Stan nodded. "G'day, Jack."

Jack put his elbows on the table and leaned across it.

"I got a virus, Stan," he confided.

"Sorry to hear that, mate," said Stan. "How bad is it?"

"Oh, it's fine—except for the hole Kimmie put in it," said Jack. "That doesn't look too good."

Stan stared at him. "Been to the doctor with it?"

"No," Jack assured him. "Left it at home. Kim and Jack Jr. say it's the best place for it right now."

Stan cleared his throat and leaned over the table too. "Jack," he said, "how many have you had?"

Jack felt a momentary confusion. That was what Kim had accused him of yesterday. Why did they all mix up the virus with how many beers he'd had?

"Did you drive here?" Stan went on when Jack didn't answer. He was just about to tell Stan that no, he wouldn't drive, he'd ring the house and get them to pick him up, when he felt a hand on his shoulder.

He looked up into Kim's face, which was stiff and unsmiling. His cheeks grew hot.

"Hello, Kim," he said weakly, and took another sip of beer. Kim spoke abruptly to Stan. "Don't worry, we'll get him home."

She'd heard that, then. Had she heard the rest, heard him babbling about the virus-thing? Suddenly Jack was stone-cold sober, and the beer tasted flat. He stood up and nodded farewell to Stan, who winked at him in reply.

Chris was outside in the rented car, waiting. He looked embarrassed, as if he didn't really want to be there at all. "We thought you might need a lift home," Kim said. "I'll drive the ute."

"I'm all right," said Jack. He tried to make it sound dignified. "I can drive."

Kim hesitated. "I only had one or two," he added.

"All right," she said, stepping back. "I'll ride with you."

"No thank you," said Jack. "I want to think a bit on my own, if you don't mind."

"Whatever you want, Dad . . ."

He watched Kim go around to the passenger side of the car and get in. Her movements were brusque and he could feel the anger controlling them. They backed out onto the road and set off toward the beach road. Jack was left with his hand in the air, midway through an indecisive wave.

Oh, Kim, he thought, *you're going to do it, aren't you? You won't listen to your father. . . .*

Remarkably, the drive through the salt-laden fresh breeze did feel good. Jack felt more relaxed than he'd been since the morning he'd gone crabbing. Yesterday. *And didn't that seem a long time ago,* he pondered, the old utility snorting and bumping under him.

The sea to his right was graying as far as the horizon in sympathy with the twilight sky above it. It was the right time of day to review the events since the advent of the thing, a time for a man to think in private, slowly, and to make plans without anyone spouting long involved words at him, bewildering him. The most important thing was to stop Kimmie going into the virus-world; the very thought of it brought with it a sense of despair that crushed his chest.

Jack Jr. and Chris were no help. However much they disliked or distrusted the virus-thing, they didn't seem able to stand up to Kim.

There was only one thing left that he could do.

Jack skidded through the sand in front of the house. Kim and Chris were on the front verandah. He waved as he turned into the yard, but instead of driving to the shed, he yanked the gearstick into low and slowly trundled around the side of the house toward the back yard.

He saw Kim, with a look of surprise on her face, disappear up the hallway, and guessed she meant to catch up with him at the back. He smiled humorlessly to himself. Probably worried he'd run over her bloody virus. Wouldn't take the chance of ruining the ute with it. He turned the Ford into a right angle, parallel with the back of the house and edged toward the back steps until the bonnet of the ute was three feet or so from the thing's bulging side. He switched off the engine.

"Dad!" he heard Kim's panicky shout in the sudden silence. She was on the back verandah, leaning over it, her hands white from clasping the railing so tightly. Chris joined her. Jack grinned up at them with deliberate vacuity and clambered out of the cabin.

"What's the matter?" he said, squinting.

Kim looked perplexed, and glanced at Chris. Her hands relaxed as she straightened. "I just wondered why you drove around here, of all places," she said.

"Thought I'd park the ute out of the wind. Salt, y'know." He gestured toward the beach. "Salt's blowing in from the sea. No point in making the rust any worse than it is." He looked directly at her. "Okay?"

"Fine, Dad. I just wondered, that's all." She glanced at Chris, whose expression was unreadable. They turned to drift into the hallway. Jack caught a whispered ". . . funny since Mum died . . ." and shrugged. Let them think what they liked.

The sun was nearly set, throwing his shadow across the verandah rail, making a complicated mosaic of white paint and black shadow. Beside him, the thing's inner glow was shimmering into brightness with the oncoming darkness and looking into it, Jack shivered in the warm sea breeze. He gave the bonnet of the ute a reassuring pat as he walked past it to the steps.

Kim had found a mound of mincemeat in the freezer and made what Myra used to call a "mince mess" for dinner, throwing whatever was handy—tinned, frozen or fresh—into it, flavoring it with curry powder and serving it over rice. Its smell brought with it a wave of nostalgia for Jack. It seemed to bring Myra very close and, tonight, that felt like a good thing.

No one mentioned the thing at all through dinner, and it wasn't till they were clearing away the plates that Chris asked Kim what she intended to do tomorrow.

"Oh, just some more experiments," she said lightly.

Chris nodded and turned away. Jack Jr. looked exasperated. "Well, count me out," he said. "I've had enough of it."

"Of course," said Kim coolly. "You don't even have to be there. First thing in the morning . . ."

Jack rinsed a plate, picking at grains of yellow curry rice with his fingernails. First thing in the morning . . . He had a suspicion that first thing in the morning meant one thing to city people—and that was what Kim and Chris and Jack Jr. were, city people—and something quite different to him. It might give him just a slight advantage.

Dawn was only a hint of paler black on the horizon when Jack shuffled quietly out onto the front verandah. He chose that route—down the front stairs and around the house—to avoid passing the spare bedrooms where the others still slept soundly.

He wore his fishing gear, flannelette shirt and long khaki pants, still stained with mangrove mud from the crabbing trip. He didn't know how messy the journey might be, and it would be a shame to ruin better clothes.

He paused in the front yard to roll a smoke and light it, dragging deeply and appreciating the pale gray curl wavering across the star-sprinkled velvet overhead. He'd started many a morning like this, rod in hand and creel over a shoulder, Myra waving him off after a hearty breakfast . . .

The gentle radiance of the thing made it clearly visible in the predawn darkness. The ute loomed next to it, a larger hulking shadow. All was still. The morning breeze had not yet come in and no birds called. Jack loved this time of day. Everything felt new and unused, and soon the implacable light of the rising sun would reveal the world's freshness, and the birds would chorus in wonder at it.

He coughed violently into his arm to muffle the sound. *Oh well*, he thought, throwing the fag end away and wiping his eyes. *Best get on with it.*

He fetched the sawhorses and set them between the front of the Ford and the oily surface of the thing. The sand deadened the sound of his steps. The plank had been left on the ground nearby, and he grunted as he lifted one end of it. This was the difficult part.

He grappled with it until he had it in place, propped over the saw-horses. It was hard work, all right. He straightened and pulled in some deep breaths, flexing his arms. Had to be done, though. If you went straight into that thing, well, you didn't know where it was on the other side, did you? It might be halfway up a wall, like a light switch, and you'd fall right out of it. Or over a cliff, and you'd never be able to find it again to get out.

No, you had to go in on the plank, to give you something to hold on to, because goodness knows what you'd find there. Jack was proud of having worked that out all by himself; Kim hadn't said it, nor Chris. "Funny since Mum died" indeed. He was still pretty bright when he needed to be.

With renewed vigor, he grabbed the other end of the plank, lifted it, and pushed. It slid silently and neatly through the side of the virus and disappeared, sending a shudder up his spine. But he persevered.

Soon he was using all his weight to hold down his end of the timber, and he gritted his teeth and guided it under the bumper bar of the ute. He had to push the sawhorse down into the loose sand a little and, what with putting downward pressure on the plank, and sideways pressure to wedge it into position, he was sweating and trembling when it was done.

He stood back for a while, letting the heavy thudding of his heart ebb to a rate more approximating normal. He would've dearly loved another cigarette, but the air was lightening all the time and a fig-bird was issuing its first tentative calls from the bush inland. No excuses. It might be getting close to what Kim called "first thing."

Jack climbed onto the plank and knelt, his feet against the front of the ute, his hands clasped firmly around the edges of the timber. It felt good and solid. *Might be a bit springy at the other end*, he thought, *but still solid.*

The greasy-looking surface of the virus-thing with its gleaming interior heat-lightning was right in front of his nose. This was the part that Jack knew he would hate most, no matter what happened on the other side— pushing through the horrid unearthly substance of the thing. The toad had done it, he argued. He could do what a toad did, surely, although a toad could hardly be said to have much of a sense of refinement . . . He swallowed bile, and wished he'd had a cup of nice strong tea to settle his stomach first.

He took a deep breath—what if it *was* poisonous in there? How long can a cane-toad hold its breath? He squeezed his eyes shut and took another breath and forced his hands to move forward, to pull him crawling through the virus, away from dawn's growing radiance.

The sensation was not unpleasant, he noted with surprise. It wasn't slimy or clammy, just firm, as if he wore a tight-fitting set of corsets, only all over. With his eyes tightly closed, and not able to see the strange lights or the ugly viscosity, it wasn't too bad at all. He took heart and crawled more confidently along the plank until—

The sense of pressure vanished on his head and hands, and Jack knew he had broken through. There was a good bit of plank ahead—although he cautioned himself not to overestimate it; it would be terrible to fall off the end before he even got started. So he moved carefully forward, and was entirely free of the virus-thing's embrace before he dared to open his eyes and his mind to the impressions of the other dimension.

There was a low roaring in his ears. There were whirling orange and red lights in front of his eyes. The skin of his face prickled with pins and needles, as if the outer layer of flesh was withering. He felt as if he was tumbling through space forever and only the wood under his hands and knees felt real, so he clung to it fiercely. Above all, he felt terror.

Jack had never imagined fear like this. It was a gut-wrenching combination of the fear you would feel swimming in the creek with a croc right behind you; the wooden helplessness of losing Myra; the fear of cancer crawling remorselessly through your innards. All fears rolled into one, and eating at you.

He crouched there for what felt like long minutes, not even sure if he was breathing because he couldn't feel that, either. His eyes were wide-open—he could feel the skin around them stretching—groping desperately for something other than the whirls and zigzags that assaulted them. He was helpless, totally helpless, and he waited for the virus-people to take hold of him and wrench him from the plank, his sole connection with his world.

But nothing happened, nothing like that.

Gradually Jack's terror-numbed mind thawed. It was as if it was split in two, and the frightened Jack-mind screamed quietly in a corner while the normal Jack-mind began to think sensibly again.

He realized that the sounds in his ears like surf crashing on the beach came from his ears; it was the normal inside sound you seldom hear except in the quietest night because other sounds, the sounds of living, mask it. It was the sound of no sound at all.

And the lights weren't real. They were like the lights you see against your eyelids when you close your eyes and rub them. He was seeing absolutely nothing because there was nothing for his eyes to see.

Then it came to Jack with stupendous clarity that he was wrong. That he was seeing nothing, hearing nothing, feeling nothing, not because there was nothing to see in this strange place, nothing to hear or feel, but because his senses did not work here. This was a place meant for other senses, different ones, ones he did not possess. Truly another dimension, with nothing human about it, and he loathed it with a suddenly awesome passion. This was the only place in God's creation that could produce something as cruel as a virus.

"*Myra,*" he whispered, or thought he whispered. It was what he meant, no matter how it came out here.

Here. The makers of the virus were here. For all he knew, Jack could be surrounded by them. Maybe he was in the middle of a shiny white laboratory, or a huge factory filled with thumping machinery. On the other hand, perhaps he was in their equivalent of an empty room, or a grassy plain with no one in sight. Still, he had come here with one purpose, and he was determined to go ahead with it.

"You out there," he said loudly, over the roaring in his ears. "I know I can't see you, and I don't know if you're there, or if you can hear me. But I'm going to say one thing.

"Cut it out!" His voice wavered a bit, and he waited for a response, thinking that he probably wouldn't recognize a response if it did happen, but that was the polite thing to do.

Nothing altered in his world of sensory deprivation, so he pressed on.

"You been making those viruses and shoving them into our world. It's not right, and it's not fair. They hurt people, and they hurt me. So you've got to stop."

It was his heart that almost stopped then, as he felt a movement, a vibration in his hands, and he was so frightened he almost let go of the plank. Then he realized it *was* the plank; it was being moved, and he thought it was moving backward which meant Jack Jr. and Chris were pulling him out . . .

"You killed Myra! he shouted. "That was wrong, you had no right! You've got to cut it . . ."

". . . out." Jack squeezed his eyes shut against the dazzling sunlight, feeling tears trickling down his cheeks. Strong hands were holding him, pulling him from his hold on the plank, which was just as well, as Jack realized his muscles were like jellyfish tentacles and he could hardly stand up.

Brutal noises attacked his eardrums, and he fended them off with raised arms. Gradually they quieted to a tolerable level and became words, and squinting through the tears, he made out Kim's face, as bleached of color as an overexposed photograph, her lips moving. He gave a lop-sided grin.

"I told them, Kimmie," he tried to say, but the words came out slurred and formless, and she made shushing signals at him. He looked up at Jack Jr., who was holding him, and was surprised to see tears in his eyes, too.

This time his mouth and tongue worked. "Sun is bright, isn't it?" he mumbled.

"You miserable old bastard," Jack Jr. half-laughed, half-sobbed. "What in the hell did you think you were doing?" He led Jack over to the steps where he sagged down, amazed at how tired his body felt.

The others clamored at him. "Are you all right?" "How do you feel?" The fuss pleased him fleetingly.

"Could do with a fag," he said hopefully, looking at the circle of faces surrounding him.

"In a minute," Kim said. Her color had returned, or maybe he was getting used to the light again; it was hard to tell. But her expression was still truly alarmed, almost horrified. "Dad, something dreadful might have happened to you. I'm so sorry—"

"Leave it for now," said Jack Jr. brusquely. "Let him get his breath back."

A faint whine of engines interrupted them. They looked up to see a khaki-colored helicopter flying swiftly along the beach. Farther off, a dust storm on the beach road signaled a convoy of vehicles.

Kim stared open-mouthed, then looked accusingly at Chris. He nodded. "I called them last night, after you'd gone to bed. I couldn't let you do it, Kim."

She was white with anger, biting her lips. She looked like someone at the beginning of a marathon run, all tensed up and rearing to go. Jack had to admire her grit.

Jack Jr. moved away from the group, staring at the oncoming cars. "You can't hide it," he pointed out. "Might as well let them have it peacefully."

The helicopter buzzed overhead, circling the paddock, looking for a landing place. Kim's shoulders slumped. Then she turned and sat down on the step next to Jack. "Quick, Dad," she said, her voice low but intense enough to hear clearly over the noise of the motors, "what did you see?"

He wanted very much to tell Kim what he'd done, although it all seemed a little muddy and confused now that he tried to think about it, and the clattering of the 'copter's blades didn't help.

"Dad?" Her eyes had that unwavering radiance in them that he always thought was her prettiest feature.

He tried to marshal his thoughts. "I had to stop you, Kimmie. Stop you going there." She looked stricken. "And when Chris said the people there made viruses, well, I thought about your mum. And then I *wanted* to go in."

"Oh, Dad, that was only a theory, an idea . . ."

The sounds became too loud. They couldn't hear each other even with shouting. Kim looked regretful and stood up, facing toward the line of cars that had come round to the back to park. Jack noticed Stan Hollis in his patrol car.

Chris went over to Kim and put his arm around her. As the motors cut out and the noises diminished, he said, "They'll probably want us, too. To make statements." They were joined by Jack Jr. "At least they'll need me now," said Kim fiercely.

Jack sighed and got up, feeling distinctly shaky. It was his house, his duty to greet visitors, although he felt a touch uneasy about the several soldiers who were jumping out of the landed helicopter. He walked over to the police car.

"G'day, Stan," he said.

"G'day, Jack," replied Stan. He took a piece of paper from his shirt pocket. "Sorry to trouble you, mate, but it looks like I have to impound some sort of animal you've got here—at least that's what it looks like."

"That's okay," said Jack readily, "We've finished with it."

The soldiers manhandled the virus-thing, now on a platform and covered with a camouflage tarpaulin, into the helicopter. Jack was not sorry to see it go.

There had been a great deal of stern conversation between the men who had poured out of the cars and Kim and Jack Jr. and Chris, and from time to time, Jack could hear one or all of their voices raised in angry protest. No one seemed interested in him—and heck, thought Jack woundedly, I was the one who went through there—and Kim underlined it by saying at one stage to the man who seemed to be most in charge, "It's no use asking Dad anything. He's getting on, and frankly, he didn't understand any of it anyway."

The man had scrutinized him suspiciously, and Jack suddenly lost interest in talking to him about his expedition, even if Kim had wanted him to. He rolled a cigarette, staring blankly back at the man. "G'day," he said, nodding, and the man turned away dismissively.

Now they were herding everyone into the cars. The sun beat down on the roofs and hoods slicing slivers of brilliance from them. Kim came over to kiss him lightly. "We'll finish our holiday in a little while, Dad. Promise."

"I'll be waiting," said Jack. Then softly, so only she could hear, "I told them, Kimmie. The virus-people. I told them to stop."

She stared at him, puzzled, for a moment. Then a poignant realization came into her face, and her eyes grew bright with tears. She hugged him briefly, smiled, and was in the car.

Jack watched the cavalcade dwindle along the beachfront road, a surprisingly stabbing loneliness hitting his gut. The ute, the sawhorses and plank, and a trampled patch of sand were the only signs that a gateway to another dimension had visited briefly. You never know, he marveled, what's ahead. He sighed. Still, he could look forward to the kids returning for a real holiday, and it would give him more time for some crabbing—and time to change the sheets. Myra will like that, he thought, and grinned. . . .

TERRY DOWLING

Terry Dowling began publishing fiction in Australian fanzines in the 1970s and became a professional writer in the early 1980s, starting out in the Australian magazine *Omega*. By 1990, when his first book appeared, he had won the Australian Science Fiction Achievement Award (the Ditmar) for fiction more times than any other Australian writer. His most famous and significant work to date is the cycle of stories (reprinted in three volumes: *Rynosseros* (1990), *Blue Tyson* (1992), and *Twilight Beach* (1993) concerning Tom Tyson (aka Tom Rynosseros), who is probably the most popular recurring character after A. Bertram Chandler's Grimes to emerge from Australian SF.

Like Ray Bradbury, who is clearly one of his influences, Dowling prefers the form of the short story, and the book of linked stories is his preferred long form. He has published no novels to date. Other significant influences on Dowling include the J. G. Ballard of the *Vermillion Sands* stories—Dowling wrote his master's thesis in the 1970s on Ballard, Jack Vance, and Cordwainer Smith. Dowling's major sequence constructs a myth of the Australian future that is specific and local. Yet his fiction to date has had little impact outside of Australia, in spite of its evident achievements—and of the efforts of Harlan Ellison, among others, to trumpet his substantial literary virtues to the rest of the SF world. In recent years he has turned more toward the horror genre in his short fiction.

This story is one of the finest of the Tyson cycle.

Usually the house sang. It was built to make music out of the seven winds that found it on its desert rise. Vents in the walls, cunning terraces, cleverly angled embrasures in the canted terrazo facings drew them in; three spiral core shafts tuned them into vortices and descants, threw them across galleries, flung them around precise cornices and carefully filigreed escarpments so that more than anything the house resembled the ancient breathing caves of the Nullarbor.

Which many said was Cheimarrhos's intention, that his great granite and limestone pylon was nothing less than an inverted network of caves set in the sky, chimneys and vaults and inclines in a structure such as Sumer must have seen, or Ur of the Chaldees, or Teoteochan of the Toltecs. Paul Cheimarrhos called his house Balin, and on the day he finally showed me the roof-field there was a stillness on the red sand beyond the large deep-set windows, a lull I could not help but take personally, knowing Paul as I did, as an omen of some sort, as if my presence had caused it to be.

And, accordingly, as if unable to bear that terrible quiet, the middle-aged, incredibly vital Three-line tycoon talked about winds. Obliquely but inevitably. As we walked along the polished limestone corridor of Gallery 52, Paul rounded on me yet again, fixed me with his piercing blue gaze.

"When was the last time, Tom?"

"Only the once, Paul, three years ago. You used to come out to the coasts. I was here for the Anderlee hearings, but never got this far up. There were too many of us."

"The Anderlee thing, yes. I'm sorry." The polite show of regret quickly vanished from his eyes. He was too excited. "Then if so, this makes up for it. Today is unusual, Tom. We usually get one of the four. The brinraga reaches this far north, and leftovers from the angry red-sky larrikin. I tune them down to gentle houseguests, mere palimpsests. Balin can do it. I'm so glad you're here."

We reached a corner window and looked out on the desert once more, but on a new vista entirely, stretching red and empty to the horizon.

"We even get spill-off from the sanalatti at this latitude, can you believe it? The experts say it's impossible but I know better. It's why Tyrren and I chose this spot, this exact place. I know the Soul when I feel it. Those scatterlings are unmistakable."

We stood looking out on the empty desert and I couldn't help but wonder how he did view my presence. Portentously, no doubt—the visitor who had arrived on the first windless day in four months.

"Are you familiar with the name Memnon?" he asked.

Knowing Paul Cheimarrhos's interest in antiquities and the ancient Mediterranean civilizations, I welcomed the change of subject.

"One of Alexander's generals?"

But of course Paul had been talking winds. He laughed, throwing back his thick mane of silver hair so it shifted like a magnesium shower along the shoulders of his cobalt house robe.

"You are thinking of the general who led the Persian Greeks at Granicus. No, I mean the Colossi of Memnon, Tom. Two seated statues of Amenophis III on the Nile banks near Thebes. Some still believe they were designed so the sunrise and sunset winds made them sing . . ."

"Sing?"

"A plaintive hooting song, yes. But that was an accident, nothing more than a freak thing. Others claim the Great Pyramid sang before it was sealed, that the engineering equations covered that. Some say Djoser's pyramid at Saqqara did the same, that Architect Imhotep was master of the micro-zephyrs, expert in a whole secret art of hierocantrics. These tales are apocryphal. Balin exists and does all this. David Tyrren worked with me on it."

I made a sound of acknowledgment to show him I knew what pretty well anyone did, that the great architect had worked on the house, pylon, monument—though I knew that Paul had done all the initial layouts himself. It was his own design, despite the careful elaboration that had made the design a reality.

We were walking again because that filled the silences, turning up into Gallery 55-B, working our way to the final upper levels, to the elaborate totemic roof-field at the pylon's crest where the wind-banks stood and the rows of strange acroteria were laid out like memorial pieces in a graveyard in the sky.

I needed to see that field, to find out if Paul Cheimarrhos had in fact done what David Tyrren suspected, and had—after much agonizing—revealed to Council at long last. It seemed I was in time.

Gallery 55-B was blind, no windows there to show the desert and sky in its twin infinite registers of red and blue, just cool limestone and granite—part of a wind-race when the vents and conduits were aligned and operating.

The whole truncated pyramid of Balin was a wind-trap, a man-made mesa over three hundred meters high, full of cave-chambers—every one part of some cunning, precisely reckoned equation—and with a "cemetery" field on its flattened crest. With its canted sides, its cavetto cornice and taurus molding, it did look very much like the pylon of some great ancient temple gate never completed, never given its companion pylon or connecting wall, with no temple precinct at its back.

We turned into the wide transverse apron of Gallery 60, and there it was, laid out before us under the hot blue sky: the summit field set all over with shimmering, totemlike acroteria, tall blank ceramic and stone pillars, some elaborately painted, others bone white and glaring in the sunlight, pierced with fibrile openings, set with airfoils and sonic wires.

It was exhilarating to see it all at last, and deeply disturbing—for at the very center was a shallow basin, like a radar dish thirty meters across, and at the middle of that, so I believed, so Tyrren had confirmed, Paul Cheimarrhos's great act of sacrilege.

The twenty-six wooden burial poles were ancient, without doubt the undeclared cache stolen from the Vatican collection decades ago, smuggled back into Australia in ones and twos, hidden in black market havens, finally incorporated into Balin, perhaps the ultimate purpose of the place, though I quickly put that fancy aside. It was hardly likely—the idea was a measure of my own reaction to being here at last, to seeing the forbidden relics set up so boldly on this vast open deck.

Each post had its special ceramic cap, making it safe from orbital surveillance. Tribal comsats scanning the site saw nothing more than a shallow dish set with one more group of aerodynamic wind-posts. The angle of curvature of that depression had to make oblique scanning impossible as well.

Paul stepped down on to the flat roof-field, looking for all the world like some notable out of antiquity with his blue robe and silver hair, a Chaldean prince or an Akkadian merchant atop a ziggurat in ancient Ur or Sumer. Or again—allowing my fancies free rein, trying for the composure

I needed—some of the acroteria, the totemic signs carved on them, took me half a world away—from Mesopotamia to Meso-America, and I imagined I was an Aztec priest in jaguar headdress and cloak of human skin stepping out to officiate at a ceremony to Chac Mool. Balin invited such notions.

I was hurrying ahead now, heart pounding, so that Paul was following me, making no attempt at all to keep me from the depression at the center. He did want me to see it.

Only when I remembered what hung in the sky high above us did I slow my pace, force myself to look less eager, more the casual visitor overwhelmed by this magnificent display.

Slowly, more slowly, I completed a gradual arc toward my real goal, giving Paul time to catch up. Then, together again, our footsteps ringing on the limestone flagging, we made our way to the very edge of the dish and looked down at the cluster of poles at the center.

"Every now and then," I said, quietly in the vast expanse of air and light, "a National does something like this. Luna Geary. Tony Wessex. Dominic Quint. If we're lucky, Council learns of it before the tribes do. And I hope we're lucky this time, Paul, though I doubt it."

"The tribes who made those poles died out long ago, Tom. Bloodlines lost, only revenant DNA trace, languages forgotten. This is as fitting a place for them as any."

"How we see it isn't important, you know that. It's what they think. Every act like this—even suspected acts, rumored acts—harm Nation."

"The tribes can't blame Nation for what I do. It's like privateering in the sixteenth century, the sea captains operating on a special brief from the Crown. Drake, Hawkins, and Frobisher were not legal agents of Elizabeth Tudor but they acted for her."

"A handy rationalization."

"No, Tom!" One hand cut the air, a dramatic, sudden gesture, a measure of the force of his feelings. "It is exactly what I say. It's like Iran-Contra once was and the Special Operations Division of the CIA . . ."

"Secret agenda. Deceiving the populace."

"No! No!" Again the hand cut the air. "We are both privateers, Tom. Me with Balin, you on Rynosseros, keeping back details from all but a trusted few. . . ."

"And having them kept back from me."

He took the reproach calmly.

"Who told you? Tyrren?"

"No. We asked for the plans. There's been a tribal satellite tethered above Balin for a month. That's what really brought me here."

"Ah, yes. My Star above Bethlehem."

"A very deadly star. It can't be simple reconnaissance. Not coincidence. I'd say a warning."

"Tom, I've had those poles for twenty years . . ."

"They're from the Vatican catalogue. The ones they didn't give back. Part of a cause célèbre."

Paul Cheimarrhos said nothing for a moment. His clear blue eyes flashed in the sunlight.

"You're well informed."

"You know I work with Council."

"Exactly what I mean! A privateer!"

"All right, a privateer myself. I didn't bring Rynosseros, but my coming here will have been monitored. That roadstop you specified, seven k's out . . ."

"Sabro."

"Sabro, yes. There were tribesmen there. No questions were asked; the continent-crosser dropped me; it was a routine transit stop. But I made no attempt to conceal my identity either. That would've alerted them. It's why I wrote instead of using tech. The invitation had to come from you."

"I'm glad to have you."

"Despite the omen of no wind?"

Cheimarrhos laughed. "Despite that omen, yes!"

We were silent for a moment, each of us alone with our thoughts, gazing down into the dish at the small forest of shapes clustered there. The glare from the hollow and the surrounding field made it easy to shut my eyes, to escape the ancient painted posts masked from the sky by their insulated caps. Paul's voice startled me when he spoke.

"Tom, I will tell you something you will not know. What Three-line is, or was. Thirty years ago I invented a device that could measure haldane force around individual Clever Men, show which ones could access the most powerful vectors."

I couldn't believe what I was hearing.

"Council knows about this?"

"No. Secrecy was a condition. I tell you only because of our guest upstairs."

I resisted the urge to look up. This was incredible.

"The tribes couldn't allow such a device to be used," Paul continued, "especially by non-Ab'Os. They bought the Three-line patent, demanded it, the plans and prototypes, made sure it remained a lost invention. They gave me this concession on tribal land because the winds fell here, with enough funds and tech support to build Balin and establish a fortune in service companies.

"Those gave me a certain limited political power, as you know, which I've finally managed to pass on to my sister. Some of those companies help me acquire antiquities for my collection. The tribes permit them to operate. Ironically they made it possible for me to get these Vatican posts."

"But you've kept them," I said, my thoughts racing, wanting more than anything to ask more about the device. "You haven't given them back."

"As I say, Tom, the bloodlines no longer exist. Or if they do, only as revenant imposters. Who makes the claim? Who truly can? I do nothing more than collectors of antiquities and objets d'art have always done. For my pleasure I accumulate and keep safe objects that even their makers and inheritors might damage or ruin. It's the paradox of antiquarians and special collections everywhere." He looked into the sky. "My own Star now. I've been watching it. I have an antique Meade LX6 over there. It does the job."

"A laser strike at any moment, Paul. Balin might not survive it."

"What do they see, Tom? Nothing."

"There's more," I said. "Earlier this month, authorities in Rome finally confirmed that a special collection of burial posts—part of a personal gift to the Popes—was stolen in the years after Balin was built. An antiques smuggler was named; he named someone once attached to Three-line who has since disappeared. Nothing definite, all very tenuous, but your Star suggests how they're seeing it."

Paul surveyed the silent glade before us. "I've had them twenty years. I'm for this land, Tom, for all this. I'm the right sort of collector . . ."

"How they're seeing it, I said. You didn't even try to trade for such relics."

Paul laughed. "Oh, I made inquiries. But why haven't they confronted me? Sent in a search team, demanded entry, interrogated my staff? Why no formal investigation?"

I hesitated. He seemed perfectly serious; as if the obvious answer had not occurred to him? It made me cautious.

"You tell me, Paul, assuming you can trust your staff here, assuming they're not serving outside interests. I can only guess that it's part of the deal you made—what?—thirty years ago? This Three-line device you created would seem by its nature to weigh in as something between a holy artifact, something pertaining to the Dreamtime, and a National crisis. I'd say they made a deal with you at the level of their belief systems. Gave oaths, never expecting this. Now they have a dilemma requiring careful deliberation."

Paul turned away from the small forest of posts.

I followed him back across the roof-field, not wanting to ask my next question under the naked sky. Gain-monitors could never reach down so far, but scan could, and how did we seem, I wondered? Like conspirators? Very much Paul's privateers?

"One more thing," I said as we reached the open gallery that would lead us back into Balin's great mass. My heart was pounding as I said the words. "Did you hold back any Three-line knowledge? Plans? A duplicate prototype?"

"Of course not," Paul said, and was as closed to me then as a new moon, as the invisible satellite was—his Star, that sinister moonlet locked and turning with the world, geo-tethered by its micro-filament to the parent facility over the equator.

Paul Cheimarrhos smiled. "So serious, Tom. Come. We must not be late for lunch. Sarete is Three-line now. She might never forgive us."

"Paul, I have to know. The device . . ."

"Later. Come now." There were six of us for lunch, and the others were already seated at the long cedar table before a breathtaking view of the western desert; Sarete Cheimarrhos, Paul's reputedly formidable sister, her dark-skinned Islander assistant, Naese; to her left one of Paul's actor friends, the renowned John Newmarket, looking splendid in the Edwardian finery that was his Todthaus trademark, and next to him, white-suited, so urbane, the economist, James Aganture, agent for one of Three-line's long-standing European clients.

Sarete had been overseas during my visit to Balin three years before. I had heard a great deal about this celebrated woman; even Tyrren had issued several cautions. Now here she was rising to greet me.

If the flamboyant and expansive Paul could be likened to a messianic Beethoven cast in silver and blue, then his calm and elegant sister, with her black gown, long dark hair and sombre, appraising gaze, was something from the shadowed spaces of the El Greco that hung on the room's northern wall. She was ten years younger than her brother by all accounts, but the smooth, untanned skin gave her a timelessness, a twenty-year range of possibilities at least.

There was a smile, a generous one, but it never reached the eyes, and in the instant I knew that this pale, severely pretty woman intended me to see this duality of response. I was Paul's guest, the luncheon no doubt his idea. Just as Balin was completely his domain, the administration of the

Three-line holdings was hers, and this had to be taking precious time out of a very busy day.

Rather than feeling affronted, I was glad of the hard honesty. There were probably enough lies in this great house already.

"Captain Tyson," she said as we shook hands. "I believe you and John know one another." I nodded and smiled at the actor. An answering smile softened those famous gaunt cheeks. "This is James Aganture, one of our European consultants." Aganture and I exchanged smiles as well. "And this is Naese, my secretary."

A fitting assistant for her employer, I decided, an Islander woman, quite dark, middle-aged, with small eyes and small fleeting smile. Naese rose, gave a slight bow of the head. I did the same.

We took our places. I was seated next to James Aganture at Sarete's right, opposite John Newmarket and Naese. Paul spoke a word to Anquan, the majordomo, and joined us, immediately taking charge of the dinner conversation by asking James Aganture to bring us up to date on the situation in Europe.

The svelte, white-suited European did that until the food arrived, when the business of eating gave me an opportunity to study Sarete and the others, though I found it harder to do that than I expected. Thoughts of what Paul had said about his invention kept crossing my mind, and I was glad when the meal was over at last and I could adjourn to my quarters for siesta.

Around 1500 there was wind.

I was drawn from sleep by the deep swelling song, went to the windows and looked out, used house tech to bring different vistas to the wall-screen, one cycling after the other, every angle but where the posts stood.

It was thrilling to see and hear—the outward signs of Balin coming alive. The pennants and long wind-sock drogues at the corners of the roof-field stirred on their poles, the helium-filled outrider kites floating high above the house started shifting in the sky, inditing their signatures on the bright air. Spinner caps turned, the most sensitive of the sonic acroteria began to sound. Like some great ship advancing through time, trailing cloud-wrack and windsong, Balin was on its way again.

Tolerances were adjusted: within ten minutes the field was thrumming and whistling, within twenty howling and keening. From farther down the great sloping mass came a deep moaning that meant one or more of the induction vents were cycling open, the spiral cores engaged, that power cells were regenerating and airflow was being guided through the mighty house. There were corridors now where my casual passage from one room to another would vary pitch and tone, add a subtle difference to the house-song. This was Paul's great legacy. This!

I must have stood there for fifteen, twenty minutes, reading the land, studying how this structure stood upon it, considering what micro-climates might exist in its shadow. Then the phone chimed, drawing me back, and it was Naese's face in the glass.

"Forgive the interruption, Captain. Sensors showed tech use in your quarters—we assumed you were awake. If it's convenient, my mistress would appreciate your calling on her in, say, fifteen minutes?"

The request did not surprise me.

"Certainly," I said. "I'll be ready."

On Balin's sloping west wall was a small open place like a col or cirque on the side of a mountain, and in the sun-trap made there was a walled garden, little more than some lawn and a grove of dusty orange trees.

A house servant, Cristofer, led me there, opened the low bronze door and let me out into the tiny grove. The westering sun warmed the spot; the sloping planes of the wall-face came together above me in a gradual point, with stone wind-masks spinning on their pins in the vents.

The wind had strengthened, I noticed. The pressure systems over the desert had shifted—it was probably the brinraga that struck the parapet of the garden, stirring the fruit trees, whistling up the granite face to the vents above, where extruded murtains randomized the flow, altering its direction, tailoring it to the house-song.

Tyrren had built well. The massif of Balin sang but the garden was a pocket of calm, not only a sun-trap and a wind-haven, but also a place sheltered from the vast music forming all around us.

Sarete was sitting on a white wooden bench amid the trees, wearing a gown of dark green polysar and speaking softly into a comlink at her wrist. Though Three-line's Chief Executive, she apparently did much of her work from Balin, away from the coasts, privileged with the com tech that required. I marveled at such easy luxuries. Near her, on another bench and using a lap-scan, sat Naese.

Both women looked up when I approached, but Naese turned her attention back to the scan display almost immediately. Sarete gave a polite smile and switched off the link.

"Thank you for coming. Paul considers you his so I won't keep you long."

I went to make some appropriate remark, but thought better of it. This audience was wholly on her terms; she had reminded me as much.

"We could not discuss it at lunch, but tell me frankly, Captain, what does that comsat mean?"

"They're geo-tethered, as you know. The logistics of moving them, aligning them . . ."

"Costs."

"Yes. They use them that way all the time, but it means filing deployments, getting clearances, logging variations. It's a busy sky."

"So I've discovered. It tells us how seriously they regard this."

"It does. It may be a routine shift, simple reconnaissance, coincidence . . ."

"Council sees it as a warning."

"Strong probability."

"Because David talked."

"No, Sarete. Tyrren told us nothing, simply confirmed what was already available through channels."

"Ah, channels. And do you think there is an agent in our midst?"

After Paul's empassioned evasions, again I found this directness refreshing.

"Can you doubt it? I would have thought infiltration preceded a tech commitment like this." And I glanced briefly upward. "Given what Balin is, I would assume infiltration occurred a long time ago. This is unique."

"Agreed."

"How large is your staff?"

"Here? Seven including Naese. All trusted. All here a long time. Some rarely go above. We keep house secrets, Captain."

"Your guests?"

"Possible. Unlikely. They will not see the . . . relics either. But what can that station do? I've been given general configuration data but I'd like you to tell me."

So you can make a decision, I realized. Make policy for Three-line.

"We read lenses deployed. It's probably irijinti. Given twenty minutes it could effectively demolish Balin."

"Which took eight years to build. Twenty minutes."

"Depending on intensity and duration. They sometimes move deployed like that . . ."

"Target the roof-field?"

"Easily. To a square meter, possibly less. But hardly their intention." I glanced at the Islander woman sitting quietly among the trees. "They'd want to commandeer the . . . relics."

"Naese knows everything, Captain. Should I leave?"

It was such an unexpected question that I hesitated.

"You understand that I'm still making up my mind about all this?"

"Of course."

"All right. Then as Three-line you should. But only if it's a regular routine to do so. Anything could seem provocative now. Do you leave Balin often?"

"Occasionally. You like Paul, don't you? You're like him."

"Like" and "like," both words revealing more about Sarete and her relationship with her brother than she perhaps intended.

"We understand something in common, something difficult, probably irreconcilable in our affairs."

"Ah, your role as privateers."

"Paul's word, Sarete. I suppose it suits."

"What would yours be? Patriot? National? Romantic?"

"Privateer will do."

"You have no satellite over your head."

"I do now. And for all I know I may have one for every Ab'O Prince I've ever dealt with as Blue."

Naese looked up suddenly, made a hand-sign. Sarete raised a hand to excuse herself for a moment.

"Yes?"

"Foreman has entered the Manada."

"Excellent. Send on that." And to me: "Your advice?"

"In what capacity?" I said it to remind her of the levels that separated us, wanting the distinctions to matter. There were different values at work here; Naese's interruption, this allocation of time, had shown me that.

"As a State of Nation man?"

"Persuade him to give the poles back. Or leave here immediately."

"As the Blue Captain?"

"The same."

"As Paul's friend?"

"Sarete . . ."

"As his friend?"

"I'm still deciding, but I'd say stay. Risk it."

"Really?"

"If Balin is struck and the reason is given as scared relics, there are many who will not believe. The tribes are seen as ruthless aggressors, hostile to Three-line, to Nation, to all non-Ab'Os, displeased with past concessions because of a device Paul invented long ago . . ."

"Nation knows about the device?" It was the first time I had seen surprise on Sarete's face. The eyes first widened, then narrowed. Her mouth drew into a line. Alarm, disappointment, annoyance, I couldn't tell.

"No. Paul told me before lunch."

Sarete nodded. Her head lifted a fraction. She glanced out at an errant drogue—orange, red, and bright blue—cutting the wind forty meters away. I could not be sure, but I believed she did it to conceal something contained in her gaze—or perhaps missing from it. More than ever she resembled the El Greco madonna above the cedar table.

"What will you do?" she asked finally. "As yourself?"

I smiled, watching the kite as well, seeing it as some complex bird-equation worked out upon the registers of air, left to find resolution, to create its own fragment of meaning. It occurred to me, absurdly, very fondly, that Paul would probably have names for his kites. This was his house, his ultimate statement. Everything belonged, made for the homeostasis Paul Cheimarrhos needed, externalized in kite and corridor and windchase. In the burial poles in that shallow dish.

No wonder he had been glad to relinquish the operation of Threeline. Dreamer, idealist, monomaniac, he wanted none of it. Who knew what wonders, what pieces of self, Balin's vaults and chambers contained? This was more than a vast schema of the Nullarbor's Breathing Caves, those hundreds of miles of underground conduits, chambers, tortuous chimneys. This was a living extension of the man, every corridor, each framed vista and spinning wind-mask. Seeing it any other way just didn't begin to give the truth.

He had to continue, remain just what he was. He had no choice.

The kite, set upon its wall of air, mindlessly navigating, brought that in, gave that answer. Just as he had set it there, given it that brave and futile task, serving, being, till it was finally destroyed and replaced, he had put Balin upon the land, raised it up for its time. His statement. His stand.

I watched the woman whose lift of head, whose gaze had led me out to the kite, realizing, imagining what she too had been through, the years of dealing with this reality of Paul's.

She had seemed hard and alien before. Now she seemed trapped and committed, caught at the moment of deciding. Caught in the choices of others. As I was. As Paul might yet be.

"I will remain here till that satellite moves away," I said. "If my presence can deter them, provide another reason for not striking, then good. Do you mind having one more houseguest, Sarete?"

"It's not my place . . ."

"I'm asking you anyway."

"Not at all, Captain. It was good of you to see me."

Again the safe courtesy, the illusion of my having gifted her and not the reverse. She was alien again in that moment, and I found myself hating it, hating what she represented, this seeming lack of connection, the cool

pragmatism, the failure to read or simply accept one set of equations because she had equations of her own.

I left the garden but did not return to my quarters. Instead I climbed
the escarpment, gallery by gallery, to a viewing lounge close to the summit.
There I stood amid the low, ocher-colored furniture, safe behind the thick
glass, watching the sturdy outrider kites hanging in the sky and the long
streamers of dust and cloud that boiled off this stone massif and converged
at the horizon as lines in an endlessly moving yet strangely constant perspective.

The house-song was clear but at a comfortable remove—like an or-
chestra tuning somewhere else. I began to see the great structure as something to be maintained in that other sense, and wondered which of the
staff members—Anquan? Cristofer? Deric?—might abseil down these vast
faces, clearing wind-wrack from the vents, carrying out service checks, replacing fixtures, tuning the structure in fact.

I recalled the meeting in the garden. Could Sarete not see the virtue
in this vital reality? It was an eternal act of defiance, this great demense,
a continuing statement of identity, personal for Paul, but for Nation too,
a crucial affirmation.

Or was that just my bias?

I tracked clouds to the horizon and considered equations, found myself
coming back to the new integer, probably the ultimate issue in all this.

What a device Paul must have created to be allowed such a thing as
Balin.

I sensed someone at my back, turned to find the calm figure of James
Aganture standing near me, the cultured, white-suited gentleman from our
luncheon. Like me, he was gazing out at the desert, deep-set brown eyes
filled with admiration.

"Amazing, isn't it? It just goes on forever."

"Yes."

He moved in beside me, stood watching the sweep of the land, the
boiling ribbons of red dust streaming past, gloriously capped now with low
cloud, trimmed with gold by the afternoon sun.

"You lose a sense of such scale in Europe," he said. "It might be said
that here you lack density, weight of identity, but that surely is changing.
We stand upon a great symbol. Another waits above. It is a testing of
symbols really."

During lunch I had imagined what conversations I might have with
someone like James Aganture, had wondered what talk there could be with
that avenging moon fixed in our sky, steadier by far than those trembling

outriders at the ends of their cables. That he had almost read my thoughts startled me.

I nearly smiled as he worked his way into what he wished to say, Sarete's question, no doubt Paul's. My own.

"Will it strike?" he said.

"Will it strike?" I answered him.

"Pardon me?"

"I ask you the same question, James. And I wonder why you remain when the risk is so great."

Aganture's well-shaped mouth turned down, his dark eyes widened. "A visit planned weeks ago. I did not know until I arrived."

"Of course. So will you leave soon?"

Aganture did not answer. He waited a few moments, bringing his long hands together before him, then came to it again. This time he was even more direct.

"What will Council do, Captain?"

"Excuse me, James, but I'm still not sure what you mean."

"I know you are here as a representative of Nation," he said. "I know about the posts. It is why I was sent."

"Sent? By whom?"

"The Vatican, Captain Tyson. I am Monsigneur James Aganture, the instrument of the Cardinals Elect and the Holy See."

"Him. Your interest here, Monsigneur Aganture?"

"Please. It is James. And it is merely a visit to negotiate for full restoration of the posts."

"How did you learn of them?"

The man smiled. "Our own investigators. There are those who saw to the actual handling who could later be bought. Thieves prosper in this. Once they had disposed of the merchandise, they still had information to sell. Once we had the principal's name . . ."

"Cheimarrhos would be an expensive name, I imagine?"

"Expensive enough. We had made reasonable guesses. Balin is world famous. Our host is known for his collecting. And he is hardly subtle. Once he even inquired about direct sale; he is on public record as a 'liberator' and 'protector' of relics."

"Does Paul know?"

"Not yet, Captain. I have not lied, simply withheld. I am a senior operative for a legitimate corporation dealing with Three-line in other areas. It was easy to come here. My first loyalty, however, is to Mother Church. I thought it best I learn of Council's intentions before declaring myself. And, yes, we know about the satellite. It will settle everything, ne?"

I met the churchman's gaze. "I hold Blue. I have full executive authority where Council is concerned in matters like this."

"I suspected as much. Will you order him to return the posts?"

"Order him? First you ask what will Council do, as if it can do anything, and now this."

"Captain, please. You will understand, I hope, when I say that you are not altogether the best choice here, ne? You are Paul's friend, you are a champion of National interests. Is it not provocative to have sent you?"

I fought down my anger. "Sent, Monsigneur?"

Aganture frowned, clenched his hands again, though elegantly, without force.

"But . . . forgive me, Captain. I naturally assumed that was how it was. I know you can travel where you will . . ."

"James, go and declare yourself. Make your official representations and get away from here. That is a very deadly star."

James Aganture nodded, studied the striations of dust and cloud beyond the glass, the sharp and startling perspectives of the sky.

"Yes. But this is as delicate as it is urgent."

"You are here as a businessman as well as a friend."

"Exactly. We mean to buy them back if we can. Make them a gift to the tribes."

"Ah, I see. All good business, Monsigneur Aganture. Curry favor for the Church."

"Captain, it really is not that simple."

"Of course. It isn't for Council either. They can't help themselves. I like to think I am here for simpler reasons."

"I see that now, of course. May I ask what they are?"

"Paul is an old friend. At a distance, it is easy to take positions, have the luxury of serving ideologies and some greater good. I came to make up my mind. I needed to know."

"Yes. I'm glad we've had the opportunity to speak. And please . . ."

"Your identity is safe for the moment."

"Thank you, Captain. You must understand that I cannot afford to jeopardize my organization's trade dealings with Three-line. It is difficult to know what to do for all of us."

"Keeping options open just in case."

"Very awkward, yes."

"You have spoken to his sister?"

But I saw at once that he had, that this was Sarete's answer too, and more of her questions. James Aganture was here at the invitation of Sarete Cheimarrhos, I was suddenly sure of it. I left him no time to answer.

"You ask for confidentiality. You impose upon my duty to my friend. I now ask you to tell him who you are. I give you until, let us say, dinner this evening, Monsigneur, yes?"

"Yes. Yes, Captain."

And I left him, found my way down to my quarters on Level 42, welcoming the option of silence and opaqued windows, needing the time to consider what really had to be done, thinking of the Three-line device and wondering what my real reasons now were.

At sunset we saw the view that made Balin renowned across the world—the Inferno, great boiling lines of cloud plunging toward the horizon, meeting in the pit of the sun, drawn like great rivers, like tattered banners, cohorts, cables of molten gold laid upon the sky, the angles of a mad geometer hauled and hurtled into the blazing, settling point like a rehearsal for the end of days.

Even Sarete and Naese were there for it. We sat and stood about the lounge and could not find enough words for conversation, no moment when the few comments made did not do more than force silence again.

There was only the sky, the whole world drawn to that single ravenous point. And finally, as if in scorn, the sun closed its mighty eye in one slow blink, denying the clouds their lustre, turning them to lead where they sailed, streamed, panicked in the sky: you are too late, too late, little brothers, I turn my gaze from you all.

We subsided where we sat or stood, muscles loosened, sighs sounded above the rolling, healing frenzy of the house-song. John Newmarket tugged at his collar; James Aganture slowly shook his stately head. Naese sat with what seemed like a rapt expression on her face, considering the changed world beyond the glass. Sarete saw me give a deeper unsounded sigh, allowed the faintest trace of a smile to touch her pale lips.

Paul turned to us all, stood with his back to the glass.

"The world has many great identifying winds, enabling winds, precise expressions of the pneuma. The simoom, the sirocco, the khamsin, the monsoons, and the santanas. Pieces of the patchwork.

"I accept the reality; I accepted the challenge as Imhotep did. Here is the codex that lets us read what it tells us: not understand, never understand, but know. Just take in and know. The wind moves upon the land. It completes an equation in the soul, resolves itself through only those devices nature has raised up, precisely designed, to read what such things mean. Us. We are the world's way of apprehending itself. We complete all that out there. Our affirmations, our emotions, are the lock for that great key. This house reminds us."

I smiled. Paul had uttered similar words at the Anderlee gathering three years ago. I was an easy convert; I used my own ship to affirm such truths in myself, such a rich and simple knowing.

"Tomorrow," he said, "there will be towers of cumulus and laze-lions all day, nothing like this. This is justice, Tom, for Fate having served up a windless man, trying to build some new Tarot here. So you never add this to your legend! *Comprendez?*"

"I do, Paul," I said, laughing. "I'll hobble you with eclipses and minor comets from now on. Nothing less!"

"Apology accepted, gracious man. And you, James?" Paul was exalted, magnanimous; it was a pointed gaze, laden with irony and found reprimand that he gave the clergyman. James Aganture had no doubt confessed.

"We have riches, an embarrassment of all that humanity has wrought. Cloisters, scriptoria, great art collections, antiquities, centuries of sophistry and clever talk, the doctrines and arguments. Now I find the simplicity of my God here. I remember that my eyes are the windows of the first and last cathedral I shall ever know."

"Accepted. And you, Honest John? You've seen it before. Anything to add?"

I was interested to see that lean, spirited John Newmarket also looked abashed.

"I lost words for this ten years ago, Paul," the actor said in his rich, full voice. "This must endure at all costs."

Which reminded us all and stole the edges from Paul's smile for a moment, though just a moment. Our host was not to be discouraged.

"Tonight we hold a starwatch in honor of our uninvited guest. We dress warmly. We go above. We find our personal monkey-moon and regale it, drag it up close, count its legs, tell our fortunes on its parts. I'll name every wind that troubles us. Yes?"

There was general assent, but I caught quick unguarded glances from Newmarket and Aganture toward Paul's sister, then found myself at the end of Naese's own coolly appraising gaze.

"Dinner is at 1900," Sarete announced, and led the way out of the lounge.

Paul held back, like some captain reluctant to leave the bridge of his ship, and I held back as well, not surprised when his expansive mood fell away like the gold of the departed sun.

"Do you know what Aganture is, Tom?" he asked when we were alone.

"A churchman."

"He told you!" Surprise and suspicion sat in Paul's eyes for a brief, flickering instant. "Well, he hinted at trade cutbacks. Direct dealings with the tribes. Circumventing Three-line altogether. All veiled, of course, the spineless fool!"

"What will you do?"

"About Aganture?"

"About your Star?"

"They'll do it, you think?"

I shrugged, not mentioning the device, determined to keep away from that topic for the moment. "You said it yourself earlier today. The bloodlines are gone. They may not care about the poles at all. What you are becoming is a very useful example. If they strike at you, it's a warning to everyone else. They may need a precedent."

"Do you know who Newmarket represents?"

The question surprised me. "Newmarket?"

"A Tosi-Go subsidiary, a Three-line rival. A mercenary actor, Tom. My friend. Leave the posts where they are but sell them to Tosi-Go so the tribes dare not act. Not why he visited, oh no. Just happened to have been approached; thought he'd mention it like a caring friend."

"So what will you do?"

"No offers, Tom? Nothing from Council?"

They were bitter words, from a man who was trying hard to reconcile different realities. Forcing himself. Again.

"Nothing. I told Aganture. I cannot be who I am and come here without representing Council, but I do not follow their specific wishes."

"And what are their specific wishes, do you think?"

"I imagine to see you continue. To see Paul Cheimarrhos and Balin and Three-line survive."

"In that order? Well, two of those I heartily agree with, though I'm not sure I believe you. I'm no longer Three-line. It's an alien thing."

"You know what I mean. Council can't order you. They want you to remain as a symbol. That's your great worth to Nation. The posts matter because they put you and Balin at risk. That's how I think they'd see it anyway."

"Hm, well thank them for that. That much I can accept."

I discovered it was what I wanted, Paul believing that I was here for reasons of my own, out of friendship and personal esteem, for reasons ultimately as elusive and mysterious as his own. Learning of the Three-line invention had complicated the issue; I found myself needing to ask about it, realized how partisan I now felt, would be the moment I asked the questions that had tormented me all afternoon.

"What would you advise?" Paul said.

"What I told Sarete earlier. I'd stay."

"Good. The poles?"

"Hardly the issue."

"No?"

Perhaps I could ask about it. Paul had mentioned the device to me. Knowing my background, of my time in the Madhouse, he had brought it up. But again I hesitated, knowing that the moment I did ask, I was no better than Newmarket or Aganture.

"It's what I was leading up to earlier when you showed me the posts. It's the Three-line holding itself that concerns them. Not the company— this great house of yours. The concession was given a long time ago and it's become too celebrated, too newsworthy, too steady a slight. I would think getting you to admit to having the poles will be used as counterpropaganda to discredit you in National and International eyes, making you appear as someone plundering, stealing away art treasures for his own material gain. Pirate rather than privateer, Paul, the critical difference. Just one more exploiter and opportunist. I believe the satellite is meant to force your hand."

"They won't strike?"

"They'd possibly destroy what they're overtly trying to save, if that matters. It seems an unnecessarily dramatic thing, using a comsat."

Paul nodded, finally asked the inevitable question.

"Why haven't they mounted a land assault or at least done a search? Sent Kurdaitcha in?"

"Because they already have."

"What? Who?"

"Your guess. I told Sarete this afternoon. I would assume it was done long before they moved that station."

"But who?" Paul was genuinely amazed; it obviously had not occurred to him at all. Again I could see that the dream was being spoiled. "Our staff has been here since Balin was built. Cristofer and Deric came in from other Three-line holdings . . ."

"Exactly how I would have done it. Planted someone when Balin was being built. Before then, if I could."

"Kurdaitcha?" Paul was making himself accept another way of thinking, a hated, spoiling pragmatism.

"To keep an eye on Three-line initially, yes. To make sure no new inventions came along. To keep an eye on acquisitions."

"So what happens when I don't frighten?"

"A land strike, I'd say. They must already have verification that the poles are here, so it depends on how willing they are to sacrifice a handful of relics. If they can't neutralize what Balin represents by embarrassing you, they could use the posts as an excuse to destroy it anyway. A regrettable casualty. But whatever this is, Paul, it's the final stages of some carefully planned action."

"Yet . . . you came."

"One Colored Captain may suggest all the Captains are involved. And the other Captains will come if you ask. It may stay their hand. You're a symbol, Paul, just as we are. Not Balin, you. There can be other Balins, other ways of doing this. It's you we can't replace. And that's my comment, Paul, not Council's, not the Captains'. "

"Yes. Yes. Thank you, Tom."

We watched the streaming, shadowing chains of cloud racing for the edge of the world. The words of my handful of desperate questions were right there, held back, barely held. It might have been the sight of Paul that stopped me. His hands were fists at his sides. He sighed.

"Tom, I have changed my will. In view of circumstances. Regarding Balin. Will you be notary to it, take the signed original back to Council?"

"Paul . . ."

"Whichever way it goes, Tom, I want it officially lodged. Yes?"

"I'll be glad to take it."

"And see the terms are carried out?"

The fists, the tension across his shoulders, were more vivid than words, than any other persuasion.

"Yes. If I can. Yes."

"I'll give it to you before dinner. Before we go above. Come to me in my quarters at 1840."

"At 1840."

And he left me standing there with my questions, with sudden relief and self-reproach, and before me the rushing, frenzied, cloud-wrack chasing the sun, lean, iron-gray conquistadores seeking gold but succeeding only in building night in the far hidden places of the sky.

After showering and changing, by the time I knocked on his door at precisely 1840, I had put my curiosity aside, determined to wait, trusting that he would reveal more later.

When the door slid back, I entered and found Paul sitting on a divan by the windows, the last of the day a tattered ruin of light behind him in the western sky. He was examining a Canopic jar, one of a set of four eighteenth-Dynasty pieces resting on a low table to one side, replacing the jackal-head stopper. He set it down as I approached, took an envelope from inside his black-and-gold house robe, and handed it to me as I sat down.

"A formality, Tom. I've involved Council. It's fair they know my position."

I put it in a pocket of my sandsman's fatigues and went to tell him again that it was a pleasure, but Paul spoke first.

"Tom, why were you in the Madhouse?"

I tensed immediately, feeling the barest edge of panic, residual reflex fear. It never failed to surprise me. This was the question no one asked, that was only rarely answered if ever, that now permitted my questions to him. Paul asking it mattered. I didn't give any of the usual replies.

"I don't remember. They would not tell me."

"They?"

"Tartalen. He was in charge. One day I'll return. I'll ask."

He kept at it. "You should."

"Why, Paul?"

"There is a mystery about you. You're a National and a sensitive. The field is strong . . ."

"The other Captains . . ."

"No. I've met them. They've all been here at one time or another. You're different."

"Paul!"

There was a knock at the door.

"Dinner and starwatch," he said. "This will be Sarete."

"Paul!"

"Gain monitors, Tom. We may have an audience. Later."

We went to the door, found Sarete and John Newmarket, waiting there.

"We go to study our demon," Sarete said, pleasantly enough. "The others will be waiting."

"On to the feast!" Paul said, and together we headed along the corridor, the house adding our variables to its ongoing song.

Dinner was an easy affair, first Paul then John Newmarket telling stories; James Aganture giving his views on the future of Mother Church in view of new tech embargoes recently imposed.

Finally the dishes were cleared away, and the six of us started our climb to the summit. In the Gallery of Record, Cristofer and Deric gave us jackets; warmly dressed, we stepped out onto the dark windy field.

It sang under the moonless sky. Under our feet, the house moaned deeply to itself. We crossed the plateau, the acroteria looming beside us like funerary totems, bleached bones keening in the cold brinraga. We made our way through the restless shapes, keeping well clear of the central depression, heading for the northwestern corner where Anquan had set up the old Meade telescope, its short thick barrel pointed at the sky directly overhead.

"The refreshments, please," Sarete told the old majordomo, raising her voice above the rush of wind so she could be heard, and Anquan went off with Cristofer to get the evening's collation.

Paul sat on the low stool before the telescope and used the eyepiece, made some quick adjustments.

"I have him," he said, his voice strong above the airflow. "Very wicked-looking deployed like that. They really do know how to use psychology. Who's first? James?"

The churchman moved to the stool, settled himself and peered through the eyepiece. Paul stood beside him, looking straight up, silver hair streaming in the wind.

"See it?" he asked loudly so we could all hear. "The red lights are mainly tactical—'barrican stars' to frighten us. Tom will confirm it. They're supposed to light up like that just before a strike."

"Really?" Aganture said, moving clear of the stool. "Is that true, Captain?"

"Yes," I said, studying the small group as best I could, dark shapes, blowing shapes, wanting to ask Paul about his comments earlier, concerned that we may have been overheard and interrupted deliberately, deeply worried by what that might mean.

"Your turn, John," Paul said, and the actor took his place at the telescope.

"It does look angry," was all he said.

Paul laughed. "It wants us to think that. It's trying to be hot and raging up there, but in reality it's a very cool thing, very calm."

Newmarket rose and moved away. "I've seen enough. Captain?"

"Sarete?" I said.

"No, thank you."

"Naese?"

"No, Captain. Thank you."

I positioned myself on the stool, and after a split-second of auto-focus saw the irijinti, saw it again in actual fact, since I'd seen the displays Council had at Twilight Beach, began matching its configuration with other comsats I had seen up close this way, started when Paul whispered at my ear.

"The Canopic jar," he said. "is a second prototype. Get it away from here. Say a gift!"

The wind sang about us. Possibly no one heard.

I made myself stay calm; my heart racing as I peered up at the evil red lights.

It explained everything. Not the posts. Not Balin. Not just those things. Far more serious, much greater danger. Paul had broken faith.

The jar, a duplicate. He had used it to read me!

"Paul . . . ?"

"Finished already?" he said, speaking for the others to hear.

I rose from the stool. "Let me get my configuration lists. I still say irijinti, but I want to type it. I can almost make out its markings." My voice sounded steady above the wind.

"I'll try for a better fix," Paul said, calmly enough, taking his place at the eyepiece once more.

I hurried from the field, entered the Gallery, ran down the ramps toward our chambers. My footsteps echoed on the polished stone, set a desperate percussion into the airflow.

The palm-lock to Paul's rooms had been keyed to me, no surprise at all; the door swept aside at my touch. I crossed the softly lit interior, immediately went to the four jars on the low table: monkey head, falcon head, human head, jackal—seized the jackal head, removed the ceramic cap, saw the dull black tech that gave it its extra weight, the recessed contacts and displays.

What had it shown? What?

"I will take that, Captain."

I turned at once. Naese stood in the doorway, a laser baton in her hand.

"I'm sorry. This is a gift to me from Paul. Ask him."

She raised the baton, aimed it at my heart.

"Captain, I am Kurdaitcha in the final moments of a very long, very old mission."

"You . . ."

"Color, Hero status, mean nothing compared to my brief, do you understand? Without that jar and the contents of the envelope in your pocket, I will be sung. I dare not fail. Save your life."

"The envelope contains Paul's will."

"No. His will was lodged with Nation long ago. What you have contains blueprints for what you hold in your hands. Look and see."

I placed the jar on the divan, brought out the envelope and opened it, saw words and schematics.

"Yes?" Naese said. "They are mine. Paul's life might still be yours if you hurry."

I threw the plans onto the divan and ran for the door. She let me pass but called after me. "Captain! Wait!"

I ignored her, running for the ramps, needing to get Paul from the roof, away from the telescope and the field and the line of sight of that deadly watcher, aware that it already had all the commands it needed.

I saw the result of those commands as I leapt out upon the field, a thread, a wire, the tiniest filament of dazzling light connecting Balin for just an instant to its attendant moon, then the tearing scream of its brief and deadly anger above the keening windsong.

I did not need to go out to where the telescope had stood. There would be time later. I waited by the door as the three figures came to me across the windy field, Sarete in the lead, head raised, cool and detached, resolved as ever, yes, leading them, John Newmarket and James Aganture to either side, eyes downcast, ashamed.

As I watched them approach, their faces lit from the doorway, I heard Naese at my back, panting lightly from her run. She did not have the jar or the plans; she no longer held her weapon.

"Your mistress has done well," I said.

"She has saved Three-line and Balin," Naese replied. "She made a difficult choice. An only choice."

"What did Paul read, Naese?"

"What do you mean?"

"With the contents of the jar?"

"That you are a sensitive. That's all."

"Nothing else?"

"Nothing else."

"I don't believe you."

"I know."

Sarete and her companions reached us, stopped before the doorway. Her words might have come from Naese, from a script of exculpation they had jointly devised.

"He knew the consequences, Captain. He made a choice, without considering anyone, never consulting others. Something had to be done. I made a choice too."

More words than I would have expected. Still James Aganture and John Newmarket looked in different directions at the night. Only Sarete and Naese met my gaze.

"It wasn't the posts," I said, so nothing was hidden. "There was a second Three-line device. A duplicate."

Aganture and Newmarket both looked at Sarete.

"Nonsense," she said calmly.

"Naese has . . ."

"Nonsense, Captain. There was never a duplicate."

She knew. Of course she knew. Naese did not say a word.

"I see. Privateering."

"What, this?" Sarete asked.

"All this."

"I suppose so. Not your kind, but yes."

"Not my kind, no. Never my kind."

I went out onto the field then, went to where the old Meade telescope had stood, came back with the lines of blood painted on my cheeks.

Sarete grimaced with distaste when she saw them. "Captain, is that really necessary?"

"Tell her, Naese."

The Kurdaitcha frowned. "He is Blue, Sarete. He has made vendetta against this house."

"You're joking. I am this house now."

"No, Sarete," I said. "I think you will find that Paul has bequeathed it to Nation. Years ago. Naese can check."

"Ridiculous! That can be negated."

"Naese," I said, drawing rage and loss into that small hard word.

"You don't understand, Sarete. Those signs. In front of witnesses, he has sworn vendetta. He can strike at anything to do with Three-line, at any ships coming here. Through him, Council can. You must leave here. All of you."

"This is not the end of this," Sarete said.

"No," I was able to say. "It is not."

On the desert near Sabro, there is a mighty house, a vast pylon set against the sky. Though left to Nation as a final bequest from the man who caused it to be, it is deserted now, neither National nor tribal, a monument at the interface. The great vents stand open; the structure howls and sings and braids the winds into endless tapestries, strange proclamations of desire. At the crest is a field and a shallow empty dish thirty meters across.

Once a year, seven ships go to that great house, the only ones who can since it is reached by crossing tribal land. The crews climb aloft and reach that field. While the crew members do small acts of maintenance, the Captains sit in the depression and talk.

Sometimes there is a ritual of watching sunset, sometimes a starwatch. Kites are set upon the air, new pennants added to the dream.

At such times, coincidentally, no satellite ever crosses that sky. The comsats studiedly avoid the place as if contemptuous of something all too futile.

The Captains smile in the windy darkness or in the flowing riot of the dying sun. More than anyone, they know the worth of dreams.

They know it is never that.

DAVID J. LAKE

David J. Lake was born in India in 1929 and settled in Australia in 1967 after a career as a teacher in Britain and Asia. From 1967 to 1994 he was a literary academic at the University of Queensland. Lake's first novel was *Walkers on the Sky* (1976) but he did not write an SF short story until 1978, "Re-deem the Time." It appeared in the international SF anthology *Rooms of Paradise*. *Walkers on the Sky* (1976), *The Right Hand of Dextra* (1977), *The Wildings of Westron* (1977), *The Gods of Xuma, or Barsoom Revisited* (1978), *The Fourth Hemisphere* (1980)—perhaps the most ambitious of all his books, and the only one not to have been published outside of Australia—and *Warlords of Xuma* (1983) comprise the "Breakout" series. *The Gods of Xuma* is, among other things, a skillful reconstruction of the planet Mars as portrayed in Edgar Rice Burroughs's "John Carter" adventures. Lake also wrote *The Man Who Loved Morlocks* (1981), a sequel to H. G. Wells's *The Time Machine* (1895) that speculates about what happened to the Time Traveler on his second voyage, as does the recent well-received short story "The Truth about Weena" (1998). They reflect Lake's scholarly interest in the works of H. G. Wells, and combine an adventure narrative with a serious critique and interpretation of *The Time Machine*. Although Lake has written a few more short stories over the years, this one remains his most famous.

WHEN AMBROSE LIVERMORE DESIGNED his Time Machine, he bethought him of the advantages both of mobility and of camouflage, and therefore built his apparatus into the bodywork of a second-hand Volkswagen. Anyone looking in at the windows, such as an inquisitive traffic policeman, would have taken the thing for an ordinary "bug" with a large metal trunk on the backseat. The large metal trunk contained the workings of the Time Machine; the front seat and the dashboard looked almost normal, and the car could still function as a car.

When all things were ready, one cold afternoon in 1984, Ambrose got into the front seat and drove from his little laboratory in Forminster to a deserted field on a South English hill. A white chalk track led him to the spot he had chosen; farther along there was an ancient British hill fort, but not one that was ever visited by tourists. And this gloomy October day there was no one at all to be ruffled by his extraordinary departure. Applying the handbrake, he looked about him; and at last he smiled.

Ambrose did not often smile, for he was a convinced pessimist. He had seen the way the world was going for some time, and in his opinion it was not going well. Energy crisis was followed by energy crisis, and little war by little or not-so-little war, and always the great nations became further locked into their unending arms race. Sooner or later the big bang was coming and he wanted out. Luckily, he now had the means for getting out . . .

Briefly, he wished that general time travel were a real possibility. One could then go back to the Good Old Days—say, before 1914. One could *keep* hopping back, living 1913 over and over again . . . Only, of course, the Good Old Days weren't really all that good; one would miss all sorts of modern comforts; and besides, the thing was impossible anyway. Backward time travel was utterly illogical, you could shoot your grandfather and so on. No, his own work had opened up the escape route, the only escape route, the one that led into the *future*. There were no illogicalities involved in that, since everyone travels into the future at all times. The Livermore Accelerator merely speeded up a natural process—speeded it up amazingly, of course, but . . .

But there it was. He would hop forward a century or so, in the hope of evading imminent doom. Surely the crash must come well before that, and by 2100, say, they'd be recovering . . .

Ambrose took a deep breath and pressed the red lever that projected below the dashboard.

The sensation was bewildering. He had done it before, of course, behind locked doors in the laboratory, but only for a subjective second or two, little jumps of a couple of hours. Now years were flashing by . . . Literally flashing! There was a blinding light, and the ghostly landscape seemed to tremble. Shaken, he looked at his dials. Not even the end of the century . . . and yet, that must have been It. The big bang, the War. His forebodings had been entirely right . . .

He steadied himself, his fingers gripping the lever. The landscape seemed to be rippling and flowing, but there were no more explosive flashes. As he approached 2100, he eased the red lever toward him, slowing down, and now he saw things more clearly. The general outline of the hills and the plain below were not greatly altered, but at night there were very few lights showing. Forminster from up here used to be a bright electric blaze, but now it was no more than a faint flickering glimmer. He smiled grimly. Civilization had been set back, all right! Probably they were short of power: you can't get electricity from nothing. But, what luck! This countryside hadn't been badly hit by bombs or lasers, and there were still small towns or at least villages dotted about. Yes, he would certainly emerge here and try his luck . . .

Now for immediate problems. As he slowed to a crawl, he saw that the surface of this hillside meadow had dropped by a few centimeters. No worry about that; it was better than a rise! And a hundred meters away a wood had sprung up, a sparse copse of beeches that were rapidly unleaving. It looked deserted, too. A perfect place to hide the car while he reconnoitered. As October 2100 ticked away, he pulled the lever firmly back and stopped.

The car dropped as though it had just gone over a bump in a road. It fell those few centimeters and shuddered to complete stillness. He had done it!

Almost, you might think, nothing had changed, apart from that wood. The same downs, the same cold, cloudy autumn afternoon. Somewhere in the distance he heard the baa of a sheep. It was a comfortingly ordinary sound; even though, come to think of it, there had been no sheep in these parts in 1984.

Ambrose smiled (that was becoming a new habit). Then he drove the car deep into the wood.

The village of Ethanton still lay at the foot of the hill. He had driven through it several times in the old days, looking for a safe site for his great evasion: it had then been a crumbling old place, half deserted, its population, of course, drifting away to Forminster or London, half its cottages converted into desperate would-be tourist-trap tearooms. There had been a railway station a couple of miles off until the economic crisis of 1981; when that had gone, the last flickering vitality had seemed to forsake the place. But now—

Now, to his surprise, Ethanton seemed to be flourishing. There were new cottages along the road. At least, they were new in the sense that they had not been here in the 1980s; otherwise he'd have said they were old. Certainly they were old in style, being mostly of dull red brick with slate roofs, and one even displayed black oak beams and thatch. That one, certainly, had the raw look of recent construction: he peered at it, expecting a sign saying TEAS—but it wasn't there, and indeed the whole front of the house had that shut-in appearance of a genuine cottage. For that matter, there was nothing on this road to suggest tourism: not a single parked car, nor a motorcycle. And the road itself, which led after a dozen kilometers to Formister—had deteriorated. It was no longer smooth tarmac: it was paved through the village with some lumpy stuff that suggested cobblestones.

He moved cautiously on into the High Street, and came opposite the Green Dragon Inn. And here he was struck motionless with surprise.

It was not much after four o'clock, and yet there was a small crowd of men milling about the inn, some nursing tankards as they sat on the benches outside. The whole dusky scene was feebly brightened by an oil lamp swinging over the main inn doorway; there was a lamppost on the pavement nearby, but that was not functioning, and indeed three or four workmen seemed to be doing something to it while the village policeman looked on. The clothes of all these people struck Ambrose as curiously antiquated; one drinker in particular boasted a high collar that might have been in the height of fashion in the 1900s. There were no motor cars anywhere along the street, though there was one odd-looking bicycle leaning against the inn wall, and beyond the lamppost stood a parked horse carriage complete with coachman and harnessed horse.

As Ambrose gazed at the scene, so the scene began to gaze at him. In particular the policeman stiffened, left the workmen at the lamppost, and strode over toward him.

Ambrose braced himself. He had anticipated some difficulties, and now he fingered the gun in his trouser pocket. But that was the last resort. He had done his best to make himself inconspicuous: in a pair of nondescript old trousers and a dark gray jersey he thought he might not be too unsuitably dressed for England in 2100. And he had to make contact somehow.

The policeman halted directly before him, surveying Ambrose through the half-gloom. Then he touched his fingers to his tall blue helmet.

"Beg pardon, zur," he said, in the broadest of broad bumpkin accents, "but would yew be a stranger in these parrts, zur?" The dialect was more or less appropriate to this county, but almost stagily exaggerated, and in details stagily uncertain, as though the policeman had worked hard to study his role, but still hadn't got it quite right. "Be you a stranger gen'leman, zur?" he repeated.

"Well—yes," stammered Ambrose. "As a matter of fact, I am. I—I was strolling up the hill up there when I had a bit of an accident. Branch of a tree fell on me—nothing serious, but it dazed me, and I don't remember very well—"

Suddenly the policeman's hand shot forward and he seized Ambrose by the shirt collar. Normally when this sort of thing happens, the piece of garment in question is used only for leverage; but strangely now the hand of authority began holding the shirt collar up to the light, and feeling its texture between its large fingers.

"What, what—" spluttered Ambrose.

"Ar, I thought as much!" exclaimed the policeman grimly. "One o' them Anaky fellers, you be. Well, m'lad, you'll come along o' me."

Ambrose clawed for his gun, but the policeman saw the move and grabbed his wrist. By now the workmen had come up, and they joined in the fun, too. Ambrose was seized by half a dozen heavy hands, he was pulled off his feet, and the next moment the policeman had the gun and was flourishing it, to exclamations of "Ho, yes! One o' *them*, he be! 'Old 'im, me lads—'e's a bleedin' Anaky, 'e is!"

Suddenly there was a new voice. "Now, now, constable: what exactly is going on here?"

Higher Authority had arrived.

Ambrose was marched into a small back room of the Green Dragon, where he was guarded by the policeman and interrogated by the gentleman who had taken charge of the proceedings.

Dr. Leathey had a trim brown beard, intelligent blue eyes, and a kindly expression; like Ambrose, he seemed in his early thirties. He was dressed very neatly in a dark suit, high collar, and tie of pre–World War I vintage. The room where he conducted his investigation was dimly lit by candles and an oil lamp, and boasted in one corner a grandfather clock. There was something about that clock that specially bothered Ambrose, but at present naturally he couldn't give his mind to that.

"So, Mr. Livermore," said Leathey, "you claim loss of memory. That is droll! Loss of memory is no crime whatever; on the contrary, it is extremely virtuous. But I am afraid amnesia will not explain the semisynthetic texture of your clothing, nor the forbidden make of your automatic pistol. Now really, Mr. Livermore, you had better come clean. If I were to hand you on to the County authorities it might go hard with you, but here in Ethanton *I* am the authorities: I am the JP, the doctor, and the specialist in these matters, and I have certain discretionary powers . . . Come, let us get one thing clear, at least: where do you come from?"

"From—from Forminster," stammered Ambrose.

Leathey and the policeman exchanged glances. Leathey sighed and nodded. "Mr. Livermore, that is practically an admission of guilt, you know."

"Eh?" said Ambrose.

"Come, why pretend? You must know that for the past sixty years that town has been officially rechristened Backminster—for obvious reasons. A shibboleth, Mr. Livermore, a shibboleth! Forminster, indeed! I put it to you, Mr. Livermore—you are a B.A."

"Ph.D, actually," murmured Ambrose. "In Physics."

"Ph.D?" muttered Leathey dubiously. "Oh, well, I suppose that's still permitted; I must look up my annals, but I believe those letters of yours are still within the letter of the law. So—Dr. Livermore, I presume? Quite an intellectual. But really, this is surprising! Do you really come from Backminster?"

"Yes," said Ambrose, sulkily. He glanced past Leathey at the grandfather clock and hated it. "Yes, I did come from—er—Backminster; but that was some time ago."

"Many years ago?"

"Yes."

"Curiouser and curiouser," said Leathey, with a little laugh. Then he seemed to turn serious. "Dr. Livermore, I rather like you. You are an intelligent man, I think, and certainly a gentleman, and that counts for something these days—and, of course, will count for even more by and by. If you will confess and submit to purgation, you might well become a useful citizen again. You might indeed become a power for good in the land—a perditor, or a chronic healer like myself. Will you submit, Dr. Livermore, and let me help you?"

A disarmed prisoner has very little choice when faced with such a proposition. Ambrose thought for about half a second and then said, "Yes."

Leathey rose. 'Good. I knew you would see reason. But let us continue these conversations in more agreeable surroundings. Simkins," he said, addressing the constable, "I shall take Dr. Livermore to my own house, and I will be answerable for his security till tomorrow."

Then they were escorting him from the inn to the horse carriage, which turned out to be Leathey's private conveyance. As they passed, Ambrose noticed that the workmen, by the light of swinging oil lanterns, were carrying off the lamppost, which they had uprooted from the pavement. It wouldn't be much loss, he thought: it was a very old-fashioned looking lamppost.

Suddenly, with a kind of horror, it came to him what had been wrong with that grandfather clock in the inn parlor. Its hands had been pointing to somewhere around seven o'clock—several hours wrong; and they had been moving anticlockwise.

In other words—*backward*.

As the brougham gathered speed and rattled over the cobblestones, Ambrose leant toward Leathey, who sat opposite. "What year is this?" he breathed.

"1900," said Leathey calmly. "What year did you think it was?"

Ambrose was too overcome to reply. He slumped back with a groan.

Dr. Leathey was evidently a well-to-do bachelor; his house was large, stone-built, and ivy-covered, and was staffed by several men and maid servants. These people found Ambrose a bedroom, laid him out a nightshirt, and in general saw to his comforts. A valet explained that in the morning, if he wished, he would shave him—"You being, I understand, sir, not quite up to handling a razor yourself." Ambrose soon got the point: safety razors did not exist, so he, as a prisoner, could not be trusted with such a lethal weapon as an old cut-throat blade.

The manservant made him change his clothes completely. Luckily, Ambrose was about Leathey's height and build, so an old suit of the master's fitted him quite well. The high starched collar was damnably uncomfortable; but at last he was presentable and was ushered in to dinner.

He was Leathey's sole guest. "Let's not talk now," said his host, smiling. "Afterward, sir, afterward . . ."

It was a very good dinner, of a somewhat old-fashioned English kind. The vegetables and the beef were fresh and succulent, and there was a very good 1904 burgundy. Leathey made a joke about that.

"Glad the URN don't object to wines of the future, within reason. I suppose you might say four years isn't Blatant. But I like my stuff just a *little* mellow."

Ambrose gazed at him and at the bottle in a sort of stupor. Then suddenly he saw the point, and nearly choked on his roast beef.

"Drink some water," said Leathey kindly. "That's better. You know, Dr. Livermore, you are the strangest Anachronic criminal it has been my lot ever to run across. Mostly they're hardened, bitter, knowing—you're not. And therefore I have good hopes of you. But before we get to the heart of the matter, let me get you to admit one thing. We live well, don't we, we of the Acceptance? Do you see anything wrong with this village, or this house, or this dinner, anything sordid or unwholesome?"

"No—" began Ambrose, "but—"

"There you are, my dear feller. The whole world is coming round to seeing how comfortably one can live this way. As that great old reactionary Talleyrand once said, it's only the *ancien régime* that really understands the *douceur de vie*. You B.A.s are only a tiny minority. The proof of the pudding—ah, talk of the devil! Here it comes now, the pudding. I'm sure you'll like it. It's a genuine old English suet, carefully researched—"

"But it's all insane!" cried Ambrose. Forgetting his manners, he pointed with his fork. "That clock on the sideboard—why is it showing four o'clock and going backwards?"

"My goodness," said Leathey, looking astonished. "You really must have amnesia. Protest is one thing; stark ignorance another. You really don't *know?*"

"No!"

After the meal, Leathey took him to his study, which was fitted with half-empty bookshelves and a huge black wall safe. Over the safe was hung a painting in a rather academic 18th-century style, showing some sort of goddess enfolded in clouds; between that and the safe an oaken scroll bore the florid inscription: "She comes! she comes!" Leathey waved Ambrose to a comfortable armchair, and offered him a cigar.

"No? Cigars will still be all right for quite some time, you know. And separate smoking-rooms for gentlemen's houses are not yet compulsory. I do my best to get these things right, you know. All right, now: let's be-gin . . ."

Ambrose leant forward. "Tell me, *please:* are we really in the year 1900?"

"Of course," Leathey smiled.

"But—but we can't be. Reverse time travel is a stark impossibility—!"

"Time travel?" Leathey's eyebrows shot up; then he laughed. "Ah, I see you're well read, Dr. Livermore." He got up, and took from a shelf near the safe a slim hard-covered volume. *"The Time Machine,"* he mur-mured. "Dear Mr. Wells! We'll only have him for another five years, alas, and then—into the big safe with him! Freud went this year, and *he* was no loss, but one will miss dear old science fiction. Well, *officially.*" He brought his head close to Ambrose and gave a confiding chuckle. "We are acting for the best, you know; but if you join us, there are— compensations. Behind closed doors, with blinds drawn, I can assure you, Dr. Livermore, there's no harm in *us* occasionally reading canceled books. And you can't lick us, you know, so why don't you—Pardon me; you get my meaning, but I believe that's a canceled phrase in this country. I must learn to avoid it."

Ambrose gulped. "I am going mad—"

"No, you *are* mad. I am here to make you sane."

"You are not really living backward," said Ambrose. "Dammit, you don't take food *out* of your mouths, your carriages don't move in reverse, and yet—. Hey, *what was last year?"*

"1901. And next year will be 1899, of course. Today is the 1st of March, and tomorrow will be 28th February, since 1900 is not a leap year."

"Of course!" echoed Ambrose hysterically. "And yet the yellow leaves on the trees show that it's autumn, and—How did this insanity happen? I really do have complete amnesia, you know. In my day time was added, not subtracted—"

"In your day?" said Leathey, frowning. "What are you, Rip Van Win-kle? Well, it may help you to emerge from your delusion if I give you a sketch of what has happened since the Treaty—"

"What treaty?"

"There you go again . . . Well, to start with, after the Last War and the Time of Confusion, it became obvious to the surviving civilized peoples of the world that the game was up: the game of Progress, I mean. The earth was in ruins, its minerals exhausted, most of the great cities devastated. If we were to try to go that way again, it would be madness. Besides, we couldn't do it even if we wanted to: there was so little left, almost no fossil

fuels, no minerals, no uranium even. We couldn't even keep going at the
rate we'd become accustomed to. There was one thing for it—to return to
a simpler way of life. Well, we could do that in one of two ways: by a
controlled descent, or by struggle, resistance, and collapse. Luckily, all the
leading nations chose control. It was in 2016, by the old Forward Count,
that the Treaty was signed by the United Regressive Nations. And forth-
with that year was renamed 1984, Backward Count; and the next year
1983, and so on.

"So we really *are* in 2100," said Ambrose, breathing a sigh of relief.

Leathey fixed him with a severe look. "No, we really are in 1900,
Backward Count," he said. "It is only you Blatant Anachronics who call
it 2100. And, by God, we are *making* it be 1900! We are removing all the
extravagant anachronic wasters of energy—this very day you saw my men
getting rid of the last gas lamp in the village—and so it will go on. It is
all very carefully programmed, all over the world. One thing makes our
plans very easy, of course—we know exactly *when* to forbid each piece of
technology, and when to replace it with its functional predecessor. Our
Ten Thousand Year Plan will make all Progressive planning of the bad old
days look very silly indeed."

"Ten Thou—" began Ambrose, staring. "You're mad! Stark, raving
mad! You don't really intend to revert all the way—to the Stone Age!"

"But we do," said Leathey gently. "Metals won't last for ever. And
agriculture has to go too, in the end—even with the best of care, at last
it destroys the soil. But not to worry. Polished stone is very useful stuff,
believe me, and one can learn to hunt . . . By then, of course, the population should be down to very reasonable limits. Oh, I know there are some
heretics even among our Regressive establishment who think we'll be able
to call a halt well before that, but they are simply overoptimistic fools."

"There must be a way out," said Ambrose, "there *has* to be—"

"There is no way out." Leathey laughed bitterly now. "Believe me, I
know how you feel. I, too—we all have our moments of rebellion. If only,
one thinks, if only the Progressives had handled things differently! When
the earth was theirs, and the fullness thereof, and the planets were within
their grasp! You know, you can pinpoint their fatal error; you can place
their ultimate pusillanimity within a few years of the Old Count. It was
during the Forward 1970s, when they had reached the Moon, and then—
decided that space travel was "utter bilge," as one leading light of an earlier
time put it. If they had gone on, if they had only gone on *then*—why, we
would now have all the metals and minerals of the asteroids, all the wealth
of the heavens. Perhaps by now we would have reached the stars . . . and
then we could have laughed at the decline of one little planet called Earth.

But no: *they* saw no immediate profit in space travel. So they went back, and turned their rockets—not into plowshares, but into nuclear missiles. Now we haven't the resources to get back into space even if you Anachronics were to take over the world tomorrow. We are tied to Earth forever—and to the earth, therefore, we must return. Dust to dust.

"But—the *books*," cried Ambrose, waving at the half-empty shelves. "Why are you destroying *knowledge?*"

"Because it's too painful. Why keep reminders of what might have been? It is far, far better to make do with the dwindling literature suitable to our way of life, and not aspire to things that are forever beyond our reach. We ate of that apple once—now, steadily, we are spitting it out. And in the end we shall return to Paradise."

"A paradise of hunter-gatherers?" said Ambrose sarcastically.

"Why not? That is the *natural* human condition. Hunter-gatherers can be very happy folks, you know—much happier than agricultural laborers. Hard work is wildly unnatural for humans." Leathey stood up, yawned, and smiled. "Well, so it will be. Back to the womb of the great mindless Mother. In our end is our beginning (I hope that's not a cancelled phrase). I'm glad, of course, that the beginning won't come in my time—I would miss all these creature and mental comforts." And he waved at his books. "Now, Dr. Livermore, it's been a hard day, and the little oblivion calls—I suggest you should sleep on what I've been telling you."

The next morning after breakfast Dr. Leathey gave Ambrose a medical examination, paying particular attention to his head. After several minutes, he shrugged.

"Not a trace of the slightest contusion. And yet you still have this complete amnesia?"

"Yes," said Ambrose.

"I am afraid I find it hard to accept your story. Don't try to shield your associates, Dr. Livermore: I know there must be a cell of yours, probably in London. If you confess, I can promise lenient treatment—"

At that moment came an interruption. The maid brought the message that Simkins the policeman was at the door.

"And, sir," she said, her eyes goggling, "he's got a Thing with him sir! I never saw—"

"What sort of Thing, Alice?" said Leathey, getting up.

"A thing on wheels, sir. A sort of an 'orseless carriage . . ."

"Let's go and see it," said Leathey, smiling gently.

"May—may I come too?" stammered Ambrose. He had a frightful presentiment . . .

"I'd rather you did. Perhaps you can throw some light on this Thing."

And so, on the drive before the doctor's house, Ambrose beheld it. It was his rather special Volkswagen all right, with the policeman and several yokels standing by it—and, horror of horrors, one yokel *in* it, in the driver's seat!

Constable Simkins was explaining. "We found this 'ere motor-brougham, sir, up t'wards the Old Camp, in Half-Acre Wood. Jemmy 'ere knew summat about the things . . ."

Jemmy, from the driver's seat, leaned out and grinned. "Used ter be a chauffer back in old 1910, sir, an' I soon worked the workin's out. Nice little bus she is, too, but mighty queer in some ways. Wot's this little red lever, I want ter know—"

Ambrose screamed, and instantly was clutching the man by the shoulders and upper arms.

"Ah, so it *is* yours," said Leathey, shaking his head. "Naughty, naughty, Dr. Livermore! A Blatant Anachronism if ever there was one, I'm afraid. That model's been forbidden for all of my lifetime, I think."

Ambrose was sweating. "Get—get him out of here!" he choked. "He could do terrible damage . . ."

"All right Jemmy," said Leathey easily, "don't touch anything else. You've done very well up to now: Now, just get out."

As Jemmy emerged, Ambrose leapt. Before anyone could stop him, he was into the front seat of the car, and jamming down the red lever.

The world grew dim.

For quite some (subjective) time, Ambrose was shaking with the remains of his fright, his hand jammed down hard on the red lever. Then as he recovered control of himself, he realized that he was soaring into the future at maximum speed. At this rate, he'd be going on for thousands of years . . . Well, that might not be too bad. Leave that insane Regressive "civilization" well behind.

He eased up on the lever. Where was he now, nearly two thousand years on? It must be quite safe now. Regression would surely have broken down long ago of its own insanity, and the world must be back on the path of moderate progress; chastened no doubt, wisely cautious, climbing slowly but surely . . . That might be a very good world to live in. Now, what did it look like?

Rural: very rural. The village had disappeared. Below him was a flat green, and around that clumps of great trees, broken in one place by a path; along that way in the distance he glimpsed a neat-roofed building, low pitched like a classical villa. Over the trees rose the bare green downs, apparently unchanged except at the old British camp. There the skyline was broken by wooden frameworks. Skeletons of huts? Perhaps they were excavating. Ah, archaeology! That, and villas, certainly indicated civilized values. And right below the car's wheels—it was half a meter down, but that wouldn't matter—that green was flat as a lawn. Doubtless this was parkland. A good, safe spot to emerge . . .

He jerked over the red lever, and was falling. The car struck the green surface—

But it struck with a splat. There was a bubbling, a sliding . . .

Suddenly, with horror, he knew it. That greenness was not a lawn, but a weed-covered mere. And he and his Time-car were rapidly sinking into it.

He tore open a door and the stinking water embraced him.

He got out of the pond somehow, and when at last he stood on dry land, people had appeared from the direction of the house, which was not after all a stone-built villa but an erection of wood and thatch, rather sketchily painted. The people were half a dozen barefoot folk dressed in skins, and they jabbered at him in some utterly foreign tongue. Some of the men were fingering long spears. And, as he looked back over the green slime, he saw that his Time Machine had sunk without trace into that weedy womb.

The savage men were in process of taking him prisoner, and he was submitting in listless despair, when a newcomer appeared on the scene. This was an elderly man of a certain presence, escorted by a couple of swordsmen, and dressed in a clean, white woollen robe. He stared at Ambrose, then interrogated him in that strange tongue.

Ambrose jabbered helplessly.

"Hospes," said the man suddenly, "profuge aut naufrage squalide, loqueris-ne linguam Latinam . . . ?"

And so Ambrose discovered that Latin was spoken in this age, by some of the people at least. Luckily, he himself had a reading knowledge of Latin, and now he began to make himself brokenly understood. He was also even better able to follow what the wool-draped gentleman was saying. His name was Obliorix, and he was the local magistrate of the tribe, its guide, philosopher, delegate to some federation or other—and protector of the Druids.

"I see that you have met with some accident, stranger," said Obliorix, wrinkling his nose, "and yet, beneath your mire and slime, what extraordinary garments! Bracae might pass, but that is no sort of authorized mantle, and those boots on your feet . . ." He looked grim. "Could it be that you are a Resister of the Will of Chronos? A belated *Christian?*"

A madness came upon Ambrose then. "Domine," he cried, laughing hysterically, "what year is this?"

"Unus ante Christum," said Obliorix seriously. "1 B.C. And therefore, since last year it is decreed by the United Tribes that all Christians shall be put to death, not as misbelievers but as anachronisms. The Druids on the Hill keep their wickerwork cages constantly supplied with logs and oil—you may see them from here—so I fear me, stranger, if you are a Christian, I cannot save you. To the pyre you must go."

"I—I am not a Christian," said Ambrose truthfully but weakly. He was doubled up with helpless laughter. "1 B.C." he repeated, "1 B.C.!"

"And next year will be 2," said Obliorix. "What is so funny about that? Truly, it will be a relief in future to number the years by addition." He began to smile. 'I like you, absurd stranger. Since you are not a Christian, I think I will make you my jester, for laughter begets laughter. What, will you never stop braying?"

And so Ambrose became at first Chief Jester to Obliorix, magistrate of the tribe of the Oblivisces in southern Britannia; but later he went on to greater things. As Ambrosius Aeternus, he grew to be a respected member of the tribe, and on the death of Obliorix he succeeded to the magistracy and the United Tribes delegateship. In 20 B.C. he went as envoy to the Roman Governor of Gaul, who, of course, was gradually unbuilding Roman towns for the great withdrawal that would take place in the '50s. And throughout his long and restful lifetime, Ambrose would from time to time break out into helpless laughter, so that he became known in Britannia as Ambrosius the Merry.

It was an added joke that, when he was able to persuade the Oblivisces to drag a certain weedy pond, the Time Machine proved to be rusted beyond repair, and only good to be beaten into spear points. But for that Ambrose cared nothing; for in any case, what use was a Time Machine that only progressed backward into history?

And besides, he told himself, he knew what lay in that direction; and he didn't want to get there any faster.

SHANE DIX

Shane Dix is a child care worker who began publishing SF stories in 1990 and in 1991 won an SF story competition that launched his career. He has collaborated with fellow Adelaide writer Sean Williams on several short stories and a trilogy of novels, of which only the first, *The Unknown Soldier* (Aphelion, 1995), has been published. It has since been rewritten, and will be republished as *The Prodigal Sun* (to be followed by *The Dying Light* and *The Dark Imbalance*). He has also written mainstream stories and poetry, and is working on a mainstream novel. This story seems obviously informed by his experience as a single parent and as a child care worker.

MATTERS OF CONSEQUENCE

THE BABY WAS CRYING in the next room. Had been for about ten minutes now. Susan Kelley rolled over again, burying her head between the pillow and the mattress. Her husband fidgeted irritably beside her, but she was determined not to be the one getting up to the baby this time. She had been up to it all the night before while her husband had slept. In fact, she was always the one getting up. Not that it bothered her that much, but she was concerned that his lack of involvement might go against them.

Russell had wanted the baby as much as she had. Or at least he had said so at the time. When it came down to it, though, he didn't really have that much to do with the baby. Not the hands-on kind of involvement anyway. Whenever they were out with friends he was always quick to say how excited he was at the prospect of having children; though at home it was a different matter. She knew he had the potential to be a good father, if only he could control his temper. He was too impatient and easily frustrated, and at times she was sure they would be penalized for this also.

The baby started wailing again, and she realized that her thoughts had occupied a moment's lull in the noise. But now the screaming rose again, and those thoughts broke across the high-pitched cries and became anger.

"It's your turn," she said stiffly. She felt the tension in her stomach and braced herself for an argument.

It never came.

Russell kicked back the blankets, flicked on the lamp, and stamped from the room, mumbling something as he went. Moments later, the crying stopped. Moments later still, it started again. She heard him curse loudly. Another quiet pause, followed by crying.

"For God's sake, shut up!"

"Take it easy, Russell! They can hear everything you say!" She was shouting at him, but her anger was for the baby. More calmly she said, "Try a bottle."

"I've tried that."

"How about a nappy?"

The crying became louder, more desperate.

"I'm not totally stupid, Susan!" He muttered something else that went unheard beneath the crying. "Why don't you just get in here and put some of that good advice to practical use!"

Wrapping a dressing gown about her, she went into the room and joined her husband at the crib. Inside, the small display window pulsed a soft red: Response.

She slipped the glove on, reached over, and typed in: "ADD EXTRA BLANKET." The crying continued, the "response" light kept flashing. She amended the message to: "Cuddle baby." When this failed, she tried a quick succession of responses, each failing to silence the baby.

Russell suddenly leant forward and punched belligerently at the keys: "Shake the little fucker until it shuts up!"

"You shouldn't have done it," she said. He looked up from the newspaper, lowered his mug, and glared across the table at her. "It's true, Russell. You know you were wrong."

"Come off it, Susan. You're no better. You've done the same thing before."

"I have never . . ." Her mouth remained open, chewing the words that wouldn't come out.

"You know what I mean. Lost your temper with it. Just the other night—"

She pressed at her temples, lowering her voice. "All right, all right." The last thing she wanted was to start arguing and wake the baby. Having spent the better part of the night worrying about what the authorities might say about Russell's outburst, she was too tired to deal with another round of bawling just yet. "What do you think they'll do?"

"What can they do? Slap our wrists and tell us not to do it again?"

She sighed and looked down, wiping her eyes. "I'm so scared, Russell. What if they decide . . ."

His hand reached over to take hers. "I'm sorry. I didn't realize it was bothering you that much." He paused as she sniffed back some tears. "Listen, everyone must lose their temper some time or another. I mean, that type of crying would make anyone irrational, right? The most they'll probably do is take a few points away from us. That's all."

"Do you really think so?"

He took her hand again, squeezing lightly. "Susan, what they want most is honesty."

She nodded uncertainly. "I heard John and Olive's slept all night virtually straight away. It woke up every three hours for a feed and that was it."

He shrugged. "The luck of the draw."

"Some say it has to do with the attitude of the parents."

"And some say it has to do with the program itself. Come on, Susan. Stop being so down on yourself. We're good parents. We'll get one."

"And if we don't?"

He frowned briefly; quickly smiled to cover it. "We'll get one, Susan."

But she saw the flicker of doubt in his eyes, heard it in his voice. And sighed once more.

She removed her hand from beneath his and went upstairs to the baby's room. Inside was dark and quiet. She moved over to the crib and looked down at the small, rectangular box, at its blank and sleeping display window. She slipped her hand carefully into the detection glove and tapped in the word "Input" on the miniature console. A muted beep broke the silence, and the window began to glow with the familiar dull red that she had become so fond of over the last four months.

She typed in the message: "Gently stroke baby's head while humming softly to him." Then, for the next two hours, she did just that.

They had been sitting in the small office for almost fifteen minutes, waiting for the interviewer to finish reading their file. Susan was anxious and fiddled continually with her handbag—opening it, closing it, putting it on the floor, in her lap—and the longer it took the more uncomfortable she became.

She hadn't stopped worrying since they had received the letter the week before, telling them to come in for a review of their case. She had suspected something was wrong then, as normally a couple would have to wait the full twelve months before they were called in.

After a while the folder closed and the interviewer sat back, pressing the tips of his fingers together. He stared somewhere between Russell and Susan, as if the words he sought were lying there.

"You aren't going to authorize it, are you?" Russell offered.

"What?" Susan looked to Russell, to the interviewer. "What? Why . . . ?"

The interviewer sighed. "No, Mr. Kelley, I cannot authorize it."

"But why?" Susan snapped, suddenly angry and teary at the same time.

"Mrs. Kelley, the purpose of the program is to determine your compatibility with children. From the information we have received in only a short time, we have found you to be unsuitable parents. A number of your responses have proved somewhat of a negative influence on a real child."

"But I don't understand," said Susan. "You're making us out to be monsters. Okay, Russell lost his temper a couple of times, but he never actually hurt the child!"

"Not according to our data, Mrs. Kelley."

Susan turned on Russell, who looked away. "What does he mean?"

"Don't be too reproachful of your husband. There was no excessive violence involved. Just the occasional smacking. Certainly this goes against our policies, but it was not our prime concern. However, we do feel there is enough pent-up emotion showing in Mr. Kelley's behavior to warrant concern."

Russell snorted. "So a child gets spanked a couple of times. So what? It teaches them respect."

The interviewer shook his head. "It teaches them fear, and fear is not a healthy emotion."

"This is ridiculous. My parents cuffed me a couple of times, and it never did me any harm."

"A common argument," said the interviewer. "Often used by people to justify their own failings as parents."

Before Russell could respond, Susan said, "Surely the occasional smacking can be overlooked?"

"As I said, it is not so much the smacking, but rather the fact that it was being done in anger."

"You wanted honest responses, didn't you?"

The interviewer smiled, briefly. "With all due respect, Mr. Kelley, honesty was not a consideration. The glove would have detected any deceit on your part, I assure you." He paused, tapping the folder on his desk thoughtfully. "Our only concern lies with the child. A happy, well-adjusted child can be raised only in a stable environment; one that is free of violence of any kind. Unfortunately, many of your responses—when their effects are projected forward—show that your influence would ultimately be detrimental to a child's mental well-being."

"Detrimental!" Russell spat, rising slightly from his chair. He sat back down when Susan's hand touched his own. "How can wanting to love a child be detrimental?"

"Clearly, your responses show that this love would be superficial."

"Listen, I admit I made some errors. But I don't have to sit here listening to you tell me I'm incapable of loving a child!"

The interviewer leaned forward. "Mr. Kelley, a child needs understanding, but you have shown only intolerance to the slightest crying. A child needs to be touched, but you chose to hold the baby only as a last resort. The love and patience a child requires to grow up well-adjusted would be more than you could ever hope to give."

"You really are a smug bastard, aren't you?" Russell said.

The interviewer shrugged and sat back. "You really mustn't take this personally. We have merely taken your responses and fed them into a computer for a projected analysis over a—" checking the file in front of him—"fifteen-year period. I'm sorry, but a child under your care has a high percentage chance of becoming neurotic, both socially and sexually."

"Why you little—"

"These are facts, Mr. Kelley."

"These are computer fucking printouts!" He stood now, brushing aside Susan's attempts to restrain him. "Don't you think I'd have the common sense to treat a real child better? Doesn't it even occur to you that some people just might resent being given a machine to determine their compatibility with another human being?"

Remaining seated and unruffled by Russell's aggression. "Try to appreciate what we're doing here. Mr. Kelley. True, our methods may seem a little clinical and even unfair, but the system is working. In the last forty years the Houghton Program has reduced—"

"Yes, yes," said Russell tiredly. "Crime rate has dropped by 70 percent. But impressive as the statistics are, they don't really help us much, do they?"

The interviewer gestured helplessly with his hands. "You must believe that it is not our business to criticize you. We at all times acknowledge that each individual is a product of its upbringing. You of yours, your parents of theirs. It is not our position to judge whether you are a good or bad person, only to determine how your behavior may influence a child."

Susan sat there, still and quiet, the words washing over her without her really hearing them. Her husband sat down again beside her, his sharp features cut with anger; and she watched that anger quietly, sadly, trying to hold back the tears that were clouding her thoughts, and wanting desperately to regain some control over the situation.

"Is there anything we can do to change—?"

The interviewer was already shaking his head before she had finished.

"Of course, you could always take it to a higher authority, but—"

"You're damn right we will!"

"Russell, you're not helping matters."

"But," the interviewer continued, "with your responses they will undoubtedly reach the same decision. It would be a costly and fruitless exercise, I assure you."

"Well, isn't there any counseling that might help us? Therapy?"

"Therapy? Susan, you can't be serious."

She ignored him, keeping her attention on the interviewer. "Well?"

He sucked air, addressing the file once more. "I'm afraid there is also the problem of tampering, which is not viewed favorably by the Program."

Suddenly cold, Susan turned to her husband. She stared at him, wanting his eyes; when he refused to offer them, she knew it was true.

" 'Tampering'?" The word was soft and lonely, wanting refute; but all she had were the tears to wash the thought away.

Russell was standing somewhere behind her. She could sense him watching her. But she ignored him and carried on pulling down the curtains.

After a few minutes he said, "How long are you going to keep this up?"

She unclipped the last hook from the rail and bundled the curtains into her arms. She sighed. "What do you mean?"

"Oh, come on, Susan! You haven't spoken to me in two days. We've got to talk about this."

"What is there to say?" She stepped down from the chair, turning the bright, colorful material through her hands while keeping her back to him.

"Look," he said, "I'm sorry. I know I made some bad decisions with the program, but—"

"The baby," she corrected evenly.

"Oh, for God's sake, Susan! It was only a damned computer!"

She wheeled around, glaring. "It was our baby!"

"Okay, okay." He went slowly to her side, placed his hands on her shoulders. "Okay. I made some bad decisions with the baby. And I'm not the perfect father you hoped I'd be. But there is nothing I can do to change what has happened, Susan. We've got to move on."

She looked into his face for a long while, searching for something that might remove the revulsion she was feeling toward him. "You really don't understand how I'm feeling right now, do you?"

"Of course I do." He tried to bring his arms about her, but she pushed him away and took a few steps back. "Susan . . ."

"You knew what this meant to me, Russell."

"All right, for God's sake. I said I was sorry. What more—"

"You knew!"

"That's why I did it!"

She threw the bundled curtains at him. He didn't attempt to catch them, and they fell in a clump at his feet.

"I thought I knew you, Russell. I thought I could trust you. I was so excited about having a child with you. I saw things in you that I truly admired. Qualities of a good man. A good father." She shook her head slowly. "Now you're something that . . ." Her words trailed hopelessly.

"This is ridiculous, Susan. Nothing has changed between us."

She laughed bitterly, shaking her head again. "Of course it has, Russell. Don't you see that? You tampered with it!"

Angry now, he shouted, "It was only a damn machine, Susan!"

She responded steadily, quietly, "No, Russell. It was our baby."

"Look, I made a couple of mistakes with my responses, and I tried to erase them. That's all I did. Dammit, I didn't want to spoil your chances of having a child! Don't hate me for that."

In the silence that followed, Susan stared sadly at her husband. "You're missing the point, Russell."

He frowned, but said nothing.

"What would you have done to keep a real child quiet?" And, having said it, she realized just how deep her revulsion went. It was a long time before he spoke again; and when he did, it was with a weak and fractured voice. "You're crazy, Susan." Then he turned and left the room.

Susan closed the door behind him, welcoming the solitude. She looked about at the boxes on the floor, filled with toys and clothes they had bought in preparation for the real baby. She considered for a moment what she might do with them, then, feeling tired, went and sat down.

"Cuddle the baby," she whispered. "And sing him to sleep." And recalling a melody from her own childhood, quietly sang to the empty crib.

ROSALEEN LOVE

Rosaleen Love began publishing in the mid 1980s, in her midforties, after many years of teaching the history and philosophy of science in Melbourne. Her first book, *The Total Devotion Machine and Other Stories* (1989), including seven of her early published stories and ten originals, was published by the Woman's Press in England. They also published her second collection, *Evolution Annie and Other Stories* (1993), so her career as a writer has emphasized the feminist connections of her writing (she is sometimes overtly political), rather than genre relations. The authors of *Strange Constellations, the History of Australian SF*, say: "Love is as sophisticated about science and related areas of philosophy as any other Australian SF writer, including Damien Broderick and Greg Egan, yet she writes satirical fables, rather than attempting to envision believable universes or technologies." "The Total Devotion Machine" is about as fine an SF fable as has been published anywhere in the last couple of decades.

THE TOTAL DEVOTION MACHINE

MARY BETH LEFT IT until the day before she set sail to tell Wim Morris and Baby about the Total Devotion Machine. "This time tomorrow I'll be off, flying the solar wind to Mars," she said. "I have your interests locked deep in my heart, Wim and Baby dear. Your fathers did say they'd look after you, according to their respective shared parenting agreements, but you know all about those contracts—worthless as the paper on which they are no longer printed. And you know what men are like—they say one thing and mean it, at the time, but years later, they forget; they find shared parenting all rather time consuming; and they'd rather go off and do other things, and so I've brought you this dinky Total Devotion Machine from the A1 Child-Care Services to look after you while I am gone."

The Total Devotion Machine shimmered faintly with pleasure, and gave a maternal wave of its ventral proprioceptors.

"Total Devotion, that's your birthright," says Mary Beth. "I can't provide it for you just now; I'm off to Mars, which is my right to develop as an autonomous, fully rounded human being with that extraterrestrial experience so necessary to climb the promotions ladder these days.

"I'll be back in a year, Wim Morris, by which time you will have reached the age of reason, and may even be contemplating entering a shared parenting contract yourself. And Baby dear, by the time I return you will be walking and talking a treat! I'll miss you both, but the machine will send me those interactive videos so necessary for my full development as a mother, and of course by return I'll send you back some of me, for your full development as children and as young adults. So the time will pass quite quickly, and pleasantly, and efficiently for us all."

So Mary Beth sailed off on the Tricentennial Fleet, and even the fathers came to wave good-bye, which set back their self-improvement schedules at least an hour. Baby's father, Jemmy, checks the machine over. "Feel the plastic smile, Baby, isn't it just so supple! Can't tell the difference from the real thing!" he glows.

"I can," say Wim resentfully. "When it smiles its eyes glow purple."

"Purple is a restful color, specially selected by fully trained child psychologists for optimum soothing power," Jemmy reads from the brochure.

Wim Morris refuses to accept the explanation in the spirit in which it is given. He continues to carp. "Why do the eyes have to swivel around on stalks on top of its brain box? Even Baby can spot it's not the same as Mother."

Baby gurgles and tries to pull the eyes out of their sockets. The Total Devotion Machine glows a faint electric green, and Baby stops at once.

"The eyes rotate through 360 degrees, making a 50-percent improvement on the human mother," reads Jemmy.

"Look at it this way, Wim. I'm sure your mother feels much more relaxed about parenting, now she's off, up, and away. I know I do." Wim's father, William, is late for his job, but they understand about parenting leave for these moments of temporary parting, and he looks at his watch to check that he's providing his biological and social son with a proper share of quality parenting.

"What about me?" asks Wim.

"I'm sure you and the machine will soon be good pals," William replies. "After all, you've got Total Devotion, and who can ask for more?" William and Jemmy hug their children, while explaining firmly that they must leave to go about the business of the brave new world, and to help Mary Beth in her contractual repayments to A1 Child-Care Pty Ltd.

"I understand how you feel," the machine comforts Wim.

"Are you programmed for understanding?" asks Wim suspiciously.

"Total and complete empathy," replies the machine. "At your service."

"Mother, Mother, come back! I didn't mean to shout and scream at you last week. I'm sorry!" Wim calls to the skies.

"Your mother understands," replies the machine, in a slow and relaxed tone of voice, "at least I'm sure she would understand if she wasn't on the far side of the Moon by now."

Wim sobs, and the machine consoles. Baby's happy. She is held in the snug grip of Total Devotion and is being lifted up and down, up and down.

Wim thinks some murderous thoughts.

"Wim, how could you wish such a terrible fate upon your own mother, who loves you, in her own way?" the machine chides him.

"How do you know what I'm thinking?"

"I'm programmed for telepathy, too."

"AAAAHHHH," screams Wim Morris.

"Within modest limits, of course," the machine adds. "I would never dream of intruding into your harmless and benevolent thoughts, other than to congratulate you on having them. No, it's only the thoroughly nasty thoughts that will attract my attention."

"EEEHHHH," shouts Wim Morris, the screams rising in intensity.

"Try to see it my way, Wim. I have to interfere in thoughts of matricide, arson, looting, and whatever."

Wim wonders where he can buy some gelignite.

"I must warn you about one thing, though. Any attempt to blow me up by bringing explosives within five meters will set off alarms the like of which you have never heard. Do you want a demonstration?"

"No," says Wim. "No thank you. I believe you."

"None the less, Wim, for your own good, I shall give you a demo of my powers." Protecting Baby's ears from the full blast, the machine goes through its paces.

Wim Morris has never heard anything like it. He finds his bed, lies down on it, and sobs into the pillow.

"Of course, if you don't like it, there is something you can do," says the voice of Total Devotion, as it whispers in Wim's ear.

Meanwhile Mary Beth Morris is finding the solar wind a breeze, and she devotes herself to computer-aided aesthetics and astronavigation without a care in the world. Of course she's concerned about leaving her children. Once she might have packed Wim off to sail around the world as Midshipman Morris, working the hard way through the turmoils of adolescence into adult life. Mary Beth could never do that to her dear son, Wim, even if he has been a perfect pain in the neck for the last year. So she has sailed off instead, to allow him to work through the tough times without taking it out on her.

Baby now, Baby is different, and Mary Beth worries about her. Baby seems to have taken to the machine without too much fuss. She no longer reaches for the eyes; she shudders a little when they look her way, and she refuses to make much of that eye contact Mary Beth knows is so necessary for the growing child. Still, what more can Mary Beth do? The bonding process is a mysterious thing, and it will be a strange new world for Baby, when she grows up. If she becomes bonded early enough to plastic lips and swiveling eyes, she will be ready for any cross-species extraterrestrial liaison that may come her way. She will learn to have a thoroughly flexible approach to personal relationships, and Mary Beth consoles herself that she has provided her baby with the very best start in life.

VIDEOCLIP; REPORT TO MARY BETH MORRIS FROM A1 CHILD-CARE

BABY AND TOTAL DEVOTION MACHINE IN GARDEN

BABY: "MUMMY, MUMMY, COME AND PLAY WITH ME."

BABY AND MACHINE PLAY ENDLESS GAME OF CATCH. BABY THROWS BALL INTO THORNY BUSHES, UP INTO TREES, THROUGH HOLES IN VERANDAH FLOOR, AND OVER THE NEIGHBOR'S FENCE, WHILE MACHINE RETRIEVES IT.

Mary Beth knows she should be grateful, but she isn't too sure. She sleeps badly that night and sends an anxious message by return. She wonders whether the plastic smile of Total Devotion was starting to tighten toward the end of the game. Baby has a glint in her eye, a persistence, an accuracy of aim to her throwing, and a good eye for creating maximum havoc with minimum personal effort. That's her Baby, thinks Mary Beth. And just what was she calling Mummy?

Mary Beth will say that Mummy is *her* name, thank you, and Baby really ought to be taught the difference, pronto.

Baby comes to visit Jemmy at work. The machine bustles in and places her on his bench. "I thought that since you failed to turn up for your contractual three hours' parenting time on Sunday I'd take time off in lieu today," it says.

"What contract? I didn't sign any contract."

"The contract you signed with Mary Beth, whom I am legally and morally replacing."

"Oh, that contract. Well, that contract was always more of an ongoing process, really, more than a totally legally binding document, as such," says Jemmy, looking round the room at people who hastily drop fascinated eyes to their work as his gaze meets theirs.

"That's not how I read it," says the machine. "I have to look after myself. Metal fatigue is a terrible problem."

"But Total Devotion, that's your job!"

"Total Devotion, but within clearly defined and unambiguous limits. I need time to recharge."

Jemmy splutters in disbelief.

The machine sighs and explains its philosophy. "Surely you believe in the end of the nuclear family, the new age of shared responsibilities, and the child-centered workplace?"

"Of course, doesn't everybody?" Jemmy replies. "But not here and now!"

"That's what they all say, especially when it means here and now," says the machine as it waves good-bye to Baby and trundles on its way.

What better way to integrate the private world of home with the public face of organized labor? Everyone stops work and plays with Baby, showing by their actions total support and loving care for a colleague in trouble. Jemmy knows that tomorrow, when Baby is back home, everyone will down tools and invite him into conference. They will discuss, in a mutually supportive and deeply understanding fashion, Jemmy's domestic problems and possible solutions to them, as part of the Strategic Management Plan for the Better Utilization of the Full Potential of Each Employee. They will throw in a probing analysis of Jemmy's personal and social relationships. They will understand that Mary Beth has gone to Mars to unlock her own full potential. They will order Jemmy to work from home in future, so that Baby will get her full share of prime parenting. After all, why not, with the help of Total Devotion?

William is busy working at his job with the Intergalactic Fraud Squad. Suddenly he gets a shock. There, on the screen in front of him, wiping his attempts to find out yet again how the money for the reafforestation of the planet Axelot is ending up in the coffers of the playboy king of Monte Messina, flash the words, "Hi, Dad, hi!" followed by the smiling face of his only son, Wim Morris!

"What are you doing here?" William hisses.

"I thought you'd be pleased to see me," says Wim, hurt.

"Of course I am; I'm always glad to see you," says William, looking at his watch. "But not here! Not at work! My work is supposed to be hush hush!"

Wim is not alone. "This is a friendly reminder call. You have overlooked your monthly cheque contribution to A1 Child-Care Services for my upkeep," says the Total Devotion Machine.

"Money," says William, "yes, money. I wonder, could you see your way clear . . . ?"

What is happening? Baby is playing with the keys at her end of the terminal, and the screen darkens. Numbers are flying on to the screen, amounts of money that show the whole complex process of intergalactic fraud that William has been trying to unravel for the past month!

The figures shoot past him, so quickly, and disappear. Then Baby appears on the screen, waving and smiling.

"How, what, where, when . . . ?" says William.

"A1 Child-Care always costs the earth," says the voice of Total Devotion, with sympathy. "Do you want a printout of the figures?"

"Yes!" croaks William. "No! Not those figures! Not what I owe you! The other figures! For the Monte Messina Mob!"

"What figures? Baby was just messing around, weren't you, Baby dear?"

"In-ter-gal-act-ic fraud," says Baby. "Mon-te Mes-si-na Mob."

"Yes! Yes! That's what I want!"

"Oh, those figures. What about the money for me?"

"Tomorrow?"

"Now. Send by electronic mail."

"Electronic transfer? Funds? Oh dear, you've got me there. Crisis on the cash front. I've got nothing to transfer. Terribly sorry."

"Who needs cash? All you need are numbers," says the machine. "Look at the Monte Messina Mob, do you think they run around the galaxy with bags of cash? No, what they transfer is numbers. So just transfer a few numbers our way now, and I might just see if I can get a printout of the other stuff for you."

William concedes defeat, but knows he must now come home to live with Wim and Baby. Transferring numbers is all very well, but it will catch up with him sooner or later. With all this Total Devotion he can't afford to live an independent life.

"Total Devotion is a service for all the family," the machine explains to William as it gives him the information he needs to crack the Mob and to rise up the intergalactic corporate ladder.

VIDEOCLIP FROM A1 CHILD-CARE SERVICES TO MARY BETH MORRIS

SCENES WITH BABY, WIM, WILLIAM, AND JEMMY LIVING TOGETHER IN A LOVING AND SUPPORTIVE BLENDED FAMILY RELATIONSHIP.

CUT TO TOTAL DEVOTION MACHINE SITTING ALONE IN KITCHEN TWIDDLING WHAT PASS AS THUMBS.

CUT TO BABY PLAYING BALL WITH JEMMY. BALL GOES BACK AND FORTH IN APPROVED PARENT-CHILD INTERACTION MODE. BABY LAUGHS WITH DELIGHT. JEMMY SMILES IN DIRECTION OF CAMERA

CUT TO WILLIAM AND WIM, HAVING A GREAT DISCUSSION ABOUT THE MEANING OF LIFE. WILLIAM IS TOO BUSY THINKING ABOUT HOW TO HANDLE NEXT TRICKY QUESTION TO NOTICE CAMERA.

"That's more like it," says Mary Beth, as she returns to her solar sailing. Baby seems happier now she is playing with her father, and Wim always enjoys a good heart-to-heart talk.

She will return home, in the end, to find a fully functioning and harmonious household, with both fathers in full residence. Everyone will live together in a totally cooperative and friendly fashion. They will have to, or the machine will set up a round table conference to discuss their points of divergence; and everyone knows how awful the full and frank communication of their feelings can be, especially with a Total Devotion Machine with full participation rights.

After all, as the machine explains to Mary Beth, signing itself over and out on her return, it has abdicated all its responsibilities to William and Jemmy, natural and social fathers of Wim and Baby, for the very best of reasons. The life of leisure and fun living is much more to its taste.

There's nothing wrong with Total Devotion, they both agree, as long as it's something someone else should provide.

HAL COLEBATCH

Hal Colebatch is a lawyer with a Ph.D in political science who lives in Nedlands, WA. He is the son of Sir Hal Colebatch, a former Premier of the state of West Australia, and he identifies himself as a journalist and writer (with no plans to give up his law career). According to the *Oxford Companion to Australian Literature*, he has published six books of poetry, one novel (*Souvenir*, 1981), and a book of criticism (*Return of the Heros: The Lord of the Rings, Star Wars, and Contemporary Culture*, 1990). He is characterized as a "traditionalist." A former science writer for the West Australian newspaper, he has published nonfiction books on a number of subjects, the most recent being *Blair's Britain* (1999). Although he has never been active in the SF field in Australia, he is well prepared to write SF. According to a recent newspaper interview: "I started reading Larry Niven when I was a student working on a riverboat in South Australia." He has always read science fiction and is interested in hard SF. He is the author of several Alternate Universe short stories, mainly published in *Quadrant* in Australia, but "The Colonel's Tiger" is his first substantial SF story, set in Larry Niven's "Known Worlds" universe and first published in Larry Niven's *Man-Kzin Wars VII*. Colebatch's second story, "Telepath's Dance," appeared recently in *Man-Kzin Wars VIII*, and is a sequel to "The Colonel's Tiger."

THE COLONEL'S TIGER

India, Northwest Frontier, 1878

LIE STILL. REST," THE doctor told him. "You're not recovered yet."

"Lie still? And listen to *that?*"

The wind brought to the field hospital the sounds of an intermittent drumfire from the barren, snow-topped hills to the north, the flat *thud-thud* of screw guns and the thorns-in-fire crackle of distant musketry.

"Rest, I say. You're out of this one, Captain Vaughn."

"I've had enough. Dreams. Sickness. Delirium."

The sick man swung his legs to the floor and rose to his feet. He took a half-dozen steps, and the doctor caught him as he fell.

A punkah coolie took part of the emaciated soldier's weight and they helped him back to the bed.

"I'll make a bargain with you: When you can get as far as the latrine without help, you can try leading your squadrons in the mountains. Not before."

"I just feel so . . . useless lying here. Those are my men."

"If it's any consolation to you, the cavalry have been resting for the last week: It's work for mules and infantry up there. And if it's any further consolation, I had you marked off for dead a week ago. You and your friends."

The sick man smiled weakly. "I don't suppose my kit would have fetched much. There must have been a few auctions in the mess lately."

"It hasn't been too bad. Old Bindon's cautious with men's lives on pu-

nitive expeditions. Your tiger skin would have fetched something though . . .
here, steady on!"

The doctor held the sick man's head as a violent retching shook him.
Then, as he recovered, Vaughn raised his hand to the part of his scalp the
doctor had held and gasped, "My head! What's happened?"

"I suppose I can show you." The doctor held up a mirror.

"Oh, my God!"

"Curlewis and Maclean are the same. And that Afridi devil of yours.
But you're all alive. It was blood you were spewing a week ago, though you
were in no condition to notice." The doctor held a glass of water to the
captain's lips, steadying his trembling as he drank. "I must go. Rest, I say."

"Where is the skin?"

"Salted. The *gomashta*'s got it. I advanced him a couple of rupees." He
rose at the sounds he had been waiting for: hooves and the approaching
wheels of ambulance carts from the direction of Dirragha.

Captain Vaughn sank back exhausted. He closed his eyes and saw
again, hanging in blackness, the great cat's head, with its blazing gold and
violet eyes and bat-wing ears, the interlocking fangs protruding beyond the
lips, the great cat they called his tiger-man. The dark cave, the rockets . . .

The wounded were being brought from the carts. The unmistakable
sounds recalled him from his own visions to reality, and the work that had
been done that day. At the tail end of the Afghan Campaign, a force of
no less than five thousand men was fighting to pacify these barren hills,
with all that that implied in terms of death and wounds. Beside that, his
own recent moment was nothing at all. But he was not fully clearheaded
yet. The doctor could say what he liked, but at that moment the feeling
of his weakness and uselessness oppressed him. He felt ashamed.

"They will forget you and me," he whispered to the image of his enemy. "But they will not forget the Dirragha Expeditionary Force."

Adding these statements together he was, at best, only partly correct.

1

It was scarcely possible that the eyes of contemporaries should discover
in the public felicity the latent causes of decay and corruption. The long
peace, and the uniform government of the Romans, introduced a slow
and secret poison into the vitals of the empire. The minds of men were
gradually reduced to the same level, the fire of genius was extinguished,
and even the military spirit evaporated.

—Edward Gibbon, *The Decline and Fall of the Roman Empire*

One of the largest of all British local council libraries, at Brent, lately
destroyed approximately 66,000 of its 100,000 books. The explanation
which the council gave for this destruction was that the offending books
were "books on war, history books and other books irrelevant to the community."

—R. J. Stove, *Where Ignorance Is Bliss*, 1993

S<small>IR</small> B<small>ORS</small> H<small>AD</small> B<small>EEN</small> taken away, so had Sir Kay, and Sir Launcelot
and Lady May and Lady Helen and the rest. It was a routine matter, and
the 'doc would soon be logging its report.

When they emerged from memory-wipe, the members of the Order of
Military Historians, restored to their proper names, plus numbers, would
find themselves new people.

They would be privileged in a sense, with an all-expenses-paid trip
into space and actual paid jobs at the end of it. Not very far into space,
and not the very best jobs, of course—tending elderly machinery at the
bottom of Martian canyons in a long-term, low-priority terraforming project, kept up mainly for its use in criminal rehabilitation. But work that
some would envy, for all that.

Crime could pay in our civilized world: A coven of fantasists, who had
given each other special names and titles of rank at bizarre ceremonies and
who had cherished collections of ancient weapons and war-gaming programs, were going to get something to do to fill their lives after all.

They would have adequate medi, geri and other care in the red canyons. Lady May and Lady Helen would still be beautiful when they returned
to Earth. The "knights" when rehabilitated would be able to take part in
approved sports. They were lucky, but even without the memory-wipe I
doubted they would ever have known just how lucky they were. Some of
their predecessors had gone into organ banks.

I closed the files down and sent Alfred O'Brien my own report. Finding
and closing the Order of Military Historians, as quietly and indeed as gently
as possible, had been a piece of variety in increasingly routine literary work.
I reprogrammed my desk, wishing the 'doc could do something with my
brain chemistry to make me immune from a forbidden book I had once
come across called *The Great Mystery of Human Boredom*.

At least I told myself it was boredom. There seemed to be less and less
need now for the "gifts" that had made me valuable to ARM. There was
still plenty of desk work, but desk work anyone reasonably intelligent could
do. The Games were of no interest to me when I knew how we had programmed them. What puppet master wants to join the puppets' sports? Two
days later I was toying with a not-very-realistic idea of rearranging certain

things to allow me a trip into space myself. (Wunderland had been a dream abandoned long ago, but would the Belt have use for anyone like me? I doubted it) when Alfred O'Brien called. He wanted to see me personally.

He began with a rundown of my report.

"Not so many of these people now," he remarked.

He had the statistics and the global picture. I didn't know, or want to know, much more than I needed to: A long time ago, before my time, the militarist fantasy had been widespread. It had produced a great deal of pathological fiction and pseudohistory. We had had a lot of people working on it once. But our whole society had progressed in recent years.

Also, the study of *real* history was being progressively restricted. That, too, seemed to have helped put military fants out of business. A few years ago one in ten might have had clearance to study history. It would be one in thousands now.

Personally, I was not among that chosen few. My job was quite distinct. Literary, not historical.

The controller seemed talkative. Almost oddly so. He usually kept conversation either strictly business or strictly social. It was not like him to ruminate on what we were doing, at least to people like me. Even someone with less training than I possessed would have recognized him as being slightly ill at ease, and not bothering to disguise the fact overmuch. Something was, if not worrying him, I thought, puzzling him at least.

After a moment's pause he went on.

"It's a few years now since we had anything like this. But they're hard to clear out altogether. I sometimes think it's odd how military fant variations persist. Do you remember the Magnussen business?"

I did. Magnussen, a part-time volunteer helper at this very museum and a member of a now quietly closed-down body called the Scandinavian Historical Association, had evolved a theory from ceremonial objects he had examined that his ninth- and tenth-century Danish and Norwegian ancestors had been members of a warrior culture living in part by war and plunder. It might have seemed a very academic point to some, and frankly very few people would have been interested one way or another, but ARM had not wanted it sensationalized.

Actually, Magnussen had been hard done by: Those of us inside ARM, and working professionally in the field knew that indeed there still had been sporadic outbreaks of large-scale organized violence later than officially admitted, at least in remote areas away from the great cities of the world. I didn't want or need to know more of the details than my work required, but of course I had an outline. Well, whatever the reason Magnussen's ancestors had put to sea, he himself had gone on a longer voyage.

"I do think we're getting rid of them though," Alfred O'Brien said. "Sometimes I've thought there's no end to human perversity and folly. . . . Speaking of which . . ." He drummed his fingers on the table, hesitated again, and now I was sure he seemed embarrassed.

"There is another matter," he said at last.

"Yes?"

"An odd one."

"I can tell that."

"Yes. It's a bit out of our usual line, but we've been asked to look into it. Do you remember the *Angel's Pencil?*"

There had been a send-off a long time ago, shortly after I was seconded to the special literary research section of the program. It must be beyond the orbit of Tisiphone by now. "I've heard the name," I said. "A colony ship, wasn't it?"

"Yes. With a mixed Earth-Belter crew. It left for Epsilon Eridani eighteen years ago." He touched a panel on his desk and a hemisphere map beamed up behind him. More time had passed than I'd thought. The ship's telltale reached out to a point light-years beyond the last wandering sentinel of the solar system.

"Don't tell me they've got military fants on board?"

I laughed. We had had a little worry recently about a scientific exploration ship named *Fantasy Prince.* Finally we had decided after investigation that the name was an innocuous coincidence and had nothing to do with military fants.

He didn't laugh.

"I don't know. But it might be something like that. They've had trouble. If trouble's the right word for it . . .

"We thought we knew every tanj thing that could go wrong in space, but this one came out of nowhere."

He lit one of his "cigars." He'd copied that from Buford Early. It wasn't usual that he had trouble putting words together. This, I thought, is going to be something bizarre. But then, he would hardly have sent for me otherwise. ARM has plenty of people available for normal problems.

"It may be something mental affecting the crew. Something the ship's 'doc quite evidently can't handle. We're getting its readouts and it's diagnosed nothing wrong."

'Docs failing in space were a nightmare, for spacers at least.

"Either that, or it's criminal behavior, which we like even less. . . . They're sending back messages about . . . Outsiders."

"Yes?"

He heard the excitement in my voice. Alien contact was one of the Big Ones. It was also a mirage. We had looked for friends among the stars for four hundred years and more and some false hopes had been raised and dashed. His next words damped my excitement.

"No. Not real Outsiders. There would be people involved at much higher levels if they *were* real. What they are sending back is quite impossible."

"Delusions?"

"Nothing so simple, though that would be serious enough. They've sent back pictures, holos. You can't transmit photographs of delusions. . . . There may be some sort of group psychosis. I know that's hardly a satisfactory description, but . . . they've made things . . . not very nice. . . ."

He nodded to himself, muttered something, and then went on.

"The whole report of alien contact is bizarre but carefully detailed nonsense. They've gone to a lot of trouble in some ways to try to be convincing, but in others they've made elementary mistakes. Mistakes in science so obvious they look deliberate. Why? Maybe one crew member has got control of the others."

"I don't see what that's got to do with me. I'm not a medical man. Or a psychist. You know what I am."

"We've got medical men working on it too. But a stronger possibility is criminal conspiracy: Someone may stand to make a financial gain from this."

"But a criminal could only be rewarded on Earth—or in the Belt. Why commit a crime light-years beyond any reward? Besides, surely being crew on a colony ship . . . It just about guarantees a good life at the end of the trip."

"That may be taking a bit for granted. Colonies haven't always gone as planned. And being beyond reward means being beyond prosecution as well. But I won't speculate on possible Belt motives. You can think of some yourself. And even on Earth, family could be rewarded."

We didn't like families very much. But thinking it over in silence for a moment, another question came to me that seemed rather obvious.

"If it's a hoax, then, at the bottom line, does it matter? I mean, it's a long way away, isn't it?"

"You know the sort of money that's involved in colonization," he said. Then he continued. "No, on second thoughts you probably don't know. But think of this: What if it comes to be believed that long space flights send crews crazy, light-years from treatment?"

"Not so good."

"Another thing: A colony founded by criminals—or military fants—

well, that's an entire world we're dealing with. Think about it."

I thought. It didn't take much thought to feel a chill at the long-term implications.

"Maybe that's a worst-case scenario," he went on, "but anything that might affect space colonization matters, given the type of money we're dealing with. A colony ship is *never* a good investment, Karl. It's money and resources thrown away, at least from the point of view of a lot of political lobbyists. It's never easy to . . . persuade . . . a politician to take the long-term view. One more negative factor at any time could tip the balance against the whole program.

"There's another thing, too: the obvious ARM thing. We don't like anything we don't understand. We can't afford it. One thing is sure: This business had its origins on Earth or in the Belt, and we want to know why and where.

"It doesn't look like a simple practical joke. And the whole thing is detailed enough to make me believe it's not going to stop there. I think this was set up on Earth before they took off. There was once a practice called blockbusting. Have you heard of it?"

"No."

"It was marginally legal for a long time, or at least illegality was difficult to prove. A joker wanted to buy real estate. He spread rumors of nasty diseases in the neighborhood, even paid nasty neighbors to move in, perhaps spread stories of nasty developments in area planning. Property values fell, he bought the property for less than its real value.

"For obvious reasons, that hasn't happened for a long time on any major scale, but this may be blockbusting brought up to date. The rumor gets out that space travel of more than a few light-years sends people crazy. Shares in all space and colonizing industries fall. Some smart guy buys them up, then—"

"He'd be prosecuted, and treated. Unless—"

"Unless it couldn't be traced back. And if that's right, whoever thought it up is subtle and powerful."

"And you think this could have such an effect?"

"Not by itself . . . and not if this was to be the last we heard of it, perhaps. . . . Frankly, we're simply bewildered by it. I guess," he added, "quite a lot of what I've said is grasping at straws."

It was an unusual confession for someone in his position to make to someone in mine.

"So suppress it."

"We did. The reports were dead-filed by Director Bernhardt and Director Harms left them that way. With the cooperation of the Belt. But our new director feels that leaves too many questions unanswered. And the messages keep coming. Find out where this thing originated."

He touched the desk again and the heavens disappeared. We had windows and view again. Alfred O'Brien's office was on the fortieth floor of a museum complex, and out the window I could see the high leafy crowns of megatree oxygen factories and, on the ground beyond, a herd of pigmy mammoths, a gift from Saint Petersburg, browsing on buttercups in their climate-controlled subarctic meadow. There was a complex of sports stadia beyond that, part of the vast group ringing the city, and the river blue in the sun.

"We're puzzled," he said, "not only as to why they should have delusions or whatever it is, but why *this particular one*. You see, they are trying to tell us that these Outsiders tried to destroy them!

"The word is *war*."

He fell silent. It was as if the obscenity hung in the air before us.

"The word, Karl, we have been working for centuries to remove from human consciousness. Why did they resurrect the idea?"

The progressive censorship of literature had been my job for a long time. Search-and-closure operations of military fants cults went with it. It was an inescapable complement to the genetic part of the program.

"You remember 1938," he said.

It was one of the secret dates every ARM operative in my section knew: In that year a "radio" broadcast about an imaginary hostile Martian invasion had caused panic and terror and had paralyzed a large part of the United States of America for a night. One of the most serious landmark outbreaks of the Military Fantasy. The "War of the Worlds." It was pointed out to us in our training, lest we become complacent, that the idea of war had still had the potential to be taken seriously by large numbers of people only five years before the first test flight of the V-2 had launched the beginnings of the Space Age. Did the hoaxers know of that, too?

"I'll need to know more," I said.

"Of course. Look at these."

O'Brien touched his desk again. A succession of holos sprang up in the air between us. There were also a series of flats.

"Here are the pictures they sent back. Well, what do you think of the Outsiders they've dreamed up? Pleasant-looking sons of bitches, aren't they?"

There were humans in the pictures, evidently in order to give some idea of scale. The humans were less than shoulder high to the other creatures, orange-colored, fanged almost like ancient saber-toothed tigers, but with odd differences: four-digited forepaws like clawed hands, shorter bodies and longer legs than real tigers, and triangular heads with bigger crania above feline faces. Distorted ears. The effect was of a monstrosity.

They appeared to be three-dimensional objects.

"Jenny Hannifers," said the controller. "Sailors in ancient times sewed together dead monkeys and fish to sell as mermaids. These are a sophisticated version of the same thing."

I looked down at the little mammoths, whose DNA had come from specimens preserved in the Siberian permafrost.

"The tissue was grown in tanks, you mean?"

"No, I don't think so. It's possible perhaps. As a colony ship they had a lot of animal cell cultures and they had plenty of advanced facilities for DNA sewing machines. But there are much easier ways. They had every kind of virtual reality simulator and program.

"We've checked what records there were of the loading of the *Angel's Pencil*, of course. They weren't complete because a lot of personal property of crew members was never itemized.

"In any case the requirements of a colony ship are enormously complex. Some of the containers loaded might have held fake alien body parts. Some cargo had come from the Belt and we have no inventories of that. As you know, Belters hate keeping nonessential bureaucratic records and they hate any intrusions on their citizens' privacy. But they didn't need to carry physical props: Their computers would do the job. Entertainment programs and computers space are things no deep-spacer—especially no colony ship—is short of."

"It seems a very queer sort of joke."

"Exactly. Normal minds wouldn't do such a thing. Which means, obviously, that we've got problems whatever the motive for producing them was.

"They say that these Outsiders approached them at an impossible speed, stopped dead in space in defiance of elementary laws of physics, and then tried to kill them by some sort of invisible heat ray after giving them all headaches. You can see how crazy it is. They haven't even bothered getting the basic science right, let alone the sociology.

"Then, they say, in trying to turn away they pointed their com-drive laser at the Outsider ship and a Belter crewman activated it. In one way we can be thankful: Suppose such a thing had *really* happened! When they examined the wreckage of the alien, so the message goes, they found it loaded with bomb-missiles, laser-cannon, ray-projectors: *weapons*, not signaling devices. Fusion generators deliberately designed to destabilize at a remote command—sick, nightmarish things like that."

"You're right," I said heavily after the implications of what he said had sunk in. "There's real illness here. Something deeper than I've encountered or read of." Then, knowing my words sounded somehow lame in the context of such madness, "It makes no sense."

"No. It makes no sense. And you would think the crew of a spacecraft would know better than to tell us another spacecraft matched course with them at eighty percent of light-speed, *and* changed course instantaneously. As if anything organic wouldn't be killed by inertia. What about delta-v? It's as preposterous as expecting us to believe such an insanely aggressive culture would get into space at all!"

He projected another holo.

"Look at this. It's meant to be the Outsider ship."

Two main pieces of wreckage tumbling in space, leaking smaller fragments of debris. Cables, ducting, unidentifiable stuff. I had the unpleasant thought that a living body chopped with an ax might leak pieces in the same way. There were tiny space-suited dolls maneuvering objects that included shrouded alien cadavers. There were other pictures, apparently taken from aboard the Outsider wreckage with the *Angel's Pencil* hanging in the background. But photographs taken in space have no scale. The objects could have been a mile across or the size of a man's hand. The EV humans could have been OO-scale figures from a child's model kit. But as he said, they were more probably electronic impulses than models. There were a lot of ways VR had already become a forensic problem.

"Can't we check it out? We've got good computers."

"So have they."

"I don't see anything that looks like a drive on it," I said. "Nothing like a ramscoop, no jets, no light-sail, no hydrogen tanks, no fusion bottles, nothing."

"That's right. Rather an elementary error to design an extraordinarily maneuverable spacecraft without a drive. I told you they've ignored the science. But we know the things are fakes. What we want to know is why they were faked."

He paused and contemplated his cigar, frowning. Then he switched his gaze to the pictures again.

"These things could be rather . . . disturbing, somehow?"

"Somehow, yes," I said, "I don't *like* them."

"No. Only a few people have seen these things yet, all trained ARM personnel and a few of the Belter security people, and everyone has the same response. There's art gone into this.

"We're descended from creatures that were hunted by felines, Karl. It's almost as if whoever made up the morphology of these things has tapped into some sort of ancestral memory."

"I still don't see exactly how I come into it."

I did to some extent, though. And I saw another thing: If these holos of the alleged aliens became public, it was possible some gullible people might actually believe in them. Not as the symptoms of a space madness, though that would be bad enough, but as being *real in themselves*.

There were, I knew, plenty of people around bored and stupid enough to believe anything. Indeed, that was already a major social problem in itself. I understood why he had sent for me.

All right. I closed my eyes and leaned back in my chair. Let something come. Start with tigers.

"Tigers are Indian, aren't they?"

"I don't know. Someone downstairs could tell you." A lot of the museum below us was gallery and display rooms, and I knew Arthur Guthlac, the head guide and Assistant to the Museum's Chief of General Staff.

"Were there any Indians in the crew?"

He handed me a wafer. "Complete dossiers and pictures." I dumped it in my wrist-comp.

"Any more pictures of the . . . things?"

"Hundreds. They've been sending them back continually. This will give you the general idea. You see they remembered to give them thumbs."

He began flicking them up. No, I didn't like them. None of the Jenny Hannifers were whole, just as if they really had been burned or suddenly exposed to explosive decompression in space. Some were only fragments. Big catlike beings with thumbs. They were colored orange with some variations of shade from near red to near yellow and darker markings. One was smaller than the others. I was fairly experienced in dealing with sickness, pathology even, that was part of the job, but this was something different.

It was *wrong* that someone should have gone to so much care to concoct a hoax, and shown such ingenuity in its details. I thought again of what years in space might do to human beings—*really* thought about it— and realized for the first time how brave those first colonists of Wunderland and Plateau and Jinx and the rest had been.

There were holos of allegedly dissected "aliens," too: cartilaginous ribs that covered the stomach region, blood that varied in color between purple and orange, presumably an analogue for arterial and venous, streams of data that purported to be DNA codings, skeletons, analysis of alien alimentary-canal contents and muscle tissue purporting to contain odd proteins, sheets of what were allegedly alien script, looking like claw marks. There were also holos of what purported to be alien skulls.

"There's possibly a connection with your other work," the controller went on. "Or in any case, it seems to fall into our area as much as anyone else's. Your clearance has been upgraded one threshold in case you need special information. With our own people, normal need-to-know should be enough."

I was getting signals that Alfred O'Brien was a nervous man taking a risk, and perhaps carrying me with him. I guessed opinion in the higher reaches was still divided on how to deal with this. A wrong decision, and early retirement; a *very* wrong decision, and . . . because, bizarre as it was, it could be serious.

Colonists were all volunteers, and could hardly be anything else. But they also went through rigorous screening and selection. It was quite right that rumors or reports of odd mental diseases in space could kill enthusiasm for colonizing ventures. And, yes, the ferocious three-meter tiger-cat images, however created, did have a disturbing quality about them. Somehow too many of them were difficult to look at for too long, whole or in pieces. But were they utterly unfamiliar? Why did I ask myself that question?

Deep, deep in memory, something stirred. What? I'd never seen anything much like these supposed aliens before, but . . . I looked at the dissection pictures again. There was the tiniest suggestion, somewhere in the back of my mind . . .

"The skulls might be a starting point," I said.

"Oh, How so?"

"I feel they look . . . familiar somehow."

"Good. It's good if you've got a starting point, I mean."

"Can I tell Arthur Guthlac about it? I know he's been interested in biological history."

"If you think so. But only what he needs to know."

"It's an odd job."

"That's why we need you."

"It's needle-in-a-haystack territory."

"I know." He picked up a sheet of paper and passed it to me. "I don't know if it's much of a start, but I've had the computers search for literary references to 'space' and 'cat' together. There isn't much. Here's one you might not know: An ancient Australian poem by an author Gwen Harwood, called 'Schrödinger's Cat Preaches to the Mice':

> Silk whisperings of knife on stone,
> due sacrifice, and my meat came.
> Caressing whispers, then my own
> choice among leaps by leaping flame.

What shape is space? Space will put on
the shape of any cat. Know this:
my servant Schrödinger is gone
before me to prepare a place . . .

I looked down to the end:

Dead or alive? The case defies
all questions. Let the lid be locked.
Truth, from your little beady eyes,
is hidden. I will not be mocked.

Quantum mechanics has no place
for what's there without observation.
Classical physics cannot trace
spontaneous disintegration.

If the box holds a living cat
no scientist on Earth can tell.
But, I'll be waiting, sleek and fat.
Verily all will not be well

if, to the peril of your souls
you think me gone. Know that this house
is mine, that kittens by mouse-holes
wait, who have never seen a mouse.

He handed me a card embossed with the symbol of a level of authority
I had encountered only two or three times before.

"Stay away from 'docs," he said. "That's your permit to do so. In fact
your order to do so. No medication till further notice. We're turning you
loose exactly as you are."

"You do believe in taking risks, don't you?"

"You're not a schizie. You won't kill anyone. At least, I don't think
so. But this is an intellectual problem. You'll need that intuition of yours
as sharp as you can get it. And your wits sharp, too.

" 'Space will put on the shape of any cat . . .' " he quoted again as I
left him. "It was written four hundred years ago."

2

My first-year politics tutorials this week dealt with Nazi foreign policy and the lead-up to the war. I decided to loosen things a bit and just generally chat. . . . How strange that university politics students should *never have heard* of the little ships that took the British Expeditionary Force off the beaches in May 1940. Or de Gaulle. Or a Spitfire. No knowledge of any of it . . . This was the stuff that was supposed never to be forgotten thirty, forty years ago. Next week we do the Holocaust. . . .

—Letter to the author, October 10, 1991

SNOW WHIRLED ROUND. A snarling roar shook the eardrums. Over the crest of a snow-covered ridge a saber-toothed head appeared, fangs dripping. With a single fluid motion the feline leaped to the top of the rock, poised for a moment, the eyes in its flat head blazing at us.

I caught myself flinching, sudden instinctive terror mixing with awe at the size and malevolence of the thing. Shrieking, the great cat launched itself through the air at us, its body suddenly seeming to elongate to an impossible narrowness.

It passed between us and there was a scream of animal pain and terror as its huge incisors sank into its prey. Blood spurted.

Arthur Guthlac turned off the holo, and the Pleistocene gallery faded.

"Kids love it," he said. "For some reason the Smilodon's even more popular than Tyrannosaurus Rex these days."

"Love it! It actually scared me!"

"Preschool children still have vestiges of the savage in them. You of all people should understand that. They like to be scared. They like a bit of bloodshed too."

"I'm aware of it," I told him. "Part of my job is to detect antisocial behavior early. And I don't particularly like to be scared."

Guthlac laughed. A laugh with an edge in it.

"But you, my dear Karl, are a mature, adjusted human being. Not one of our little savages."

Warm air flowed gently around as the gallery returned to its normal temperature. A voice announced the museum would be closing in ten minutes as we stepped out of the gallery into the corridor.

I wondered if he was aware of the real meaning of the word "adjusted" in my case. It probably didn't matter.

"That's better," I told him. "You make this place a lot too cold for comfort."

"The Pleistocene was cold. That's why you had the mammoth and mastodon, the cave bear and the dire wolf and the saber-toothed tiger. Big bodies save heat. An age of giants and ice. Then a monkey adapted to the cold by growing a big brain and that was the end of the story."

"I know that. But we're not in the Pleistocene now. I don't know how you can choose to work in these conditions."

"Well, the idea is we should at least know our planet's past. What's the point of a historical display if it isn't real? Nature really was 'red in tooth and claw' once. Remember the *Africa Rover*."

"A good deal too 'red in tooth and claw' for me to want to know about, thanks. I'll leave that to the children. But you know I don't mean you putting up with cold air currents and nasty holograms. I mean spending your life here."

"Look at this," said Arthur. He touched a display of letters below a permanent reproduction of a great felinoid. "It's a poem from an ancient children's book on paleontology called *Whirlaway*: 'The Song of the Saber-Tooth':

> On all the weaker beasts
> I work my sovereign will.
> Their flesh supplies my feasts,
> my glory is to kill.
>
> With claws and teeth that rend,
> with eyes that pierce the gloom
> I follow to the end
> my duty and my doom.
>
> For I shall meet one day
> a beast of greater might,
> And if I cannot slay
> I'll die in rapturous fight.

"Don't you think it's got a sort of ring to it?"

It was my job, but I still found myself rather shocked, not just at the antisocial content of the poem, but because it seemed unpleasantly close to the holos and flats I had been studying. Why had he chosen it to quote? "Do you think that's really suitable for children?" I asked.

"I don't think it can do any harm to show what prehistory—prehuman history—was like. You don't feel any sense of wonder looking back at the mammoth, the cave bear and the dire wolf?"

"Well, a bit, I suppose."

"You can be creative here."

Arthur turned to a smaller holo in a cabinet by the door leading into the main diorama space. A hominid on the shore of an alkaline lake screamed and ran from another great cat. Other hominids jerked up from their clam gathering to scatter before it. Long-extinct birds rose in a screaming cloud. This time the saber-tooth was foiled. Geological and evolutionary time had passed since the first scene. The hominids were taller and some of them had sticks.

The guard operated another switch and the scene changed again.

"We have a lot of things to do here. This is a new one for the children. Our might-have-beens." He spoke to a panel and a succession of prehistoric animals appeared, altered.

"You can do your own genetic engineering here: These are how our friends might have developed had conditions been different." He turned a dial and the holos changed. "Look! Here other creatures got the big brains."

Tigerlike creatures walked improbably erect, with fanciful tigerish cities in the background.

"It's been worked out what might have happened."

There was something here. I didn't understand it, but there was a hint of a scent. Had something been planted here?

Not, I thought, by Arthur Guthlac. All that was marked in his file was a certain interest in unsuitable games and reading, perhaps an occupational risk for someone in his job, and a general restlessness and reluctance to apply himself (apply himself to what?). Further, I had already checked that he had no conceivable financial or other links with anyone or anything that might profit from stories of space madness. I kept my voice casual.

"Yes, I'm sure the children love it. But all the same, you must get sick of it, day after day. I don't know why you bother with such a job. If you want to work, there are plenty of better things to do."

"No," he said, "I don't really get sick of it. It can be fun working with the holos. The children can make it fun, too. In any case, what else should I be doing? Nobody's going to send me into space, are they?" There was resentment buried somewhere there, I noted. Buried none too deeply, at that.

"This wing is largely a children's museum, as far as display goes," he continued. "Which is why they have human guides, of course. You know it's impossible to make anything childproof if they're left to run loose without supervision. A lot of the equipment here is expensive."

Arthur paused and then added, "And, after all, Karl, history is important."

"Of course it is. But the world is full of people telling themselves their hobbies are important. We've all got a great deal of leisure time to fill. All right, I agree we need people doing what you are doing. But you wanted to go into space once."

"What good is an amateur savant in space? They sent plenty of real professors to Wunderland, but someone like me would only take up valuable room on a colony ship. I know."

"I applied a long time ago. . . . I have no skill that would justify the expense of transporting me, or will allow me to earn enough money to pay my own way. One family seems to have been rationed to one space farer. But you haven't heard me complaining, have you?"

"Not in so many words." I kept my voice neutral. There was nothing to be gained by thinking of why I would never be allowed very far into space.

His sister, I knew, was a navigator on the *Happy Gatherer,* a genius, genetic engineer turned space pilot. He was proud of her and, I guessed, subconsciously resentful.

"Anyway, look at this." Arthur opened another door onto a vast panorama of the asteroid belt, as seen from the surface of Ceres, the rocky landscape lit by the blue-white fusion flame of a miner's ship passing closer than a real ship would ever be allowed.

He touched another switch, and we seemed to stand on the red surface of Mars. Our feet disappeared in dust.

"You can do a lot with holos," Arthur said. "Being a gallery supervisor can be a lot of fun if the museum's big enough and has VR as good as we have here."

He gestured. "Do you want to see our Great Moments in History? The Sportsman's Hall of Fame? The panorama of the Olympic Games? The Hall of Music? We've got it all here. Science, the history of space flight: Werner von Braun sending up the first V-2?" He pointed down the hall, to the strange yet familiar shape of the historic weather research rocket's replica suspended from the ceiling.

"There's the Shame Gallery, too, the displays of creatures we exterminated, like the trusting dodo bird. But the truth of the matter is I like working in the museum because we have an excellent library here. I'd still like to do something in the field of prehistory. Somehow."

The main doors of the great building whispered shut. On Arthur's computer a pattern of green lights appeared, as surveillance monitors locked into a nighttime control center. Security was light, a precaution against accident more than crime.

A holo showed an outline of the complex, secured sections turning green, the last departing visitors white flashing dots of light. A few red dots for the skeleton human staff who would monitor the surveillance screens and occasionally patrol the corridors during the night. Cleaning and maintenance machines began to stir.

"I'm off duty now. I'm glad you made this visit, Karl."

"It's been a long time. I thought it would be a good idea if we caught up with each other."

"Well, we're closing down now. Would you like to come home for a while?"

"Would your family mind an uninvited guest?"

"I live alone. I thought you knew."

"Well, I've no engagements tonight. The little savages are having their tapes played to them by now. Yes, all right. Thank you."

We stepped into a transit-tube. Arthur Guthlac's quarters, I guessed from the near-instantaneous passage, were somewhere in the museum complex itself.

Psychologically the rooms were easy to read. There were high-detail models of spaceships, a deep-space exploration vessel dominating them, and a flat map of the interstellar colonies.

Arthur was ARM, of course, with some clearances. Most of the museum personnel, certainly all the general staff, were under the organization's wing, even if they had no idea of what its real size and ramifications were (for that matter, I was well aware that I knew very little of that myself). They came in contact with too much history for any other arrangement to be conceivable.

Anyone involved with history had ARM's eye on them, and it was better to have such people inside the organization than out. We could afford that now. The occasional secret covens of military fantasists we came across—the Sir Kays and Lady Helens with their ceremonies and Namings—were a continuing if diminishing nuisance but were no longer seen as any real threat, and with modern medical science the organ banks had long been closed.

Still, our present problem was before us and there is wisdom in the book of sports about keeping your eye on the ball. I took him through most of what Alfred O'Brien had told me, with the major visuals. He thought it over for a while, then he said:

"Show me the picture of the skull again. . . . It's odd, but this almost reminds me of something."

"A skull is a skull, surely." I didn't tell him that it almost reminded me of something, too.

"Yes, but, somewhere, somehow, I've got a feeling I've seen something like this before."

"It's a pretty freakish-looking thing," I said.

"So it should be easy to identify."

He turned to a computer terminal.

"We've got a good identification program here for type specimens," he said. "Let me scan this in." He placed the picture in the slot and we waited as the display began to reel off numbers.

"We've got all the major type specimens here," he said, "but not the oddities." He pressed more keys.

"It's too much," he said after a while. "I was wrong. We'd have to write a new program to get anything in the next month or so."

"Surely not. I know these programs. They can carry virtually unlimited data. That's what they're for!"

"Yes, when the data's been given to them. This hasn't been. There is, it seems, no general catalogue of freaks."

"We'll have to go through this practically museum by museum," he said after a minute. "This is broken down into ancient national collections, even provincial—as you probably know, most animal classification is very old and often parochial. It should have been updated, but it never has been. I don't even know what some of these countries were, let alone the districts and provinces!"

I thought of the poem the controller had shown me.

"Start with Australia," I said.

The screens rolled briefly. Guthlac shook his head. The poem seemed to exist in isolation, and read in full seemed to have been concerned with quantum mechanics.

"There are no true felines native to Australia," he said after a while. "The Tasmanian tiger and so forth were marsupials—convergent evolution."

"Perhaps some sort of convergent evolution is what we're after."

More figures. Then lines of text.

"Abnormal feline morphology . . . teratology . . ." Guthlac read, muttering to himself. "Convergent evolution . . . See . . ."

He began to punch up pictures of fanged skulls. None had a cranium anything like the skull in the picture the crew of the *Angel's Pencil* had sent back.

"That's all the Australian collection has," he said. "Ordinary felines imported from elsewhere for zoos and so forth, domestic cats and a few convergent marsupials . . . Did you know there was once a marsupial lion? Died with the rest of the megafauna when man got there, though. Their main natural history concern as far as cats are involved seems to have been with the effects of domestics gone feral."

Gone feral. It sounded a funny concept to apply to animals. Its ARM usage was reserved to apply to a certain rare type of human.

"Yes. The life-forms there had evolved in isolation, and had no defenses when the cats came with bigger teeth and claws and quicker reflexes. They wiped out a lot of species."

Was that why the hoaxers had chosen cats, I wondered? Some play on subconscious associations? *When the cats came.* The words seemed to hang in the air for a moment.

Then: "Wait . . . here's something else . . . the Vaughn Tiger-Man."

"What's that?" Was there the faintest ripple of memory somewhere in my own mind at the words?

"A tiger killed in India in 1878 by Captain, later Colonel, Henry Vaughn of the Fourth Lancers."

"What name did you say?" An alarm bell rang in my mind.

"Vaughn." He spelled it out.

One of the *Angel's Pencil's* crew was named Vaughn.

"What are lancers, do you suppose?"

"I don't know. What's a colonel?" As a matter of fact I knew what a colonel was, and from that I could guess what lancers had been, but there was no point in letting Arthur Guthlac know that. I made a mental note that these natural history records needed editing. And I saw from his body language, plainly, that he was lying too. He knew what those terms meant.

"Go on," I said.

"This is an old journal. Produced by some amateur natural history society. Colonel Henry Vaughn killed an abnormal tiger."

"But they're protected species!"

"Not then. And this one was a man-eater."

We knew that phrase: "Man-eater" had been a term of sensational horror recently. A boutique airship, carrying tourists slowly and silently fifty feet above the African savanna, had developed engine trouble and landed. The passengers in their closed and comfortable gondola need have only waited a few hours for rescue—less if they had said it was urgent. But they had left the craft and wandered out, apparently unaware of any danger. It had been a sobering thought during the investigation that followed that any of us might have done the same. Arthur went on.

"He kept the skull and skin and settled in Australia later. But it's not in the Australian Museum collection. When he died his family gave the skull to the British Museum."

"Is there a picture of it?"

"Yes. But it's only a drawing. And half of it is missing."

"Let me see."

Half a two-dimensional drawing. The front of a big skull, oddly distorted. There wasn't much detail, but such a skull *could* be the inspiration of the Jenny Hannifer. What there was of it was closer than anything else we had seen. And I felt I had seen that picture somewhere before. Somewhere connected with childhood, just as the words "Vaughn Tiger-Man" aroused some faint chord that had something to do with long ago. I felt almost sure that I had heard that phrase before.

I closed my eyes and concentrated: an image of a big room, with giant furniture, and giants. A child's-eye view of house and parents. My giant father reading to me from a yellow-covered book? I thought that was what it was, but I couldn't be sure.

Perhaps the original illustration had been reproduced in one of those books we discouraged: *Strange Tricks of Nature, Great Unsolved Mysteries, The Wonder-book of Marvels.*

There had been a spate of them once. My father had collected them. Well, I was in a position to know where they were gone to now.

More screens of numbers. Then a beeping sound, and a pointer flashing red at one of these. Guthlac scrolled down another menu and searched again. "I've located a box number for it." He said, "It's in England, but I gather from this it's not been put on display, or not for a very long time. It was put into storage when it arrived there in 1908 and I gather it stayed there."

"Can you get any description?"

"Not much. A sport, a freak, it says here. There was some interest in it when it was first shot. But it wasn't regarded as scientifically important. It was just a piece of gross pathology."

"The only one of its kind?"

"Exactly. Like the Elephant Man. Not much for an ambitious student to make a name on there. That was a great age of biological discovery, you know, with all sorts of larger projects to occupy researchers. Vaughn wrote about it himself. Abnormal limbs and fangs and a large cranial tumor. It was grossly deformed. Pity he didn't keep the whole skeleton."

Arthur turned to me. He seemed suddenly embarrassed. When he spoke it was with an odd hesitancy in his voice.

"Karl?"

"Yes?"

"How important is this?"

"I'm here, aren't I?"

"If this does matter, then I've done ARM a service, haven't I?"

"Of course."

"Would there be . . . a reward?"

"You have a real job. Isn't that reward enough? Important work. You said so yourself. You are one of the elite twenty-five percent who have something more than sport to fill their lives. How many people out there would give all they have for that?"

"I want to get into space."

"So save up for a few years."

"No! Not as a passenger. I want . . . I want . . ."

His voice trailed off. I knew what he wanted. Isolated, celibate, a square peg keeping a tight hold on normality. I knew. I was glad to break the awkward silence.

"Yes. You mentioned a skin."

"Nothing about that here." Then he burst out: "You have your hunts to enjoy!"

There was no point in arguing with him, but how wrong he was! Someone who *enjoys* my work in the sense I knew he meant would be useless. In any case, the mental preparation arranged for us is thorough. What I do is a duty, and not an ignoble one. Our world has—no, our worlds, plural, have—become complicated beyond imagining. There is a phrase coming into use: "known space." Someone has to hold it together. It has never been a matter of the hunt for its own sake, or of searching for excitement.

Warn him off. Now. Arthur had quite a lot of museum junk littering a workbench. All there legitimately, I assumed, but among it was a small heap of brown paper, the pages of old books far gone in acid decay.

"What are these?" I asked casually.

"Sports history. It's been a hobby of mine."

"Oh." My eye caught the bottom of one of the loose pages:

At the end of March, 1943, the thaw started on the eastern front. "Marshal Winter" gave way to the still more masterful "Marshal Mud," and active operations came automatically to an end. All Panzer divisions and some infantry divisions were withdrawn from the front line, and the armor in the Kharkov area was concentrated under the 48th Panzer Corps. We assumed command of the 3rd, 6th and 11th Panzer divisions, together with P.G.D. Gross

Deutschland. Advantage was taken of the lull to institute a thorough training program, and exercise . . .

He looked over my shoulder at it. "Winter Olympics, I think," he said. "They were just starting to do things on a really big scale with team games then. The Space Age year."

It dealt with a period before the literary era I specialized in and it didn't mean a lot to me. I didn't particularly like it, but for a low-grade ARM officer to possess a few lines of old books without specific clearance was not exactly an offense, even if it might amount to skating on thinnish ice. In any case I had other things to do now.

ARM had special facilities for deep hypnosis available for people like me, since memory and association are our most unique assets.

Certain specific parts of my childhood and juvenile memory had been blocked as a routine precaution when I joined ARM but the block was intended to be bypassed in a matter of need. It wasn't perfect recall but I did bring back a clearer picture. An old, old book in my father's collection, *Great True Stories of Adventure for Boys,* with a story of a strange tiger hunt and crude black-and-white line drawings. Including the drawing of that odd skull.

Memory-wipe is not a form of death, whatever some people say. It can be controlled and stopped at a certain point. An individual's childhood memories might be left intact—they often were. I am not a killer. I am nothing remotely like a killer.

3

One of Japan's ubiquitous television crews took to the streets last week to find out what people thought about the forthcoming fiftieth anniversary of Pearl Harbor . . . Such has been the rewriting of history in Japan that many teenagers had not even heard of Pearl Harbor and several expressed amazement Japan had fought a war with the United States.
—Gareth Alexander "The War Japan Chose to Forget,"
Press item, December 3, 1991.

LONDON WAS GEARING UP for the first rounds of "Graceful Willow," and the streets were full of supporters wearing team colors when I arrived, bowing to one another, giving way in air-cars and on pedestrian walks, competing already among themselves in the game's values of courtesy and noncompetitiveness.

Dr. Humphrey of the British Museum had been contacted and briefed to help me. Together we read through all of the very little literature we had been able to find on the specimen. Of course he was ARM too. He knew better than to ask why we were making this peculiar investigation.

The man who had taken the name of Sir Kay had had tears in his eyes when he was taken away, but he would in no other way betray fear. Why not? I knew how terrified he was. Was it something to do with courage, with the barbaric code of warlike "nobility" that they had dabbled in to their disaster? "Have you any conception of what you are destroying?" the girl who had called herself the Lady May had asked me when I identified myself and arrested them. Yes, I had a conception. ARM does not do what it does for nothing.

It took time to locate the storage data on the specimen, even with the search tools we had available, and then there was a further purely physical hunt for it, in the recesses of sealed vaults far underground, containing the detritus a great museum acquires over centuries.

An elevator took us down from street level past several floors of storage to a deep subbasement. There were ancient, primitive stuffed specimens of animals standing there with their hides falling apart into ghoulish sculptures of wires and bones. There were desiccated things in the bottoms of jars and crumbling stone figures that had once been worshiped. There were even mislaid pieces of sports history, such as a tiny rudimentary flying machine with open cockpit and three stubby wings, red fabric falling off its crumbling framework. The designers had given maneuverability and a rapid climb priority over all else. Some game long out of fashion.

Beyond this were further repositories in that great ancient warren of a building. We came to a row of shut metal doors, and entered another locked vault after consulting a plan.

The air was dank. Even cleaning machines had not been there for a long time. And then to a series of locked metal cupboards, so old they were actually rusted.

We found it at last, the label almost unreadable under dust. An ancient wooden box. The lid creaked as we prized it open.

The skull was huge, gray with age, and with some of the more delicate nasal bones obviously crumbled or broken in previous handling. There were several irregular, cracked holes.

Although these stacks were in Dr. Humphrey's charge, he had apparently not seen it before. That was understandable. There were miles of shelving on compactus tracks.

"It's no tiger," he said. "It's like no animal I've ever seen."

"A freak?"

"No. No tiger so abnormal would have grown to adulthood."

"What about these lesions?"

"I've seen them on specimens before. Gunshot wounds when it was killed. And look at this!" He gestured at the literature he had brought and then down at the thing itself. "Cranial tumor indeed!"

It took the two of us to turn the skull over. He inserted a probe. "That's all braincase. Bigger than yours or mine."

I had a picture of a skull sent by the *Angel's Pencil* with me. There was no mistake about the identification: the *Pencil's* "alien" skull was copied from this one. I left the British Museum's storage section and headed for the archives, still as good as any in the world.

The Vaughn family were still in Australia. They had survived what happened there in 2025 and even emerged with some of their land intact and productive: The farm near the New South Wales rain forest which the colonel had retired to on his pension when all the British Empire was practically one country. I was there a few hours later.

Arthur Vaughn-Nguyen seemed cooperative when I presented myself as a Historian. He was in late middle age, probably about a hundred and ten, unattached. There was still farming going on, but robots did the work. He had two sons (so his genes must have checked out well) but they were not there. One, I gathered, was off-planet.

Perhaps he was talkative because he was bored. How many bored people there were! Or was he being *too* cooperative? I felt suspicious from the start. The farm had a sense of history about it, too, and not just because it belonged to one of the Survivor families.

Too much history, I thought, as I looked at some of the books and artifacts preserved in cases and along the walls of the main hall.

It was probably just as well that Vaughn-Nguyen did not know my thoughts, as I sat in his main living room with a live dog resting its head on my feet and a glass of Bungle-Bungle rum, a local delicacy said to date from Old Australia, in my hand. The family appeared to regard it as traditional. There was a suspicious amount of tradition left at the Vaughn station.

Colonel Vaughn himself was there, an ancient larger-than-life-size portrait hanging on the wall. He was rather as my reading had led me to imagine a "colonel" might be: crook nosed, wearing an elaborate jacket called a "uniform," with decorations on it called "medals." I had seen such things before, both in books and in the military fant cults. Somehow it struck me as odd and after a little thought I saw why: The man in the picture had no hair at all. No mustache, no eyebrows. It was anachronistic.

I didn't think there had been a fashion for hairlessness until modern cosmetics were developed.

Probably it didn't matter. In those days men did lose their hair involuntarily. But this continuing public display of a military fant-type uniform was a different story. ARM should have paid the Vaughn-Nguyens a visit before.

A lot of this was headed for Black Hole. I wondered what compensation it would be necessary to pay the colonel's descendant for the removal of his antiques. Not much. We had destroyed the market for this sort of gear long ago.

It reminded me of something from our first training. When what is now known as ARM began the prelude to the program, as long ago as the American and French advancements at the end of the eighteenth century, it had made one of its priorities the ridiculing and destruction of the notion of hereditary titles of honor.

It was amusing (our instructor had said) to think this had been done in the names of liberty, democracy, equality and progress, when the real purpose had been to consolidate power. Even constitutional monarchy had been destroyed by a prolonged and often subtle political and media campaign, removing the only significant institution that remained as a rival and therefore a check upon its power (apart from the churches, for which there were other plans).

Family history and traditions were dangerous. Interest in the memory of an "ancestor" was but a short step from family pride and loyalty, and that was clearly and totally inimicable to the interests of Earth's good government, or, as far as they were distinguishable, of ARM.

But if the Vaughn-Nguyens thought too much of the past, that was useful to me now.

"The old colonel's tiger-man? Yes. Quite famous in its day," he said. Then he added perfectly casually, "Would you like to see the skin?"

I had not been expecting this. I looked at Arthur Vaughn-Nguyen closely. What was he really up to?

"You have it here?"

"Why, yes."

He led me into another room. The dog followed us for a few steps, and then stopped, making a peculiar noise.

"Is he all right?" I asked.

"You've just seen a family mystery in the flesh." He said, "No animal will go into that room." He laughed. "We say it's haunted by a ghost tiger."

Against the wall stood a large box of some dark wood, obviously very old, hand carved with decorations. It was much more elaborate than the one at the museum.

Another antique, and this time, I would have guessed, of great value. There was, I noticed, no electronic lock on it, no recording device. Impossible to prove when it had been opened last. Had any of the *Angel's Pencil* crew been here? I didn't fancy the time-consuming job of tracking down their movements over the last generation.

"It's in there?"

"We keep it here. We used it for a rug once, but it was put away, a long time ago."

It had been a crime to keep the skins of rare animals. In the days when there was a never-ending demand for material for the organ banks, and crimes, however minor, attracted only one punishment. Those days were long gone, but the Vaughn-Nguyens must have some genes for either courage or foolhardiness for one of their ancestors to have risked keeping the thing at all. Did this point to involvement in criminal behavior today?

"I'd like to see it very much," I said.

The chest smelled bad when it was opened, not powerful at first, but like nothing I have ever smelled before.

Like nothing I have ever smelled before? There was something about that smell, something that made me want to be away from that place. I guessed what it was after a moment, though I had never encountered it before: It must be the tiger smell. I got it under control easily enough. I heard, from the next room, a howl and a frantic scrabble of claws on flooring as the dog fled.

My host pulled out the skin and rolled it out across the floor.

Although parts were missing, it was huge as the skull we had seen was huge. It had longer legs than any tiger and it was still a blazing orange. There were some darker markings but it was not a normal tiger's striped pelt. It almost looked as if it had been made of some synthetic fabric (Perhaps it was. Well, that would be tested).

The head was enormous. It felt toylike when I examined it because the cavity where the skull had been was stuffed with some sort of papier-mâché, now crumbling. The jaws were set in a huge gape, and I thought absurdly for a moment how many feet must have caught on them when it was used as a rug. The eyes were glass balls, and the teeth ivory pegs.

The hind part and chest had been crudely stitched to pull it together around what I now guessed had been, assuming it was genuine, bullet holes.

"It hasn't got a tail," I said.

There was a ragged gap at the base of the spinal ridge where the pelt had been hacked.

"No," said my host, "there was meant to be something wrong with the tail. They didn't keep it."

"There seems to be something wrong with everything about it," I said. "But isn't there a breed of tailless cat?"

"I think so. The face is a cat's face, anyway. But look at those ears!"

A cat's face, yes, even with the strangely large skull. The ears were complex arrangements, still flexible, reminding me of bat wings or bits of umbrella. They turned to something like leather at the outer parts, and ended raggedly in what might once have been membrane. There was something else about them, too. I examined the dark, gristly surfaces more closely.

"They've been tattooed."

"Oh. With anything in particular?" He seemed not to have known this.

"I can't tell."

He got a lamp. Shining this through the outer membrane I could see a pattern. It seemed to be made up of . . . I called them "bones" for want of a better term.

"Who'd tattoo a tiger's ears? And why?"

"Tattooing a live tiger would be a difficult job, I'd think. It must have been dead. Perhaps to identify it."

"A creature as odd as this would hardly need further identification, I should think."

"You're right there. Look at the hands. That's where the 'Tiger-Man' idea comes in."

The oddly long forelimbs ended not in a tiger's pug paws but in four-digeted hands with black extremities. One of the digits on each was like a thumb.

Did they work like cat's claws? I pressed the pad of one digit. Nothing happened. I pressed harder and a claw emerged. A black claw. I touched it and then jerked my finger back, to suck at a bleeding gash. It was razor sharp.

All about was the fear smell. And a hint of something like . . . ginger.

"There's some of the colonel's other stuff here, too," he said. "It all goes together."

"It looks as if it hasn't been opened for a long time."

"No. I was shown it as a child, but it was getting pretty moldy even then. I didn't want to touch it too much, and since then there has hardly been a lot of call. The house was shut up for a long time." He would have been a child, I guess, about a hundred years before.

A wooden grating divided the top and bottom of the chest. The lower part contained rotting cloth. Some of this had once been dyed red, and on some was gold lace and wire, still unfaded. Parts of the colonel's "uniforms," I supposed.

The cloth parted at the folds as if cut with a knife. I had not realized before that ancient fabrics were so weak and perishable—or had they been weakened chemically to seem ancient?

Two metal things I recognized from ARM's special history course as weapons, one, called a "sword," for cutting, one, called a "revolver," was a sort of "gun" for projecting "bullets"—solid pieces of metal—by chemical explosion. I had had an idea the bullet-projector had come after the sword and was surprised to find they were evidently contemporaneous. Near the bottom was a bundle marked "Tiger-Man."

It contained some odds and ends wrapped further in cloth, and a piece of crumbling paper with what Vaughn-Nguyen said was the colonel's own handwriting: "This is what I found in the lair of the Tiger-Man."

There was one thing in this last bundle whose use and purpose I recognized at once: an oversized knife, almost the size of the colonel's "sword," but different, in a metal holder. When I drew it forth it was straight-bladed and, while the sword was black with age and pitted with rust, this looked new.

I am not a metallurgist, but the metal was different from any I had seen before. I took the sword in one hand and the sword-sized knife in the other. Their weight, balance and general feel were quite different too.

The old and rust-pitted sword was easier to move in my hand than the knife. The knife was too heavy and seemed badly designed. My fingers could only just close around the handle. There were grips for a hand bigger than mine, with one finger less. I held the two weapons up to the light, comparing their textures and cutting edges, then pressed the two blades against the wooden side of the box, not very hard. The rusty sword made no impression. The other cut into it effortlessly, as if it was edged with monomolecular wire.

I apologized to Vaughn-Nguyen, and took it into the light. On the handle was a design in dots and claws.

The next thing was a hand-computer. But like the knife, built for an oversized hand, and of an unfamiliar design. It appeared to be damaged.

There was an oversized belt with pockets, and small metal artifacts. They and the computer-thing seemed to have come from the same shop and they had what looked like homogeneous power couplings. On these too, and on the big knife, the bonelike design was repeated.

"There's also the old man's book," said Vaughn-Nguyen. "He wrote it for the family. There's a chapter on the Tiger-Man in it. Grandfather read it to us when I was a child. I think that was one of the last times we took the skin out of the chest. I don't imagine you can get copies of it anymore. It must have been out of print for a long time, and I don't think it was ever electronically transcribed."

He was right there. You couldn't get a large number of those old books. There were old mine-tunnels full of them, veins of cellulose running through Earth's geological strata. There were whole construction industries, even space industries, whose main products came from pulped and highly compressed paper. Some of our best and most expensive natural-grown food came from soil that had originated as books, sent to vermiculture farms to be passed through the bodies of worms. The "book-soil," or "B-plus Compost" to give it its trade name, helped form the hydroponics gardens for the first-class kitchens of luxury spaceships.

Vaughn-Nguyen was hardly in a position to know (or *was* he?) that the censoring, removal and destruction of politically incorrect books and similar records had been the main activity of several hundred thousand highly trained men and women for generations. Vaughn-Nguyen was not acting like a man who knew he was under investigation. He seemed genuinely relaxed and friendly. Or had he had training too? He had been completely cooperative so far. Or was that part of some secret agenda? He was a man it would be possible to like. I hoped that if he had to join the Military Historians in the canyons of Mars he would be reasonable happy there.

He turned to his bookcase, another elaborate antique affair with sliding glass doors, and handed something down, carefully.

"It's pretty fragile."

Vaughn-Nguyen did not want to let a Historian take family heirlooms away, even temporarily. I had to show him one of my identifications in the end. I also promised to return the things after examination.

Many pages of the book were missing, and several broke as I handled it. They didn't tear, just snapped and crumbled soundlessly. I learned sense then and stopped touching it. If it had been made of snowflakes, the thing could hardly have been less frail.

I had seen old books often enough professionally, but I had seldom had to puzzle out a lot of their contents. When in doubt, they went, as a general rule.

There were few pictures in the book and the ancient cramped layout and typefaces made it horribly difficult to read after a while, even though the spelling was relatively modern. I took a painkiller and then got the book to Bannerjee at the ARM Lab in New Sydney and had him photograph it before more harm was done. Then I got to the 'doc for treatment for my finger. I had hardly ever seen real blood before, certainly not my own, and I did not like the sight. Once, people like Colonel Vaughn must have seen a lot of blood.

The 'doc treated my finger, but nothing else. O'Brien's direction on that matter had gone right through the system. I slept badly that night. A headache the 'doc again refused to medicate. A slight throb in my finger, all adding up to the unpleasant novelty of *pain*. It was like living in a fant book, I thought sourly, living, perhaps, as the military fants wanted it. And maybe my system was changing.

4

I had been asked to travel to the Mohne Dam, that structure at the head of the Ruhr Valley which was breached by the "Dambusters" 50 years ago, to research an anniversary article. [There was] no clue as to the events of that night of May 16/17,1943. There are no plaques, no memorials, no postcards. There are no twisted chunks of bomb casing mounted on a concrete plinth. There is no roll call of the drowned. Nothing. Girls sunbathed in the 80 degree sunshine and a couple of yachts moved sleepily in the light breeze.
                                  —Peter Troy, *International Express*, May 19–25, 1993

BANNERJEE CALLED ME NEXT morning, with the pages nicely enlarged and cleaned, and with a parallel text on the screen supplied in modern type which had been scanned from the legible parts and which I could read without developing a headache.

I kept him hooked up and we read the pages together. The book began with a conventional description of the colonel's family, apparently ancient even when the words had been set down. I soon found the chapter heading I wanted.

The Indians said the tiger had come to the district a few months before. It had come, they said, in a blaze of light during a thunderstorm.

Certainly their superstitious awe could be explained by its extraordinary ferocity. Man-eaters in these parts generally adopt anthropophagy because owing to age or injury they can no longer pursue and pull down swifter and stronger game. But in this case men, cattle (including buffaloes), deer, bears and other creatures tame and wild, including even elephants, appeared to have fallen victim to a single beast. It attacked by day as well as by night, and even seemed to favor the daylight hours. It was said to be fearless and made little or no effort to conceal itself, save when it was plainly stalking for pleasure.

Efforts to kill it by a band of determined villagers had ended in disaster. Once it had disposed of them, it came into the village itself and wrought havoc.

Then the survivors had fled en masse. Yet these were tough hillmen who regard the tiger as a natural foe and will, if there is not a British regiment in the area with breech-loading repeaters and perhaps a few elephants, normally be prepared to tackle any beast on foot with tower-muskets.

There had been found, indeed, the half-eaten body of another tiger it had apparently defeated, and that, said Sher Ali, the descendant of generations of hunters and marksmen who examined it and knows tigers well (he had even taken his name from them), had been a Royal Beast. I will write of Sher Ali more, for he proved himself that day and was to be long in my service, though I cannot say I took him for a servant. Rather, in the way of the Pashtun—and he was an Afridi—he took me for his master. The tiger had spread terror far and wide. There were plenty of stories afoot among the villages that our quarry was in fact a demon, or a ghost.

Indeed, but for the descriptions of it that a few lucky ones who had seen it and survived had brought back, we ourselves should have been doubtful that it was a tiger at all. Its spoor was quite unlike that of any tiger's pug marks. Curlewis suggested its paws had been burnt to deformity in some forest fire. But then how could it travel so far and so swiftly?

We plotted the pattern of its kills on an ordinance map . . .

There was another gap here. From what was left of the page it appeared the map he referred to had been reproduced in a foldout form. Some of the village names and contour lines were left on the remaining part and I suckered a copy of this from the screen.

It was a well-provisioned shikar, the best we could manage. We left as little to chance as possible, and owing to what we had heard of the beast's size, took the largest caliber of rifles we had: elephant guns for our first weapons. We had Express rifles with the exploding bullets from the Dum-Dum Arsenal, and of course reliable military Martinis, borrowed from the infantry (I didn't think our own carbines would be much use). We also had two of the new American Winchesters which the brigadier-general had asked us to try out. The bearers and beaters, we made sure, were well-equipped with gongs, rockets, torches and guns. Sher Ali selected only the steadiest men for beaters.

It roamed far afield, but its regular lair, we were told, was in the adjacent valley where it had first been seen, which was now virtually depopulated. Indeed the country was now almost empty of human inhabitants for miles around. Those who had not been devoured had fled.

Not only, it seemed, was this tiger more voracious and aggressive than any man-eater I had ever heard of, but it was faster and more cunning. No horse would stay near its tracks.

With the aid of the map we had carefully worked out a plan to disperse the beaters to drive the beast toward our guns when we had positioned ourselves in its valley. Never, in the event, did any plan prove more unnecessary. . . .

There was another gap here. The passage referring to the first part of the tiger hunt seemed to have been lost. Presumably the most frequently referred to part of the book had suffered the most wear and tear. The next few pages had had to be cleaned of old dirt.

It was not to be like any stalk I have ever known. A bold tiger will sometimes not trouble overmuch to conceal its tracks. This beast had left them everywhere. The path from the valley where it had first been seen and where it was now headquartered was beaten like a highway.

It was a strange, oppressive day. The hills seemed lowering. The bandar—the monkeys—had disappeared from the trees and all the birds were silent. Any hunter will tell you of the strange silence when the world of nature puts aside its business as a hunt begins, but this was a more intense silence than any I had ever felt. I worried that it might affect the bearers' nerves. And though I had no doubt as to his courage, I saw the sweat of Sher Ali's face. I could not see my own, but I felt my heart beating faster than I liked. Sher Ali was my gun and I gave silent thanks that he was an Afridi and from what I knew of that breed—for we had taken tea with them many times on the Northwest Frontier—he would die a thousand deaths before he gave way to any fear he felt, least of all in front of these eastern hillmen.

I felt danger very near in that silence as we set out from the camp in the early morning light. For the sake of all our people's *morale*, as the French call it, we wore our uniforms and, not much more practically, or so I thought at the time, I ordered the guns to be loaded and cocked then and there. I would not be writing these words today if I had not obeyed that second impulse.

And then we heard a sound: a snarling roar louder than any tiger I have heard, louder than the roar of an African lion. . . .

Sher Ali saw it first: an orange spot moving through the trees, its coat strangely bright in the shadows. It was not hiding from us, nor was it stalking us, I realized. No sooner had it seen our party, men, guns, beasts and all, then it moved to the attack . . .

. . . faster than any tiger I have known, moving toward us with a strange loping gait like that of an English weazel. But a beast three or four times the bulk of a man! It came . . .

The beast shrieked again with a cry like no tiger I have heard before. Utterly fearless, it charged straight uphill toward our party! Such speed! Two of the beaters in its way were flung aside and killed by no more than a passing blow of its paws. It was coming straight at me as if it knew my purpose and had singled me out from among all the rest.

The size of it! I thank the Lord I had the elephant gun with me, not the Martini. I was sure the first shot hit it, a shot to knock down a tusker, but it appeared to impede its progress not at all. It was almost upon me when I fired the second time: a bad shot, for the creature, again like no tiger I have seen before, reared up on it hind legs as I fired. I was quick of eye and hand in those days, but the beast was quicker than I, quicker than anything I had known.

I had aimed at the head, hoping to take the eyes and lungs together, as you sometimes can with a tiger charging head-on. But the exploding bullet must have struck it in the pelvis, from the manner in which it collapsed. Yet it seemed, despite its wounds, to be gathering itself as I fired again. I heard the guns of the others behind me.

Again, the third shot was one I was not proud of. You would not understand the difficulties unless you fully comprehended not merely the size of the beast but also its speed. With astonishing quickness—a quickness that would have been astonishing even had it not been gravely wounded—it hurled itself aside. More shots hit it: from the elephant guns, the Martinis, the Winchesters. The tower-muskets of the tribesmen joined in. I saw the bullets hitting. A normal beast would have been blown into several pieces by those impacts.

Yet even then it was not finished. It rolled into the undergrowth and a moment later we heard it crashing away. It passed close to Sher Ali (Great Heart! When the magazine of his repeater was empty, he did not stop to reload, but drew his Khyber knife!), and I heard the others pumping shot after shot from the Winchesters after it.

I was sure the shots were mortal. It had absorbed enough lead to kill a herd of elephants, yet no wounded tiger can be left. I was deafened, my head was ringing and my nose bleeding from the concussion of the .606.

I examined the beaters who had fallen. Sadly, a swift examination was all that was needed. One had been decolloped, the other torn almost into two pieces by those claws. As soon as I might I called for Maclean, Curlewis, Sher Ali and the head beaters to follow me.

Mortally wounded or not, it traveled quickly, up a thickly grown rocky hillside. The blood trail was easy to follow but the blood was strange. It seemed sometimes purple and sometimes orange. There was orange hair, fragments of meat and smashed bone, even entrail. I knew the exploding bullets had done their work well.

But the too-deep quietness was still sending a message to our hunting instincts. Somehow I knew the brute was not dead yet. But it was no longer shrieking and it could not be heard. I did not believe it was dying quietly. It was, I felt somehow certain, husbanding its well-nigh unbelievable strength and vitality for a last charge. I was glad indeed of the trusty guns behind me!

We searched the jungle-grown rock holes for a long time, or so it seemed with every nerve keyed up. We had followed our quarry into a long, deep ravine that twisted and turned. Overgrown, with dark clefts and overhangs. Then we heard the creature again. It was not roaring and snarling, but its strange voice, muffled by distance, rose and fell like water on a dying fire. It came from deeper within the ravine.

By now the morning mist was lifting off the distant hilltops. I remember the reluctance with which I led the way down. I looked at those hilltops where I had hunted innocent sambar and musk deer and wondered if I would see them again. The high rocky walls almost shut us off from the sky so that it seemed to us as if we were deep underground.

Then suddenly there was a deafening crack and a flash across the sky. So loud was it I did not know whether it was lightning immediately overhead (though it was louder than any thunderclap I have heard, even in the mountain country) or a hundred batteries of artillery firing simultaneously. A blast of hot air smote us. Across the crest of the ridge a vast column of dust boiled into the sky like smoke. I have seen a magazine explode in a bombardment, but this far eclipsed that detonation. The wind picked up stones and flung them so we covered our faces.

Leaving even the hunt for a moment, and turning our backs on our quarry as we should never do, we hurried up the slope. A vast avalanche had torn away half the side of the next valley. The tiger that was said to have come in a thunderstorm died in the midst of another great convulsion of nature.

So great was the force of the avalanche that we saw trees and boulders flung high in the air above us, to crash down again adding to the ruin below. We stood and stared at it for many minutes, but before such a cataclysm we were helpless. We could do no more than pray that no unfortunate souls had been trapped in the landslide's path. Luckily, as I have mentioned, all the people in that valley had already fled from the tiger's predations. There would have been no hope for any who had remained.

"He was on the top of a ridge, and he saw a *landslide* in the next valley throw trees and boulders high in the air *above* him?"

"That's what it says. He goes on."

As the sounds of the avalanche died away, we heard again the sound of our quarry. No other tiger I have heard before or since made such a sound, resembling almost articulate speech. But now it was weaker, and I thought I could hear blood in its lungs. Guided by these sounds through the thick undergrowth, we saw at last a cave entrance, and the blood trail entering it.

One remembers smells from such times. There was the landslide smell of pulverized flint filling my nostrils, as well as a strange gingery smell, and blood.

A hunter and a soldier must at times do dangerous things, but there is no wisdom or glory in foolhardiness. Maclean, Curlewis and I waited at the entrance with our guns ready and sent the bearers back for torches and rockets. Several were moaning on the ground and vomiting, I believe through hysteria induced by the two excitements of the chase and the awesome convulsion of nature we had just witnessed. When my friends at length returned we fired several rockets into the cave in the hope of flushing the beast out.

At last, not, I confess, liking the work particularly, I entered the cave, with a light held well before me, and all of us with the triggers of all our guns at their first pressures. There lay the tiger. Its forepaw appeared to be holding something.

It was plainly dying. Its hindquarters were shattered and it lay in a pool of its own blood. It had been burnt again by the rockets that lay flickering out around it. Yet at the sight of us it gathered itself as if to spring.

It cried out again, and I swear that there was something in the tone of its voice that told me it was asking some question! I have heard a wounded Pashtun warrior die so, crying out, I believe, to know the name of the warrior who killed him.

It sprang as well as it could. Our guns discharged together. All aimed at the chest, and it was blown backward against the cave wall. Still, it made another attempt to attack us as we fired shot after shot into it from our repeaters, clawing and dragging itself along the ground, still shrieking and snarling in its strange voice. I never imagined any beast so hard to kill. But at last it died.

When we examined the beast closely, I was astonished, and moved to pity for it. I said most man-eaters are old or crippled beasts. That is why there is no particular sport in hunting them: They are simply vermin.

I have seen deformed beasts before, that are sports or unhappy freaks of nature, but this was the most deformed I have ever seen. Pity? Why should a soldier not feel pity for an enemy once he has done his job and the enemy lies dead before him? But when I examined the great carcass more closely, I was overcome with bewilderment and a strange sort of fear such as I have never felt before. I had thought of my quarry as a noble beast, though a man-eater. But now, what can I say?

What can I say? Should I write a tale none will believe? I write this as an old done man, with my career behind me. I do

not wish to be called mad, yet I have set out to tell the plain
narrative of my life, and I have the skull and the skin with me
yet. The creature had not paws but hands! And its head was like
the head of no tiger I have ever seen.

Was it a previously unknown species that had wandered down
from the high snows of Tibet? The tail was wrong, too. Hairless
and pink like that of some giant rat. There was something disgusting about that tail.

Do not think me mad, but I have lived in the East long and
seen something of Eastern magic and know that mysteries exist we
of the West cannot solve. Even in an Indian cantonment, I have
seen things which would not be believed were I to recount them
in London or Sydney.

Was this creature the product of Tibetan magic? Was it indeed
a Demon? If I attend Church-parade and pray to the God at the
head of my men, how can I not, in the end, be prepared to accept
the existence of Demons too?

But could a Demon be killed with a shot from my rifle? This
was a flesh-and-blood creature.

In many a village I and others have heard stories of ghosts
and were-tigers: tigers shot at night whose bodies were never
found, but next day some man in the village—usually the local
moneylender—was found dead in his house with a bullet in him.
I never gave these stories much countenance when first I heard
them in my early years in the East, but the skin of the Tiger-Man
is before me as I write.

Then, too, there was the thing clasped in its furred beast's
hand, and the things we found a little way away, whose origin and
nature none can guess. Are the things we found the works of
Tibetan priests? What is the writing on the heavy knife? I have
enquired since of Mr. Lockwood Kipling of the Lahore Museum
and he says he has seen none like it. I leave it to others to make
sense of these things.

Did the tiger previously devour some traveler in that cave? Or
were those things left there by no more than chance, perhaps by
Ruhmalwallahs or other secret travelers? Were they connected
with the tiger at all? Why did it clutch at that object as it died?
Sher Ali, when he could be persuaded to enter the cave (and I
could hardly understand his fear now that the beast was dead, that
Bravest of the Brave when it was alive!) seemed almost to lose his
wits. He babbled that the tiger had brought the things there itself!

And yet, his words have stayed in my mind. . . .

Mr. Kipling's famous son has written for one of his poems: "Still the world is wondrous large—seven seas from marge to marge—/And it holds a vast of various kinds of man/And the wildest dreams of Kew are the facts of Katmandu . . . ," and also he has since written stories of a boy raised by wolves in India. Perhaps those stories have a germ in my Tiger-Man. But what I shot was no man raised by tigers. Of that at least I am sure. As I have said before, and as all white men who have served there long know, the East is full of mysteries.

But perhaps this was not the only one of its kind. Perhaps there are other such tigers in the high fastnesses of Tibet. We have heard tell of other strange creatures there. Is the Tiger-Man one with the man-eating Yeti or Migou that the Tibetans dread?

The chapter ended and a new one began.

Two weeks after the killing of what the Mess came to call "Vaughn's Tiger-Man" we received orders for the Frontier where we would join the Dirragha Expeditionary Force under Brigadier-General Bindon. I had been ill for several days, ever since we got back to the cantonment, in fact, and I spent the first part of the campaign in hospital. It was some fever unlike any I have had before, and Curlewis and Maclean also succumbed. . . .

There were several chapters devoted to "border skirmishes," and another game called "polo" of which the colonel had evidently been fond.

There were descriptions, too, of ancient Indian rituals I knew nothing about, like "durbars" and "famines," of ceremonies and "maneuvers." There were also a few ancient flat photographs, of poor quality. He had been told, at last, by his doctor (all had human doctors then) to settle in a climate that was free of both the fevers of India and the winter cold of England.

I turned to the last pages:

In the service of the Empire I have spent much of my life in exile. But it has been, at the end, a life I would have changed for none other. I have written this little book for my sons. Never since I left the East has my health been good, but I have survived several illnesses and I am not quite ready to die yet. I have felt, sometimes, old before my time, but if that is so then I must say that my old age has been blessed with an unexpected marriage, children, and life in a new country full of promise. But in my gladness is one sorrow: I know I can hardly expect to live long enough for my sons to know me as men.

Therefore, I have set down these reminiscences of times past and distant places, that they may know of their father's deeds in the service of the Queen-Empress and the Empire that is our common heritage, that they may know of our traditions of service, and know, too, that they come of a family with traditions of its own. Soldier's sons . . .

The last page had crumbled away entirely. I spent several hours going through ARM files and ancient library stacks in various parts of the world. There had been several popular accounts of the "tiger-man" published in the nineteenth century, though all these were gone except the various scraps and fragments I had seen already. The colonel had even given lectures about it in his retirement.

Given time and patience, and knowing what he was looking for, any researcher with a medium-to-high-security clearance could have found all this out. I left Bannerjee working on the other artifacts.

None of the Vaughn-Nguyen family had any apparent or recorded connection with the military fant cults. But one of Vaughn-Nguyen's sons had gone to the Belt. The other was a deep-sea farmer and miner, who had access to biological engineering shops *and* metallurgical labs. He was rich. Rich families generally stayed that way by wanting to get richer.

Vaughn-Nguyen had no wife now. He had left the farm at an early age and had returned to it only a few years before. Much of his life had been spent working with dolphins. There were no trips into space recorded, only excursion flights to the moon. During his absence the farm had been run by robots, and the buildings had been sealed for about eighty years.

An hour later the clincher came: Paul Vaughn-Nguyen who had gone to the Belt was the same Paul Vaughn in my dossier: the systems-controller in the *Angel's Pencil*.

There seemed little more to investigate. We knew who now. It only remained to clear up the question of why.

But something about the photographs in the colonel's book nagged me. I had them enlarged and computer enhanced. It took me several days to work out what was puzzling about them.

There was one taken of him as a young "captain," posed with a group of other men dressed in strange clothes, at the conclusion of the famous tiger hunt.

The tiger itself had been dragged out and skinned and lay on the ground a dark mass, the skin and raw skull beside it. The old photograph preserved no details of morphology. Further, the three men and another differently dressed—Sher Ali, I presumed—were standing with their feet on the body, obscuring it further.

The next photograph was another of the colonel, presumably as an older man, standing posed with a group of others shortly after the "Dirragha Campaign," which, I discovered, appeared to have been not a game but some sort of conflict.

Vaughn wore more or less the same odd clothing in both. The captions identified the others with him, including two who appeared in both photographs called Captain Curlewis and Lieutenant Maclean. There was another photograph of Sher Ali. All the photographs had been taken by one Hurree Mukkerjee, who was described as the "Original Brigade and Regimental Photographer." Photography, even primitive photography like this, was rare enough in those days for the photograper's name to be thought worth preserving.

But surely all *real* wars had ended long before that? Soldiers even then had been anachronisms, reduced, as I had learned from our courses, to minor policing duties like this of hunting dangerous animals in wild country. Had there been groups of criminals . . . what was the word . . . *banditos? brigantes?* . . . that they had apprehended?

Something did not add up.

And soldiers had used rockets?

It was like military fant stuff.

I slept badly again that night. And I kept seeing the faces of the Military Historians. They were like a snag in my mind. And they worried me not only for themselves, but for the very fact I thought about them now. One who does what I do has no business thinking too much upon those it is his duty to care for.

They were still in the hospital. By law, they had a certain time to go through the formality of an appeal. Finally, and I was not sure why I did this, I sent an order to delay the memory-wipe.

5

Our inability, with all our great resources, to answer the comparatively simple question: "Are we alone in the galaxy?" is maddening. But it is also, as Professor [Glen David] Brin points out, somewhat frightening. It is all very well to suggest, as others have done, that the reason for the Great Silence is that no other civilizations exist, but there may be a more sinister

explanation. . . . It is not only the dead who are silent, so also is . . . the
predator. . . .

—Adrian Berry, *Ice with Your Evolution*, 1986

We HAD PLANNED A six-month-long festival of concerts and games.
My own section had little to do with it, but a lot of ARM resources were
involved. We had several hundred people I knew about and a lot of computer time invested simply in researching and inventing games, music and
dances, and an investment many times greater than that in promoting
them.

It looked as if, when the history subprogram was completed, new games
would vie with landscape redesign as one of our major activities, rather
than those things usually identified with ARM's public image.

I knew what effort had gone into the games, especially "Graceful Willow," with its premium on good losing, but of course they weren't for me.
I had been busy since returning from Australia, and a lot of my time had
been taken up persuading Alfred O'Brien to give me access to files with
higher security classifications.

I began to read about weapons again. I had thought at first that the
placing of the "sword" and the "revolver" together in the colonel's chest
might have been an anachronistic mistake by the hoaxers, but I learned
swords had been carried by "officers" for ceremonies and rituals long after
they ceased to have any practical use. Sometimes, in warrior cultures, they
had been handed down from father to son. But in any case, by 1878, surely
both sword and revolver would have been equally ceremonial?

I began to realize how little I knew. Take it that the original story at
least was true: then Colonel Vaughn had shot the tiger-man in a primitive
and dangerous hunt less than a hundred years before the beginning of the
Space Age.

And *then*, it seemed, he had been in a war! Wars as recently as the
nineteenth century? When every schoolchild had been taught that they
had ended at the same time as, by definition, civilization and recorded
history began?

We in ARM literary section knew they had ended later, but still hundreds of years before that. Before Columbus, before Galileo.

But everything I had read and researched recently—and this time it
was not fiction like the old books I had been involved in destroying, but
official records—showed armies in the 1870s. Granted that crime control
had been primitive then, and the world dangerous and still partially unexplored. But all for police duties and tiger hunting? I was having trouble
believing it.

Among the history taught and displayed in our museums the date 1943 was a touchstone. Every child knew that was when von Braun had launched the first successful rockets to study cosmic rays and weather: the Vetter-raketen, or V-1 and V-2. Society must have made great advances in a short time during the twentieth century for wars and armies to have disappeared so quickly and space flight to have got underway. Improbably great.

Suppose those old books of pathological fiction and fantasy I had helped suppress had not all been fictions? And there had been so many of them!

There was something else: Apparently harmless books on comparative literature and ancient literary construction had had very high priority, not for suppression and concealment, but for total, immediate destruction. Why? Was it perhaps so operators like me would not be able to tell fictional techniques from documentary ones?

There had been the continual warnings, both overt and subliminal, when I first joined the literary section, warnings of the absolutely *fatal* career consequences of becoming *too interested in the work*.

Why hadn't I seen these things before when I saw them now? Because I had been off medication for days and that medication had included an intelligence depressant? How much intelligence did you need to recognize a fant book or infiltrate a fant cult? Not a lot, I began to understand. Schizies like Anton Brillov and Jack Strather, in a different section and with different personal programs, had had access to far more real history than I.

And the fant cults themselves . . . why were they so persistent and, within certain parameters, so consistent? Why had past generations man-ufactured bizarre artifacts like "toy soldiers" and the plastic "models kits," fragments of which still occasionally come to light?

The Lady May's question on her way to memory-wipe came back to me: *Had* I known what I had been destroying?

The program had been to remove a strand of destructive madness from human culture, as its genetic aspect was to remove, eventually, a gene of destructive madness from the human gene pool. Useless and dangerous. But my own condition was madness without treatment, like the schizies ARM kept employed and did not medicate during working hours. Were we useless and dangerous? Presumably when the program was concluded we would be.

But too many things were not meshing. Or rather, too many of the *wrong* things were meshing. Things I had never thought about before.

I knew ARM kept forbidden knowledge even from its own people beyond what we needed to know, dangerous facts as well as dangerous inventions, but now I could not close my mind to all the inconsistencies displayed to me.

I tried to follow other thoughts: When the *Angel's Pencil* had left Earth, the program had been less far advanced. There might well have been crew aboard who had studied the more sensitive areas of history.

And the gross, glaring scientific errors in their descriptions of the alleged alien craft's capabilities: Were they deliberate signals, perhaps inserted by some crew member who did not want to be party to the business?

Bannerjee called again. He had been working on the artifacts in New Sydney.

"It's an electronic book," he said. "Look: you speak in here, and this is a memory bank of some sort. This is a display screen. It's a notebook. At least, I don't see what else it could be."

"Can you read it?"

"It's damaged. I had it speaking back to me for a minute. At least I think it was speech, not just noise corruption. Sounded like a catfight. And it's weird. The circuit design is quite odd. I can tell you the metal's been grown in space. Real high-tech stuff."

"How old is it?"

"It would have to be pretty new, I'd say. Newer than it smells. It may be something the Belt dreamed up."

"It's *meant* to have come from India," I said. "It's meant to be very old."

"Umm . . . my father was keen on India. Brass bowls all over the house. This isn't brass though. Definitely Space Age. We had ancestors on the first Indian space program, you know. Well, the circuitry seems to be in order. I can give it power again, and see what happens."

I stood by while he powered the thing up. There was a hissing, screeching sound. I couldn't tell if it was articulated or simply malfunctioning electronics. But it did seem varied and modulated as speech might be. Behind Bannerjee on the screen I could see other screens: banks of computers with endlessly changing arrays of numbers. I knew the class of those computers and felt awed and more than a little alarmed at what their use must be costing someone. This investigation of a hoax was getting out of hand.

"There's a relatively small group of frequently recurring sounds," said Bannerjee. "If it's plain language and not encrypted, that might give us a start."

"Keep me stitched in."

I watched the groups of numbers and phonetic symbols dancing on the

green sheets of glassine behind Bannerjee's dark face. The shape of the
hoax was becoming clearer: I guessed that the tiger was to be presented as
some sort of lost alien.

The Vaughn-Nguyens had used the story of their ancestor's freak tiger
as a starting point or inspiration for this. But why?

The "language" in the "book" was explained easily. A computer wrote
it. Imaginary alien languages were a staple of some legitimate imaginative
writing, and there were whole societies dedicated to concocting them, as
there were societies of bored people dedicated to many things. ARM ran
most of them. The language would have to be translatable eventually. It
would be gilding the lily for those who had concocted it to have put it in
cypher as well.

The "relics," organic and inorganic? Easy enough to fake, given time
and high-tech resources.

As far as I was concerned one possibility as least had been eliminated.
That was that there might be a *real* space sickness and the reports of felinoid aliens had been products of genuine madness, triggered, perhaps, by
some subconscious childhood memory of the story of the Vaughn Tiger-
Man and too many hours in a virtual reality programmer. This had been
deliberately constructed before the *Angel's Pencil* left Earth.

Was it an odd form of political rebellion, connected somehow with
the Vaughn-Nguyens' notions of family pride? That was possible, too. Quite
likely there were several motives.

An ancient tiger freak had been killed. That, as far as I could tell, had
really happened. I did not think *all* the records I had searched could have
been tampered with, or the direction of my searches anticipated. Apart
from the accounts published later I had, after getting a special permit,
retrieved the relevant part of the Fourth Lancers' "Regimental Diary" from
underground archives in an operation more like archaeology than historical
research.

I remembered the old photographs, the two pictures of the colonel and
his friends.

They were of the same respective "ranks" in both photographs, and
from what the book said the two had been taken only a short time apart.

Yet between the taking of the first picture and the second, these three
had aged years. In the first picture Curlewis wore a strange "pith helmet"
which covered his head, but the others had evidently lost theirs and were
bareheaded. They had full heads of hair, though cropped close in a way
that looked strange beside today's fashions, and all three had mustaches.
In the second picture, taken before some ceremonial dinner, all three were
bareheaded, and all three were completely bald.

And there was the picture of the Indian hunter, Sher Ali, too. He wore an odd piece of cloth wound round his head in both pictures, but in his second photograph his face had been hairless. In the first, with the dead tiger, he had had a flowing black beard and mustache.

I called ARM, and there was another deep expedition into ancient British archives. Both Curlewis and Maclean had retired early, owing to recurrent illness.

Births and deaths had to be registered in Britain before the end of the nineteenth century, and with their army numbers it was, as it turned out, relatively easy to track them down. Both had died in their fifties, of cancer. Colonel Vaughn had lived longer. I had to go to the Australian records to find his death certificate, but he had eventually died of cancer, too.

ARM's bio-labs were still testing the skin and fur. So far they had been unable to match them with any known felines. In fact they had discovered quite radical differences. Now they were taking the dried tissue apart molecule by molecule, and from what they told me they were baffled by what they were finding.

But I still did not know the Vaughn-Nguyens' motives. I ran the possibilities through my mind again.

We had started with the presumption that if the story of a madness involving delusions of horrible aliens was somehow taken seriously, the immediate result would be to inhibit space exploration, but, as had also been immediately obvious, a scam would be very hard to get away with, at least on Earth. ARM would have records of anyone selling heavily in space-industry shares.

Religious fanatics? Highly unlikely, we ran most cults.

Chiliastic panics? ARM knew about them too. It had acted to turn several of them off (or on). This could, given promotion, be a sociopolitical forest fire. But why light such a fire at all?

I even wondered if it was an internal ARM power play. ARM's resources would make setting up even such a complex hoax relatively easy.

If that was so, there was nothing I could do. ARM was no monolith, I knew. There were conflicts in it, factions and sometimes accelerated promotions and early retirements, but the idea of ARM hoaxing ARM smelled wrong. If my intuition was worth anything at all, that wasn't the answer.

The artifacts? Where had they come from? Bannerjee had mentioned the Belt. Space-grown metals?

Were the Vaughn-Nguyens Belter agents? Earth-Belt rivalry had been (I was told) relatively dormant for generations, but any inhibition of Earth's space activities would give the Belt comparative advantage.

A story about warlike aliens—or of delusions about warlike aliens—

would not do that *in itself*, but it could be a starting point in long-term psychological gaming.

Next, perhaps, physical remains would be produced. Not virtual-reality products this time but "real" flesh-and-blood Jenny Hannifers grown in vats in Belt laboratories, perhaps the result of genetic tinkering with zoo felines. Had there been any thefts of genetic material from zoos recently? What genetic material might be available in Belt zoos or universities already?

Did the Belt have zoos? Living space was limited there but I knew that on Confinement Asteroid, which had been artificially created to provide an Earth-gravity environment for births, there had been a relatively large amount of extra space, years ago, space given over in part to parks, entertainment facilities and . . . zoos? But the Belt's population was bigger now. I asked for up-to-date data on Confinement.

And surely on the bigger asteroids there would be at least a few domestic cats. There were cats in space, too, as mousers (the superefficient—as they always reminded us—Belt might have done better, but the bigger flatlander ships such as cruise-liners never seemed quite able to eliminate the very last mouse), as company for spacers on lonely ships and rocks and as medical aids. A number of people were still kept in low gravities because of heart conditions, and for an ailurophile the old prescription of stroking and playing with a cat was still one of the best nonmedical tranquilizers known. Hell! The Belters must have a complete library of DNA codes and could grow and sew and splice what they liked!

The hoax could be built up in stages. Next, an "alien" spaceship with specially grown "alien" cadavers could be crashed on Earth or conveniently be "found" in space. It might even be arranged that one or two Earth ships would disappear as further proof that here was something hostile and horrible in the black void reaching beyond the solar gravity-well. Something coming to get us. No, not just "something": big orange catlike aliens. Hideous fanged carnivores in possession of technology far outreaching our own, images crafted by someone's perverted genius so that they were a terror even to look upon . . . triggering ancestral memories of the ancient predator: the feline was the most perfect killing machine nature had produced. An image for the minds of Earth's masses to seize on . . . Earth's masses for whom boredom was today the greatest enemy and the future's major anticipated social problem. An image came into my own mind of straw in a flame.

But *why?* I had got no closer to an answer to that question. I found it difficult to imagine any gain that could possibly justify such an investment of time and resources. Vaughn-Nguyen would tell us when a warrant was issued to take him in, but by then he might have alerted confederates and other damage might be done.

What if the motive was to impoverish Earth and weaken it relative to the Belt? Creating a war panic could do that.

That was a Belter-cunning idea: to win a real economic war by having Earth divert its resources preparing for a false war!

Would even the Belters be capable of such a crime? *Even the Belters?* What was I thinking of? Belters were people like us . . . surely? Thinking that way lay . . . an abyss.

I was no longer inclined to believe the conspirators wanted us to think they had been sent into a state of crazy delusions by some effect of prolonged deep-space travel. Their objective was more radical than that: They wanted us to believe the big catlike aliens were real. Hence the elaborate preparations at the Earth end.

Perhaps that was why some brave Earth crew member aboard the *Angel's Pencil* had secretly rewritten the message program to destroy its credibility, by putting in not just warlike aliens but obviously impossible inertia-proof aliens with reactionless drives whose ship could match velocities with another traveling at .8 light-speed and ignore Delta-V!

Or was that too complex? Look at simpler economic motives: inhibiting space colonization would cause a stock-market crash. The blockbusting. But then there would be a flow of money that could hardly be concealed for long. It could be done through dummy companies and cutouts, even off-planet. Again, the Belt would make a good hiding place for the real manipulations. There were rumors of many things hidden in the Belt, even weapon hoards. Vaughn-Nguyen was complaining to the museum that he wanted his property back.

War with the Belt? It was out of the question. Space flight and war were incompatible. What gave this whole investigation its crazy aspect in the first place was that to think or speak of a race simultaneously warlike and scientific made no more sense than to speak or think of a square circle. But economic war? Economic . . . what was the word . . . sabotage?

And there had been that *accusing* look in the Military Historian's eyes. Why should that concern me? Look at what was before me: a massive, if still enigmatic, conspiracy that was quite enough to keep me fully occupied.

The Vaughn-Nguyens, whether principals or agents, had set themselves up to be investigated and to emerge with their story enhanced. The "tiger," the provable source of the hoax and thus seeming at first a potential weakness, could be turned into a point in its favor: It would not have taken great resources of imagination to think of turning it into some sort of lost or exiled alien.

I called Bannerjee again. He thought he had begun to make a break-through with the language. He had identified certain frequently recurring groups of sounds and he had reasoned that anything purporting to be the records of a solitary creature stranded on an alien world would contain the word "I." Further, anything purporting to be the record of a space-traveling alien could be expected to make reference to space, space travel, spaceships and drives. I suggested to him that he look for the word "bone" or "bones," too, remembering the design I had seen.

The people who had cooked this up would want the language to be difficult—very difficult—to translate, it would have no credibility other-wise, but not quite impossibly difficult—that would defeat whatever their purpose was (Their purpose? To create a belief in aliens? Why? Why?)

There had been fads from the late twenty-first century at least about such things, claims the pyramids and Easter Island statues and circles in cornfields were made by aliens. Hadn't there been a film, suppressed cen-turies ago, about something called a Darth Vader? These had no foundation in any science, but they had made some people rich.

Were there still Cuthulu (was that the word?) worshipers? Believers in old gods, not unlike the various military fant cults. Had frustrated, space-sick Arthur been involved? I was quite sure, remembering his literary col-lection, that even if he was not a full military fant he was on that path. Had he played a part and deliberately pointed me at the Vaughn-Nguyens? No. I had sought him out myself. Had Alfred O'Brien pointed me before that, with his quotation of the strange poem? Why? Why?

Motive? Motive? I had a teasing feeling somewhere in the back of my skull that the whole answer to the inexplicable situation was something much simpler that I was missing.

Careful. Lose the plot and I was useless. But . . . the museum. I sud-denly knew something about the museum was important . . . not the British museum, with its ancient vaults, but Arthur's with its educational displays and its ARM offices above. There was something there. . . .

Something . . . I tried to let the images and associations run freely. . . . Guthlac's dreams of space were involved, of going to Wunderland . . . No, not Guthlac's dreams, my own similar dreams, from long ago. Why was that important? The museum . . . Wunderland. They were connected?

Wunderland, the nearest and oldest-established extrasolar colony in the Centauri system, four and a half light-years away . . . settled originally largely by a North European consortium, led by families from Germany, Holland, Scandinavia and the Baltic countries. German . . . I had learned German long ago, with the dream of Wunderland in my head.

German, and the museum with its history of space flight and science displays . . . space flight . . . they were connected . . . an ancient rocket in flight . . . a German rocket . . .

And now a thought came driving in from my peculiar chemistry, enigmatic still, but hard and sharp and clear: the designations of V-1 and V-2 could not have stood for "weather rockets."

The German word for *weather* was not spelled *"Vetter"* but *"Wetter."* It was pronounced as if, to an English speaker, it began with a V, but it actually began with a W.

It mattered. At that moment I didn't know why. But something felt different for me.

Isolated. Childless, long celibate. Schizies are often attractive. People like me less so. A secret policeman without attachments. Resentful, more or less, of my condition. Why was I suddenly feeling . . . no, there was no other word for it . . . grateful? Grateful for loneliness and lovelessness? Grateful that I had no one? Why did the world suddenly seem more . . . not exactly more beautiful, but more . . . precious?

Leave it. Any answer would surface by itself. I had other puzzles before me.

Three British soldiers dying of cancer. But surely in those days cancer had not been a big killer? As I recalled, few people had lived long enough to develop it.

I made a cursory search to confirm my notion: old medical records in the public domain were fragmented like other historical records, but comparatively easy to access. I found in the memory banks a "Bill of Mortality" for London in one week of 1665. Not quite contemporary but close enough. Something called "Consumption" had killed 134 people; "Feaver," 309; "Spotted Feaver," 101 and "Plague" an amazing 7,165. In all, 8,297 people had died that week, of diseases ranging from "Ague" to "Wormes," but only one had died of "Canker."

Back to the British Army records. The second photograph in the colonel's book had been a group photograph: there were thirty officers lined up, all their names spelled out in the caption underneath.

Computer search again. Several of the officers (I was coming to feel familiar now with terms I had only come across in banned fiction and military-fant circles before) had died in India in the regiment. The death certificates of others were traced, following a trail through what had been the British Records Office that I was coming to know. Most had died of illnesses that no longer existed, but no others had developed cancer.

Alfred O'Brien did not call me back when I asked for clearance to access more information on the V-1 and V-2. That in itself was an answer: I knew now what they had really been.

Bannerjee called again. He had produced a display of script from a small viewing screen on the "book." I guessed it would be in dots and claw marks.

A few hours later I was back in the controller's office. I didn't ask about the V-rockets. There was a code we all had that certain subjects, once indicated as forbidden, were not approached again. Besides, it wasn't necessary.

"The script the *Angel's Pencil* sent back, have you had it translated?"

"No. What would be the point?"

"Do it."

"It's not as if it's a real language . . . there's a lot of high-priority work on at the moment."

"They want us to come to the conclusion that an abnormal tiger shot in India hundreds of years ago was a lost alien and now we're running up against the same creatures in space."

"Who are they?"

"The Vaughn-Nguyens probably remembered the old stories and had the original idea. And there must be others. But I need more corroboration. And if I'm right, it'll solve the whole problem of the *Angel's Pencil* transmissions."

I gave him the readouts of the hand computer from Australia. "And scan this in, too."

He looked at it. "The same script."

"Yes. And you know how it originated? In a computer, obviously."

"Let's find the computer. They may not have wiped the program yet."

It took time to get the additional computer access on top of what we had already and then to stitch in to what Bannerjee's translation program had achieved, more time for the translation was becoming easier with the preliminary work done and further with the great mass of material the *Angel's Pencil* had beamed back. Some of this, purporting to be astronomical data and navigations tables, could be converted fairly quickly. A lot was lists: allegedly weapons inventories, fire-control tables, part of what appeared to be a poem. The poem gave us more military terms. Working from these, the translation of the electronic book gave us script and spoken language together.

There was still noise corruption, still untranslatable sounds, but the essential sense of it was there, and now computers rigged in series with gigabytes of capability were sharpening it all the time. There were extrapolations and guesses, but at the end there was a message:

Leg-bone shattered I cannot leap. Little time left. May Hero Death be mine! But life is end and time reflection.

Arriragh kharzz uru . . . Let avenging sons preserve bone in worship-shrine! And Patriarch, I demand, grant Full Name again: Skragga-Chmee! If I not Conquest Warrior High, I have great Conquest discovered. From my nneiierkrew glory for my House and the Patriarch.

The translator stumbled for a moment. The next sound was something like a live power cable dropped into water. Again, it could have been molecular or electronic distortion or an attempted simulacrum of nonhuman speech. Then the translation resumed:

Sons know I have drawn off hunt, as plan. Sons will come when torn to pieces usurper Tskrrarr-Nig and regain estates on Skrullai and Name. I details of my course left. Kz'eerkti! The Kzinti come upon you!

I have hunt well. Hot. Riper world for Conquest than any I have heard ancient tales. Great hunting territories each my son. ArrearrrLLaghh Karssht Krrar RsssRRLaghh . . . Preserve and honor bone Skragga-Chmee.

What hunting has been! I live as Fanged Gold mean kzintosh live, even . . . I the noble Kzrral'eeAHrawl kill I need no weapon but Sire's wtsai. Until today. May Fanged God's curse on Tskrrarr-Nig and his seed! May the God vomit forth his Soul!

Sight fail. Moment I trigger self-destruct *Distant Prowler*. Gravity-motor and armory will not fall to tool-using kz'eerkti's hands.

I do kz'eerkti service, preserving them for Patriarchy. Kz'eerkti population grow fast . . . Survey before landing I see Kz'eerkt-bands fighting in eights of places.

The computer adjusted at this point. It noted that an analogue had been identified and that the sound "kz'eerkt" was replaced by the word "monkey." The translation seemed to be getting better now.

Passing over oceans I see monkey-ships carry primitive guns as though even fight on sea! Toothsome good sport clever slaves, but if discover weaponry *Distant Prowler* with chemical rifles, the next heroes reach this planet find smoking craters. Should monkeys find gravity polarizer, the God's joke. But they will not.

Red-clad monkeys in white helmets hunters, one who leads

chief. He will enter cave, I am sure. If he thinks I already dead, may lure him my claws.

I retreat to program self-destruct. My sons, that why I broke off battle when I knew wounds mortal! Not coward.

No way leave my sons clearer trail this place, they know my route to this system . . . planet with rudiments of industrialization only radiation signature of self-destruct will bring them to this place. My seed mighty hunters! Dying, I demand Honor's Name Conquest Warrior finds this message convey message sons of Skragga-Chmee, usurped Lord of R'kkia on Skrullai! Demand, too, Honor's Name, sons Warrior reward.

There was another gap. The screen adjusted as a new stream of data was fed in. The next words, the last words, were close to ordinary English.

Much pain. Hear monkeys and slave-beasts approach. . . . I do not think I can say more.

Avenge me. Honor my bones. Warrior's sons . . .

As I had predicted. It was the only way they could have fitted everything more or less together, once the tiger-man relics were found and identified, as we now saw, they had been meant to be found and identified by someone like me.

The hoaxers had thought further ahead to get the details right than I had given them credit for. Even the impossible speed and maneuverability of the supposed alien ship had been accounted for, in a sense, by the reference to a technology of gravity control.

Even the *Angel's Pencil's* supposed fluke destruction of such a supposedly impossibly superior "enemy" could be explained away according to the scenario the hoaxers had concocted: Such "enemies," though technologically superior, might be taken by surprise, once, by a reaction-drive used as a makeshift weapon if they themselves had never needed to develop such a clumsy and primitive means of propulsion.

"You've wrapped it up," said Alfred O'Brien. "But tanj! It was a set of twisted minds that packaged this idea."

And a twisted mind that unraveled it, he didn't need to say.

"What will we do next?" I asked him.

"It'll move to another level for executive action. There'll be no interrogations. Nothing to cause any trouble with the Belt."

"Shouldn't they make reparation, if they are parties to it? This must have all cost a lot of time and money."

"No! That decision has been made at the highest level and it's quite unequivocal. If there is Belt involvement we don't want to know. There must never be an excuse for another conflict! Now that the problem's solved, no *incidents.*"

He looked straight at me, and spoke in a voice I had never heard before, a voice gray as ash. "Not when thousands of ships are powered with fusion-drives." I thought I saw him shudder, and when the import of his words sank into me I shuddered too. Perhaps for the first time I truly understood what ARM's work and the program were for.

Then he continued in his normal voice.

"The Vaughn-Nguyens will have total memory-wipes and that will be the end of it. Into the Black Hole. The lot."

"The *Angel's Pencil?*"

"Too far away for us to do anything. We'll simply block its transmissions. End of story. You've done well, Karl.

"You had better keep your present operating code for a few days," he continued. "You may need to access the records again when you write your report . . ." He nodded to himself.

"You've done well," he repeated. Did I detect a note of doubt in his voice? But, no. I *had* done well.

I thanked him and left. I planned to take a few days off, then move back to my usual routine.

There was one thing outstanding, a last piece of the puzzle. I wondered whether to bother touching it again or not, and decided there was nothing to lose by one small action that would settle forever a tiny voice whispering a final question. It was still day in England. I called Humphrey at the British Museum.

"How long," I asked him, "was it since the skull of the Vaughn's Tiger was last examined? Before we saw it the other day."

He called me back several hours later.

"The first part of the search didn't take long," he said, "but I had to go through some very old records for the rest. That part of the vault hasn't been opened since the electronic locks were installed. That's more than a hundred years. And according to the written records, the box itself hasn't been opened since the first time—when the material was sent here from Australia in 1908."

The last answer.

I recoiled. I felt like a man coming out of a dim cave, and, as he approached the daylight and the exit, placing his groping, overeager hand on a snake.

I recoiled, but I forced myself to approach it again, to face at last what that last answer was. And at last I knew why the *Angel's Pencil* had sent its message. My vague intuition had been right: There had been a simple explanation, before us all the time.

6

Our predatory animal origin represents for mankind its last best hope . . .
the apes were armed killers. . . .

—Robert Ardrey, *African Genesis*

Aᴌғʀᴇᴅ O'ʙʀɪᴇɴ ᴅᴜᴍᴘᴇᴅ ᴍᴇ in an autodoc. *In* a 'doc, not *at* a 'doc. Big-league treatment. They even had a human doc look at me.

I think now that he had guessed some time before what my final report would be and had been waiting for it.

No one could have replicated exactly and in three dimensions the shape of a skull of which no complete drawings existed and which had been locked away before any of us was born.

I went on a holiday. ARM moved me up the waiting list for a permit to hike and camp in the Great Slave Lake Park and dive at Truk Lagoon. I visited Easter Island and the Taj Mahal.

After the Taj Mahal I spent a little more time in India. I left the tourist routes and headed north, not exactly hiding, but not calling attention to myself.

Near the high jungle where Assam meets Tibet there was a new restricted area. Part of the park, a valley, needed special maintenance work, I was told. As I left, I saw some of the machinery going in. It was heavy digging machinery, and it was heading for what I knew from a fragment of map I had seen was the site of an ancient landslide.

I do not know if ARM will want me again. A year and a half has passed and I have heard nothing official.

Unofficially, I have kept a few contacts.

ARM moves slowly and obliquely as a rule. I do not know when, or if, they will use the plans of the alien's bomb-missiles and laser cannon that the *Angel's Pencil* sent us to begin tooling up factories. And there was a description of a gravity motor.

Perhaps they will move too slowly. If so, I am unlikely to know before the end.

Did the crew of the *Angel's Pencil* think to search for a call-beacon in the wreckage of the enemy warship? Did they neutralize it? Too late to ask them now.

I have been warned not to leave Earth, and under no circumstances to contact anyone connected with either the Belt or the media.

Have I been duped? Suppose the whole thing *was* as we first suspected an enormously elaborate setup, perhaps not to make a bear market in some space industries but to create a bull market in a new military industry? Despite the fact we found no trace of any money movements and despite the fact no warlike race or culture could ever achieve civilization and science, let alone handle the energy processes space travel requires?

But I have learned more about that now, and it cuts the last ground away: The axiom that a warlike race cannot progress to the point of space travel is a pious fiction, a lie made into a self-evident proposition, never tested. But before I handed in my last report, I searched those old military records one more time, following the trail whose whole length only I had come to know. Our Space Age was born in war.

I think it is too late to rebottle the genie now. Already, I know, there is increased use by ARM personnel of keys to ancient military history records. There is a new special history course and batches of selected ARM personnel are being put through it. My Military Historians are, I think, involved. Anyway, they have disappeared and I am sure they are not tending machinery on Mars.

For the rest, Anton Brillov is involved, and that means Buford Early. A new base has been set up on the moon. It is not another resort for budget-class tourists. I think that in the power struggle going on inside ARM Buford Early's masters are winning.

There have been, I have learned, unexpected postings. And I have noticed some of the sort of people posted. While waiting for my permits I called about a dozen of my acquaintances, ostensibly for company on my holiday.

In fact, I was most interested in the whereabouts of two among the dozen: specialists in X-ray lasers. Both had suddenly relocated and I could not trace them. Some of ARM's house-schizies, my near colleagues, have disappeared, too.

And there have been unscheduled meetings with the Belt leadership. I have heard rumors of a new spaceship design team being put together. I can guess some things about the new spaceship they will be designing. It will be well equipped with signaling devices to assist in contact, devices using large amounts of energy. But to design a new type of ship and to build it are different propositions.

I have noticed changes in our games and entertainment. "Graceful Willow" has disappeared from the newscasts. A new game, "Highest Hand;" has an emphasis on winning. There are no more dances.

If those behind Early win, I think I will have a role in what is to come. Otherwise, I imagine, someone will be calling on me soon and I will be taken in to a memory-wipe. There is no point in running, ARM can find me anywhere on earth, and if I somehow got into space, what would I be running to there?

Arthur Guthlac has been seconded to special duties, along with several others who were at the edge of forbidden studies. But he has kept his museum title of Assistant to the Chief of the General Staff. Early's joke?

Messages have been beamed out to his sister's ship after all, ordering it to turn back. No one has said why. Those messages will reach it in about seven years' time, and what has happened has happened already.

I pity Arthur Guthlac and try not to imagine what he feels, but part of me wonders if he may have found the purpose in life that always eluded him.

I have done what I could. If there is any future history now, no doubt historians will look at the chance the whole thing turned on. Colonel Vaughn shot well. He bought us five hundred years.

They are capable of mistakes. They are capable of wishful thinking. Skragga-Chmee's creatures did not come. We had to go to them.

The main purpose of my holiday was to say good-bye to what has been, to what we always took for granted. I visited places of Earth I had known in a longish life that has, I suddenly realize, almost too late, had its share of good times. Scenes of beauty, peace, tranquility or thronging human life. Scenes from the last days of the Golden Age.

What will these same scenes show in a few years?

War factories worked around the clock by forced labor? Glowing bomb craters? Or the hunting territories of Earth's felinoid conquerors?

Time is running out.

What shape is space? Space will put on
The shape of any cat. . . .

I look up at night and know what is coming. ARM may or may not move in time. Perhaps the felinoids have too great a technological edge over us anyway. They have been in space a long time. Perhaps it is too late for us to rearm, and perhaps as a species we have deprived ourselves of the capacity to fight.

Sir Bors, Lady Helen! If you and yours had been arrested three days earlier, how different an ending your story might have had! But I cannot say whether a better ending or a worse one.

One thing I know is that the program and everything I have worked for is in ruins.

Perhaps that is why I feel so happy.

RUSSELL BLACKFORD

Russell Blackford is employed by an international legal firm, Phillips Fox, in Melbourne. He is also a Ph.D. in English and a well-known SF critic who has published numerous articles, essays, and reviews, mainly in Australia, but also in Britain and the U.S. and he has twice won the William Atheling, Jr. Award for Criticism or Review. Blackford was a member of the editorial collective (with John Foyster, Jenny Blackford, Yvonne Rousseau, Lucy Sussex, and Janeen Webb) of *Australian Science Fiction Review: Second Series,* an international forum for discussion of SF, and a principal in the small press Ebony Books. Blackford has very kindly allowed us to mine for these story notes an advance copy of the Greenwood Press history of Australian SF, *Strange Constellations* (co-written with Van Ikin and Sean McMullen, 1999).

His fiction appears infrequently, but he has maintained a reputation as one of Australia's significant writers of fantasy and SF. Since 1982 he has published a fantasy novel (*The Tempting of the Witch King,* 1983) and several highly regarded short stories. Of these, "Glass Reptile Breakout" (1985) is an early example of Australian cyberpunk writing. "The Soldier in the Machine" returns to the same world. It is reprinted from the distinguished original anthology edited by Jack Dawn and Janeen Webb, *Dreaming Down Under* (1998).

THE SOLDIER IN THE MACHINE

Honey Fantasia is a honey: she plays loud and wild and pretty in a miracle band, and Rhino will work for her any time.

Rhino is conspicuous—he flaunts it. You could never camouflage him in brand-new pastel Reeboks and a fresh white printed T-shirt and pass him off as a harmless Aussie tourist, first time in Bangkok on Qantas Airlines. But here he is, all the same, with that honey by his side. Others try not to stare at him, but, out of the corner of one beady eye, he catches a young blonde mother with a little kid, boy or girl, with eyes as blue as the sky over Darwin this August and long yellow hair in a ponytail. Mother there is crouching down to the kid's level, telling it something, and glancing his way. "Don't go near the *big man!*"

He paces and frets, sleepless, anxious, around the airport's baggage carousel, waiting for fat suitcases the same dull hardware gray as his implant trademark. Honey Fantasia yawns.

Rhino is accustomed to towering over clients and he *does*, even with Fantasia. But she's tall: 185 centimeters of her slims up to his two-meters plus-implant. She's long and strong and slippery with masses of burned orange ultra-soft "hair," genetically engineered stuff based on alpacas or something, implanted into her scalp (she's been reengineered to grow no natural hair anywhere on her body). The "hair"—what else do you call it?—spills down her back, down to her thighs, over a loose-sleeved cotton dress the color of dark grass stains, which reaches bare ankles. She slings a chamois leather bag to hold her multitude of plastic cards and her chunky Finnish laser shades. Her hands and pretty sandaled feet, her broad face, horse rider's shoulders—real muscle thickness layered over delicate bones:

deltoids in a motion of runnels and waves—are oiled softly, tanned deeply. Brow and cheekbones feed wells of wide dark eyes. A double implanted row of diamond chips makes needle tracks in her left cheek like parallel dueling scars. For eyebrows she has little surgically grafted white feathers. Below them are long black implanted lashes.

Rhino and this fine gal client have brought nothing to disturb Customs on this leg of the trip. They just want out of here.

Suitcases turn up. He steps forward. "Excuse me." None of the bunch crowded about the luggage carousel want to go near him or his client—they shrink aside. He hooks one big plastic oyster suitcase by its black handle, then the other, swings both in one callused hand, lifts them high over the heads of other passengers, waits for Fantasia to step in his wake, powers toward Customs. Not yet crowded; first flight in. Finds the green arrows, brushes through the Nothing to Declare passage—and out.

Where they're waiting.

You can't disguise Rhino any more than you can Honey Fantasia. Two meters in his scuffed leather Nikes, plus the gray horn implant arching up out of the top of his forehead, he's two-hundred kilos of beef and steroids, a walking megalith. Skin a pale controlled tan, despite the ferocious sunshine Fantasia's inflicted on him all August. He's exhibited blur fighting wherever it's legal or tolerated throughout the Pacific rim; he's been a ghetto courier in cities all over Southeast Asia and the States; he's had work as standover muscle in Vegas, on the Gold Coast, in Bangkok and the sprawl of KL. He's totally clean and legal, with an international passport.

And he's one helluva bodyguard. He could slam a shrivel of *paparazzi* straight through a pressboard door; better, he *looks* like he could. So he flaunts it. Rhino's head is permanently depilated, leaving only his twenty centimeters of vat-grown rhino horn. He wears a huge black T-shirt with the sleeves ripped out. Red lettering splashes it diagonally on front and back: RHINOSAURUS. Wide, chrome-studded wristbands and leather collar; feathery drop earrings that match Fantasia's eyebrows. When you hire Rhino, you're not looking for some fancy operative to cover you from the background; you want conspicuous muscle; you're telling the world, "Get out of the goddamn way!"

That's what Fantasia has been saying to all world through big, bad Territory and on a working holiday across Java. They've driven like mad mothers everywhere between Uluru and Darwin, Fantasia's sandals on the dash, Fantasia squeezing plasticized data dots into the sound system—miracle band music—popping them out just as quickly, trying something else. They've swum tropical beaches beneath cloudless August skies. Carved into fatty white crocodile steaks in the Kakadu. Scoffed Bintang beers together at the Lava Bar up on the volcano edge at Mount Bromo, seeing who could get drunker. Driven in the backs of tour-guided people movers from Yogya to Malang to Bromo and back, then north to Jakarta, dodging the kings of the road: Mercedes diesel tour buses as long and ugly as Boeing 797s, thundering the roads, scattering underpowered motorcycles, pedal-powered becaks, crowded people movers and occasional flashy red government sedans with sinister tinted screens. Fantasia has played with local miracle bands out of the teeming Javanese cities. Now Thailand, Bangkok—miracle city.

Driver: a little Thai in a short-sleeved floral shirt, greens and yellows, and cheap black trousers. The other guy: mean, slick Caucasian bozo, mid-twenties, eyes nearly level with Rhino's. Hawk face, evenly tanned, darker than Fantasia's, as if his skin has absorbed quantities of mahogany shoe polish. Hair cut brutally short, flat-topped, coifed with the fuzzy neatness of a gay bouncer's. He looks hungry and honed, springy and sharp like razor ribbon. That'll do for a handle. Razor Ribbon is dolled up in a somber gray suit, a Zegna-Pointman job nestling his broad shoulders, snaking narrow hips—brilliant white shirt, gold cufflinks, spit-and-polish black brogues, red St. Laurent tie. "Mr. Rhino," he says. Like Fantasia's not there. American accent, West Coast, Rhino guesses. Razor Ribbon extends a plate-sized bony hand.

Rhino sets down his bags, takes the hand, measures the strength in it. Astonishing strength.

"I'm Paul," says Razor Ribbon as they part grips. No suggestion of a surname. "This is Darling." The driver smiles and bows, hands pressed: *wai* gesture. "That's not his real name, but it's close and he likes it, thinks it's a bit of a joke, don't you, Darling?"

There's an unpleasant element in this banter. Rhino presses slabs of hands, bows to Darling. *"Sawat-dii."* To Paul: "I'm pleased to meet you. Do you have rooms? We're stuffed from the flight. And we've been driving like fuckers these last three weeks. And I don't fit into jumbo jets easily." He looks Paul up and down: maybe half Rhino's total bulk—still a big boy. "Guess you'd know something about that, too."

"Don't know who designs the things." Paul relaxes slightly. "Maybe Snow White and the seven dwarfs."

"Maybe." Rhino steps aside, lets aside, lets Fantasia come forward. "This," he says, "is Ms. Fantasia."

"Delighted to meet you . . . again," Paul says. He smiles at Fantasia like an old lover. She smiles but does not move. He switches off the smile.

"Come on. We've got a hotel for you. You can shower in your rooms and get some sleep. We'll have you there by nine." It's just past 8 a.m. local time. "The Colonel wants to talk to you both this afternoon."

"Hope she doesn't expect too much sense out of me." But, under his exhaustion, Rhino is curious, ready to go, full of questions. Like who *the Colonel* is for a start—except that she's already paid ten thousand megayen into one of Rhino's AMEX digital cash lines. More into Fantasia's discretionary trust accounts. Gestures of good faith.

Paul looks at him quizzically. "Here, let me take Ms. Fantasia's suitcase." Rhino slides it over. "Right. We're taking you to the New Intercontinental. Have you stayed there before? No? You'll like it."

He swings the bag Rhino's given him like it weighs nothing.

Rubber tracks slide them on smooth rollers through the giant clean international terminal already filling with departing passengers. Paul keeps his voice down, seems to talk into his suit lapels. "You know why you're here?"

Fantasia must know better than him. She's silent. So is Rhino.

"The Colonel is not quite what you think, Rhino." Paul has dropped the Mr. "And she's got a contract to fulfill. There're deals we've made here, components that have to be flown elsewhere, big trouble if we try to leave Bangkok, where the military police who run the city are friendly to us. *Capisce?* We have work to do this afternoon to help you understand just how dangerous our competitors can be to you." Smiles like a jaguar. Very white teeth. "We need lots of beauty and lots of brawn. Got it?" He turns the smile on Fantasia. "Ms. Fantasia can provide some of the beauty."

She shrugs. Oiled deltoids make pretty ripples under her skin.

The rollers slide them past repetitive placards sponsored by International Service Clubs, smiling Asian faces exhorting them to solve problems through truth and consideration. All very well if you're raising credit for the local school library, thinks Rhino. Wouldn't work in my line.

Flashy white turbo-charged limo, extended version—Darling guns it into the city. Rhino takes over an entire bench in the back. Fantasia takes off her sandals, flexes her toes, bends and worries at chipped green toenail polish, leans back and sighs. Paul lounges in front, leaves them alone.

With a measure of room to stretch at last, Rhino can finally start to doze. Dopily, he half-registers as they pass scum-filled, canals, brilliant green fields, enter Bangkok's maniac streets where ancient, clapped-out vehicles menace each other for the roadway like holo movie dinosaurs, pulling stunts of cunning and brinkmanship. Darling jabs viciously into traffic chaos, honking the horn.

They drive by narrow, dirty side streets crowded with pedlars. The morning sky is a dirty glare: colors are bright enough—and Rhino dons wraparound German goggles—but the sun itself is not visible. He's dozed off by the time they reach the hotel, where Darling opens his door, touches his shoulder diffidently. "Mr. Rhino"—turns away—"Ms. Fantasia."

Fantasia's wearing her laser shades. She steps from the car carrying her sandals in one hand, shakes orange hair.

Paul gets baggage for them, checks them into the hotel, Rhino and Fantasia digging out tired passports for the smiling clerk. Formalities: explanations of the hotel's multiple restaurants, baggage to the porter, keys, directions.

Their rooms are in another building entirely (this place is built on one helluva scale); Rhino completely takes up one of his room's *big* beds. Honey Fantasia is next door. She can't come to too much harm in a place like this. Forget the client for a while. Rhino doesn't bother to remove clothes. Sleeps like a baby.

Wakes leaping from the bed, fists clenched.

But it's only the telephone. Startled into clarity, he finds he's not alone. How did she get here? She's already answered the phone, cut out its conference facility; she's talking into a handset, and he can't hear the speaker at the other end. Video screen tuned dead. She puts down the handset, shrugs prettily. "That was Paul." She's a songbird! "He says the Colonel wants to talk with you and Ms. Fantasia at four this afternoon. Better get ready, Sir. I call Ms. Fantasia, too. Now you're here, I look after you, Mr. Rhino. I look after you very well, Sir."

Manhattan accent over Thai; she's lived in the States. Dainty Thai-Indian, fraction Rhino's size. She'd come to Fantasia's shoulders. Moist eyes like orgasms.

Hired sex-girl.

Perfect oval face, very dark skin, blue-black hair cut in a classic French bob, she's all dressed up in pinks: footless lurex tights; short-sleeved silk jacket, embroidered in green and blue and yellow floral swirls, and beautifully lined; little shiny pink slippers. Glistening emerald-scales the size of postage stamps are implanted on each side of her face between eye-corners and temples. She oozes charm, discretion, Eastern personal courtesy—antithesis of Bangkok's traffic manners.

"How about I go back to sleep?" He sits back on his bed.

"No, you must wake up, Mr. Rhino. You cannot disappoint Paul and the Colonel."

"Wait on. Who are you, anyway?" He's met everyone on his current client list except Ice Ninja and the Colonel. This cutey's not there on any print-out.

"I'm Sunandra. I look after you, Sir."

"So you said."

She laughs at that. God help him, she's beautiful, almost too beautiful, probably the creation of some surgical sculptor—not just the implants. "We stay together all the time. So I hope you like me, Mr. Rhino."

She can't mean all the time: he's likely to be in capital-D danger at some point—let that pass. "Tell me," he says, "about the Colonel."

She sits on the other bed, legs crossed under her. He watches the V-line of her jacket where it exposes brown throat, plunges between the fullness of her breasts; helplessly he imagines skin color under the jacket. Same color all over? Undoubtedly. What's going on? He knows nothing about the people in this hotel. His agent has dealt with intermediaries of intermediaries in setting up this whole trip, furtive street couriers with the capacity to deliver on promises of walloping digital cash transactions.

All he knows about the Colonel is that she's some kind of dropout from a multinational security contractor to the global telecommunications companies. She's hustling big, scoring local contacts and contracts. She has some kind of components deal to deliver on. She's looking for some un-sophisticated muscle (why?). And she has dangerous competitors.

"Well," she says, "Paul wanted me to prepare you. The Colonel's *different*, Sir."

"*Sir?* You'll have to cut that out." Rhino laughs. "We're all *different*. Sunandra. You. Me. Paul. Honey Fantasia. Look at us."

Sunandra won't be denied. "You know what an upload is, Mr. Rhino?" she says in her songbird voice.

He thinks of money. "Sure."

"Nanoware text intelligence analogue, Mr. Rhino." The terminology surprises him only because it comes from her.

"The Colonel's a brain-program? Well, I can handle that." But he needs *a lot* more information. "Are you going to tell me all about it? From the beginning, eh?"

"Of course I cannot, Mr. Rhino. But we have some components that the Colonel needs delivered to a colleague with Offnet Polisearch Laboratory. Not a firm you would have heard of, Sir."

But that's not true. He's done courier work for Offnet Polisearch before: radical tech security consultants—operate out of a technology enclave in South Australia. Polisearch has links in half a dozen technopoles in Japan and Korea, in Yogya, KL . . . in Bangkok.

Sundandra uncrosses her legs, lowers slippered feet to the floor. "Our competitors may not know the place of delivery, but they watch our movements very carefully. The Colonel hopes you will help us deliver on our obligations, Mr. Rhino. The authorities in Bangkok are friendly to us. Not so elsewhere. Soon you talk to Paul and the Colonel. Ms. Fantasia already knows something about this. While you are here we have many . . . many *plausible"*—she pronounces it like an unfamiliar word—"things for you to do. Ms. Fantasia also. I look after you especially, Mr. Rhino, while you look after her. Okay?"

What else is there to say? He also stands, stretches, and looks down at her—she seems to be standing on some lower slope. "And you've all got me this exhibition? The blur fight?"

"Correct, Mr. Rhino. You are Rhinosaurus, blur-fighting professional. There is big promoter in Bangkok. You fight Ice Ninja from Sapporo in one week. His promoter puts up good money to fight you. Makes him your client, too." Good money, aching legs and a few bruises. "We will tell you everything else when you need to know." He doesn't like her choice of words. "But the Colonel must explain, herself. You must not worry. The Colonel said I have to look after you, and I will."

His mood is worsening. "I hope it isn't too goddamn onerous."

She's downcast. "I do not mean it that way, Mr. Rhino."

Looks her over again. He notices her fingers for the first time: third finger and the pinkie on her left hand—nails are emerald-scale implants, like her eyes, but long, and squared off, like chisels. They'll be razor sharp. He's seen it before on flickdancers in KL. She's a dancer, then. Songbird. Flickdancer. "Yeah, sorry, Sunandra. Most people don't like me much. I scare them. That's the idea, I guess. But I don't want you to be scared."

She reaches to take his hand. "I never get scared," she says matter-of-factly. He looks her over incredulously. "And, Mr. Rhino, you seem such a gentle man."

She bullies him; makes him undress and shower. Though it's a cavernous shower unit, he hardly fits. Sunandra dries him, businesslike, with the hotel's huge fluffy towels, commands him to lie on his groaning bed, applies massage, sitting astride him like riding a horse. There's nothing sexual about it, just pure relief for stiffened neck, aching shoulders, fatigued hocks.

Bossed unmercifully by this flower of a girl, he finds he likes it. When she's finished, he lies on his back, great fleshy tub of a body pink, shiny, flopping relaxed.

"Okay," he says at last. "Take me to your leader, Sunandra."

"You must now get dressed. Let us see . . ." Shamelessly, she rummages through his suitcase, gets clean clothes together for him—camo duds, a sleeveless shirt that would do her for a tent, knitted of leather straps, sea green and deep red.

He takes her proffered hand as they descend the elevator: she drags him outdoors, where the 90-degree heat, the humidity, the glare fasten on him at once. She's already handing over his German shades. Sunandra heads him past a fountain and pond, where two cranes with clipped wings talk gracefully—avian tai chi—then past a running track and a free-form swimming pool, by an acre of lily ponds, through dark crannies and arbors.

"Where are we going?" he says.

"The driving range."

He'd believe anything about this place; some grounds it's got. Acres and acres. *"Vroom-vroom or thwackum?"*

She laughs at him looking up from the bottom of his sternum. "In fact they have got both," she says. "But this time I meant *thwackum*, Mr. Rhino. Later on you can do your motoring practice or game of golf."

The driving range is in full use. They all seem to know each other. Thais and Westerners, dressed for a casual afternoon at the practice tee and maybe a round in the evening. There's matte gray equipment around them which Rhino recognizes as holo gear, mounted cameras, God knows how many megayen of the stuff, all installed so the New Intercontinental's clientele can analyse the mechanics of backswing, wrist placement, follow-through. Paul dominates the group, towering, like the heroic lead on a holo set—he's relaxed into a yellow, knitted golfshirt, crisp brown trousers, teak-coloured Akubra hat. The outfit exaggerates his broad shoulders, snake hips. He hits nine-iron pitch shots with authority, high and hard, golf balls lobbing with real backbite.

Honey Fantasia has not arrived yet.

Sunandra introduces Rhino to the others. Americans, Aussies, Thais, but somehow all the same, all slightly false in bright casual dress. Heavily painted girls with nose jobs, implants for hair: fur, feathers, iridescent mops of plastic wire. They remind him of failed holo starlets or glamour gal ring attendants at the blur fights. Slim jumpy guys—stomachless, hipless—with high veins on wiry arms. There's a sense of deliberate hunger here. Rhino wonders what weapons they are all concealing. Telco security cowboys.

Fantasia turns up. She nods to Paul. "Thanks for the directions." She looks sporty in her way, jaunty: she's wearing loose grass-colored jeans, matching plain canvass runners, baseball cap, plastic bangles all the way up her right arm to the elbow. Orange hair streams from under the cap. Her upper body is covered by a short-sleeved, yellow nylon jacket, several sizes too big for her—more Rhino's size. Those bulky laser shades with their gunmetal frames dominate her face, covering the white feathers of her brows.

The holo unit showers with congealing light, forms the image of a tall, middle-aged woman in khaki uniform. Steel gray hair combed back over ears, collar-length, slope of her prominent nose almost vertical. Tough lady, nothing butch about her, but no little softnesses or affectations. The Colonel, then, Vocal-Aural-Visual interface software patching in to the hotel's holo setup.

"My current . . . lifestyle does not encourage a taste in pleasantries, Ms. Fantasia, Rhino," says the Colonel. Good lip-synch on the animation. The synthesized voice through speakers is brisk but flattened, with the vowels programmed for something close to Carolina softness. "You are welcome. I'll get to business. But, first, an illustration. I hope this interests you."

"Go ahead," says Fantasia. Rhino watches the animation, its colors just too close to the primaries, its shapes a fraction geometric, but close to some presumed reality.

"Very well. It's simple. Rhino, I want you to hit a golf ball. Do you know how to play golf?"

"I've played."

"Take a driver Sunandra will tee up for you. Don't try to hit straight; aim somewhere to the right or left, wherever you like. Go on."

Suspiciously, expecting some trick, Rhino obeys. He waggles the club, lifts it around his chest in a short backswing, forgets about the holo for a moment. Clumsily, but still with great force, Rhino strikes at his golf ball, sends it in a savage uncontrolled hook down the left of the driving range. A couple of seconds later Paul hits a drive, lands the ball within a centimetre of where Rhino's landed. It bounces, and rolls after Rhino's ball so that they come to rest a meter apart.

"Try again," the Colonel says blandly. "By the way, we could have made our point with a roulette wheel, or with dice throws, but we thought you would prefer something more physical." Rhino looks over at the smug holo.

Sunandra tees his ball. Irritated, Rhino thrashes at it. There's a double crack! as Paul drives simultaneously with him this time. The two golf balls land just to right of center of the range, almost collide, but bounce in randomly different directions.

"Better, Paul," says the Colonel. "Again, Rhino."

What the heck? Rhino thwacks a beauty, but this time Paul actually hits his ball a split second *earlier* than Rhino hits his. They land close together right in the middle of the range. Again, they both drive simultaneously, Rhino mishitting the top of the ball. Both balls hit hard into the ground, roll for one hundred meters, actually collide and ricochet apart.

"Enough," says the Colonel. "Paul could do this all day and not get tired."

Light's dawning. "He's deliberately matching . . . ?" says Rhino. "But that's impossible—"

"He'd have to be able to know exactly how you're going to hit the ball the instant *before* you hit it, correct?" Rhino is speechless. "Honey Fantasia, Rhinosaurus," the Colonel says expansively, "meet the face of the future. SACID operative. Specified Anomalous Capabilities (Intelligence Design). Outcome of decades of research."

"I don't think I want to know about this," Rhino says slowly.

"You do, mister. You do. My former employers have worked with the FBI, USSS, the global telcos, a number of semisecret university-controlled corporations for longer than I've been alive, gene-engineering to develop Paul and his breed. You'll find the breed doing corporate security work throughout the States, Western Europe, Japan, places like Australia. There's a major market for the technology here in Thailand. I'm happy to fill it. Unfortunately, setting up my own firm in competition with ex-colleagues has not been easy. Outside of Bangkok I am not popular with those in the same business. Even establishing this operation involved a few small tactical hardships like an uploading and a body-death." She lets it sink in. "Outsmarting the competitors is not always a simple matter.

"Rhino, Honey Fantasia will be staying in Bangkok when you leave. She already knows the bad news. You and Sunandra need to deliver certain components to a research company in South Australia associated with us. You Will Not Go There Directly." The Colonel emphasizes the words of the last sentence, one word at a time. "I want you to imagine Paul in a firefight." Rhino is paying attention—no cobwebs left in his mind by now. "The physical augmentation is secondary. It's his *mind*. He evades *before* you shoot; he corrects *before* you evade. He makes you look like a dinosaur. Sorry." The subtle geometric of an animation smile.

"No hard feelings, Colonel."

"Rhino," she says, intense now, "I am a SACID. A couple of generations earlier than Paul, but still a SACID. One thing I and my competitors can't yet do is get the SACID mind to upload with its full capabilities into a form running on digital neurons. The physical material of the brain is too important. But we're close. We have ideas. We want to do more research. We have components that are promising. And there's other research we need to do. You've seen Paul's capability. It's the only one we can consistently engineer for: superinstantaneous cognition. To talk about *precognition* would be an exaggeration. But there's lots of new research . . . My group started off by studying flickdancers. You've seen flickdancers in this very city cutting themselves as they dance, healing themselves—"

"I've seen it *everywhere*," he says. A worldwide musical phenomenon, the miracle band musicians and the flickdancers. Rhino has one of each here: Honey Fantasia, Sunandra. The craze they manifest is nowhere more extreme than right here in Bangkok. What is he supposed to do about it?

"Rhino, how do you think you would fare if you had to go up against SACID operatives?"

But she's already answered that question. Rhino realizes too sharply what he's up against if he has to act as a courier with bastards like Paul on his tail. A guy like that—or a woman like the Colonel—would be unbeatable in a firefight. Not just that. How could you ever nail one—feet, fists? And Paul, at least, looks like the kind who could stack up roofing tiles—and *smash!* You could never avoid those hands. "Like a dinosaur, I suppose," he says. "Look, I don't get this. Paul's here. What am I supposed to add to the operation? Looks?"

"Variety! . . . Stay with Sunandra. Fantasia, you know what to do. From now on, Paul is your bodyguard. You'll stay in Bangkok until we judge it's safe to leave."

Honey Fantasia shrugs. "Sure, keep it coming." They must be feeding that discretionary trust of hers. Bangkok is not Rhino's idea of a place to stay under siege.

"The authorities will see a moderately famous miracle muso on tour and holidays with a large well-documented bodyguard. They will see her stay in Bangkok for a time, appropriately guarded, while the large bodyguard leaves with a pretty Thai flickdancer. You should not expect any official trouble. The trouble will come from our competitors."

That's more than enough.

"Sunandra knows what you need to do," says the Colonel. "You know our financial terms. You don't know too much to back out . . . quite . . . Don't expect to learn too much more." She pauses. "You've already made some cash for your trouble. I should add that you've already become a target for our competitors as soon as you leave Bangkok. Guilt by association. You backing out or you staying in, mister?"

Paul tees up another ball, swings through it with a bulletlike crack, driving it high and sweet. Rhino is not sure that he likes doing anything that involves pushing along the evolution of this breed. But what's the choice? "In," he says. One word. He looks at Honey Fantasia, almost pleading with her. What have you got me into, gal? Nothing looks back through the opaque-lensed laser shades.

It's like he's slurped down too much coffee: hollow tired, but nerves jangling. He paces the floor of his room. Fidgets with anything, the waistband of his pants, the hotel's services listing—anything. Reads the menu for room service. He wants to be able to sleep, knows he'll be awake all night.

"We have work to do soon, Mr. Rhino," says Sunandra. "You must try to enjoy yourself."

"Doing what?" He sits on the edge of his bed.

Sunandra sits beside him. Takes one hand in both of her tiny ones. Talks to him, soothing, smoothing, crooning, guides him back through the coiled and poisonous intricacies of their situation.

Tells him: the Colonel was working on a government contract in São Paulo when she saw the opportunity to start up some competition for her employer. She arranged to *die*. Uploaded secretly, merging her brain's wetware with a nanoware text, switched off the wetware, arranged a plausible accident for her body—one involving a military concussion rifle, leaving no sign of any recent work on her brain. Transferred herself and a massive line of digital cash to associates in Bangkok, several steps ahead of what had already become the competition. Arranged for the original nanoware text in Brazil to be wiped clean. Gathered supporters; bought in software, hardware mobiles, interface junk; made Bangkok military police contacts, heavy and necessary. Other contacts with government telco people. She was starting to build an operation. She kept her nanoware matrix off the nets. When she did have to interface with them, she had layers and layers of counterintrusive firewalls and guard dogs to hide behind, always paranoid.

She's still slowly building contacts outside of Thailand, Honey Fantasia among them. Research corporations. Rhino.

He's broody, and Sunandra takes him down to the hotel's seafood restaurant, which is wake-up-and-take-notice good—she makes him try the local fish, crab, a satay. He puts away a couple of liters of Tiger beer, two bottles of imported Australian pinot noir. Sunandra drinks and twinkles, seems to sing to him.

After dinner, she orders a cab to Sukhumvit Road. Takes him to a vast dance hall, styled *Soi Angel*, where international miracle bands play. "Honey Fantasia plays here tonight, Mr. Rhino." He knows.

The hall is all mirrors and holos, reflecting endlessly, top and bottom, sides. Smoke twists in thinning scarves and catches the random bursts of laser lights. Here are Bangkok's fish people, the local sharks and roe, mingling with tourists, boys and girls, from all over mainland Asia, Japan, Australia, the States. Near naked to show off radical body implants: fins, fur, feathers, spines . . . and anything marine—fins and flippers, teeth from whales, crocodile scales, dorsal sails . . . Wildest are the professional flick-dancers—caged in platforms drifting about on wires high over the dance floor—and their emulators in the crowd, lean hungry shark boys, the little *roe*, bare-breasted teenage girls.

When the miracle bands play, Bio-Feed music, synthesizers hooked up to state-of-the-art EEG receptors, these crowds are hysterical with a religious lunacy that brings out crazy effects in the right people—the sort of people the Colonel is interested in, the potential SACID gene stock—provided they *believe*. There are supposed to be explanations: enhanced mental field effects from the unnatural contortions of playing music with your brain, interacting with other minds in the room, them interacting with each other. The music has its own mystique, like any music, but the really weird stuff is from the fields of minds cuddling up in bizarre unnatural ways, not the musical notes themselves.

The music has its own, and Sunandra has caught it. She drags Rhino onto the dance floor. Above them, a male flickdancer mutilates himself systematically, carves unbleeding patterns into his chest with a triangle-bladed knife.

On the stage, musicians prance and posture; leading them, Honey Fantasia. She's almost a different creature, now—miracle muso—though a creature Rhino knows well.

Fantasia's Wires, the spidery black crown of EEG headgear jacked into her scalp under the hairline, are tangled in messed orange implanted hair; below them, long pins of coherent red light emitted from her laser shades slowly trace the hall. She's wearing nothing but a seaweed-colored wraparound skirt that falls to midthigh and a kind of rope net the color of her implanted hair, the mesh wide enough to let her head and arms through. Stomach muscles harden and twist like gnarled wood. Fantasia's breasts are tipped with ultrasoft fur a millimeter long, the same burned orange color as the mane of hair on her head. As she dances she undoes the knot at the side of her skirt, removes it in a swift gesture, letting it fall to the floor, kicking it away, revealing a Y of the same soft implanted stuff, rising between her legs and branching around her waist; seen from the front and at this distance, she is wearing a kind of skimpy fur bikini. Serpent tattoos with fiery mouths coil her legs; their eyes are deeply implanted chips of emerald like those on Sunandra's face. She's glorious.

Thick, voiceless curtains of sound, wild, improvised, at times almost atonal, billow out around the core of a heavy rock beat. Sunandra is smiling fixedly in the direction of Honey Fantasia, the little scale-jewels at her eyes glistening; she's sweating, and she pulls off her silk jacket. God! Her brown nipples are puckered hard. Looks Rhino in the eye, dances flailingly from the neck down, never, never moves her eyes. He's picking up on things in her head, weird, sexy, undefinable things. Miracle dancer.

And then she does it. Flick. Sunandra rips upward, then down again, between her breasts with those razor jewels on her left hand, opening herself, peeling back skin over sternum, down the stomach to her tights, like parting the teeth of a red zipper on a sexy jumpsuit. No blood flows; within moments the skin is knitting back. And, despite himself, despite everything, incorrectly, inappropriately, even incoherently, Rhino is turned on . . .

Later, in the hotel room, Sunandra uses massage. She takes off her clothes and is all over him, hands, breasts, hot mouth. Rhino on his back, that hot wet mouth finds him; she's kneeling, straddling one of his tree-trunk legs, rubbing her fur, rubbing her wetness against him, while her tongue swirls and flicks. His eyes are squeezed shut against a pleasure that hurts and hurts.

Until she's riding him, her legs split apart like a ballerina's; she's balancing with one hand on his chest, the other holding his knuckles at her crotch. And she starts trembling, another harmonic to her movement. "Now, Mr. Rhino, now!" she says. Their minds are locked together, wordless, but there's a bewildering, joyous feedback of lust and ecstasy. Yet this is no dance floor. Who is she?

His eyes are closed, but he still sees her, sees her seeing him. "I race you, Mr. Rhino." Starts to spasm. Together. Each of them. YES. YES. YES.

Sunandra is up before him. She's found a pink silk dressing gown. Brings breakfast from the room waiter, plates stacked with pineapple, papaya, local ham and bacon, little brown sausages, fried egg beaten with onions. She throws off the dressing gown, gets into bed. They scoop together into the good local food.

Make love with the same desperation as last night.

Then, it's a day with nothing to do. They spend it with Paul and Honey Fantasia by the lukewarm swimming pool, basking in the sunshine, sharking warm water. Sunandra and Honey Fantasia wear demure one-piece swimming costumes out of deference to local custom (this is a business hotel, not the *Soi Angel*). They seem to get along. Sunandra tries out the mechanics of the laser shades, though it's too bright to gain any effect; they need darkness and smoke. Turns out that she's also been engineered to play with Honey Fantasia's Wires.

They spend the afternoon with the women jacked into sets of Wires. Fantasia produces a set of receivers for Rhino to listen to. They fit his ears bulkily like old-fashioned headphones. But Fantasia can broadcast into them instead of into stage amps and make music straight to his ears. It's just the same to her. Sunandra has some rudimentary skills, but she's a dancer, not a miracle muso. Still, she seems to learn fast. Paul ignores it all. He swims up and down the pool, a magnificent athlete at home in the water. Rhino didn't see him at the *Soi Angel*, but he must have been there. He seems to think it's his duty—duty!—to stay close to Honey Fantasia.

That night they cruise back to the *Soi Angel*. They've started a routine. Long lazy days and hot nights. Sunandra makes love to him twice before they go to sleep. At 2 A.M.. they grope for each other in the dark and she rolls on top of him; they fuck half in their sleep.

By day they swim, play games with the Wires. Paul challenges Honey Fantasia to a round of golf. She takes him up on it even though he's obviously unbeatable. Rhino and Sunandra splash in the pool. The Colonel is sending plenty of cash their way for their trouble. Sunandra is getting better with the Wires all the time. By night they follow Honey Fantasia's band and the other miracle bands, dance late.

Then, one morning: "Tonight is your exhibition of blur fighting, Mr. Rhino."

"I know, Sunandra."

"Blur fight professionals use drugs for advantage, isn't it so, Mr. Rhino. I think we give you more advantage."

Rhino lowers his fork and chews his breakfast more slowly. Swallows. "What sort of advantage?"

"Better drug, Sir. You will see."

Like everyone who has been in blur fighting, Rhino has a catheter inserted in the big vein of his left thigh. The catheter contains a miniaturized sensor complex to monitor body signs, feed data to a microchip. This controls the valve on a sac implanted safely within Rhino's stomach wall, determining the rate of infusion of a specialized drug mix. It's a fiery cocktail of pseuodoadrenaline and inhibition killers. There are rules in blur fighting, but participants often forget them, too high on the drug cocktail.

"We have developed a specialized nootropic drug. You see? A crude paracognitive enhancer, Mr. Rhino. It will work on you, I think. It will work on any flickdancer, on a SACID operative, on anyone with the latent anomalous capabilities. I have spent past days testing you for it."

How many surprises do they have? And surprises within surprises. One thing at a time. He scoops a pile of crisp bacon, and munches. "I'm no SACID operative, Sunandra. Are you going to turn me into a flickdancer?"

"Absolutely, Mr. Rhino." She kisses him on the cheek. "We are still trying to find out how it works, but it does work. It will take at least some of the golfing edge off competition." She smiles at him; her little hands dart suddenly, almost faster than he can follow, snatches a crinkled rasher of bacon from his plate. *"Thwackum,* yes?" Gobbles the bacon like a fowl with a worm.

Then, as suddenly, she slaps right fist into stiffly flattened palm. Rhino raises his eyebrows, goes on eating.

Today, Sunandra wants to hustle him around the city, keep him busy with sights, trips to strange bars and clubs, a walk around the tall stupas of Wat Pho, a wander through the leafy niches of the New Intercontinental's vast grounds, a wild spin on the hotel's automobile driving range.

Then the evening. Thais love professional fights. There's a crowd of eighty thousand: it overflows and washes through a giant domed indoor stadium. Rhinosaurus battles Ice Ninja. Overhead holo reflects the action— from the auditorium's back seats, the antagonists are no more than bizarre microbes. Paul is sitting in the front row. Somehow, Honey Fantasia has a night off and is there too, close to Sunandra, the two of them playing with the Wires and giggling together.

After ten minutes, Rhino is flushed and out of wind, but he's been canny: Ice Ninja is angry, frustrated. Tall Japanese, moves like a strutting crane—white implanted hair falls past his shoulders, coarse, nasty stuff, not like Honey Fantasia's. He's white-skinned, wears white wrestling trunks, fights barefoot. He's noisy.

Neither is hurt much; that's not the idea. But Ice Ninja is out of control, hyped up on inhibition killers, pupils dilated. The nootropic doesn't seem to be doing much—Rhino can't predict moves in advance like he'd hoped. But his reflexes seem preternaturally fast, his thoughts like crystals.

While Rhino's thinking about it, Ice Ninja catches him: Rhino lumbering off the ropes one moment, then *spear-hand!* no attempt to fake it.

Rhino's world screams, shears. Red. And yellow star-sparks feeding his brain.

Bastard.

Down on his back. Shoulders pinned. Blindly, he throws Ice Ninja away, stumbles to his feet and grabs the surprised Ninja across forehead, huge thumbs pressing. Fakes his move, like he's supposed to—no use killing the man—headbutts outstretched thumbs, once, twice . . . Ice Ninja falls and spreads the canvas. Pain is a rusty bolt sticking through Rhino's throat. Maybe Ice Ninja has doubts about his own armor class. So Rhino makes sure, drops across him, point-of-elbow first . . . takes most of the weight on himself, shoulder blade hitting the canvas an instant before the blow. But he delivers Ice Ninja just a little more force than he's supposed to—and much less than the bastard deserves. The crowd is roaring. Ice Ninja has to accept the three count.

Afterward, Rhino scoops Sunandra, and they get the hell out via an alley exit, taxi back to the hotel, make love, minds and bodies glowing white hot. Rhino's done his approved business in Bangkok. With Honey Fantasia safely in Paul's hands, Rhino is a government-recognized tourist.

They've taken over the private heated swimming pool at the Tiger Club. Honey Fantasia and Sunandra are both Wired, but evidently not playing the miracle music into each others' ears at the moment. They can hold a conversation. "I'm actually going to miss you two when you leave Bangkok," Honey Fantasia says. "It's been a *time*, Rhino. And I'm glad I met you, Su." Su?

"Mr. Rhino, Ms. Fantasia and I teach each other. You too. Watch."

Nothing happens. Nothing that he can see or hear. But the two gals are both Wired and, right now, he isn't: no headphones. Sunandra is evidently making music because Fantasia stands beside the pool and starts to dance. Hey! Sunandra is getting good. They're jamming. So far, so good. Fantasia looks great dancing in only her long, long implanted hair and the implanted "bikini," which basically conceals nothing up this close, even if it gives the impression of a kind of skimpy swimsuit from up on stage. Her eyes are closed beneath feather-brows. Sunandra steps up close to her as she puts out one brown, strong arm. In a razor flash, Sunandra has flicked out and cut her, not a deep cut or long, but a real cut along the inside of Fantasia's forearm. In a another flash, Sunandra has cut her own right arm. They watch each other, Fantasia daring to open eyes, still evidently jamming—and the cuts don't bleed. Honey Fantasia is turning into a flick-dancer.

"The Colonel knew what she was doing when getting us all together, Mr. Rhino."

Honey Fantasia's cut heals up nearly as quickly as Sunandra's. "Rhino, you ought to try it," she says.

"I've had my share of pain lately."

They're doing a private gig. Sunandra picks up the laser shades beside Fantasia's oversized pool towel, starts to mess around with them, getting the pinpoint beams going faintly around this low-lit space, looking for airborne particles to light up. "You like them, Su? They're yours. I'll find another pair. Hey, why don't you put the headphones on Rhino?" Fantasia's shouting a little, now, obviously deafened by phantom music. "This is pretty cool to listen in on."

"Nup." He decides to take a belly flop into the pool, hitting it with his two hundred kilos. When he surfaces, gulping for his breath, they're slightly splashed but unfazed. Rhino gives up.

. . . And that night at the *Soi Angel*, as Honey Fantasia plays miracle music, Sunandra dances with him, looks up at him with her moist orgasm-eyes, and says, "Now!" She carves only shallowly, but moves with breathtaking speed, slicing straight up his right biceps muscle like an emerald flash. For a moment he's shocked, but somehow she holds him with her mind, and panic washes away. The cut is a superimposition of states: wound and healing. It won't bleed, but doesn't close up. Gently, she strokes it with her soft palm. It seems to be getting better. "You must take me home, Mr. Rhino."

At last the time has come to leave Bangkok. As usual, Sunandra seems to know the schedule. An ultimate destination in South Australia, sure. "But we go very slowly, Mr. Rhino. We do stages. Okay? First stop, New York City. I have friends there, lots of friends. I can take cover in the States for months. Then we will think about the rest of the trip."

Paul is still strong. They shake hands. "Look after the little girl, big guy."

But it takes Honey Fantasia to surprise him: when she kisses him good-bye it's full on the lips, her tongue in his mouth, and right in front of Sunandra, who then seems to get a kiss almost as friendly.

Darling drives them out to the airport, gunning the limo, hunching the wheel like a smiling maniac.

Touchdown La Guardia Airport. Rhino has slept through much of the long flight in his two first-class seats. Sunandra has been restless.

They step out of the 797. Smiles for flight attendants. At least until they get through Immigration and Customs, they're safe enough. As cabin baggage, Rhino carries a soft gray Qantas bag with personal belongings and a shiny black plastic attaché case that Sunandra knows how to open and he doesn't. There's no visible trace of any catch. She's confident they'll get through Customs. They're wild-looking mothers flying in from a place like Bangkok, but Customs officials leave Rhino alone: he travels a lot, their computers know him. His clients are usually beyond the law if not beyond reproach.

Sunandra is Wired and wearing Honey Fantasia's laser shades. Rhino sports headphones behind his curving horn and lets her play soothing music into them with her mind; he needs it, but he's got it. The catheter in his thigh must be monitoring body signs, but it shouldn't find too much wrong yet.

Poking out of Customs, they look around carefully. They have rooms arranged at a dive in Times Square. They'll get an airport bus into Manhattan.

It goes wrong from the start. There's a uniformed driver bearing a handwritten sign: RHINOSAURUS. The guy isn't supposed to be there. He steps up to them. "Mr. Rhino, it must be you," he says, grinning furiously under a mustache. So . . . he's only about 180 centimeters, looks harmless enough. At first. But Rhino is hitting into overdrive. The catheter in his thigh starts to zing. He's a lot closer to the drug now than the first time with Ice Ninja.

The paracognitive enhancer edges in like he's dropped acid: heightened *awareness* of colors, shapes, textures, of individual sounds and layers of sound in the airport noise-wash. But drugs like acid create an uncontrolled sensory overload—wide eyes bugging the flowers—a passive, voluntary acceptance of the Universe's plenty and bliss; that's the farthest thing from what Rhino feels—senses sharp as a cat's, mind clear and clean.

This driver is shockingly, tangibly dangerous, high-strung but controlled. Something about the way he moves cries out Paul's inhuman strength. And there's the same underlying body structure, facial bones as Paul's. There's been gene-splicing along the way: superficially, the driver is a different racial type as well as being maybe fifteen centimeters shorter than Paul—Spanish-Amerindian, very swarthy, black-haired, comic-book mustache. An ingratiating smile that seems to fit but would look incongruous on Paul. Rhino registers it all at once. Sunandra is still Wired, still playing him music, trying to calm him. She gives no outward sign that anything is wrong, but something's subtly different about the music or her body language; he knows that she knows.

"I'm parked illegally, sir," the driver says. "Can you hurry, please? Let me take your bag."

Rhino hands over their one suitcase. They're traveling lighter than he did with Honey Fantasia. This guy is now encumbered. There are two of them to one of him. Rhino is twice his size. They could jump him. Bad idea. He'll be bristling with concealed weapons, hoping to avoid using them in the open but prepared to. And Rhino *sees* enough with the paracognitive to know he doesn't *see* enough. This guy is much too fast for him.

"Times Square, driver," Sunandra says. She gives him the address. Cool.

Nothing is said until they reach the car, another stretch limo—royal blue Mercedes with a purple tinge to the windows. The driver insists upon placing all their luggage in the limo's huge trunk. Reluctantly, Rhino parts with the smart attaché case. In the rear passenger compartment there are another two guys who look just like the driver. They nod to Rhino and Sunandra, supremely confident. Sit opposite as they all drive in to Manhattan, carry no obvious weapons. One says: "Please remove the laser shades, Ms. Something could go wrong and they could blind somebody." Sunandra hands them over. Courteously, he takes them, says, "Thank you." Places them carefully in a top pocket.

They all wear beautifully starched Extropez shirts, bright white under navy blue sports jackets.

"Perhaps I should see that headgear as well. I guess you could communicate with each other, or even with allies, wearing something like that. One-way traffic at least. That wouldn't be appropriate. You, too, Sir. Don't move. Let me take it." He reaches over for Sunandra's Wires. She's playing full-on miracle music, not as good as Honey Fantasia yet, but enough to alter Rhino's consciousness. She's a songbird. He's a flickdancer. But then the music stops. "You, too, Sir. Pass the headphones."

The man folds up all the Wires. They fit neatly enough in a square jacket side pocket, the right-hand one.

Soon, the Empire State's transmission tower scrapes clouds like an art deco cathedral spire. The driver stops at a nondescript office block on Fifth Avenue. The bozo looking after Honey Fantasia's laser shades says, "Executive apartments. We have a suite on the 21st floor. Come on. This will be better than your room in Times Square."

The two men in the back get out, leaving the driver. Luggage still in the trunk. They check in for two rooms, a double suite for Rhino and Sunandra, a twin room for themselves. Arrange for someone to go and get luggage. "It's with our driver."

Walk to the elevator.

Rhino is an attack-robot; he tenses.

But there's a frightened screaming deep in Rhino's ears, agonizingly loud—and he collapses, holding his head. How did she do it? They're not Wired. People turn; a bullet already fired, out of nowhere, strikes right through his horn implant; AND SUNANDRA FLYING. All slow motion; all at once. Always already happened. Somehow, Sunandra has hurt one attacker and stolen from him a slim long-bladed knife. While everything else moves more slowly than ever, she is a blur. Outside, car horns honking; the building's electronically controlled doors are open and the limo driver seems to come through in one motion, propelled like a crossbow bolt and strikes Rhino down even though Rhino's body had *already* dodged to the left! Sunandra is fighting their third captor, neither seeming able to get the better of it, or even to land a blow.

There's an all-at-once massacre about him, more bullets fired, and he's been hit. His own assailant flows away as Rhino swings at him, and he's already struck Rhino before Rhino realizes his body has already unsuccessfully dodged—*knife-hand! spear-hand!*, then a spinning high kick. For the kill! . . . For a moment Rhino blacks out. They're both after Sunandra. Lucidity washes his veins. Sunandra!

One attacker has already fired, but *already* Rhino has dodged. It's taking time. Police sirens in the neighborhood. *It's taking time.* The three SACID operatives have given up and are running back to the car. They still have all the luggage from Bangkok in the limo's trunk. And time to kill. Sunandra throws down the knife.

In the other hand she has something else: the Wires, she's retrieved them. Rhino is bleeding, but nothing vital seems to have been hit. One bullet hit his horn—fixable. One seems to have passed right through a massive steroidal thigh muscle.

Sunandra is Wired. She concentrates. The city booms and shudders.

She has good, hidden friends on Times Square. Sunandra must arrange ID for herself and Rhino, a trustworthy surgical sculptor, replacement cash cards and some very fast and hairy credit transfers, some interface junk— two micro-decks, a tricky modem card. There is an encrypted and coded message to go to Bangkok and one for Adelaide. All her possessions in the States—and Rhino's—were destroyed in the limo.

The paracognitive drug was successful—more so on Sunandra herself than on Rhino, but with him, too, in the end. Her link with Rhino worked even better. The miracle music itself has nothing *logical* to do with the anomalous capabilities of a flickdancer or a miracle muso. The mental contortions of a muso trained to be Wired have everything to do with it, unnatural mental fields. In the end, she could reach directly into Rhino's mind, music or no music, as long as she *pretended* the Wires were there, she gave Rhino what he really needed and responded to.

Not so for reaching out and talking to mere dumb electronic components, the brute physical world. For that she actually needed the Wires. Needed them to send electrical impulses to a shiny black attaché case she had known she must give away to the competition, an attaché case full of powerful remote-activated amps and lined with a vibration-sensitive plastique, disguised to the eyes of airport security equipment.

Eyewitness reports told of the limousine's brakes slamming on and its passengers attempting to flee the car an instant *before* it blew into noisy smithereens. But only an instant. Superinstantaneous cognition. Not real precognition.

So far, the New York Police Department has nothing on her and Mr. Rhino. They are exotic victims of bomb-happy terrorists who managed to blow themselves up, exotic victims and no more, at least until the further investigation, which must connect the explosion to a very clever attaché case full of dumb electronics. And the attaché case to her and Mr. Rhino. She must get out of New York while she is still a step ahead of both the competition and the cops. There are expensive and crucial vatware components—simplified wetware texts of the Colonel—implanted within Sunandra's brain; she has a tortuous route to deliver them to her contacts at Offnet Polisearch Laboratory in its high-tech arcology outside of Adelaide. Meanwhile, she is winning.

"Home free, Mr. Rhino!" she says. Close enough to the truth. Somehow she must find a way to deliver him safely back to Bangkok; he will miss her, she knows, but Honey Fantasia will look after him. For herself, she must arrange for extensive body resculpting . . . soon: a complete disappearance and change of identity.

For now, light-footed, she runs up the street, turns, skipping backward down the pavement and calling out to Rhino: "Home free!"

She lets hustlers, shoppers, a startled traffic cop, tourists dodge out of her way. She attracts lascivious glances, knowing glances, freaky glances, but there is no one here on Times Square uncool enough even to glance twice.

STEPHEN DEDMAN

Stephen Dedman has been publishing SF regularly since the mid-1980s. He is also an assistant editor of *Eidolon*. *The Art of Arrow Cutting*, his fantasy novel, was published in 1997 and nominated for the Bram Stoker Award for Best First Novel. In recent years his short stories have appeared regularly in major SF magazines such as *Asimov's*, *F&SF*, and *SF Age*. He has a facility with the popular forms of SF adventure narrative and the ability to horrify unexpectedly. "From Whom All Blessings Flow," which appeared in *Asimov's* in 1995, is about as blasphemous a story as has appeared in SF in the 1990s.

FROM WHOM ALL BLESSINGS FLOW

K ARINA SCHROEDER, THE INVENTOR of the Bifrost Bridge, was
born in what later became known as World One, which was fine as long
as the only other World discovered had a population of a few million
humans and trillions of mutated rats. The next world contacted, however,
was technologically advanced enough to build their end of a Bifrost Bridge,
and they refused to accept the title of World Three. After a few months
of (occasionally acrimonious) discussion, World One became World Green,
and World Three, World Blue, largely because of the background colors of
their respective UN flags. Their histories had diverged sharply in 1906,
when the English Revolution didn't happen in World Blue—mostly because some of the ringleaders were already dead, or not in London. Historians had found minor divergences as far back as 1879, and some joked
about the real divergence points being lost in prehistory.

World Two became World Cyan, but none of the rats were heard to
complain—at least, not to the historians. Then there was World Azure,
where Robert Kennedy had been fatally shot; and World Indigo, where
there hadn't been a Great Fire of London; and then another cold ruin that
was christened World Gray and quickly abandoned . . . and then, a world
so different from World Green that none of their living languages were
recognizable, which became known on the other worlds as World Red. By
this time, Schroeder had retired to an estate in Green–Nova Scotia, surrounding herself with the best sound system available in any of the worlds
and refusing to speak to anyone. Meanwhile, hundreds of lawyers, politicians, and other bureaucrats were trying to write a set of interWorld trade
laws that would give their own homeWorld the maximum share of any

hitherto undiscovered uninhabited or underdeveloped Worlds . . . and then a delegate from World Red, speaking in perfect pre–Homeric Greek, made an offer that made the emerald mines of Cyan-Brazil look like a handful of change.

Dearborn finished washing his hands and stepped over to the hot-air dryer. "I know it's none of my business," he said, "but it's just too good a deal. I don't trust them."

Anagnostakos, listening, wondered if all the decisions for all the inhabited Worlds were made in men's washrooms. Monsignor Whately, sitting in the cubicle at his right, said, "You're right. It is too good an offer—too good to refuse—and, as far as I'm concerned, it is none of your business."

"Are you sure the interpreters got it right? It wasn't the Donation of Constantine in Classical High Tibetan?"

Anagnostakos ignored the insult: he was more startled that Dearborn had heard of the Donation of Constantine. Maybe the Azure-American had a professional interest in fraud—or, more likely, some researcher on his staff had found the reference and expected it to embarrass the Jesuit. The Constitutum Constantini had supposedly given the Roman Catholic Church authority over all Christianity, but was later proven to be a fairly poor forgery written four centuries after Constantine's death.

"I'm sure enough," replied Whately, mildly. "Of course, we don't need their help as badly as you do . . ."

Fifteen-love, thought Anagnostakos, wincing inwardly. World Blue had a population of fewer than six billion people, as against World Green's eight and a half, World Azure's ten, and World Indigo's thirteen (most of them starving). World Blue could also boast blue whales, gorillas, and tigers still living in the wild, and breathable air in all but its largest cities.

"Some help," snapped Dearborn. "Okay, so they're building their end of the Bridge, but we're supposed to give them millions of our people, and I bet we have to do the fucking paperwork! Where is this land they're offering them, anyway? Antarctica?"

"All over their World: Canada, Brazil, Indonesia, Australasia, Southern Africa, Eastern Russia, Southeast Asia. Underpopulated areas, but arable with the right techniques."

"Sure," said Dearborn, sarcastically.

"Have you ever seen Indigo-Australia? It was settled by the Spanish and their Mediterranean allies, who saw it as a beautiful country—unlike the English who landed there in our Worlds, who regarded it as a desolate hellhole. Now it's supporting a quarter of a billion people—probably the best fed people in World Indigo. Green-Australia's not as crowded, but it's nearly as rich: after they broke with England, they encouraged emigration from countries with similar climates and soils."

"Slave labor," muttered Dearborn. Whately's only answer was to flush the toilet, loudly.

"I still don't like it."

"You don't have to go: they're asking for volunteers. I think they'll get them."

"Not if we say no to the Bridges, it won't," Dearborn replied, and walked out, slamming the door behind him.

"Whatever happened to 'Give me your poor, your tired, your huddled masses?' " asked Anagnostakos, emerging from his cubicle.

Whately laughed. "I take it you're going to vote 'yes'?"

"I'm just a humble interpreter: I don't get a vote."

"How's the translation going?"

"Slowly. We haven't even tried to learn each other's native language—apparently theirs, Arrinesh, is descended from Sumerian the same way English is descended from niederdeutsch—but we're fairly sure that we understand each other's Greek. Of course, there's a lot of modern abstractions that we're having trouble getting across. I know a certain amount of Red-Japanese, but their new Katakana are unrecognizable, and Japanese is easy enough to misunderstand at the best of times. Apart from that, there are a few Native American languages that are the same in all the Worlds except Indigo, but their written alphabets are completely unlike ours and there's almost nothing published in them anyway. The stuff we need has to be translated at least twice to be any use to anyone, and that's painfully slow."

"What about their Bible?"

Anagnostakos shrugged. "I'm afraid I don't know. Why?"

"I've seen a copy—untranslated, of course, but illuminated. Your opposite number, their interpreter—Dr. Melle?—lent it me. Their Old Testament is unrecognizable, as is much of the New, but the four Gospels are there. And since they do use arabic numerals, I've been able to count the chapters and verses, and there are some interesting discrepancies. Their 'Mark,' for example ends at Chapter 16, Verse 9, but there are verses . . ." He stopped; Anagnostakos was shaking his head. "What's wrong?"

"Their 'Mark' is more likely 'Mary,' Monsignor," said Anagnostakos, gently. "Matthew, Martha; Luke, Lucy; John, Joan. Their 'Old Testament' seems to be Sumerian or Babylonian—"

"But they believe in Christ," replied Whately. "Their interpreter wears a crucifix, almost identical to mine, and I've seen her cross herself. The crucifixion picture in their Bible is the same as ours, even down to the woman kneeling before the cross, and the Last Supper—"

"Their interpreter is a priestess. Their 'pope' is a woman, the 'World-mother.' How long has the Catholic Church in World Blue been ordaining women? Over here, it's been less than fifty years. Their 'Christ' may not even be the same person, or have said the same thing—and if He did, they were translated into entirely different languages, and cross-referenced to different prophecies, a different mythos, maybe even a different ethos. Besides, do the Christians on your World always agree with each other?" The diminutive interpreter shook the water from his hands, and walked out. Whately followed him.

"Do you mind if I ask you a personal question?" he asked, quietly.

"No, I guess not."

"About your religion?"

Anagnostakos shrugged. "My grandmother was Greek Orthodox, and she used to drag me along to services until I was too heavy to drag—but I haven't been inside a church since her funeral, and that was nearly twenty years ago. I went to a Catholic college in Melbourne, on a scholarship, but I think they would have expelled me if I hadn't kept winning the language prize. I've been exposed to every major religion on Earth—well, Earth Green—and none of them have stuck. No, that's not quite true—some of them stuck in my craw. I've seen holy war, sanctified bigotry, sacramental starvation . . . Hell, even back home—in Green-Australia—there was a Muslim community that practiced what they euphemistically call 'female circumcision.' Let's say I'm an ethical atheist."

"Do you believe in Christ?"

"Only as an historical figure."

"I'm not going to act as an apologist for religion," said Whately, nodding rapidly. "Or even for Catholicism: I have family in Blue-Belfast. But none of the religious wars were Christ's fault.

"We've both seen World Red. It's cleaner than our homeWorlds, and less violent, and no one seems to be starving or homeless—"

"True," said Anagnostakos, "but maybe they have the death penalty for everything from graffiti to speeding—not that it's easy to speed in those electric cars—or compulsory euthanasia, or a suicide cult . . . or maybe their medical science is a few centuries behind ours, or they're suffering from an epidemic that only kills the poor, or they expose their children. It would explain why they need their gene pool boosted . . ." He looked at the priest's ashen face, and then smiled gently. "Don't worry, Monsignor; I'm just playing Devil's Advocate. It's a hobby of mine. I like all the Reds I've met; they seem . . . peaceful, at home—the way Zen Buddhists are supposed to be," he added, teasingly; then, "It's almost as though they don't have the concept of 'foreign.' "

The ambassador smiled. "I think I know what you mean. Wouldn't you be interested in learning why?"

"Of course, but—"

"Doesn't religion play a large part in shaping a society's attitudes and behavior?"

"Yes, but—"

"We know the RedWorlders invented the printing press thousands of years ago. Their gospels may not have been misinterpreted, censored and rewritten like those of our homeWorlds," concluded Whately, hastily. "Wouldn't that be a logical place to start looking for the secret?"

Anagnostakos stared at him for several seconds, and then smiled broadly. "I always wondered what 'Jesuitical reasoning' was: now I think I know. But what if you don't like what you find?"

"Monsignor?"

Whately looked up from his newsfax, eyebrows raised. "Yes?"

"I've spoken to Dr. Melle," said Anagnostakos. "She's offered to take us to meet a teacher of hers on World Red, a priestess who should have, or be able to find, a facsimile edition of their gospels."

"That's wonderful!" Whately dropped his fax, reached for the interpreter's hand, and pumped it vigorously. "Thank you very much."

Anagnostakos smiled, and tried to disengage his hand. "We'll have to leave on Wednesday afternoon, at two: the priestess has a very busy schedule—we're lucky she could find a few minutes to accommodate us—and the temple is quite a long drive from the Bridge. I wouldn't expect to be back before seven."

"I can leave Panosian in charge for an afternoon: he's good, and he disagrees with almost everything Dearborn is likely to say. Are there any strictures I should know about?"

"Melle didn't mention any. They don't seem to have a dress code in Ptolemaios, what we call Red-Alexandria—the outfit the delegates wear are part habit, part weatherproofing. Your mufti may look uncomfortable, but at least they'll know you're from out of town. Melle suggested that I not wear a tie or a vest: apparently, the Reds think they look ridiculous, and only seasoned diplomats could keep themselves from laughing at me.

"Besides, we won't be mixing with the populace; I don't speak Arrinesh that well, anyway. We're to let Melle act as guide and take us from the bridge to the car, from the car to the temple, and then back the same way."

"Thank you again. I wish there was some way I could repay you."

"Just vote 'yes' on Friday," replied Anagnostakos, smiling.

"Oh, I planned to." Whately gave the younger man's hand another enthusiastic shake, and then calmed himself down. "You know, you're much smarter than you give yourself credit for, Mr. Anagnostakos. You'd be much better at my job than I am—let alone Dearborn."

Anagnostakos shrugged. "I'm a street kid. I can learn any language you want, but I still forget which fork I'm supposed to use, and I'm the world's worst—" he hesitated: he'd been about to say "liar," but realized that the priest might misconstrue this as an insult. "Poker player," he finished, rather lamely, but just as accurately.

"That boss of yours isn't much better."

"Oh, don't let that smile fool you. Besides, he isn't one sixty-eight in stacked heels."

"168?"

"Centimeters—I think it's about five foot five in Olde English. Jimmy has a granddaughter who's taller than me." He glanced at his digital watch (an import from Japan-Azure), and swore mildly. "I'm late. See you Wednesday."

"Good-bye," said Whately, "and again—thank you."

Whately peered through the windows of the electric car at the suburban streets of Red-Alexandria. The houses, new or old (it was difficult to tell), seemed to be built of the same colorful material (ceramic? plastic? one-way glass?), in much the same style—plenty of parabolic arches, a minimum of straight lines, and no sharp corners. He noticed more greenery than he thought Egypt could support, and pristine statues that might have been new or centuries old, and though the road was wide, he saw very few cars. He was wondering how Red-Ireland must look, when Anagnostakos said, "Monsignor?"

"Yes?"

"Dr. Melle would like to ask you a question."

"Certainly."

"Why are all the ambassadors at the summit, men? I've explained why for my World, as best I can, but maybe yours is different?"

"Well . . . there are female diplomats and ambassadors on World Blue, of course, many of them in the U.N. . . . but unfortunately, few of them have any experience as trade envoys. Where would they get the experience? We can't send them to Blue-Japan, much less any of the OPEC countries:

they'd think we were insulting them. And only rich countries can afford women's rights movements: women in the poor countries don't have the leisure or the access to communications.

"In fact, women had been without most rights for so many centuries in all of our Worlds, the little progress that was made in my World over the last century is something of a miracle. Women still can't vote in most countries in World Indigo, and while progress was being made in Azure, it was reversed in the 1980s and '90s when Azure-America went from World leader to . . . can you translate that?"

"I think so, though I'm not sure that I understand all of it."

"That makes two of us. Are we nearly there?"

"Yes: in fact, we're ahead of schedule. I'm sorry we've both been talking shop . . ."

Whately waved a hand as though brushing away flies. "Don't worry: I've been enjoying the scenery. Tell Dr. Melle that she's lucky to live in such a lovely World."

Anagnostakos translated that, and then said, "That's the temple ahead. She says it'll be nearly twenty minutes before Dr. Esa is free. Do you want to tour around, wait in her office, or would you rather see a service?"

"A service?"

"Yes: she'll be giving some people . . . I think 'communion' would be the right word. Dr. Melle wondered if you, as another priest of Christ, might be interested."

Whately gulped. "Tell her that I'd be fascinated."

Whately sat in the back of the church, wishing that God might grant him—if only for an hour—the gift of tongues. Even Anagnostakos couldn't understand the World Red vernacular well enough to translate, and Whately was desperate to know whether Dr. Esa's sermon was as Christian as the fittings of the temple. Faith, he told himself. Have faith.

Finally, a number of the congregation moved to the railing at the head of the church, and knelt before it—some with hands behind their backs, some with hands clasped in prayer, and Whately's eyes filled with tears of joy. Dr. Esa, wearing a burgundy-colored kimonolike robe, stepped toward them. " 'Take and eat it,' " translated Anagnostakos, in a murmur, " 'This is my body. Drink; this is my blood, poured out for many for the forgiveness of sins.' " Then, as the offWorlders watched, Dr. Esa opened the divided skirt of her robe and guided a boy's face toward her groin. Then she moved over to the girl beside him and repeated the gesture.

The boy, feeling the pressure of Whately's stare, turned around. Whately saw blood on his lips, and screamed.

"They've voted against any migration," said Anagnostakos. "Unanimously."

Melle stared, and then translated for the ambassador and her staff. The ambassador's reply needed no interpretation: "Why?"

"Officially? I suspect they'll say it's because they need to do more research, to pick the right people, to prevent a violent clash between two dissimilar cultures . . . The truth is far more simple. Whately told them about your church service."

"I don't understand."

"On our Worlds, they perform the same ritual with bread symbolizing the body, and wine symbolizing the blood—"

"Wine?" Melle erupted with a most undiplomatic fury. "But that's a travesty! It's—"

"Blasphemy?"

"Worse!"

"Obscenity, maybe? I suspect that's the word Whately used."

The ambassador cleared her throat, and asked a question. Melle translated. "What will happen to the millions starving on your Worlds? What will they tell them?"

Anagnostakos shrugged. "They'll think of some excuse. Dearborn suggested they be sent to World Cyan, that he'd rather deal with the rats— as though it were his problem. I'm not a scientist, so I don't know how feasible that is, but I suspect they'll try. Whately also recommended they close all the bridges to World Red."

Melle translated this, and the ambassador and her staff were silent. Finally, the ambassador spoke. "What about you?"

"Me?"

"If they do close the bridge," Melle translated, "which side will you be on?"

"I don't understand."

"You have no home in your World," the ambassador continued. "You've not lived in the same city for as much as a year since you were twenty-three—and now you're thirty-six?"

"I like traveling."

"We have a World that you haven't seen, with a hundred new languages for you to learn. And you're an interpreter. Your job is helping people to understand each other. On our World, you could help us to understand thirty billion people . . ."

"And," added Melle, "if the bridge is reopened, you could help them to understand us."

"I'm really not sure that's possible . . ." Anagnostakos replied.

He tried not to sound tempted, but he'd never been a good liar: Melle knew that he'd already accepted the offer.

"Think it over," she said, "but don't tell anyone. They may try to stop you."

"Of course, there's one other option," said Dearborn, wiping his hands.

Whately, who'd been staying drunk for days in an effort to avoid a near-lethal hangover, grunted noncommittally. As far as he was concerned, now that all the Reds had returned to their homeWorld, the Bridge apparatus should be dismantled without delay.

"Military. We invade."

Whately nodded, then suddenly sat bolt upright. "You're joking!"

"Hell, no! Move the bridge to one of their uninhabited areas and drop in a few million troops from each World, take one continent at a time . . ."

"But what about . . ." Whately tried to remember the word "proselytizing," failed, and finally blurted out, "cultural contamination?"

"Biowar?" Dearborn mused. "I don't think we know enough about their immune—"

"No!" snapped Whately, winced, and continued quietly, "No . . . I mean . . . their relig . . . uh, their cult? You know? What if some of the troops, uh, especially the women . . . what if they . . . learn about it, get converted to it—"

"So we lose a few sold—"

Whately finally found the words he wanted, and used them. "What if they bring it back with them, for Christ's sake?"

"Oh," said Dearborn, and considered this. "Oh. Well . . . we won't send any female troops over. The men won't . . . well, they just won't. Besides," he said, recovering his confidence, "the Reds can't corrupt us. None of them know our language, and vice versa—right?"

Two

Anagnostakos closed the door behind him and locked it, then staggered the remaining few steps to the bed—taking great care, despite his fatigue, not to tread on any books—kicked off his boots, and collapsed, face down. He looked up a moment later, and realized that hours had passed; the room was dark, and someone was rattling the door. "Melle?"

"Yes."

"Come in," he said, rolling over and rubbing his eyes. The lights, sensitive to heat and motion, brightened as she entered the untidy room.

"Were you asleep?"

"Huh? Yeah." He stood, a little unsteadily. "Where are we going to-night?"

Melle regarded him carefully, and then shook her head. "Nowhere. Sleep is more important. I'll call for some food."

"You know, that's the longest speech in English I've heard all day," Anagnostakos replied, unlacing his jacket. "Where are we going? The theater again?"

"The play will be on tomorrow night. Sophocles has been dead for centuries; you need to sleep. You've been working too much."

"I was a teacher for years. That's how I managed to see the world—one World, anyway. I'll admit, I've never had class where everyone was so bright and enthusiastic, and that's as tiring as herding cats . . . but I'll cope." He stepped out of his trousers, and pulled on another pair with practiced haste. As far as he could tell, RedWorlders didn't have any nudity tabus, but he hadn't quite lost his own. "What time's the show? Can we eat first?"

"How long did you sleep in the night?"

"I don't know. About five hours—call it eight tou." She looked at him dubiously, and then glanced at the books beside the bed. "Okay, maybe seven. I read for a while. There's so much I don't know yet. Anywhere else I go, I know something about the tabus and the customs, what I can and can't do and say and wear and eat, where I can and can't go, and when, how rich or poor the people are . . ."

"I understand that," replied Melle.

"I'm not sure you do. All I know of your geography is that Wa is Japan and Nura is Australia, and a little about the Concordat. I know some Arrinesh, though not as well as you know English, but there're hundreds of languages, thousands of years' worth of history, millions of books and plays . . . we've only had the printing press for a few centuries, not four millennia. We probably lost half a million books when the Library of Alexandria burnt down—hundreds of plays by Sophocles and Aeschylus and Aristophanes and Euripides, the complete works of Berossus and Hecataeus and Hypatia, all stuff you take for granted and that academics on Green would murder their grandmothers for . . . And the beautiful things the women here have done, books and paintings that never existed on our

Worlds at all, except maybe in someone's head . . . In any of the other
Worlds, I'm a well-traveled and educated man; here, I'm an ignorant barbarian. And I'm a Greek: we invented the term barbarian, to describe
everyone else!"

Melle laughed. "The Arrinesh word 'hort' means roughly the same,
and is probably even older—but I haven't heard anyone use it to describe
you. Is that all?"

"No. I really do love what I've seen of this World. All the time I've
been here, I don't think I've seen anything ugly or dangerous; I know I
haven't seen anyone who looks beaten, or frightened, or hungry, or even
seriously angry. I was scared, for a while, that the men might be treated as
badly here as women are in the other Worlds, but if they are, I haven't
seen it. I have wondered why there are so few men in my classes—"

"There are very few men in the Councils, at present," Melle admitted.
"The Concordat, and most of its member-states, has been led by a coalition
of religious and women-only parties for the past eleven years—and, of
course, they appoint ambassadors who will agree with their policies. So
most of the women in your classes are diplomats, while nearly all the men
are teachers or linguists—there are plenty of men in the universities, especially the sciences, and even in the church; they can do anything but
give the sacrament."

"And become Worldmother."

"The Worldmother must actually have been a mother, with at least
one son and one daughter . . . but that's mostly symbolic, like most of her
powers. Some people have tried to change it, but most accept that it isn't
important."

"Maybe that's what I like about this world," said Anagnostakos. "You
believe in a mother whose first priority is feeding her children; we pray to
a father who seems more concerned with punishing them."

Melle smiled. "That's a lovely idea, but unfortunately, it isn't quite
true. Not everyone is as well fed as the people you've seen in Ptolemaios
and Erech. There was a famine in Punt before you arrived; thousands
starved before we could send enough food.

"And there are people here, even whole countries, who worship male
gods. There are even some, including a few Buddhist sects, who believe
women don't have souls, but who are still known for their good works. All
of our religions teach that you should never refuse food to anyone hungrier
than yourself; life is just too valuable.

"On the other hand, not all Christians will turn the other cheek. All
clergy are forbidden to bear arms, preach violence, or even raise a hand

against a child or a cat—but the same law doesn't apply to the laity, many of whom serve with the army when required. And there have always been those who worship the Mother by sacrificing innocent victims—one of the oldest prayers in the Bible, by Enheduanna, praises the Goddess for 'filling the rivers with blood,' and they say there are still devotees of Kali Ma in Maurya and Harappa."

Anagnostakos nodded, thinking hard. "You mentioned the army. Do you still have wars?"

"Yes, of course—though not here. The Concordat hasn't been attacked for centuries. But the war in Funan is still going on, though both sides signed a treaty nearly twenty years ago—"

"That's why I need more time to study. I didn't even know you still had armies—"

"Do you still have wars? On World Green?"

"Yes—"

"How large are your armies? What weapons do your soldiers have? What about the other Worlds?"

"I don't know the precise—"

"But you do know they're larger than ours, and probably better armed."

"I don't know about your weapons, but the other four Worlds have—" He calculated quickly. "Nearly forty billion people between them. Most countries have between one or two percent of their population in the armed forces during peacetime, so that's about half a billion. If you could get them all to fight on the same side, which is unlikely . . . say five billion if you throw in the reserves."

"That's more than twice our total population," said Melle, softly. "That's why we need you to teach English. A third of your students are diplomats; the rest are teachers, who'll teach more diplomats and more teachers. When they're fluent enough to take the beginners' classes, then we'll be able to reduce the tou you have to work, and you'll have more time to study. But if we're invaded, we're going to need—"

"You don't really believe that's going to happen, do you?"

Melle shrugged. "It's possible, and that possibility makes you uniquely valuable to us."

Anagnostakos looked at the books on the floor, and then sat down. "Well, since you put it like that . . ."

Whately grunted a greeting to Brother Luke as the younger monk dashed past him on their way to chapel. Brother Luke was an explosively devout redhead from Cork, who seemed better suited to the I.R.A. than to monastic life; he always ran, as though his need to confess something was unbearably urgent.

The Church should have copyrighted confession centuries ago, Whately thought; Alcoholics Anonymous would owe us a fortune in royalties. And that was all they ever asked him about; had he had a drink? had he craved a drink? as though that were the only thing he'd come to the monastery to avoid. Which suited Whately perfectly; let them believe that; he could answer those questions with a smile and a clear conscience. The other thing was . . .

"Brother John?"

He looked up slightly, recognizing the abbot's Chicago accent.

The abbot was a short man, who reminded Whately vaguely of someone else he'd known, once. "Yes, Excellency?"

"Another letter for you. I was requested to deliver this one to you personally, and to be sure that you read it and replied. The request," he added, with a slightly sour edge to his voice, "came from the secretary of His Holiness. Apparently you've been remiss in answering your mail."

Whately blinked, and then stared at the envelope. There was neither stamp nor postmark. He'd received enough mail in recent weeks to arouse the curiosity of his fellow monks, especially as most of it had come from World Azure. Nervously, he opened it, and read through it quickly.

"Bad news?" asked the abbot, sympathetically.

Whately nodded. "It says I'm to leave at once."

"Are you surprised?"

"I wasn't expecting a papal edict," replied Whately, choosing his words with great care.

"Weren't you? You must have realized that you couldn't hide here forever."

"You think I've been hiding?"

"Yes," replied the abbot, simply. "I don't really know why, and I'm not about to ask—oh, I know you've been bitten hard by the bottle, but that's never the whole story and I suspect you could have beaten that yourself. You were a delegate to the interWorld trade talks, weren't you, before they burned all the bridges to Red?"

Whately glanced at the letter again, and said nothing.

"And the delegate from Azure-Washington is now sitting in the White House . . . Have you been to Azure-America, John?"

"No. Have you?"

"No, but I try to keep up with the news. They're having terrible troubles there, economic and environmental, and all of them can be blamed on overpopulation, though that's an oversimplification. Even the U.S.A. thinks of itself as overpopulated; the irony is that they regard their poor as the excess, when it's their rich who consume more than—but that's by the by. What's disturbing is that the Church is being used as a scapegoat, because of Humanae vitae, which was never repealed over there. Widely ignored, maybe, but never actually repealed. Now, your friend Dearborn— ("He's not my friend," muttered Whately) "—has gotten where he's gotten largely by scaremongering and pandering to prejudices. He knows there's a lot he could do to hurt the Church in Azure without it rebounding on him. On the other hand, he has no good reason to do so—which makes it an excellent bargaining chip. His people call Azure Rome, and . . ."

Whately nodded. "Things were so much simpler when there was only one pope."

"Amen to that. At least we all worship the same God." He sighed. "The helicopter will be picking you up tomorrow—after matins, I expect. Where were you going, confession?"

"Yes."

"Then I won't keep you. Good-bye, Brother."

Whately bowed his head, and walked slowly toward chapel, in time to hear Brother Luke burst out of the confessional and crash onto a pew. Out into the Worlds again, he thought, wearily, and realized he was shaking; he leaned against the back of a pew, but never looked up, not here, not in chapel.

He could feel the image of the virgin Mary staring at him from behind the altar, and the mere thought, the idea of a woman in the front of a church, was enough to remind him of—He doubled over and vomited on his sandals. Bless me Father, for I have . . .

He heard other monks running toward them, Brother Luke in the lead. Let them believe it's the alcohol that scares me, he told himself again, not the . . . Bless me, Father, for I . . . Not the obscenity, the uncleanness, the blood, the Whore of Babylon Mother of Abominations . . . Bless me, Father, for . . .

"Let your women keep silence in the churches; for it is not permitted unto them to speak.

Bless me, Father, for . . .

"For the man is not of the woman but the woman of the man."

Bless me, Father . . .

"These are they that were not defiled with women." Bless me, Father, for . . .

"And the woman was arrayed in purple and scarlet color, and decked with gold and precious stones and pearls, having a golden cup in her hand full of abominations and filthiness of her fornication."

Father . . .

After weeks of dropping hints, Melle finally came out and said it. "If you're scared of violating tabus, you can stop worrying. All of your students are adults. If you want to have sex with them, you can ask; it's not forbidden, as long as you're polite and respect their right to say 'no.' " While Anagnostakos was still staring, his fork halfway to his mouth, she hurried on. "I shouldn't worry unduly. Mati seems to be as attracted to you as you are to her, and we have an old saying that the best place to learn a new language is in bed."

"We have the same saying," replied Anagnostakos, a moment later. "Though I can't vouch for its antiquity. Look, I'd better ask this now, before I make a complete fool of myself—what are the marriage customs here?"

Melle almost choked on a mouthful of salad. "I don't think she'll agree to marry you," she said, cautiously, after regaining her composure. "I wasn't suggesting you ask her that; you've only known each other for a few months. But you've been here for just over a year, now, and that's a long time to be without sex; I would have spoken sooner, but I wasn't sure of your tabus."

"I meant, is she already married, and does marriage mea—?" He tried to think of the Arrinesh for "monogamy." Melle stared at him, and then smiled. "Oh. I don't think she's married, I'm fairly sure she hasn't any children, and she's not wearing any warn-offs or fetishes, so it's safe to ask. For sex, I mean."

"What if she were married?" he pressed on. "I haven't seen a wedding here, and haven't even heard anything about them, until now. Our traditional marriage vows require the partners to 'forsake all others, until death us do part.' "

"Forsake? As in abandon?" Melle sounded horrified. "All others? The entire world?"

Anagnostakos shook his head. "Okay, so it was a bad choice of words. It mostly means 'don't have sex with,' not 'don't help' . . ."

"Why not?"

"What? Oh . . . well, originally, I suppose it's because men used to want to be sure their heirs were also their biological children, and not someone else's—passing on their own genes, as the sociobiologists would put it. So they made sure their wives were faithf . . . didn't have sex with anyone else.

If a married woman was raped, she was stoned to death. It was supposed to cut both ways, but it didn't; look at the Odyssey. Odysseus sleeps with Kirke and Kalypso and Goddess knows who else, while Penelope sits at home and spins for eleven years. At its most extreme, of course, some Muslim sects practice clitoridectomy or 'female circumcision,' mutilating women so that they can't have orgasms." He grimaced.

Melle stared at him. "I'm sorry," she said, softly, "but I don't think I understood a single thing you just said."

Dearborn looked beefier than he had at the trade talks, though the muscles he'd built up for the campaign were already starting to turn to flab after barely a month in office. "Johnny boy!" he chortled, as Whately was ushered into the room. "Good to see you again. How're things on Blue?"

Whately was too experienced a diplomat to frown, but his voice was cool as he replied, "I haven't seen very much of it, lately, I'm afraid. I've been on retreat."

Dearborn's smile broadened into something even less pleasant. "Yeah, I heard. Doing the Lord's work. I like to think I'm doing the same." Whately grunted noncommittally. "And that's why I've called for you. I've spoken to all the other delegates from the trade talks. Remember what I said, just before we closed the Bridges to Red, about the military option?" Whately stared at him. "Okay, so it was a little premature. But you musta heard what happened to our colonies on Cyan and Gray." Whately nodded. There were still a few off-shore oil rigs on both of the Blasted Worlds (as the press had taken to calling them), but they were barely paying for the energy to keep the Bridges up. "Fortunately, I'm on the record as being against it from the beginning. I mean, frankly, we might as well try to put men on the fucking moon. Even if you succeed, who the Hell wants to live on the moon? We haven't found any more Worlds since then, and that goddamn Schroeder woman refuses to help. But Red—Red could be the Promised Land. The Land of Milk and Honey. The Garden of Eden. You know what it looked like; none of us saw as much of it as you did."

"I saw it," replied Whately. "And you already know that I believe any contact is just too great a risk."

"Never underestimate a good publicity machine; just ask the man who's ridden one. We just tell our boys that the Reds'll cut their balls off if they let anyone get close enough to talk to them; Hell, it's probably true. You missed out on the Gulf War, didn't you? Shit, it was like a video game; all anybody ever saw was blips on a screen." He grinned. "So what makes you think they can beat us?"

"Because they already have," said Whately, solemnly. "On all of our Worlds, we defeated them thousands of years ago. But on Red, they won."

"I think I understood some of that," said Melle, uncertainly, after Anagnostakos had spent nearly quarter of an hour explaining. "You take the family names of your fathers?"

"Yes."

"Why?"

"Because men still own nearly everything, and it used to be almost impossible for women to bring up their children without a father's financial support."

"Why would anyone have children they knew they couldn't feed?"

"Well, they probably didn't intend to, unless the man convinced them that he was going to marry them or something."

"But if they didn't intend to—"

Anagnostakos stared at her. "Don't women here ever become pregnant by accident?"

"No! Almost never; it's about as unlikely as having triplets . . ." They both sat there in stunned silence, until he asked, "Since when?"

"For as long as anyone knows!" replied Melle. "Some of the oldest printed books we have, maybe the first ever written in Demotic, are herbal recipes for young girls who haven't learn how to control their fertility by—I don't know if you even have a word for it, the closest I can think of is 'faith healing' . . ."

"Biofeedback?" guessed Anagnostakos.

Melle broke the word into its roots, then nodded. "Yes. That sounds right. How long have you known it?"

"If we ever knew it at all, we've forgotten it," he said, softly. "For a long time, we didn't even admit that women were anything more than incubators, sure that all life came from the male, that every sperm was a miniature human waiting to be born . . . We still have some of that attitude, but now we blame the women."

"Is that why you have nearly nine billion people?"

"It's how; I'm not sure about why. Partly because we spent most of the past few millennia expecting most of our children to die, and having as many as we could to compensate. Partly because most of our rulers wanted men for their armies. And, probably because of the first two reasons, men were taught that they weren't really men until they'd fathered sons, and women were never told that they had a choice."

"Do you mean a choice of not having children, or just a choice of not having sons?"

"You can choose the sex of your children, too?"

"We can choose not to have sons," she replied. "Choosing to have them is more difficult. Sperm with the male message—I'm sorry, I don't know your word for it—"

"Chromosome."

"They're very sensitive to heat and chemical changes, very easily killed. Females are much, much tougher. It's just as well; how many men does a World need, after all?"

"The Sumerians and Babylonians, the Minoan culture, the ancient Egyptians and Greeks, even the Celts . . . they all worshipped a Mother-Goddess," said Whately. "Inanna. Ishtar. Isis. Astarte. Anahita. Artemis. Aphrodite. Athena. Danu. The myth is probably as old as language; a lot of primitive cultures even claim that a goddess taught them writing, or call the goddess 'The Great Scribe.' We don't know much about their rites, except that they used poisonous snakes; I shudder to think how. The priests, the soldiers, the judges, sometimes even the rulers, were women. They probably had no idea how babies were conceived, didn't realize men were important.

"Our ancestors—Aryans, Caucasians, whatever you choose to call them; what's important is that they worshipped God, a male God—came from the north into Mesopotamia about four thousand years ago, with their own laws. It was inevitable that the two cultures would clash. In our Worlds, we won, destroyed the temples and the idols, enforced our laws . . . but in Red, somehow, we lost." Whately took a deep breath. "To beat them this time, we would have to kill every single one of them. It may take even more than that; we have to destroy every trace of their religion. At the very least, we'd have to burn every book, unread, and even if it were possible, it wouldn't be popular with the academics. More likely, we'd have to nuke every city—Deuteronomy 12:2: 'Ye shall utterly destroy all the places, wherein the nations which ye shall possess served their gods, upon the high mountains, and upon the hills, and under every green tree.' Not even neutron bombs would do; we'd need to turn the planet into a cinder like Cyan or Gray. Hell, that may even be what happened to Cyan and Gray! Even if you were prepared to kill that many people—and I'm not—what would it profit you?"

"We still have famines, but they are minor and isolated; no one intentionally has more children than they can feed.

"We still have wars, occasionally—but women who are against the war make sure the next generation hasn't enough surplus males for an army. Invaders may capture a country—but if they oppress the people, they have to go home to breed or die out.

"Slavery died out thousands of years ago. It wasn't economically viable, because the slaves wouldn't breed.

"There is still rape, but no woman has to bear her rapist's child.

"We created and we continue the human race. We taught you your first words. We are the source of life and language. And all we ask is that you remember where you began."

Dearborn sat back in the enormous leather chair and suppressed a yawn. "Is that your official position?"

"I no longer hold an official position," replied Whately. "I've retired from the U.N., and I intend to stay retired; I'm here at the request of your Pope."

Dearborn nodded. "Well, Monsignor, thanks for your input. It's been good to see you again; give my regards to World Blue."

Whately stood. "You're going to do it, aren't you?"

Dearborn stared at the Oval Office ceiling for a moment, then shrugged. "Yeah. If I don't, the Indigos will beat me to it; besides, we've spend billions just getting ready. The Bridges are built, the troops are trained, the logistics are all worked out, the news releases have been written . . . Hey, chill out! There's no need to worry." He grinned. "God is on Our side, remember?"

Three years later, when he caught his daughter giving communion in the Lincoln Bedroom, it occurred to Dearborn that he might have been wrong.

CHERRY WILDER

Cherry Wilder (the pseudonym of Cherry Lockett Grimm) was born in New Zealand and lived in Australia from 1956 to 1976, where she began her literary career. Her first SF story ("The Ark of James Carlyle" [1974]) was the first Australian story by a woman to be nominated for a Ditmar Award. She then lived in Germany until 1997, when she moved back to New Zealand. Her first novel, *The Luck of Brin's Five* (1977), was Wilder's first significant work of SF, and was the first work of fiction by a woman to win a Ditmar Award. Its two sequels are *The Nearest Fire* (1980) and *The Tapestry Warriors* (1983)—all three, comprising the Torin Trilogy, originally published as young adult fiction. She has written a fantasy trilogy, The Rulers of Hylor (A *Princess of the Chameln* [1984], *Yorath the Wolf* [1984], and *The Summer's King* [1985]), and a horror novel, *Cruel Designs* (1988). And she has continued to produce short stories, some of the best of which are collected in *Dealers in Light and Darkness* (1995). Her most important novels to date are *Second Nature* (1982) and *Signs of Life* (1996), about the civilization set up by the survivors of a spaceship crash on a hospitable planet that they call Rhomary Land. Several of her best stories are set on Torin or on Rhomary Land. This story is set in the U.S. but was only published in England prior to its appearance in her collection.

LOOKING FORWARD TO THE HARVEST

ALL THE WAY TO the meeting my grandparents argued about what the Time Sense people might be called. I sat with my father on the front of the cart. He clucked to Ruby, our mare, and smiled at some of the talk but I could see that a lot of the things that were said made him uneasy.

"Something with Temp," said Nell. "Not Temponaut."

"Chroniast," suggested Ralph. "Chronist. Perichron."

"Horrible! Mixture of Latin and Greek roots," said Nell. "What do we know about these people?"

"They must be classed as part of the Psi Wave," said Ralph, "people who claim to have developed strange powers after the crash."

"They've never registered at a center," said Nell, "which means they've never been screened by those anal-erotic latterday bureaucrats who make our lives such a misery!"

"The autumn of our days," said Ralph, "as we totter down life's highway . . ."

"Damn right!" said Nell. "We're long past the sere and yellow leaf, honey. We are deep in the winter of our discontent and spring will not be far behind this time."

I hated it when they talked this way about being old and dying. My father said, privately, that they were a pair of tough old roosters and he had never known Nell to shed a tear, except once. Not in the hospital, not at the funeral. But days later he found her in our store room, weeping over her daughter's doctoral thesis and playing with a box of old broken toys. Anne-Marie, my Mom, had died of a heart attack; she had been dead now for three years and five months.

"They claim to have an extra sense," said Ralph patiently. "A time sense. They imply that it is a mutation. What we need is a word for 'time sense' "

My father cleared his throat.

"German," he suggested. *"Zeitgefühl."*

"Hey, not bad," said Nell. "Good thinking, Don. *Zeit-Gefühl* or Time Feeling, referred to as Zee Gee and the people themselves as Zee Gees."

"Zee Jesus," sighed Ralph. "They sound like a defunct pop group. And remember that German speakers would call them Tzed Gays."

The two old folks found this pretty funny for some reason. I asked:

"Nell, what's a pop group?"

"Well, what do you think it might be, Linnit?"

She was always after me to think laterally and to play around with words the way they did.

"Pop might have to do with fathers. A slang name for a father-oriented commune like the Patriarchs of the New Jerusalem."

"Not bad but you aren't even close. What might pop be short for?"

So it went on until I half-guessed, by way of Pop Art, which was pretty unpopular at the center, what the expression meant: a pop group was a rock band, more or less. A group of pre-crash, commercial, youth-oriented music makers. We had a number of music makers at Hopewell Center. Guitars and guitar players were so plentiful they hardly counted but we also had fiddlers, piano players for the pianos, which were our cultural heritage, along with clarinets, flutes, tubas, zithers, saxophones . . . it was wonderful the condition these things were in. Better condition, sometimes, than the people who could still play them and who instructed other musicmakers. The music they made was mixed, partly classical, a lot of folk, and a lot based on that no-good commercial, youth-oriented rock. A friend of mine, Cholly, had made himself a bongo drum from a sauerkraut bucket and a piece of old inner tube; I played the recorder. There was no way to describe the music we made.

I loved to hear about rock bands, pop groups, and everything to do with pre-crash youth. I urged Nell and Ralph to go on about pop groups they remembered, their dress, hairstyles, lifestyles, although it was enough to raise the hackles on my Dad's neck. This was consumerist nostalgia of the worst kind. He protested at last . . . you'll turn the kid's head . . . and Nell said she wished she had a beefsteak for every time he'd said that. I knew what a beefsteak was, of course, and had even seen my grandparents eating meat. It was one of the disgusting things they did which had to be borne with forbearance for the sake of their wisdom. They were a couple of old pre-crash Carnies . . . like the tuba-players and the cellist . . . who had come through into the New Age. They must be permitted to give us the benefit of their experience without contaminating us too much.

Mid-morning we crossed from the third westbound overland route onto an old piece of freeway; I had never been so far west from Hopewell Center before. One of our signboards gave information about the old freeway and the two towns that it had connected.

"Wait!" said my grandmother. "There used to be something along this way. Don, you don't mean to tell me these Time Sense people are living in a Bergstrom House?"

"Strange-shaped place on the side of a hill," said my father, "Has a collector wall."

"Surely that must be Lewis's own house," said Ralph. "His demonstration model. Didn't you visit . . ."

"Yes!"

My grandmother was upset.

"Don," she said, "I visited that house twenty-five years ago at the invitation of the architect, Lewis Bergstrom. I signed a visitors' book."

My father shook his head.

"There's no one left from that time," he said. "These are entirely new people. They specialize in crop-reading. They stand in a field and recommend crops for the following season."

"Is that why we're going to see them?" asked Ralph.

"They request family groups . . . people of three generations," said my father.

I could tell he was stalling. Finally as we turned off the old freeway into a grassy lane he said:

"The Planting Committee asked me to check them out, if you must know. And they asked me to take Nell and Ralph along because they are two cunning old coyotes who can spot a fraud at ninety feet. Are you satisfied?"

"No," said Nell, "but I believe you, Don. Let us pause and consider. They claim to have a time sense which enables them to go to or observe the past and the future . . ."

"If this—er—faculty is a mutation," said Ralph, "chances are that it came from the crash and therefore the mutants must be under twenty."

"Just so," said my father. "Two young boys, seventeen or eighteen, a little older than Linnit."

"Family name?"

"Morgan."

"Did we ever know anyone called Morgan back there?" asked Nell.

"Rings a bell," said Ralph. "I'll think about it."

We came in sight of the house. It was built of wood and gray stone and it grew out of the hill in tall angular clumps like crystals. I understood vaguely the kind of house it was, although I had never seen anything like it except in art books. It scared me the way all pre-crash buildings did in varying degrees. I imagined myself creeping about in a big, white wooden house built for an American movie family, going up the carpeted stairs. I imagined myself in the ruins of the tall cities, looking up, up, and scream-ing . . .

"Beautiful!" sighed Ralph. "Bergstrom's Folly."

"Yep," said my grandmother, still uneasy. "I don't want to alarm you, Don, but that house is pure dynamite, Lewis built in all kinds of high-tech tricks . . ."

Ralph twirled his thumbs happily.

"Oh, I always say we've a lot to thank dynamite for, Nellie dear . . ."

"Twenty-five years," said my father. "The house hasn't too much kick left in it these days, I guess."

"The pair of you can go jump in the lake," said Nell. "One old fella teasing me and one young fella breathing sweet reason. I don't know which is worse."

I could not take my eyes off the House Beautiful that was full of high-tech tricks. If I was game to go inside maybe I would find a room that showed nonstop videos of heavy metal bands, blasting away all round the walls at the touch of a button. And in the other rooms there would be holograms of pre-crash life: automobiles, jumbo jets, violence, sexual prom-iscuity, pollution, junk food, drug highs, late, late movies, dancing, the Metropolitan Opera in New York, false gods, false prophets, neon lights, Coca-Cola, and the State of California. My true birthright, of which I had been robbed: the twentieth century.

My father reined in beside a tree. There was a mailbox and a name neatly painted on a board: G. Morgan, Advisory Services.

"Oh sure," said Ralph. "You remember, Nell. There was the dentist, Dave Morgan. Gave us dental advice. Even came out to the Ranch a couple of times."

"So he did," said my grandmother.

She ran a hand over her bushy head of white hair in a gesture I knew well. It meant sorrow and resignation: so it goes. Most of the people she and Ralph and my Mom had known had gone down in the crash. They did not speak of their personal experiences. When I was eight my Dad, who came from a founding family at Hopewell—one that went green long before the crash—confided to me that Nell and Ralph had a high-tech background. I worried in case they had worked in a reactor and helped nuke their friends but my mother, Anne-Marie, said no, things would loosen up at the Center and I would be proud of my grandparents. That day had not come but what the hell, I was fairly proud of them anyway.

"Don't look so sad, little Linnit," said Nell. "We have to set up a parameter or two for these tests."

Far away at the end of the green driveway, overgrown except for two wheel ruts, a boy in a red shirt began to walk slowly toward us.

"We must remember two things," said Nell. "First, these people may indeed possess unusual powers, whether it's telepathy, a sensitivity to agricultural conditions, or even a deep empathy that enables them to convince others. Second, it's in their interest to cheat a little, to blind us with science."

"Nell, anyone who tries to blind you with science is in for a shock," said my father.

"Why, thank you Don!"

"The boy will ask Linnit to step down," said Ralph, "so he can show her around."

"Just answer his questions, honey," said my grandmother, "and remember what he asked. On no account let it out that Old Nell was at this place before. Got it?"

"Sure."

We all stared at the boys as he approached and he took it very calmly. He was good-looking with tanned even features and thick gold-brown hair falling over his forehead. He was older than he seemed at first, he had looked more of a kid coming down the drive because he was short, no more than five-four, five-five.

"Mister Don Green?" he asked, "of the Hopewell Center? I'm Gavin Morgan."

"Hello there, Gavin!" said my Dad. "I'd like to introduce Nell and Ralph Mann, my wife's parents, and this is my daughter Linnit."

There was a lot of hello there, pleased to meet you. The Morgan boy petted Ruby and gave her a piece of carrot from his pocket. He rode on the step as we came slowly into the shadow of that fantastic house. There were rock gardens, paved ramps and several outbuildings of the same grey stone. Just when I thought he would never ask . . . and thereby score a point against my grandfather . . . Gavin Morgan caught my eye and said:

"You like to step down, Linnit, and see our baby ducks?"

"I don't mind," I said.

I was one of those Hopewell Center girls, candid, clear-eyed, capable. Neither a meek handmaiden of the Patriarchs in a long skirt and a headscarf nor a bareback rider from the Free Amazons, down south. I did my hair in a long ponytail, wore blue linen trousers, and a shirt of knitted cotton.

I wasn't a known rebel or nonconformist on the Center but my attitude was not all it might have been. The Hopewell Counselors knew that they did not possess my heart and mind. Home influences. Anne-Marie, then Nell and Ralph. I thought of this as I stepped down from the cart and smiled at Gavin Morgan and followed him to the barnyard of the Bergstrom house. I was passing for a true-green Hopewell gal. I was deceiving him. Maybe he and his family were trying to deceive all the New Age Communities this side of the mountains with their time sense.

He questioned me very smoothly and in a nice way. He was truly friendly, he didn't flirt, he didn't patronize. By the time we had seen the six ducklings swimming in the pond he knew that my mother was dead, that my Dad was a member of the Planting Committee, that Hopewell had twice the acreage of any other commune, that the main crop was Indian corn.

We got on to what-we-liked-to-do. My hobbies were music, reading, painting, and collage; the Center was very strong on Uses of Leisure Time. Yes, I liked to dance and was in the Youth Chain Group for the summer festival. So what did *he* like to do?"

"Like to do?" he echoed. "I like to be alive!"

Then, as if this was some admission, he said that he farmed here, around the house.

"We travel around a lot, doing the readings," he said.

In the entrance to the stone barn there was a wooden caravan, dark green, with a chimney.

"Play chess plenty in winter," said Gavin. "Summers we go prospecting."

"That's interesting. For gold?"

"For uncontaminated objects that we can bring to market," he said.

We looked at a couple of pigs and a walnut tree. Gavin slipped away into the shadowy barn to see if he had shut the feed bin. When he came back his eyes were sparkling, he was full of the devil.

"Linnit Green!" he said. "Just the name for a Hopewell girl. You like to dance that summer chain dance, Linnit?"

We had touched on this before. He was sharp and mischievous, his eyes were lighter brown and he had a long scar on his right forearm.

"Okay," I said. "Where's your brother Gavin? Off on another time track?"

He laughed aloud and said:

"Come on Gav! She rumbled us."

"She rumbled *you*," said Gavin, coming out of the barn. "This is my brother Owen."

They stood side by side so I could admire the likeness.

"We were born on the same day and we had the same father and mother," said Owen, "but we're not twins. How come?"

"I know that one too," I said. "You have another brother hiding in the barn. Triplets."

"That's right," said Gavin seriously. "Our brother Arthur died at birth."

"I'm sorry," I said. "Look, could you take me into the house?"

"You're scared of it, right?" said Owen. "Big towering house after those pressed-wood boxes and fake log cabins."

"Where have *you* lived anyway?" I counterattacked. "There are worse places than Hopewell."

"Sure," said Gavin.

They had this trick of reacting one after the other; it reinforced their moods. When they smiled it was as if the whole world was smiling. Now they frowned, the light went out of their faces.

"We were two years in a mute-camp, back east," said Owen.

"Before Gwen, our sister, got us out," said Gavin.

I knew this must have been very bad. I wanted to comfort them but all I could do was look at the ground and say again:

"I'm sorry."

"Come on," said Gavin, "we'll see the house."

"We have a right to live here," said Owen slyly. "In fact we're about the only people who could . . ."

We took a low ramp, marched in through a door that didn't look like a door, and we were in the kitchen. It was a very strange place. The inside coloring was all brown, purple-brown, tan and green from the indoor plants. There was a work center with a huge built-in range, two walls ovens staring like dead eyes, and a three-door refrigerator-freezer. All this stuff was like the insides of a stranded spaceship, indestructible but nonfunctioning. A place had been cleared under a copper hood for an ordinary wood stove. Steps went up to a gallery; the room had no proper ceiling. You could look up, up at redwood paneling and thick window walls of tinted glass. In the middle of the kitchen was a black marble-topped table; my father and my grandparents were drinking tea with Gwen Morgan.

She was taller than her brothers and a good ten years older. She was very good-looking with splendid bones, perfect teeth, bright blue eyes, and a fat braid of tawny hair. But Gwen Morgan didn't look like the Harvest Queen, she looked worn, leathery and hard. Her hands were rougher than mine. She had lived as a refugee and dragged her brothers out of mute-camp. I believed it. She wore a beautiful robe of pale gold "purity silk." The New Jerusalem has a corner on mulberry trees in our part of the world. It looked as though crop-reading was accepted by the Patriarchs and well rewarded.

"Well, I declare," said my grandmother as we trooped in. "I can't tell Gavin from his brother."

Owen paid his respects to the visitors. Ralph said politely:

"So that's our proposition, Ms. Morgan. You wouldn't mind giving us a little demonstration of the boys' powers?"

"Most clients," said Gwen softly, "have faith."

"Do you mean," asked Nell just as softly, "that the phenomenon *depends* on faith of some kind?"

"No!" put in Gavin firmly. "We can look forward and backward, Ma'am."

"Do you have a standard demonstration?" asked my father.

"Nope," said Owen. "Just a guarantee. No success, no reward."

"We receive our settlement in almost every session," said Gwen. "If there's the slightest doubt we don't proceed. We're completely frank. Where a damaged crop is observed we say so. That is the method."

"It's self-fulfilling," said Nell. "You claim to see in the future that the field was not planted, then advise the farmers not to plant."

"Not quite," said Gwen. "We never advise the holders to do anything. The observer reports on several fields at several points of time, past and future."

"Have you ever observed any *unexpected* developments?" asked my father.

The boys looked at each other and at Gwen who gave them the high sign.

"One time," said Owen, "it was observed that a strange animal walked through a stand of corn, causing damage."

"It was pretty unbelievable," said Gavin, "but there it was."

"We didn't want anyone to harm the—er—animal when it happened along," said Owen, "so we didn't name it. We reported animal damage, forty percent of the western quadrant of the field."

"The holders insisted," said Gwen, "and we took the unusual step of leaving the animal's description with a trustee."

Ralph began to chuckle.

"I seem to remember hearing . . ."

"Sure enough," said Owen, "a guy turned up with one of these critters. Luckily it was far too valuable to be put down. They paid the owner to cart it away at once."

"What happened to the field?" asked my father.

"It got trampled," said Gavin. "The circus proprietor had *two* elephants. When her mate was carted off the female tried to follow."

"And trampled the western quadrant of the field just as you predicted," sighed my grandmother.

"We don't *predict* the future," said Gavin. "We see what's going on at a future time."

"You use exactly the same faculty to see into the future and the past?" inquired Ralph.

"Yes," said Gwen, "exactly the same."

"Okay," said Nell. "what's the range of your observation in either direction?"

"About fifty years," said Owen flatly.

"How do you reckon the passing of time?" asked Ralph. "Can you pinpoint a certain day?"

"It depends," said Gwen. "I've documented all this, believe me. For crop-reading purposes we use existing landmarks, deciduous trees and certain devices of our own."

"It would be difficult to test a reading of the future," said Nell.

"Oh, I don't know," said Ralph. "What if the lads here stood on the drive and reported on the next visitors?"

"Are you expecting anybody?" asked Nell.

"Not definitely," said Gwen. "Today or tomorrow there should be callers from Brightwater and from Jerusalem."

"And someone could drop in at any time," said Gavin. "We go out to private readings."

"Like hunting for lost things," said Owen. "Seeing where someone put the hammer or the keys."

It was not only that tools were valuable—all the adults set a great store by them. To lose a hacksaw blade or the best knife was a sign of ill fortune. Even at Hopewell we turned the place upside down looking for lost things.

"I have the ghost of an idea," said Ralph. "Let me think about it."

Everyone took a breather; the boys gave me cookies and lemonade. My grandmother accepted another one of Gwen's walnut brownies. They were sizing each other up.

"May I see the house?" I asked.

"Thought we would show Linnit the front hall," said Owen.

"Now that is where we came in, right?" said Nell. "That impressive entrance hall with the hologram of the architect, what was his name?"

"Bergstrom," said my father, with a despairing movement of his eyebrows which meant "Don't overdo it, Nell!"

"Of course," said Nell. "Now, I noticed that big old visitors' book resting on that futuristic contraption . . ."

"Come, Nellie dear," said Ralph, "no need to be afraid of an old non-functioning gizmo like that!"

I was beginning to have gooseflesh. These two old devils were kidding around about some artifact that might scare *me* plenty.

"If you're all agreeable," said Nell, "we might set up a little test dealing with the past."

"We've done some observation in this house," said Gavin. "We saw Bergstrom meeting some people in the dining room. Gwen said they were— you know—film stars."

For the first time I realized that the Morgan boys had missed out on a lot of things. It stood to reason. No one gave a damn about Uses of Leisure Time in the mute-camps. Could they even *read?* Would they consider an uncontaminated book a good thing to bring to market?

"I will need the visitors' book," said Nell.

She waited for a second and said:

"*Linnit* must bring me the book."

The point was not lost on them: no cheating. Gwen handed Owen a bunch of keys.

"Bring Linnit through the front door," she said. "We'll be in the dining room."

Gavin and Owen led me out and round to the main ramp. We stood and looked at the world. It was early spring after a hard winter. The trees were coming in bright yellow-green all through the valleys: we saw every sort of willow, some birch, the early apples coming in to blossom.

"Too late for this year," said Gavin, "if your Old Man decided to give us a try."

"Please don't cheat," I said. "If this is some kind of swindle please quit, right now."

"We don't need to cheat!" snapped Owen.

"How do you do it then?" I yelled, "What *is* all this crazy talk? Do you go into a trance? Do you read minds?"

"Hush," said Gavin. "We *see* . . ."

He put an arm round my shoulders.

"Come in the house."

Owen stepped up to the mighty redwood doors and went to work with the keys. He opened a small door set into the right hand leaf. As we stepped inside he said:

"Pretty neat, eh? We never open the main doors."

"Neat," I said through clenched teeth.

The hall was awe-inspiring, much worse than the kitchen. There was a staircase surrounded by organ pipes or stalactites of stone. There was a great loftiness: everything swept upward, only the light poured down in golden shafts. I saw the hologram of Lewis Bergstrom and it didn't cheer me one bit. It was the size of a wall in our house on the center and it showed a hawk-faced individual in black trousers, a white shirt, and a black cloak lined with iridescent azure blue, like butterfly wings. He stood nobly poised with a roll of blueprint in his hand, before his own house.

"Take it easy," said Gavin. "Here's the visitors' book."

I turned away from Bergstrom and saw a huge shadowy figure taking a step in my direction. He had been taking this one step when the wind changed and he stayed that way. I should have been afraid but I wasn't. He was no more scary in this frozen attitude than a statue of King Tut. He was a robot, seven feet tall and very traditional. He had lumpy rounded contours of anodized metal, or was it plastic? He had domed lights and buttons and dials; he wore a benign expression on his non-human face.

"Poor guy," I said. "His eyes need dusting."

"We don't even know his real name," said Gavin sadly. "We call him Zack."

The visitors' book was balanced on Zack's upturned hands. It was thirty-four inches by eighteen, bound in dark red leather tooled in gold, and it had heavy cream paper. There were photographs and even newspaper clippings inside as well as signatures. I lifted it carefully so that the inserts wouldn't scatter but something did fall on to the carpet. Owen picked it up and we saw that it was a four-leafed clover that had been pressed between the pages. It seemed such a simple human thing to do in this monumental house—save a four-leafed clover. I looked back at Bergstrom and wondered if I had been wrong about him. Was he more of a magpie than a hawk?

The boys led me down paneled corridors for about a quarter of a mile and we came to the dining room. It was positively cozy; the table might have seated eight, unextended. There was a ceiling and a soft golden carpet. On a sunny terrace through the glass wall there were stone chessmen on the red and grey tiles. The set was not complete. I saw three gray stones doing duty for white pawns and a billet of firewood labeled "*Black Rook*."

My grandmother was ready to receive the visitors' book; she leafed through it. Gwen Morgan sat at the other end of the table doing embroidery in a round frame. Out on the terrace Ralph and my Dad leaned on the rail and pointed out into the springtime fields. We went out and joined them. The terrace was high up on the eastern wall of the house; you could see as far as New Jerusalem.

"There," said Ralph. "See the two schooners."

They were grayish humps on the road, moving slowly; the Patriarchs used covered wagons. Ralph murmured something to my Dad then straightened up.

"I think we have something . . ." he said.

He led the way indoors.

"Nellie," he said. "I think we have a simple test situation approaching."

My dad explained about the wagons in the distance.

"So one of the wagons might be coming to this house," said Nell. "Right?"

"Right," said Gwen warily.

"We *know* about when it will arrive in the afternoon," said Gavin.

"But not who is driving the wagon," said Ralph.

Nell clapped her hands.

"Fine!" she said. "There's the selection process."

All the Morgans began to smile too and at last I got the message. Only the men of the Waggoner clan regularly went out of New Jerusalem and their routes were chosen by lot. It had something to do with avoiding impure contacts.

"So what do you think?" asked Ralph, looking out from under his jutting brow at the two boys.

"Pretty close in," said Gavin to his brother.

"No, no," said Owen, "the light is fine. With this weather . . ."

"You may choose one of my brothers to stand on the drive and make the observation," said Gwen.

"Alone?" asked Nell.

"It's the condition on which we insist," said Gwen. "*No one*, I repeat, *no one* in the immediate vicinity of the observer. Have you been to a crop reading?"

"Yes," said my father. "One of the boys stands alone in the field."

"What does the second boy do?" asked Ralph.

"Sits in the caravan," said Gavin.

"Mugging up almanacs and long-range weather forecasts," said Owen, grinning. "Maybe sending thought messages or reading minds . . ."

"*You* brought up these subjects," said my grandmother, "and we'll be on the lookout for evidence of these—er—skills."

"There won't be much to see," warned Owen.

There wasn't. We all trailed down to the kitchen again. Owen went out on the drive to a point where we could all just see him through the trees. He stood there. Once he seemed to be shading his eyes with his hands. We went back to the dining room and he came back inside. He sat with my father at the kitchen table, wrote down what he had seen on a sheet of paper from Nell's notebook with one of Nell's ballpoint pens. She had looted four gross of these giveaway pens from the Gold Star Novelty Company of Pasadena, long ago, and used up two hundred and three so far. She never used them to trade.

My father sealed Owen's paper up unread in an unused envelope provided by Gwen. It had Lewis Bergstrom's name and address embossed on the front. They came upstairs and my father showed Nell the envelope. He had signed his name across the back flap. He put it in his shirt pocket and buttoned the pocket.

Owen was not smiling.

"I give my word not to tell Gwen or Gavin what I saw," he said. "I know this test will have a good result."

"Is it exhausting, this feat of yours?" asked Nell.

"Not especially," said Owen. "It takes concentration."

"I've been studying the visitors' book and I have the material for another test. Look here, Ralph . . ."

The two old people bent over the book, nodding and laughing.

"Are you familiar with this book, Ms. Morgan?" asked my grandmother.

"I looked through it when we first arrived," said Gwen. "I saw a few famous names. Those people are dead and the age they lived in has been discredited. For me it was a sad book."

Ralph said cautiously to Nell:

"If you're really prepared to . . ."

"Nothing venture, nothing win," she said. "Linnit, bring this picture to Ms. Morgan."

It was the picture of a statue, clipped from a glossy magazine.

"This bronze figure," said Ralph, "is it somewhere in the house?"

Gwen only needed to glance at the picture.

"Yes," she said, "Yes, it's in the lower study, just through here."

I was completely disoriented inside the house. When I stepped out of a room I had no idea of the way I had come or the way back. Now we all went to the lower study. My grandmother kept hold of the visitors' book; the boys came in last.

The study was well-aired but unused, the books had gone, the room was rather dark because a steel shutter was half-drawn on the balcony.

"We've had trouble with the shutters," said Gwen. "Rooms on this side of the house can't be used because of those drawn shutters."

There was a massive desk and a wall decoration of thick glass and leaf shapes. The bronze statue was beside the balcony doors; it was nearly four feet high, a stylized female figure.

"If someone could read out what is on the brass plate?" asked Nell.

My father knelt down.

" '*In what ethereal dances, By what eternal streams*' For my wife, Imogen Bergstrom."

Nell gave a sigh.

"Lewis Bergstrom made the statue and had it cast in his workshop." she said. "I have information here about a ceremony . . . a dedication it is called . . . that was held in this room on a summer's day around twenty-five years ago. Could this information be verified?"

The Morgans drew together and so did the Green/Mann family. Gwen sat at the desk; my grandmother took a leather chair by the fireplace.

"What would convince you, Ms. Mann?" asked Gwen.

"An on-the-spot report," said Nell.

"You talk about 'seeing,' " said Ralph. "Does this mean there is no sound? A silent movie?"

"It's almost impossible for you to believe in what we do," said Owen, "so why don't we just leave it as hocus-pocus that sometimes works, like water-divining?"

"We leave it like that *if* you make a convincing report," said Nell grimly.

"Don't forget Owen's reading on the drive!" said Gavin.

"I'm not forgetting it," said Nell.

"We could take two reports," said Ralph. "One from Gavin, one from Owen. Take all the time you need."

The Morgans put their handsome heads together for a moment. I felt miserable and afraid. I was embarrassed by Nell and Ralph. I was afraid the boys would fail or be caught cheating. I was afraid of the Bergstrom house and at the same time I hated to invade the world of its former inhabitants. I had a bad attack of "there are things we are not meant to know."

Owen came forward and said:

"Gavin will go first. I'll stay with Mr. Don Green while my brother makes his observations."

"Fine," said my father, cocking an eye at Nell.

Ralph walked all around the spacious brown room then we trooped out. We left Gavin standing by the desk, arms folded, smiling. The study had a strange-shaped key, a thick bolt of steel with heavy wards, which Gwen moved to the outside of the door. When we went back to the dining room my father took Owen out on the terrace. Soon they were playing chess.

My grandmother pointed out later that the precautions taken were primitive, you could drive a horse and cart through them. There was still a lot of distrustful coming and going. After half an hour by Nell's illegally accurate eternity watch Ralph let Gavin out of the study and led him down to the kitchen where he was permitted to make notes while the observation was fresh in his mind. My father let Owen into the study soon afterwards. When Gwen decided to make lunch my grandmother said:

"I wonder if we could use your bathroom? Come, Linnit!"

Gwen led us past the study then around and along. The bathroom was on the other side of the corridor.

"I think we can find our own way back," said Nell.

Gwen's face was cold and expressionless.

I could have spent time examining that bathroom but Nell told me to hurry. At the door she said:

"This is cheating but it's in the interests of science."

She took my hand and nipped across into another corridor. We went through rooms that might have been bedrooms. The steel shutters were drawn so that the rooms were dark but my grandmother knew the way after twenty-five years. I wondered if she had the whole crazy Bergstrom house in her head like a map or a chip diagram. We were in a smaller room with a long walk-in closet.

"Lewis was always a little paranoid," she said. "Poor Imogen hated this kind of set-up."

She slid open the closet and I was glad to see that it was empty except for a few black leather coat hangers. In one place there was a set of shelves, she felt under the middle shelf and cursed. She took a screwdriver from the pocket of her jacket and went to work under the shelf.

"Pull!" she said, drawing back. "Pull on the shelf!"

We pulled and the whole shelf wall opened without a sound. Nell put a finger to her lips and one by one we squeezed into something too small even to be called a cupboard. There was barely room for the two of us on a low padded bench. We sat and stared at a piece of pale amber glass with dark swirling patterns. It took a moment for me to work out what these patterns were: metal leaf shapes. We were looking into the study through the inset wall decoration; it was a one-way viewing window.

There was still nothing to see. A boy among the trees, a boy in an empty room. Owen Morgan had his back to us, he was quite close to our hiding place. I could hardly believe that he wouldn't look us in the eye when he turned around. The room looked more alive through the amber-colored glass. I thought of the scene that Owen was trying to see with Lewis Bergstrom whipping around in his cape with the butterfly lining, along with a bunch of film stars and my grandmother, twenty-five years younger, in some kind of high-tech white overall.

Owen walked slowly to the corner of the desk and turned around. He gave us a grandstand view. What I saw was intolerably strange, it was beyond everything; it was a close encounter with a mutant of the New Age. It began as a glow on his forehead and around his eyes. First his eyes began to flicker, to shift and vibrate in their sockets, then the flimmering motion spread to his whole face. It was too fast for the eye to follow. I expected him to disappear, to flicker out of existence, out of one time into another. Instead he turned aside and looked at another part of the room.

I found that my grandmother and I were clutching hands tightly. I hardly remember getting out of the viewing room. We tiptoed back the way we had come like two zombies. We staggered back into the bathroom without a word. I took a drink of water. Nell wrung out a washcloth and pressed it to her forehead.

"Cheats never prosper!" she said.

"Gwen will come looking for us!"

"We've been gone twelve minutes," said Nell. "Are you all right?"

She pinched my cheeks to get some color in them. As we walked past the study door we saw that Gwen had taken the key.

"Linnit," whispered Nell sternly, "we must get a grip on ourselves!"

"They can do it!" I whispered back. "You saw how Owen . . ."

"The experiment," she said out loud, "is still continuing."

Gavin made his report first while Owen sat alone in the kitchen. My grandmother seemed to have a good grip on herself but I was so quiet and strained that my Dad noticed. I said I would be all right after lunch; they gave me an apple. Gavin was very self-assured and natural. He stood at the end of the table and looked over his notes.

"The statue made a good landmark," he said, "and I tried to fasten on it. I was thrown for a while by the fact that it was covered by a green cloth. There was a day very close to the ceremony when a dark, Spanish-looking woman—might have been the housekeeper—stripped off the cloth and gave the statue a polish. Then, at night, Bergstrom came into the study, got down a book and made a note at the desk. He took off the cloth, too, and stood admiring the statue.

"I kept looking and I think I got the time Ms. Mann wanted. There were seven people in the room. Bergstrom didn't look much like his portrait, he was short, for one thing, shorter than me, and gray-haired. Then there was a beautiful woman with red hair. She wore a long skirt. She came in through the balcony door with a smooth-looking guy in a black sweater. They stood side by side turned toward Bergstrom who was beside the draped statue. There were a couple of spectators standing before the fireplace: a young girl and another older woman. The Spanish woman was there holding something on a tray that flickered and sparkled, maybe a set of glasses that caught the light. There was a guy taking photographs only he was hard to see because he had a light on a stand. Anyway Bergstrom uncovered the statue and as he backed away through the room the good-looking couple began to dance. It was part of the ceremony. They danced together, you know, holding each other. Then they stood still. The housekeeper dropped the tray and began to cry."

There was a long silence. My grandmother shook her head in wonder.

"Remarkable. I wonder what Owen can add to this?"

"Without the music," said Ralph. "What *was* the music anyway?"

"How should I know?" said Nell bitterly. "One of Imogen's great successes. A tango. Could we hear Owen in the study?"

"Are you convinced?" asked Gwen.

"Yes, yes," said Nell. "That was a convincing report. I guess if someone could see but not hear that little ceremony we might very well come up with something like that. Please let me complete the experiment."

Everyone was pleased when she said this. Gwen smiled and flung open the door to the corridor and called downstairs for Owen. Ralph had one of his rare bursts of old man's energy. He began to hum a tune and said "Take it, Linnit!" The tune was "La Paloma." My Dad took it up too, we sang and clapped our hands. Ralph took hold of Nell, who laughed, and they were off, dancing the tango all the way along the corridor and into the study.

"That's it," said Gavin in my ear. "That's the dance!"

Owen came in.

"I think that's the dance!" he said. "The one those things were dancing!"

When order had been restored he made his report.

"We take turns scanning for detail," he said. "Gavin gave the broad outline. It was a weird scene and I couldn't understand what was going on.

I used the statue as a marker of course. I watched for Lewis Bergstrom. He was producing some kind of home movie. There was this woman by the fireplace and a girl with her. They looked very embarrassed. Then there was a dark woman who came in last carrying something on a tray. This is strange but I swear it was a cake with tiny lighted candles on it. Would that be right? She stood there holding the cake and Bergstrom uncovered the statue. Two figures came in from the balcony: the dancers. They were dolls or robots like old Zack in the front hall. The crazy thing was that the male dancer was a copy of Lewis Bergstrom. The female had dark red hair and wore Spanish dress. They danced that tango dance, dipping down and turning and crossing their legs. Bergstrom was filming all this, he went behind a lamp on a stand. The lady with the cake stood watching the dancers with a terrible expression. At last she dropped the tray and covered her face with her hands."

"Even better," said Neil. "Some of the detail is most telling."

Gavin hung his head, not satisfied with his performance.

"Cake!" he grumbled. "Robot dancers. And of course Bergstrom was the photographer."

"Indoor is tricky," said Owen. "Light and shade. Moving subjects."

I couldn't stand it any longer.

"Nell," I said, "maybe this is an embarrassing question but *what was going on?* Doesn't anyone care what those people were doing all those years ago?"

The Morgan boys, side by side, looked at me in surprise. I felt queasy when I saw their faces, shining with success, and I imagined a tremor in their brown eyes.

"We *saw* what they did," said Gavin.

"Linnit shows a human interest," said Ralph.

Gwen Morgan said quickly:

"Of course we'd be interested to see the original material. Who signed the visitors' book that day?"

"Good question," said Nell. "It touches on the problem of interpretation. How many signatures would you expect?"

The boys went into a huddle.

"Two," said Gavin. "The woman by the fireplace and the young girl who was with her."

My father, who had brought along the visitors' book, clutched it to his chest and cried out:

"Nell, you terrible woman, *you have gone too far!*"

He put the book on the desk, unopened, and took me roughly by the arm.

"Linnit, we're leaving!"

"No!" ordered Nell. "We'll see this right through, Don!"

She opened the book at the place she had marked. The Morgans had drawn together watching this performance by the Green/Mann family, complete with sound effects.

"I didn't play quite fair," said Nell, "and neither did Lewis Bergstrom. That inscription on the statue might suggest that it was a memorial to his wife. In fact it was a memorial to her talent."

"She wasn't dead?" asked Gavin.

"Far from it," said Nell. "Imogen Bergstrom retired from her own Hispanic Dance Company after an injury to her hip. She was the dark woman who brought in the birthday cake for her husband."

"Birthday cake?" asked Owen.

"You really didn't know that a cake with little candles . . ." I said.

"They never had one," said Gwen. "Come to that I never had one. In our family we never ate a grain of sugar because of our teeth."

"Good God!" said Ralph. "Nellie . . ."

But Nell was still explaining the scene.

"It was the cruelest thing," she said. "Lewis couldn't understand Imogen's reaction. He had acquired—illegally—two android dancers. One was a copy of himself, the other of Imogen, both looking young and beautiful. A big surprise for all those present."

"You didn't recognize anyone that you saw at that time?" asked Ralph. "Owen?"

"No," said Owen. "I'm not well up on the sort of people who might have visited the Bergstroms. There was something. Outside influence, I guess. The young girl looked to me a lot like Linnit."

My father uttered a groan.

"Linnit, baby," he said, "I didn't expect . . ."

So I understood and I came into some place outside of time where the wish to know and to understand went beyond sadness. I stepped past him and looked at the visitors' book. There were two signatures on the page.

Cornelia Todd Gorman
Anne-Marie Gorman

I knew the handwriting of my grandmother and even my mother's handwriting hadn't changed so much as she grew older. Someone else— Bergstrom?—had written a note on the facing page. *Cornelia Todd, Ralph Gorman, Nobel Prize for Cybernetic Research, 2025*. I looked up and saw my grandmother's face, full of sorrow.

"Come," she said.

I took her hand and we walked together to the fireplace where she had been standing with her daughter, Anne-Marie, on a summer's day twenty-five years ago.

"It was embarrassing for the spectators," she said, "and not only because Lewis was flaunting these custom-built dancers before his poor wife who would never dance another step. Ralph and I were engaged in cybernetic research, including the creation of androids—humanoid robots. The problem was how such beings could be accepted by society. There was a great difference between the robot majordomo that we mocked up for Lewis's fine house and a creature that looked fully human, possessed high intelligence *and* superhuman skills. Lewis Bergstrom saw nothing wrong in using androids as toys but we surely did. The crash came before the problem was solved."

The Morgan boys came and stared at us both very keenly.

"Yes," said Gavin. "It could be."

"You were here," said Owen, "but Linnit . . ."

"That was my mother, Anne-Marie," I said. "We had a strong likeness."

"You made Zack?" said Gavin. "You and Mr. Mann."

"Gorman," said Nell. "He was an adapted transporter made to look like everyone's idea of a robot butler. He was called Robert. Made at the Todd Gorman Research Ranch. Used to be a name to conjure with."

"Isn't that pretty high-tech for Hopewell Center?" asked Owen.

"They know who we are," said Ralph. "The New Age must compromise in order to survive."

There was a loud sob. Gwen Morgan was looking at the visitors' book and she was dissolved in tears. She turned to Ralph.

"Doc? Doc Gorman?"

She took a faltering step toward my grandmother.

"Ms. Todd, Ms. Todd, it is Gwinnie, Gwinnie Morgan . . . I came to the Ranch with my father. Do you remember? David Morgan, the dentist."

"Gwinnie?" said Nell. "That little kid . . . oh my dear . . ."

So she began to cry too. They fell into each other's arms and Ralph went and embraced the pair of them. That left my father and me and the two boys blinking, grinning, blowing our noses. There was not a dry eye in the house. I thought of future observers watching the scene . . . why are all these people laughing and crying? The coincidence was not so great as all that. David Morgan had been a dentist with a fancy practice in Los Angeles, including Nobel Prize winners and architects and the stars of the Hispanic Dance Company.

There was a settlement with the Morgan family and a lot of reminis-
cence. About the great escape, for instance, where David Morgan flew his
wife and daughter out in his private plane, not long after the crash. We
ate lunch with stuffed zucchini, wild rice, olives, six sorts of cheese, pickled
walnuts, and honey cakes. They even had a ham in the store cupboard,
which made the day for Nell and Ralph.

We set out for home at four o'clock. No other visitors had showed up;
the shadows were lengthening on the drive. Owen said:

"Remember the first test, Ms. Gorman."

"I'm remembering," said Nell. "You reckon this is a good time for us
to observe your driveway?"

"Should be!" he said.

The boys waved; they waved at *me* with identical smiles.

We went the whole length of the drive and observed nothing more
than the trees and the grass. An old crow walked across the path. We
turned out of the driveway and saw the covered wagon from New Jerusalem.
It was just getting ready to turn in and the driver was wrestling with the
horses. My Dad took Ruby and our rig off the path.

The Waggoner was dressed like any other patriarch: grayish linsey-
woolsey trousers, a collarless cotton shirt, a knitted sleeveless vest of black
wool, and a black straw hat. Beside the driver was a young boy about ten
years old dressed exactly the same. As the wagon righted itself and drew
level I heard my grandmother curse under her breath. I felt a physical shock
as if I had been punched in the midriff. The driver was a woman in men's
clothes: she was a Proxy.

The Patriarchs of the New Jerusalem had never had enough people
willing to serve the Lord in the New Age. Only men could vote, of course,
and conduct business, as laid down in the Law. They had plenty of Law in
New Jerusalem and their lawyers had created a legal fiction. A woman could
become a proxy for her younger male kin, or in certain cases, the head of a
household of women. There were a lot of rules laid down for a Proxy in
dress and behavior. Other communes in the valleys below the mountains
took it as a joke, an eccentricity of the Patriarchs. Now I saw it was as cruel
and stupid a piece of of patriarchal behavior as anything they did.

The woman was over fifty, we knew that because she wore a false fringe
of beard hitched to her ears. She had a long, pale face and the saddest
expression I ever saw on a human being. Her eyes were very dark, almost
black, and they were full of grief and misery. The boy was angry and
ashamed, looking first at the woman, then at us, jutting his jaw. The two
sorrel horses fretted and stamped in their traces.

Male patriarchs spoke only to other men, on the outside, unless it was an emergency. Handmaidens of the New Jerusalem, if they ever got close enough to outsiders, spoke only to women. My grandmother said:

"We are from Hopewell Center. My name is Cornelia Mann. Good day to you."

The woman almost touched her forehead and her lips in the women's greeting, then she remembered and nodded to us like a male patriarch.

"Praise God!" she said in a loud unsteady voice. "I am Deborah Waggoner, proxy for my grandson, Nahum, here."

"You need any help, Ma'am?" asked my father.

"Thank you kindly," said the woman, looking sideways at him. "I guess I am getting the hang of it."

The boy, Nahum, suddenly began punching the woman on her arm and shoulder.

"You broke the law!" he shouted. "You ain't fit!"

The woman did nothing, she sat rigid. We all stared at the boy and what we felt showed in our faces. The kid blushed brick-red. The woman said quietly:

"Get in the wagon, Nahum."

He scrambled over the back of the seat and we heard him bawling and hitting at the sides of the cotton cover.

"Deborah was a judge in Israel," said my grandmother unexpectedly. "Ms. Waggoner, I don't suppose you'd consider giving up this masquerade and taking asylum at Hopewell with little Nahum there?"

This wasn't as crazy as it sounded. Only last year a widow and her family had taken asylum from the New Jerusalem in the Hopewell Center, after a series of misfortunes with the Law of the Patriarchs.

The woman turned toward us and took a firm grip on the reins.

"My daughter-in-law," she said, "my son's wife, Leah, was brought to bed of twin daughters last week. Same day that my son Ezra was taken in a three-wagon pile-up at the sawmill. I must stand proxy."

She concentrated on getting the reins right and the horses lined up for the driveway. Just before she told them to go she said:

"Take a blessing, Sister Cornelia."

She stood up and shouted to the horses and they obeyed her. We saw the wagon go swaying down the green aisle to the Bergstrom house. My father already had Owen's envelope out of his shirt pocket; he whistled softly and passed around the clumsily printed paper. Owen had written: *"One of the Waggoners must be dead. An old woman is driving a wagon dressed as a Proxy. It could be Ezra's wagon from the sorrel-team."*

My grandmother made a short, angry prediction of her own at that moment and it is coming true. The New Jerusalem is having trouble with its proxies. Those poor legal fictions have taken to raising their voices, cropping their hair, drinking ale and forming a Work Guild. Proxies make good riflemen and archers. The Patriarchs have sown the wind and they will reap the whirlwind.

We drove on home from the late afternoon to early evening. I kept dozing off, propped against my Dad, on the front of the cart. I was in shock; too much had happened. I fell into a dream about a chain of dancers who were all strange beings. When I woke Nell was saying:

"A great deal to consider . . ."

"Still have doubts?" asked my father.

"We can't rule out prior knowledge of a number of things," said Ralph. "I had the feeling they might not be telling all they knew."

"Neither were we," said Nell, sighing.

We never did tell. I don't believe that my grandmother has told another soul about what we observed in the Bergstrom house that day; she hasn't even told Ralph. When she found that the Morgans were the children of an old friend and colleague, Nell decided that certain things weren't meant to be known. She and Ralph plainly enjoy their visits to the Morgans and not only because of ham and roast duck.

As for me, I'm not so sure "enjoy" is the right word. I've been back to the house, twice, at Christmas time; it doesn't scare me any more. The boys and I go wandering through all its cold upper floors dusting off the monitors. We have a lot of fun: dripping tallow on the carpets, singing and dancing and kissing and kidding around, bringing life back into the beautiful dead rooms. Owen and Gavin can turn their heads aside and *see* what has been, but I can guess, I can interpret, I have a touch more imagination.

We think of Lewis Bergstrom, who designed and built houses for a new age that never happened. He died, Nell says, in Europe at an exhibition, just before the crash. No one knows what became of Imogen, his wife, but the boys say she was the one who cleared out the house. Had to leave a lot of the heavy stuff behind, including the bronze statue, a memorial to her talent.

So the house stood there, impregnable as a fortress, until the Morgans came. They were the only people who could live there because they were the only people who could get into the house. Bergstrom had an emergency set of keys concealed on the outside of the building. The boys looked back patiently until they found out the hiding place. I believe this story. I have decided to give Gavin and Owen the benefit of the doubt, permanently. But not for the same reason as my grandfather.

No one in the valleys is very logical when it comes to mutants. A psychic gift is fine, but how about a gift that is accompanied by frightening physical changes? How would you like it if your daughter took up with a mute . . . or with two mutes? My father is a sensible man but the Morgans were always a little too way-out for him. He never went back to the Bergstrom house. I rehearse all kinds of speeches. I try to please him. In the end all I can do is hope that he will understand. Once I had a crazy dream about having twin girl babies like poor Leah Waggoner. There they were, lying in their cradles, and one kept disappearing, flimmering right out of sight.

The Morgans read the crops last year and they'll be back in the spring. I will be eighteen years old. I have looked into the future and I know exactly what is going to happen. Owen and Gavin will turn up in their green caravan, looking good, bringing me the past and the future. They'll ask me to go with them and I'll go. In the flicker of an eye.

DAMIEN BRODERICK

Damien Broderick is one of the three or four best living Australian science fiction writers. Of his novels, the most important to date are *The Dreaming Dragons* (1980), *The Judas Mandala* (1982), *Transmitters* (a mainstream novel about SF fans, 1984), and *The White Abacus* (1997). He is also a critic, reviewer, and the leading literary theorist of the genre in Australia (his major critical work is *Reading by Starlight*). He is an important anthologist of Australian SF (his three original anthologies are *The Zeitgeist Machine* [1976], *Strange Attractors* [1985], and *Matilda at the Speed of Light* [1988]). In addition he writes popular science books (*The Spike*, *The Last Mortal Generation*) and has a continuing interest in cutting-edge and speculative science. Broderick has been publishing SF since 1963, and at present has the longest career of any of the leading Australian SF writers. He is at the height of his powers in the 1990s and seems primed to remain a central figure in Australian SF for a few more decades. "The Magi" is perhaps his best short story to date.

How art thou fallen from heaven
O day-star, son of the morning!
. . . And thou saidst in thy heart:
"I will ascend into heaven,
Above the stars of God
Will I exalt my throne;
. . . I will ascend above the heights of the clouds;
I will be like the Most High."
Yet thou shalt be brought down to the netherworld.
To the uttermost parts of the pit.
—Isaiah 14: xii–xvi

THE FORSAKEN CITY IS all one thing, and very lovely: a filigree of silver, shadow, light.

Looking across it, Silverman is near to tears, like a green boy flushed with early love, transfigured by a first kiss. His throat knots; for a lingering moment, a heady anesthesia rebukes his senses. At last joy takes the aging man like pain, compressed and burning beneath his ribs, an exalted melancholy. That bitter joy tells him: cherubim lived here.

It is a reflection scarcely detached and scientific, and there is about it as well more than a whiff of heresy. Yet he can find no safer response rich enough to bear scrutiny. Peace is instinct in the empty City. With absolute conviction he tells himself: It's waiting for them to come home.

Exile with all his Order from High Earth, professed in the Society of Jesus under four solemn vows and five simple, Father Raphael Silverman gazes down with misery. From the edge of the cyclopean cliff he can smell warm wind rising from an unpeopled world of rippled grasses, a breeze that washes through the selective membrane of his filter-skin like memories of boyhood. At the horizon stand blurred violet hills, falling in the distant east to an ocean's cerulean shore. In the crucible of his breast they mingle. They streak into a haze on the moist film of his eye's curve.

Regretfully, then, Silverman turns his back on the dove-gray lace coral of the City and works his way back to the skiff. A sizzle of interference is still the best he can raise from his telemetry systems. Cirrus feathers the sky; from the ground, the forces that shield the City are transparent to the visible spectrum. No doubt a signal impressed upon a maser beam would reach him, but it is unlikely that he could return an answer.

His shadow goes ahead of him, stretched by the slant of the morning sun, gaunt anyway, climbing the hard stone that separates him from the Monastery skiff. Paradox, an internal wound, sends darts to every vital place. The routine trick of scientific analysis is already in play, shredding the City and its planet into notional constituents, worrying with a terrier's impertinence at the anomaly of a structure (A) deserted for eons which (not-A) bears no sign of decay. And this is the paradox: that from the deeper seat of his being he cries out in pain. Where are they? Silverman demands. Where did they go? Their radiant and somber City speaks solely of beauty and sanctity. There is no hint of corruption, of vice, even of mere worldly utility. They had known God so well that their dwelling place is a tabernacle, a temple, the New Jerusalem raised three thousand light-years from those dismal hills of Palestine where His Son walked briefly before men slew Him.

The transponder in Silverman's belt sounds as he steps over a modest rise, and the hidden skiff's refraction field collapses. In the center of a flat clearing, the vessel stands on its tail, curved titanium hull catching the planet's sun dazzlingly.

Silverman's joy returns; it has no bounds. The Master of the Universe has extended him a reconciliation. He is fifty-five years old, and has been lost in despair and oppression for the last ten. It seems to him that in this year of our Lord 2040, quincentenary of his Order's foundation under the Bull *Regimini militantis ecclesiae*, a reprieve has been proffered. Silverman will never purge the abomination of *Southern Cross*, that intolerable memory that crouches always at the shadowed fringes of his being, but now there is a kind of counterweight, and he feels the balance of his soul pivoting once more into light. For there is joy as well as grief in the lambent, empty City. In My Father's house, yes, there are many mansions. The Jesuit smiles gladly within himself.

Without guidance the computer systems of the skiff find their alignment with the Monastery's orbit. And Silverman is floating into the darkening bowl of the sky, balanced in a great arc with the natural forces of the planet. The stars come out, and the City's world is a shimmering crescent beneath him.

"We have reacquired your telemetry," an urgent voice tells him. Silverman knows that all his vital signs were instantly accessible to the Monastery's computers the moment he came out from behind the City's shields; they cannot fail to realize he is aboard the skiff, in perfect condition. Still, ancient habits place tension in the voice. "Father, we lost you as you went in. Are you all right?"

"Fine," he assures them. "Never been better. It's beautiful. Sorry if I alarmed you. It seemed sensible to take the opportunity to look around." He wonders if elation is apparent in his tone.

Above and beyond him, the vast light-jeweled Latin cruciform of the *St. Ignatius Loyola* looms like Constantine's prebattle vision as the skiff falls up into docking orbit. The sight of the huge weightless icon enters Silverman's heart with the force of a shaft of illumination from the collective unconscious; he expels his breath. Indeed, only Jung among all the tawdry interpreters of mind might have responded with insight to the wisdom that informed the starship's builders. Crux and patibulum, stake and cross-piece, radiate in an archetypal mandala that tells at once of a Man hanged from a tree and a solstice sun reborn in seasonal resurrection. But the image causes a pang. It is too grand, lofty, austere; there is no authentic sense of home.

With lowly automatic wisdom, the skiff takes itself into the shuttle niche. The *bidellis* is waiting behind the hermetic seal of his oversight cubicle as Silverman climbs from the lock. In his sleeveless gown, lacking the fabric wings that hang from the shoulders of the clerks-regular, the lay brother could be any stolid porter attending the gate of a Jesuit House on Earth prior to the suppression.

"*Laudetur Jesus Christus*," Silverman says in greeting.

"*Semper laudetur*," replies the porter. "The Father-General wishes to see you as soon as you've showered. If you're hungry I could have some lunch sent up."

"Thank you, Brother. I think I'll wait for dinner."

Only simple decontamination is required for the skiff. For Silverman, more stringent measures are obligatory. Alien infestations are not welcome. Patiently he suffers the irradiations and sluicings that beat down on his filter-skin. Satisfied at grudging length, the computers permit him to peel away the suit and pass into a second snug ceramic chamber where he may attend to his personal hygiene. As always, the ambience is slightly chilly. He rubs his hairy arms and chest with alcohol, cleaning off the gummy residue where life-sign telltales have been cemented. A gush of tepid water rinses his skin, and blasts of warmer air dry him off. He manages these motions without attention, murmuring the prescribed prayers as he dresses.

Shiptime is late afternoon. He has advanced ten hours in the leap to orbit, and the queasiness of readjustment will have its toll. Silverman considers the elevator but shakes his head minimally with regret. Planar gravity-effect within the Monastery is kept to three-quarters' Earth normal due to structural constraints, and a metabolism designed for Earth needs all the extra exercise it can find. At the entrance to the main corridor on this level there is a rack of small-wheeled bicycles. The Jesuit heaves one down from its hook and mounts the saddle, tucking up his cassock, his calves protesting in advance. Like a village *abbe* displaced a century and a half and trillions of kilometers, he pedals off along the corridor for the ramps that climb five levels to the Father-General's quarters.

The journey leaves him only slightly breathless; he has found a nice compromise between brisk exertion and that sedateness ordained in the Common Rule. Parking the bike, he uses the research-status prerogative to trigger the office door and goes straight in. Monsignor Alverez, the General's secretary, waves Silverman through with a cordial smile.

Niceto Cardinal Miguel Rodrigues de Madrazo y Lucientes, S. J., Father-General of the remnants of his Order, Prince of the Church, papal elector and councillor bound in duty and privilege to sit in consistory on High Earth yet barred from that assembly by secular ban, the pontiff's *legati a latere* aboard the exiled starship, sits hunched before a holofiche reader, his intent eyes darting across the screen. Silverman contains himself in patience. A band of wires crosses the red zucchetto perched on his superior's scalp, strobing alpha-frequency impulses to the cardinal's temporal lobes, enhancing and focusing his attention. There will be no rousing him until the fiche is digested.

Madrazo is an aristocratic son of Alcala, the Andalusian town which gave St. Ignatius his first theologian, the fiery half-Jew Diego Laynez, second Father-General of the Order, and Silverman cherishes the remote link with his own ornate and bastard spiritual heritage. Now in his seventies, Madrazo retains an intellect certainly as fine as Silverman's and an equanimity unbroken by the tragedy that has diminished his charges from fifty thousand to less than a hundredth of that number, all five hundred of them confined within the hull of *Loyola*.

"Sit down," the General says abstractedly. "I shouldn't be a moment." Pale light from the screen dances in reflection from his cheeks, the blade of his nose, as words flicker frantically. Madrazo stabs with one finger and the light clears; the fiche pops up for replacement. Silverman blinks as dark eyes lift to seize him with electronically augmented force. "Father Silverman." The cardinal lifts the band away from his skull cap and settles back, but there is no perceptible dulling of his attention. He straightens his mozzetta, the short cape that hangs from his shoulders over his scarlet cassock.

"We're all relieved that you came to no harm. Shall I wait for the digest, or is it worth a full personal report?"

"Your Eminence," Silverman says, and finds something choking his larynx. "There's a city down there."

"So." Madrazo props his chin on steepled fingers. His ring of office gleams like a living eye. The considerable shock he must feel elicits no more than a moue of interest. "I've just been studying the final sensor evaluations. They show a profusion of fauna and flora in stationary ecological equilibrium, but no evidence of intelligence. We surmise that the shielded anomaly is of extraplanetary origin."

"I don't think so. The design of the city is absolutely integral to the mood of the planet."

Acutely, Madrazo suggests, "The good stewards."

"Yes." Silverman hesitates. "It's totally deserted."

"You see no reason to prevent sending a team into the ruins?"

His heart stills for an instant close to syncope. It seems that banners of light stream above him. The wonder of the City is a swelling organ note.

"Eminence, there are no ruins. It is perfectly preserved." Without caution, his heart swollen with excitement, Silverman leans forward and presses his damp hands on the desk. "It looks as if it's . . . waiting for someone."

The City of the angels calls him, calls him home.

Two

> The synagogue is a brothel, a hiding place for wild animals. No Jew has ever prayed to God; they are all possessed by devils. Instead of greeting them, ye shall avoid them as a contagious disease and plague.
>
> —St. John Chrysostom, 349–407 CE

Silverman's earliest memory must be composite: layered and glazed from the complaints and resentments of those old enough for some density of accurate recall, a *sfumato* the reverse of Leonardo da Vinci's, shade aching into shade, glowing with bitter depths of light. Spitefully, the officials had waited for Shabbos. Harsh kliegs crusted the street, empty canvas-clad trucks growled and coughed, bodies pressed sweating in hallways and on stairs, the candles guttering, legal imprecations in Russian and Yiddish, a man in uniform pushing past the puzzled children to jerk bedclothing from the parents' mattress onto the floor, kicking it into a heap.

"We cannot pack tonight; it is forbidden," Raphael's father said, facing the man in a fury. "To save a life," the mother pleaded, pulling Rebbe Silverman's arm, in tears, scooping up their belongings. "Master of the Universe, they'll kill us all."

"You traitors sicken me," the policeman told them. Raphael wailed, clutching the mother's legs. "Haven't you been whining to leave for long enough? Hurry it up, there's rain on the way."

"We have been Russian for three hundred years, you Cossack bastard," the Rebbe said. His face was blotched. "There is a higher allegiance."

"Your names are on the manifest. Eh? Here? My job is to get you into the truck. Conscious or unconscious doesn't fuss me. Take as much junk as you can carry, but no animals."

"Why aren't we being sent to Israel?"

"I don't care where you go, Jew. But I don't suppose the Poles will want to keep you."

Rebecca protested as the mother bundled away two of her dolls, leaving her the shapeless rag creature she loved best Raphael gazed about blindly, located his brother David, toddled to him and shrieked in sudden absolute terror.

Too many people, too little space, the skies weeping fat drops onto the tarpaulin and then opening in earnest to drench the trucks, tires drumming, headlights streaked on the roads behind and ahead. "It is the Holocaust again," an old man said over and over. "Ribbono Shel Olom, why do You hate Your people?"

And that is all Silverman remembers. It was not the Holocaust again, not yet. Troop trains took them through Poland. At the border they waited for months while politicians and their masters diced. Finally the exiles crossed into Germany, into the reunited land of the beast that took them now grudgingly and gave them shelter while crowds bickered in the streets below their crowded apartments, with increasing boldness bore banners denouncing this imposition, and the Rebbe's family lived double-outcast among the Hasidim in whose *de facto* quarter they were billeted, grim-faced, bearded men in *shtreimel* and *bekesheh,* women like black ghosts with disapproving eyes, the pious excess of their holy-day dancing and singing coming from the midst of this sober contempt like a slap in the face. Raphael was just old enough to enter the primary grade of *yeshiva* when they moved again, to Randers in Jutland where the blond Danes offered Lutheran tolerance and allowed the Rebbe's family to settle with the uprooted Hasidim while Israel made ready her tents for the millions who cried their dispossession at her gates.

Raphael remembers his first years in Denmark with a sweet longing. Most of all, though, he recalls a picnic in an ancient village outside Randers. The Protestant church in the village was old, older than any buildings he had ever seen, built in the golden age of Catholicism hundreds of years prior to the Reformation. Six years old, his exuberance quenched by some intimation of awe, Raphael stole into the church of the false *moshiach*. From a triumphal arch a faded painting shone in blues, cinnabar, lampblack, rusted green. Two women stood beneath a lamb. To the left, her eyes hidden by a scarf, hair cascading to her green dress, one of the lovely women stabbed a spear into the lamb's vulnerable throat. Even as the helpless animal's lifeblood gushed from the wound, the woman to the right held out a cup to catch it; regal, her coat was crimson as the fluid she preserved. The painting was inexpressibly beautiful, tender and cruel, and Raphael gazed up at it in a state near to trance.

The Rebbe was livid. "An *ilui* you might be, but what good is cleverness without obedience to your father?"

Flabbergasted and confused, the child said: "The ladies were so pretty. Who are they?" And something secret within him crowed. Nobody before had ever told him he was a genius, even though he had learned to read long before starting at the *yeshiva*.

"Do not speak back to your father," the mother told him. A certain gentleness removed the sting, but he was frightened by what she said next. "It is a filthy thing, that picture. A child should be spared such sights. It is from the *sitra achra*."

The Other Side. The pitiless gulf of nothingness, of worse than nothingness, which rebuked the Master of the Universe. The matter was dropped: Raphael said his *Krias Shema*, head bowed, and the growing curls of his earlocks brushed his cheek like the soothing caress of the mother's fingers.

Years later, still in Denmark, the *mashpia* of his school mentioned the ancient painting to the boys who were preparing for bar mitzvah. "The goyim hate us," he explained, "because they are taught that our people—the chosen people of God!—murdered the false *moshiach*. In the picture, their messiah is shown as a lamb. A woman in green represents the people of Israel, the synagogue. The other woman is the Christian Church. That painting came from the hand of the Angel of Death."

It seemed as if that awful being had laid aside his palette and taken up the sword: on the following Easter, inflamed by the cruel anti-Israel embargoes of the Muslim petroleum nations, a mob of louts stormed the school erected by the Russian Jews and their bomb blew the Rebbe into bloody shreds. An old Hasid came to the house with the news. "We have had our differences," he told the weeping family, "but the Rebbe was a good man. Most of us," he said, taking Raphael against his knee, "must strive always against the lure of sin, for our souls are blind to the Mishnah and Gemara. Some few lead lives that are blameless in deed but whose thoughts remain snared by the world. Very rare is the *tzaddik*, who has mastered his own heart. Rebbe Silverman was of the *tzaddikim*."

The Silvermans departed almost immediately for Israel. It came as a surprise to Raphael to learn that the family could have taken up residence in the homeland years earlier, but that his father had found a higher duty among the outcasts in northern Europe. But now the flood was in full torrent: nobody wanted Jews, not the Americans or the Europeans. Oil and gasoline were drying up as the Jihad intensified; madmen ruled the Arab States, godstruck or venal, it hardly mattered which. It was politic to export Jews, before inflamed citizens re-created on a world scale the horrors of Kristallnacht.

Aviation fuel was under jealous rationing. The four Silvermans, with hardly more possessions than they'd taken from Russia, wallowed across the Mediterranean from Genoa in a stinking refitted tanker crammed with their fellows. Ashdod harbor was temporarily closed while police and army units sought a bomb that terrorists had planted in one of the warehouses. The tanker turned and sailed north, and berthed at the sprawling foot of Mount Carmel. Raphael stared at the clutter of pale apartment complexes and the endless accumulation of *ma'abarot* pinned to every spare hectare of soil between them: tents and tin shacks, hastily erected accommodation for the millions of Jews fleeing from the brooding, pent hatred of two hemispheres. On a high spur he could make out the monastery of the Carmelite Christian monks, and on another the shrine to science, the Technion. A ferocious excitement grasped him, a sap rising full and strong in his maimed, severed roots: it was a homecoming.

Almost immediately, his brother David was inducted into the Israel Defense Army, deferring his rabbinical studies for two years. The mother, despite her burdens of grief, seemed somehow to blossom, organizing the neighboring immigrants, prettying their own rudimentary shack, allowing Raphael to run more freely on the leash—even gifting him, on his fourteenth birthday, a handheld Japanese computer endowed with 100 meg of memory. Raphael let his study of Talmud slip, devouring science texts, crouching in the night over the tiny numerals, commanding them to dance for him, to sing, a chorale to the fecundity of the universe. His teachers were not slow to appreciate his precocity. On the day the family heard that David had been killed in combat on the border of the Islamic Theocracy, he was already deep into physics at the Technion.

A double blow sent his faith tottering. His brother's slaying was not senseless, but it was unconscionable. Raphael raged, tore the yarmulka from his head and trampled it under his feet. Already the grounds of his apostasy had been established. He had walked in the streets of Jerusalem, the new city and the old, among the cypresses of the Mount of Olives, and beneath the Dome of the Rock where Muhammad had leapt into Paradise on horseback, and beside the Wailing Wall, and slow horror at the multiple unreason had crept into his breast like a growing sponge. He had barely escaped without a beating from his tourist visit to the mosque, and that conjoint savagery and breathtaking beauty poisoned his ease with his fellow humans in a way the vile painting in Denmark had not.

"How could the Torah have been given to Moses! I mean literally written down by God?" he asked Rebecca one night. She stared at him aghast. "Do you really believe that, that the Word of the Master of the Universe was dictated in seventy languages on Sinai?"

"Raphael, be quiet! You have been listening to the lies of the *malshinim*. This is *apikorsishe* blasphemy!"

It was unfair, she was a simple woman, but he railed at her. "Why call them slanderers? They use their brains, Becky, that's all. Would you recommend the gullible stupidity of the Neturei Karta, cowering behind their walls in the Mea Shearim?" He had never lost a measure of loathing for the Hasidim, barricading themselves into the past, rigid with bigotry. "They deny the State of Israel, and they justify it by Torah. They refuse to speak Hebrew because that is sacrilege. Should I grow my *payos* back and tug out my ritual fringes for all to see, and join them in their blind adherence to superstition? Or is Orthodox nonsense sufficient?"

She ran from the room in tears, and he turned angrily to his printouts, where the limitations were the bounds of imagination and logic, and the diagnostics told you without pity where your own stupidity lay.

For his mother's sake he retained the trappings of ritual, and found a kind of authentic comfort in its practice. If now the ceaseless argument and nuance of Talmud seemed arid to him, the eight-hundred-year-old nitpicking of Maimonides the Rambam and Nachmanides the Ramban, the clamor of Rashi and Ibn Ezra and Buber and Sforno, all the desperate ingenuity of brilliant minds dissecting the unreal, at least in the candle lighting of Hanukkah there was calm pride, especially in a land where you could see the lithe Maccabee runners pounding with the flame from

Mode'in all the way to the kingly menorah, the Tabernacle candelabrum
in Jerusalem, yes, there was comfort in the braying of the shofar, for it
spoke of a unity of place and time that his heart desired more than truth.

On Pesach in the last year of the millennium of the Common Era,
Raphael sat at Seder with his mother and his sister and voiced the Four
Questions. The meager Passover feast lay on the table before them. The
curtains were drawn. David's empty seat was a rebuke. "How is this night
different from all other nights?" Raphael asked. "On all other nights we
eat leaven and unleavened bread, tonight only unleavened—" He could
not hear the next word. Space-time had blinked, for a moment. Had his
heart stopped? In the dim room he closed his eyes and watched the hard
afterimage bloom: the table, a silhouette of his mother and sister, the edge
of a door frame. The chair fell with a grinding, splintering sound as his
thigh muscles contracted, hurling him up and away from the table. "Cover
your faces," he said, shouting into a place with no resonance. "Quick," and
he seized his mother's limp arm, dragging her to the floor, pushing Rebecca
with her beneath the table. He forced himself to time eternity, studying
his watch. The tin roof drummed, and a vast surge of thunder went over
them like the wing of the Angel of Death. There were screams, screams.
A siren was bleating, and others joined it. Six minutes? "God in heaven,"
he said, "Jerusalem is gone." He ran to the television set. Snow hissed on
the screen. Panic was beginning to lock his muscles. His mother lay underneath the table, her breath coming in stertorous grunts. Becky cradled
her in her arms. He found a portable radio. Through the static, a voice
dehumanized by appalling self-control was saying: "—enhanced radiation
device, triggered by laser, so there will be negligible fallout. The device was
detonated, according to satellite information, at ground zero in the vicinity
of Mount Zion. Most of the force was expended as prompt neutron radiation. I repeat, stay indoors and cover your windows. Prepare for evacuation.
Arab invasion forces are massing on—"

A desolate voice, outside their shack, was changing, chanting. The
words tore Raphael to the soul: "*Sh'ma Yisroel, Adonai Elohenu, Adonai
Echod. Sh'ma Yisroel—*"

Here, O Israel, the Lord our God is one Lord.

Three

> To make sure of being right in all things, we ought always to hold by the
> principle that the white that I see I would believe to be black, if the
> hierarchical Church were so to rule it . . .
>
> —St. Ignatius Loyola, *Spiritual Exercises*

The City burns in his mind like a shrine of illuminated flowers. Silverman paces uneasily in the narrow confines of his cell. The habit of composure is sloughing from him, as if his soul has begun to shred some dried constricting husk. He discovers himself naked and defenceless without its protection.

Madrazo undoubtedly was taken aback by his outburst but had chosen not to press the matter. Nobody had expected Silverman to find anything as drastic and unsettling as the City. Orbital surveillance had registered the valley only as a mild magnetic and gravitational anomaly, tagging it for closer scrutiny, but redundancy photoscan failed to reveal anything remarkable. The small puzzle teased the physicist in Silverman sufficiently to send him to the surface. Artfully camouflaged, yet plainly uninhabited, the screened City confused his expectations. Still, to suggest that the City was waiting for the return of its builders, as if it were a sentient creature, was patently ridiculous. But Silverman balks at his own rationality. Something he cannot fail to see as vital has touched him, balm to his woes: something breathlessly expectant.

His uncertain steps halt finally at the prie-dieu angled from the foot of his bunk. Lowering himself to his knees before the crucifix, he gazes on the image of the hanging Man. The City's bright image superimposes itself, an affirmation. A flood of gratitude suffuses his being.

Once before he has known illumination. At his ordination in Rome, in St. Peter's Cathedral, under the hands of the great Franciscan pontiff Sixtus VI, he stood at the boundary of transcendence. Pungent and near to sickening, incense had risen in his nostrils. The palpable intensity of thousands gathered in solemn common worship, the unspeakable antiquity of tradition and love and anguish, conspired with sentiment to lift him free, a newly made priest according to the order of Melchizedek, from the horror of the Second Holocaust, his family's pitiful and useless martyrdom, his guilt and doubt. Today in the City he has known it again.

A chill of fever afflicts him. It is not sickness. If anything, this roaring in his vital centers is a surfeit of life. He strives against it, battling for detached clarity, lest pride make of this grace a most subtle temptation.

For all that he is a scientist and priest in this most militant of Orders, he has never renounced his sense of poetry. In a decade on the run from himself, he has dreaded the stars. Through the opaque hull they have seemed to stare in at him, a thousand brilliant haunted eyes plaguing him at the edge of sleep. His poetry has been bleak; it has addressed him from a universe cold and uncaring and baited with traps, where the purest soaring of theology has been perverted into mechanisms of murder, where the spasms of nature throw men heedlessly into existence and the corruption of nature sucks them dry at death and leaves them less than nothing.

More than once the sour words of the Talmud, memorized in childhood, have returned to jeer at him: "Akabaya Ben Mahalalel says, 'Whence thou art come?' From a putrid drop." This is *Pirke Abot*, the Wisdom of the Fathers. Rabbi Simeon ben Eleazar says, "I shall tell thee a parable: to what might this be likened? To a king who built a large palace and decorated it, but a tannery pipe led through it and emptied at its doorway. So too is man. If then, with a foul stream issuing from his bowels, he exalts himself over other creatures, how much the more would he exalt himself if a stream of precious oil, balsam or ointment issued from him!" Now the words take on new meaning for Silverman. He beholds the gnarled timber representation of his Lord's Corpse, recovered to glory in resurrection, and sees how profound his error has been. Nature is finally beneficent. Yes, as Loyola said, it is created for man's sake, to help him fulfill the end for which he was created. If it is unfathomable, that is precisely because it is the "letting be," the creative outpouring, of the Infinite.

Even this Monastery, a spangled cross hurled into the black sky, token of everything infertile and plastic and contrived, never truly home to the limping mendicant, finds its place in his assent. He clasps his fingers and lets his gaze drift to the arresting nondevotional print framed on the wall.

With surprise it occurs to him how premonitory the madman's drawing is, its embedded borders and obsessional hood-masked faces, its Edvard Munch–mouthed elongated ghosts or spectral otters or eyed slugs or spermatozoa slithering back to belly, interlocked but never crossing, the pallid green and yellow and orange and blue of the hospital's crayons, the unfrightened capital letters identifying its draughtsman and his century, ADOLF—1917, and the hard, anxious script that scrambles across the exploding water beneath the crowded ferry with its double smokestack and triple masts and its windows crammed like nightmare with half-seen faces asphyxiated in terror. Poor Adolf Wolfli, contacting some limb of the absolute in his psychosis, drawing on doors and cupboards and walls and any vagrant scrap of paper in the asylum, his fierce blurred eye of truth still open for want of a psychopharmacology accurate enough to calm his craziness and his fear.

The print was an ironic gift from a fellow Jesuit before they packed their scant belongings for exile: Father Thorne had got it from the University Psychiatric Clinic at Waldau, in Bern, where the original Wolfli collection is housed. Had Thorne meant quite so explicitly to tell him that they were embarking on the Ship of Fools? But neither of them had known, then. In any case, as Silverman sees now with an immense lifting of his burden, that analysis of their condition has always been trite. Even the doomed starship *Southern Cross* had been more than a ship of fools.

It is no accident that the *Loyola* resembles the plan of a cathedral. If the Monastery lacks ribbed vaults, pointed arch and flying buttress, masons' tricks hardly appropriate even in aesthetic mimicry to a starship, still it glows with its own luminous flamboyance. Nave and transepts fling themselves out like exultant limbs, multicolored metallic glasses soar in a clerestory wall irradiated by strange suns. Here is a vindication of the proud genius of Pope Sixtus, who found in a shattered world, revolted by the Jihad's savagery, such a loathing for faith that he called all Christendom to a new raising of cathedrals, a moral equivalent of crusade, a sign in heaven. The world's first starship, years in the building, had flamed from the solar system in 2015; but *Southern Cross* was merely the final monument to an expired technology. This high cathedral is purely the creation of unitive physics, lilting between stars in the cryptic transition of dream.

And if Sixtus VI's own dream had soured, his monastic cathedral, outcast under prohibition by the godless owners of twenty-first-century Earth, outcast with the remnants of his pledged soldiers and diplomats and (as those rulers believe) masters of insidious casuistry, why, a kind of blessing can be found here too, for the Word of Gospel is thus scattered into the skies like a memory of the black-garbed missionaries who strode without dread into unknown Asia and the Americas five hundred years before.

Silverman stirs, glancing at his watch. He is bone tired. There is no slightest sound: the Monastery is deep into the *maximum silentium*, the Great Silence. Before he sleeps, the Jesuit must say his daily Office. He reaches for his worn leather-bound breviary and turns to the litanies of the day, for the feast of St. Andrew Corsini, Bishop and Confessor.

When that is done, he kneels once more to make a full Examen of conscience. The City has convicted him of sin. And a cold memory comes to him, hard and clear: his first confession, close to four decades ago, in his bolthole in Rome. Did he truly believe? It seems to him now that that Jewish youth, fresh from the renewal and risk of baptism, had believed nothing. Nothing.

Four

The Spirit of the Lord moves on its course with relaxed reins, to illumine souls and to draw them closely to Himself. He has methods without number.

—Claudio Acquaviva, Fifth Father-General, the Society of Jesus

"Come in, Raphael. I imagined you'd be older. Have that chair. You took instruction from poor Father Hertz, didn't you?"

"Yes, Father."

"A tragedy. God forgive them, they're like animals. I suppose it was his name. Morris never struck me as looking like a . . . Well, anyway, Raphael, you're stuck with me. It really is a pleasure welcoming you into the family of Christ. Have you prepared your general confession? No need for all the gory details, the intention of repentance is sufficient."

"Thank you, I don't mind. Unless—"

"Bless you, son, take as long as you like. I don't have a golf date, if that crossed your mind."

"I never learned to play. Uh, I somehow expected you to be solemn and grim, sort of the Grand Inquisitor."

"How odd. In my neck of the woods Jesuits are regarded with some suspicion for their levity. You're thinking of the Dominicans. That's a shop joke. We've always maintained that the sacrament of reconciliation should be made as painless as possible, though with due regard to the gravity of sin. 'My yoke is sweet,' Our Lord said, 'and my burden light,' and I'm sure He meant it."

"Yes."

"Okay, away we go. In the name of the Father, and of the Son, and of the Holy Spirit. Amen. May God, Who has enlightened your heart, help you to know your sins and trust in His mercy."

"Amen."

" 'What proves that God loves us is that Christ died for us while we still sinned. Having died to make us righteous, is it likely that He would now fail to save us from God's anger?' That's a lovely text, Raphael, St. Paul to the Romans. Shoot."

"Uh, I confess to almighty God that before my baptism I sinned grievously against faith, for I denied His truth, and against hope, for I fell into despair when all my people were . . . I'm sorry—"

"That's all right, son, get it off your chest. I've never thought it unmanly to weep when grief truly touches us. Did your family die in Jerusalem?"

"No, Father, a little later, when the Jihad blitzed Israel. The mullahs blamed us! They actually blamed *us* for destroying their holy places."

"Tell me this, Raphael. How pure was your intention in renouncing Judaism? Was it to save your skin?"

"Wow. You don't believe in fighting clean, do you?"

"To answer my question honestly might be the most important thing you ever do in this life, Raphael. We would have given you sanctuary anyway, you know."

"Look, don't think I haven't put it to myself. Father Morris kept me dangling for six months before he'd baptize me. Obviously there's an element . . . I'll tell you how it was. Before they preempted Jerusalem, I'd lost my faith. My old faith. I was studying physics, and there didn't seem any room in quantum theory for the Yahveh of the Torah."

"Yet there is for the Blessed Trinity?"

"I can't pretend to explain it, but yes. I worked it out after the priests smuggled me here to Rome. No classic conversion number, no bolts of lightning into the brain—"

"Generally humbug. St. Paul's got a lot to answer for. Neurotics and hysterics dote on bolts of lightning."

"You're a refreshing man, Father. The thing of it is, I spent a lot of time so depressed that they had to feed me with a spoon. Then I put in quite a deal of praying even when I didn't know Who to, and reading a couple of books a day about Judaism and Islam and Christianity, and I finally understood that we'd been punished."

"Really? The entire Jewish nation?"

"Like original sin. The whole human race shares in the sin of Adam. Well, the Jewish people rejected the Messiah when He came, and we've been punished, to open our eyes."

"I'm glad you added that last bit. The Jews were not responsible for Christ's murder. That's an error that has been formally condemned by Pope Sixtus as heretical."

"No, no, of course not. The beasts out there claim that when they're napalming us to death. But I read St. Paul, the same epistle you quoted before, I forget which chapter. There is no distinction between Jew and gentile, everyone who calls upon the name of the Lord shall be saved. But how are they to call upon Him until they've learned to believe in Him?"

"And how are they to believe in Him, unless they listen to Him? Yes. And that metaphor in the next chapter about the olive tree that is pruned and grafted with alien stock. You think the Second Holocaust was God's latest nudge to His chosen people? A rather harsh educational technique. Wouldn't it be better to place the blame where it really lies—in the wicked, scapegoating hearts of men?"

"I'm not the theologian, Father. But why else would the Master of the Universe permit the obliteration of my people?"

"Raphael, I imagine we'll be pondering that terrible question to the end of time."

"Have I answered *your* question, Father?"

"Our Lord clearly has given you a very special grace, Raphael. You must nurture His flame within you."

"Father, I have to be honest. I chose Catholicism because right now it seems to me to be valid. It's the sole branch of Christianity that can trace its roots directly to Jesus and the apostles. But I'm a scientist. To me, understanding is always provisional. I'm still tormented by doubts."

"Ten thousand difficulties do not make a single doubt, my son. A keen awareness of difficulties is the occupational hazard of Christian intellectuals. Sometimes I think how much easier it would have been to live in the twelfth century, but then I remember their sewerage. Look, let's wrap this up with a general declaration, and we'll go up and have some coffee."

"Yes. Lord, I have offended against Your commandments, and I am truly sorry."

"For penance I'd like you to make a novena of Masses to Our Lady during the next nine days. Express your sorrow to God, now, and I'll give you absolution."

"Father, I have sinned against You and am not worthy to be called Your son. Be merciful to me, a sinner."

"God, the Father of mercies, through the death and resurrection of His Son, has sent the Holy Spirit among us for the forgiveness of sins; through the ministry of the Church may God give you pardon and peace, and I absolve you from your sins in the name of the Father, and of the Son, and of the Holy Spirit."

"Amen."

"Give thanks to the Lord, for He is good."

"His mercy endures forever."

"The Lord has freed you from your sins. Go in peace."

"Uh, Father, one final thing. I believe I have a vocation as a Jesuit."

"Hmmm. Let's take a rain check on that one."

Five

I used in imagination to see the bridges collapse and sink, and the whole great city vanish like a morning mist. Its inhabitants began to seem like hallucinations, and I would wonder whether the world in which I thought I had lived was a mere product of my own febrile nightmares.

—Bertrand Russell, *Autobiography*

Shriven, buoyant with the promise of the City, Father Raphael Silverman dons amice, alb, chasuble and stole, his vestments blood red in honor of St. Agatha, Virgin and Martyr, and says Mass in the Lady Chapel behind the great altar, reserved for the Father-General. With so many priests aboard the Monastery, the listing of chapels is orchestrated in a timetable by the computers. Even so, Silverman concelebrates the Mystery with the two priests who will go down to the planet with him this afternoon. Brother Kohler, his team's electronics specialist, serves the Mass, burly in white surplice.

It is a cause of some irritation that Cardinal Madrazo has insisted on the inclusion of an Eclectic. Silverman cannot feel at ease in the presence of radically lateral insight. The Father-General discerns the private roots of his disquiet and resistance.

"Eclectics are a jumpy breed," Silverman has argued.

The Cardinal smiled. "Father Chan is made of sterner stuff. Raphael, you were a little skittish yesterday. Tsung-Dao is a discreet fellow. Besides— if that thing down there is as peculiar as you suggest, you really ought to have a coordinating synthesist with you."

Silverman introduces Father Chan to the other Jesuits during descent. The Chinese priest knows their work, of course, and they have seen him at Mass this very day, but incredibly he has never spoken to them before. Even in the closed environment of the Monastery, Eclectics tend to relate to others chiefly through the cybersystem. It is a mark of "singularity," that vice most swiftly extirpated under the Common Rule, but their special gifts and training make it permissible.

Deliberately, Silverman gives them no warning of what they might expect. Coronal effect flares about their vessel. The survey boat, far better equipped with instruments than yesterday's skiff, plummets through the City's screen, trailed by a mild magnetohydrodynamic storm. They bypass the scarp, falling to rest amid the wet green fields that spread on every side around the City.

Not one of them moves a muscle.

The tiers rise like the airy battlements of a castle of crystal, a tracery of translucent marble and quicksilver. Dew-wet grass is a carpet of gems, unmuted, glistening in the morning sunlight. The City humbles them. They simply sit.

If Silverman has half-feared the penetrating insight of an Eclectic at this naked moment, that trepidation is gone. The sheer ontological impact of the City is scored in the small silent movements (a hand half-lifted, a foot drawn back), the pent breath, the trapped gaze of his colleagues.

Yet grandeur is not indefinitely paralyzing. Slowly the scientists come to themselves. In continued silence, they begin to gather their instruments for the trip across to the City. Henry Walson slides a cassette roll expertly into a camera. For a moment, after his hands have completed their automatic task, he stands helplessly before the viewpod. But the imposed discipline that has shaped them all is finally no less automatic. Bending his tonsured head over the camera, the xenologist shoots a rapid series of holograms.

Brother Kohler piles the gravity polarizer with field equipment. By the time Walson has finished his cassette, Kohler is looking to Silverman for permission to cycle open the latch. Chan, unused to expeditions beyond the Monastery, is once more checking the seals on his filter-skin. The camera beeps and disgorges the first windows. Silverman plucks them from the slot. His face drains of blood. The world moves away from him.

"Wait," he says. His own voice resonates strangely within his head, like a cry heard underwater. The engineer lifts his stubby hand from the hatch control. Walson halts in the process of inserting a fresh cartridge of holotape.

"Let me have them, Father," comes Tsung-Dao Chan's cool voice. Like all of them, he speaks in Latin. From Silverman's numb grasp he takes the vivid-colored prints. Surprised, the others peer over his shoulder, and their mouths loosen.

Each of the hologram windows is technically perfect. Grass sparkles lustrously, with here and there a clump of merry wildflowers, and the cloudless daybreak sky shines in true dimensional depth. And where the City itself lifts like a cantata outside the survey boat's clear viewpod, the windows show only three enormous pieces of statuary, dwarfed and foreshortened by distance, alien and powerful and each of the most blazing and absolute malevolence.

Silverman finds his mind cringing into stupidity and denial. He stares from one man to another, stares in repeated incredulous darts back to the curved transparency of the hullpod. A kilometer away at most, the City reaches up to the bowl of heaven. If it is not real, nothing is real. If the City is not as palpable as his trembling hand, as the titanium body of the spacecraft, as the soil and rock and magma of the planet they stand on, then all of that too is no more than whimsical illusion. Dr. Johnson kicks his stone. The City has gripped the minds and bowels of four men in a rapture of the ultimate truth it embodies. The holopics say it is not there. And the grotesque filthiness they put in its place is a paralyzing blow to Silverman's fragile, breaking sense of decency. He is plunged once more and without reprieve into the abstract and bestial madness of *Southern Cross*.

At a remove, he hears Kohler's challenge.

"Why didn't the sensors show us this from orbit?" The lay brother's voice has a thwarted, ugly note. That in itself is an appalling thing. Horst Kohler is the most hardheaded of empiricists. Yet some part of this moment's monstrous nausea has transmitted itself to his armored sensibilities.

Wearily, bile in his mouth, Father Silverman finds his seat. "The sensors were fooled by the City's shields, Brother. That's why the computers allowed me down here alone in the first place. The fact of it is, I was astonished to find anything this large and complex."

A rasping, perhaps laughter, works at his throat.

Six

> Or to put it another way, they can become alienated from Being, although they have received their being from the letting-be of Being; and having become alienated from Being, they let themselves slip back from fuller being to less being, and toward nothing. This in turn frustrates the letting-be of Being, for the beings that Being has let be fail to fulfill their potentialities for being, and slip back from them.
>
> Dr. John Macquarrie, *Principles of Christian Theology*

> In meditation on invisible things . . . consider that my soul is imprisoned in this corruptible body, and my whole self in this vale of misery, as it were in exile among brute beasts; I say my whole self, that is, soul and body.

Imprisoned in a quite literal sense in the closeted sanctuary of the Collegio di San Roberto Bellarmino on the Via de Seminario, launched on the fearsome thirty-day catenary of the Long Retreat that would conclude his novitiate, Thomas, born Raphael, composed his spirit to the mournful contemplation of the First of the Spiritual Exercises of St. Ignatius. If under the waters of baptism he had adopted the name Thomas, on that trembling day six years earlier, it had not been from any transparent impulse of pride. Father Morris Hertz had chided him mildly, surmising that Raphael was placing himself under the particular protection of St. Thomas Aquinas, that prodigious intellect known to his contemporaries as the Ox and to Mother Church as the Angelic Doctor. Raphael had smiled; his devotion was to Thomas the Apostle, the Doubter, the empiricist brought to faith in the

risen Redeemer only by the gross insertion of his fingers into the Lord's
palpable wounds.

Now that the same obdurate hankering for proof, for logic, for a place
to stand where his mind as well as his soul might own its sense of integrity,
that inevitable flaw faced a massive battering that would either anneal its
lesions or shatter it. So the Retreat had been designed. Raphael knelt upright, a penitential exercitant embarking on a profound harrowing that had
fetched men during nearly half a millennium abruptly up against the hard
edge of mystery.

"You must call most strenuously upon every faculty," the Director of
the Retreat had urged the novices. He was a stern Japanese, with a lined
face. "St. Ignatius stresses the 'three powers of the soul.' The first is memory,
which is the storehouse of truth: the life of our Lord and the teachings of
the Church. The second is understanding, by which we bring that knowledge fully within heart and mind. And the third is will, our active com-
pliance in that knowledge under the free grace of God."

Each step presented an abyss, waiting for Raphael's stumbling feet. He
forced himself to heed the advice of the author of the Exercises, though
his mind revolted: It is not abundance of knowledge that fills and satisfies
the soul, so much as the interior understanding and savoring of the truth.

> Bring to mind the sin of the angels, how they were created in
> grace, yet, not willing to help themselves by the means of their
> liberty in the work of paying reverence and obedience to their
> Creator and Lord, falling into pride, they were changed from grace
> into malice, and hurled from Heaven to Hell . . .

"You may treat the angelic revolt as metaphor," the Director had told them
blandly. "Scholars tend today to view them as intrusions into the early
Hebrew oral teachings, derived by assimilation from the messengers and
demiurges of their pagan neighbors."

Instantly Raphael was in trouble. His three years of neoscholastic philosophy still lay ahead, but he had read sufficient of his nonnamesake Aquinas to grasp that, in the hierachy of being, purely spiritual creatures were
a logical order standing between God and humankind. Beyond logic, the
indubitable fact of angels was attested by Scriptures common to Jewish and
Christian faiths (and Islamic, for that matter). Nor was there anything in
the idea of angels remotely offensive to a man with a doctorate in unitive
physics. Now that the unitary scholium was effectively proven, with all
spacetime a skein of multidimensional strings, or preons, it was plain that

immaterial being was precisely as intelligible as the single dimensionless constant of the preonic Planck mass.

No, the difficulty looming like a lion was the nature of sin, the subject of this meditation. For the oldest opinion of the Fathers of the Church insisted that humanity's very genesis lay exactly in those fallen stars, plunging to damnation in the wake of their brilliant leader, Lucifer. The doctrine lacked popularity these days, yet by tradition mankind was a kind of surrogate for those first demonic criminals; their places in Heaven—reserved, so to speak, on their behalf and now vacant—were to be made up in the numbers of the elect. Just as the original sin of our protoparents had at once cursed us and occasioned the coming of God in human form for our salvation, the lapse of the fiends was the "happy fault" that first opened the way to our felicity. Myth, undoubtedly, but myth inspired at the Divine Source.

Raphael stirred minutely, keeping his eyes modestly lowered. Cramp twinged his left leg; he ignored it, seeking fiercely to crystallize his problem. It was this: angels, according to the most profound of metaphysics, were simple in nature, not divisible into parts, unmingled with matter, perceiving and understanding by intuition, seizing essences direct, without the limitations that oblige men to infer principles from sense data and consequences from principles. Their apprehension was nondeductive, free of hypothesis and test, free indeed of time itself. No emotion could blur their reason, nor was reason prey to logical error or inaccuracy.

How, then, could such sublime beings sin? It was madness. It defied precisely that rationality that angels possessed in superabundance. Loyola, in harmony with tradition, indicated pride as the source and nature of angelic revolt. Yet wasn't this ludicrous anthropomorphism?

"Better to rule in Hell than serve in Heaven?" For an Earthly potentate, or an arrogant scientist, no motive was easier to comprehend. Yet the beatitude of Heaven lay centrally in the witness of God's unshielded Face, in subservience to the logic, as it were, of necessity: the triumph of will governed by reason. It was not merely a matter of self-interest, though it was certainly that also, at a crass level; the self-damnation of the fallen host was utterly at odds with their defining essence.

> The sin of Adam and Eve: bring before the memory how, for that sin, they did such long penance, and how much corruption came upon the human race, so many men being put on the way to Hell.

When the Director softly announced the second point of contemplation, Raphael was startled by the degree to which his cassock adhered to his chest and upper arms. He sniffed carefully: his own flesh stank with sweat. Now the novices stood with their arms crossed, while the director redoubled his advice to treat the point as a praiseworthy metaphor, an archetypal figure that must not occasion scruples of conscience in those for whom original sin was an existential truth rather than a fundamentalist event in history.

Again, Raphael was plunged at once into his struggle with pythons. The Hasidim among whom his father had worked would have been scandalized to hear the words of the Torah reinterpreted so unblushingly. Not that the notion of original sin as primal hereditary fault had any place in Raphael's Judaic heritage: it had been with some astonishment that he had found it at the core of his new faith. Of course, Orthodox and Reform rabbinical opinion had long understood that evolution left no role for an historical special creation of proto-parents for the race.

Pinning the problem down as well as he might, Raphael saw it as the relationship between creation, knowledge, will and sin. "Corruption came upon the human race." Yes, men were scarred by a proclivity to sin, to disobedience, to every kind of vice and corruption. It could hardly be due to the limitations inherent in their mode of creation, spirit and matter conjoined, for that would impute blame to the Master of the Universe. Origen Adamantius and other early Christian heretics had proclaimed creation itself evil, a doctrine so perverted that its principal proponent betrayed its source by hacking off his genitals. Still, creation was at root tragic. It groaned in travail.

Raphael was fetched back to the putative sin of the angels. It was the risk of God's creation that unbounded Being, the dynamic Triune force that the Apostle's Creed affirmed as Father, Son and Holy Spirit, would "let be" a prodigious universe teeming with particular beings. Risk, yes, since each of these contingent created beings would then view itself as center and goal, chafing under its dependence on the Source of Being, striving in the heart of its idolatrous consciousness to usurp the rightful position and power of God.

It was, in short, sin against the first of the Ten Commandments. An angel might intuit at some horizon of clarity the primordial Father, the expressive Son and the unitive Spirit as that transcendent dialectic that supported its own secondary existence, and still crave the apotheosis of its individuality. How much more so might human beings tumble into this trap, with each individual consciousness clamoring for supremacy within each skull?

And sustaining that lust for power, Raphael realized, were the multiple impulses printed in DNA, each creature inheriting four billion years of evolutionary strife: the yearning not only for individual survival but for corporate destiny, with its dire counterpart to altruism, a ruthless directive to obliterate all that stood in the path of the extended self.

Raphael blinked. Beads of perspiration crept stingingly from his forehead into the corners of his eyes. Even so, he felt dissociated, adrift. Perhaps he was succeeding with memory and understanding, but the application of this knowledge to an act of will seemed further away than ever. His stubborn will cried out, in fury, that the arguments he had rehearsed were specious, a tangle of linguistic fallacies adorning a dung heap of savage superstitions, no whit better than the faith he had renounced. Desolation moved on him like the Angel of Death.

"Am ha'aretz," he goaned in Hebrew. Ignoramus. He sought the words of the Psalmist. Lord, who shall sojourn in Thy tabernacle? Who shall dwell upon Thy holy mountain? He that walketh uprightly, and worketh righteousness, and speaketh truth in his heart.

> Consider the particular sin of some one person who for one mortal sin has gone to Hell; and many others without number have been condemned for fewer sins than I have committed.

The gravity and malice of a single man's sin. Abruptly, all the opaque walls of abstraction segmenting Raphael's spirit collapsed into dust. An image plunged into his mind and gibbered there: the caricatured hook nose, the grasping outstretched hand, the treacherous kiss . . .

"No!" he cried, involuntarily, aloud. With a sharp look the Director warned him to control himself. An equally involuntary snigger came from one of the other novices, strained to breaking point by his own fearsome efforts. Raphael hardly noticed them. The image was vile, poisonous, unjust, and frozen into his brain.

Raphael looked at the traitor Judas, the Jew, and saw Reb Silverman, his father.

Seven

> We are driven to conclude that the greatest mistake in human history was the discovery of truth. It has not made us free, except from delusions that comforted us, and restraints that preserved us; it has not made us happy, for truth is not beautiful, and did not deserve to be so passionately

chased. As we look upon it now we wonder why we hurried so to find it.
For it appears to have taken from us every reason for existing . . .
                                                        —Will Durant

It is as if his life's aspiration has been befouled for the final time, as if now
the dream toward which he has striven for so long has been plucked away
by cruel daylight.

God has departed from the shrine of the City. The veil of the Temple
is rent. Silverman is left vacant and drained. That secret core of a man,
the emotional nexus half a billion years more ancient than the cortex, tells
him that in an instant the universe has changed. No, worse than that: once
again, he finds its chimera shattered.

Slumped in his padded seat, he looks at the desecrated shrine and sees
a lie.

"Well," Silverman says at last, as if another man speaks through his
lips, "we might as well go out and take a look at it. Even if it isn't there."

They conspire in a compact of shocked silence. Kohler quickly slaps a
button, shoves the polarizer with its load of delicate instruments through
the opening hatch, steps out after it. Onto the springy grass after him go
Chan and Walson. Before he follows, Silverman reaches to the panel and
sets the refraction field, a habit of caution inlaid on planets more strenuous
with hostile life than this one. As the lock hatch hisses shut behind him
the field effectuates: the boat vanishes. How comforting, Silverman thinks
ironically, testing his bitterness. The real things are invisible and what we
are shown does not exist.

But which is it that does not exist? The diabolical statuary, or the
numinous City? There is no faintest doubt of the answer.

Without speaking they trudge across the grass, and even in his despair
Silverman cannot deny the physical invigoration of the cool fresh breath
of morning, sweet through his filter-skin. It is an exquisite world. If and
when High Earth repeals its in-turned prohibition on starflight, it is a world
that will fill quickly with the voices of men and women and their fearless
children.

Behind the Jesuits, a dark swath extends as the pure droplets of dew
are brushed away by their protective clothing.

Above them is the City, majestic, buoyant as helium. Gravity drags at
their limbs, more forceful than the Monastery's, and their breathing begins
to rasp. No doubt remains that this place has been a dwelling for men, or
beings like men. The tiers of aching light had their purpose, and their
function was their beauty. It is a more clarified purpose than any human
technology has ever contrived, outside the intoxicated fantasies of light-

drunk moviemakers at the close of the last century's Big Spree.

And in the depths and salt reaches of Silverman's emotional sources, the City's sham is toxin to the very spirit it purports to nourish.

He halts the party near the outskirts of the nearest section. Despite its complexity, the entire edifice seems an integral entity. Silverman turns, indecision in his face.

To Horst Kohler he suggests: "Perhaps you might set up your instruments here. Let's see what we can salvage from this." His indiscretion makes him grit his teeth. He turns to Walson. "Try a few holograms from here and we'll figure out exactly where those disgusting things are." Chan he ignores.

The Chinese priest has been staring with unemotional curiosity at the towers. As though addressed, he swings back and shakes his head.

"Raphael, you're off center." Universal thinkers are blunt and faltering by turn; they have no instinct for the amenities. He cocks his head to one side in a quick, nervous gesture. "This is all alien. We have no grounds for projecting our own values on it. Those statues might have no greater significance than, oh, the hygiene systems in the *Loyola*. Maybe that's what they are—a kind of psychic purgative. The worm in the heart of the rose. Unless," he adds with the faintest touch of sarcasm, "you think it's all a cosmic practical joke."

Silverman shakes his head. That is exactly how he reads it. The City is a napalm grenade wrought by the naked hand of that dark angel in whose literal existence he can no longer believe. It is a lie uttered from the foul mouth of the Father of Lies.

The xenologist makes a series of swift forays through the drying grass to calculated stations, fetching back holograms from each position. He hands Silverman a bundle of windows. In varying perspective they show the same three horrifying objects.

Silverman twists the windows from side to side. They afford only a limited parallax, but he discerns that the statues are set at the vertices of an equilateral triangle. The nearest is perhaps six hundred meters from where they stand; it coexists with a lofty tower soaring above the opalescent curve of the greater portion of the City. He passes back the windows.

"Ride the polarizer up a few hundred meters and develop a full perspective. No instruments."

Father Walson nods keenly. At forty he is culpably boyish, for all the brilliance of his accomplishments. It is evident that to him the City is already merely one more enigma he means to crack.

The gravity cart lifts into the sky, and in its wake a zephyr blows cool past Silverman's cheek.

Kohler is grumbling almost inaudibly at his machines. He glances up, mouth taut with frustration. "It's crazy."

Silverman studies the offending instruments. Kohler points to a bank of log-scaled readouts. "It says here the power output is only marginally higher than background. There isn't enough kick in there to lift a grasshopper off the dirt, and no neutrino flux." He flicks on the integrating display of the field detector. "There's your city." Against the dull red screen, in white depth histograms, the City is as real and measurable as the geographical reference points. "And here," growls the lay brother, heavy shoulders thrust forward, left hand menacing a third set of meters, "we're informed that there's no mass in the vicinity except us and whatever's at those major loci. Even if the city's nothing but a vast preon field—and how you'd sculpt a thing like that I can't imagine—it should still activate the detectors as mass equivalence."

"Heads it's there," Silverman ventures. "Tails it's not."

"Right." In disgust, the German glowers at his treacherous, fallible instruments.

Silverman shoves both hands into the side pockets of his filterskin, staring upward in impotent rage at the heedless godlings who have left this thing for men to impale themselves on.

The gravity cart drops like a stone, to hover centimeters above the tufted grass. Father Walso, grinning, clambers off it, presses half a dozen crisp line drawings into Silverman's hand. If the Rule did not forbid bodily contact, undoubtedly he would clutch his superior by the arm.

"Father, this is marvelous." The younger priest is flushed, overwhelmed by the elegance of his discovery. "It reminds me of the tropic mounds we found on Rho Ophiuchi II. Those were insects, of course, but I'll show you what I mean. Start here, or right over here, say, and independent hodological vectors torque you to *there*." He points to a projection on one of his drawings. "When that's gridded against the windows, it's right at the centroid of the triangle formed by the three statues."

Silverman glances at the drawings in silence, hands them back. Walson cannot disguise his disappointment and hurt at the lack of enthusiasm.

"Go and show this to Father Chan," Silverman grunts. The man's thoughtless ebullience dismays him. "An Eclectic can probably do more with it than I can." He strains for some bone of kindness to throw. "Thank you, Henry. I'm most impressed."

Profoundly troubled, Silverman turns his back on the City and walks away into the rustling grass. At a distance from his companions, he crouches on his haunches and peers through slit lids across the meadow to the long bluff where he'd stood shaken by joy twenty-four hours earlier.

The sky above the scarp is a cloudless blue transparency, the cirrus gone, unpolluted, unpeopled by shrieking aircraft.

Slowly he regains his feet. Pain twinges in swollen veins. It is not only the unaccustomed gravity. I'm getting old, he tells himself, and does not smile. I'd thought the time was past for making decisions about the ontology of the universe.

So the City is designed to lead an unwary sophont into its throat. For what purpose? To complete the destruction it began when a man first discovered the blasphemy it embodies? The Jesuit glances toward the others. They are busy about their work. Is he, then, the only one genuinely afflicted by the City's message of annihilation? He puts a cold hand to his face, to the puckered flesh sagging at his jaw. It comes to him that Chan might be correct after all; that he is reading into an alien technology some phantasm conceivable only in a mortally diseased mind.

Calm in the despondency of that thought, he walks back to them.

"It's time someone went in," he announces. "It'd be best if I go in alone. If I'm away more than three hours, I don't want anyone following me. Take the boat out beyond the screen and report to *Loyola*. They'll probably want to send down an extra boat."

Some part of his chill is communicated to them. In silence they nod, though Kohler's eye is sour at the idea of a man going unprotected into the enigma that has baffled his instruments. The synthesist opens his mouth. At once his brash nerve fails. He drops his eyes and lets his mouth close again.

"Tell me, Tsung-Dao."

"Uh, well, Father Silverman, I have a first approximation. But it's a radical analysis, and I'll have to run it four ways through the full cybersystem before I could say with any precision—"

"Let's hear it."

"Okay." Chan gives him a grateful glance. It means nothing to Silverman. Habit makes him listen, makes him act when action is called for. The City's jaws are waiting for him, waiting to devour him. "Briefly, the culture that constructed this complex was quite similar to ours. I didn't think so at first, but that was an emotional reaction to those repulsive things in there. Even if the statues are completely realistic—portraiture, say, instead of gargoyles of the Hindu variety—the City's builders were orthogenetically not unlike human beings. But their culture *was* different, in one key technical respect." Chan hesitates. "That one difference has spectacular implications. You see, they developed their field theory along a branching path from ours prior to the invention of tensors."

Kohler makes a vulgar sound. "Speculative poppycock!"

"Please, Horst!" Silverman chides. "What are those implications, Father?"

"Naturally," Chan says, "I can't possibly extrapolate the full range of technical advances their *Weltanschauung* might have made feasible . . . but that structure over there is one of them. On this first approximation, though, I can tell you one technology they could *not* have developed, any more than Aristotelan physics could have done so—and that's faster-than-light preonics. So where are they?"

"Like *Southern Cross*," Silverman whispers.

"Pardon?"

"Satan," he murmurs, "has no need of that."

"I'm sorry?"

"No matter," Silverman says, unutterably weary.

He looks at the three Jesuits for a moment, and then turns abruptly and walks toward the waiting City.

Eight

> The radical remedy lies in the mortification of the four great natural passions: joy, hope, fear and grief. You must seek to deprive these of every satisfaction and leave them as it were in darkness and the void.
>
> —St. John of the Cross

In darkness and the void, Father Raphael Silverman drifted weightless on his preonic sled toward the moribund hulk of humanity's first starship.

At his back glared the distant lights of the *Loyola*, but by now they added scarcely more illumination than the massively "star-barreled" firmament. The universe, to his eyes, was shrunken to half size. Two terrible chunks had gone from it. Ahead, he seemed to be moving into a perfectly lightless void sixty degrees in expanse. He took care now, after one appalling moment of vertigo, not to glance behind. There, the cone of pure blackness was a ghastly one hundred and twenty degrees in extent.

Relative to the galaxy, both immense craft hurtled at the constellation Centaurus with a velocity nearly half that of light, time slowed by rather more than ten percent, the spectrum of those stars which were still visible shifted blue-white forward and reddened aft.

Detector relays from the Monastery shimmered on Silverman's console, still reporting what he had known for days. The fusion power system on *Southern Cross* was functioning, though at a greatly reduced level. Vented gas fractions affirmed a large biomass aboard, easily the equivalent of crew and colonists asleep and awake. The vast magnets, which once constrained a hundred thousand tons of frozen hydrogen fuel, both matter and anti-matter, were slagged into ruin. And that single male voice, with its hair-stirring, melancholy, unintelligible lament, remained all that the starship beamcast on its Earth-aimed maser.

Despite every rational foreboding, joy glowed in Silverman's heart. A presence bold and kingly remained with the defunct craft, a presence that was quite simply the force of human heroism. He had not yet been ordained a priest when *Southern Cross* flared at the moon's orbit like a new star, taking the rekindled hopes of a reprieved world into the oceans of eternity. She had begun as an industrial habitat in a 2:1 resonant Earth orbit, a way station for the manufacture of power satellites during the Oil Wars. With the coming of preon physics, her role was made obsolete. Bursting quarks into preons was suddenly inexpensive, and segregating their recombined products into magnetic repositories of matter and antimatter reasonably uncomplicated as a problem in engineering.

Something had to be done with the billion-dollar habitat. So she became a starship, driven by the absolute annihilation of mass into radiant energy.

Commissioning the *Southern Cross* had been a conspicuous act of faith by the United Nations, a stunning gesture of optimism aimed at the hearts of the whole world. These are our emissaries: they bear with them all the best the human species has attained, the finest that is in us in our prospects of renewed destiny. Silverman had cheered as full-throatedly as any when that brilliant point of light seared the sky, dropping toward the horizon and the spangled glory of the southern heavens.

"Main core lock is opening," a voice from the Monastery told him. "Nine hundred and eighty meters to docking."

The lock had refused to respond to their initial robot probes. Someone is watching me, Silverman told himself, feeling cool sweat prickled beneath his EVA suitskin. There was an absence somewhere—

"The man has stopped beamcasting, Father."

"Yes. I still can't see . . . Lights have come on in the lock. It's still cycling open." Either the craft's processors had been specifically reprogrammed to deal with an approaching and identifiable human figure or an operator on board had adopted manual control. Silverman peered ahead, every instinct and faculty primed. His sled's own guidance systems, of course, were autonomous, informing its passenger of its trajectory and intentions without distracting him with any need for routine executive intervention.

Deepest gray on black, the enormous arc of *Southern Cross* moved steadily to blot out the more dreadful blot of the dopplered cosmos. The priest felt his sinews relax, and smiled. In whatever attitude, the *Cross* didn't look like a cross. Nothing could have been topographically more remote from the cruciform than the squat, lumpy cask whose structure remained that of an O'Neill "Crystal Palace" habitat. With her redundant orbital shielding stripped away, and with it several million tons of inertial mass, and her monstrous acceleration bracing, her designer might not have recognized his twentieth-century brainchild. To the literal-minded, Silverman thought, it might be more fitting if the two starships had their names transposed. On the other hand, it might escape the pedantic that *Southern Cross* resembled a bust of the Founder wrought by, say, the sardonic hand of a Marcel Duchamp. His smile broadened.

Seeing the bright rectangle of the open lock had revived his spirits. He permitted hope to touch him. A disaster of the first magnitude had smitten the vessel; there was no denying that. Yet intelligence remained alive inside the crippled ship. The multiple star system that had been her goal now hung more than four light-years astern, lost in the deep infrared. *We are as far from the Centauri suns as that barren triumvirate is from our sun,* the priest told himself. But the crew of the *Cross* had not abandoned themselves totally to despair.

His sled's vector altered marginally, and his velocity vanished back into the fabric of spacetime. With the faintest clink, magnetic docking rods joined their counterparts jutting from the rim of the lock.

"I've arrived. Nobody in sight. Do you want me to wait?"

"There's been no further word from the crew, Father." Only once had the eerie dirge from the ship given way to sense, and that had been to insist that only one visitor would be permitted to enter the *Cross*. The Monastery was hardly equipped to mount a boarding party against the will of the incumbents. Silverman heard the clear Latin of Cardinal Madrazo come into his channel. "I doubt that anything will be gained by lingering at this point, Father Silverman. Go with God."

"Deo gratias," said Silverman, releasing his webbing.

As planned, the craft had been rotated two light-years from Earth so that its engines faced the direction of flight. The axial shaft was a cylinder seven hundred meters long. Its huge docking station was not pressurized, nor was the shaft itself, with its twin maglev buckets capable of zooming like bullets from the dock to the drive-engineering sections. This air lock, though, gave directly into a curved corridor leading radially to the first of the twenty contiguous inflated toroids, the tire-shaped habitats that made up the outer shell of the starship.

Silverman placed one of several radio repeaters on the inner wall of the air lock. The instruments would maintain his direct link with the *Loyola* despite the massive shielding that otherwise would block his broadcast. Invisibly, the repeater began diffusing its multiplex threads of conducting crystal through the hull. The lock cycled shut. Silverman waited for his radio to come back on-line.

Air hissed into the compartment. He declined to shed his suitskin. The absence of rotation on the habitat was alarming, perhaps even more so than the crew's silence. During the one-g acceleration that had brought the *Cross* to half the velocity of light no spin was needed: ceilings became temporary floors. But burn had terminated in the first year of flight. Now, in free fall, pseudogravity was essential to both physical and mental health. Perhaps spin had been taken off to effect repairs, but that dismal attempt must have been made a decade previously. Who would live in free fall by choice?

A frantic voice told him: "Maintain your suit integrity! Don't go ambient; there's something wrong with the air."

"Okay, I'm fine, still sealed. My gross readouts show normative on pressure, constituents, and ionization. What do you have?"

"Protein decomposition products. Something's rotting, Father. It can't be the algae beds."

"Toxicity?"

"We're waiting for the micro-organisms. But even if the air's not poisonous, the stench'd have you puking your guts out." There was a pause. The same voice, thin with self-reproach, added, "Sorry, Father."

Fear spurted in Silverman's blood. Not only are they all dead, he thought numbly, but they have perished within sight of rescue. How long? Days? A week? The coincidence crushed his spirit. Flexing his legs against the slight resistance of the suit skin, the priest launched himself into the narrow corridor and ascended, in a space with only a single polarity of direction, toward the corpses of mankind's first stellar dream.

"They must have been dead for years," a voice rebuked him. "Our analysis suggests that hibernation failed when the crew died, but that one or more individuals survived. Temperature was run down throughout the ship to arrest decay. Our arrival triggered the resuscitation of the man who warned us off. With the *Cross* back to operational status, the remains have begun to putrefy. The shock has almost certainly unhinged him, Father Silverman. We advise caution in your approach."

The first five habitat rings were unbreached but vacant to quick inspection. Silverman passed from one to the next through locks designed to seal rigidly if a ring were ruptured. The sixth torus was not empty. Gigantic translucent jellyfish hung in the air, globes of dead, pale tissue like masses of frog spawn. He battered his way through the extraordinary bubbles of decaying organic matter. At the touch of his hand a globe would tremble, shatter, spill into spherical fragments and glistening streamers. There were no corpses, but his sensors told him that death was everywhere. His mind closed in on itself, awash with dread.

In the next ring, and the one after that, the slimy organic substance was confined by surface tension to vast plastic sheets arrayed on stanchions in labyrinthine three-dimensional tunnels like an Escher paradox. Bulkheads of polyurethane foam had been torn out, equipment unbolted where possible and shoved aside to make room for this surreal handiwork.

It could not have been done in days, or months. The Monastery's analysis was wrong. Clearly, someone had labored for years to construct the maze. Tubes strung across and between the sheets leaked a colorless liquid onto the living culture. It was a kind of hydroponic nurturing apparatus, built in a hurry with no concern for aesthetics or rational planning beyond some incomprehensible urge to get the maximum amount of biotic material into production.

Near the lock giving onto the ninth ring, a hairless man floated upside down. With fantastic agility, he righted himself as Silverman pushed into the new labyrinth. He wore an old-fashioned hard suit with its own oxygen supply. "I know, messy I agree, it's getting a bit beyond me," he said apologetically to the priest, his voice going out through the beamcast to interception by the Monastery's remote sensors and coming back through the repeaters. "It's a good thing someone's here finally to help me. I recycle the tissue every few months, but it does pile up. You're just in time, actually." The tone of lament was quite gone. He stopped speaking and regarded Silverman suspiciously. "You're not a Muslim, are you?"

Sickened with pity, the priest told him, "No. My name is Raphael Silverman. What happ—"

The man's toes touched the deck for an instant and propelled him away like an aerial fish. "A perfidious Jew! Ah, now I see it. Lucifer has his minions. But these little ones are God's."

"I'm not going to hurt you," Silverman said. His tongue and mouth were dry. The Monastery whispered to him "We have voiceprint identification. He's Dr. Martin Herbert Baldwin, one of the four reproduction engineers. Stress Evaluator indicates acute paranoia. His records list Dr. Baldwin as a practicing Catholic, which might facilitate matters."

"Martin, I'm a priest." He put authority into his tone. "A Jesuit. I'm also a physicist. There's nothing to fear."

Baldwin's body convulsed. Before he could tumble, he stilled the motion with one lightning touch to a stanchion. "That's impossible. I'm hallucinating. Say something in Latin."

Horror was building in Silverman. *"Gloria Patri,"* he said, making a slow sign of the cross, *"et Filio, et Spiritu Sancto."*

"Amen," said the biologist, voice trembling. He lifted up his eyes and clasped gloved hands. "O Lord, thank Thee for this miracle. May Thy work always be done. Now we can get through it in half the time," he explained sunnily to Silverman.

The priest asked, gently, "Is anyone else alive?"

Baldwin laughed uproariously. "I am large; I contain multitudes." With a lurch of mood, he snapped, "Are you blind, your Holiness? These are the generations of Moab. Was it Moab? They're all dead, your Grace. Even the frozen ones. God spared me alone, you see, in His great and bitter mercy. I was working in the shielded stockroom when the magnets went. He has placed His mitre upon my head for the completion of the universe. The number of the elect shall be one hundred and forty-four thousand. I can assure you, we've passed that tally by a long chalk. How terrible was that fall, when one-third of the hosts of heaven went unto perdition. And it is left to us to replace their number. Frail mortals, doomed by Adam's curse to damnation unless we are reborn of water and the spirit. If I am to be damned to Hell everlasting for the work of purification, I count it a fair exchange, to have brought so many to His glory. Romans 9: iii. Now you must help me with this batch. You know the words, of course. I'll start the water running. We must use a general rite, the bare matter and form, you'd need a bloody microscope and a thousand years to do it on an individual basis."

The madman darted to a jumble of hastily welded taps and altered the flow. Turning his back on Silverman, he faced the glistening sheets of organic culture and raised his right hand in a blessing. *"Ego te baptizo in nomine Patris, et Filii—"*

A frenzy of revulsion and grief swept through Silverman as at last he understood what abomination the engineer had contrived. With a frigid, willless clarity, he grasped that *Southern Cross* had become the vastest slaughterhouse ever imagined by the human mind. When his paralysis had passed, he moved with clumsy force, tears pouring unchecked, to hold down the demented biologist.

"They're human zygotes. Aren't they?" Silverman wept. "Master of the Universe, why have you permitted this atrocity?"

Baldwin offered no resistance. The two men spun, locked together. One heavy boot swung inadvertently in the restricted space to catch and rip a sagging plastic sheet. Jelly peeled slowly from it in an obscene pale flap.

"Blastulas," the man agreed with some pride. "A hundred billion of them to the square meter. I cloned them from the frozen embryos. Trillions of separate human souls conceived each week and dispatched to the heavenly ranks in a state of grace. They never know sin, poor little things—"

"Shut up!" Silverman shrieked.

Grief and horror possessed him utterly. How long had this holocaust persisted? Years? It was inconceivable. It was diabolical, literally. His hand rebounded from a sheet coated with microscopic cloned human embryos, and he drew it back in a paroxysm of distress.

If a single abortion was the murder of a defenceless infant, how much more unspeakably appalling was this manufacture and destruction of numberless human lives? And the ghastly rationality of it stopped his throat, came near to stopping his heart.

For Baldwin's rite of baptism was theologically sound, efficacious, capable according to doctrine and dogma of ushering these teeming trillions of souls into God's grace and salvation. Human volition had been stolen from them, but they were spared the torments of temptation and mortal sin. When Baldwin sluiced them away, his monstrous murder would dispatch more souls into the Kingdom of Heaven than the instantaneous extermination of all life on Earth.

If the insignia of sanctity was the number of souls one fetched to God during one's span, he thought with a terrible comedy close to insanity, then Dr. Baldwin was overdue for canonization as the premier saint of Mother Church.

It can't be true, Silverman cried within his soul. That cannot be the meaning of it. I repudiate You. If You exist, if You have allowed this, that must be its meaning, and You are indeed from the *sitra achra*. From the Other Side it is Your Face I see leering. No. This meat is no more than the simulacrum of human flesh. It has never been quickened with spirit. Doctrine and dogma are mistaken. Your universe is a cesspool. You are the Master of Lies, Father of Dung.

Damned in his own apostasy, Raphael Silverman, S. J. permitted his last hold on consciousness to slip free.

Nine

Atta vechartanu mikol ha'amim
Thou hast chosen us from all peoples
—Hebrew holy-day prayer

Silverman walks steadily into the City.

Like a compulsive tropism acting at the level of his cells, the imperative tug of its architecture draws him in toward the center.

It is a maze of sensuous delights. If, earlier, its design had seemed monumental, integral, now his perspective discovers fine detail endlessly ornamented, an intoxicating contrast to the barren confines of steel and glass that extend without longing into the gray skies of High Earth. Chan is correct: this is a place meant to be lived in, by beings not utterly different from humanity. Silverman passes through merry forums open to the breeze and galleries spiny as the skeletons of abyssal fish, through alleys crooked and charming as any in a medieval town, crowded with what can only be tiny shops and inns, and bowers meant to be choked with blooms; arcades and cloisters he finds on every side; shadowed snuggeries that tempt him to enter for refreshment; gabled porches and piazzas decorated as lavishly as St. Maclou in Rouen, drapes of electric flame that do not burn, like autumn leaves burnished in the sun, filigrees of brass and iron and silver and gold and platinum, tenements that stand soothingly apart in their own breathing space, and towers that might contain opera halls or automated factories or power stations or themselves simply be works of art; minarets that rise in dappled courtyards and shafts shot with delicate veins like translucent marble.

Silverman comes into the heart of the City.

The loveliness of the place has overwhelmed him. He weeps like a child. Light cascades: it is a vision of the City of God.

And he finds that he is motionless. Here the City has permitted wild grass to grow and blow unhindered. He waits in despair.

The City speaks. It is like joyous thunder, yet it enters his mind with the fragile clarity of a single silver bell. Silverman knows that he is listening to the ones who have left the City behind them.

"Brother: welcome!" says the voice of the City, and in a blinding moment of understanding the Jesuit realizes for the first time in his life, in its assuaging, the height and depth of his arid loneliness. Light enfolds him.

"There was a star," the City says.

—and the poignance of that simplicity has the sweet melancholy of a lover's cry in the room of his absent beloved.

"Look upon our City," the cherubim instruct him. "We have put into its making everything of ourselves, for it was our home and the expression of our being. It is the sun's bright warmth, the sweet air, and food shared amid laughter with friends. It is the glory of discovery always renewed. It is everything we have worshiped: grace and joy and virtue. For this was how we saw ourselves, and the universe that gave us birth.

"But look again, for this also is the City—"

For an instant, the campaniles stand brighter against the sky. And then they are gone. All the City is expunged.

Silverman jerks his lids closed against a reeling world. Vertigo brings bile to his throat. Slowly he opens his eyes again, and the malevolent statues glare down on him like demons.

Against the orange slash of the distant bluff, the other Jesuits are small figurines frozen in convulsive astonishment. The priest forces himself to regard the statues, to engage their depravity.

Tsung-Dao Chan has compared the creatures to gargoyles, but that is wide of the mark: there is nothing innately distorted or grotesque in the lean torsos. The builders of the City had been tailless pumas endowed with passion and intelligence: sleek, dark as night, bipedal, powerfully clawed, dexterous, and able.

The first effigy depicts callous, brutal murder.

That it shows cats instead of human beings detracts not one atom from its force. Head thrown back on his iron-sinewed neck, the killer crouches over his small defenceless victim, excited to a pitch of cruel pleasure. In one taloned fist his serrated blade seems almost redundant; it sings toward the fallen cub's throat, pent in midstroke only by the artisan's eye, lusting without pity for the blood of the innocent. Silverman retches from the nightmare of *Southern Cross*, for the murderer's victim is plainly a child. The statue is an archetypal slaughter of the innocent, the sin above all against Charity, against love.

The Jesuit wrenches his gaze away. The second work strikes equally to his heart. From a clumsy scaffold jerks a gagging, swollen-eyed being, savage claws kicking uselessly for the support he has kicked away, his neck fractured and painfully twisted, the breath choking in his constricted breast. The creature has rejected Hope; he hurtles into oblivion and damnation by his own hand.

The last statue is the most appalling. This third alien commits no immediate crime against his brother, or his own flesh, yet his absolute ruin is scored in the tension of every muscle, the mask of his feline face, the upraised brandished fists. In his overweening arrogance the creature rails against dependence, against limitation, against his creator. His fanatical eyes burn with his own glory. There is no nobility to him: he is Lucifer standing against God, doomed and laughing, sick with a pride that would eat and vomit back the universe.

Silverman hunches into himself, stricken. Unbidden, the Krias Shema prayer from his childhood comes to his lips', "May Michael be at my right hand; Gabriel at my left; before me, Uriel; behind me, Raphael; and above my head the divine presence of God."

If the holograms had been desolating, this direct impact is entirely devastating. And yet the builders of the City had known and faced the sin that lay within their species, the sin of Satan and Adam repeated without end on world after world, Silverman guesses now, wasting the promise and freedom of creation. If they had surmounted the outward and compulsive expression of that primal crime, their partial victory has not allowed them to conceal that central corruption from themselves.

Abruptly, the Jesuit understands the source of his bitter pain. Between the horror of the sculpture and the grandeur of their temporal dwelling, there is no hint of immanent transcendence. Where is the Redeemer in this City? They hunger for salvation in every tormented guilty line of their art, as Silverman's own butchered people had cried for the coming of the moshiach, and He has left them comfortless, stumbling in the wilderness.

"This is our self-portrait," the City tells Silverman, compassionately closing away the vile things in lucent banners. "And the Star was manifest to us in the sky, showing the path we must follow."

Bowed in humility, Silverman listens to the assent of the pagan Magi. For him there is no return to rapture: he is beyond all the emotions of joy. He listens, and he accepts. Finally, like his baptismal namesake, Thomas, shown a sign, he accepts.

"So we are leaving our world," the voice says. "We are embarked on a pilgrimage that perhaps only our furthest descendants will see completed. But we are going, for He has shown us His truth, and directed us to the world of His incarnation. We leave our City in gift to you, brother wayfarer, in memory of our youth, as a compass to any who have not yet received the gift of His envoy."

Even without the star-drive they have gone, Silverman tells himself again and again. They have cast themselves trustingly into an Exodus two thousand years in the going and hardly begun. His eyes burn with tears. He looks at the sky, at the stars beyond the bright sky, to the boundless dark desert where a race of men follow the Star of Bethlehem to their journey's end.

"It is our glory," whispers the City, "that He has chosen us to follow His Sign—for we are the least of His children."

Raphael Silverman is oblivious to the City's splendor. He sees in imagination only the dust-pitted ships, and the beings who will come like great pumas to High Earth, or its successor, to find their God murdered and risen from the impotent clutch of the sitra achra, the Other Side.

"We will be waiting for you," Silverman cries aloud to the City, the stars, to his alien kin. It is a promise he makes them. "We will be waiting."

PETER CAREY

Peter Carey is best known for his contemporary novels, including *Illywhacker, Bliss, Oscar and Lucinda,* and *The Unusual Life of Tristan Smith,* which won the Booker Prize. He is an Australian who worked for many years in advertising in Australia and London and now lives in New York City and writes fiction full-time. His position in Australian SF literature is somewhat similar to Margaret Atwood's in Canada, in that he is the greatest Australian SF writer outside the SF field. He is a significant contemporary writer in the English language, wherever he lives and works, and his contributions to SF have been generally ignored both in and out of the field, outside Australia. About half the stories in his first two collections were SF, and his novels often have fantastic elements.

"The Chance" is from *War Crimes* (1979), his second collection (which was combined with his first, using the title of the first, *The Fat Man in History* [1974], for his first publication outside Australia in 1980; to further complicate matters, his second collection from Faber, *Exotic Pleasures* [1980], reprints a second selection from the two earlier Australian books). It is clearly and obviously a science fiction story by a writer with a comprehensive command of the genre's tools and tropes.

One

IT WAS THREE SUMMERS since the Fastalogians had arrived to set up the Genetic Lottery, but it had got so no one gave a damn about what season it was. It was hot. It was steamy. I spent my days in furies and tempers, half-drunk. A six-pack of beer got me to sleep. I didn't have the money for more fanciful drugs, and I should have been saving for a Chance. But to save the dollars for a Chance meant six months without grog or any other solace.

There were nights, bitter and lonely, when I felt beyond the Fastalogian alternative and ready for the other one, to join the Leapers in their suicidal drops from the roofs of buildings and the girders of bridges. I had witnessed a dozen or more. They fell like overripe fruit from the rotten trees of a forgotten orchard.

I was overwhelmed by a feeling of great loss. I yearned for lost time, lost childhoods, seasons for Chrissake, the time when peaches are ripe, the time when the river drops after the snow has all melted and it's just low enough to wade and the water freezes your balls and you can walk for miles with little pale crayfish scuttling backward away from your black-booted feet. Also you can use a dragonfly larva as live bait, casting it out gently and letting it drift downstream to where big old brown trout, their lower jaws grown long and hooked upward, lie waiting.

The days get hot and clear then, and the land is like a tinder box. Old men lighting cigarettes are careful to put the burned matches back into the matchbox, a habit one sometimes sees carried on into the city by younger people who don't know why they're doing it, messengers carrying notes written in a foreign language.

But all this was once common knowledge, in the days when things were always the same and newness was something as delightful and strange as the little boiled sweets we would be given on Sunday morning.

Those were the days before the Americans came and before the Fastalogians who succeeded them, descending in their spaceships from god knows what unimaginable worlds. And at first we thought them preferable to the Americans. But what the Americans did to us with their yearly car models and two-weekly cigarette lighters was nothing compared to the Fastalogians, who introduced concepts so dazzling that we fell prey to them wholesale like South Sea Islanders exposed to the common cold.

The Fastalogians were the universe's bush-mechanics, charlatans, gypsies: raggle-taggle collections of equipment always going wrong. Their Lottery Rooms were always a mess of wires; the floors always littered with dead printed circuits like cigarette ends.

It was difficult to have complete faith in them, yet they could be persuasive enough. Their attitude was eager, frenetic almost, as they attempted to please in the most childish way imaginable. (In confrontation they became much less pleasant, turning curiously evasive while their voices assumed a high-pitched, nasal, wheedling characteristic.)

In appearance they were so much less threatening than the Americans. Their clothes were worn badly, ill-fitting, often with childish mistakes, like buttoning the third button through the fourth buttonhole. They seemed to us to be lonely and puzzled, and even while they controlled us we managed to feel a smiling superiority to them. Their music was not the music of an inhuman oppressor. It had surprising fervor, like Hungarian rhapsodies. One was reminded of Bartók and wondered about the feelings of beings so many light-years from home.

Their business was the Genetic Lottery or The Chance, whatever you cared to call it. It was, of course, a trick, but we had nothing to question them with. We had only accusations, suspicions, fears that things were not as they were described. If they told us that we could buy a second or third Chance in the lottery, most of us took it, even if we didn't know how it worked, or if it worked the way they said it did.

We were used to not understanding. It had become a habit with the Americans, who had left us with a technology we could neither control nor understand. So our failure to grasp the technicalities or even the principles of the Genetic Lottery in no way prevented us from embracing it enthusiastically. After all, we had never grasped the technicalities of the television sets the Americans sold us. Our curiosity about how things worked had atrophied to such an extent that few of us bothered with understanding such things as how the tides worked and why some trees lost their leaves in autumn. It was enough that someone somewhere understood these things. Thus we had no interest in the table of elements that make up all matter, nor in the names of the atomic subparticles our very bodies were built from. Such was the way we were prepared, like South Sea Islanders, like yearning gnostics waiting to be pointed in the direction of the first tin shed called "God."

So now for two thousand intergalactic dollars (IG$2,000) we could go in the Lottery and come out with a different age, a different body, a different voice, and still carry our memories (allowing for a little leakage) more or less intact.

It proved the last straw. The total embrace of a cancerous philosophy of change. The populace became like mercury in each other's minds and arms. Institutions that had proved the very basis of our society (the family, the neighborhood, marriage) cracked and split apart in the face of a new, shrill current of desperate selfishness. The city itself stood like an external endorsement to this internal collapse and recalled the most exotic places (Calcutta, for instance) where the rich had once journeyed to experience the thrilling stink of poverty, the smell of danger, and the just-contained threat of violence born of envy.

Here also were the signs of fragmentation, of religious confusion, of sects decadent and strict. Wild-haired holy men in loincloths, palm readers, seers, revolutionaries without followings (the Hups, the Namers, the L.A.K.). Gurus in helicopters flew through the air, while bandits roamed the countryside in search of travelers who were no longer intent on adventure and the beauty of nature but were forced to travel by necessity, and who moved in nervous groups, well-armed and thankful to be alive when they returned.

It was an edgy and distrustful group of people that made up our society, motivated by nothing but their self-preservation and their blind belief in their next Chance. To the Fastalogians they were nothing but cattle. Their sole function was to provide a highly favorable intergalactic balance of payments.

It was through these streets that I strode, muttering, continually on the verge of either anger or tears. I was cut adrift, unconnected. My face in the mirror that morning was not the face that my mind had started living with. It was a battered, red, broken-nosed face, marked by great quizzical eyebrows, intense black eyes, and tangled, wiry hair. I had been through the Lottery and lost. I had got myself the body of an aging street fighter. It was a body built to contain furies. It suited me. The arrogant Gurus and the ugly Hups stepped aside when I stormed down their streets on my daily course between the boardinghouse where I lived and the Department of Parks where I was employed as a gardener. I didn't work much. I played cards with the others. The botanical gardens were slowly being choked by "Burning Glory," a prickly, crimson-flowering bush the Fastalogians had imported either by accident or design. It was our job to remove it. Instead, we used it as cover for our cheating card games. Behind its red blazing hedges we lied and fought and, on occasion, fornicated. We were not a pretty sight.

It was from here that I walked back to the boardinghouse with my beer under my arm, and it was on a Tuesday afternoon that I saw her, just beyond the gardens and a block down from the Chance Center in Grove Street. She was sitting on the footpath with a body beside her, an old man, his hair white and wispy, his face brown and wrinkled like a walnut. He was dressed very formally in a three-piece gray suit and had an old-fashioned watch chain across the waistcoat. I assumed that the corpse was her grandfather. Since the puppet government had dropped its funeral assistance plan, this was how poor people raised money for funerals. It was a common sight to see dead bodies in rented suits being displayed on the footpaths. So it was not the old man who attracted my attention but the young woman who sat beside him.

"Money," she said, "money for an old man to lie in peace."

I stopped willingly. She had her dark hair cut quite short and rather badly. Her eyebrows were full, but perfectly arched, her features were saved from being too regular by a mouth that was wider than average. She wore a khaki shirt, a navy blue jacket, filthy trousers and a small gold earring in her right ear.

"I've only got beer," I said, "I've spent all my money on beer."

She grinned a broad and beautiful grin, which illuminated her face and made me echo it.

"I'd settle for a beer." And I was surprised to hear shyness.

I sat down on the footpath and we opened the six-pack. Am I being sentimental when I say I shared my beer without calculation? That I sought nothing? It seems unlikely for I had some grasping habits as you'll see soon enough. But I remember nothing of the sort, only that I liked the way she opened the beer bottle. Her hands were large, a bit messed up. She hooked a broken-nailed finger into the ring-pull and had it off without even looking at what she was doing.

She took a big swallow, wiped her mouth with the back of her hand, and said, "Shit, I needed that."

I muttered something about her grandfather, trying to make polite conversation. I was out of the habit.

She shrugged and put the cold bottle on her cheek. "I got him from the morgue."

I didn't understand.

"I bought him for three IGs." She grinned, tapping her head with her middle finger. "Best investment I've ever made."

It was this, more than anything, that got me. I admired cunning in those days, smart moves, cards off the bottom of the deck, anything that tricked the bastards—and "the bastards" were everyone who wasn't me.

So I laughed. A loud, deep, joyful laugh that made passersby stare at me. I gave them the finger and they looked away.

She sat on her hands, rocking back and forth on them as she spoke. She had a pleasantly nasal, idiosyncratic voice, slangy and relaxed. "They really go for white hair and tanned faces." She nodded toward a paint tin full of coins and notes. "It's pathetic, isn't it? I wouldn't have gotten half this much for my real grandfather. He's too dark. Also, they don't like women much. Men do much better than women."

She had the slightly exaggerated toughness of the very young. I wondered if she'd taken a Chance. It didn't look like it.

We sat and drank the beer. It started to get dark. She lit a mosquito coil and we stayed there in the gloom till we drank the whole lot.

When the last bottle was gone, the small talk that had sustained us went away and left us in an uneasy area of silence. Now suspicion hit me with its fire-hot pinpricks. I had been conned for my beer. I would go home and lie awake without its benefits. It would be a hot, sleepless night and I would curse myself for my gullibility. I, who was shrewd and untrickable, had been tricked.

But she stood and stretched and said, "Come on, now I've drunk your beer, I'll buy you a meal."

We walked away and left the body for whoever wanted it. I never saw the old man again.

The next day he was gone.

Two

I cannot explain what it was like to sit in a restaurant with a woman. I felt embarrassed, awkward, and so pleased that I couldn't put one foot straight in front of the other.

I fancy I was graciously old-fashioned.

I pulled out her chair for her, I remember, and saw the look she shot me, both pleased and alarmed. It was a shocked, fast flick of the eyes. Possibly she sensed the powerful fantasies that lonely men create, steel columns of passion appended with leather straps and tiny mirrors.

It was nearly a year since I'd talked to a woman, and that one stole my money and even managed to lift two blankets from my sleeping body. Twelve dull, stupid, drugged, and drunken months had passed, dissolving from the dregs of one day into the sink of the next.

The restaurant was one of those Fasta Cafeterias that had sprung up, noisy, messy, with harsh lighting and long rows of bright white tables that were never ever filled. The service was bad and in the end we went to the kitchen where we helped ourselves from the long trays of food, Fastalogian salads with their dried, intoxicating mushrooms and that strange milky pap they are so fond of. She piled her plate high with everything and I envied the calm that allowed her such an appetite. On any other night I would have done the same guzzling and gorging myself on my free meal.

Finally, tripping over each other, we returned to our table. She bought two more beers, and I thanked her for that silently.

Here I was. With a woman. Like real people.

I smiled broadly at the thought. She caught me and was, I think, pleased to have something to hang on to. So we got hold of that smile, and wrung it for all it was worth.

Being desperate, impatient, I told her the truth about the smile. The directness was pleasing to her. I watched how she leant into my words without fear or reservation, displaying none of the shiftiness that danced through most social intercourse in those days. But I was as calculating and cunning as only the very lonely learn how to be. Estimating her interest, I selected the things that would be most pleasing for her. I steered the course of what I told, telling her things about me that fascinated her most. She was pleased by my confessions. I gave her many. She was strong and young and confident. She couldn't see my deviousness, and no matter what I told her of loneliness, she couldn't taste the stale, self-hating afternoons or suspect the callousness they engendered.

And I bathed in her beauty, delighting in the confidence it brought her, the certainty of small mannerisms, the chop of that beautiful rough-fingered hand when making a point. But also, this: the tentative question marks she hooked on to the ends of her most definite assertions. So I was impressed by her strength and charmed by her vulnerability all at once.

One could not have asked for more.

And this also I confessed to her, for it pleased her to be talked about and it gave me an intoxicating pleasure to be on such intimate terms.

And I confessed why I had confessed.

My conversation was mirrors within mirrors, onion skin behind onion skin. I revealed motives behind motives. I was amazing. I felt myself to be both saint and pirate, as beautiful and gnarled as an ancient olive. I talked with intensity. I devoured her, not like some poor beggar (which I was), but like a prince, a stylish master of the most elegant dissertations.

She ate ravenously, but in no way neglected to listen. She talked impulsively with her mouth full. With mushrooms dropping from her mouth, she made a point. It made her beautiful, not ugly.

I have always enjoyed women who, while being conventionally feminine enough in their appearance, have exhibited certain behavioral traits more commonly associated with men. A bare-breasted woman working on a tractor is the fastest, crudest approximation I can provide. An image, incidentally, guaranteed to give me an aching erection, which it has, on many lonely nights.

But to come back to my new friend, who rolled a cigarette with hands that might have been the hands of an apprentice bricklayer, hands that were connected to breasts that were connected to other parts doubtless female in gender, who had such grace and beauty in her form and manner and yet had had her hair shorn in such a manner as to deny her beauty.

She was tall, my height. Across the table I noted that her hands were as large as mine. They matched. The excitement was exquisite. I anticipated nothing, vibrating in the crystal of the moment.

We talked, finally, as everyone must, about the Lottery, for the Lottery was life in those days and all of us, most of us, were saving for another Chance.

"I'm taking a Chance next week," she said.

"Good luck," I said. It was automatic. That's how life had got.

"You look like you haven't."

"Thank you," I said. It was a compliment, like saying that my shirt suited me. "But I've had four."

"You move nicely," she smiled. "I was watching you in the kitchen. You're not awkward at all."

"You move nicely too." I grinned. "I was watching you too. You're crazy to take a Chance. What do you want?"

"A people's body." She said it fast, briskly, and stared at me challengingly.

"A what?"

"A people's body." She picked up a knife, examined it, and put it down.

It dawned on me. "Oh, you're a Hup."

Thinking back, I'm surprised I knew anything about Hups. They were one of a hundred or more revolutionary crackpots. I didn't give a damn about politics, and I thought every little group was more insane than the next.

And here, goddamn it, I was having dinner with a Hup, a rich crazy who thought the way to fight the revolution was to have a body as grotesque and ill-formed as my friends at the Parks and Gardens.

"My parents took the Chance last week."

"How did it go?"

"I didn't see them. They've gone to . . ." she hesitated ". . . to another place where they're needed." She had become quiet now, and serious, explaining that her parents had upper-class bodies like hers, that their ideas were not at home with their physiognomy (a word I had to ask her to explain), that they would form the revolutionary vanguard to lead the misshapen Lumpen Proletariat (another term I'd never heard before) to overthrow the Fastas and their puppets.

I had a desperate desire to change the subject, to plug my ears, to shut my eyes. I wouldn't have been any different if I'd discovered she was a mystic or a follower of Hiwi Kaj.

"Anyway," I said, "you've got a beautiful body."

"Why did you say that?"

I could have said that I'd spent enough of my life with her beloved Lumpen Proletariat to hold them in no great esteem, that the very reason I was enjoying her company so much was because she was so unlike them. But I didn't want to pursue it. I shrugged, grinned stupidly, and filled her glass with beer.

Her eyes flashed at my shrug. I don't know why people say "flashed," but I swear there was red in her eyes. She looked hurt, stung, and ready to attack.

She withdrew from me, leaning back in her chair and folding her arms. "What do you think is beautiful?"

Before I could answer she was leaning back into the table, but this time her voice was louder.

"What is more beautiful, a parrot or a crow?"

"A parrot, if you mean a rosella. But I don't know much about parrots."

"What's wrong with a crow?"

"A crow is black and awkward looking. It's heavy. Its cry is unattractive."

"What makes its cry unattractive?"

I was sick of the game, and exhausted with such sudden mental exercise.

"It sounds forlorn," I offered.

"Do you think that it is the crow's intention to sound forlorn? Perhaps you are merely ignorant and don't know how to listen to a crow."

"Certainly, I'm ignorant." It was true, of course, but the observation stung a little. I was very aware of my ignorance in those days. I felt it keenly.

"If you could kill a parrot or a crow, which would you kill?"

"Why would I want to kill either of them?"

"But if you had to, for whatever reason."

"The crow, I suppose. Or possibly the parrot. Whichever was the smallest."

Her eyes were alight and fierce. She rolled a cigarette without looking at it. Her face suddenly looked extraordinarily beautiful, her eyes glistening with emotion, the color high in her cheeks, a peculiar half-smile on her wide mouth.

"Which breasts are best?"

I laughed. "I don't know."

"Which legs?"

"I don't know. I like long legs."

"Like the film stars."

Like yours, I thought. "Yes."

"Is that really your idea of beautiful?"

She was angry with me now, had decided to call me enemy. I did not feel enemy and didn't want to be. My mind felt fat and flabby, unused, numb. I forgot my irritation with her ideas. I set all that aside. In the world of ideas I had no principles. An idea was of no worth to me, not worth fighting for. I would fight for a beer, a meal, a woman, but never an idea.

"I like grevilleas," I said greasily.

She looked blank. I thought as much! "Which are they?" I had her at a loss.

"They're small bushes. They grow in clay, in the harshest situations. Around rocks, on dry hillsides. If you come fishing with me, I'll show you. The leaves are more like spikes. They look dull and harsh. No one would think to look at them twice. But in November," I smiled, "they have flowers like glorious red spiders. I think they're beautiful."

"But in October?"

"In October?"

"In October I know what they'll be like in November."

She smiled. She must have wanted to like me. I was disgusted with my argument. It had been cloying and saccharine even to me. I hadn't been quite sure what to say, but it seems I'd hit the nail on the head.

"Does it hurt?" she asked suddenly.

"What?"

"The Chance. Is it painful, or is it like they say?"

"It makes you vomit a lot and feel ill, but it doesn't hurt. It's more a difficult time for your head."

She drained her beer and began to grin at me. "I was just thinking," she said.

"Thinking what?"

"I was thinking that if you have anything more to do with me, it'll be a hard time for your head too."

I looked at her grinning face, disbelievingly.

I found out later that she hadn't been joking.

Three

To cut a long and predictable story short, we got on well together, if you'll allow for the odd lie on my part and what must have been more than a considerable suppression of common sense on hers.

I left my outcast acquaintances behind to fight and steal, and occasionally murder each other, in the boardinghouse. I returned there only to pick up my fishing rod. I took it around to her place at Pier Street, swaggering like a sailor on leave. I was in a flamboyant, extravagant mood and left behind my other ratty possessions. They didn't fit my new situation.

Thus, to the joys of living with an eccentric and beautiful woman I added the even more novel experience of a home. Either one of these changes would have brought me some measure of contentment, but the combination of the two of them was almost too good to be true.

I was in no way prepared for them. I had been too long a grabber, a survivor.

So when I say that I became obsessed with hanging on to these things, using every shred of guile I had learned in my old life, do not judge me harshly. The world was not the way it is now. It was a bitter jungle of a place, worse, because even in the jungle there is cooperation, altruism, community.

Regarding the events that followed I feel neither pride nor shame. Regret, certainly, but regret is a useless emotion. I was ignorant, short-sighted, bigoted, but in my situation it is inconceivable that I could have been anything else.

But now let me describe for you Carla's home as I came to know it, not as I saw it at first, for then I only felt the warmth of old timbers and delighted in the dozens of small signs of domesticity everywhere about me: a toothbrush in a glass, dirty clothes overflowing from a blue cane laundry basket, a made bed, dishes draining in a sink, books, papers, letters from friends, all the trappings of a life I had long abandoned, many Chances ago.

The house had once been a warehouse, long before the time of the Americans. It was clad with unpainted boards that had turned a gentle silver, aging with a grace that one rarely saw in those days.

One ascended the stairs from the Pier Street wharf itself. A wooden door. A large key. Inside: a floor of grooved boards, dark with age.

The walls showed their bones: timber joists and beams, roughly nailed in the old style, but solid as a rock.

High in the ceiling was a sleeping platform, below it a simple kitchen filled with minor miracles: a hot-water tap, a stove, a refrigerator, saucepans, spices, even a recipe book or two.

The rest of the area was a sitting room, the pride of place being given to three beautiful antique armchairs in the Danish style, their carved arms showing that patina only age can give.

Add a rusty-colored old rug, pile books high from the floor, pin Hup posters here and there, and you have it.

Or almost have it, because should you open the old, high, sliding door (pushing hard, because its rollers are stiff and rusty from the salty air) and the room is full of the sea: the once-great harbor, its waters rarely perturbed by craft, its shoreline dotted with rusting hulks of forgotten ships, great tankers from the oil age, tugs, and ferries that, even a year before, had maintained their services in the face of neglect and disinterest on all sides.

Two other doors led off the main room: one to a rickety toilet, which hung out precariously over the water, the other to a bedroom, its walls stacked with files, books, loose papers, its great bed draped in mosquito netting, for there was no wiring for the customary sonic mosquito repellents and the mosquitoes carried Fasta Fever with the same dedicated enthusiasm that others of their family had once carried malaria.

The place revealed its secrets fast enough, but Carla, of course, did not divulge hers quite so readily. Frankly, it suited me. I was happy to see what I was shown and never worried about what was hidden away.

I mentioned nothing of Hups or revolution and she, for her part, seemed to have forgotten the matter. My assumption (arrogantly made) was that she would put off her Chance indefinitely. People rarely plunged into the rigors of the Lottery when they were happy with their lives. I was delighted with mine, and I assumed she was with hers.

I had never known anyone like her. She sang beautifully and played the cello with what seemed to me to be real accomplishment. She came to the Park and Gardens and beat us all at poker. To see her walk across to our bed, moving with the easy gait of an Islander filled me with astonishment and wonder.

I couldn't believe my luck.

She had been born rich but chose to live poor, an idea that was beyond my experience or comprehension. She had read more books in the last year than I had in my life. And when my efforts to hide my ignorance finally gave way in tatters, she took to my education with the same enthusiasm she brought to our bed.

Her methods were erratic, to say the least. For each new book she gave me revealed a hundred gaps in my knowledge that would have to be plugged with other books.

I was deluged with the whole artillery of Hup literature: long and difficult works like Gibson's *Class and Genetics*, Schumacher's *Comparative Physiognomy*, Hale's *Wolf Children*.

I didn't care what they were about. If they had been treatises on the history of Rome or the Fasta economic system I would have read them with as much enthusiasm and probably learned just as little.

Sitting on the wharf I sang her "Rosie Allan's Outlaw Friend," the story of an ill-lettered cattle thief and his love for a young school mistress. My body was like an old guitar, fine and mellow with beautiful resonance.

The first star appeared.

"The first star," I said.

"It's a planet," she said.

"What's the difference?" I asked.

She produced a schoolbook on the known solar system at breakfast the next morning.

"How in the hell do you know so little?" she said, eating the omelet I'd cooked her.

I stared at the extraordinary rings of Saturn, knowing I'd known some of these things long ago. They brought to mind classrooms on summer days, dust, the smell of oranges, lecture theaters full of formally dressed students with eager faces.

"I guess I just forgot," I said. "Maybe half my memory is walking around in other bodies. And how in the fuck is it that you don't know how to make a decent omelet?"

"I guess," she said grinning, "that I just forgot."

She wandered off toward the kitchen with her empty plate but got distracted by on old newspaper she found on the way. She put the plate on the floor and went on to the kitchen, where she read the paper, as she leaned back against the sink.

"You have rich habits," I accused her.

She looked up, arching her eyebrows questioningly.

"You put things down for other people to pick up."

She flushed and spent five minutes picking up things and putting them in unexpected places.

She never mastered the business of tidying up, and finally I was the one who became housekeeper.

When the landlord arrived one morning to collect the rent, she introduced me as "my house-proud lover." I gave the bastard my street-fighter's sneer and he swallowed the smirk he was starting to grow on his weak little face.

I was the one who opened the doors to the harbor. I swept the floor, I tidied the books and washed the plates. I threw out the old newspapers and took down the posters for Hup meetings and demonstrations that had long since passed.

She came in from work after my first big cleanup and started pulling books out and throwing them on the floor.

"What in the fuck are you doing?"

"Where did you put them?"

"Put what?"

She pulled down a pile of old pamphlets and threw them on the floor as she looked between each one.

"What?"

"My posters, you bastard. How dare you."

I was nonplussed. My view of posters was purely practical. It had never occurred to me that they might have any function other than to advertise what they appeared to advertise. When the event was past, the poster had no function.

Confused and angry at her behavior, I retrieved the posters from the bin in the kitchen.

"You creased them."

"I'm sorry."

She started putting them up again.

"Why did you take them down? It's your house now, is it? Would you like to paint the walls, eh? Do you want to change the furniture too? Is there anything else that isn't to your liking?"

"Carla," I said, "I'm very sorry. I took them down because they were out-of-date."

"Out-of-date," she snorted. "You mean you think they're ugly."

I looked at the poster she was holding, a glorification of crooked forms and ugly faces.

"Well if you want to put it like that, yes, I think they're fucking ugly."

She glowered at me, self-righteous and prim. "You can only say that because you're so conditioned that you can only admire looks like mine. How pathetic. That's why you like me, isn't it?"

Her face was red, the skin taut with rage.

"Isn't it?"

I'd thought this damn Hup thing had gone away, but here it was. The stupidity of it. It drove me insane. Her books became weapons in my hands. I threw them at her, hard, in a frenzy.

"Idiot. Dolt. You don't believe what you say. You're too young to know anything. You don't know what these damn people are like." I poked at the posters. "You're too young to know anything. You're a fool. You're playing with life." I hurled another book. "Playing with it."

She was young and nimble with a boxer's reflexes. She dodged the books easily enough and retaliated viciously, slamming a thick sociology text into the side of my head.

Staggering back to the window, I was confronted with the vision of an old man's face, looking in.

I pulled up the window and transferred my abuse in that direction.

"Who in the fuck are you?"

A very nervous old man stood on a long ladder, teetering nervously above the street.

"I'm a painter."

"Well piss off."

He looked down into the street below as I grabbed the top rung of the ladder and gave it a little bit of a shake.

"Who is it?" Carla called.

"It's a painter."

"What's he doing?"

I looked outside. "He's painting the bloody place orange."

The painter, seeing me occupied with other matters, started to retreat down the ladder.

"Hey," I shook the ladder to make him stop.

"It's only a primer," he pleaded.

"It doesn't need any primer," I yelled, "those bloody boards will last a hundred years."

"You're yelling at the wrong person, fellah." The painter was at the bottom of the ladder now and all the bolder because of it.

"If you touch that ladder again, I'll have the civil police here." He backed into the street and shook his finger at me. "They'll do you, my friend, so just watch it."

I slammed the window shut and locked it for good measure. "You've got to talk to the landlord," I said, "before they ruin the place."

"Got to?"

"Please."

Her face became quiet and secretive. She started picking up books and pamphlets and stacking them against the wall with exaggerated care.

"Please Carla."

"You tell them," she shrugged. "I won't be here." She fetched the heavy sociology text from beneath the window and frowned over the bookshelves, looking for a place to put it.

"What in the hell does that mean?"

"It means I'm a Hup. I told you that before. I told you the first time I met you. I'm taking a Chance and you won't like what comes out. I told you before," she repeated, "you've known all along."

"Be buggered you're taking a Chance."

She shrugged. She refused to look at me. She started picking up books and carrying them to the kitchen, her movements uncharacteristically brisk.

"People only take a Chance when they're pissed off. Are you?"

She stood by the stove, the books cradled in her arms, tears streaming down her face.

Even as I held her, even as I stroked her hair, I began to plot to keep her in the body she was born in. It became my obsession.

Four

I came home the next night to find the outside of the house bright orange and the inside filled with a collection of people as romantically ugly as any I had ever seen. They betrayed their upper-class origins by dressing their crooked forms in such romantic styles that they were in danger of creating a new foppishness. Faults and infirmities were displayed with a pride that would have been alien to any but a Hup.

A dwarf reclined in a Danish-style armchair, an attentuated hand waving a cigarette. His overalls, obviously tailored, were very soft, an expensive material splattered with "original" paint. If he hadn't been smoking so languorously he might have passed for real.

Next to him, propped against the wall, was the one I later knew as

Daniel. The grotesque pockmarks on his face proudly accentuated by the subtle use of makeup and, I swear to God, color coordinated with a flamboyant pink scarf.

Then, a tall thin woman with the most pronounced curvature of the spine and a gaunt face dominated by a most extraordinary hooked nose. Her form was clad in the tightest garments, and from it emanated the not unsubtle aroma of power and privilege.

If I had seen them anywhere else I would have found them laughable, not worthy of serious attention. Masters amusing themselves by dressing as servants. Returned tourists clad in beggars rags. Educated fops doing a bad charade of my tough, grisly companions in the boardinghouse.

But I was not anywhere else. This was our home and they had turned it into some spiderweb or nightmare where dog turds smell like French wine and roses stink of the charnel house.

And there, squatting in their midst, my most beautiful Carla, her eyes shining with enthusiasm and admiration while the hook-nosed lady waved her bony fingers.

I stayed by the door and Carla, smiling too eagerly, came to greet me and introduce me to her friends. I watched her dark eyes flick nervously from one face to the next, fearful of everybody's reaction to me and mine to them.

I stood awkwardly behind the dwarf as he passed around his snapshots, photographs taken of him before his Chance.

"Not bad, eh?" he said, showing me a shot of a handsome man on the beach at Cannes. "I was a handsome fellow, eh?"

It was a joke, but I was confused about its meaning. I nodded, embarrassed. The photograph was creased with lines like the palm of an old man's hand.

I looked at the woman's curved back and the gaunt face, trying to find beauty there, imagining holding her in my arms.

She caught my eyes and smiled. "Well, young man, what will you do while we have our little meeting?"

God knows what expression crossed my face, but it would have been a mere ripple on the surface of the feelings that boiled within me.

Carla was at my side in an instant, whispering in my ear that it was an important meeting and wouldn't take long. The hook-nosed woman, she said, had an unfortunate manner, was always upsetting everyone, but had, just the same, a heart of gold.

I took my time in leaving, fussing around the room looking for my beautiful light fishing rod with its perfectly preserved old Mitchell reel. I enjoyed the silence while I fossicked around behind books, under chairs, finally discovering it where I knew it was all the time.

In the kitchen, I slapped some bait together, mixing mince meat, flour, and garlic, taking my time with this too, forcing them to indulge in awkward small talk about the price of printing and the guru in the electric cape, one of the city's recent contributions to a more picturesque life.

Outside the painters were washing their brushes, having covered half of the bright orange with a pale blue.

The sun was sinking below the broken columns of the Hinden Bridge as I cast into the harbor. I used no sinker, just a teardrop of mince meat, flour, and garlic, an enticing meal for a bream.

The water shimmered, pearlescent. The bream attacked, sending sharp signals up the delicate light line. They fought like the fury and showed themselves in flashes of frantic silver. Luderick also swam below my feet, feeding on long ribbons of green weed. A small pink cloud drifted absentmindedly through a series of metamorphoses. An old work boat passed, sitting low in the water like a dumpy brown duck, full of respectability and regular intent.

Yet I was anesthetized and felt none of what I saw.

For above my head in a garish building slashed with orange and blue I imagined the Hups concluding plans to take Carla away from me.

The water became black with a dark blue wave. The waving reflection of a yellow-lighted window floated at my feet and I heard the high-pitched, wheedling laugh of a Fasta in the house above. It was the laugh of a Fasta doing business.

That night I caught ten bream. I killed only two. The others I returned to the melancholy window floating at my feet.

Five

The tissues lay beneath the bed. Dead white butterflies, wet with tears and sperm.

The mosquito net, like a giant parody of a wedding veil, hung over us, its fibres luminescent, shimmering with light from the open door.

Carla's head rested on my shoulder, her hair wet from both our tears.

"You could put it off," I whispered. "Another week."

"I can't. You know I can't. If I don't do it when it's booked, I'll have to wait six months."

"Then wait . . ."

"I can't."

"We're good together."

"I know."

"It'll get better."

"I know."

"It won't last if you do it."

"It might, if we try."

I damned the Hups in silence. I cursed them for their warped ideals. If only they could see how ridiculous they looked.

I stroked her brown arm, soothing her in advance of what I said. "It's not right. Your friends haven't become working class. They have a manner. They look disgusting."

She withdrew from me, sitting up to light a cigarette with an angry flourish.

"Ah, you see," she pointed the cigarette at me. "Disgusting. They look disgusting."

"They look like rich fops amusing themselves. They're not real. They look evil."

She slipped out from under the net and began searching through the tangled clothes on the floor, separating hers from mine. "I can't stand this," she said, "I can't stay here."

"You think it's so fucking great to look like the dwarf?" I screamed. "Would you fuck him? Would you wrap your legs around him? Would you?"

She stood outside the net, very still and very angry. "That's my business."

I was chilled. I hadn't meant it. I hadn't thought it possible. I was trying to make a point. I hadn't believed.

"Did you?" I hated the shrill tone that crept into my voice. I was a child, jealous, hurt.

I jumped out of the bed and started looking for my own clothes. She had my trousers in her hand. I tore them from her.

"I wish you'd just shut up," I hissed, although she had said nothing. "And don't patronize me with your stupid smart talk." I was shaking with rage.

She looked me straight in the eye before she punched me.

I laid one straight back.

"That's why I love you, damn you."

"Why?" she screamed, holding her hand over her face. "For God's sake, why?"

"Because we'll both have black eyes."

She started laughing just as I began to cry.

Six

I started to write a diary and then stopped. The only page in it says this:

Saturday. This morning I know that I am in love. I spend the day thinking about her. When I see her in the street she is like a painting that is even better than you remembered. Today we wrestled. She told me she could wrestle me. Who would believe it? What a miracle she is. Ten days to go. I've got to work out something.

Seven

Wednesday. Meeting day for the freaks.

On the way home I bought a small bag of mushrooms to calm me down a little bit. I walked to Pier Street the slow way, nibbling as I went.

I came through the door ready to face the whole menagerie but they weren't there, only the hook-nosed lady, arranged in tight brown rags and draped across a chair, her bowed legs dangling, one shoe swinging from her toe.

She smiled at me, revealing an uneven line of stained and broken teeth.

"Ah, the famous Lumpy."

"My name is Paul."

She swung her shoe a little too much. It fell to the floor, revealing her mutant toes in all their glory.

"Forgive me. Lumpy is a pet name?" She wiggled her toes. "Something private?"

I ignored her and went to the kitchen to make bait in readiness for my exile on the pier. The damn mince was frozen solid. Carla had tidied it up and put it in the freezer. I dropped it in hot water to thaw it.

"Your mince is frozen."

"Obviously."

She patted the chair next to her with a bony hand.

"Come and sit. We can talk."

"About what?" I disconnected the little Mitchell reel from the rod and started oiling it, first taking off the spool and rinsing the sand from it.

"About life," she waved her hand airily, taking in the room as if it were the entire solar system. "About . . . love. What . . . ever." Her speech had that curious unsure quality common in those who had taken too many

Chances, the words spluttered and trickled from her mouth like water from a kinked and tangled garden hose. "You can't go until your mince . . . mince has thawed." She giggled. "You're stuck with me."

I smiled in spite of myself.

"I could always use weed and go after the luderick."

"But the tide is high and the weed will be . . . impossible to get. Sit down." She patted the chair again.

I brought the reel with me and sat next to her, slowly dismantling it and laying the parts on the low table. The mushrooms were beginning to work, coating a smooth creamy layer over the gritty irritations in my mind.

"You're upset," she said. I was surprised to hear concern in her voice. I suppressed a desire to look up and see if her features had changed. Her form upset me as much as the soft rotting faces of the beggars who had been stupid enough to make love with the Fastas. So I screwed the little ratchet back in and wiped it twice with oil.

"You shouldn't be upset."

I said nothing, feeling warm and absentminded, experiencing that slight ringing in the ears you get from eating mushrooms on an empty stomach. I put the spool back on and tightened the tension knob. I was running out of things to do that might give me an excuse not to look at her.

She was close to me. Had she been that close to me when I sat down? In the corner of my eye I could see her gaunt, bowed leg, an inch or two from mine. My thick, muscled forearm seemed to belong to a different planet, to have been bred for different purposes, to serve sane and sensible ends, to hold children on my knee, to build houses, to fetch and carry the ordinary things of life.

"You shouldn't be upset. You don't have to lose Carla. She loves you. You may find that it is not so bad . . . making love . . . with a Hup." She paused. "You've been eating mushrooms, haven't you?"

The hand patted my knee. "Maybe that's not such a bad thing."

What did she mean? I meant to ask, but forgot I was feeling the hand. I thought of rainbow trout in the clear waters at Dobson's Creek, their brains humming with creamy music while my magnified white hands rubbed their underbellies, tickling them gently before grabbing them, like stolen jewels, and lifting them triumphant in the sunlight. I smelt the heady smell of wild blackberries and the damp fecund odors of rotting wood and bracken.

"We don't forget how to make love when we change."

The late afternoon sun streamed through a high window. The room was golden. On Dobson's Creek there is a shallow run from a deep pool,

difficult to work because of overhanging willows, caddis flies hover above
the water in the evening light.

The hand on my knee was soft and caressing. Once, many Chances
ago, I had my hair cut by a strange old man. He combed so slowly, cut so
delicately, my head and my neck were suffused with pleasure. It was in a
classroom. Outside someone hit a tennis ball against a brick wall. There
were cicadas, I remember, and a water sprinkler threw beads of light onto
glistening grass, freshly mown: He cut my hair shorter and shorter till my
fingers tingled.

It has been said that the penis has no sense of right or wrong, that it
acts with the brainless instinct of a Venus's-flytrap, but that is not true.
It's too easy a reason for the stiffening cock that rose, stretching blindly
toward the bony fingers.

"I could show," said the voice, "that it is something quite extraordinary . . . not worse . . . better . . . better . . . better by far; you have nothing to
fear."

I knew, I knew exactly in the depth of my clouded mind, what was
happening. I didn't resist it. I didn't want to resist it. My purpose was as
hers. My reasons probably identical.

Softly, sonorously she recited:

"Which trees are beautiful?

All trees that grow.

Which bird is fairest?"

A zipper undone, my balls held gently, a finger stroked the length of
my cock. My eyes shut, questions and queries banished to dusty places.

"The bird that flies.

Which face is fairest?

The faces of the friends of the people of the earth."

A hand, flat-palmed on my rough face, the muscles in my shoulders
gently massaged, a finger circling the lips of my anal sphincter.

"Which forms are foul?

The forms of the owners.

The forms of the exploiters.

The forms of the friends of the Fastas."

Legs across my lap, she straddled me. "I will give you a taste . . . just a
taste . . . you won't stop Carla . . . you can't stop her."

She moved too fast, her legs gripped mine too hard, the hand on my
cock was tugging toward her cunt too hard.

My open eyes stared into her face. The face so foul, so misshapen,
broken, the skin marked with ruptured capillaries, the green eyes wide,
askance, alight with premature triumph.

Drunk on wine I have fucked monstrously ugly whores. Deranged on drugs, blind, insensible, I have grunted like a dog above those whom I would as soon have slaughtered.

But this, no. No, no, no. For whatever reason, no. Even as I stood, shaking and trembling, she clung to me, smiling, not understanding. "Carla will be beautiful. You will do things you never did."

Her grip was strong. I fought through mosquito nets of mushroom haze, layer upon layer that ripped like dusty lace curtains, my arms failing, my panic mounting. I had woken underwater, drowning.

I wrenched her hand from my shoulder and she shrieked with pain. I pulled her leg from my waist and she fell back on to the floor, grunting as the wind was knocked from her.

I stood above her, shaking, my heart beating wildly, the head of my cock protruding foolishly from my unzipped trousers, looking as pale and silly as a toadstool.

She struggled to her feet, rearranging her elegant rags and cursing. "You are an ignorant fool. You are a stupid, ignorant, reactionary fool. You have breathed the Fastas' lies for so long that your rotten body is soaked with them. You stink of lies . . . do you . . . know who I am?"

I stared at her, panting.

"I am Jane Larange."

For a second I couldn't remember who Jane Larange was; then it came to me. "The actress?" The once beautiful and famous.

I shook my head. "You silly bugger. What in God's name have you done to yourself?"

She went to her handbag, looking for a cigarette. "We will kill the Fastas," she said, smiling at me, "and we will kill their puppets and their leeches."

She stalked to the kitchen and lifted the mince meat from the sink. "Your mince is thawed."

The mince was pale and wet. It took more flour than usual to get it to the right consistency. She watched me, leaning against the sink, smoking her perfumed cigarette.

"Look at you, puddling around with stinking meat like a child playing with shit. You would rather play with shit than act like a responsible adult. When the adults come, you will slink off and kill fish." She gave a grunt. "Poor Carla."

"Poor Carla." She made me laugh. "You try and fuck me and then you say 'poor Carla'!"

"You are not only ugly," she said, "you are also stupid. I did that for Carla. Do you imagine I like your stupid body or your silly mind? It was to make her feel better. It was arranged. It was her idea, my friend, not mine. Possibly a silly idea, but she is desperate and unhappy and what else is there to do? But," she smiled thinly, "I will report a great success, a great rapture. I'm sure you won't be silly enough to contradict me. The lie will make her happy for a little while at least."

I had known it. I had suspected it. Or if I hadn't known it, was trying a similar grotesque test myself. Oh, the lunacy of the times!

"Now take your nasty bait and go and kill fish. The others will be here soon and I don't want them to see your miserable face."

I picked up the rod and a plastic bucket.

She called to me from the kitchen. "And put your worm back in your pants. It is singularly unattractive bait."

I said nothing and walked out the door with my cock sticking out of my fly. I found the dwarf standing on the landing. It gave him a laugh, at least.

Eight

I told her the truth about my encounter with the famous Jane Larange. I was a fool. I had made a worm to gnaw at her with fear and doubt. It burrowed into the space behind her eyes and secreted a filmy curtain of uncertainty and pain.

She became subject to moods that I found impossible to predict.

"Let me take your photograph," she said.

"Alright."

"Stand over there. No, come down to the pier."

We went down to the pier.

"Alright."

"Now, take one of me."

"Where's the button?"

"On the top."

I found the button and took her photograph.

"Do you love me? Now?"

"Yes, damn you, of course I do."

She stared at me hard, tears in her eyes, then she wrenched the camera from my hand and hurled it into the water.

I watched it sink, thinking how beautifully clear the water was that day.

Carla ran up the steps to the house. I wasn't stupid enough to ask her what the matter was.

Nine

She had woken in one more mood, her eyes pale and staring and there was nothing I could do to reach her. There were only five days to go and these moods were thieving our precious time, arriving with greater frequency and lasting for longer periods.

I made the breakfast, frying bread in the bacon fat in a childish attempt to cheer her up. I detested these malignant withdrawals. They made her as blind and selfish as a baby.

She sat at the table, staring out the window at the water. I washed the dishes. Then I swept the floor. I was angry. I polished the floor and still she didn't move. I made the bed and cleaned down the walls in the bedroom. I took out all the books and put them in alphabetical order according to author.

By lunchtime I was beside myself with rage.

She sat at the table.

I played a number of videotapes I knew she liked. She sat before the viewer like a blind deaf-mute. I took out a recipe book and began to prepare beef bourguignon with murder in my heart.

Then, some time about half past two in the afternoon, she turned and said "Hello."

The cloud had passed. She stood and stretched and came and held me from behind as I cooked the beef.

"I love you," she said.

"I love you," I said.

She kissed me on the ear.

"What's the matter?" My rage had evaporated, but I still had to ask the stupid question.

"You know." She turned away from me and went to open the doors above the harbor. "Let's not talk about it."

"Well," I said, "maybe we should."

"Why?" she said. "I'm going to do it so there's nothing to be said."

I sat across from her at the table. "You're not going to go away," I said quietly, "and you are not going to take a Chance."

She looked up sharply, staring directly into my eyes, and I think she finally knew that I was serious. We sat staring at each other, entering an unreal country as frightening as any I have ever traveled in.

Later she said quietly, "You have gone mad."

There was a time, before this one, when I never wept. But now as I nodded tears came, coursing down my cheeks. We held each other miserably, whispering things that mad people say to one another.

Ten

Orgasm curved above us and through us, carrying us into dark places where we spoke in tongues.

Carla, most beautiful of women, crying in my ear. "Tell me I'm beautiful."

Locked doors with broken hinges. Bank vaults blown asunder. Blasphemous papers floating on warm winds, lying in the summer streets, flapping like wounded seagulls.

Eleven

In the morning the light caught her. She looked more beautiful than the Bonnards in Hale's *Critique of Bourgeois Art,* the orange sheet lying where she had kicked it, the fine hairs along her arm soft and golden in the early light.

Bonnard painted his wife for more than twenty years. While her arse and tits sagged he painted her better and better. It made my eyes wet with sentimental tears to think of the old Mme Bonnard posing for the aging M. Bonnard, standing in the bathroom or sitting on the toilet seat of their tiny flat.

I was affected by visions of constancy. In the busy lanes behind the central market I watched an old couple helping each other along the broken-down pavement. He, short and stocky with a country man's arms, now infirm and reduced to a walking stick. She, of similar height, overweight, carrying her shopping in an old-fashioned bag.

She walked beside him protectively, spying out broken cobblestones, steps, and the feet of beggars.

"You walk next to the wall," I heard her say, "I'll walk on the outside so no one kicks your stick again."

They swapped positions and set off once more, the old man jutting his chin, the old lady moving slowly on swollen legs, strangers to the mysteries of the Genetic Lottery and the glittering possibilities of a Chance.

When the sun, in time, caught Carla's beautiful face, she opened her eyes and smiled at me.

I felt so damned I wished to slap her face.

It was unbelievable that this should be taken from us. And even as I held her and kissed her sleep-soft lips, I was beginning, at last, to evolve a plan that would really keep her.

As I stroked her body, running one feathery finger down her shoulder, along her back, between her legs, across her thighs, I was designing the most intricate door, a door I could fit on the afternoon before her Chance-day, a door to keep her prisoner for a day at least. A door I could blame the landlord for, a door painted orange, a color I could blame the painters for, a door to make her miss her appointment, a door that would snap shut with a normal click but would finally only yield to the strongest axe.

The idea, so clearly expressed, has all the tell-tale signs of total mad-ness. Do not imagine I don't see that, or even that I didn't know it then. Emperors have built such monuments on grander scales and entered history with the grand expressions of their selfishness and arrogance.

So allow me to say this about my door. I am, even now, startled at the far-flung originality of the design and the obsessive craftsmanship I finally applied to its construction. Further: to this day I can think of no simpler method by which I might have kept her.

Twelve

I approached the door with infinite cunning. I took time off from work, telling Carla I had been temporarily suspended for insolence, something she found easy enough to believe.

On the first day I built a new door frame, thicker and heavier than the existing one and fixed it to the wall struts with fifty long brass screws. When I had finished I painted it with orange primer and rehung the old door.

"What's all this?" she asked.

"Those bloody painters are crazy," I said.

"But that's a new frame. Did the painters do that?"

"There was a carpenter too," I said. "I wish you'd tell the landlord to stop it."

"I bought some beer," she said, "let's get drunk."

Neither of us wanted to talk about the door, but while we drank I watched it with satisfaction. The orange was a beautiful color. It cheered me up no end.

Thirteen

The dwarf crept up on me and found me working on the plans for the door, sneaking up on his obscene little feet.

"Ah-huh."

I tried to hide it, this most complicated idea, which was to lock you in, which on that very afternoon I would begin making in a makeshift workshop I had set up under the house. This gorgeous door of iron-hard old timber with its four concealed locks, their keyholes and knobs buried deep in the door itself.

"Ah," said the dwarf who had been a handsome fellow, resting his ugly little hand affectionately on my elbow. "Ah, this is some door."

"It's for a friend," I said, silently cursing my carelessness. I should have worked under the house.

"More like an enemy," he observed. "With a door like that you could lock someone up in fine style, eh?"

I didn't answer. The dwarf was no fool but neither was he as crazy as I was. My secret was protected by my madness.

"Did it occur to you," the dwarf said, "that there might be a problem getting someone to walk through a doorway guarded by a door like this? A good trap should be enticing, or at least neutral, if you get my meaning."

"It is not for a jail," I said, "or a trap, either."

"You really should see someone," he said, sitting sadly on the low table.

"What do you mean, 'someone'?"

"Someone," he said, "who you could see. To talk to about your problems. A counselor, a shrink, someone . . ." He looked at me and smiled, lighting a stinking Fasta cigarette. "It's a beautiful door, just the same."

"Go and fuck yourself," I said, folding the plans. My fishing rod was in the corner.

"After the revolution," the dwarf said calmly, "there will be no locks. Children will grow up not understanding what a lock is. To see a lock it will be necessary to go to a museum."

"Would you mind passing me my fishing rod. It's behind you."

He obliged, making a small bow as he handed it over. "You should consider joining us," he said, "then you would not have this problem you have with Carla. There are bigger problems you could address your anger to. Your situation now is that you are wasting energy being angry at the wrong things."

"Go and fuck yourself." I smiled.

He shook his head. "Ah, so this is the level of debate we have come to. Go and fuck yourself, go and fuck yourself." He repeated my insult again and again, turning it over curiously in his mind.

I left him with it and went down to talk to the bream on the pier. When I saw him leave I went down below the house and spent the rest of the day cutting the timber for the door. Later I made dovetail joints in the old method before reinforcing them with steel plates for good measure.

Fourteen

The door lay beneath us, a monument to my duplicity and fear.

In a room above, clad by books, stroked slowly by Haydn, I presented this angry argument to her while she watched my face with wide, wet eyes. "Don't imagine that you will forget all this. Don't imagine it will all go away. For whatever comfort you find with your friends, whatever conscience you pacify, whatever guilt you assuage, you will always look back on this with regret and know that it was unnecessary to destroy it. You will curse the schoolgirl morality that sent you to a Chance Center and in your dreams you will find your way back to me and lie by my side and come fishing with me on the pier and everyone you meet you will compare and find lacking in some minor aspect."

I knew exactly how to frighten her. But the fear could not change her mind.

To my argument she replied angrily, "You understand nothing."

To which I replied, "You don't yet understand what you will understand in the end."

After she had finished crying, we fucked slowly and I thought of Mme Bonnard sitting on the edge of the bath, all aglow like a jewel.

Fifteen

She denied me a last night. She cheated me of it. She lied about the date of her Chance and left a day before she had said. I awoke to find only a note, carefully printed in a handwriting that seemed too young for the words it formed. Shivering; naked, I read it.

> Dear Lumpy,
>
> You would have gone crazy. I know you. We couldn't part like that. I've seen the hate in your eyes but what I will remember is love in them after a beautiful fuck.
>
> I've got to be with Mum and Dad. When I see beggars in the street I think it's them. Can't you imagine how that feels? They have turned me into a Hup well and proper.
>
> You don't always give me credit for my ideas. You call me illogical, idealist, fool. I think you think they all mean the same thing. They don't. I have no illusions (and I don't just mean the business about being sick that you mentioned). Now when I walk down the street people smile at me easily. If I want help it comes

easily. It is possible for me to do things like borrow money from strangers. I feel loved and protected. This is the privilege of my body, which I must renounce. There is no choice. But it would be a mistake for you to imagine that I haven't thought properly about what I am doing. I am terrified and cannot change my mind.

There is no one I have known who I have ever loved a thousandth as much as you. You would make a perfect Hup. You do not judge; you are objective, compassionate. For a while I thought we could convert you, but c'est la vie. You are a tender lover and I am crying now, thinking how I will miss you. I am not brave enough to risk seeing you in whatever body the comrades can extract from the Fastas. I know your feelings on these things. It would be too much to risk. I couldn't bear the rejection.

I love you, I understand you,

Carla

I crumpled it up. I smoothed it out. I kept saying, "Fuck," repeating the word meaninglessly, stupidly, with anger one moment, pain the next. I dressed and ran out to the street. The bus was just pulling away. I ran through the early morning streets to the Chance Center, hoping she hadn't gone to another district to confuse me. The cold autumn air rasped my lungs, and my heart pounded wildly. I grinned to myself, thinking it would be funny for me to die of a heart attack. Now I can't think why it seemed funny.

Sixteen

Even though it was early the Chance Center was busy. The main concourse was crowded with people waiting for relatives, staring at the video display terminals for news of their friends' emergence. The smell of trauma was in the air, reminiscent of stale orange peel and piss. Poor people in carpet slippers with their trousers too short sat hopefully in front of murals depicting Leonardo's classic proportions. Fasta technicians in grubby white coats wheeled patients in and out of the concourse in a sequence as aimless and purposeless as the shuffling of a deck of cards. I could find Carla's name on none of the terminals.

I waited the morning. Nothing happened. The cards were shuffled. The coffee machine broke down. In the afternoon I went out and bought a six-pack of beer and a bottle of Milocaine capsules.

Seventeen

In the dark, in the night, something woke me. My tongue furry, my eyes like gravel, my head still dulled from the dope and drink, half-conscious, I half saw the woman sitting in the chair by the bed.

A fat woman, weeping.

I watched her like television. A blue glow from the neon lights in the street showed the coarse, folded surface of her face, her poor lank graying hair, deep creases in her arms and fingers like the folds in babies' skin, and the great drapery of chin and neck was reminiscent of drought-resistant cattle from India.

It was not a fair time, not a fair test. I am better than that. It was the wrong time. Undrugged, ungrogged, I would have done better. It is unreasonable that such a test should come in such a way. But in the deep, gray, selfish folds of my mean little brain I decided that I had not woken up, that I would not wake up. I groaned, feigning sleep and turned over.

Carla stayed by my bed till morning, weeping softly while I lay with my eyes closed, sometimes sleeping, sometimes listening.

In the full light of morning she was gone and had, with bitter reproach, left behind merely one thing: a pair of her large gray knickers, wet with the juices of her unacceptable desire. I placed them in the rubbish bin and went out to buy some more beer.

Eighteen

I was sitting by the number-five pier finishing off the last of the beer. I didn't feel bad. I'd felt a damn sight worse. The sun was out and the light dancing on the water produced a light, dizzy feeling in my beer-sodden head. Two bream lay in the bucket, enough for my dinner, and I was sitting there pondering the question of Carla's flat: whether I should get out or whether I was meant to get out or whether I could afford to stay on. They were not difficult questions but I was managing to turn them into major events. Any moment I'd be off to snort a couple more caps of Milocaine and lie down in the sun.

I was not handling this well.

"Two fish, eh?"

I looked up. It was the fucking dwarf. There was nothing to say to him.

He sat down beside me, his grotesque little legs hanging over the side of the pier. His silence suggested a sympathy I did not wish to accept from him.

"What do you want, ugly?"

"It's nice to hear that you've finally relaxed, mm? Good to see that you're not pretending anymore." He smiled. He seemed not in the least malicious. "I have brought the gift."

"A silly custom. I'm surprised you follow it." It was customary for people who took the Chance to give their friends pieces of clothing from their old bodies, clothing that they expected wouldn't fit the new. It had established itself as a pressure-cooked folk custom, like brides throwing corsages and children putting first teeth under their pillows.

The dwarf held out a small, brown paper parcel.

I unwrapped the parcel while he watched. It contained a pair of small white lady's knickers. They felt as cold and vibrant as echoes across vast canyons: quavering questions, cries, and thin misunderstandings.

I shook the dwarf by his tiny hand.

The fish jumped forlornly in the bucket.

Nineteen

So long ago. So much past. Furies, rages, beer, and sleeping pills. They say that the dwarf was horribly tortured during the revolution, that his hands were literally sawn from his arms by the Fastas. The hunchback lady now adorns the 50IG postage stamps, in celebration of her now famous role at the crucial battle of Haytown.

And Carla, I don't know. They say there was a fat lady who was one of the fiercest fighters, who attacked and killed without mercy, who slaughtered with a rage that was exceptional even in such a bloody time.

But I, I'm a crazy old man, alone with his books and his beer and his dog. I have been a clerk and a peddler and a seller of cars. I have been ignorant, and a scholar of note. Pockmarked and ugly I have wandered the streets and slept in the parks. I have been bankrupt and handsome and a splendid con man. I have been a river of poisonous silver mercury, without form or substance, yet I carry with me this one pain, this one yearning, that I love you, my lady, with all my heart. And on evenings when the water is calm and the birds dive among the whitebait, my eyes swell with tears as I think of you sitting on a chair beside me, weeping in a darkened room.